I0760828

# THE SACRED BAND

AUTHOR'S CUT EDITION

JANET & CHRIS MORRIS

**Perseid Press**
P.O. Box 584
Centerville MA 02632

**The Sacred Band**



First Kerlak Publishing hardcover printing: 2011
First Perseid trade edition: December 2012
First Perseid Kindle edition: December 2012

Cover and illustration art: Feuerbach: *Amazonenschlacht* (detail), 1873
Cover image © Perseid Press
Cover design: Roy Mauritsen
Book design: Marie Pitrat



Kindle ISBN-13: 978-0-09887550-1-7
Trade: ISBN-13: 978-1-948602-51-8
Hardcover: ISBN-13: 978-1-948602-50-1

Library of Congress Control Number: 2011926942

Published in the United States of America

**Related Works by Janet Morris and Chris Morris**

*Tempus* (1987), Janet Morris

*Beyond Sanctuary* (1985), Janet Morris

*Beyond the Veil* (1985), Janet Morris

*Beyond Wizardwall* (1986), Janet Morris

*City at the Edge of Time* (1988), Janet & Chris Morris

*Tempus Unbound* (1989), Janet & Chris Morris

*Storm Seed* (1990), Janet & Chris Morris

*The Sacred Band* (2010), Janet Morris & Chris Morris

*The Fish, the Fighters and the Song-girl* (2012),
Janet Morris & Chris Morris

## *Contents*


| | |
|---|---|
| *Chapter 1: Cheating the Fates* | *1* |
| *Chapter 2: Mercy from the Heavens* | *11* |
| *Chapter 3: Blink of the God's Eye* | *19* |
| *Chapter 4: Two Gods Storming* | *31* |
| *Chapter 5: Stepsons and Mothers* | *37* |
| *Chapter 6: Breath of the Gods* | *43* |
| *Chapter 7: Dreams of Gods and Glory* | *55* |
| *Chapter 8: God-given Right* | *65* |
| *Chapter 9: Anger of the Gods* | *79* |
| *Chapter 10: Ancient Remedy* | *93* |
| *Chapter 11: Waiting for the Gods* | *105* |
| *Chapter 12: Damned in Sanctuary* | *119* |
| *Chapter 13: The Fated Dead* | *125* |
| *Chapter 14: Love, War and Harmony* | *131* |
| *Chapter 15: Gods and Heroes* | *147* |
| *Chapter 16: Gift of Heaven* | *153* |
| *Chapter 17: Whiplash from the Gods* | *165* |
| *Chapter 18: Playing the Gods' Games* | *181* |

*Chapter 19: Test of Fates* 197

*Chapter 20: Divine Lovers and Beloveds* 211

*Chapter 21: Evening Parade* 219

*Chapter 22: Playing With Powers* 229

*Chapter 23: Gods and Fates* 249

*Chapter 24: Wake of the Dream Lord* 255

*Chapter 25: Weapon of the God* 267

*Chapter 26: No Mercy* 283

*Chapter 27: Bright Sky, Fated Share* 295

*Chapter 28: Shock Troops of the Gods* 309

*Chapter 29: What You Pay For What You Pray For* 325

*Chapter 30: The Blessed One* 343

*Chapter 31: Proof of Heaven* 351

*Chapter 32: Ancient Weapon* 363

*Chapter 33: Dreams of Immortality* 381

*Chapter 34: Son of the Storm God* 399

*Chapter 35: God and Goddess, Oath and Honor* 413

*Chapter 36: Grace of the Goddess* 431

*Chapter 37: Echoes of Chaeronea* 449

*Chapter 38: When Gods and Men and Fates Contest* 459

*Chapter 39: God to God, Man to Man* 489

*Chapter 40: Three God Night* 507

*Chapter 41: Death Comes Shambling After* 549

*Chapter 42: Echo of War* 587

*Chapter 43: Battle of Your Dreams* 607

*Chapter 44: All Fall Down* 665

*Chapter 45: The Way Up and the Way Down* 701

*Chapter 46: Life and Everlasting Glory* 711

*Authors' Notes and Acknowledgements* xiii

JANET & CHRIS
MORRIS

## *Chapter 1: Cheating the Fates*

"Who are you?" asks the sentry in a hushed tone, eye-whites and teeth catching a quick spill of starlight down his helmet's thin nosepiece. On this deep blue night, nothing stirs but torches snapping in the camp beyond. "Why are you here?"

"Critias. Sacred Band business," Crit replies, watching for a glimmer of light behind the Theban sentry, a fleeting gleam or deeper dark to show him the sword and shield of this man's partner. Never mind it: this is a pair's left-side leader, momentarily alone, awkwardly surprised, sidling rightward and feeling vulnerable on his open side.

"*Whose* Sacred Band? All ours are here with us." Eye-whites again: this sentry is searching for his partner, somewhere in the dark.

"Ours. The Sacred Band of Stepsons." Crit's voice catches in his throat. Behind him, Critias can hear his own squadron (clink of harness, snort and hoofbeat: his sworn partner; ten pairs of Stepson cavalry; one hell-wheeled chariot from a foreign land) – strangers all, in this place called Chaeronea.

"What do you want?" demands the sentry; wary, with danger all around. Tonight, this sentry's Sacred Band of Thebes is three hundred strong. Tomorrow, they will be obliterated.

Someday, under a statue of a lion, two hundred fifty-four of their skeletons will be recovered. And this sentry's dust will be there.

Someday.

Crit wished he didn't know it. But his commander had told him so.

"What do you *want?"* the sentry repeats, too challenging, too suspicious: impatient; ready to escalate, right hand on hilt and the other signaling his partner nearby, hidden in the dark.

*Don't, boy. Draw that sword on your left hip now and everything changes – for the worse, for you and all your brothers.* Crit flexes his fingers but keeps both arms relaxed at his sides: his squadron, at his back, is more than warning enough.

"Our cadre – *our* Sacred Band – might fight beside you here," Crit answers calmly. "Thousands wait across the valley, looking to make an end to you. You could use some help." *In the morning, Macedonian forces shatter your front lines. Facing their long-speared phalanxes, your support troops desert, leaving your Band to die alone. But I can't tell you that.* "My commander, Tempus – the Riddler, favorite of the storm god – wants to speak with yours."

So Crit has just introduced a god into this conversation. Well and good. Forewarned might be forearmed, for these Thebans, because the storm god *is* here – always is wherever Tempus is.

Meddling from Enlil, storm god of the armies. Too little, too late for these doomed fighters. Divine intervention? A small mercy? Perhaps. But only for some. Not all. Not many. This sortie is a whim: the dark humor of his commander, a man the god immortalized, catching up Crit's soul one more time – along with everybody else's.

The Riddler's hell-wheeled chariot starts rolling forward: slowly, slowly, horses snorting; no threat imminent; coming abreast at a jigging walk; driving up on a wet wind rising, which flaps Crit's mantle around his calves. Tempus has waited long enough and wants, now, to make his presence felt.

"Right here, Crit," says the Riddler, a sighing shift of gravel in his softest voice, a gentle tone reserved for horses and the truly damned.

Now the sentry's partner unwraps from gloom on his right and speaks so low Crit can't catch the words, with the wind picking up and the chariot rattling. The second sentry goes running, greaves and leather squeaking, sandals slapping, clank of metal. Above, the blue-black sky starts to lose its milky road of glittering stars: clouds boiling up, building a danker dark.

*What are we doing here, trying to save the fated dead?*

The nearest of Tempus's chariot horses is slobbering on Crit's right shoulder. Crit's partner, Straton, grabs the team's rein from the other side. One of the blacks screams a challenge to some horse, somewhere, but doesn't raise its head.

Critias knows what these Thebans see (these dead-men-to-be), keeping watch on their last sunrise to come – guesses how it seems to them, when they peer into the chariot's car: chariot and black horses such as none here have seen but on temple walls; his commander's massive strength at the reins with his right-side partner standing by in that car forged by the lord of dream and shadow. In a Sacred Band, the charioteer is always senior: the Thebans know who is who now. Gold rims glisten on chariot wheels, on ancient demons decorating the dream-forged car bearing the Riddler – called Tempus the Obscure, the Black, the Sleepless One – keeper of all their fates, heroic in form, with eyes that can bring a man back from hell. One more time.

Tempus has Stealth, called Nikodemos, beside him, who's been to that hell and back how many times for the Riddler?

A clean-limbed, balanced force, Niko is Tempus's right-side partner and an avatar of the storm god Enlil in his own right, if reluctantly.

These two want to save forty-six fighters from the Sacred Band of Thebes, twenty-three pairs whose skeletons won't lie under a stone lion for later men to find or poets to extol. Why? To staff a mission. And Critias, executive officer of the Sacred Band of Stepsons, had agreed – at the time. When it hadn't seemed so outrageous to interfere; to rescue paired fighters from a distant place and time where they are about to die, shoulder to shoulder, with honor, just as their oath-bond demands.

*If the result is fixed, why fight at all?*

Maybe these (someday missing) twenty-three Theban pairs just cut and ran, made new lives, had children.... Maybe they still would. Still could. But Crit didn't think so.

The sentry's partner comes back with a bigger, older man on a blowing warhorse and a slighter man, jogging beside: more doomed lovers of the god – or goddess – if not of each other.

Crit raises his right arm shoulder-high, taking the left-hand chariot horse by the bit. This signal, on its own, brings up all the mounted Sacred Band of Stepsons swathed in dark behind them. Good thing, with the wind getting up, and the storm god of heaven about to make a statement of his own. Crit felt better with the Stepsons' horses up around him, although his partner Straton rode a horse resurrected by a witch. Considering so many ghosts-to-be, the single ghost horse of the Stepsons troubled Crit less tonight.

The Theban commander (or the man they sent to parlay) rides up close, stout little warhorse between his knees. They must know their doom, this Sacred Band of lovers. They'd won a lot, triumphed ten to one, some said; three to one, for certain: they'd made Thebes great, a mighty power. But this next battle will be their last. Any reconnaissance could tell you what awaited on the morning. Lots. You didn't even need to be able to count that high, when faced with thousands of enemies a valley away, and more behind them. Lots and lots.

Tempus said to that doomed man, in a voice like gravel coursing downhill, "You speak for them, all of yours?"

"I do. Theagenes." No title, no rank; no need for all that now.

This Theban's helmet was fierce, crested, almond-eyed, lips and chin showing through a narrow vertical slit. Theagenes's mantle blew over his horse's croup in the rising wind. You couldn't see what he thought of that chariot from hell, but the crouched way he sat his horse and urged it forward, motioning his partner to stay back, told Crit the message was received.

"You wanted me?" the Theban asks the Riddler.

"I did. I do. Tempus." His commander's voice growls deep in his throat, acknowledging the deadly situation. But not defeat. The Riddler was trying to save something, where precious little could be saved. "Our storm god Enlil says you can use a little help. And your goddess Harmony agrees."

That brought the helmeted Theagenes on his scrappy horse up so close Critias could judge the breathing of the other man, deep and cautious, this leader of this other Sacred Band of soon-to-be dead. "If the gods sent you to fight here, then the gods are fools," says Theagenes, words very soft, just a rasp that won't carry, careful not to dishearten his men, behind. "What's the price for this help? There always is one."

"The price?" Softer still, the Riddler answers: "You'll lose all your pairs tomorrow, every one." He snaps his reins. The chariot horses, with Crit and Strat in tow, move closer to the Theban: one step; two; and halt.

"Then why are you here? We don't need help counting. You came to tell me this, Tempus, Riddler – whoever? What's the point?"

"The point is life. Let me spare twenty-three pairs of yours destined to die on tomorrow's battleplain and all my Sacred Band will stay and fight beside you, till the end. And I, myself. And mine. And what price there is for that, you and yours will not pay it." Tempus's head inclined to his partner, almost imperceptibly: Nikodemos, motionless, attentive beside him like a ready falcon or a hunting dog. "I've eleven pairs here of mine…and this chariot. I promise it's enough for what's in store. We'll see to all the rites, as you want them. And some will be left who remember. I'll take twenty-three pairs of yours away with me."

"Take them where? Not to the fields of Elysion, from the look of you. To Hades? They can get there on their own, it seems, directly."

"Not to safety. You know better. But to a chance at life. To fight on other days. To carry on."

From the rear, in the midst of the Sacred Band of Stepsons, at the worst possible moment, a boy of theirs pushes his horse through the waiting cavalry, making riders move and mounts clarion and challenge. Nikodemos, beside Tempus, shifts in the car and motions sharply: be *still*. Someone back there stopped the youthful Stepson, before he intruded where boys had no right to be. Crit heard a thump. Then stillness in the ranks: discipline snapped tight again.

"To carry on?" Theagenes repeated, disbelieving, ready for death, inured to hope.

Before Tempus can reply, the storm god has his say and lightning flares sky-wide. Thunder breaks loose above, clouds blocking the road to heaven that had shined softly in the stars.

There's almost no time between blinding-white slashing of the sky and thunderclap. Horses squeal and neigh.

In the bright sheet lightning, men and horses moving slowly are revealed, coming up softly – not quite sneaking – from the other Sacred Band's tents, leather wraps upon their horses' hooves. This tactic didn't affront Critias; he would have done the same. Survival has its own etiquette.

And what do the Theban hoplites see in this extended rending of the sky, this white-bright glory of Enlil's lightning? The future, but not theirs: paired cavalry fighters; formed ranks of armored death; grim men on their tall horses with lightning limning weapons tailored to the task; men spoiling for a fight if the gods allowed – the Sacred Band of Stepsons, out from shadows and the dark.

So it could go another way, yet. Crit whistles his unit to readiness, but doubts the need: everybody knows the danger here; none underestimates his peril. Horses shy in the brilliant light. Never had so many of his been so spooked by so little. Then the dark resumes it hegemony over them all. It would be a relief to fight against, rather than beside, this other Sacred Band, doomed to the man in any case, just to break the tension.

*But that isn't what the Riddler wants, or what the storm god of the armies wants, or what Niko's maat, his mystery of balance and justice, wants. Or we wouldn't be here. Now.* Was all this really just about putting together a new Sacred Squadron, a Band to send down to Sanctuary, a thieves' world where none of the veteran Stepsons would willingly return? To Sanctuary, where the gods themselves had said the Band had done enough, and relieved them of their service there? Critias hated Sanctuary more than anyplace he'd ever been. But now they had young warriors who needed seasoning: some with blood hot for vengeance and some with the blood of gods in their veins, some with kin in that hellhole called Sanctuary – which was like calling a witch a priest. Sanctuary would train these boys like no place else could. And Tempus had never said they were done there.

Now Tempus waits and watches, unhelmeted, just staring back at Theagenes with those long, slitted eyes; not responding to Theagenes's *'To carry on?'* Words repeated, for clarification, by a man locked in the confounding gaze of Crit's commander.

Crit was neither witch nor priest, not god-bound or, he hoped, god-damned. He was unmagical, at best unflappable even in the face of Tempus or the unknown, but this mission froze his tongue and made his breath come fast. Crit was just a soldier. He couldn't figure odds when dicing with the gods. He held on to the lead-horse's bit and its outside rein with one hand and his shortsword's pommel with the other and waited, to see what this Theban Sacred Band would do. The gods themselves were in this, up to their high-handed tricks, or Lord Storm's lightning and thunder wouldn't come illuminating this camp like a fête day when the doomed fighters in those tents ought to be getting a good night's sleep – not sneaking up through the dark, rousted and ready.

"Not to safety," the Riddler finally says once more. "To fight on other days. To carry on."

Then this Theagenes sighs, "Not to safety. For Harmony. Wanting neither too much to live nor too much to die."

*Their code, this strange Sacred Band. Not sworn to a tutelary god such as Enlil, but to a goddess, 'Harmony.' More like Niko's 'maat.'*

And Tempus speaks then, words from deep inside, "As the gods decree."

Now Theagenes repeats what the Riddler has offered: "But to fight on other days. To carry on. That, I can accept for them. And gladly," agrees this man who knows the coming dawn will be his last.

If Crit weren't so nervous that the Theban fighters ambling up might start a skirmish here tonight, he'd have wept for them. But here they came, this other Sacred Band, slipping through the night, so unconcernedly harmonious and quiet as they surrounded his Stepsons, deploying left wing and right, before and behind, all wolfish and keen.

So just in time the Riddler said, "Done," and stepped down from the chariot's car to take Theagenes's hand. Blades snicked from scabbards behind Crit; spears hefted protectively; arrows nocked and, above, thunder pealed like applause from heaven. "Crit," said the Riddler over his shoulder. "Niko. You know what to do."

Somewhere in the night, a lone wolf howled. And got an answer.

## *Chapter 2: Mercy from the Heavens*

*So, Enlil, lord of storm and bloodbath, how do You like this fight so far?* Tempus asked the god in his head and got no reply but deep breathing and grunting like the fighters make where they fall. The battle is all around, though, and the god likes battle well enough that Tempus can barely keep his chariot and right-side partner in mind as Enlil looks down from heaven and out of his eyes and everywhere is shrieking and bleeding and dark death hurtling through the skies as man tries something new and deadly against his brother.

Arrows arcing. Long spears, thunking into flesh. Men stagger backward, impaled, screaming. War, then and now, no difference: here, today, the name and the work of the long spear is Death; none can stand before it.

Arrows whiz by his head. Niko jostles him, using his shield to protect Tempus although the god will surely see to his servant. Sharp cavalry wedge breaks the Theban line. Long spears piercing, glittering in the sunlight. Men and horses screaming. Maneuvers carefully drilled, impossible to complete. Waves of death breaking on the Chaeronean plain. So many falling, piled one upon the other. Bloody mud so slick that horses skid and stumble. And his Stepsons, bright Stepsons in the thick of it: cavalry, where such cavalry has never been before. Here Macedonians try tactics on Thebans that will kill so many now…and multitudes more, later – powering a war like none ever seen in all the days of man – and make a boy an emperor...later.

*Is this what You, Lord Storm, really want? Is this what You, Enlil, storm god of the armies, want to see and see and see again? Again and again? And want? Again and again?*

No answer from Enlil, god of the battlefield. The god is too close today, his supernal mind bloody and full of dark purpose, rending and tearing away all but souls. The god is so high in him; hardly separate from him; a mind in his mind; strength beyond mortal comprehension: celestial rage loosed. The man can't say now where Tempus ends and Enlil begins. Hoofbeats thundering. Long spears, thunking into flesh. Men staggering backward, impaled, groaning.

Maybe this time he has pushed the god too far, opened up too much, asked too much of a force that sees no difference between good and evil, right and wrong, but loves conflict and change and the steering of all things through all things by strife…. *War is all, and king of all….*

Today, Tempus is perhaps more god than man, his humanity more submerged than it has ever been before when the god takes his flesh and empowers it. It can't be helped. Or maybe it will *be* the help. Man here is learning a catechism about how to use a horse in battle and how to field fighters in a newer way. Infantry all around, the honorable dying in a multitude before the onslaught of the dishonorable. An object lesson the world does not soon forget, when the great are taken down by the lowly, when artifice and infamy, with no soul involved (just precision), routs brains and heart and honor.

Glory wears a dreadful face today as war takes a different turn. Long spear, thunking into flesh. A youth staggers backward, impaled, whimpering. Spear pierces flesh between the nipples: mortal strike. Swords slash necks and arms. A shield-holding line drifts right, each protecting his open side. Too many open sides. Too many. Sharp phalanx just being born: an unholy advantage – new and deadly, sparking strategies so much newer and deadlier still.

The Sacred Band of Thebes, heroes all, are holding steady, each pair fielded, intentionally, with the stronger bonded to the weaker; each pair tight together while the enemy – so many, many, with gross force of numbers – overcomes their inspired battle. Sometimes, not even inspiration is enough.

*Look to the souls of Your own soldiers, God, who labor in Thine awful cause.* Tempus hasn't come here to lose lives. He's come to save them. In the press, wild eyes popping, dying breaths sigh from the mouths of men who have screamed their throats dry. He has no horse under him, no god-given advantage of man and horse becoming something more. But his sharp-bladed chariot wheels still take their toll. And the edges on the bladed axle cut deep like scythes as Niko, beside him, blocks arrows and knocks spears away with his shield, protecting them both with keen eye and steady arm. On a horse, Tempus's god-given speed transfers to his mount, but not through the reins or the car of a chariot. So time is slow for him, waiting for Death to pick and choose his way across this foretold battlefield, where today bravery loses the fight to guile, and civilization bows to brutality once again.

Whooshing, clashing, ring, and bellow. Death is all around. And his rightman, steady on, a dark sick look in hazel eyes, stays in the chariot with him because this Sacred Band of Thebes needs all the help Tempus's fighters can provide (and more), while their own fight is drawing to a close against an enemy coming on like ants at a feast, unending. Long spears, thunking into flesh. Men staggering backward, impaled, moaning.

Some of his Stepsons have crossbows: these, too, an unfair advantage in this moment; but the least advantage his Stepsons need, on such a dark day where Courage is driven off the battlefield by the hordes of Lust; while Chaos reigns, and righteous battle is punished and brought low by overwhelming force. Entrails are strewn everywhere, pieces of limbs glistening among them. Blinded men crawl away. Theban Sacred Banders, crouched over slain partners, are holding out until the last.

It won't be long now until the eerie quiet falls that signals victory for one, annihilation for the other. But it's not over yet. Now Strife is here, bearing down with her awful mouth open wide, keening. Fear follows, stinking, her bowels loose and horrid. And Death rides his own chariot, while Slaughter and Carnage flank him, shambling beside. Here Panic reigns. Talk is impossible over the din.

*Time to go.* Both reins in his left hand, Tempus touches Niko's shoulder. Niko's shield comes up and Niko half-falls against him, trying to block a long, long spear from Tempus's gut – and succeeding.

Beyond the remnant of the Sacred Band of Thebes, surrounded by his own Sacred Band of Stepsons, a whirlwind is forming. His partner Niko sees it now, as Tempus heads their chariot team that way. Stepson maneuver codes ring out, called by Critias, by Straton, and by Niko when he can. The chariot, a tempting target, makes Tempus and Niko vulnerable. He wishes they had brought their mounts, unsure now that the chariot was a risk worth taking in this battle that is, for him, about saving twenty-three pairs of fighters – and about respect for the honored dead and the about-to-be dead.

Supported by Stepson cavalry, the surviving Thebans fight on, feet planted firmly on the earth. Theban past and future, ruined together, are ending together: enemies stream toward them, a constant onslaught; unstoppable, insurmountable.

Long spears, thunking into flesh. Men staggering backward, impaled, groaning. Innovation, all the difference today.

The Stepsons form up, trying to herd the pairs of Thebans to safety, toward the whirlwind on the banks of the river Cephissus. Their goddess Harmony rises up beside them, touches Thebans with her soft hand – and the remaining Thebans argue, in the midst of battle.

Now, despite all, so few of them will leave….

Tempus sees his own youngest Stepsons, callow youths with the fire of battle lust in their eyes, just blooded. Slashed and speared, youth gets up to throw itself again into the fray. Why? Always pushing their limits. Testing their courage. Judging their mettle. For the look in the eyes of their comrades. For the black stare in the eyes of their enemies once life has fled. *Don't stare too long in the eyes of the newly dead, young fighters, Thebans and my own.* Was this the right choice, or only one more horrific moment in the annals of wrong?

Tempus has his sword, god-given, and it glows with sanctification of his battle. He strikes whenever he can, leaning out, long and low, against this craven enemy who deserves no better than a slit belly, time to think about what was done while entrails slowly spill. But few come near this chariot. The arm-long blades on its axle, twisting and cutting everything as wheels spin fast, and his shortsword susurrusing, and his god-given speed make the chariot too costly a target, here and now. Long spear, thunking into flesh. Another man staggers backward, impaled, sobbing.

With hand-sign, he indicates to Niko where they need to go. Bleeding from arms and legs, kicking spearpoints and broken arrows and a few mangled limbs from the car, his Stepson passes on those orders.

Now the portal to another place is open for the Sacred Bands and his men are closing ranks. They'd drilled this twenty, fifty times. Straton has the ghost horse, impervious to all, and guards the portal with the bay who can't die or bleed, and who takes exception to anything and all that might harm its rider. It would be easier, from the look of it (because there was no talking in the dying and wailing and clatter of weapons and prayers called out to heaven from so many throats) to rid the field of enemies than to get those Thebans to break their ranks – even for salvation.

So be it: who would come, would come. He gave the signal. And Critias, with a flash of contorted face and devotion to duty beyond what any could ask, was trying to reason with the remnants of the Sacred Band of Thebes. There are so few Thebans left alive (fathers and sons, paired brothers and lovers and friends). So many more dead: such a muddle of still flesh and blood, with that forgotten look that bodies have when life has fled. One with so many arrows in him he looks like a porcupine. One man's head, detached, wears a wistful look as it stares at the sky.

Tempus sees a few men go through the portal into safety, into a shimmering in the whirlwind that swallows men and horses whole.

He sees the Theban Sacred Banders ceded him by providence: honest men, principled and brave beyond need and even what the gods require. *Maat* and justice allow only so much. Only so many favors can be had from the all-knowing gods. He couldn't save them all, or history itself would be embattled. He had a few. He and Enlil had wheedled a few from the pitiless Fates, a bit of mercy from the heavens. It must be enough.

He caught Crit's imploring gaze, nodded, stretched out his arm and pointed: and took a spear in the chest that Niko hadn't seen coming. Dark, and deep pain. Long spear, thunking into flesh. Man staggering backward, impaled. This spear goes where it can do the most harm, aimed by an arm and an eye that knows just where to strike and how to strike. It touches his heart. He feels the cold. Then, despite his god-given speed and Enlil's grace, strength is fleeing. Nikodemos pushes him down into the car and stands over him, grabbing the reins and his sword before he drops it.

*So, god of war and bloodbath, where art Thou today? Whose side do You fight on, Lord Storm? On the side of might or on the side of right?* For both sides were on the battleplain this day. And the god, rustling inside him, doesn't say a word, but looks, and looks, and at length makes clouds to darken the day and to take him away, and his away….

Red and black cover him, and a deeper, more abiding cold.

*

When he woke, when consciousness rushed back in a blinding flash, it was as they pulled the spearhead out. "Where?" he croaked, gritting it to mask his pain.

"Safe. Rest, Riddler," he heard. Niko's voice was very low.

"How many lost? And found?" he wanted to know, asking questions of the grainy dark. He would heal. He always did.

"None lost of ours…yet. Found, of theirs…enough." Stealth, called Nikodemos, has iron in his voice. Tempus would be protected, better shielded from whatever the Stepson thought threatening, if love could heal and save.

"We have to go back, do their rites," Tempus croaked. He had made a solemn promise. His word is binding. He tried to sit up, fell back. Weakness was unaccustomed. Strange, because the god was in him, yet – just a rustling, but truly there.

"Riddler, it's taken care of. Rest awhile." He heard Critias, near at hand, who always handled everything thrown at him.

"Make a light."

"It's not dark in here, Riddler. Bright as the god's eye," Straton said, with an empathy that chilled him. They were all using his war name, when the danger should be past.

*"Ace, keep shut,"* Niko whispered urgently to Straton.

"Why can't I see?"

"Commander, we don't know," Stealth said. "It will pass."

Where and how his fighters were, his right-side partner's tone said, was not his problem – not just now.

## *Chapter 3: Blink of the God's Eye*

A man as angry as Nikodemos was, in the aftermath of the Theban rescue gone awry, didn't belong among the civilized. And the island of Lemuria was the most civilized place Niko had ever been: a city-state with towering citadel, power unchallengeable behind its sheer seaside walls. Nikodemos was a secular adept of the Bandaran mystery of *maat* – of transcendent perception, equilibrium and mystic calm. He was failing himself and all *maat's* precepts if he lost control of his temper, of his balance or his heart.

So once back safe, if not sound, on New Year's Day in Lemuria, he quietly ordered the Sacred Band of Stepsons and the new Theban Sacred Band, all twenty-three pairs, to make ready for an unspecified sortie as soon as they were fit to fight. Seeing hell in his eyes and muscles jump in his angular jaw, his flesh wounds unbandaged and scabbing up willy-nilly, Stepsons went scurrying through the whitewashed barracks and the town below, preparing for they knew not what. Meanwhile, Niko chased after his temper, trying to get it under control. But he couldn't catch it. There was too much unrest in his soul.

Now nearly all knew he was planning a mission. He didn't tell them where. But Crit knew where, had to know.

And Straton knew. Soon Cime the Free Agent, the Riddler's woman who ruled as "Evening Star" in timeless Lemuria, must be told that he was taking the Sacred Band to Sanctuary.

This was the foray the Riddler intended, after all. When Niko had briefed Critias and Straton, they'd stared at him in disbelief. But they would implement his orders. He was the Riddler's right-side partner; his word bound the Band like law while their commander lay abed.

Ignoring deeper wounds (his own, his seasoned fighters') that needed tending, he called the three youngest Stepsons out of their barracks and told them they were lucky to be alive, dressing them down savagely for not holding steady in the ranks. Their eyes, wide and shocky; their faces, cut and bruised; their hands, trembling, told him they'd learned something on the Chaeronean battleplain. What they'd learned was nowhere near enough. These three Bandaran- trained youths were his responsibility; he couldn't leave them to their own devices. He'd sponsored them, first on Bandara with the secular adepts, and now in Tempus's Sacred Band.

So he got his best horse and he drilled the trainees on the practice field until the sun set, and had the veteran, Gayle, take over from him then. "All night long," he told his broad and sturdy Stepson, once a 3rd Commando fighter and among his most studied masters of the crueler arts. "Until they drop in their tracks. And tomorrow, all day long. I want them disciplined."

And he left, wishing he could find something to hack to pieces.

Then he had to face the Riddler's woman up at Pinnacle House in that uncanny palace of hers, with indoor trees and arcane windows to take you anywhere in the blink of a god's eye. Up he went as the sun was setting, a supplicant on a pilgrimage, seeking absolution in that vast and vaulted hall of glass and stone where multicolored streamers hung from rafters, tattered standards from forgotten wars.

His own cowardice shamed him. He should have come here sooner. Cime would have all their hides for bedspreads. But Stealth, called Nikodemos, had a rage in him so deep he'd spent years in the misty isles of Bandara trying to tame it. Now it was loose, anger aimed at the gods themselves. He'd had to wait until he could trust himself with Cime: they never were easy with each other. She'd almost seduced him once. He couldn't trust her. Her relations with his left-side leader were beyond his ken.

"I'm here to see the Evening Star," he said when a jowly servant with black dogs on either side opened up the huge oak doors.

"Come in, Lord Nikodemos," the man bid him. They all knew he'd wed a princess, years ago, and was royalty in his own right – if he cared to return to the city at the edge of time. He didn't care if he ever went back there. Those were other days, other hurts that fed his anger; but none as deep as these, today.

How was he going to tell Cime how badly he'd failed, what a botch he'd made of this mission of mercy that Tempus had decreed?

Niko was led by the padding servant and the dogs through marble halls, all red and black and white, to her sanctum. Cime was the Riddler's sister, some said: a gray-eyed beauty, her black hair silvered, wearing silk and leather and a look on her diamond-shaped face as if she'd seen a ghost. Ageless, Cime was, as long as he'd known her; as they all were here, while in Lemuria's embrace. She seemed thirty. He'd heard she was far beyond three hundred years of age. She had a deeper beauty than mortals do, a fabled power, and a voice always full of seduction. Always.

Always, but not today. She knew at first glance that something was very wrong. Perhaps she sensed his misery. Or she'd heard whispers. She was braced and guarded.

"What is it, Niko?" Voice too sharp, edgy. She looked him up and down and found him wanting. Three huge black dogs milled around her feet; some said they changed to humans when she chose. "What happened?"

So he had to own to it. He squared his shoulders and sucked in a breath. As she came up close, he bowed his head to look into those gray eyes his commander loved so well. "We fouled up. I did. He got hurt. Badly, maybe. And the god…is not helping him today."

She said nothing, but ran full-tilt past him down the hall, like a sprite or a goddess bent on vengeance. She'd know where Niko would have put him.

He had to run after her. And he never caught her till they got to where the Riddler lay.

When they reached the Stepsons' billet, everyone was there who had no incapacitating wounds or pressing duties. Even a couple of Thebans waited (walking wounded in kirtles and mantles, hair shorn, alike as father and son, eyes so full of loss they barely noticed what they saw), helmets under their arms. Stepsons saw Cime, then Niko, come running and parted the crowd for them, squinting at them as if from a hundred miles away. No one talked. All stood back. It wasn't a good day, everybody knew.

He tried to guide Cime to the sickroom. She shook him off – a sharp, dismissive shrug. Inside, Strat and Crit sat on the Riddler's either side with a bucket full of bloody rags and murder in their eyes. Whitewashed walls seemed too close, the simple bed of his commander's office cell too hard.

Tempus just lay there, unseeing, a wound bubbling in his chest that should be mortal. But wasn't – yet. Niko clutches that hope like his dream-forged sword.

Cime pulled two rods down from her hair and it tumbled around her face. Even Niko stepped back involuntarily. All three Stepsons in this room know what those diamond rods can do: suck your soul, suck your life, and leave you empty, lost, or worse. What else they did was between her and the powers that she served.

"Well," Cime said, still at the foot of the Riddler's sick-bed, diamond rods in fists on either hip, "now you've done it, haven't you, all you fools? Tempus, can you hear me?"

"Life to you, Cime," said the Riddler from his bed, "and everlasting glory." He smiled his humorless kill-smile, just a tightening at the corners of his mouth.

The last thing Cime would do was acknowledge the Sacred Band greeting. "Get out of here, Stepsons. I'll see to him. You three have done quite enough today: all of you and your feckless, treacherous god."

And with that, she banished them. Niko hoped this banishment was not forever, but who could say?

The last thing he saw was Cime striding to the bed. The last thing he heard was Tempus's voice, rattling deep in his chest, saying, "Sister, don't bait the god today."

*

"So we're still going. Tomorrow. With the Riddler or without him," Niko told Critias and Straton, three days later, out by the bullpen where Stepsons worked their horses in the bright morning light. The sea wind was gentle; the sky was blue and clear; and nothing about this morning matched Niko's mood.

Crit kept silent, running a hand through his dark, feathery hair, never looking up. He had a bandage on his right forearm and one on his right thigh, both spotted with red and pink, stiff and yellow toward the edges.

Strat replied, "Whatever you say, Stealth." Taciturn, stolid Strat, with his wide forehead scabbed up into his sandy hair, spread his scraped hands and dropped them to his sides. His left eye was swollen half shut; his left cheek lacerated, bruised: fresh souvenirs from Chaeronea. On his arms, deep cuts were healing, flushed and angry, covered with grease. Straton, nearly Tempus's size, still had a bad left shoulder from Sanctuary duty, long ago and far away. These new war wounds were insignificant compared to what Strat, the Stepsons' interrogator, had suffered at the hands of a necromant in Sanctuary ten years past. The witch haunted Straton yet.

Niko knew that was bothering Crit, who still hadn't said a word. Critias didn't want Strat going back to Sanctuary, not while the witch lived there. But only Tempus could rescind Niko's order, and Cime wouldn't let any of the Stepsons see the Riddler.

Niko told Straton, "Ace, bring those three Bandaran trainees to me, and the senior Theban after I'm done with them." Niko needed to talk to Crit in private, without Straton there. Strat left, glancing back once over his damaged shoulder at the two of them.

Beyond Crit, in the circular bullpen, was Sync, rangy and dark, working one of the black sons of Tempus's gray Trôs stallion. The colt bucked and bugled to any mare near enough to hear. Several nickered back, from paddocks nearby. Critias looked up, pretending to judge the training. "Nice colt, Stealth. Yours, isn't he?"

Niko said to Critias, "Take him, Fox. He's yours." It couldn't matter less today, although colts of the Band's senior stallion were highly prized. What mattered was the Riddler. What mattered was Crit's partner, Straton.

"I don't need him, Stealth," Crit said, his face carefully arranged, and turned to him. *Or anything from you.* Unsaid, but clear as the sky above.

"Then don't take him. Doesn't matter." What mattered was that all three of them were using war names among themselves, a sign of tensions high and aggression reined tight. "What are we going to do about Ace?" Niko asked. "That witch of his in Sanctuary might be more than we can handle." Niko knew all about witches, and witchery, and the compulsion in your soul you couldn't fight.

"He says she'll be no problem. He wants to go." Crit's eyes slapped him across the face. "Not a smart move, this mission. Not now, for any of us." He came one step closer.

"It's Tempus's mission, not mine. What he wanted."

"Not if he can't...go." Crit was Tempus's executive officer. He had the rank, if he pulled it, to make a schism out of this. "Why go now? To help that god-sired brat, Kouras, cage his temper? So Arton can meet his mommy? So Sham, the wizard-boy, can have an outing? To teach the remnants of the Theban Sacred Band how to get along without their brothers? That lot is grieving so, it will take more than new horses and new tactics to heal them. And it'll take longer than I want to stay at the world's anus to wet-nurse them."

"We go where the commander says we go. We do what he wants done."

The colt hit the boards with his hooves and charged Sync, in the middle of the pen. A whip cracked. The colt surrendered, stopped, and went back to the rail, ears pinned, eyes rolling.

"Who knows what he wants today? Not you. Not me. He's not seeing anyone. Strat doesn't need this trip. Neither do I. Somebody's got to stay here with the Riddler – if *she'll* let us near him." Now Crit took two more steps toward Niko and jabbed a finger at his chest. "*You* should stay." The finger withdrew, but Critias was too full of truth to stop. "This is your mess. Running away won't solve it."

Niko took a deep breath and grabbed his temper. "If you'll have them ready to travel, two days hence, we'll leave," he said. *If:* a small opening for compromise, an acknowledgement of rank necessary with this man, who was protective of his partner, Strat – and everything else teetering on the edge of oblivion here. None of them had ever seen the Riddler take so long to heal, if heal he would.

Damn the Theban Sacred Band and all it had cost them. But Niko had command, and command must not be wasted, not spent foolishly, nor respect and camaraderie lost in anger. Niko's mouth was full of barbs. "I'm going to take those Bandaran-trained boys." Crit would never understand Bandaran stricture. Or care. "And the Thebans, and the best Stepsons who'll sojourn. And leave some in Sanctuary a year or two, if I can. Come with me, or stay behind. This is no time to argue."

Now it was out, open discord.

Crit said, "*Time?* Stealth, you haven't even had *time* to look in on your own wounded Stepsons. What would the Riddler say to that?" then turned on his heel and walked away, his long stride giving Niko no chance to stop him unless he wanted to run after Crit like a penitent child.

Too much anger. Too much helplessness. Too much grief. Niko couldn't bring himself to meet with the Thebans yet. He knew he should, but he couldn't face the ghosts in their eyes. So Crit had had to do it. If Tempus didn't recover, then what? The Sacred Band would be at Cime's mercy. They served at

Tempus's pleasure. All this talk of Niko being Tempus's inheritor was only that…talk.

He went to see his sable mare. Then, on foot, he fled the walled citadel and went down to the shore, through the town where nothing ever had been wrong before, where people lived happy lives free from want and the worst thing that ever happened was a bar fight among Stepsons or moldy hay coming in from surrounding farms.

Tempus and he had brought horses down here to work them in the surf on better days. He was too angry even to think, too taut and regretful to bring the mare. He might make another mistake. The mistake he had made was a worse error than he'd ever thought a man could survive.

Would the Riddler live? See again? Walk again? Lead again? None of them could get in to visit, to find out.

Niko's fury, at himself and the gods, was driving him, he knew, as it had driven him for so long before he'd joined the Stepsons. He'd lost one partner soon after, then a second. He couldn't lose another. Tempus was supposed to be eternal. At least, everyone said he was. Had they so angered the gods, trying to save the Thebans, the fated dead, that Tempus would be taken from them?

Niko walked knee-deep into the surf as if the tide could cool his anger. Long ago, his rage had driven him to *maat*, his discipline of will and equilibrium, justice and balance, and those had driven him on, to the Sacred Band and the Riddler's service, where he was – finally and correctly, he thought – Tempus's right-side partner, learning day by day what his commander had to teach. He was, at long last and great cost, an avatar of Enlil on his own. With the Riddler hurt, his anger was nearly ungovernable.

*Long spear, thunking into flesh. Man staggering backward, impaled, groaning.*

He whispered to the surf, "Help me help him." Only pounding waves answered.

Thebans. These unlucky Thebans were bringing their fate home to roost here, looking dazed and amputated, full of silent grief for their lost brothers and the entire world they'd known. *Better off than dead.* He would take them to Sanctuary, the most luckless town he'd ever seen. They would fit right in there.

And he and Straton, Tempus's two witch-cursed Stepsons, would face their fears – or their doom. It didn't seem to matter. *Greater dooms win greater destinies.* This, his commander had taught him.

The next day, after Niko had gone to Cime, helmet in hand, begging assistance and pleading for mercy, apologizing until he thought his heart would break, she relented and let him see the Riddler.

*

Not long after that, Niko rode beside Tempus as the commander, still healing, led his Sacred Band of Stepsons on their best horses into Lemuria's mystic portal. And out again, to emerge – by dint of Cime's Lemurian power – right onto Sanctuary's northwest shore, with every boy-soldier and Theban bringing up the rear, just as the Riddler had planned.

Once Tempus's vision returned, by Enlil's grace, the Evening Star couldn't interfere with the commander's wishes. Niko sympathized. No one could.

Steady drizzle falls. The sky above is restless with scudding clouds. A furious storm masses behind them, out to sea, throwing black spears of rain down from heaven's walls. Dark waves flee inland, surly, breaking on the beach.

Riding toward the ochre walls of Sanctuary on his sable mare, with the Riddler beside him on his gray Trôs horse, Niko catches Tempus's eye.

Tempus stares back, baring his teeth: "Enlil rides with us, Niko. Every step of the way."

Wet wind blows like the breath of the gods on Niko's neck. Rain falls harder. Thunder cracks as distant lightning skewers the sea.

Since the storm is coming near, and his commander sitting easily on his horse, Niko doesn't doubt the Riddler's word. Enlil, ancient storm god of the armies, is with them; and Vashanka, the local storm god; and Niko's *maat*. And perhaps even the Theban goddess, Harmony, daughter of Ares and Aphrodite. Good. They will need every man and god and skill among them in this hellhole. Even his sable mare knows it. She raises her head and challenges the heavens as they jog along, the Stepsons two by two, Crit and Strat close behind: sixty-six fighters, all told, come into the city-state of Sanctuary through the Gate of Justice. *Maat* is justice, as well as balance. In all the years he'd served here, Niko had never ridden through this gate. Maybe it will be lucky for them this time, with a child of Sanctuary's storm god, a warlock's son, a seer and all the saved Sacred Band of Thebes in tow. But Niko isn't counting on it.

## *Chapter 4: Two Gods Storming*

Drought has clutched Sanctuary in her withering hand, year after year. Now comes the storm, its squalls howling off the sea, whipping the waves high, swamping boats and rocking the ships of Sanctuary's young navy so seamen rush to weigh anchor and ride out the gale as best they may.

Parched earth and fields cracked open from drought can't absorb all this rain, where ground has turned so hard that horses' coffin bones bruise year-round and a body needs an axe to dig a hole. The runoff steals topsoil from the fields and moves it, silting creeks, turning ponds into lakes and crops into waste. Pastures flood and granaries give up their stores to the ruin of salt and water. When the storm passes, then clean-up will begin: broken trees and wrecked wagons can be dragged from roads, roofs repaired, wells cleaned of drowned rat and cat. *If* the storm ever stops. *If* the fierce gale abates. *If* the sun comes back in the gray-black sky and the gray-black sea stops churning up its contents to strew the shore with sea wrack and jellyfish and sharks and whales and worse.

*If.*

Around walled Sanctuary, the storm swells the White and Red Foal rivers till they burst their banks and lap against cellar, step and statue. The seaborne storm soughs and blows and whistles and sings its salty song, so that those old enough to remember wizard weather take shelter in their attics, digging out old, half-forgotten warding charms.

But this storm is no wizard's work, some say, for no charm or ward forfends it. Sixty-six Stepsons have come riding into Sanctuary, some say, bringing the storm and the wrath of the storm gods down upon them all. The gods are angry at Sanctuary, some say, for becoming too irreverent: a lesson must be taught.

All this time, the rain rains harder and the gale gusts fiercer. In the palace, a priest called Torch orders sandbags laid. Meanwhile, the oligarchic council tries the power of prayer and prays as it has never prayed before.

Down on Wideway and up past the docks, word of the Stepsons' coming spreads like the swelling tide of brackish water and people worry for their lives. Mothers hug their children tight and caution maiden daughters, while older women stare out their windows with dreamy eyes, remembering days gone by.

On the Street of Red Lanterns, at Amoli's Lily Garden and Phoebe's Inn, whores bolt their doors. At the Aphrodisia House, a harlot named Shawme, dreaming of heroes, peeks out her shutters but sees only the wild wind, swirling rain in arabesques as if invisible lovers dance amid the storm. The storm sees the girl and caresses her face, then moves on.

In the Bazaar where the city-guard captain, Walegrin, has taken down a soggy awning from outside his sister's shop, a blousy S'danzo seeress named Illyra reads her cards. She looks up at her big brother and says, "Arton is coming. My boy is coming home," but she is not smiling, not in the face of this awful storm.

Walegrin, soaked to his sandy braids and needing to get back out there among his men, says, "What else, Illyra? I know that look."

"Death, reversed. A son of the storm god. A son of sorcery. A son of fate. The Three of Swords, reversed." Hoops shiver madly in her ears as she lunges toward her brother, grabbing him tight. "Don't go back out there tonight, Walegrin. Don't."

Nevertheless, the city guard's captain goes back to his garrison, hoping that someday his sister (who'd lost two children and adopted a third) would mend. Fortunetelling was a poor living where magic didn't work. The storm sees the soldier at his duty where guardsmen heft sandbags to stem the tide and goes another way, whistling.

Meanwhile at the mercenary hostel north of town, in its common room where dusty weapons from bygone wars hang on rufous walls, sixty-six fighters make themselves at home, filling bowls from the sideboard with possets of curdled milk and wine and honey while Straton works out stabling and the order of the watch.

"We'll get it, the three of us, whatever stuff you want, sir," says Shamshi, the boldest and oldest of the young guard, to Straton, who has assignments to make from his customary corner table.

It's crowded in the common room. Strat hasn't seen it like this since recruitment for the war on Wizardwall was under way. Today, it was crowded with men of his. There weren't half a dozen other mercenaries here when the Stepsons had arrived, just the eye-patched guildhall master and a cook to see to things. Somehow they were managing to find a bed for every man and a stall for every horse. Now Strat was sending out the seasoned pairs to help with bulwarks, road-clearing, and general citizen-saving in the storm.

"Shamshi, take this list, then, and Arton and Gyskouras, and this…." Strat pulled a fat purse from under his woolen chlamys. "Bring back what you can. And mind those horses, in the rain. The Riddler will have your guts for bowstrings if you lame one." Fair-haired Shamshi was already backing away, a flush in his cheeks, head down, wizard-gray eyes on his feet, as if the young Stepson were bowing his way out of an audience with a king. "And come right back."

No chance of that, a fool would know. Strat stripped off his chlamys and flung it on a bench. Niko was out at the old Stepsons' barracks, assessing the stabling: eighty stalls comprised the stables – four barns for twenty horses each: two in line, parallel to the front gates; one perpendicular on either side. Plenty of work, to refurbish those. Crit was managing a hundred things, as Crit was wont to do. Straton was keeping watch over the Thebans (who'd roached their hair in mourning and wandered about, dazed, wounded and bruised, holding on to one another). The split in his scalp itched, where a curved shortsword had cleaved his helmet and kissed him deep. *Long spears, thunking into flesh. Men staggering backward, impaled, moaning.*

And, of course, Strat was watching over the man upstairs. The Riddler was holed up in his old corner room, resting. What did it mean? The commander never slept, could work every man of them into the grave. Or could once.

Was there something, as Niko and Crit thought, unlucky about the Thebans? Did the Fates, who predestined all men's lives, take offense at saving these? But this storm was a consecration, wasn't it, of their mission? Straton read it so. The guildhall master said they'd broken the drought here, riding in with two storm gods squalling in the Stepsons' wake. There'd been a *long* drought here. The Sanctuarites should be happy with the rain the storm gods brought. Maybe they would be, when the emergency relief crews got done.

No use wondering, with so much left to do. The storm-lashing this little city was taking was just a portion of its due, to Straton's way of thinking. And the omen of storm was always the best of signs for Tempus and his Stepsons, a sanctification of this, or any, foray. If you are a man of the Riddler's, in good standing with the Sacred Band of Stepsons, any storm is bound to clear your way.

Or at least Strat hoped so, because he'd just sent Sync and Gayle down by the White Foal Bridge, where Crit had made Straton promise, under any circumstances, *not* to go – where the necromant Ischade once kept a small, unassuming house; where Straton had gone too many evenings, ten years past. And where he went in his dreams, sometimes, still.

He rubs his left shoulder, twice arrow-shot, never right but not too bad today; his scalp wound plagues him worse, scabs pulling on his hair. Sync and Gayle would see to that house, and any in it, to rescuing anyone who needed help down where the White Foal River found the restless dead another home. Although the witch who lived in his dreams needed no man's help, and never would.

He decided he'd go see his ghost horse in the stable out back, the ghost horse *she* gave him. The ghost horse needed to know that they weren't going back down there.

Not this time.

## *Chapter 5: Stepsons and Mothers*

The summer storm was easing up – not stopping yet but not boxing your ears or slashing you across the face or snatching the breath from your nostrils – when Arton finally convinced Gyskouras and Shamshi to cut through the Bazaar.

"Over here. This way," Arton urged the other two trainees, guiding his horse around the wreckage of a produce stall. Some daylight remained, even if the light had that pearly quality of supernal tantrums abating. The sky, no longer boiling like a stewpot, was just a featureless mass of wall cloud. This was as he had foreseen it.

*Time to find my mother.*

All had unfolded in accord with his foreknowledge. They had money and horses. They were away from the senior staff, young Stepsons loose on the town. After facing so much death on the Chaeronean battleplain, Arton needed to know if his foresight was right: if his mother was still alive. War seared its specter into your memory. Doubled the beat of your heart. Humbled you because it would take you if it could. Living had become very important, the only thing that mattered. His blackened eye; his scored cheek; his left forearm and hand, blistered from hefting his wicker-framed bronze shield: none of these mattered. The bragging rights he'd so wanted didn't matter. Breathing mattered.

The battle had shaken all three of them. Life seemed so fragile, each Sacred Band fighter so vulnerable. They were being as brave as they could manage to be.

Gyskouras, called 'Kouras' by his friends, sidled his chestnut horse close to Arton's bay. Red-haired, green-eyed Gyskouras, chin attempting a beard, was Arton's childhood friend. They'd gone to Bandara together and now were Stepsons together. Kouras was the son of the storm god Vashanka and a temple dancer, so everyone said.

Arton wasn't anything special in Bandaran terms or in any other terms: he could part the veil, sometimes; see the future, a little; but often didn't understand what he saw in time for it to do much good. He hadn't foreseen how terrifying the Chaeronean battleplain would be. *Long spears, thunking into flesh. Men stagger backward, impaled, crying.* Arton had a hawkish nose, sharp chin, dark hair, and eyes that gave him a predatory look: from this, his war name, 'Hawk,' had come. But not his foresight, nor Kouras's god-blood, nor Shamshi's warlock lineage seemed protection enough after Chaeronea.

"Is this it, Hawk?" Kouras said under his breath. Kouras had taken a cut on his neck where an arrow grazed him, a spear wound on his hip, and a long slice down his arm from a sword's bite. But Kouras healed like lightning: you could hardly see angry flesh around his scabs, today.

"It? I think so," Arton replied, softer than his horse's complaint when it couldn't grab an apple from among the leaves and casks and kegs and crates littering the street.

Where the street widened, Shamshi brought his horse up to theirs; rain dripped off his helmet. Sham, of all three, had taken the worst wounds on the battlefield, but no arrow through his thigh or long gash on his shoulder fazed him; the spear that should have ripped apart his lung was somehow turned aside by armor; it was as if he felt no pain from any wound he took.

Now they were riding three abreast through fabled Sanctuary, boys in Stepsons' clothing with weapons on their hips.

"Is *what* 'it?' You think *what's* so, Arton?" Sham snapped. Sham was still angry and defensive about misbehaving in the ranks, earning all three of them two days and nights of punitive drill.

Shamshi was handsome, with pale hair and the body of a man, not a youth. On Bandara, Sham had mastered several mysteries and was said to have the makings of a formidable adept. Sharp, careful, always wanting to lead, was Sham. But Arton didn't trust Sham. And Sham trusted only himself. "Well, Arton? Speak *up,*" Sham demanded. "Are you lost? This street isn't on Straton's list."

"We're going to find Arton's mother now," Kouras announced, using that 'son of the god' voice that made his wispy beard immaterial. Sham wouldn't argue with Kouras, not directly. Kouras had a berserker streak when aroused. The wall cloud above pulsed bright. Twice.

"Well…so *be* it," Sham retorted. "Just make sure Stealth hears that I'm saying, here and now, it's not on our list and if we weren't ordered to stick together, I wouldn't be doing this."

"Noted. For the record," Kouras said, a veiled rebuke.

*For the record in eternity of what we do and what we say, that never can be altered:* Bandaran protocol. "For the balance of the thing," Arton chimed in, completing the ritual statement. He didn't add that in his premonition Sham was with them when he found his mother, therefore Sham must come along.

And then they were there: at the S'danzo seeress's shop – where Arton's life and his destiny had begun. The shop matched his vision: small and somewhat drab, a bit poor with rot in its wooden steps. Only the awning out front was missing. The awning should be there.... Arton slipped off his bay; Kouras got off his chestnut. They tied their horses to a hitching post by the steps.

Sham didn't dismount. He eyed the fortuneteller's sign. Straddling the blue roan, he scowled down at them, his swordsman's shoulders squared and his helmeted head cocked: "You're going to use the Stepsons' money? *For this?* Get your fortune told?" Sham was contrary by nature. "Stealth will drill us till we can't see straight. I want no part of this...." The roan began backing up, obedient to his shifting weight and one soft cluck, a touch of rein.

Kouras said, "You'll come or be damned, Sham." Thunder rumbled.

Arton shivered. It was never good when Kouras talked like that, cursed like that: son of the storm god. Lightning flickered on the other side of town. Rain spattered down Kouras's face, off his arms, glistening like oil poured out for the gods. No one knew if Gyskouras's curses were merely talk. Or more. Arton shivered again.

Shamshi grumbled under his breath, dismounting from the roan's off side. How much older was Sham? Four years? Five? Kouras was nearly as tall, but heavier-made, with big bones that belied a natural grace. Arton was slighter, compact: just a peasant boy who'd gotten into Bandara and then the Stepsons on a fluke and Kouras's coattails.

"In we go, then, God Child. And let it be on your head," Sham teased harshly.

Kouras looked away, into the blowing rain, muscles ticcing on his fuzzy jaw.

The threesome climbed up the steps, Arton in the lead. Arton knocked. Knocked again. A little brass peephole opened. It closed. Someone muttered behind the pine door. Then the door creaked open like a sepulcher.

A woman stood there. Was this she? What did they look like to her? Three young wet Stepsons on the prowl, weapons at the ready. Belatedly, Arton wished he'd worn his helmet, like the other boys: in it, he looked more impressive than he was. But it hurt his bruises and it was full of rainwater, hanging upside down from his horse's saddle.

"Yes?" said the woman. She made his heart beat fast, so beautiful was she, all bright colors and deep soft eyes, curly hair and long circles of gold in each ear, buxom and young and…. Arton blinked and a matron, tired, swollen-eyed, with mud on her skirt, stood there. But the gold circles hanging from her ears were the same. She peered at him. "Are you coming in, soldiers? We're not really scrying today, but I can…will…."

Arton said, "We want to see the seeress."

Kouras said, "Are you the S'danzo, Illyra?"

Sham said, "Can we get this over with? Come in out of the rain? This scruffy fellow here might be your son, Arton – if you're Illyra."

The woman said, "Yes. Oh. Well. Do come in, then," as if sons showed up on her doorstep every day.

Then she fainted into Arton's arms.

## *Chapter 6: Breath of the Gods*

On the Chaeronean battleplain, the remnants of the Sacred Band of Thebes saw the spear impale Tempus. They saw him fall. Yet now he lives.

*Wanting neither too much to live nor too much to die.* Tough talk. The Thebans were not so tough now, in Sanctuary, ripped away from all they'd known and all they'd cherished but life itself and one another.

As he rode his dappled Trôs horse south along the White Foal through summer streets, blessedly alone on this warm gray morning, Tempus knew he'd been right to do it: to bring his new Sacred Banders here where everything was always wrong, where venal fools played at small men's games and battles even smaller.

Sanctuary is changed, a mere decade's difference, nothing very daunting to a man who's seen centuries come and go. The streets wind the same way; people scrabbling for a living scramble now, as people always do, to reestablish normal life in a wild storm's wake.

The Sacred Band of Thebes needed Sanctuary, a place to acclimate and integrate with his Stepsons. Here they would learn new ways: burn their dead as Stepsons do; thank new gods; and meet new challenges where honor and glory are enough. They were his now, and would step up to even greater things: fight for life itself and everlasting freedom of the human spirit. But not yet. Like Sanctuary, throwing off the damage of the storm, they needed to put their backs into tomorrow, not cry for yesterday.

The Thebans must heal, to join with his greater Sacred Band. Damaged and wounded, ripped and sundered, they sojourned now in a strange new country. At least they were not in the country of the dead. They needed a place to live, to renew their pride, to forgive each other and their pain – not feel guilty that they'd kept the breath of the gods in their nostrils while their brothers had died. *Long spears, thunking into flesh. Men staggering backward, impaled, screaming.*

How had he thought he could do so much without an awful cost? '*Let me spare twenty-three pairs of yours destined for tomorrow's battleplain, and all my Sacred Band will stay and fight beside you, till the end. And I, myself. And mine. And what price there is for that, you and yours will not pay it.*' No matter, it was done. And this thieves' world couldn't care a whit where a man was from or what strange tongue he spoke or ways he had, as long as he was useful.

Drab and sullen Sanctuary would teach them much, toughen them up and grow them up while they learned to sing a different song. They were not in the beautiful hills of home now.

Tempus's horse knew the way to Aphrodisia House; the clip-clop of its long stride soothed him. Peepers chirped far off. When he got there, he'd invite Molin Torchholder to come and have a talk. Meeting Torchholder, the priest, at a brothel seemed fitting. The Street of Red Lanterns was full of debris, broken shops and shattered dreams and young men cleaning up in gangs, hoping for tips better than coppers from the madams. Niko would be unhappy, left behind, but Tempus was not a child to be tended. A wind blew in off the disgruntled sea, memory of the storm.

He wore shabby leather duty gear, helmet hanging from his saddle, nothing to identify him. Yet men scurried off and women grabbed their children: an armored, mounted mercenary in these streets should not be underestimated, even early in the day, before the taverns opened. And the Trôs under him was all warhorse, impossible to misconstrue.

Three city guardsmen, sweating in the muggy air, emerged from behind a wagon of sandbags. They barred his path, spread-legged across the whorehold's narrow street. One was big, heavy, with sandy war braids and a captain's badge on his shoulder. *Perfect*. "Need help, Citizen?" the city guard's captain, Walegrin, said.

Sanctuary was too curious, these days. But never mind. Tempus halted his horse. He let the city guard look him over, waiting for recognition to dawn in Walegrin's eyes.

Then it did: "I'll be damned and resurrected. Look what the storm blew in." Walegrin came two steps closer. "Is there a revolution set for Ilsday? An undead festival? Palace coup in the offing? The Prince/Governor's fled to Ranke. Nobody's here but the oligarchs and us simple folk. What could the likes of you want here?" Flashing a cautionary hand-sign to the two men flanking him, both brashly fingering their hilts, Walegrin took one more step toward Tempus.

The Trôs pinned its ears, bunching its muscles under him, ready to spring forward at a touch of leg. He patted its dappled shoulder. "Good to see you too, Walegrin. Ask Torch to meet me in Aphrodisia House. At your soonest pleasure. And come yourself, if you wish." He signaled his horse to walk on. It snapped at Walegrin as it came abreast. The soldier backed off. The horse walked by.

Everything on the street was fraught with menace that could yet turn deadly. His back crawled, riding away from the city guard toward the whorehouse of his choice. These locals were up to their necks in muck-pits overflowing and looters and every kind of fool out to take advantage in the storm's wake.

But no arrows chased him, only the occasional dog. He drop-tied the Trôs horse outside Aphrodisia House, rather than ride it up the stairs as he fleetingly, rebelliously, so wanted to do. Thieves' paradise or not, a fool trying to steal that horse would find he had hell by the reins.

Inside, the fleshy Madam Myrtis took one look at him, blinked, and then primped herself in his path, all powdered breasts, perfume and musk. "It's too early, sir, for my girls…." She stared. Put her hand to her throat. Her whole faced jiggled and she said, "But for you, of course…whatever you require...." Whispers on the upstairs landing: young girls and boys peeking between the balusters, giggling, hands over their mouths.

"A quiet room to talk to a man or two." Rooms here were much safer than in the palace or any tavern in town. He was trembling, an unexpected wash of weakness. His chest hurt; muscles spasmed across his breast. *Damn the gods and their games.*

Myrtis took him to a room that smelled of smoke with a round table and six chairs and left him without another word. He sat heavily, Cime's voice ringing in his ears: "*How could you let this happen, Tempus? How could these Thebans be worth so much? Oh, gods, what have they done to you? What are we going to do now?*" He had never heard her so frightened, not in all their centuries. But once he'd nearly lost her, and he recalled how he'd felt then: to be the one who must find a way where there was none, to save your beloved from certain death; to save your future; to buy another day, or ten, or a thousand, from the ruthless Fates. Even though he couldn't see her face, she'd made him feel profligate, an utter fool.

The wound in his chest hurts so much now that his heart is threatening to stop. Again.

He puts his head in both his hands, elbows on the table, and just breathes. *God, leave off. Take me or don't, but be done with Your anger and this game.* He thinks he knows what Enlil wants, but he has preparations yet to make. And the god is not talking to him today.

Some thousand beats of blood in his ears later, the door opened. "Torch," he said.

"Don't get up," said Molin Torchholder, the priest who was half Nisi warlock, and swished to a seat in a commotion of robes.

"I wasn't going to."

Behind Torchholder, the blond city-guard captain took up a position outside the open door. "Close that." Torch motioned and the door swung shut. "What is this, Tempus? To what do we owe the pleasure, after so very long?" A decade of age and line and spotted skin on Torch's face reminded Tempus of just how long.

"I want to buy or lease the old Stepsons' barracks. I'll be billeting sixty to a hundred fighters here, as in times gone by. You can hire them, or others will." He sat back, praying his body would cooperate, crossing his arms over his chest. Under his chiton and his leather armor, it feels as if the wound is seeping. What if blood leaks out, runs down his leg, onto the chair, the floor, for anyone to see?

"Meaning we're going to need you – and yours?"

"Meaning someone will. So say the gods. You might, if we can agree a price."

So they haggled: Torchholder set a price for Tempus's purchase of the barracks and the hundred surrounding acres; Tempus set a price for the hire of the Band by the month and year and a statement of work listing responsibilities for stability operations.

Costs were argued, apportioned. The Band would augment the city guard as necessary but manage its own missions; be on call to discharge Sanctuary's ground-based military treaty responsibilities and defend the city-state in emergencies. Expeditionary warfare and countering magic or sorcerous incursions were agreed to be outside the scope of work. The palace would provide funding, logistical support, materiel and equipment; the Band would provide strategic planning, personnel and implementation for crisis management as well as peacekeeping, including site security for public events on a cost-plus basis. Tactics, techniques and procedures were left to the discretion of the Sacred Band.

When water had been brought and they had all but come to terms, there was a disturbance outside. And then that disturbance was inside, under wraps:

"Niko, join us. Torch, you remember Stealth, my right-side partner." Nikodemos came to stand by Tempus, behind his seat, only a brush of his hand on the Riddler's shoulder and his empty eyes showing his temper.

The palace priest, who had been Sanctuary's actual ruler for so long, looked up at Nikodemos and shook his head, a tiny movement. "Now I believe it, that you've brought that whole accursed Sacred Band of yours. You know magic is in decline here, these days. No troubles with witches or warlocks. No work for this...kind...of fighter."

"This is not the old Band, or at least not all. Be gentle with my new fighters, Torch. For your city's sake and your own."

"I think we have an agreement, Tempus. Your hire's set," said the priest.

*There's the breath of the gods on these dice. Go carefully, Molin.* "Fine, the deal's done. Torch, you'll be happy to know that your storm god Vashanka has returned, within his son, Gyskouras – your scheme, fulfilled. Let's hope the god and youth find you pleasing in their sight." Torchholder had arranged the god's ritual rape of a temple dancer, years ago: Gyskouras was the issue of that mating. "And the youth is with my Sacred Band."

"Oh?" said the priest. "*Oh.* I see."

"Riddler," said Niko at the same moment in a whisper, "I need to speak with you."

"We're finished here," said Tempus. And they were.

Outside, Niko's sable mare, tied to the post, had her tail over her back, winking lewdly at his Trôs and nickering come-hither propositions. This was a whorehouse, after all. If those two horses had been any closer or poorly trained, there'd have been a breeding in the street. Tempus climbed up on the Trôs and had to remind it of its job. His chest felt better; he hadn't left a trail of blood behind; at least the god had spared him that humiliation.

"Commander, there's a problem with the trainees."

"Then put it right, Niko." Stealth was sheepish, coming after him and finding nothing wrong. "We're moving out to the old Stepsons' barracks in the morning. Send Sync and Gayle out to see what else we'll need to do there."

"This will be the third time we've moved in there," Nikodemos reminded him, eyes searching: judging how he rode, watching where they went, and not daring to ask what he wanted to know – how Tempus was healing.

"It's better, every day," he told Niko without being asked. He hoped it was, this wound, which would have killed him if he'd been mortal. The god was never slow to heal his avatar unless he was very angry. "We need to deploy the Band, get those Thebans where they can do more than mourn their dead. Have a funerary rite of our own out there, so those who came away with us can say farewell to those who stayed behind."

For all the fated dead: maybe that would placate the angry gods. Maybe.

*

On the afternoon chosen for the funerary rites of remembrance, the sun blazed bright in a clear blue sky over the Stepsons' barracks, so familiar from former times. They could not have chosen a better day for this, Tempus thought. Although the Thebans will honor men whose bodies lie back in Chaeronea, this rite is necessary for the survivors: the grief of the living will go to heaven on the balefire.

Out in back of the training ground with its rail fence, where Stepsons drilled Theban Sacred Banders and each other, beyond the ancient amphitheater, all was nearly ready for the ceremony. Grass, so bright green it was nearly blue, gave its sweet-smelling thanks for the rain. On the hill, past the copse, the stone altar of the storm god was being prepared. Men labored around the pyre, others on the empty ceremonial bier – some briskly, some gingerly (those hurt or still dazed).

Three men were dragging a tree limb toward the altar to add to the pyre when one, a Stepson, dropped in his tracks. The Theban pair with him called out for help, gesticulating.

Men came running, shouting, crowding. When Tempus got there, pushing the curious aside, it was too late. One of his own Stepsons, half a Sacred Band pair, was dead: lying flat on his back; sightless eyes open, staring at the sky.

"What happened?" Tempus asks, bands of pain crushing his chest.

"My partner and I were right beside him, pulling this branch. He just sighed and crumpled. Died as he fell, probably," a Theban replies, nudging the nearby branch with a sandaled foot.

"Who are you?"

"Charon; and this is Lysis," says the older Theban, heavy-set and strong with a square jaw, motioning to the young partner at his side.

The youngster with him speaks up, quavering, as Stepsons and Thebans gather closer around the corpse and Crit shoulders through with Straton: "We didn't do anything to him. It's not our fault…."

Charon, the elder Theban, his hair shorn in mourning, is a man of at least forty. His partner is less than half his age, wild-eyed from the shock of unexpected loss heaped upon abiding grief: Inexplicable death: fortune's disfavor.

"All of mine stand back," Charon says. "Give these men room." The Thebans widen their circle, each staring at the sudden corpse.

Crit kneels down, runs his hands over the dead man's head.

Straton does the same. They whisper.

Crit cranes his neck. "Riddler, it's Deon, Ari's partner. He took a bad blow to the head, on the battleplain. You can feel the bump. Big as my elbow. It took a while to finish him, that's all."

*That's all.* Nearly all the greater Sacred Band is here now, silent and grave; Stepsons next to Thebans, united by the tragedy of Deon's body crumpled in the grass.

"We'll put him on the pyre," Niko murmurs, once he's shoved through the crowd and come up on Tempus's right.

"Ari's with the trainees, getting supplies. I'll send someone to get him." And even more quietly: "Our new Sacred Banders will see what happens when one of ours goes to heaven. 'What is common, we must do.'" Niko quotes what Tempus has taught him.

*Now we'll have Deon, a real body for our funerary pyre after all, not just memories of the absent dead.*

So it goes that way, when the pyre is all made, the fire lit, and every Theban has cast a lock of hair, a piece of gear, a favorite treasure, and said his goodbyes to absent friends before the flames roaring high in the dusk as if to touch the sunset sky.

Then Tempus steps up and says the words for his Stepson, Deon, with Deon's grief-stricken partner, Ari, by his side. Nikodemos stands by the two of them. Straton and Crit and all the friends of this departing member of his Sacred Band are there as well. Everyone repeats: "Joy to you, Stepson, and everlasting glory."

Into the middle of the fire, where the body lies, comes the shade of Abarsis, Slaughter Priest, and takes Deon in his arms. The spirit of the dead Stepson clings to Abarsis's neck.

While the Theban Sacred Band pairs are awe-struck and murmuring, Abarsis locks his eyes on Tempus and smiles a soft, sad smile. "Life to you, beloved Riddler," says the shade, "and everlasting glory." Abarsis looks from Tempus to Niko. "Tempus, Niko, it is hard to battle anger, for whatever it wants it pays from the soul. Let this fire consume your anger and make of it an offering to the god."

And the flames take two shades, Abarsis and Deon, to heaven.

As the pairs walk away in hushed silence to drink or game or prayer or duty, and the fire burns down and the stars come out, Nikodemos approaches Tempus where he consoles Ari, his grieving Stepson, and others wait their turn.

Tempus breaks away to join him. Some creature rustles in the grass and moves on, unseen.

"Commander, did Abarsis speak to you? I thought he did."

"He said, 'It is hard to battle anger, for whatever it wants it pays from the soul.' Did he not say it to you?" This warning from the Stepsons' patron shade is one of Tempus's own sayings, from his days as Herakleitos, before he left Ephesus; before the curse….

"He did. I just…wasn't sure I really heard it. Or that you heard it. Or that we both heard the same."

"The god still loves us, Niko. Gods and men honor those who have fought in battle." Although not the only way to interpret this visit from Abarsis, at least it is one way, the time-honored way.

Then they see the Theban, Charon, consoling all his friends, young and old (touching arms, squeezing shoulders, embracing the distraught), helping where he can as tears finally flow freely, now that the remnants of this band of brothers have time to grieve among their own. Forty-six fighters, mourning their two hundred and fifty-four lost heroes: it's critically important that the survivors not lose heart.

*In change is rest.*

As he had thought it long ago, he thinks it again. Perhaps healing can begin now. They have seen Tempus, alive and 'well' among them, a miracle in their terms. They have seen the shade who loves the Stepsons take a soul to heaven.

Now, if the gods allow, his Thebans can start to mend, and rejoin the living.

## *Chapter 7: Dreams of Gods and Glory*

*Long spear, thunking into flesh. Man staggering backward, impaled, groaning.*

Niko is sweating when he wakes in his bed in sopping sheets, as tangled as his dream of the battleplain. *It is hard to battle anger, for whatever it wants, it pays from the soul,* said Abarsis from the flames. Whenever Abarsis appears, Niko has strange dreams. Niko is never at ease with dreams, stays as far as he can from the dream lord's realm. Now Abarsis has come and chastised him – and the Riddler – for their anger. Niko was, is, and always will be a weapon of the god, nothing more. But he dreams about Chaeronea too much.

Enough. He picks at the scabs on his arms, reminders from the battle; first absently, then roughly; then pulls them off altogether: let's start anew.

He gets out his summer duty gear: worn linen and leather armor bossed with bronze; soft low boots; his belt with knife, throwing stars and service sword; helmet and shield. Stored nearby in another trunk are the cuirass, sword, shield, helm and dirk given him by Aškelon, regent of the seventh sphere, entelechy of dreams. The dream-forged panoply is far too much weaponry for Sanctuary, at least today.

The trainees must be dealt with, soon. And the Thebans. Time to unite the Sacred Band – Thebans with his people: one unit, one heart, one swing through life. As he'd promised the Riddler they would do.

Crit is cranky when Niko finds him, parchment and wax and stylus strewn across his desk in his dim and musty room. "Stealth, why don't you stay here and do all this, and I'll go take your duty?" Crit's eyes are bleary with weariness. Billeting sixty-six fighters for a long stay means renewing old contacts, provisioning, accounts, and more. He has a week of new beard.

They were in the slaver's old house, where the offices once were and are again. Mold crawled across the ceiling. Ghosts lurked in every nook and cranny, debts unpaid of blood and pain from former times. And joy as well, if a man but looked for it. And glory, hard-won, of a rarefied kind. "We're doing well combining the troops," Niko offered. "But I promised Tempus I'd deal with trainees today. And the Thebans. Still want to trade duty?"

"No, no. That's fine. You go do that. And I'll make sure your mare has dinner in her stall when you get back." Crit got up, wearing just a chiton and a work-belt, and walked him to the door: "Can I put Ari with that Shamshi boy? Sham needs a partner. Ari's loss of Deon will be hard to mend; they were more than friends."

Bad time. Wrong question. "You don't need to remind me. I've lost two partners." *And will not lose another.* "But I don't know what we've got there, in Sham. Let's take those three trainees with us to the Street of Red lanterns tomorrow night. If you like what you see, Crit, it's up to you." Niko was careful not to overstep: Crit customarily assigned new partners after pairs were broken by death.

"I'll go with you, but that isn't what I'm asking." Crit wouldn't let it rest. Tempus's executive officer was all attention now that the real question of Shamshi's fitness to serve was broached. "Your three Bandaran boys went into town with Stepsons' money and orders, spent twice what they should, prowled the streets too long, and came back too late with too little. Straton is *not* pleased. Sham's the eldest."

"I know. I'm sorry. They'll do better. Sham will."

In Crit's mind, as in Niko's, the three trainees were Niko's responsibility – and Shamshi, of the three, the most liable when things went wrong.

"Your Bandaran boys need to be treated like the others, Niko. I can't manage the squadron this way, with Thebans needing one thing and Bandarans something else, and Stepsons outnumbered. All my senior pairs have problems about this posting as it is."

"You mean, Strat has problems." *Here, where the pair has had troubles before.*

"You deal with the commander. I'll deal with Strat. That's not what's on the table."

They were standing face to face now, in the doorway where the sunlight slanted through, under the overhang – bodies speaking volumes, opposed. They were about the same size and weight, if push came to shove.

Niko took a deep breath. *Too much anger.* When had they lost one another? "I heard Strat sent Sync and Gayle down to the White Foal River where that necromant of his used to live. You chase away your ghosts, I'll chase away mine, and we won't have a problem." He struggled to blunt the edge in his voice. "If you and Strat have troubles, or he does – like before – you come to me. I'll help, just among us three." The ghost horse was the Band's keepsake from those days, an apt reminder of all that had happened here.

And none of that could be allowed to happen again. "What's Tempus *really* doing, here?" Crit finally asked.

"Ask him, not me."

*

In the sunshine behind the barracks, Niko found the Thebans out where Sync, the Band's rangy horse-tamer, was giving lessons in cavalry tactics, Stepson-style. Since that style was the most demanding and deadly yet devised, the Thebans were rapt, attentive, while one of their own fighters spun a warhorse in the ring so fast that horse and rider blurred.

"Sync, I need Charon," Niko called.

Summoned, the heavy-set Charon came jogging, his young Lysis following along like a golden puppy at his heels. Both had spiky growths of new hair starting, just shadows on their skulls. "Only you," said Niko to Charon, the apparent leader of the Thebans. The youngster looked as if he'd been slapped.

"Lysis is my son," said Charon, as if that mattered. He wore a Stepson-issue chiton, leggings because of the lessons under way, and boots.

Niko stared until the youth backed up, all the way to the fence.

"How are your fighters, Charon?" Niko set off for the altar on the hill.

Charon followed, then came abreast. "As well as any men would be, ripped away from everything they know and love. With all their brothers dead at Chaeronea."

The play of veins across the Theban's big hands caught Niko's attention: rough-hewn, weathered, and strong.

"They *are* your fighters, aren't they?"

"They are Harmony's. Or they were." The older man was muscled and still vital; he watched the ground as they climbed. "Perhaps they're yours now, Nikodemos. Or your Riddler's. Or your god's."

"But you speak for them."

"I'm the oldest. The most senior. It means nothing now."

"It means everything. Your judgment is unquestioned by your fighters. They follow your lead. You know their hearts. So…help us save what can be saved and what can be carried forward."

They had nearly reached the hilltop, where the black char was, where the shade of Abarsis had appeared to all the gathered Sacred Band, Stepsons and Thebans alike.

Charon looked at him obliquely; then faced him: "Help you how, when everything here is so different? They ask me who and what you are, you Stepsons."

"Help us make the two Bands one. As for who and what we are, what you saw on the battleplain is what we are: the Sacred Band of Stepsons."

"Does this storm god of yours really speak to your commander? Appear, like the spirit in the flames? Will that shade of yours take our fallen up to Elysion from your pyres, in their turn? Or somewhere else?"

"If Tempus says the storm god speaks to him, then it is so. When Enlil appears, it's in a storm. As for your dead, and what power will take their souls, or where…I don't know. Abarsis has always taken every soul of our Sacred Band to heaven, no matter where our slain fighters come from, or what god they love – if any."

An eagle circled overhead, hunting. Its shadow fell over him, then moved on, right to left. Niko shivered: a good omen for what was said here. But there was no use trying to explain *maat* to this Theban, not yet; perhaps not ever.

"Are we hostages? Conscripts? Our goddess, Harmony, is she here with us?" Charon's craggy face worked.

"You aren't hostages, not conscripts. Go or stay, but with all your hearts. As for your goddess…only you know if she is here with you."

"Do you expect us to swear allegiance to your storm god? Serve him? Serve you? What happens if we don't?"

Very carefully, Niko trod this ground. "My commander has been a favorite of one storm god or another for a very long time. We fighters are sworn to our commander, to the Stepsons, the greater Sacred Band, to one another, to our partners – not to a god or place. What we hold sacred is honor, justice, and glory. You need not swear allegiance to our storm god, to serve with us. Fighters are among us from many lands, with many gods and many beliefs. Believe as you will. What is between a man and his god is theirs alone to say."

It was so risky – not what the Riddler wanted, who'd already risked so much and paid so much for these men; paid even a Stepson's life – to let these Thebans think they could walk away. "As for serving us, and what happens if you don't…. What do you imagine was agreed on that Chaeronean battleplain? Your commander and mine came to terms." Niko sought Charon's guarded eyes. "We kept our bargain. You all live, you Thebans, you fated dead. And a Stepson gave his life for it. So you can remember. So you can fight on other days. So you can fight beside us, equal and among us. Our word is binding."

Then they stood silent before the burned-out pyre, where nothing remained but a few charred and ruined trinkets: a hilt; a broken blade half-melted; a female statuette or two.

Charon gazed into the ashes of the pyre, unspeaking, blinking hard. Niko sent his senses questing. This Charon's spirit was turbulent, dark with loss, purple like the cuts and bruises on his arms and under his eyes: so much bloodshed, so much anguish, so little time to heal. Beyond the altar, a doe and a spotted fawn looked up, saw them, and leaped away.

Charon said slowly, "In this new world, this day and forever, then, we are not only Thebans – we are all Stepsons. We are all one Sacred Band. If you will have us. And mine will fight by yours, henceforth, as brothers." Charon raised his head and extended his hand.

*Forever.* Charon didn't realize how true that might come to be. Niko clasped hands with the other man, embraced him, stepped back, and said, "To the death, shoulder to shoulder, with honor. That's still the same. And always will be. Life to you, Stepson, and everlasting glory."

"And to you, Nikodemos, my new brother." The words were thick, coming out in that strange, lilting accent; words sometimes difficult to decipher, secured at such great cost across a sea of time and grief.

So it was not over, with a goddess who might or might not be here in the mix, trying to come to terms with their jealous war god. Niko could not guess what would be in heaven. But in Sanctuary, things were finally well begun. At last, he had something to tell the Riddler that might help to heal him. And he had something to tell Ari: that Ari's dead partner, Deon, had not sacrificed in vain, but shown these Thebans how to climb to heaven. And he had forty-six Theban fighters to swear into the service of the Riddler, into his Sacred Band of Stepsons.

Disciplining the Bandaran trainees would have to wait.

The Sacred Band ceremonies were going to take all day long.

*

When the rites were done and the Thebans no longer a group apart, but sworn to the commander, the Stepsons, and greater Sacred Band, the Riddler decreed a feast for that evening. So Niko, with Crit and Straton, scrambled to attend to preparations. Four lambs and four pigs and a steer were secured and butchered, and firepits were built on a spot near the copse. Wine and beer were brought in from the town, and fruit and sweets and all manner of delights. The meat was turned on spits above the fire and the men came up as they would. No celebration had ever been held at the Stepsons' barracks, so there were not tables enough or benches enough or cups or plates enough for all.

Fighters ate sitting on the ground, in the cool tender grass, from boards in their laps, or held food in their fingers, or sawed chunks of juicy meat off the carcasses with their knives. The smoke smelled sweet, mixed with wafting jasmine. Somewhere, peacocks cried like babies, nightingales sang, and crickets chirped. It seemed to Niko like a night of triumph on a long campaign, like a camp after battle with torches lit and flickering all around and men swapping songs and stories, arms over one another's shoulders or standing about in little groups, gazing at the fire in the dark. And in a way, it was.

Crit came over, with Strat and the Riddler himself, while Niko was trying to talk to Ari. Niko had met Ari in Tyse long ago, and reminded him of the night they scuffled outside an inn there, below the town.

Ari was saying, "…I'll never forget riding away with you, Stealth, after you took down those Rankans with throwing stars. I thought we'd die there, quarrels in our backs, you for what you did and me for bearing witness." Near the fire, two young raccoons sat on fence posts, feasting on moths drawn to the light.

Crit had fought beside Ari in the wizard wars, and said, "Of all the Tysians who joined us, you always were the best tactician, Ari, so it must have been one tough night, if you say so."

"I say so," said the bereft Sacred Bander and then subsided, staring past them at the feast.

Beyond him, Strat and the Riddler conferred, huge in the fire-lit dark. Niko knew where Crit was leading things: Crit was intent on partnering Ari with Shamshi. Niko put his food aside and got up. "We're going into town tomorrow night, to Aphrodisia House, Ari. Come if you like. We're taking those trainees of mine to see if there might be men hiding in those boys."

And he left Ari with Crit, who was pushing things too fast, Niko thought. Ari's partner was barely departed, a new spirit finding its place in heaven.

But in the end, on the following evening they all rode out together to the Street of Red Lanterns: Niko and Tempus, Strat and Crit and Ari, with the three intimidated trainees bringing up the rear on young horses from the string that needed night seasoning. Bats flew by, beating the air and spooking the trainees' mounts, but no one was unhorsed. When they got to Aphrodisia House, Niko still hadn't had a chance to speak with Tempus alone about Sham, and the other trainees, and the Thebans.

So when the others went up the stairs, Niko held back, seeing to his green horse.

Tempus came up behind him so quietly he didn't hear the footsteps over the stamping and blowing of their mounts: "What, Stealth?"

He jumped. Then turned, embarrassed at being startled, snuck up on like a drunken youth. So he spoke boldly: "Crit wants to pair Ari with Sham. I don't think so."

"Why not?" On either side of Aphrodisia House's door, torches *whapped* in the night, throwing shadows, masking the Riddler's expression. "For Ari's sake or Sham's? Or does your *maat* say no?" Not a good start to this, from Tempus's tone.

"Maybe for *maat's* sake. Maybe it's just too soon." It was only instinct, if a strong one, that Sham was a problem. But Niko had bigger problems, he thought: "Commander, how do you…that is, are you pleased with the Thebans? Will they help us, do you think? Is the storm god pleased? Do you feel…?" His concerns were intrusive, beyond his station. *Will the god forgive us now? Let you heal as you have always healed before?* He couldn't ask, didn't dare. His commander's injury was his fault.

"Better." Tempus's armored eyes showing no hint of what lay behind them. The Riddler touched him on the shoulder briefly, just a pat. "Let's see what these boys are made of."

So up they went, into the brothel, late in the evening with the night all around and so many memories from times gone by, flooding Niko's brain and chilling his heart.

## *Chapter 8: God-given Right*

"I can't believe we're really here, Hawk," whispered Gyskouras to Arton. He was looking around at the clientele; at the girls at the bar; at more girls seductively lounging on burgundy chairs and couches in the brothel's ground floor salon. "And here with *them.*" Kouras gestured over his shoulder at the Riddler and his right-side partner, Stealth, coming in the door during the second watch of the night in light mantles with weapons underneath, as if they owned the place.

Arton couldn't believe it either, from the look on his face.

Sham had a different look, calculatingly perfect, where he stood close to Ari, the bereaved Sacred Bander with his curly black hair, black eyes and blacker spirits.

Kouras watched the senior Stepsons as closely as he could, these sons of the armies. How did they command the room without speaking? How did they make people give way before them?

These heroes, seasoned and formidable, controlled everyone and everything in the salon as if by god-given right. Fox, called Critias, and Ace, called Straton, made a quick circuit of the ground floor, inspecting everything, professionally unobtrusive. And nodded once. Then Fox and Stealth (attentive, honed sharp and economical like panthers are, lean muscle rippling) cleared places for the group at the bar. Next, Ace and the Riddler stepped up to the bar, dominating all the space around them, solid as city walls and towering nearly as large, making everyone else seem smaller.

Lesser men already in the room quietly left it. Women sidled toward the stairs until the buxom madam shooed the girls back in, to be appraised and apportioned.

Then a girl came downstairs and Kouras couldn't hear or see anything else but the pad of her bare feet and the rustle of her soft blue dress with copper beads weighing down its hem. The beads tinkled and the girl, her brown hair curling at her throat, moved through the room as if she floated on a cloud. Around her was an opalescent glow. Kouras forgot about the Sacred Band, about Arton and Arton's newly discovered mother, about everything but this girl who must pass by him to get to the couches where other harlots already posed provocatively.

He was just about to go claim her when Sham stepped into her path, bold as a grown man. Kouras didn't know why, but rage filled him.

Now everything becomes preternaturally clear: he sees the Stepsons at the bar, talking to the madam; he sees the girl's eyes dart around the room; and he sees Sham, holding out his hand to her.

And then he is there, somehow interceding, putting his body between Sham and the girl. Her blue eyes look up at him, fearful, shy, and concerned. He hears himself say, "You're mine, tonight."

Sham, behind him, says something he doesn't catch and touches his arm.

He shakes off the touch irritably, not bothering to turn to face the intrusion. The girl hasn't said a word. Her eyes are soft and shy.

Now she does: "I'm Shawme."

"I'm Kouras." Over her shoulder, he sees the Riddler, and Stealth, elbows on the bar at their backs, watching him closely, their heads together.

He felt a hand on his shoulder – Sham's. He heard Straton say, "There's plenty for all. No fighting. Rules of the house." The touch on his shoulder went away. He could hear Straton and Sham, moving off.

Then his fingers grasped her wrist and he couldn't even feel the floor beneath his feet. The next thing he knew, the most beautiful girl in the world was leading him up the stairs and no one seemed to mind a bit.

*

Arton stood transfixed by the murals on the bordello's walls, depicting things he'd never thought about, and some things he'd thought about too much. What would his newfound mother, Illyra, say if she could see him now? The murals were a guidebook of what to do and how to do it. This was how he'd been begotten. There was nothing wrong in it. But some of what was painted here in bright colors behind the couches and divans was not gentle, or kind. Some were things he'd never thought could be done among women and men.

"Have a drink, warfighter?" said a voice beside him in the middle of the room. The woman standing there, her breasts pushed up nearly to her chin, was old enough to be his mother and smelled moist, like soiled sheets. "Come along. Take a seat."

Miserably, he followed until they reached a round table with three girls seated there. Then he realized this old lady didn't aim to claim him.

The three girls giggled, rubbing their arms, showing their legs.

"What to drink?" asked the old serving woman.

He didn't know what to say, so he said, "Whatever they're having." He slid into a seat between two of them.

They were rolling up leaves sprinkled with powder, and lighting the leafy tubes from the table's candle. "Here, war-fighter," said the closest girl, a sharp-faced blond. "Smoke some. Like this." She demonstrated.

He did. Colors sharpened; his pulse slowed. When he could breathe again, exhaling, he saw the entire Sacred Band leadership leaning on the bar and watching all with obvious amusement that he wished he shared.

Wine came in four goblets. Each girl got one, and so did he.

He drank fast, hoping for courage.

The sharp-faced girl said, "You have to pick one of us, fighter."

Her red-haired friend smirked, "Or take all three upstairs."

A girl with light brown curls (so like his mother's) interceded. "Or choose another," she said kindly, waving her hand at the couches nearby. "Anybody here. Even the all-night girls, the famous ones." Her voice was wistful; her dress was green. "The madam says, anything you boys want, you get. Anything." This girl's brown eyes were exotic, dusted with gold. She couldn't be much older than he was. Her mouth was soft, under its red paint. Her cheeks flushed.

Other girls on couches preened and stretched provocatively as Ari and Sham walked by. Sham said, "Looks like you've got a bed full," as he passed, and pulled on a lock of Arton's hair.

The redhead at Arton's table tapped ash into the candle's pool of wax, her eyes flickering to the big fighters at the bar.

"Come on, Stepson – smoke's on the house, so's the wine, so are we. Make your choice. Your bosses are waiting for you three to pick someone, before they will."

All three women looked at him like cats cornering a mouse. Desperately, Arton said to the kind girl with the brown curls, "If you'd like, we could…" What did you say, propositioning a harlot? How did you ask a girl to go upstairs?

Then his foresight blasted him, blinding him to the here and now: he saw a brown-curled girl, lying in a watery ditch, her white skin bruised and muddy. As quickly as it came, the vision was gone. If he took her up the stairs, was that the result? Or if he didn't?

All three were watching him, and so were the Stepsons at the bar. He said, "Please, come with me," in a quavering voice, formally holding out his hand to the brown-curled girl. Her skin was white again, not covered with mud and bruises like the skin of the girl in his inner sight.

She gave a happy giggle, grasping his hand. Up they went, past the bar, past Nikodemos and Tempus, wreathed in blue smoke, staring frankly after them.

There were so many stairs.

Her scent was heady. His palms were sweating. Her hips were switching, muscles moving provocatively under the thin silk. His blood was thudding in his ears. Here were more doors than stairs, door after door after door. Then she tugged him to and through one, and pulled him toward a huge, low bed with a bronze mirror on the opposite wall. She let go of his hand to smooth the ruddy velvet bedclothes.

He had to say it: "I don't want to…do anything. I want to talk, just talk. For now."

She stopped. She turned to him, her hands already at the laces on her dress. "What's wrong? Did I do something wrong?" Her face crumpled.

He was afraid she was going to cry. There was no place to sit but on the bed, except one wooden chair. How could he tell her? *Could* he tell her? He hadn't been able to tell his mother that he could see the future.

He remembered Illyra's face, wrinkled from all the life she'd led, how guarded she had been when she regained consciousness in his arms. She couldn't '*see*' him, his mother had said. She never could. His fate was hidden from her. And then she'd hung on him and wept and wept and wept, telling him there was nothing she could do, there'd never been anything she could do to help him. All of this transpired while Kouras and Sham stood around in the little shop's front room, hearing every word.

He wasn't going to be that way. His life wouldn't turn out that way. He wasn't going to let his bit of talent break him, fill him with fear and helplessness, undermine his nerve and imperil his future. He was a Stepson, a Bandaran initiate. He could get out of destiny's way, bring fortune to heel. He knew he could. Someday. Eventually.

Foresight: his gift and curse. He must make it serve him, make it be what he wanted it to be. Starting today. Or he'd end up like his mother, paralyzed with fear, plagued by prescience, bowed by the weight of knowing too much and not being able to change anything.

So he sat on the girl's bed and patted the velvet beside him. "Sit here. What's your name?" He wouldn't let his foresight be the end of her, if her end was what he'd seen. She wasn't yet dead in his vision. He knew quite well, after Chaeronea, what death looked like. "Where are you from? How did you come to be here?"

"Tifeta," she replied. "My name is Tifeta. I'm from Azehur. My parents moved here when I was three."

His mother would want him to do the best he could for this girl whose life was at risk. Somehow.

So he began trying very hard to have another vision, see a better future for this girl, Tifeta; a safe direction, a path to take this innocent out of harm's way. The more he tried to see a different fate, the less the girl in his vision looked like Tifeta. But he couldn't banish from his inner sight entirely that vision of a brown-curled girl dying in the mud: so still, so sad, so clear.

*

Sham's brown-haired girl was already writhing under him when lightning seared the sky and thunder shook the whorehouse. His harlot squealed. Three more lightning bolts split the dark outside the window and cracks of thunder followed, so close they seemed right overhead: Kouras was having a good time down the hall.

The girl under him froze, tensing to flee like a terrified dog seeking shelter from the storm. He grabbed her wrists. "Don't mind that. It's just Kouras, finishing up, I bet." No rain followed. No lightning flashed again or thunder rolled across the sky. "Stay still."

But the brown-haired whore wouldn't stay still. And he liked it that she struggled under him. He liked holding her little wrists. He pulled them above her head and got both her wrists in one hand. Better. She wriggled under him. Definitely better. He shifted his weight, thrust one knee between her legs and slapped her, hard, across the face. Her head snapped to the right; brown hair fell across her eyes, across the pillow.

"I said, stay still."

She mewled. A drop of blood formed at the corner of her mouth, trying to drip down her chin: red blood against white skin. Her breasts heaved under him; her breath came faster and faster. He put his knee harder into the slick between her thighs. She arched up, her head still turned away. Was she hysterical, really struggling, or playing at it? He didn't know. But he wanted her feelings to be real, not a game, not just a drama bought and paid for by the Stepsons. It mustn't be a game for her.

He was about to make everything very real for her.

Unforgettable.

She was sweating now, trembling. He got his knee out from between her legs and thrust himself down hard. He put all his force into her, pulling her wrists up and up, moving her as he wished with his body's strength. She moaned and quaked more as he got his other hand under her spine at the waist and bent her back, forcing his way where he wanted to go. He wouldn't let it be a game for her. And then something in him roused to wakefulness.

His mind reached for hers; caught hers. He tasted her fear and fed it with not just his body's strength, but with his mind's strength. Perhaps she thought he was just a boy. Perhaps she respected only the money she'd been paid for this.

He sent her mind to Chaeronea, where bodies lay bleeding and broken, heaped one upon the other. Close enough to hell, that vision was, full of purple haze and swollen bodies: *Long spears, thunking into flesh. Men staggering backward, impaled, moaning.*

She started to weep real tears, then sob so that her whole body shook. He had found a way to reach her, after all. He tried something more, entranced by this new skill he was just learning. He envisioned her dying; pictured her lying in a ditch, covered with mud; naked, dirty water between her legs.

She spasmed. She struggled hard, throwing herself left, then right, trying to find life amid the death his mind promised her. Then everything exploded into a rage he couldn't control, and he dimly heard her wailing.

Eventually he regained control – of her, of himself. He didn't know how long it had taken. He was sure someone would be pounding on the door by now. He let go of her wrists and stoppered her mouth.

She slapped at his back and scratched him, but not hard enough to matter. Then she gave up, lying as still as the dead under him, still as still could be, breath rasping and her eyes huge.

One more time, he reached into her mind, and this time he let her taste the grave. She whimpered, afraid to move. Her fear took him over passion's edge and he was done. Spent. She was no longer interesting. He let her go and rolled away, breathing deeply.

She didn't move. The scratches she'd clawed in his back were stinging. He hunted for his clothes, his weapons. Lucky for her he hadn't thought of those before.

She took shuddering, greedy breaths. Fortunately for her, he hadn't thought to tease her with a blade. But he didn't really need one. His mind could do a better job. His talent knew just where to pierce her. He didn't like her now, at all, though earlier he'd thought she was the best of the whores available.

Still no one came pounding on the door to rescue her. She'd made enough noise to wake the dead. He said harshly, "Isn't somebody going to come up here, after all your screeching and squealing?" He still didn't know her name.

"When Tempus's men are here? *Ha.* Cries of pleasure, shrieks of pain…who can tell the difference? If you're done…just go downstairs. No one will say anything about it. No one. Please, just go…if you're done with me." Her voice was trembling pathetically, trying to indicate compliance. She had an elbow crooked across her eyes. Her belly quivered. Blood was smeared across one cheek.

And that got Sham to thinking: maybe he wasn't done with her quite yet.

And when he was, maybe he'd get a different girl and come back up here, to a different room, if the Sacred Band's largess and its timetable would allow.

*

Myrtis, the madam of Aphrodisia House, knew Tempus and what he liked; knew Niko and what he liked; knew what Strat and Crit liked; and had provided amply for each and all. Crit had no complaints on that score.

Everyone had seen the lightning and heard the thunder, before Kouras came down the stairs with his girl held close. And no rain had followed...yet.

"Did that big bang mean you hit the target?" Strat teased Kouras when the youth and girl came near. Crit kicked Straton under the table.

Kouras blushed. His red hair was disheveled and his face puffy as he led his girl past them. The two youngsters sat, hands clasped, elbows on the table between them, cheeks close together, near a window under the mural of love in the garden.

*Don't fall in love with a whore, son of the storm god.* With an effort of will, Crit stopped watching the young couple. Maybe he'd learned what he needed to know about Kouras tonight. The god told Tempus what he wanted the Riddler to know, but never spoke to Crit at all. Maybe this Kouras would be all right.

Waiting for the others, Crit and Strat were dicing, smoking and drinking in the salon, when the screaming began again. Tempus was still upstairs. Sometimes this happened when the storm god took a hand. Nobody moved. And nobody would be allowed to move. No one would interrupt the commander, if Crit and Strat had to guard the stairs personally or take them apart, board by board. But the wailing and moaning went on too long, Crit thought. Tempus was always efficient. And the sounds were from the wrong part of the upstairs, Strat was certain.

Anyway, Niko was up there yet with a virgin the madam had found for him. Ari came down to join them. The bereaved Stepson confirmed that the sounds were from Sham's room and sat in on the game of dice.

Myrtis stood silently behind her bar, picking lint off her knitted sleeve with quick, nervous fingers, while the salon emptied of everyone else but the Band and Kouras's whore.

So be it, Crit thought.

Then Arton came down by himself, his face pale, taking many backward looks. He came to the Stepsons' table and pointed up the stairs, where moaning was still faintly audible.

Arton had just opened his mouth when Crit said, "Don't say a word, unless it's about the good time you had. Just sit down here, Stepson, have a drink, join the game. Maybe we can win back the cost of breaking your maiden."

Arton sat between Ari, who was trying not to laugh, and Straton, and said, "I have to tell you what I saw…." Then the boy stopped, looking over his shoulder, back up the stairs where silence reigned.

"We know. We've seen it all before," said Ari, and clapped the young Stepson on the back.

Arton needed to learn this lesson, Crit thought, about keeping shut and waiting for events to unfold.

"No, you *don't* know," said Arton, puffing out a breath and sitting back. "I had a…premonition, you could call it – I saw a girl dying in a ditch…a vision."

"I see all sorts of things when I'm clearing my pipes," Straton told him. "Don't give it another thought."

"Well, shouldn't we do something?" Arton asked. "It hasn't happened yet."

"Exactly," Strat said.

Crit said simultaneously, "What do you suggest, when it hasn't happened yet?"

Niko came downstairs, adjusting his swordbelt, face expressionless, with Tempus right behind him. So they must have talked in the hall before coming down, Crit thought. Both sat, side by side, across from Crit and Strat. "What's the game?" Niko asked, eyeing the dice.

Crit was just about to say, when a courier from the palace came over with a wax tablet for Tempus to read and sign if acceptable.

The Riddler opened the wooden covers, read the message. He wordlessly handed it to Niko, who read it and handed it to Crit. "Well, Commander," Crit said, "are we working for Torchholder and his oligarchs this season? Or not? These terms are fair enough." Crit knew his voice was too brittle. Tempus had left him with this sack of cats to tend once before, and ridden off to Ranke with Niko close behind.

"To police what can't be policed? We are. Good practice for the Thebans, keeping order here," said the Riddler. Tempus impressed his cylinder seal and sent his assent back with the waiting courier. "We're officially in the pay of the palace, starting now. We'll have to coordinate with the city guard, but you've done that before, Crit."

Crit had done it before and sworn he'd never do it again. But when you worked for the Riddler you always did what you thought you couldn't manage, or survive.

Niko was silent. Not good. But Nikodemos would do what Tempus ordered, if that was the problem.

It wasn't. Niko said, "I'm going to go get Shamshi," very softly. "See what's to be seen."

Everybody turned to Niko.

Crit said, "You're not." Everything they'd heard could be feigned, whether sounds of pleasure or pain: all whores were actresses.

Ari said, "I'll do it. I should, if I might pair with him."

Strat said, "By Enlil's prong, let's give the boy a chance."

Tempus agreed, "Let it play out." Just then Sham came down the stairs, looking unperturbed, not even glassy-eyed or ruffled. Then the Riddler ordered, "Get the horses. Let's go."

Tempus got up from the table to talk with the madam behind her bar, Niko at his heels. That left Crit to organize the withdrawal, while the boys stared at one another appraisingly.

At dawn the next morning, Shamshi's brown-haired harlot, a girl named Dinia, was found by the city guard, dead in a ditch. Her death prompted the city guard's captain, Walegrin, to come to Critias, asking questions. But since all the whores had been alive when the Stepsons left Aphrodisia House, and since the Sacred Band was now in the employ of the palace, and since Critias was Tempus's executive officer and therefore the first to be contacted with this request for salient details (and thus able to insist that he, personally, would take Shamshi's statement), the incident was manageable and would not spin out of control.

Whether the same could be said of Shamshi, neither the Riddler, nor Niko, or Straton or Ari were sure. Crit, himself, was reserving judgment. But one thing was certain: the palace could not be allowed to interrogate a Stepson or pass judgment on a Sacred Bander; no precedent of interference could be permitted. Only the Sacred Band would judge and punish its own. The Shamshi matter must be dealt with internally.

And Arton, who had seen the future and proved his sight was true, had earned new respect among the best of the Sacred Band of Stepsons.

As for Kouras, a little lightning and thunder wouldn't get him very far in the company he was keeping these days, but it was a beginning.

## *Chapter 9: Anger of the Gods*

Today is not Tempus's best day. His chest still hurts, a sign of something very wrong between him and heaven. Ever since Chaeronea, everything he's doing seems askew. This wrongness comes from Fates angered and gods disturbed. Yet he'd pled mercy for the Theban Band before his Stepsons intervened. And won divine sanction, a bit of compassion from on high. Or so he'd thought then.

But now, in the aftermath of that battle, some strangeness in the proportion remains, a shadow over his entire Sacred Band, as if destiny itself is out of kilter. *Long spear, thunking into flesh: man staggering backward, impaled.* He was that man, that day – and still is, today. Celestial vengeance was immediate: a spear deep in his chest for his hubris, for trying to save the Thebans.

Do the Fates feel cheated or the Theban goddess, Harmony, denied? He fears so.

He has feared so little for three centuries, this tightness in his chest that won't abate is ominous. And Enlil, most jealous of war gods, keeps silent: brooding, bumping him and shoving him hither and yon, conspicuously withholding aid. Meanwhile the local storm god, Vashanka, lord of sack and pillage, rides back into Sanctuary like a mercenary hot to restore his reputation. Now Sanctuary's heavens are too crowded.

To make things worse, Vashanka's priest, Torchholder, has just arrived at the Stepsons' barracks unannounced as lightning flares and thunder rolls across the sky.

"Stay back, Torch," Tempus yells to the priest above the screams of two horses bent on mating.

Torchholder makes no reply, standing by the rail fence, looking on, wearing a superior smirk for all to see in the morning gloom.

"Why don't you bless this mating, since you're here?" Tempus's shoulder and elbow are pushed hard against the neck of the Trôs stallion, his hand jerking a chain across the stallion's nose as he leads the aroused stud toward Niko's mare. They plan to knock this mare out of heat today.

His fighters need to see, right now, that Tempus is strong enough to do what men and gods require. There has been too much coddling of their commander, who should need none under Enlil's protection. The Band takes pride in knowing the god is on their side, and this weakening of their leader has led to whispers and trepidation in the ranks.

Strat stays out of striking distance as the stallion rears, bugling, and charges the mare, lifting even Tempus briefly off the ground. Tempus's chest wound flames, threatening to rip apart.

Horses blare their lust and scream to the skies. Reproduction will not be denied. Nature has a surer plan than mortals can devise.

Grabbing up his robes, Torchholder backs along the fence to safety, away from plunging horses, and still makes no reply. Talk is useless anyway, over the din of horses vowing momentary fealty to each other.

Niko has the mare's upper lip twisted in a rope loop at one end of a wooden shaft. Straton holds her bandage-wrapped tail to the side as Tempus brings the stallion down on all fours and aims him at the mare's rump. The mare wails and stamps and the stallion trumpets as two huge horses get ready to make another. Then Nature stalls, and ardor cools.

Torchholder, intrigued, edges forward, robes dragging in the dust. Now, finally, comes a blessing from the waving hands and wriggling fingers of the Sacred Band's new patron, Vashanka's priest in Sanctuary.

Crit, darting in close, winds a rope around the mare's left front ankle, pulling her forefoot off the ground and out to one side. "Now, try it."

Despite the loops wound tight about her upper lip and her suspended foreleg, the mare tries to kick, jerking the ankle rope, and nearly goes to her knees. "Watch out," Strat warns, pulling her tail around her hip. "Here we go."

*...man staggering backward...* As dangerous as any battle is this moment when emboldened mare meets screaming stallion for the purpose of begetting, and woe to any who try to get in between.

In a rush, the stallion rears up and mounts her, teeth in her neck, front legs along her withers, pushing his horsehood desperately into her flank. No foal can result from missing the target. Tempus shoves the stallion over hard with his shoulder, grabbing the organ and guiding it. Now mating is achieved, with requisite grunts and squeals called out to the equine gods.

The priest starts forward; Tempus warns him back: the danger is not past. The stallion's tail flags and jerks while the mare leans back against him. Then he's finished, nearly collapsing on her, head drooping along her neck. Everyone relaxes. He won't bite her, nor kill those men around him. She won't bite him, now, or anybody else.

"We're done," Tempus confirms.

The big Trôs slides off Niko's mare. Straton drops her tail and takes the stallion's lead shank from Tempus. Crit frees the mare's leg and grabs hold of her head. Niko untwists the loop on her lip.

Quiet descends as two horses, passion spent, part with only a few nickers exchanged between them. The deed is done, the result yet to come, with none hurt, not man nor horse. With horses or men, some things take time. And with or without some wizard-blooded priest, this mating is truly blessed. Tempus knows the signs. The storm god, withholding so much else right now, is pleased with this. Clouds collect above; the sun goes away; the day swiftly cools. And in Tempus's head, the god shifts and rumbles, breathing deeply, watching all, as he has not done since Chaeronea. Then the god withdraws. For Tempus, time resumes its normal pace.

Niko beside him, Tempus walks over to the priest and says, "So, Torchholder, how can we help you today?"

"Help me? Keep the peace with that Sacred Band of yours, as we agreed. What are you going to do about this Shamshi boy of yours? What about this dead girl from Aphrodisia House?" said Torchholder darkly. "You're responsible to investigate this death."

"As you wish." *Better us than you. Perhaps the gods aren't so angry, today.* Tempus called out to his Stepsons leading the horses away: "Crit, Straton, come right back. We're going into town to deal with this dead whore. And send Kouras to me. Now." Tempus turned back to the priest. "Kouras is really why you're here, isn't it, Torch? To meet the son of Vashanka. And why you've hired the Band, to put the god-child under your command. Let's hope you're not disappointed."

"I won't be," said the priest.

"Eminence, Kouras is asking about his mother, the temple dancer, Seylalha," Niko said to Torch. "Tempus doesn't remember her well." Niko's astute grin came and went. "Do you still have her?"

"She's dead."

"Let me guess," Tempus said. "She died yesterday? The day before?" Tempus wouldn't put it past this priest to have killed Kouras's mother as soon as he learned the boy was alive and well and in Sanctuary. For control of Gys-kouras, possibly the future avatar of a long missing god, Molin Torchholder would pull no punches, take no chances, and spare no expense. The youth's heritage had ensured that Torchholder would hire the Band: Gyskouras was an actual son of Vashanka, the Pillager, the most ravenous and destructive of all storm gods. There was too much power in this youthful Stepson for the priest to resist. No competition for Kouras's allegiance, not even from his mother, could be tolerated by a man like Torch. "Or will his mother die before morning, or by tomorrow, latest?"

"Commander, you mistake me," protested the priest.

Niko scoffed, crossing his arms.

"I doubt it," Tempus said.

"My heart is pained that you think so ill of me," Torch rejoined. "We have a temple to Vashanka in the city and – as you well know – a chapel in the palace. He should see them. Gyskouras is more than welcome in his father's homes."

"Just remember, Torch, this young Kouras is one of ours: Niko's trainee, a member of the Sacred Band of Stepsons. We'll not let you corrupt him."

Then boyish Gyskouras, barefoot, red hair wet and combed back (sporting a few healing wounds from Chaeronea and wearing only a chiton and a shortsword on his belt), came jogging across the training field, straight to Tempus. "Commander, Straton said come to you." Acknowledging only Niko with a nod, looking neither to the left nor or the right and displaying no curiosity about the priest, the young Stepson awaited orders.

"Gyskouras, this is Molin Torchholder, priest of the god Vashanka in Sanctuary, and our patron. He knows of your mother." Tempus barely remembered Seylalha, Kouras's mother, from a ritual procreation here, long ago. "We'll leave you two to talk awhile. Not long, Kouras: We're riding into town today and, when we go, you're with us."

The look on Torch's face was worthy of a starving jackal faced with a young and tender goat.

*

The whole Band leadership wants to be with Tempus. They'd nearly lost him. They still might. He's not himself yet, and everybody knows it. Niko knows it all too well.

Like an honor guard, they go with him everywhere. The Riddler tells Niko that he thinks the Fates may be angry, the Theban goddess incensed. *Chaeronea.* Everything that feels so wrong, went wrong there. And just won't mend. Niko has never felt so close to doom.

Creaking leather, clank of iron, muffled hoofbeats on the muddy roads: Tempus and his officers coming into Sanctuary under a cloudy sky. All the best of the Stepsons ride south across the White Foal Bridge and into the Red Lanterns district to find out why a whore has died.

*Just be well, Tempus, so all of us can breathe again. Don't take risks here that can be avoided. No death worth dying awaits any man in Sanctuary, where even gods can be lost.* The storm god tells Niko's partner what he needs to know.

Niko never hears Enlil. And his commander, darkly brooding, with his wound so slowly healing (leading that breeding stallion with the god's might in him, a more than human effort) had been bent on reassuring every fighter that all was well and their commander's strength returning. Tempus wouldn't have bothered, if it were the truth.

Coming down the Street of Red Lanterns, still littered with debris from the last storm, Tempus sidles his big Trôs close to Niko's colt. The colt, crowded, squeals. "Why didn't you tell me about Sham, Niko?"

"I tried," he reminded the Riddler as the big horse jostles his colt again. No one else can hear them as they file along, two by two: Crit rides with Strat; Charon with Lysis; and Sync with Kouras, behind them. "But you were always busy. And what could I say? That he's a dark soul? I had nothing solid then.... Just my *maat*, just my gut feelings. But now I doubt he'll make a Stepson. I'm surer still he's not the pairing kind. Ari's guileless and disciplined; Shamshi is cunning and disruptive. I disagree with Crit that Ari and Sham could make a match." *There, it's said. Shamshi will do Ari harm if we force it.*

"Anything more, Niko?" The Trôs horse side-passed until Tempus's right knee brushed Niko's left and the colt squealed once more, offended, then quieted under Niko's urging, learning its lesson about keeping calm in close quarters.

Out came all the problems Niko was trying not to load onto the Riddler: "More? Ari needs a friend, a partner. Sham's not that kind. Shamshi isn't anyone's friend. And Sham was too rough with that whore, *for no reason.* We all heard it. It might have been theater from the whore, but it wasn't. He didn't kill her there and then. But he could have and he might have caused her death later." *Just heal, Tempus.*

"The partnering can wait. We'll find out what happened to this woman, or at least observe the forms. Crit has my orders. We will discipline our own, if it comes to that. And the priest will let us. Torch doesn't really care about the dead whore: he wants Gyskouras's allegiance."

Subject closed. Niko knew better than to try reopening it. But they were still close enough to talk unheard, coming past Phoebe's Inn, where Shamshi's predilections would have been well served.

The Trôs shied into Niko's black, and then other horses balked: dead snake in the road, five feet long, white-bellied, and chewed halfway through.

"Riddler, about the gods being angry? I've been feeling it. Is that why you brought these Thebans into town with us?"

"We need to fix it," said Tempus, and that was all.

At Aphrodisia House, Tempus strode in with Niko, Strat and Crit close behind. Madam Myrtis said, "She took a bath and went out walking. That's all I know." The madam's eyes were frightened. "Commander, you and your Stepsons are always welcome here. This fuss is not our doing. I saw the body. There's no sign of…murder on her, but sometimes girls just…die."

They thanked the whoremistress and got out of there, to follow Myrtis's directions to where the dead harlot was found and then to examine the body for themselves.

Coming down the steps, Crit caught Niko by the arm. "Stealth, will you track the dead girl?"

"Surely. But go slow then. Or go ahead and I'll catch up." Niko signaled toward the Thebans, and Kouras: *caution; stay back.* The Theban Charon, quick-eyed, understood and nodded, surveying all from atop a sorrel horse, Lysis astride a brown gelding close beside.

Now Niko must ignore everything, to track a dead girl's wraith in the whorehold. His horse's cadence lulls him. *Relax. Breathe deep.* But calm eludes him, in broad daylight on a Sanctuary street.

It might be too late to find the fading heat-track of this girl, when so many others have been up and down these streets today. But he'd seen the girl just last night at Aphrodisia House when she was alive. His breathing steadied; the colt he rode walked on. The sun high above came out and beat down warm, forgiving: proof of life.

Harness jingled. A breeze caught up the sound and sent it spinning, into another place – into a dark night ending, where a girl's pain-wracked track could still be found. Her heat-track was red and amber, fuzzy like wool wound round a seeress's hands, heading off toward the White Foal's edge. He kneed the horse to follow, between alleys, across a back lot, forgetful of the group. He reached the river's bank, within sight of the White Foal Bridge.

The luminous heat-track did not cross the bridge. It stopped in a ditch beside the road. And there it died, winking out like a doused flame.

Niko stopped his horse. He wasn't going any farther. The girl died here. He saw no image, no crumpled form, no struggle or attacker: just that dousing of the red and amber light. He wasn't going to seek his rest-place (his spirit's place of peace) to invite a dead girl's soul there and ask it questions. In former times, when he was better balanced, he might have caught up with a soul so newly dead. But not today. Not unless the Riddler ordered. Not unless there wasn't any other way.

He sat his horse quietly until the rest arrived. They'd taken a longer route. The dead girl had been accustomed to this part of town, knew all the shortcuts. "Here," he said, shaking off the trance. "She died right here."

Tempus got off his horse, surveyed the ground. He bent down, took mud in his fist, and nodded. Opening his hand, the Riddler looked at the mud as if it told a tale, wiped his hand on his thigh and mounted up, staring across the bridge through slitted eyes.

Critias and Straton sat unmoving on their horses, Thebans and Kouras close behind. Crit's face was stony. Straton's ghost horse reared up on both hind feet; settled; reared again, came down but jigged in place. Now Niko recognized this place: across that bridge, down that cart track on the other side, two witches once made their homes.

Across the White Foal Bridge was the place Straton had promised Critias he would never go again, where a necromant had kept an odd little house with a low iron fence. Strat had sent Sync and Gayle down here to see if the necromant's house was still standing, but they couldn't find it. The ghost horse gave an ear-splitting whinny: it wanted to go home.

Charon and his son looked from Stepson to Stepson, not knowing why battle was in the faces and the bodies of the Sanctuary veterans.

"Strat," Niko said. "I'm sorry. I didn't realize where we were."

Strat said, "No fault of yours, Niko. No fault of anyone's."

His face was stiff with self-control.

Necromants kill without leaving a sign of violence. The marks Sham had made on the harlot from Aphrodisia House, according to the whoremistress, Myrtis, were minimal, unlikely to be fatal, barely there.

*O gods, not again.* Every hair stood up on Niko's arms. Tempus and he had killed a witch, for certain, years ago. But the necromant, Ischade, might still be prowling. She'd nearly destroyed Straton once. Of all things wrong in Sanctuary, Niko knew this witch was what Critias feared the most.

*Maybe it's not the witch. Maybe the necromant had nothing to do with this. Maybe it was death touch and Shamshi after all. An elbow in the sternum, a finger jabbing at your heart, and inescapable death is delayed hours, even a day. Which is worse, a necromant, or a renegade Bandaran initiate with wizard blood? Take your pick.*

Crit, who loved his partner too much, said protectively, "Now we know what happened to that girl from Aphrodisia House." Crit's voice was bitter, his sigh deep and quavery. Stepsons had cleaned up countless corpses from witches' work on this side of town, a decade past. "So we know how our harlot died, and where. And when we see the body, we'll know at whose hands. Let's go." A necromant was an easy explanation, and Crit's preferred one, if perhaps not the right one.

Tempus looked from Crit to Strat, to Niko, and voiced what everyone was thinking: "So at least one of those witches may still live down here." The Riddler wanted to protect Sham from palace interference, to avoid a scandal involving the Band, to deal with this matter internally. And by agreement, chasing witches and warlocks for the palace was outside the Band's area of responsibility.

The Thebans were casting glances every whichway, trying to spy a witch, a specter, a supernatural threat. But they wouldn't. Not in daylight. If they found this threat, it would have found them – and they couldn't win against it with their swords.

Tempus ordered everyone out of there. They rode bunched up, east to the old Rankan garrison of cyclopean stone and cedar, where Walegrin had taken the body.

Once there, the Thebans waited outside with the horses and everyone else, including Kouras, went inside and down stone stairs to the cellar to take a look. The corpse's wicker litter was surrounded with herbs to mask the smell, laid on a heavy wooden table and covered with a gray linen shroud.

*It's just one body. Just one girl. But it's an offense against the gods, murder without reason, bereft of honor or even sense: Riddler, can't you feel the darkness in that Shamshi?* Most likely death touch – not any witch – had killed this girl.

Had there *ever* before been a renegade Bandaran initiate, a travesty sprung from the misty isles? If Sham is one now, Niko has had a hand in making him. Long ago, Niko had taken Shamshi to Bandara to save him from execution alongside his adulterous mother in Mygdon. It was a small mercy then; perhaps a mercy gone bad, here and now.

Strat held up the shroud a long time before folding it back. Crit turned the body and felt it all over, pushing at its loins, its belly, looking for signs of wounds from rape that might have killed. Tempus kept watch over his Stepsons with havoc in his eyes.

Walegrin drifted in, unspeaking, and leaned against the dank wall under a high window in this candle-lit chamber where bodies were kept until they could be claimed or burned or buried.

Kouras blanched, confronted with the ashen, cold body of a young girl he'd so recently met. "That's her," said the son of the storm god. "Sham's…chosen girl. Dinia."

"Niko?" Straton asked.

Niko didn't need to examine the corpse but he was expected to do it. Nothing here would change his mind: death touch, not witchery, made this kill. He could nearly smell it. He could nearly see it, like afterimages from lightning strikes. But he couldn't prove it. Strat's blue eyes met his, and held. They shared a special bond, the two witch-touched Stepsons.

Niko ran his hands over the cold whore amid the herbs and linen, lying on her litter, caked with mud and grit. "There's no mortal wound." He rolled her body to and fro, to be sure. "It can happen this way with the necromant." *Don't contradict the preferred version of events. It's plausible. It's what Crit wants, what the Riddler wants: someone from outside to take the blame.*

If Kouras's eyes got any bigger, they would pop from his head: ordinary life was just as dangerous as the battlefield, Kouras was learning today.

Straton frowned at Niko, then looked away. Strat had loved the witch. He might love her still.

And the moment feels so wrong to Niko that his head spins. His commander is changing destinies today. He knows what Strat wants. He knows what Crit and his commander want. He knows what his *maat* tells him. And none of these agree.

Tempus fixes him with that hellish stare and repeats what Niko said: "It can happen this way with the necromant." And waits. No one says a word. Then his commander asks him: "But did it? Niko?"

Niko can only say, "It could be the witch. Or not. I can't say for certain."

Tempus claps Straton on the back. "Straton, Crit, you know the witch's signature. Have your say. Write the words for the palace. Walegrin," Tempus turns to the garrison captain, who hasn't said a word. "A witch is at play here. Nothing new in that. Our Stepson is not at fault. Torchholder says there's no sorcery abroad. Perhaps he forgot about necromancy." He turns on his heel. "I have enough, without a witch to chase. Tell Torch we're done with this. Our agreement is specific: the Sacred Band won't fight witches or warlocks or wizards this season. You tolerate this necromant in your midst. Live with it or die with it. But don't bring it to my door. Understood?"

That tone from the Riddler, of iron being whetted or a doom being sealed, everyone understands.

Walegrin backs away and out the door, palms up before him, promising an end to the matter.

Outside in the muggy air, Tempus strode up to Charon, the Theban, and said, "This goddess of yours, Harmony – we need to deal with her. Now. Can you help us?"

"Now? Perhaps," said Charon, "we can find a way. Our deities are not like yours…. Except on the battlefield." His golden son, Lysis, looked from Tempus, to his father, and back.

"If your goddess is unhappy here, maybe we can help get her home where she belongs." The Riddler's voice may have chilled the Thebans, but it gladdened Niko's heart. It was a voice like gravel sliding downhill, like bones being crushed for marrow or chariot wheels turning, or your destiny about to take command: *Tempus as he always has been, and is again, at last.*

Then they all rode full-tilt, back toward the Sacred Band barracks in a clatter of hooves and a flurry of manes and tails and mantles, through streets where people scrambled out of their path and dove for cover, who hadn't heard so many warhorses come running in a long, long time.

## *Chapter 10: Ancient Remedy*

"Slaughter the ox, decapitate it, gut it, bone it – *don't* skin it – and leave the carcass beside Enlil's altar. Then clean up and come to the old amphitheater before first watch – all of you, no weapons, for special training. And don't make a mess out at the altar," Straton had told the three youngest Stepsons, hours ago, before midday, and now the day was nearly done.

The Sacred Band leadership had decided on a remedy for the problems surrounding Shamshi. Everyone knew what to do. Straton had interrogated Sham to make sure – not touching him, just talking with him. Niko had asked Strat to be gentle; so Strat was as gentle as he could be. It had been a long time since someone had asked him to be gentle, searching for the truth.

A young fighter's eyes, pupils wide, innocent and brave, can haunt your dreams – not like Sham's, which were guarded, cunning. Shamshi was outwardly repentant about the rape, worried. The trainee was nearly twenty, Strat estimated: old enough to fight, to kill, and to be treated as a man. His face was pinched, full of care. He knew the Sacred Band had protected him from palace interference and garrison internment. He might have preferred those to what was to come, if he'd had a choice.

Strat had questioned Shamshi painstakingly – for Niko, for himself, and for Critias. So that there would be no doubt. Because the witch, Ischade, might be involved.

"Tell me the witch isn't in this," Crit had whispered to Straton, outside the interrogation cell they'd made out of Critias's office.

"The witch isn't in this," Straton had replied, remembering when they'd exchanged these exact words before, years ago.

Straton could honestly say that the necromant had had no hand in this whore's death, so far as he could tell. He wasn't saying it to protect the witch. He was saying it because he believed it to be true. And Crit knew it.

Truth has its own ring, and those who live by it and die by it know the sound of it when they hear it. And this truth had convinced the senior staff that something must be done about the wizard boy. Truth has a way of doing that.

Now the moon was out early, full and huge while the sky still blazed blue and pink and gold. Lit torches were stuck in the ground in a circle, throwing long, distorted shadows. In that circle waited Tempus and Niko, Crit and Sync. Sync had a length of hemp rope coiled over his shoulder.

Strat took his place among them. Their circle spread out more. The Sacred Band was gathering, curious Stepsons and Thebans drifting in with the lengthening shadows of the waning day. He saw craggy Charon and his son Lysis sit beside some others on the stones ringing the amphitheater. Some stood by in groups of two or three. *Special training.* Crickets made more noise than the fighters loitering here, wondering what was coming.

Tempus has gotten out his leopard mantle, his boar's tooth helmet, and his sharkskin-hilted sword for this. His bow, mortised with a golden grip, lies close to the helmet beside him on the ground. When Tempus wore that panoply, slaughter (or at least vengeance) was on the docket of the god. Niko has his dream-forged cuirass, all his spooky panoply of weapons given him by the regent of the seventh sphere. Critias, Sync, and Strat too are wearing their ceremonial best.

Straton catches Niko's hazel eyes, flat and cold, focused somewhere miles away. All three trainees are young secular initiates from the misty isles. Only Niko knows what that really can mean to this enterprise. Not much. The innocent have nothing to fear with Tempus and Critias, Niko and Sync here, Strat thinks. And Straton, himself, is not an inconsequential force today: all to teach one young man a difficult lesson. *O gods, how did this get so far? How has it come to this?*

The moon was high above the altar on the hill when the three youths arrived, as ordered: weaponless and scrupulously clean in chitons, linen loinguards and sandals. They peered around, eyes glittering, at the unexpected audience of Sacred Banders – some so recently saved, some veteran fighters, and at those within the circle of torches. Nearly the whole Sacred Band is ranged round them, hushed and expectant.

Niko leaves the circle, moving by Strat so closely that their arms brush. His face is carefully composed, calm in the dusk and torchlight. Firelight dances on his cuirass with its demons of the elder gods, its thunderbolts; and on his shortsword, where Enlil's bulls and lions and so many primal symbols play.

This ritual is a thousand years older than Thebes or its goddess. Straton hopes the Thebans will understand. Tempus and Niko had chosen it: *for the balance of the thing.* And he and Critias and Sync had agreed.

Straton watched their commander, who in turn watched Stealth bring in the boys. Strat looked into Tempus's eyes – eyes that had seen so much worse than all would see tonight

– and shivered in the gloaming. Everyone here knows that look, except the trainees. The Stepsons all know that ageless face, relentless as the turning of the seasons; they know that proud mouth drawn tight, with black humor dancing at its corners.

Niko brought the trainees up close, bidding them be silent and take their places. They knew now that something was coming. Kouras stared straight ahead; Arton craned his neck every whichway; Shamshi strode on, the oldest, tallest and strongest of the three, pacing Niko.

"Kouras and Arton, you stand behind Tempus and Crit. Shamshi, go to the middle of the circle, please," said Niko quietly.

They did as they were told.

Then Niko took his place, closing up the circle. *Nowhere to run.* And everyone about is staring at the circle of heavily-armed fighters around an unarmed youth. The crickets seem too loud.

Straton searches the faces of the boys, who must have an inkling, by now, of what is coming. Arton waits behind Critias, and Kouras behind Tempus, without a word.

Sham, his big shoulders squared, stands easily in the middle of the circle, facing Niko, attentive. *Playing out the game, facing down the men surrounding him? Or just uncomprehending?*

Then all the senior officers put away their swords, a ceremonial statement from antiquity meaning that all is in order, and weapons not required. Sync takes his rope from his shoulder and shakes out a loop, as if he were about to catch a colt.

*Now he knows. Or guesses.*

Wild eyes darting, backing up, stopping because Crit is there, behind him. One desperate pivot, full around, and Shamshi says, "What *is* this?"

"Your lesson. One you won't forget," replies the Riddler, as Sync's loop whirls, then drops over Shamshi, down his torso, around his ankles, and jerks him from his feet. The youth yells once and then he's struggling silently in the dirt and grass.

Now they rush him, this young rapist with his Bandaran skills, whom Niko says might be able to kill you with a touch. The boy protests, loudly cursing an incoherent stream. Tempus grabs both his wrists, and holds, while Sync pulls the other way with his loop, and then Strat and Niko move in. Strat knows his part: he slaps the boy back-handed, hard across the face, and knees him in the groin, to stun him momentarily.

Together, they flip Sham onto his belly. Strat gets a knee in the small of his back. The young fighter has great strength, more than anyone expects, but has less to say now with his mouth pressed in the dirt.

Tempus holds Shamshi tight, one hand still imprisoning both wrists. It takes all five men to subdue him. Strat uses all possible care, but the boy still writhes and fights them, spitting curses.

Niko has his hands on Sham's head and neck now, doing something Bandaran that makes the youth gasp for breath, gag, and finally faint dead away. When Crit and Niko have tight holds on both of Sham's arms, Tempus lets go of his wrists. They must be careful with this perhaps unconscious wizard boy, since death touch may be in Sham's arsenal. Strat and Sync bind Sham's arms to his torso with the rope. Then all the men let go, staring around at the silent crowd.

Gyskouras and Arton are holding onto each other, still behind the circle, wondering if their turn is next.

Tempus hefts the trussed, unconscious youth and heads for the altar where the deboned ox awaits. The others from the circle follow.

Except the other two trainees, Kouras and Arton, who are rooted to the spot, until Niko says, "You're coming with us."

And everyone else traipses after them in a ragged line, up the hill to the storm god's altar and the butchered ox.

Sham is still unconscious. They rip his clothes away, then wrap him in the meaty hide and sew it around him, over his face and head, his limbs, so his legs and arms can't move. All together, they heave the hairy package up and onto the storm god's altar. It groans, a muffled sound.

Then Tempus faces the other boys and all the gathered Sacred Band. "This fighter dishonored us. Take this lesson to heart. The storm god will decide if he lives. We leave him here all night. No one touches him, or tries to free him."

Behind him, the oxhide bundle on the altar begins to struggle. Muted screams come from within. Sync, unperturbed, gathers up Sham's torn chiton and loinguard and puts them under one arm.

"If no beast eats him in the night, then we free him in the morning. The lesson's done. Punishment finished. He's cleansed by the storm god of any taint. If the god sends a bear or a wolf or a panther to tear him apart, then that is Enlil's verdict and no one interferes. But if anyone cuts him loose tonight or tries to save him, we hunt down all of them and kill them."

Tempus strides down from the hilltop with Niko, Critias, and Sync around him and they stalk through the crowd and away without another word.

Down the slope, people were beginning to talk, a careful buzzing, an uneasy chatter accompanied by nervous laughter.

Arton's eyes were streaming tears; sobs shook his shoulders. Gyskouras had a flinty, distant look; his hands were strangling one another. Strat came down the slope last and, as he passed the boys, he said, "I hope you both understand. You can*not* help him."

"But can we stay here?" said Gyskouras sullenly. "Stay with him tonight?"

"If you want to share his fate tomorrow. If you chase away the beasts, then what's the point? The storm god decides his fate, not boys."

He pushed the two of them before him, thinking that loyalty such as these two displayed was rare and precious. He'd seen it too infrequently in his life. Sham, if he lived, should be grateful for such friends.

*

Nikodemos was disturbed, now that the deed was done. He had been a slave and a bondservant when he was younger than Sham. He knew well the feeling of being helpless, his life in others' hands. Alone in his quarters, he sought and found his rest-place. From there he went deep inside Shamshi's mind, although he hated to invade another's place of safety. But the young fighter had brought this on himself. So he went, to see if something could be salvaged.

Once there – where Niko would have gone to hide, if such torture were happening to him – he found a much different place than he'd expected: this Shamshi was not intimidated; he was enraged.

He'd known that Shamshi was not an adept of *maat*, but the confused images and the darkness deep in this wizard's son were full of calculated artifice and burning ambition.

Instead of a placid meadow or a sunlit stream or mountain grove, here were images of Chaeronea, war and bloodbath embraced, exalted, magnified and memorialized. *Long spears, thunking into flesh. Men staggering backward, impaled, screaming.*

This youth had spent more time on Bandara than Niko ever had. When Nikodemos had been Arton's age, he already was a Sacred Band fighter, paired with a man nine years older. Before that he'd been a caravan guard and, before that, a single mercenary making his way in the world, dependent on his skills alone to feed him. Sham had stayed on Bandara, learning but not doing, years longer. Perhaps he'd stayed too long.

Too much beauty, too much encouragement; not enough hardship, not enough paid for what was received: a young life distorted, expectations out of balance. Of course Sham was no devotee of *maat*. This one wanted to rule, thought he was destined for greater things than mere mortals aspire to.

Niko walks on Sham's private battleplain, like the battleplain at Chaeronea, but here endless ranks of combatants are killing one another amid a purple haze and Niko cannot stay.

Niko sees a gate, barred and battered. He'd lost a fight in a place like this once, where wounds would bleed and bones would crack on a man's body in the world, no matter how far away the fight was fought from flesh and blood. One man lies here with so many arrows in him he looks like a porcupine. One unattached head wears a wistful look, just staring. *Chaeronea.*

It is not foolish to fear the darkness here. Niko backs away. *Out. Not cowardice, but self-preservation. Out.* And into a room within this youth's mind where a whore quivers while her soul leaches away. And leaches away. And away. Sham isn't here with her, but Niko understands Shamshi now, this wizard boy: it is not simple death touch that Sham is using; this is something twisted, perverted, and rare; not *of* Bandara, but harnessing Bandaran skills to power it. What he sees chills his heart, clenches icy claws around his soul and squeezes. He leaves.

He isn't going to fight a demon here, or any spawn of hell, or even a youth whose body is somewhere else, wrapped in a bloody oxhide. He backs out of there, wandering across blackened grass covered with char until he finds his path, where dark footprints lie deep in mucky ground, and follows his own spirit's tracks, out of there. *Out* of there.

When he came to himself, Niko was in his barracks room again. He was shaking all over, trembling from head to foot. He spent some time regaining his equilibrium. Then he went to see his sable mare, who usually could cheer him. But not tonight. Not with that youth tied on the altar and wolves howling and jackals gibbering.

So he went to see the Riddler. Strat and Crit and Sync were sitting there already, shadows in their eyes as deep as the moonlit night.

"What, Niko?" Tempus knew him too well.

"I…went seeking Sham in his rest-place. It's not like mine. There's no rest there, just battle. I'm not sure what we've done will help. He's very angry. What we did might make things worse. If he lives."

"If he lives or not, the storm god will decide. We'll wait together until sunrise, then go see what Enlil has wrought."

*Yes, leave it to the god. This is not a normal boy, not even a normal Bandaran adept. This is something darker. Much, much darker. And stronger. Stronger than he should be.* Niko couldn't tell them this. With the Riddler, he had chosen the ritual, fit for a black heart, but not for blacker arts. So he didn't say any more.

They had plenty of time to wonder what they might find in the morning on Enlil's altar. And to ponder what the Thebans and the youngsters would think of Stepson justice. They knew what the Stepsons would think: this rite was an ancient remedy for a timeless crime.

A while later, they heard a ruckus outside the Riddler's door. "I'll go," said Crit, signaling the others to come alert, wait and see. Violence begets violence every time. So as Critias went to open the door, shortsword drawn, Strat reached for a crossbow and nocked a bolt, covering him as he pulled the door open wide.

The two remaining trainees stood there, the seer and the storm god's son, blinking in the lamplight spilling out the door from Tempus's room. Arton, with his teeth chattering, was pulling Kouras firmly by the mantle. "Stealth, we're looking for Stealth.... We – That is, can we...? *Stealth,* can we come in, so we're not tempted to...*do* anything we shouldn't?"

Kouras wrenched free. "I'm all *right.* I *won't* go up there, I said."

Since Arton was the prescient one, Niko brought the boys inside, out of harm's way for the rest of the night.

In the morning, Sham would be alive or dead. Whatever happened with Shamshi, the wizard boy, Niko knew they would soon have to deal with Charon, his Theban Sacred Band and their goddess, Harmony. Tempus, by the look of him, had had enough of encounters deferred and confrontations postponed.

## *Chapter 11: Waiting for the Gods*

Sunrise is spilling lemon light on the hill behind the barracks when Tempus arrives on foot. His Sacred Band spreads out in his wake like a mantle in the wind. Everyone wants to know what's on the altar this morning.

The hide-wrapped bundle is nowhere to be seen. No rope lies near, cut or chewed. No meaty skin, no young fighter, no sign of rescue or struggle can be found. There is no scar of mud and trampled grass where a heavy burden has been carried off.

On the hilltop, the bright sunrise reveals only his own footprints, and those of his Stepsons, and three boys' lighter prints from the night before. Tempus sees no trough or swathe such as a body would have made being dragged away or savaged; no beast has left tracks in the mud. The altar of Enlil is pristine in the dawn: free of blood or any other sign of what took place here, as if the gods are in the game today.

*Enlil, where are You in this? On what side, for what result? Did You take him?*

The god doesn't answer Tempus.

Niko, Critias and the two trainees come up to him, where he pokes in the char from the pyre made here days ago.

The boys chatter: "Stealth, you know we didn't do anything. We were with you all night…."

Niko kicks at the char, looking at the scuff his sandal has made in the grass.

Crit hunkers down, across from Tempus: "Commander, shall we hunt? Bring Shamshi back, by whatever means, alive or dead?" Sharp eyes, bared teeth: Crit is a wolfhound on the hilltop, eager for the scent.

*Hunt.* No spoor shows anywhere. All see that. Arton and Kouras, frightened to be blamed, stick close together, following Niko like a pair of cubs. The char left in the muddy grass shows clearly: nothing human stood at this altar last night but five Stepsons with a burden; no animal came hungry and went away fed.

"Hunt? Yes, Crit. By threes and fours. Assign at least one veteran to each Theban pair. Hunt night and day. Set up drops and stations in the city. Be assiduous. Something spirited that youth away. Be prepared for anything. We may be hunted in our turn, but hunt we shall."

'*But if anyone cuts him loose tonight or tries to save him, we hunt down all of them and kill them,*' Tempus had decreed. And so they will.

Acknowledging his commander's orders, Crit takes the boys, with their many backward looks, down through the Band coming the other way, up the hill.

Niko hovers nearby, outwardly poised, watching everything with that mystic calm. Beneath it lies mayhem, begging to be loosed. Things are too numinous now for anyone's good, Tempus knows. His right-side partner wants a target to destroy, a way to make amends for his trainee gone wrong. "Stealth, what does your *maat* show you?'

Niko crouches down as if arrows are aloft, and looks around, then up, and then stares deep and hard at Tempus.

"I'll find him for you. And I'll kill him, if I can. There's a good chance no one else can. It's time."

*'If I can.'* Tempus looks closer at this young fighter who has faced so much beside him, year after year, and never faltered, never flinched.

Stealth, called Nikodemos, is the most talented man at arms Tempus has ever seen. A cold sweeps up the hill or out of Niko's flesh; or out of Tempus's heart, still twinging as skin and bone and muscle knit. "Chaeronea, Niko?"

Niko nods. "Chaeronea. The youth who wouldn't keep his place in the ranks. I still see that battle, Riddler, in my inner sight. In the light of day. Worse, in *his* rest-place."

Tempus knows that Chaeronean vision too well, but is startled to hear that Niko sees it too. *Long spears, thunking into flesh. Man staggering backward, impaled.* "I see the same. Chaeronea." Hard to admit. Harder to bear. Haunted by one battle out of so, so many battles…. Now perhaps, there is a reason for this recurring specter of the Theban martyrs: a trainee of the Band, spinning out of control, with mental skills like Niko's and wizardry in his blood. And Niko, who would risk anything for Tempus, had ventured into Shamshi's rest-place – where Tempus's rightman would least like to go.

Niko says nothing, just looks away down that hill where Thebans and Sacred Banders from a dozen other lands make their way up together. Some are coming close: harsh breathing, muttered conversation; hunched shoulders, harried looks. Tempus raises his hand and everyone stops, like magic fielded, pausing where they are.

"What, Stealth?" I *will not lose this one, Enlil, or You and I will lose each other.* Valor was in Nikodemos, unquestionable, and commitment like trees to stand or night to fall. Again he asked his right-side partner, *"What?"*

"Commander, Shamshi took Chaeronea and made it his rest-place. What kind of soul is that, who wants to walk among corpses? Sham has death touch and other disciplines…but never mastered *maat*. He may be a good fighter, but he has an awful heart. And I helped make him what he is. This problem's mine to solve."

"Don't blame yourself, Niko. Some things are truly fated. *Before* you took Shamshi to Bandara, when I visited Aškelon on Meridian, the dream lord held Sham there. Ash told me then that Shamshi was born to die young." And a sprite named Jihan, a Froth Daughter of Tempus's long acquaintance, had languished in that nightmare realm with Sham, both in thrall to Aškelon, lord of dream and shadow. "What we'll do now, Stealth, we'll do together. You're with me until I say otherwise."

The very mention of Aškelon made Niko turn his head away and shiver. The lord of Meridian must still plague Nikodemos in his dreams.

He stood up. And Niko did. And in his head, Tempus heard a rustle, then a deep breath and a low growl. *So, Enlil, our doings interest You at last. Is this to Your taste, wildly moving destiny? Did You steal that skin-wrapped boy away? Save him? Unmake him? Better, take this young fighter Niko to Your breast and hold him close. He is the hope of You and me and every one of us. Hold him fast.*

Enlil says nothing, confesses nothing, promises nothing – only breathes, a ringing and a sighing in his head.

Tempus motions again to the crowd: permission to approach, granted. *Come up and see what the gods have wrought today.*

Up come the fighters then, to take a look, to touch the char and grass, walk the hill, and find a sign. But no one finds an omen or a portent, or a trace of what has happened here.

"Charon," called Tempus to the Theban leader. "Attend us." Charon came out from among his milling men, his golden son close behind. Hair has grown out far enough on both their heads that you can see Charon's is black and the boy's is blond. They dressed like Stepsons now and moved among the troops with ease. Lucky Thebans, breathing deep of the morning air; moving freely; talking, laughing; breeze touching skin, tickling bristly hair: alive.

"Your goddess, Harmony," Tempus said, when Charon came close. "Now. My god and your goddess need to meet. Where shall we see to it, and how?"

Charon's brown eyes met his, and held. "Our goddess? She pours oil on troubled waters. She plays the flute, sings songs of love in war. Sweet daughter of Ares and Aphrodite, she brings harmonious action in war and concord in love. You think she's here?" Eye contact broken, Charon searches all around. Then his craggy face works to find a fit expression to show his son. "I have an amulet of hers and a small figure…."

Tempus, decided, says, "Bring them: and a flute, if you have one; with a small jug of oil, some water, bread and wine. Get your horses. We're going to the seashore. Niko, show him."

*

When they reached the spit where the lighthouse still stood, Enlil was all about them: black clouds and fierce thunder; purple sky like a bruise the size of heaven; storm blowing in off the sea, pounding rain against them in slaps and punches. This light had an unearthly quality. Thunderheads swallowed up the day. The wet wind knew everyone's name, calling out from a hundred throats.

The god was in him, wild and bold and pushing on his heart, which thundered like the storm. Out to the water's edge they rode, where a jetty grew barnacles and waves crashed high. Young Lysis held their horses while Tempus, Niko, and Charon, barefoot, climbed across the slippery rocks.

First, the oil; then the bread, soaked in wine, they cast upon the waters. Up and up in him Enlil came, stretching his perceptions: Too much god for Sanctuary but not for the ocean and not for Tempus today.

"Lord Storm, make this Theban goddess come to us. Make a peace with her, or charm her to your cause. You let us save these men. She did. Do not let her mock your own intention," he said aloud, invoking Enlil. Maybe Niko heard him. Maybe Charon did. Or maybe the surf swept away his words. But the god heard.

Lightning snapped across the sky: not up, or down, but from one side of heaven to the other. It snapped again, tearing through the clouds. Horses screamed, rearing. On the sandy beach the young Theban, holding all four mounts, shouted and struggled with his charges.

Charon didn't look back; he faced the sea. Solemn ritual, august words spoken: he gave the little statue of the goddess to Nikodemos, who took her in his hands and cast her to the waves. Charon pulled out a flute and began to play tremulously, a soft and lilting melody.

Tempus had the amulet of the goddess. He pulled it from his belt, almost not daring to try her on for size. But he slipped the thong over his head, gulping breath as he did so.

*Snap* went the lightning. *Growl* went the thunder. *Howl* went the wind. A tremor shook the jetty, moving the rocks under his feet. Spume climbed high from rearing waves. The flute song wavered, trilled, and then grew stronger.

Enlil said in a ringing voice inside his skull, *Bring these infidels to Me? Claim My mercy for others? Have you no need of it, yourself? I am infinite, but not infinitely patient. What, treacherous servant, do you want today? A Theban goddess? Was not Chaeronea quite enough?*

Before he could reply, the god no longer was chastising him, but was inside him, inhabiting all his flesh and scalding it. Barely, he saw Nikodemos and Charon, scrambling backward. No time to wonder what they saw. No way to mediate it, if he would.

Now a cloud reaches down from the skies and up from the sea and a cyclone builds, coming inland, questing. Deep and dark and mile upon mile it comes. The flute calls the whirlwind. The god stands inside his flesh, balanced on the sea-slapped stones.

The cyclone bends its head to the tip of the jetty. Tempus's ears pop. Then the cyclone rears up, nuzzles the sky and spins away, quick as a cat. Against the prevailing wind it retreats, drawing back, and back, sucking wind and surf along, first leaving naked sand for miles, then a calmer sea and brighter sky behind.

The flute still sings its soft song – but not from Charon's lips. Tempus barely notices Charon, on his knees, and Niko, hand shielding his eyes from a sudden sun.

On the tip of the jetty a woman sits, honey hair brushing her hips, and plays the flute in a pool of sunlight. Huge scallop shells beside her hold oil and wine and bread. She wears a lavender linen dress, not one bit wet from sea spray. There the sea no longer breaks upon the jetty, for the tide has shooed it back, revealing pure white sand around the rocks.

The woman stops playing and looks around, as if bemused. She looks at Tempus, at Niko, at the sea and the sky. "You called? Is there confusion? Some doubt or need?

Some love, or war, or love in war, at stake?" asks the goddess Harmony.

When she rises, it is as if her hair streams back forever where the sea breeze blows it.

Enlil knows what he wants to do. Tempus needs less of passion, and more of piety, for these men he's brought, but the deities will have their way. No god will go on bended knee to another.

Inside his head, and through his mouth, Enlil says, "Harmony. Here with me are your Theban faithful. Be you pleased? Then be pleasing in my sight." Tempus cannot speak so loud as this. He wishes he hadn't asked for it. But here now was the god, in front of these men, full up in him. And ready to ravish a goddess on the beach.

He had no idea how big she was, or how big he was, or how small anyone or everything else was. The sky seemed so close he could nearly touch it.

The barefoot goddess in her folds of linen took long strides toward him along the jetty, smiling.

"Enlil," said Harmony in a mellifluous voice, as if a flute could speak, "look kindly on my faithful. And you," she snapped and pointed to Charon, on his knees with his forehead to the sand, "stop grieving. Start giving thanks to me. You live to fight on other days. Ask for my protection and you shall have it. Don't ask, and the storm god of the armies will have his way."

Then she turned to Niko. "You, fighter, adept of mind, avatar of Enlil in name but not in soul: take care, or lose all you've won at such great cost." Then she faced Lysis, holding their horses: "Ah, you are truly mine, young Lysis. We bless thee." She made a pass with that milk-white hand, waving her flute. All the horses held by the boy calmed and nickered.

Her gaze returned to Tempus. “So, Enlil, you seek a *bargain?* A pact, a common deal with *me?* Come here.”

Then Tempus knew what was going to happen here. “Niko, Charon, get out of here. Go. Run. *Run. Now.*”

Mortal eyes should not see some things. Mortal flesh was not strong enough to withstand other things. But it was too late: the god and goddess were going to join, on that white bed of pristine sand, here and now, and wrestle out just who was who today in heaven.

Then the sky turned black from pillar to pillar, and privacy veiled what humans should not know.

*

“If you please,” said Harmony, the goddess of love in war and balance, in the soft sand and the tent of clouds above. “A little closer.”

“Like so?” responded Enlil, the god of bloodshed and battlefield, taking her in his arms.

Silky dark enrobed them; starry skies shed eternal light.

“What of our mortals, Storm God? And your immortalized one? What of him? Your Riddlcr, sorcly woundcd upon my battleplain? What if I don’t let you heal him?”

“Do what you wish,” nuzzled the god Enlil, breathing the sweet smell of Harmony, unwilling to cede the goddess a hostage.

“Then, I will soften my heart unto him – *if* you do not impose your rule upon my Theban faithful. My protection shall be as good as yours here and wherever my Thebans are, my sword as quick, and my heart as true.”

“There is imbalance, then,” growled the god. “I am in control here. And I am a god of war, not love.”

"So you say. Yet you covet a child of balance as your avatar, an adept of *maat* – because you know that without balance there can be no true triumph, no lasting victory. Hear me, Enlil: Balance *and* justice are my attributes. My father, Ares, is god of war, like you. Thus from war am I sprung. He made me with the goddess of love to express this truth: in war, there must be compassion. You know this in your heart. You heal your avatars. You immortalize your favorites. You show mercy. How else could you have snatched my believers from the fated battleplain?"

"*Battleplain?* A killing ground of ignominious death. I cannot condone such wanton waste of believing souls, such a massacre. A god should have more pride. Anyway," wheedled the storm god, "you agreed in principle. We only took a few. Ones the Fates won't miss."

"You forget, Enlil: my faithful *choose.* And are you so sure the Fates won't miss those you spirited away? That the Fates are not angry? Will they not try to claim my faithful yet? Destiny is unknowable. And I am disappointed: a moment of weakness from the god of war?" the goddess teases. "You are supposed to be implacable, are you not?"

"These are noble men, heroes who were dying in your name and in mine, it seems, for a lost cause. You did nothing until my avatar pled for them," the god reminded the goddess.

"And rightly so. Everything must have its price," said the goddess, unmoved. "But there is so much love – of honor, glory, one another – in these warriors. I acknowledge what you see in them. Doomed souls, all. Living on, under whose protection? Yours? Mine? You are so cruel, with only war and death to give. I shall not give up *my* faithful – not to death, or beyond."

"Mine was a moment of celestial grace, not weakness, forgivable under the circumstances. When a man begs for mercy for his brothers, without asking anything for himself, even the storm god of the armies must consider it. And mine will pay what price you ask for the salvation of your Thebans, if you but lift your eyes to me and wish it so. Even the lives of my own fighters, we will pay – life for life – if that is the price of mercy for those we saved. But valor is also worth much, and honor, and faith and the love of gods," said the war god, protective of his own.

Eventually they hammered out their bargain, on the sands of Sanctuary wrapped in black clouds of storm so soft and warm inside, so furious and fierce outside:

"There is no mercy in trading life for life. And certainly no righteousness. Mercy, once given, cannot be taken back," Harmony said.

"Mine are mine, then. Yours are yours. But these men must prove worthy. War's balance shall prevail. Nor is mercy constant, when battle looms and destiny awaits." Enlil said.

And to this both gods agreed.

*

Charon took his son under his arm, once the horses were stabled and groomed. "We really saw her…Harmony," said Lysis, his eyes aglow.

"We really saw her. She appeared, in flesh and blood," said Charon.

"Can I say so? Tell the others?" asked his son. Around the youth, horses nickered softly in their stalls, telling one another tales, munching hay in a rhythm as old as time.

"Men may not believe you, my son. But you must always say the truth, when the truth holds no danger for you or your loved ones," Charon counseled. "Now we must find the others, join the hunt."

What else they had seen – the shimmering and flickering around the Sacred Band's commander – troubled Charon. But this demigod, Tempus, had come to Chaeronea and saved them, these few remnants of the once-great Sacred Band of Thebes. If he was cruel, he was impartial, principled, and bold. This Tempus and his right-side partner, more beautiful than any man should be, fought only for uncompromising honor and glory, for a stringent code not tied to pride of place. They were mercenaries of the god of war himself. And if Tempus was more than human, then he still bled, still took wounds.

His Stepsons had intervened unbidden, ripping Charon and his Band from their destiny, from their brothers, and brought them here. *To fight on other days.* Now they lived on, in this strange country full of hero-cults, reminiscent of home but perplexingly different. And home, he and his might never be again.

The news of Harmony appearing on the jetty would soothe his fighters' hearts like a balm. The Theban Sacred Band now had a goddess as real as storm and lightning, who had grappled with the Stepsons' god, Enlil, on a beach in the light of day. Lysis had seen things today to change a man for life... for the better. Because those young eyes had looked upon so many things that would change a man for the worse, Charon was truly grateful.

He stroked his little statue of Harmony, come back to him somehow in all the confusion and the running from the storm that boiled up on the beach, and he hummed the song he'd played upon his pipe.

## *Chapter 12: Damned in Sanctuary*

A great black bird alighted in the Stepsons' path and flapped and fluttered and spun into something much, much worse. Crit's horse bugled and reared, taking six steps backward on its hind legs. He got it down on all fours just before it would have broken through the flimsy railing on White Foal Bridge, plunging them into the river in the dusk.

Straton's ghost horse stood, imperturbable, its reins loose and flapping. Strat's face was impassive while, before them, air sucked and rolled and roiled. The Theban pair behind Crit backed up their horses fast, straight off the bridge in a fine display of well-trained horse and man, and drew their swords.

"Damn," Crit muttered. "I knew it. *You*, Thebans, put those swords away and go wait for us at the intersection we just passed." Out of danger, if there is such a place right now: they'd already seen too much. Theban swords couldn't chop this thing apart.

Before him on the bridge, a dark hole in nothing at all is sealing itself with a pop. A darker figure arises from the gloaming, small and robed, only deep eyes showing in a pale, cowled face. Crit heard the *clop-clop* of Thebans on horses, following his orders, headed for safety.

*"How dare you?"* hisses the necromant, floating their way, getting bigger all the while (black eyes huge, then twice huge), until she stands, just eyes and cloak and slash of mouth, between the calm ghost horse and Crit's agitated sorrel. She puts a hand out to the ghost horse. It licks her palm.

Strat merely shivered once, silent, and felt around in his belt-pouch as if, now that the worst had happened, he was going to roll a smoke. But he didn't.

"How *dare* you?" asked Ischade again. "Blame that strumpet's death on *me.*"

Strat said, "Ischade. Let me explain." But he didn't.

Crit said, "So you're saying it *wasn't* you?" when what he wanted to say was *'Get away from my partner. Don't touch him.'* This hellish creature of the twilight, who'd done so much harm to so many, had nearly gotten Straton killed twice and left him with a crossbow-shot shoulder for a souvenir. "We thought you didn't live here anymore. If 'live' is the right word for it."

She said, "Critias, does your commander know you're out this late?" Ischade put a hand on Straton's thigh, patting him like a dog.

Crit's shortsword came *snicking* out of its scabbard before he could think.

Ischade said, "Oh, *please.*" Eyes deeper than hell flicked to Straton and back to Crit again.

Strat said, "Crit, that won't solve anything."

"It's all right, Straton." Ischade stared at Crit. As an urge to put away the sword overwhelmed him, Crit struggled briefly. Sheathing it, he felt foolish. What had he been thinking?

And here they were, in it again – up to their necks in Sanctuary's undead.

The new Sacred Banders would never understand, Crit knew. They weren't in Thebes anymore. And Sanctuary wasn't a training camp anymore, now that the necromant had surfaced. Cold bodies, lifeless in the street. Dead whore, covered with mud and bruises. And a monster of the Stepsons' making, on the loose. Night hunts and dead drops and patrolling the Maze, moving back into his old office over the Shambles stable. *Please, gods, no.*

*Sanctuary giveth and taketh away, and giveth again, and taketh away again. And again. And again.*

To get Ischade to Phoebe's Inn, where Tempus was, Straton put her up behind him on the accursed ghost horse she'd resurrected for him. Crit couldn't seem to stop all this from happening over and over, no matter how he tried: Ischade and Straton, together. If not for the Riddler, Crit never would have come back here. But Tempus looks at you and you go where you shouldn't, where no sensible man would – because he asks it, because he knows you can, and so you must.

Hell was Ischade, hell her caress: Ischade, touching his partner, still vulnerable from years before. He'd seen nothing worse on Chaeronea's battleplain than that witch with both her arms around Strat's chest, riding, riding…. And the Theban Sacred Band pair trots along behind, unknowing, only concern and caution in their eyes.

At Phoebe's, once the horses are tied outside, the Riddler must be summoned downstairs. Disturbing Tempus at times like these is not the act of a sane man, or a smart one.

The Riddler and Stealth came to the upstairs balcony's railing, regarding each of them in turn, as if from heaven's highest peak: first Straton; then Critias; then the Theban Sacred Band pair (fondling their weapons, gawking at this most arcane pleasure shop in all the whorehold, where not a girl or boy can be seen downstairs).

Then Tempus fixed upon the witch, gripped the railing until his fingers went white, and said from deep in his chest:

"Ischade. Mine are hunting one of ours, not you, on an internal matter." To make things clear. To make sure she knew he knew she wasn't to blame.

The necromant, so tiny, looked up but her cowl didn't fall back. Her cape belled out: underneath, her hands were on her hips. She didn't say a word.

*Damn, and damn, and damned again. Careful, Riddler; careful.*

Down come Tempus and Niko, taking the stairs very slowly. Behind them, a woman peeks out from under the staircase; a door slams shut back there. The Riddler and Stealth stop before the witch. Tempus says, "We thought you didn't live here anymore." Tempus is trying to avoid confrontation.

But that just makes things worse: "Never you mind where *I* live. Such cheek, after what you've done. Blaming *me* instead of your own." Somehow that sound gets caught up on a wind that can't be indoors, and spins, and spins, and echoes in Crit's head. Strat is mesmerized, entranced, his breathing shallow. *I have to get Strat away from her.*

"Madam," the Riddler says carefully, rocking back but not quite retreating. "Our apologies. You know about what happened. It was a natural assumption…given the nature of the death."

"You know who did what. So do I. *You* hunt him. And find him. Or I will. Beware, should *I* take up the hunt. And keep your Stepsons from my door, if you want pairs remaining pairs." A gust blows the front door wide and rattles every shutter; torches gutter, steady; lamplight eddies and flickers.

Niko touches the Riddler's arm. Tempus ducks his head and then says, "Let us see you home."

"There's no need." In a whorl of inky cloak and obedient shadow, she whirls and swirls away, parting the Theban pair like a sword parts limb from limb.

Niko stares at Crit and Strat with indictment or commiseration, or both. Tempus, that tiny kill-smile on his face, says, "Crit, hunt somewhere else."

## *Chapter 13: The Fated Dead*

In the stinking dark of the meaty hide wrapped around him, Shamshi had discovered a power he didn't know he had: great patience. And strength to sustain it: great stubbornness. He couldn't get the smell of dead ox out of his nose or the ire out of his heart. He never would.

He was beyond fear. He was in a withdrawal from fear, in a trance he could maintain against unbearable torture. He needed to stay in this trance, to save his mind and soul from whatever lay ahead. He was not sure, yet, whether what had hold of him was god or devil, man or beast. Or something else.

His plight was a defilement of all he revered. He had been humiliated and left to die without a chance to fight. For far too long, he relived his struggle with the Stepsons in the amphitheater. He would struggle there forever, in his dreams. Life was unfair.

*Some*thing had lifted him up and thrown him through the air as if he were as light as a feather. Some force hoisted him without arms and hurled him over the treetops.

*Some*thing had him. *Some*thing had grabbed him up. He'd screamed but it didn't matter. He wept forever. He cursed for eternity. He snarled and squirmed until his strength was spent.

Boughs were snapping around him with a sound like bones breaking, but the carcass around him cushioned the impacts. His meaty shroud careened, bounced, spun and fell. But no jaws squeezed him. No talons ripped him. Nothing tore him asunder.

He floated in darkness for so very long. Time distended, slowing. Sadness and loss overswept him. All he once was and all his hopes, his dreams, were destroyed. He was shattered. He wept until he could weep no more.

He went to his rest-place and strode the battleplain of Chaeronea, kicking corpses from his path. *Long spears, thunking into flesh. Men staggering backward, impaled, weeping.* Here vengeance was all any man desired, among the uneasy dead. So many ghosts stumbled about, lamenting. The dead here had been left behind by those who ran away. So lonely for their loved ones. So angry at their enemies. So disappointed by their companions. All of these restless dead and nearly dead and dreaming dead he'd collected here were deserted by their craven comrades, who'd fled destruction that should have been spread among so many more.

He hadn't known, until then, that most of the Theban infantry had cut and run, leaving the Sacred Band to fight alone until they died, outnumbered so many, many to one. Was it a hundred to one? So they thought, in any case. So they grieved, one and all. So they mourned, still and silent, only their minds alive, only their hearts yet feeling: the Sacred Band of Thebes, so completely, irretrievably ruined.

Shamshi's face was pressed against the yielding, bloody bag. Some part of him, struggling to breathe there, would always be wrapped in that stinking, wet and slimy hide. He would never take another breath without smelling that acrid odor, never toss his head without feeling his skin rub against sticky meat, never move his hands and feet without straining against the flesh and ropes that bound him helpless.

In his rest-place, he could still walk free. He could plan a revenge fit for warfighters, arrogant and cold. When he was eaten up and killed by whatever had him in its arms, he could still strike out. He knew he could. He had spent so many seasons on Bandara; he knew his soul could survive his body's dissolution.

But it was going to hurt like bloody hell.

*Whump.* He hit the ground, hard. And bounced, and hit again. Solid earth was beneath him. In his mind, he cut the ropes and laces binding him, slicing apart stitch after stitch. And the same ropes and laces binding him on earth gave way. He tensed to spring, to come out fighting, to face huge fangs and slashing claws of bear or panther or whatever creature had spirited him away, tossing him through the treetops, playing with him as if he were a mouse to be thrown up into the air and caught. And flung away again. And caught. And slapped. And batted and caught....

Nothing attacked him. He lay quietly inside his oxhide shroud. He was safe. He trembled there for a very long time. No huge paw smacked him senseless. No ravening bear tried to drag him away. He must get his hands free, then his feet. He tried to move. He might have been pulling his limbs away from setting mortar. Blood glued his hair to the stinky meat. On his face, his head, his limbs, his flesh stung as so much hair was pulled out, but he spread his arms wide; he freed his legs.

In a flurry, he sat up, ripping off the heavy, stinky hide and glaring around, shaking from head to foot.

It was evening, third watch or later. He couldn't see where he was. He didn't know how long he'd been here. He could smell trees and loam, overcoming the reek of the carcass's hide. Entwined with that, he smelled a cook-fire.

He sat still for a long time, joyfully breathing air filled with more than the rank smell of dead ox, fearing that movement would bring his abductor down on him. He mustn't alert whatever was so strong that it had carried him away. But nothing came growling. No giant cat, no pack of wolves descended on him. No huge bird on the wing came to rip him limb from limb or blind him or bite out his throat.

He wanted to scramble away from the hide. He dared not. Sound might alert whatever had taken him. He waited. And he waited. But no beast came to claim him. He was alone in a wood full of night noises. After a very long time he got up, crouched and naked, and then scuttled off into the woods to get as far away as he could from the reeking hide. How long had he been wrapped up, a captive? He couldn't say.

But now he was free, alive in the woods. He had no clothes, no weapons, no future rolling out before him, beckoning, day by day. A free man can plan and hope and scheme. So can a man with nothing left to lose. Revenge would be very sweet, against all the fated dead and those who sought to save them.

Something had flung him away. Was it the god, Enlil, disgusted at the horror of what had been done to him – or at what he'd done? Had he been discarded? Or had he been saved?

*Some*thing had helped him. Or he had helped himself. He was a Bandaran adept. He could kill with an elbow or a stab of his finger. He could walk broken glass or wet parchment or a gravel pond, leaving neither blood nor track or even disturbed pebbles behind. He could get into another's soul and see what was there. He could change a mind, touch a heart. He could mold a future, or ten, or a hundred. And he would do all of that.

He was alive. And he was filled with hate. But his hatred must cool. A man in search of revenge must have a plan. He had learned that lesson well on Bandara, every day when lesser men had told him what to do and how to do it.

Now and forevermore, he would do things his way.

So he snuck up on the cook-fire he'd smelled. He saw men there, horses with noses in their feed bags and crossbows still hanging from their saddles. He crouched in the bushes, marveling at his luck. These three were two Thebans and a Stepson, camped for the evening, by the look of them, stripped down to chitons in the warm summer night.

He thought one might be Ari, the black-curled, swarthy Stepson who'd lost his partner, Deon, a few days ago. Ari had gone with Shamshi and the others to Aphrodisia House; Ari had been there when Sham had chosen that benighted girl who'd caused all the trouble. In the whorehouse, Ari had patted him on the buttocks playfully, put an arm around his shoulders. Shamshi hadn't liked that: he wasn't that kind of Stepson, had no intention of becoming anyone's 'divine friend,' as the Theban Sacred Band called so close a bond. If this was that same Stepson, Ari, then it was fitting that Shamshi happened upon him. Perhaps, if this *was* Ari, it was an omen, a sign that Sham was on the proper path. He snuck carefully around, getting downwind. If the horses smelled blood, they'd alert their riders.

But no horse neighed a warning. As he approached, he whispered softly to the horses, calming them with all the mental skill he had. Panoplies by their sides, the men were talking quietly, laughing low, as soldiers will when a cook-fire burns of an evening. No Sacred Bander heard, or even glanced his way as he slid a crossbow and quiver from one saddle and throwing stars from a saddlebag.

Three of them; one of him; and he was naked, sticky and smeared with blood: surely this contest would be fair enough. He imagined serene mornings, lazy days, and slowed his pulse. He sent thoughts of tranquility to the relaxing men. He fingered the throwing stars. He shouldered the quiver. He nocked a bolt quietly. These men had never learned his disciplines. They were never on Bandara. And so they heard nothing but one another, until they heard the crossbow *thwack* into Ari's heart.

Ari drops like a stone with only one yip of surprise. Now yelling begins, and screams of rage and anguish. A shout rings out. *Too late.* Too late to stop him. Too late to find a lone attacker in the fire-lit dark. Throwing stars fly from his fingers and he shoots two more crossbow bolts. Too late for the first Theban now, who'd come so far to die. Another crossbow bolt whispers on its way, burying itself deep in the second Theban's lung. One bubbly shout rings out, from this Theban with his hands on the bolt piercing his breast. Quickly, shouting fades to burbles, to twitching on the ground beside the cook-fire. This last Theban falls atop his brother.

*Chaeronea.*

Then it's quiet but for the crackling fire, the soft stamping of the horses and the swishing of their tails.

Shamshi now has three horses, weapons, armor, and clothes. And he has a dinner, all prepared for him to eat. It will taste sweet, whatever is sizzling on the spit above those flames.

Better yet, he has his first taste of revenge upon the fated dead.

## *Chapter 14: Love, War and Harmony*

"Really, *me?* Join *you* tonight?" said Lysis wonderingly, when Arton and Kouras found Charon's son on the training field. Arton had known just where to find Lysis: with the horses. It hadn't required prescience. Behind Lysis, in the bullpen, a chestnut filly trotted aimlessly, snuffling the dirt, its workout interrupted. Sync, the Band's horse-tamer, awaited Lysis in the middle of the pen with a fist on one hip and a whip in his other hand. Arton admired Lysis, the favorite of Harmony, this golden youth about whom everyone whispered since the goddess had manifested on the jetty and blessed him.

"Really, *you.*" Kouras confirmed. "You'll need your weapons and your armor. *If* Charon agrees. Stealth said your father might come as well – join us in the hunt for Shamshi. We'll be guarding Aphrodisia House...scene of the crime." He grinned expansively and stood up tall. "Stealth will be there. We can handle anything that comes our way." Kouras's voice deepened: "Even the renegade. Can't we, Arton?"

"I hope so." Arton wasn't so sure. Things had gone very wrong and now the whole Band was hunting Shamshi, with orders to kill him on sight. And Arton and Kouras must hunt him too. Shamshi had been...one of them; on Bandara with them. Arton added, "With the storm god's favor." After what had happened, uppermost in Arton's mind was the fact that he must never, ever displease the Riddler.

Kouras repeated, "We're going to *Aphrodisia* House, Lysis. Make sure your father knows that." All Kouras could think about or talk about was Shawme, the girl he'd found at the brothel on that night when everything changed. "Stealth thinks Shamshi might go back there. So we'll be protecting the…ladies, showing our colors."

Golden afternoon sun shone down, bright like the morning they'd found the empty altar. Arton was uneasy. His prescience wasn't helping. He had vague premonitions, dark and dreadful; unclear, disquieting. Recurring snippets of Chaeronea's horror danced in his head. *Long spears, thunking into flesh. Man staggers backward, impaled, sobbing.* Maybe he could visit his mother, Illyra, again, in the city. Maybe Stealth would let him guard the Bazaar instead of the whorehouse.

Climbing the fence, Lysis ran to Sync, nearly begging permission to find his father and volunteer. The horse-tamer had been among the leadership that had disciplined Shamshi. *Rope loop, shaking down; widening, whirling….*

And now Shamshi was…where?

Arton didn't want to end up like Sham. He kept seeing Shamshi's face in his inner sight. Everyone else seemed so unmoved. Five grown men, sewing a boy into a meaty shroud that the victim had helped prepare. Slaughtering the ox and deboning its carcass had been awful at the time; now he barely cared about that. Arton would never forget the look on Sham's face. Kouras was sure that Sham was dead, spirited away by the affronted storm god.

Arton knew without a doubt that Sham wasn't dead. He could *see* Shamshi, reaching out to him. Sometimes, like now, Arton had inexplicable knowledge of distant happenings in the present; more often, he glimpsed the future. Therefore, he was sure Shamshi was alive now: present and future, running together, showing him his friend. And Arton was secretly glad. Maybe the Band would never find Sham….

Arton and Kouras hurried off to get ready for tonight's foray. In incoherent visions of Shamshi, Arton was invariably overcome by unrelenting rage and overwhelming anger. Then he'd feel the thrill of a hunter; the joy of striking terror into the hunted. Arton wasn't angry at anyone; rather, he was apprehensive, having seen the Stepsons punish one of their own. So did the fury he felt belong to Sham? Arton was glad that Stealth was leading them tonight.

As he cleaned his tack, his gear, and did his chores in the stable, Arton shied away from the whispers in his mind. He didn't want to see the future clearly – not right now, with the whole Band out hunting a youth who had so recently been one of them.

Jumbled images of the future stubbornly refused to yield any coherent guidance. He knew only that he needed to be very careful on these dark days. *Be careful.* Be careful of what? Careful of the Stepsons, so angry, out on the hunt? Of the Thebans? That was the trouble with being a seer. He never knew enough, clearly enough, soon enough to do him any good.

Tonight at Aphrodisia House he must find that same girl, Tifeta, who would be content to sit and talk with him and not make fun of him if he didn't want to do more than talk. Or he must find his mother, who surely could help him see his way past this persistent foreboding that had snatched away his courage and left confusion in its place.

*

*One door opens, another closes.* Charon knows the signs. Ever since the goddess Harmony manifested on the lighthouse spit, Thebans walk with new authority in the barracks and in the city, laughing louder, heads held high.

*'...stop grieving. Start giving thanks to me. You live to fight on other days',* the goddess had told him on the beach.

Charon gives heartfelt thanks many times a day. Now he can counsel his men better, help them with their grief better; prepare them for their future better. He makes a small shrine to Harmony in the corner of his room. Every word the goddess said and every nuance of what happened on the beach (with Harmony and Enlil; with Tempus, Nikodemos, Lysis and Charon himself) is being repeated, analyzed, dissected and turned upside down by his Theban brothers.

Harmony, tutelary goddess of the Sacred Band of Thebes, is among them here in Sanctuary. People whisper, awed. The Stepsons, not to be outdone, praise Enlil to the skies but ask privately how to pay respect to this foreign goddess. Charon is proud.

With god and goddess united – or seeming so – the greater Sacred Band takes heart. Among the Stepsons, talk of 'unlucky Thebans' is fading away. Even the storms abate. Blue skies look down on the barracks, on city walls and Sanctuary's surrounds, where the hunt for the deserter, Shamshi, is still ongoing.

There could have been no better time for Harmony to appear among them than in these days of readjustment for his Thebans; these days of worry and wrath among the Stepsons, out to destroy one of their own.

Young Lysis is the 'Blessed One,' pleasing in the sight of the goddess. His son's new skill with horses (if new it is) is the talk of the barracks. Charon's boy, Lysis, is celebrated by his brother Thebans and the friend of everyone.

So, with all these encouraging omens, Charon accepts the invitation to volunteer with his son for this foray: a Theban pair has been chosen by Nikodemos, the Stepsons' second-in-command – a high honor. He and Lysis will join the hunt tonight. Most of Charon's pairs have been detailed to the countryside, with Stepsons monitoring them (nowhere that trouble could find them), as if they were raw recruits.

Tracking down and killing a young fighter is inharmonious, onerous and sad. Nevertheless, this quarry is dangerous; the risk, very real. And the mission is honorable in the eyes of the Sacred Band of Stepsons. *Honorable battle sustains a Sacred Band.* He cannot deny his son, Lysis, this chance to face a worthy foe. Perhaps if Shamshi had had an older, wiser partner, as was the Theban custom, tragedy could have been averted. But things are as they are.

*One door closes, another opens.* The Band is closing the door on Shamshi, said to be a warlock's bastard son, and opening it wide for his Lysis, blessed by Harmony herself. Charon believes very little in sorcery, which to his mind is the realm of superstitious women, fools, the infirm, and the very old. He believes very much in the gods, in blessed Harmony, in the Fates, and in his own good fortune at having been snatched, son and all, from the jaws of death. If Lysis's mother, in far Elysion, could see them now, how happy she would be to have her son accepted, like his father, among these strangers, even into the exalted company of the Band's leadership.

Charon resolved to make the most of these opportunities brought to him by Harmony. To show his gratitude, he played her three songs, before the little altar in his room where he'd placed her statuette: one hymn to her, a paean to joy itself, and a love song fit for such a lovely day.

*

Since it meant so much to Arton, Niko agreed to let the boys go by the Bazaar on the way to Aphrodisia House. To get there from the barracks north of town, they had to enter the city through Triumph Gate, which meant riding south down General's Road, through the caravan grounds and north again to the Street of Red Lanterns. The young fighters and the Theban leader were Niko's bait to flush Shamshi from hiding. If Shamshi was about, seeing these would surely lure him. Parading Lysis, Arton, Kouras and Charon through town was not the worst of plans.

The west side was a good place for confrontation from horseback, if it came tonight. The farmer's market and caravan grounds are relatively open spaces. The Bazaar and the Red Lantern district are more built-up, more claustrophobic, and more dangerous. Nevertheless, the west side has fewer ramshackle buildings jumbled close than does the Maze, Sanctuary's chockablock slum, which lords its notoriety over the alleyways of Downwind and Shambles Cross and Ratfall, decrepitude more tumbledown and treacherous yet. Fewer alleys meant fewer rickety roosts and dilapidated hidey-holes for a sniper.

If Niko had been Shamshi, he would have fled, be miles away now in another town, another city, another land. But Niko was not Shamshi, and Niko could feel the wizard boy nearby: his bleak intention; the slither of a stalker; the occasional rattle in Niko's rest-place as Shamshi reconnoitered Niko's mental battlements. He doubted that Shamshi could assault him there and win but, with this adversary, even that was on the table.

*Spears thunking into flesh. Men staggering back, impaled, whimpering.* The battleplain of Chaeronea flashes through his mind too much, day and night – or is it the battleplain in Shamshi's rest-place?

Unless the pairs out hunting Sham caught him in the open and got very, very lucky, this renegade could wreak his vengeance on all and sundry for as long as he wished. The wizard boy might hide out in the Maze indefinitely – or slide deeper into Sanctuary's bowels (into Downwind or Shambles or Ratfall) where none might ever find him. With Sham's Bandaran skills, the renegade could track the trainees' progress, might have touched their minds by now. It remained to use Charon and the youths to make Shamshi come to Niko.

So it mattered little whether Niko herded his lambs through the streets or penned them up inside Aphrodisia House. When Shamshi was ready, when the lure was irresistible, he would come. The hunted would become the hunter.

Niko hadn't taken Charon into his confidence. Though Charon might guess, he must know nothing more than did the three young fighters. The plan was plausible. The bait must remain unknowing, lest Shamshi catch wind of the trap from the boy's thoughts, or Charon's.

*Shamshi will sense no deception, when truth is truth.*

And the boys, as well as Charon, needed this outing, in the face of so much change, so much portent, so much suddenly right and so much suddenly wrong, all at once: Theban goddess come to Sanctuary; wizard boy on the rampage.

By the time they got to the S'danzo's little fortune-telling shop and tied their horses there, night was settling, sunset fading. The Bazaar was a warren of crooked streets, flimsy stands, illicit caravanners and fly-by-night dealers, where the desperate and predatory slipped out of the nearby slums by night.

*Tell my fortune, old woman?* Perhaps he'd ask her, perhaps not. Niko had all the prophecy he needed when he looked at the Riddler and saw vigor returning, with the strength of the storm god close at hand.

Outside the poor little shop with its two torches lit to beat back the night, he stroked his mare and gave Charon some coppers to pay the seeress for the boys' fortunes. "I'll stay here with the horses. You go inside. But make it brief." Now that they were here, in this indefensible position, the back of Niko's neck was aprickle. But even if Sham pounced, Bandaran training or not, he was only one man. Shadows were legion, lengthening, merging on the dirty streets.

"Stealth, you're sure?" said Charon, avuncular with his son close by.

"Quite sure." *My fortune is in my commander's hands, and so is yours.*

Charon followed the young fighters up the steps. They knocked. The door to the fortune-teller's shop opened. Light spilled around a heavy woman's figure, out onto the half-rotted steps. If this woman could see the future, then why couldn't she improve her own lot?

"We won't be long," Charon promised from the S'danzo's doorway, and disappeared inside. The door closed with a squeak and Niko had a moment to himself.

He'd had few such moments lately for calm and reflection. Wanted none. He promised the Riddler he'd find Shamshi and kill him if he could. So Niko had chosen these young fighters, to recreate the circumstances at Aphrodisia House. To attract his quarry. Long days, sleepless nights, when so many men hunt down a youth to kill him. The commander would join the vigil, by and by.

Since the god and goddess met on the jetty, Tempus has been growing stronger and Niko more ill at ease. Some read the appearance of the deities on the beach as sanctification. Niko remembers the Theban goddess cautioning him: *'You, fighter, adept of mind, avatar of Enlil in name but not in soul: take care, or lose all you've won at such great cost.'* The meaning of her warning remains unclear.

*Show me what you mean. I don't understand.*

But maybe he does.

He needs to help Tempus. He's won nothing but a chance to put things right, after Chaeronea. Wants nothing else. Things are out of balance, teetering toward a collapse Niko can almost see but not define. Unpredictable elements are colliding, wills careening into one another: Enlil; this foreign goddess; Shamshi, the wizard boy; the necromant; a seer; the storm god's son; predestined Thebans, saved from death – or from angry Fates.

Who knew but that another hunt was underway, in the country of the gods?

One thing, weighed against all, could balance the scales: the Riddler, regaining his former mettle. His chest wound is nearly healed. No one would have said it when the commander seemed so threatened, but now Crit and Strat admit how deeply they'd been worried.

And Tempus *is* better, if not yet all he was before – before the spear that Niko couldn't block, that he wasn't fast enough to deflect. Before the sickening thud. *Long spear, thunking into flesh.*

He can't forgive himself, can't get past it. He's begun to shun sleep the way his commander does; but Nikodemos, unlike Tempus, must sleep sometime. If he sleeps, he might dream. In his dreams, he might be vulnerable to so many unfettered forces here: to the necromant; to the dream lord, whose smithery he wears tonight upon his person; even to Shamshi, who rattles the gates of his rest-place.

He must chase Chaeronea from his mind and retake control. Tempus has forgiven him; he must forgive himself. He scratches absently at recent (Chaeronean) flesh wounds, pulling layers of dead skin away from freshly-minted battle scars on both arms and on his thigh.

He talked softly to his sable mare, nonsense and endearments. She was calm, placid, and probably pregnant by now. The mating had quelled her heat, as it was meant to do. He was musing about the foal to come when he heard a step, then another, behind him. Still stroking his mare, he looked over his shoulder.

A young woman stood there, modestly cloaked, in the flickery torchlight of this mild summer night which should not hold so much portent or so much risk. She said, "What a lovely mare." Her head was bare; her hair spilled into her hood; her face was beautiful, innocent.

But Niko had been snared by beauty and innocence more than once. The Riddler had warned him to beware here. So had the Theban goddess. He wished he had waited for Tempus but the trap was his to set, the Riddler's to spring. He had his orders.

"Thank you," he said carefully.

Her soft eyes caught the torchlight and held it. "What is this horse's name?" She came closer, toward the mare.

Niko said, "She doesn't have one. She's an Aškelonian. There aren't many. In the whole Band, there's not another like her." Despite himself, his muscles tensed as this woman came up out of nowhere. Was this a witch in comely guise, coalescing out of shadow to kill him? Shamshi in disguise? He didn't think so.

"An Aškelonian mare? From the land of dream? My, my. I can well believe it. What a lucky man you are," she said, and came closer still. Her voice was musical. "But you should name her." She walked up to the horse, her hands clasped behind her. The mare raised its head. Before Niko could warn her that this was a warhorse, the young woman leaned forward, hands still clasped behind her back, and breathed into the mare's nostrils. The mare blew softly and then nickered. The woman stepped back. She was a lady, this one – not a witch, not a trollop, despite being on the street by herself so late. "It was good to see her," she said. "And you. Stepson, isn't it?"

"Stealth, called Nikodemos." He couldn't stop looking at her: so brave, so sure a woman, coming up to a strange horse and exchanging breath. "You shouldn't be out alone so late," he said, hoping she would stay. "What's your name?"

"Me? If your mare needs no name, why do I? And I am safe, never fear."

"Wait and I'll see you to your door." He didn't want to lose track of her, not yet.

But then the boys were on the S'danzo's threshold, coming out, talking and laughing, Charon behind them. All five horses milled about; he had to quiet them. When he looked up, she was gone.

He was unreasonably disappointed. She was a chance-met noblewoman, found and lost in an instant, who wouldn't even give her name to a lowly Stepson….

No matter. He had a trap to bait, a renegade to run to ground and, with luck, a battle to join.

At Aphrodisia House, once the horses were safe in the stable out back, they found the salon crowded with locals who'd grown accustomed to the Band standing around, watchful and heavily armed. Every burgundy couch and seat was taken.

When he saw Charon's eyebrow raise at painted women and boys with kohl and seashell dust around their eyes, Niko said, "It's time for Lysis to learn. He's surely old enough."

"We don't do it this way, in Thebes."

"How do you do it in Thebes?"

"In Thebes? A boy of good breeding would be mentored by an aristocrat...in war and love, in music and philosophy, to tame his fierce nature. Normally my son would have had such a Sacred Band partner – not his father – to teach him all of these, and more, and buy his panoply when he came of age. But Lysis is my youngest. His mother is in the Elysian fields. I've kept him with me." Charon was disapproving. He waved a hand at folk nuzzling one another, drinking, laughing on the plush couches and the stairs. "When it was time for women, they would be invited to the sponsor's house, after a celebration or a battle. Or there would be a temple virgin. Or an arranged marriage with property and dowry that needed sons to hold it firm."

"I'll station him outside the door, to watch the street," Niko offered, looking beyond Charon's head, where Kouras, who should be checking exits, was talking to a girl who looked familiar.

"No, let it be. He'll learn new ways here. So will I."

Outside, distant thunder rumbles low as Kouras sees Niko, waves, and comes over, a young harlot under his arm. "Stealth, called Nikodemos, favorite of the Riddler, of the Sacred Band of Stepsons," says Kouras, "this is Shawme. Shawme, this is the…my commander's right-side partner."

Niko inclines his head to her. The son of Vashanka, the local storm god, treating a whore like a lady? Molin Torchholder would not be pleased. Niko said, "Young woman, have you a problem? Can I help?" The girl looked at him through Rankan-blue eyes: there was a northern bloodline in her.

She said, "Kind sir, Kouras said I should tell you…."

"Tell me what?" He was covertly scanning the crowd, looking for anything out of place, watching Arton and Lysis talking to people and moving through groups as they should.

"I remember," Shawme said, "when I found it on the Downwind beach, when the Stepsons were here last time. I was just a young girl, starting to work here to get out of Ratfall." She held out a silvery tube, the length of her hand, which had a flat compartment along one side. "This is for you. A mage named Randal told me to give it to the Band if you ever came back. 'It surmounts evil,' he told me, 'keeps doom at bay.'"

*Randal.* Now Niko was paying attention. His former partner, Randal, was in Lemuria these days. Taking the tube she proffered, he pulled back the slide on the compartment. There were darts inside that had been in there for a long time. Darts such as these were invariably poisoned. "Thank you, Shawme. That was…what…ten years ago or more?" People here aged dependably, not like in Lemuria, where time stood still; Shawme couldn't have been more than eleven or twelve when she'd found it, from the look of her now. "And thank you, Kouras, for bringing this to me. Citizens shouldn't have dangerous toys," he said formally, cautioning. He tucked the tube into his belt.

"It was a long time ago," Shawme said wistfully. "When I lived here in Aphrodisia House."

"She has her own house now," Kouras said defensively. Outside, lightning flickered; more thunder rumbled, closer now. "Don't you, Shawme?" Her hair was black tonight. Had it been black, before? "She only works here as a favor to the Madam, on special nights."

"This isn't one of those special nights, Kouras, so far as you're concerned. You're on duty. Get back to it." *Careful, Kouras – of this harlot bearing a gift and a mage's message, both a decade old.* He turns away, to end the audience, and here are Tempus, Straton and Critias, blowing in the door on a wet wind, gusting. One look at his commander's face tells

Niko something has happened that Tempus doesn't like. Rain, beaded on their mantles, drips down onto the floor.

Patrons scatter as the Stepsons clear the bar and order drinks.

Charon and the trainees forgotten, Niko threads through the crowd, which disperses like skittering leaves. His senses fan out, showing him agitated colors dancing around Tempus, Critias, and Straton: red, yellow, white.

He meets them at the bar, sliding into the space on Tempus's right. The Riddler says, "Order something," through tight lips.

Niko does. All the Stepsons, drinks in hand, turn to watch the room.

"What's happened?" he asks, nearly in the Riddler's ear.

He'd been expecting something, like black wings coming closer, rustling overhead, these last days.

Without looking away from the couches and the tables, Tempus answers: "Sync's team found Ari and a Theban pair, dead and stripped in the uplands near the Red Foal River, horses gone. Killed with their own weapons – crossbow bolts and throwing stars. Very sloppy. We should be able to find the horses, at least, dead or alive – if we can't find Shamshi." The Riddler is enraged, barely whispering.

"Corpses were discolored, stiff," Crit adds, matter of fact.

"Stinking," Strat says. "Bellies badly bloated. Two, three days old. We started looking for them when they didn't check in with anyone." Strat is fairly growling.

Anger radiates from Tempus like physical heat, making Niko start to sweat. This means pyres tomorrow, funerary rites (both Stepson and Theban), and all the gloom and disorientation that comes with them.

Charon spies them and heads their way, cutting through the crowd like a trireme on the attack. Now they must tell

Charon that two of his are dead, probably at the hands of the renegade Stepson.

"First blood," Niko says softly, squeezing his eyes shut for a moment, struggling to remain impassive. *Ari.* Niko had known Ari since the Tyse campaign.

"But not last," Tempus promises.

"Look what Kouras found on one of the whores here." Niko pulls out the dart tube, with its poisoned darts, and shows it to Tempus. "She's had it for ten years. Randal told her to hold it for us if we returned."

"Randal." The Riddler shakes his head. "Just what we don't need here: a wizard weapon."

"Commander, what would wizards want with poison? Sorcery doesn't work here now, according to Torch. Even if it was a wizard weapon once, that poison's so old it's probably lost its power," Crit says sensibly.

"Let's hope we haven't lost ours." The Riddler's gaze now fixes on Kouras, who is studying everything from one corner of the room, arms at his sides, ready and waiting. Tempus rubs his jaw. "Give the dart tube back to Kouras. Maybe then the rain will stop."

When they went outside to get the horses, the rain had stopped and Niko's sable mare was gone.

## *Chapter 15: Gods and Heroes*

"Look at them," Lysis says to Kouras as the pyre burns low and men drift away toward the barracks, to mourn or drink or ride out to their duty. Three fighters, dead: two Thebans, Dienekes and Chlidon; one Stepson, Ari. For the first time, Abarsis, the Stepsons' patron shade, took all three fallen fighters away on smoke and flame, soul by precious soul. Tonight's ceremony was more a Stepson ritual than Theban; yet all of neither, some of both: new rites for a new and greater Sacred Band. Thebans wander about, awed but uneasy, not knowing whether their brothers are bound for far Elysion, or some other rest. Pipes sound softly in the twilight, an old Theban hymn to the dead. The oncoming night is lucent with memories. "Just *look* at them," says Lysis again.

"Look at who?" Kouras asks. He has Shawme's dart tube in his belt pouch; it feels cool to the touch. Kouras doesn't really care what Lysis has to say. Ari is with Abarsis and the storm god in heaven. Their Stepson, Ari, had died protecting those two Thebans – from Sham, probably. But not certainly. *Long spears, thunking into flesh.* So much dying and grieving. Damned Thebans. "Who are you *talking* about?"

"The Riddler and Stealth. Look at them."

Last gleam of firelight, first rays of starlight play on ceremonial panoplies as Tempus and Niko, with Straton and Critias alongside, go to get their horses in the coming dark. "I'm looking. So what? They're not coming this way. They have better things to do. Find Stealth's horse, for one." Insult added to injury, that the horse of the Band's second-in-command was stolen.

"*Those* two…they're like Odysseus and Diomedes on the night hunt," Lysis says admiringly in a muted tone. "They're like the heroes of the Iliad, with their swift-footed horses, swaggering off to battle as the gods decree."

"Like *who?* Lysis, get a grip. Hero-worship will get you killed. And they're not swaggering. They're in a hurry." Lysis might be blessed by Harmony and have his father, leader of the Thebans, watching over him here, but Sanctuary is storm god territory, as far as Kouras is concerned. Kouras is angry at the Thebans – at anything Theban. He must be careful: death always makes him want to kill something in return.

Stepsons met the Band's leaders with four prancing horses: the Riddler's two silver Trôs horses, Crit's chestnut, and the bay ghost horse. The two pairs mounted, reined around, and all four thundered away into the night, toward the city, mantles billowing out behind them. Above, the sky goes from dark blue to blue-black. Stars will be bright tonight with the fat moon rising, unhidden by clouds.

"Let's find Arton, report to Sync and go. Your father's not coming, Lysis. Sync's leading, with Gayle, until we get to town. Then we've got our own patrol. Hurry or we'll be late." They were posted to the Maze tonight, their first patrol of Sanctuary's infamous slum.

Gayle had assigned Kouras a big dun from the Stepsons' string. He didn't usually get so good a horse. The stallion is a handful, busy testing Kouras as to who is who and which of them, horse or rider, is in control. His legs were already aching. The dun wants convincing. Kouras is grateful for the dark. At least Sync and Gayle, up ahead, don't see him struggle. All the horses were reassigned tonight, because the mare was missing. Maybe Sync will let Kouras stop by Aphrodisia House to see Shawme when his shift is done. He side-passed the dun over to Arton's gelding and had to kick hard to get it done. Straton rode this horse, when he wasn't on the ghost horse. Like rider, like horse: the dun is as stubborn and immune to coercion as the big interrogator.

They were near the White Foal split when the first arrow whispered over Kouras's head. Then a second nearly struck the dun. Kouras could hear the air rushing to get out of the crossbow bolt's way. The arrow seemed slow to him, as if he could grab it in flight, just reach out and grasp it while it pushed air against his face, going by his nose.

In one motion, Sync wheeled his horse and fired a bolt, cursing. Gayle swung his mount around on Sync's right, swearing and shooting almost in unison. Kouras shot back down the trajectory of the last incoming bolt, aiming where he thought the shooter was hiding; and nocked another bolt. He couldn't see their assailant. Lysis fired next, crouching low on his horse's neck.

Then a quarrel from this hidden enemy hit Lysis in the thigh and the Theban cried out. Sliding off his horse, buttocks to mount, Kouras was already aiming his crossbow when Sync called the dismount code. Lysis, pinned by the thigh to his saddle, fumbled for another quarrel and swept the dark with his crossbow's snout before he shot back. Sync fired again. Then Gayle did. Then Kouras did.

Kouras had never heard so clearly in battle: hooves pounding dirt; girths squeaking; metal jingling; men cursing; labored breathing, grunts and whistles; shortswords rasping from scabbards; crossbows firing. Reactions of the others seem so slow to him, orders from his patrol leader superfluous.

Kouras doesn't care about Sync's orders now. He can hardly hear Sync or Gayle above the blood pounding in his ears. There's a shooter out there somewhere. He stands behind his horse, its reins under his foot, and shoots over its saddle, aiming where he thinks the quarrels are coming from, cranking his crossbow. And cranks and levers and shoots again. And again, moving with his mount as it sidles left and right.

Everyone is shooting, even Lysis. Crossbow bolts whisper by. Kouras strains his eyes to catch a glimpse of their attacker. A gleam, a telltale sign. Some flash of panoply, some movement in the dappled night. Not enough moonlight yet, but almost. *Almost.*

His heart is beating faster. He can *almost* see.... Almost feel the other shooter; almost find the enemy in the dark. He nocks one more quarrel, fires one more bolt into the trees across the road. His horse jigs, jostling his hand on the trigger. The shot goes wild.

"That's enough," Sync decrees. "Hold your fire." Kouras doesn't.

Gayle shouts, "Hold your porking fire. Everybody. Kouras, darling, that means you, too."

Kouras doesn't see Lysis at first, in the dark, but he hears him. Lysis is chattering, shocky; his voice is shaky, high and full of bravado.

As the moon finally begins to rise, Gayle swears at the quarrel in Lysis's thigh: "Porking arrow's porking-well stuck in the saddle. Hold still, Lysis. I'm going to break it off."

Lysis yelps.

"Let me go after him," Kouras implores the night, feeling like a guard dog on too short a leash. "The god will help me.

He's running. Can't you hear him? In the underbrush? I think I hit him. I know I can find him…."

"Don't argue with me, Stepson," Sync barks, in no mood for suggestions. "Follow orders, boy. I said, 'that's enough.' We stay together. Get these horses off the road. Down in the gully, there, where there's cover. I need to see how bad this wound is."

So they will be pinned down here half the night, waiting for someone (who isn't here) to shoot at them.

Mount in tow, Arton comes over to Kouras, eye-whites bright in the moonlight, saying breathlessly, "See? My mother *said:* Three of Swords, reversed – blood and conflict. Death card, upside down. *Danger.*"

"Bull's balls upside down. Danger? Facing danger is our job, Hawk. It's easy to predict trouble when there's a renegade Stepson out here, picking us off, and everybody knows it," Kouras snaps. He feels invincible, feels like the storm god himself, full of wrath and hungry for a target, something to kill. He has a grievance to redress.

Shoot at *me? Beware Sham, the wrath of the storm god. And his son.*

Above their heads, the sky clouds over completely, where before the night was utterly clear. Lightning flares, revealing everything around them, bright as day. Thunder peals. Lightning strikes and strikes again, so fast the thunder can't keep up and when thunderclaps comes rolling, they sound like remonstrance from heaven. The ground beneath them shakes and quivers. Horses rear and paw the sky, then plunge, blaring. In the bright-white flashes of lightning, Kouras can see blood streaming from Lysis's thigh, the bolt buried so deep in flesh that it goes right through and the broken shaft sticks out the other side. Thunder roars and roars and roars again.

Rain deluges them, as they scramble with their spooky horses down into the gully by the road. Lysis's arm is over Gayle's shoulder, both of them one easy target now. Lysis can't walk unaided. Kouras has to take Lysis's horse, which is terrified and neighing all the way.

Lightning cracks the sky and thunder shakes the ground once more. Now there's a whipping wind to drive the rain, to clean the wound on Lysis's skewered leg: the storm god's rain, soaking them all to the skin. And Kouras thinks, *Too late, Father. Leave off with thy lightning. Our enemy has fled. You're scaring all the horses.* Does Vashanka really hear him?

It seems so, but he's never known for certain. And god or no god, he was stuck here, by Sync's order, in a muddy ditch – with Gayle swearing a blue streak; with Arton marveling that his vision came true; with Lysis going shocky and incoherent; and with all the frightened horses, milling and neighing. No matter what the storm god wanted, there'd be no more chasing after this enemy tonight. Maybe Kouras's bolt had sped true, but there'd be no telling: any blood trail would be washed away by the torrential rain falling.

*Sham, you'd better run.*

## *Chapter 16: Gift of Heaven*

Niko hadn't gone back to the barracks with Tempus when the weather finally broke. Another long night of searching Sanctuary had turned up no trace of Niko's sable mare. The mare was no one else's responsibility: he had lost her; he must find her; not take up the Band's time, searching for one horse. He felt invaded, violated, singled out and too angry for his *maat* to help him. He needed to check the horse-traders' stalls. He was praying she might be there – or anywhere. If she were dead, there wasn't enough room in hell for the thief to hide from him. But he didn't think she was dead.

His mare should have come back when he called her. If she were anywhere near, she would have. He had gone to his rest-place and called her. He'd looked out through her eyes. He could see a stall around her, but nothing to tell him where that stall was, or if he was really sensing her alive and well, or just wishing he was.

He was riding one of Tempus's Trôs stallions, a big dapple gray like all the Trôs-breds. Perhaps one of the best horses in the world, kill-trained and experienced beyond what most horses ever learned. On the day of the funerary rites for Ari and the Theban pair, Tempus had been so kind, so understanding: the Riddler had brought out the Trôs, tacked up and ready, and handed him its reins without a word. He shouldn't have this horse, invaluable to the Band, since he'd lost them the Aškelonian mare. He'd said that. Tempus just clapped him on the shoulder, saying, "We'll find her, Niko," and went back into the barn.

Dawn was breaking, the Maze coming to life. The byways were clean, for once, washed by the downpour. Men and women swept their storefronts' debris out into the streets, maintaining the standard of the neighborhood. He rode by the Vulgar Unicorn, wondering if anyone he'd known was still there. The few he'd recognized on the streets looked so much older; and they looked at him as if they'd seen a ghost: no one aged in Lemuria, and he'd spent five years in the eternal city at the edge of time as well. So these folk all looked a decade older and he hadn't changed, except for a few more scars here and there.

He rode west toward the farmer's market, out by the caravan grounds near the White Foal River. When he got there, every horseman who saw the Trôs stared unabashedly. There were at least a dozen traders leading stock back and forth before prospective buyers. He slid off the Trôs and strolled, reins in hand, over to the nearest horse trader, squat and jowly with greasy skin and black spots on his face.

"You want to sell that horse, soldier?" said the trader in a Nisi accent. "Give you a good price. Not much of that blood around, except up in Free Nisibis, and they don't sell the ones they's got." At least there was still a Free Nisibis; Niko had fought in the war to make it so. Those Nisibisi horses were kin to his, from when the Stepsons had a stock farm there.

"He's not for sale." Three other traders had been edging close. They heard the answer to the question everyone wanted to ask and moved away, back to their canvas stalls. "I'm looking for a mare."

"A mare for *him?* I'll show you the best I've got, but I don't think you'll want her…." The best horses were always stabled closest to the town.

"Not for him. The mare I'm looking for has light brown eyes with black flecks, a black stripe down her spine, and black dapples on a gold-bay coat: sable colored. Big. Very strong. Seen her?"

The man hadn't. You could dye a hair-coat any color, though, so Niko had to look at every big mare in the market.

He didn't find her and the Trôs kept collecting admirers. People trailed the horse to see what the mercenary with the gray stallion had in mind.

When he gave up and left, he was satisfied she wasn't in the farmer's market. Heading back to the barracks, he rode north on General's Road under a sky that was blue overhead and fighting valiantly to withstand storm clouds blowing inland.

There was one thing he hadn't tried: he could ask the dream lord, his mare's breeder, for help. To do that, he'd need to find Aškelon in his dreams, or use his transcendent perception. But he wasn't calm enough. And he didn't have time to sleep, let alone dream. Not yet.

He was hoping the long ride would soothe him. The stallion single-footed along. Birds chirped and butterflies flitted; rabbits hopped in the grass to the east where, beyond, a few farms lay. Wheat and hay fields waved in the sun. He was just thinking he hadn't realized there were so many farms out this way when he heard another horse approaching from his left. Overhead, a red-tailed hawk circled, then flew leftward, its shadow in his path. Right to left, overhead, was the best of bird omina.

The Trôs didn't break gait, but gave an ear-splitting welcome to a horse coming from a side road where bushes and trees grew tall.

The oncoming horse whinnied, a high-pitched cry. He knew that whinny like he knew his own heartbeat. His pulsed raced. *Wait.* And then, there was his sable mare, a woman in leathers astride her.

The rider's long honey hair flowed freely down her back. His mare, her tipped-in ears pointing his way, started to trot toward him.

*Wait.* He almost drew his shortsword. He loosened it in its scabbard. Then he halted the Trôs, one hand on his hilt, while horse and rider came his way. His pulse slowed. His heartbeat steadied. He was acutely aware of everything around him. The wind on his face brought him the smells of meadow and hayfields nearby. Birds fluttered among the trees. Bushes bowed in the breeze along the roadside as the horse and woman approached. *Wait.*

*Wait.* Until she had closed the distance between them, until his mare and the Trôs stood nearly nose to nose.

"That's my horse you've got there," he said flatly.

"I know, Stepson," said the woman. "Your mare with no name. She turned up in my backyard yesterday morning. Since no one came to claim her, I thought to ride out to your barracks to return her."

"No need," he said. "I'll take her." This was the young noblewoman he'd met outside Illyra's fortune-telling shop in the Bazaar. She was even more beautiful than he remembered; but it had been dark that night, with torchlight flickering.

"It's a long ride back to your barracks, Stealth called Nikodemos. Come to my house and give your gray some water first. It's right down this path."

Somehow, there seemed no harm. She was correct. Tempus's gray would like a drink; deserved one, before the lengthy ride into the uplands. His anger had been replaced with relief. He had found his mare.

The woman motioned him to come along. So he followed her, keeping his stallion behind the mare's swishing tail. The woman sat a horse well. They rode up a sheltered path, around a bend, to a house with columns, white and hidden from the road. He'd had no idea that such a house was back here, but he'd been away a long time. A servant came unbidden to take their horses and water them.

Sliding off the Trôs, he loosened his horse's girth and handed over its reins. Before he let the man take his mare, he touched her all over: there was no heat in her hooves, her pasterns, her knees, or her hocks. She seemed unharmed. She whickered and butted him with her head.

"Come inside, Stealth called Nikodemos. Have some water yourself. Wait out the heat of the day."

"Thank you," he said. It would be impolite to refuse.

Inside, all was cool and airy, filled with diffuse light. She disappeared and reappeared, bringing water, wine and fruit for them. "You should eat something." The sound of her voice made it seem so. He ate some fruit while she watched.

"We shall celebrate the reunion of two loved ones." She moved like a dancer, with a fascinating grace. "Here, let me take your things."

He held on to his weapons, saying, "I won't be here long."

"Of course you won't," she said, coming up to him so close that they nearly touched.

She put her hand on his swordbelt.

He knew he should back away, get his horses, and ride out of there. *Right now.*

"I need to go." He didn't make a move. She didn't take her hand away. He knew where this was going but he couldn't find the resolve to stop it. "I have responsibilities."

"Of course you do."

This isn't his first gymkhana, not the first time he's been waylaid, but for some reason he doesn't know what to say or do this time. Her hand is still on his belt, just resting there, not asking or demanding anything. He doesn't make a move to touch her, unwilling in any way to force the issue. He is just a fighter; she is some noble lady. He can't risk being thought forward, misreading her, or displeasing her.

She smells like meadow, like new mown hay and morning sun. By now he isn't thinking of anything but her eyes, her innocent face, her smooth skin and honey hair down to her hips.

"Come, child of balance, you have all the time you need."

He is undone in a heartbeat, drowning in those wide, soft eyes.

Her fingers unbuckle his swordbelt. All the while she holds his eyes with hers, never blinking. It is impossible to resist her. There is no reason even to try.

"Stand still," she says. She runs her hands over him, caressing him here and there and everywhere. His skin flares hot wherever her fingers slide along him.

He hasn't felt such a touch in years. He hasn't let down his guard so far in forever and a day.

Somehow she was behind him and before him and he was naked. Her fingers found the grievous scars on his groin, on his buttocks. And he felt more sensation there than he had for so very long.

She says, "What's this? All these wounds?"

He says, "I got those winning." It is what he always says, on the few occasions anyone sees those scars and dares to ask about them.

She says, "You've won a lot, then."

As never before, he feels he must explain. So he does: "I'm a son of the armies. Priests did some of that to me. Politics, some. Some I got for no good reason. I have a calling – to restore balance. When balance is restored, people get hurt."

Her sweet eyes seem about to spill tears. He doesn't want that. He picks her up and kisses her eyelids. "It's all right," he says.

She is light as a feather, her honey-colored hair brushing his chest, his arms; tickling his skin, his groin, and his thighs. He carries her upstairs, to a bed as soft as clouds, in a room painted like the skies above.

He is spinning, joyously out of control, by then. He goes where she leads him, does what she tells him, and never once thinks of anything but the depth of her eyes and the beauty of her bared soul. She fits him so perfectly. He can't restrain himself. He's cut loose from everything but her. She sets him afire.

When that fire burns low, he stretches out against her, feeling safe and warm. Sleep steals over him as he lies there with her in his arms.

He doesn't know how long they slept. When he woke, she was still beside him. The sun was still shining. He had to get back to the barracks.

She walked him to his horses, soft eyes always keeping him enthralled. The horses were ready and waiting.

He couldn't think of a thing to say but, "Thank you… for taking such good care of her…and me. It's been a long time…."

"Nikodemos, be careful, now. Don't lose that mare again. Next time I might not be here to find her."

When he rode out of there, ponying his mare, he realized he still didn't know her name. So he went back to find out, and couldn't even recognize the path to her house. All he saw were overgrown bushes and a few ramshackle, deserted buildings in the fields.

*Not a witch, this time. My maat knows better. Then, what?*

He didn't have an answer.

After he got back to the barracks with his mare, he was putting her in her stall when Critias came by and leaned on the half-door. "I see you found the mare. Good. At least one thing went right today. Did you hear about Lysis getting crossbow-shot last night? Ambush. They never saw who fired on them. Not Sync's fault, but on his watch. Riddler's getting ready to go back out hunting. You might want to see him before he does."

"That bad?"

"He's not happy. And he's got his leopard-skin mantle and his boar's-tooth helmet. I just thought you should know. I saw to Lysis and Charon for you." Meaning that Niko should have been here to do it, not dallying in town on private business.

Niko vaulted the half door. "On my way."

*

Niko found all the Thebans gathered outside Charon's little room. Inside, Charon and Kouras were tending Lysis, Charon's bolt-shot son. Young fighters look like children when first they're wounded, all soft white flesh and boneless; old fighters look decrepit and all their bones show through translucent skin. This Theban father and son were no exception.

Lysis was lying on his father's pallet. He stared up at Niko with eyes full of pupil sunk deep into sockets, purple against his pallid skin; blood still seeped through the bandage on his thigh. *Long spears, thunking into flesh. Man staggers backward, impaled, groaning.*

His father, Charon, looked even worse: the injuries Charon had sustained were of the heart – of conscience, not of body – but they showed on him in every muscle and line. Deep creases in Charon's weathered face might have been rubbed with charcoal; each whisker stood out black against blanched skin.

Niko knew just how Charon felt. Someone had brought a crutch hastily whittled from maple and propped it against a wall, near a small shrine to Harmony in one corner of Charon's whitewashed room. Niko recognized the statuette, the little shells filled with oil, water and wine, and the flute from the goddess's appearance on the jetty. After letting Niko inside, Charon retreated with Kouras to a corner of the tiny room and didn't say a word.

Helmet under his arm, Niko said, "How are you, Lysis? We hear you put up a good fight. Sync was pleased. Remember: locate, fix and destroy – that's the mission with the renegade." Better to depersonalize this adversary. "You managed two out of three."

Lysis said, "Stealth, it was Kouras who put up the best fight." Over in the corner, Kouras stood taller. Too many sickbeds. Too many empty beds. Theban luck was still with the Sacred Band.

Niko said, "Nevertheless, we're looking forward to having you back in action as soon as you mend. Your Theban brothers can be proud of what you did. And so can your father." The mother was long dead. *Say something, Charon. It's your son, not your wife.*

"Thank you, Stealth," Charon said, "for coming. And thank the Riddler for us."

"He'll stop by, when he can," Niko said. There wasn't a fly or an ant on the altar with its oil and wine and water. "Kouras, do you still have that dart tube?"

Kouras brought it to Niko without a word. Niko took it to the bedside. "You'll be here a few days. We want you well armed. This is a special weapon." His fingers slid back the slide. Lysis struggled to sit up. Charon came to join Kouras by the bedside. "Look here, closely. Fifteen darts. All poisoned. Don't prick yourself; don't put the points to your tongue. Insert the dart in the tube." He did so. "Like that. Close the slide. Aim and blow through it in the direction of your enemy. The range depends on your breathing, but don't practice with the real ones. You can hit someone in this room, or twice as far away. Maybe Kouras can find you practice darts. In case your assailant tries to finish you, now you have a surprise for him. If you haven't used a dart, disarm the weapon, thus – by shaking out the dart and putting the dart away."

Charon and Lysis both reached for the dart tube. Niko gave it to the Theban youth.

"Life to you, Stepson, and everlasting glory," Niko said to Lysis.

Flushing with pride, Lysis looked up and said, "And to you, Commander."

Not quite right, but close enough.

Charon followed Niko outside: "My thanks for what you did in there."

*My job.* "He's a good young man, a credit to all Thebans."

Niko headed for the offices, where Tempus waited. Charon paced him. "I should have gone with him. Sync asked me. I had the bereaved, all the funerary aftermath…you know."

"I know. This was good for him.... Fighting without his father...." Niko rubbed his arms, where new scars prickled.

"I should have been there. I'm his left-side leader. Fighting without your partner is never good."

Niko knew that all too well. "Is there something else?"

"That weapon. It's really special?"

"Really special. If Shamshi comes for him, it may make all the difference." *If* the poison still worked; *if* it really had come from Randal into their hands; *if* Shamshi really was the attacker, and the attack was not just coincidental, random violence. "When Lysis is well and riding, I want it back."

Now Charon's color was better. He stood up straighter. "Our goddess, Harmony, will hear your praises sung tonight, Stealth called Nikodemos."

*Please, gods, no.* "You just keep me informed about Lysis's progress."

## *Chapter 17: Whiplash from the Gods*

Crit woke and knuckled sleep from bleary eyes. Place and time came back to him in bits and pieces. He was back in Sanctuary among the damned, wasn't he? Or was it all just a bad dream?

Let's see: a Stepson dropping dead on the training field after surviving Chaeronea; a whore roughed up by one of their own and then found dead in mysterious circumstances; a Stepson-trainee wrapped in hide, spirited away from Enlil's altar without a trace; his rightman back in the clutches of the witch; two Thebans and one Stepson killed with their own weapons; a young Theban shot in the leg by a hidden enemy with a Stepson crossbow; a renegade on the loose whom the best of the Sacred Band can't find, no matter how they try. Definitely Sanctuary.

And to top it all off, Shamshi, the wizard boy, is stalking the Sacred Band while the Band is hunting him.

Crit washes in the basin by his bed and shaves the beard he's let grow too long, ever since Tempus took a spear in the heart and all of them to hell with him. Again. Best to be clean-shaven in summer. The bandage on his right thigh is stiff and dirty, but smaller; he changes it, tying off the ends.

Maybe Crit should count his blessings: Stealth's good mare is stolen, or run off, and then fortuitously returned to them with all her tack and all his gear, no questions asked, or answered; Kouras is nursing a crush on a whore who comes complete with arcane weapons and gives them up without a fight; a foreign goddess appears on the lighthouse spit, grapples with the storm god in the sand, and the Thebans proclaim it a miracle; the necromant warns them to do their jobs or she will – at least now he's got a volunteer.

(Ischade, with her arms around Straton's chest, riding….)

And the rain just won't stop falling.

He puts on his loinguard, his linen and leathers, his armor. *Their commander, staggering back, impaled, groaning.* Crit had never thought he'd live to see that if he lived a thousand years. Now he can't see anything else when he shuts his eyes. And the Riddler heals, one more time. Takes mortal wounds, and rises from his sickbed with that look on his face that says he has too much to do to let death intervene. But it took so long, this time. And it took so much from their commander, this time. What about next time?

He girds on his swordbelt, grabs his helmet, his most rainproof mantle, looks around once and latches the door to his room as he leaves. The sound is too sharp, too final on this day that feels unrighteous.

Thebans are everywhere in the barracks, hovering over their wounded youngest brother, haunted and morose, worshipping their Harmony with flutes and pipes, but causing only discord. This band of lovers, saved from the Chaeronean battleplain by the Riddler and his right-side partner, bring death and destruction everywhere they go. Better that the Thebans are here in Sanctuary than in sweet Lemuria, or anywhere else Crit has been with Tempus. Is that it? Is that what Crit's commander, with a will as inscrutable as the gods', wants from this mission? For the curse to play out, for the Thebans to mend or die here, where death is cheap and everything is always wrong? Tempus says so, and looks at Crit with those hooded eyes that have seen more battlefields than Crit can count. To save something, where precious little can be saved. Again and again. To tip a balance, change destiny, trick fate.

Crit looks for Straton everywhere around the barracks and can't find him. He asks; no one knows where Straton is today. Crit gets his sorrel horse, tacks it up, and takes his shield along, using its shoulder strap to sling it on his back. Things just don't feel right. Crit has learned from serving with the Riddler: when things feel wrong, take heed.

He rides alone out the gate, toward Sanctuary. Maybe he can find some wrongs that swinging a simple sword can right. Maybe the sniper will try for Crit. A bit of honest battle would do him good, against an enemy he can see, and slash, cut into quivering chunks and vanquish. Take a leaf from Niko's book.

Crit (like so many others) will fight and die for the Riddler, eons of men and battles, trusting those long and ancient eyes. Now, by their commander's will, the Sacred Band has a home, where someday the Thebans will be welcome – someday, when their loyalty is proven. Crit wishes he were home now, a world away in far Lemuria, a place meant for changing destiny, for staging missions stretching out unending – if you're brave enough, if you're tough enough, if your faith never wavers. But no one's going home until the Thebans pass or fail the Riddler's test: get trained up, or die trying.

More than that, Tempus will not say. But the Riddler is the Riddler. If Crit can solve the riddles, maybe he can get himself and Straton out of Sanctuary, home safe and sound to Lemuria, undamned and unensorceled. Sorcery doesn't work here anymore, people say. A dust storm in a battle against evil took all the witchery away, years ago, people say.

Crit is not so sure it's true. The skies open up; rain pours down, pooling in his horse's path.

On these wet, unsettled days, Stealth has that look seen so often in the Riddler's eyes: so much held back, so little given, focused far away. Not one word about how Niko found that mare.

Critias has his job to do. He has to know. He reins around, goes back the way he just came, splashing through the mud, and asks for Niko. Stealth is in with Tempus.

No time could be better for what Crit wants to say. He ties his muddy horse outside the commander's quarters. He knocks. The sound is hollow. It echoes from the overhanging roof while rainwater runs down in streams, splashing.

Niko comes out, stubble-faced and wary, closing the door behind his back. Crit sees, over Niko's shoulder, that the commander is in there. He sluices mud off himself with the edge of his hand.

"What, Crit?" Increasingly, Niko sounds and acts like the Riddler, but his commander's rightman looks more tired today than Tempus, with epochs behind him, ever seems.

Now that he's here, and Niko is, Crit is uncertain. "Something's wrong," he says, accusing. "Something you and the commander aren't telling me. Something I need to know. And Strat's gone off somewhere in all this rain. Left no word. Does he have orders?" *If he does, why don't I know?*

Niko leans back against the door, looking somewhere over Crit's right shoulder, where the eaves end and rain torrents down, as loud as a waterfall. Thunder rumbles, far off.

Niko's eyes catch his, like a wolf grabs you by the throat. "We sent him down to ask the necromant to meet with us, set a place and time." Niko, exhausted, has that raspy edge to his voice that never bodes well. "We didn't want to trouble you. He'll be fine."

"You *what?* Gods damn it." Crit nearly struck him. His fists balled so hard his nails dug into his palms. He took three deep breaths, closed his eyes, saw the Chaeronean battleplain before his inner sight, and opened them. "How *could* you?" He turned on his heel to stride away. If Niko touched him, there'd be a scuffle in the barracks where all, even Thebans, would see.

Time stopped. His heart refused to beat. The walls around the barracks seemed higher, more like a prison. This had been a slaver's estate, before Stepsons had slid down the walls and taken it by force, long ago. Crit had been here then, a mercenary in the pay of the first Stepson, called Abarsis, the warrior-priest. Abarsis had died in that battle with a barbed spear point up under his ribs and no way to get it out. *Long spear, thunking into flesh.*

They'd snapped the haft. And Tempus had held the famed Slaughter Priest in his arms until Abarsis breathed his last. Thereafter, Tempus kept Abarsis's Sacred Band and took his war-name, 'Stepson,' for their unit. But it was a javelin, not a long spear, that day. Wasn't it? *Not the same. Not the same.*

Niko lunged, catching Crit by the shoulder, spinning him around. "Fox, don't you walk away from me." Warning. Only Strat could match Niko's prowess, when Niko first came to Tempus's service. Now? Save for the Riddler, Niko was the deadliest they had in combat, the most efficient killer of them all. "Don't ever walk away from me again." Too quietly.

Almost chest to chest they stood there. Around them, nothing moved. No one made a sound. Crit could see Niko's angular jaw work, then death's-head calm come over him; familiar scars on that almost pretty face, from battles they'd fought together. Beyond Niko was their commander's closed door. All around, in the rainstorm, too many people must be watching. Crit couldn't risk taking his eyes off Niko to look and see.

"Why Strat?" It was all Crit could think of to say. "For pity's sake, why Strat, with all these others here?" He unballed his fists; saw the marks his own nails dug in his palms as he spread his arms wide: open-handed, not threatening – just muddy and deeply chilled.

"Because she'll do it, for *him.*" Laconic. Reasonable. Niko put both hands on his hips. "Because the Riddler ordered me to send him."

As if he'd been listening, Tempus pulled back the door and said, "In here. Both of you. Right now."

Inside, everything turned grainy green; then shadows and men became distinct: all three of them, like a perfect triangle of hostility in that dark little room with only two chairs, a narrow bed, and a table covered with maps and weapons. The Riddler broke formation, seeming to tower over Crit as he strode to the open door where the rain gusted in, shut it hard and stood there, looking first at one of them, then the other, big hands in his belt.

"This stops, between you two. Now," Tempus said so softly that Crit's breathing nearly drowned out the words.

Water and mud dripped from Crit's mantle and his boots onto the floor. He could hear the drops hit the wood. The bandages on his thigh and arm were soaked; wounds underneath, aching.

Niko said, "It won't happen again," running a hand through slate-dark hair, wet and too long to be comfortable under a helmet.

"Sorry, Commander." Crit wasn't, and everybody knew.

A silence full of thumping hearts and pounding blood stretched out too long.

"All right," Tempus said, "that's the end of it." But it wasn't. "What else, Fox?"

Now that he had his audience, Crit was dumbstruck. Then he said, because he couldn't help himself: "I need to know when and where you send Straton, and why. Before you do. It's my right to know, by rank, privilege and pairbond. I would have gone with him." Muddy rivulets still dripped off him.

"Stealth didn't tell you?" Tempus shifts his attention to Niko and Crit can breathe again. "Don't do that, henceforth, either."

Niko didn't say a word but he didn't flinch or drop his head or look away.

"More?" Tempus asked Crit.

"I need to know what happened with that mare of Niko's – how he found it, where, when. It's strategic; Stepson business. I need to have all the pieces." He was wet to the bone.

"No, you don't," said Niko.

*"Nikodemos,"* Tempus said, out of patience, voice like a rockslide. "Crit, we don't think it was Shamshi. A woman found the mare and returned her to Niko. Let it go, Crit. If I think you need to know more, you'll know."

Crit choked off a laugh, a scoff. "A woman. Figures. That's all I wanted – to know if you thought the renegade was behind the mare's theft."

"Now you know. We don't think that," said Niko, crossing his arms.

"I'm going to find Strat. Unless I have other orders?"

"Go," Tempus said. He wrenched open the door so hard it slammed against the wall. Crit blundered through it.

The Riddler came out, pulling the door closed behind him, and walked with him across the muddy courtyard in the rain. "Critias, these are difficult days. It's not surprising there's tension. Build your force; don't let it splinter. You're doing a good job here, better than any could ask. This place will make or break the future for some. Expect it. There's everything to win, nothing to lose for these Thebans." Tempus squinted at the sky with its moisture-laden clouds. "The rain will stop soon."

"Is the god angry at us?" The storm god, Enlil, is always wherever Tempus is.

"Which one?" Tempus says, dark humor drawing back thin lips. "Theirs or ours? We've made something mad enough to kill, over those Thebans. That Theban Band is worth saving."

*'Is.'* Not *'was.'* Crit says nothing.

Tempus adds, "We've faced angry gods before. Worry about Shamshi. We trained him. And he wants as much of our blood as he can spill." Tempus clapped Crit on the back. "Go find your partner."

Out of there – sodden and trembling on his mount in reaction to holding so much emotion in check – Crit gave the sorrel its head and let the wet wind whip him as the horse galloped toward the city. At least he knew just where to look. Not like Niko, turning Sanctuary upside down searching for a horse that ran off to his girlfriend's house. With Niko, there was always some woman, somewhere, waiting.

The woman in Crit's sights was Ischade, but he didn't find her. He was halfway to Shambles Cross when Strat came splashing his way, alone, on his bay ghost horse. Crit was unreasonably relieved.

"Crit, let's go get a drink and wait for the rain to stop. It's nearly noon," called Strat, grinning through the mud on his face as if nothing were wrong. Strat looked innocent. The ghost horse looked guilty: no rain or mud stuck to it. Crit would look the other way, this once.

He was happy to ride along with his partner beside him, letting relief wash over him. Strat seemed undamaged. Crit felt foolish for making such a fuss.

When they pulled up outside the Vulgar Unicorn, venerable alehouse with its autoerotic sign out front, the rain had nearly stopped. They tied their horses to the rail. Crit said, "So, did you see her – the witch?"

Strat said, "They told you. Nobody wanted you to worry. I can handle it."

*Like last time? Or the time before?* For the street, this was the wrong conversation. *"Did* you see her? Get a meet?"

"She'll talk to the Riddler. Downwind Beach. Just after dusk, tomorrow. Or she'll talk to me. It's up to him."

"Or me," Crit snapped, not meaning to start anything.

Straton looked at him through frank blue Rankan eyes. "Critias, I was following orders. I still am. Yours, or theirs. Whenever, however. It'll be fine." Conciliating.

So they walked into the bar, close together, shoulders nearly brushing, tracking muddy water on the floor's shavings, as they had done so often, long ago. He caught a glimpse of the two of them in the copper mirror above the bar: they hadn't changed much or aged much, thanks to Cime's Lemurian powers. Just a pair of Stepsons on duty in the town. People made way, as in former times, and everything that had happened in the ten years since they'd left here seemed to melt away.

Halfway through their second ale, Crit said, "If you go to see her again, I'm going with you." Crit rubs his right arm; on it, Chaeronean mementos show dark against pale skin where bandage had recently been.

"Just like old times, if Enlil allows," Straton promises, invoking the god.

Perhaps not quite the most prudent turn of phrase, in Sanctuary. *Be careful what you pray for, Strat.*

*

Tempus and his rightman stole through the night, riding to their rendezvous with the necromant on the Downwind beach, out in the open where nothing could be hidden.

A sea wind began to blow. Cloudbanks, lying low all day, still threatened; the sky owned few stars to shine tonight. This sky withholding stars and even rain is an omen from some greater power, Tempus thinks.

"We wanted mercy for that other Sacred Band, those doomed souls: here it is, Niko. Do you like it so far?"

Niko is so weary he can hardly speak. His anger is profound; his *maat* barely holds it in abeyance. He's making errors. Not telling Crit before they sent Straton alone to see the witch was one: unnecessary tension.

"Yes, for the balance of the thing," says his right-side partner. "Fighters die in combat. Fighters die when things are out of balance. I still think we were right…."

Bandaran teachings, warping everything. Niko and Shamshi are both Bandaran adepts: neither is behaving predictably. Shamshi was another error shared by all: why hadn't they seen it coming?

*Fury from the heavens; fury at the gods – inseparable. The way up and the way down are one and the same.*

"The balance can get along without you for a night or two, Niko. You need to sleep."

"You don't. And you're not…yourself yet. You need me with you. You can fool the others. You can't fool me. No matter what we agreed, if you are the price for Theban souls, then I'll not pay it – or let you pay it."

"I'm better, Niko. Every day. Is it the dream lord keeping you awake?" Tempus didn't want to talk about his chest wound, closing but leaving behind keepsakes in flesh and bone. Never had Enlil let him linger so long, unrestored.

"I almost went begging to the dream lord, when the mare was missing, for help finding her. But I solved it without Aškelon's aid."

Solved it *how*, Niko wouldn't say. But Tempus knew this heart, this soul, this child of *maat*. If not Aškelon, Niko was in the grip of some other force hoping to enlist him. He'd staved off witches and the entelechy of dream, hungry for his fealty. He'd kept Enlil at arm's length, though he was an avatar of the storm god by ritual and troth. Even the foreign goddess, Harmony had seen it.

Now Enlil was petulant or had his divine hands full like the rest of them, contending with the influences sweeping in behind the Thebans. With the Thebans came the Fates, a clutch of gods, a misty underworld all their own…. Perhaps more trouble than Enlil bargained for, he who was so far away on these portentous days.

The horses clop along, toward witchery and the Downwind beach. The pair rides in silence now, each preparing for the encounter with the necromant in his own way. Tempus had chosen Sanctuary as a proving ground for the Theban band of lovers and brothers, fathers and sons. He still believes he was correct. Loyalty must be forged – to him, to his: stronger than iron, from experience, from risk – it can't be bought, or taught, or promised before the fact. Allegiance must be earned so it will hold, win or lose.

Wheedling a little mercy from the gods…. He hadn't thought the price would be so high. But honor and glory never come cheap. Before, Niko always bore the brunt of whiplash from the gods when Tempus overstepped his mandate.

This time things are different. This time it was Tempus who got hurt – and Niko, trying to protect him, not seeing traps or snares along the way. Changes in the heavens wrought changes on the earth.

His Trôs horse grunts disapprovingly, as if the stallion knows his mind. Meeting with the witch again in Sanctuary is risky, not a peril to be underestimated.

He'd hoped he was done with witches. Theomachy was quite enough to deal with, rolling down from on high and catching up fragile mortals, destroying so many, so thoughtlessly, so often.

But here they were again, out in the open under a moon coming full, nearly at the Downwind beach. You could smell the rank, briny air, rotting corpses of shark and whale thrown up by the storms to die on the sand. *Perfect.*

When they got to the rendezvous, they both dismounted and stood beside their horses. He heard the rasp of Niko's shortsword coming out of its scabbard; his dream-forged sword and scabbard made by Aškelon, regent of the seventh sphere: no small threat, even to the necromant. That sword and his own could wreak havoc on devil or demon or worse.

"What do you think?" asked Niko.

"I think we'd better solicit her nicely for her aid. Put the sword away."

He sheathed it with a careless rasp of metal, to tell Tempus he was annoyed.

Then she was there – tiny – in black, with her cloak brushing the sand. The horses snorted suspiciously and scrambled backward until they had no more rein.

"Ischade. Thank you for coming," Tempus says.

"You brought your boy. A gift? For *me?* How thoughtful, Riddler. Shall I devour him right here, or is he take-away? Would you like a piece? There's enough to share." She floats toward Niko, those huge eyes surrounded in a white, white face, just a glimmer in her cowl.

Niko curses under his breath in Nisi and shifts, not retreating. His hand is on his sword's hilt. Tempus touches his elbow and withdraws. *Hold steady.*

"You'd find him tough, unappetizing. We need your help, Ischade. You know what this is about."

Niko's cuirass, which responds to supernatural forces, is starting to heat up. Little curls of sparks run across his armor. An arm's length away, the witch stops. Her feet don't touch the dune. Her cloak's hem isn't sandy. Tempus wonders for a moment whether he could put his hand right through her, whether she is here at all.

Now she raises her eyes to his and the cowl falls back. So infrequently, that happens. Nikodemos sidesteps, nearly bolts. Tempus has seen this witch before, unrobed. He was counting on that memory of an evening's aborted passion to keep things civil among the three of them.

"Just what is it, Riddler, you'd like me to do for you tonight? Having trouble with your staff? Bad little boys, hiding in the woods? One thinks you, who fields armies, should be able to handle a delinquent boy or two. After all, you have so many of them."

Niko gritted, "Commander…." Now he backs away, as she glides another bit toward him: two steps, three. Both horses jog in place.

"I want you to find this Shamshi, touch his mind, and tell us what's there. We'll do the rest."

"That's all you want to know? Where and how to trap that child, and just what you're trapping?"

"That's all," Tempus confirms. "No pillars of fire, no magic dust, no dogs or snakes changed to men. Well within your powers."

"It's within my power to tell you what you've got right here." Instantly, she's almost upon Niko. His armor starts to glow hotter. "Oh, *pish,*" she says, touching it with a finger. A spark snaps. The armor's glow fades.

Niko says, "Commander…" one more time. Judging from his tone, a sword will follow, directly.

"No, I don't want to know anything about him. I like him just the way he is. And Straton, too, if you please: leave that one be. Unless you'll heal that left shoulder, there's nothing you can do for Strat that we want done." *Ischade, leave off.*

"I can see why. But you really should know what's sneaking into this one's head and into his bed, if he's sitting on yours and whispering in your ear."

Niko doesn't draw his weapon or move or speak again, just stands as if transfixed.

Tempus is sure that if he waved his hand before Niko's face, the boy wouldn't blink or even know. A demonstration of power that doesn't need demonstrating, from this necromant who shouldn't be so powerful, or even be here now, where there is no sorcery, by court decree and common knowledge.

"As you wish." The necromant backs off and sits down cross-legged – not in the sand, but just above it. She floats there as her eyes roll up into her head while a breeze takes her black hair and wafts it around her face.

Niko, freed from Ischade's spell, staggers a step, off balance; and recovers. "What's happening?"

Tempus shrugs. "She's doing it. Finding Shamshi."

"And the cost?" Niko wants to know.

"Don't worry, Niko. I won't give you to her for supper." *But I'd like to know what she saw in you that made her give warning. That's a goddess and a witch, both with dire warnings about you. In Sanctuary, that's a quorum.*

"This Shamshi," says the witch, "is wizard's work. And hateful." She shakes herself like a wet dog and then she's standing. "How could you have had this thing among you for so long and not known it? This boy was on *Bandara?* Got training there? *Shame,* Nikodemos, secular adept of balance. Any son of the armies should have known better."

She swirled toward Niko, closer still. And he gave back again, until he was in between their horses. "Nothing to say, Hero? It's yours to do, I believe. So why am *I* here? To hold your cloak?"

Niko just shook his head, hands spread. "We need to find him, to kill him."

"Afraid to meet him mind to mind, brave warrior? If you can't kill him, I've said before, I can. And your commander can. And my warning stands: Beware. He's seeking you. You value mercy for the sake of balance. There'll be no balance while this abomination roams free."

Now the witch rounds on Tempus. "You two woke him up, whilst the darkness in him was sleeping. This Shamshi has made a killing field into his soul's refuge. I would stalk him for the joy of it, but he's your creation. Now, is that all? I can't tell you where he strikes next, until he knows it himself."

"Will you alert us?" Tempus asks. "And at what price?"

Ischade was windswept now, just a face. "I promise, you'll know beforehand, when next he comes. As for a price, this matter's free – so far. You brought that thing to my tidy home? Turned it loose here, where I hunt? With all those tender Thebans, who should be dead, running free? Clean up after yourselves. I'm not your mother."

## *Chapter 18: Playing the Gods' Games*

"Be polite to all, friendly to none. Be professional. Be ready to kill everyone and everything. Keep your enemies at a distance, your partners close at hand. This is Sanctuary. You have crossbows: shoot early; shoot often. The only unfair fight is the one you lose. Deception is a tactic: use it. Do whatever it takes to win. Arrows are cheap; you're expensive," Sync warns the eight mounted men before him in the morning light, just inside the horse gate.

Around him, Sanctuary awakes on this first dry morning in far too many days of rain: catcalls and spiels ring loud; hawkers and children shout; fishmongers and farm wives sing out their wares. Over the morning bustle, Sync can hear the sounds of his own cavalry: squeaking leather, metal rasping, stomp and hoof-fall. He has brought eight Sacred Banders: two Theban pairs, each commanded by a veteran Stepson to make two teams of three; one would-be seer; and a son of the storm god, some say – all policing Sanctuary today.

"Everybody remember we have two drops for messages and status changes: authority's always here – above the stables in the Maze, or at Shambles Cross. Now go find me a renegade."

Both of Sync's three-man teams departed, leaving only Arton and Kouras before him. "Arton, you're with me. Kouras, you're due at the palace. Ask for Torchholder. He's expecting you. Go north, straight up Processional Way, and you'll be there. It's big and...palatial."

With a snappy salute, Kouras set out northeast on a little brown gelding, not the most suitable horse for the reputed son of Vashanka, but perhaps the local storm god would find him a better one. Sync was short three mounts and doing the best he could.

At least it wasn't raining. The sky was blue, full of white fluffy clouds and sun smiling down. On the way here, he'd seen a rainbow as the skies cleared, most unlikely omen for this hell-spawned bubo of a town. He'd given Sham's big blue roan to Arton: a lot of horse for so slight a youngster, but he needed to see how Arton was progressing as a rider. "Arton, we're going to take one more look through Caravan Square for our three missing horses. Maybe you're right. Maybe we'll find them there."

The boy muttered something self-deprecating and reined the big horse around too hard. "Easy. He's alive, you know. Use your outside leg *on* him, not in him," Sync advised while the horse reared and threw its head and Arton grabbed some mane. Sync wasn't willing to assume that Arton couldn't see the future; the trainee just couldn't foresee how a horse would react to too much leg pressure.

Shy Arton had come to him at dawn, shuffling his feet, looking in the dirt as if his fortune were displayed there, and said he'd *seen* that their three stolen horses would be in Caravan Square – at least, he'd described a place that sounded like the square. It was a better shot than no shot at all, even though Stepsons had searched that neighborhood three times over. If Sync's old unit, the Rankan 3rd Commando, had searched this thieves' world, there'd be nothing left but sticks and stones scattered around. But he was Sacred Band now, in the pay of the palace, and treading lightly.

When they arrived at Caravan Square, Sync told Arton, "Lead on." Off went the young Stepson, as sure as could be, threading the big roan through three aisles, between tents, and around two corners. Maybe he and the roan would mesh.

"Here, I think," said Arton, lips nearly blue with trepidation, young jaw set, stopping before a big green tent.

*Courageous, laying your reputation on the line on a hunch.*

"Come on, then. Let's go see."

"Me?"

"You. Don't you want to be there?"

The boy dismounted awkwardly, dropping to the ground. *Maybe a smaller horse.* Then Sync handed his own reins to Arton and led the way on foot, over to a fat, bald man loitering outside his tent, pitched between two rope lines where nondescript horses stamped, peppered with rain-rot, whisking flies away with their tails. The boy had said they'd find a green tent; this was the green tent Arton chose.

"I'm looking for cavalry mounts," Sync said to the fat man. "Heard you might have some." Armored up, with their own horses in hand, they looked like what they were: mercenaries. *And you know damned well why we're here and what we want.* Arton led their two geldings up close behind him.

"Right this way, Colonel Stepson, sir." The fat man couldn't decide whether to flee or salivate. His gelatinous face worked. Then, walking backward and breathing hard, he waddled heavily before them into the tent. Stepsons were well-funded by the palace, everyone knew. Hands like hams rubbed together; pear-shaped body straightened; heart-shaped mouth pursed in a moon of fat. This man was an Ilsig, a local:

black hair, brown eyes, flat nose. "We have several to show you…three new ones, just brought in a few days ago, and some tack that came with them…and then a few others…."

Into the tent they went: the fat man; Sync; and the boy who thought he could see the future, leading their two horses.

When Sync's eyes adjusted to the gloom, the fat man had already stopped before three horses, next to one another in temporary wooden stalls.

Before the fat man led out each horse, Sync was already certain: these were his. The bay mare had a divot in her neck from an old arrow-wound, no white markings, a remodeling splint on her right front canon. The second was a red chestnut, with a scrape on her head where her white star should have been: somebody'd skinned her there to hide the identifying mark. He touched her shoulder, ran his hand down to her left elbow: she had an old boil there; he'd treated it himself. The third horse was Ari's big brown gelding, a seasoned warhorse with too many scars to hide and a spavined left hock.

The Band had put out descriptions of all these horses through the garrison's city guard. Ari's gelding should have white on its left hind hoof and ankle, but didn't. He bent down and rubbed hoof and hair backward, then licked his fingers and tried again, while the fat man rocked in place. Sync's hand came away with a brown stain on his fingers.

He stood up and showed the horse-dealer his fingers. "These are Stepson horses." *But you knew that, you porker.*

"I traded for them in good faith," whined the fat man.

"Let's see the gear. Tell me what the man looked like. Who brought them in?"

"It wasn't a man. It was a young woman – or I thought it was." The fat fellow brushed his nose with his knuckle and slid his eyes left and upward as a man does when he's lying. "Tall, black hair, light blue eyes," said the horse-trader innocently. "Said she got them in payment for a debt." Straton, the Band's interrogator, would decide how innocent this fat man was, later.

"What did you give for them?" Here was the gear, slung over a half wall: no weapons, but the tack was Stepson issue. Sync nearly stumbled over Arton, close behind him, when he turned around. The trainee looked as if he were about to burst with excitement.

The fat man named a price. Sync offered half: "And that price includes the gear. No haggling: you're in receipt of stolen property. You don't want trouble with us. Because trouble with us never, ever stops. You do this again, and I find out, you're out of luck and out of business."

Outside the tent, ponying the three horses of their dead comrades on leads, with nearly all their tack, Sync said, "Sweet work, Stepson. What else can you do? "

Arton's eyes were shining like the sun.

*

Molin Torchholder is eminently prepared for this meeting with Gyskouras in the east wing of the palace, only a corridor away from the private chapel consecrated to the storm god, Vashanka. No one from the council of oligarchs was here so early. *Good.* This was as he planned, just as he had planned to wear his simplest red and white robes and have his prettiest boy usher the Stepson inside and then leave them. He wanted to be alone with Gyskouras for this meeting.

Sun is streaming in the library windows, pooling on the silk rugs, shining off the marble tiles. The tall oak doors open silently when the young Stepson is brought in, staring boldly at all the wealth displayed on every wall and shelf and table. The doors close, just as silently, behind him.

Molin says nothing, assessing this warfighter-to-be with the blood of a god running in his veins – or so legend has it.

"You wanted to see me," says the red-haired boy, in his armor and his leathers and his linen. Green eyes like his mother's. Broad shoulders. A firm and careful demeanor; looking all around with calculating eyes.

"Yes. I'm so pleased to see you here at last. Sit down, Gyskouras." Make a friendly face, but not too friendly. *Sit in this single chair before my desk, as I have arranged it on this day when everything will change for you. Let me tell you of all the glory that awaits you.* "There's watered wine on the sideboard, if you're thirsty."

The youth stands just within the threshold, helmet under his arm, at parade rest. "No, thank you, Eminence. If you don't mind, I'll stand."

"But I do mind. We're going to have a conversation. I will sit at my desk; you will sit in that chair." He indicates the chair sharply with his hand. *Son of the storm god, Vashanka? Or son of the Riddler?* Tempus had been the god's proxy during the ritual copulation that produced Gyskouras. Neither god nor avatar takes direction well. *It's too early to have a test of wills. You seem so very young, for those eyes to be so appraising, your demeanor so composed.*

The young Stepson strides stiffly to the chair and takes his seat, helmet in his lap. He stares at Molin through a fighter's eyes, waiting to hear what is required of him.

*Do just what you're told and the known world can be yours. Ranke is falling away, marbles turning to dust, crumbling without a strong hand or a plan.* "Thank you, Gyskouras."

"Kouras."

"Pardon?" *Mygdonia's too far north to threaten us, with Wizardwall looming in between. We're a mighty city-state, now, not a backwater. We have a navy. We have rich trade routes, richer than a boy like you can dream.*

"Everyone calls me 'Kouras.'" This boy has a voice deeper than he'd first thought, husky and audacious.

"No war name? Mine is 'Torch.'" *The Beysib invaders from the sea are gone. The Ilsig gods still sleep their geriatric sleep, fuzzily trying to remember who and what they are. Such a ripe moment, for the right man, for fate to step in....*

"No war name. Yet."

The youth tilts his head and peers harder at Molin. "If I may be so bold, Eminence, what is this about?"

"Last time we met, you asked about your mother, Seylalha. You didn't ask about your father." *And what are you, warfighter? Are you the right man? Are you our future? Or just another nail in our coffin?*

"That's right. I didn't. My mother's dead, you said."

"It was a ritual begetting, a rite performed for and with Vashanka – by his priesthood and by Tempus." *So long ago, when the gods fought here like cats and dogs and sorcery ran wild.* This son of the storm god is steady, controlled, and even handsome in a pale and bloodless sort of way: Bandaran training makes its initiates like icebergs; most of what matters is hidden below the water-line. So Molin must look deeper. "It's time you knew about your father." *Time we know if you are really the son of the storm god, Vashanka's boy, and all our hopes reborn. Or just another child of the hero-cults....*

"I'm a Stepson, in the Riddler's service. I've sworn the Sacred Band oath. I assure you, I know my father." Gyskouras's voice is sharper, now, but his body and the face hardly move. Only his green eyes flicker, more brightly colored than they were before.

"Sacred Band? Do you have a partner? Are you paired?" Sitting quietly can be harder than running miles. Molin lets his hands slide off the table, lest the boy see quivering, or perspiration, or fingers twisting one another.

"Not yet. It's not time."

"Thank the god." *If you're all they say, you never will be paired. If Vashanka, our storm god, lurks behind those eyes, then you're just the one we need.*

"Eminence? *What* did you say?"

"Let me be frank." Molin never is. He comes around his desk and sits on it, close enough to reach out and touch this boy who stays so still, like a marble statue of a fighter or a warrior-priest or a god. *Or am I seeing only what I hope to see, need to see, since Sanctuary's gods are so weak, so old, and, at this strange time, so disengaged?* "If you are what people think you are – a true son of Vashanka, our long-missing storm god – then Sanctuary's arms will open wide to welcome you. All we have will be yours."

Gyskouras gets up, puts his helmet under his arm, and looks Molin in the eye. They are barely an arm's length apart. *"If?* This isn't humorous to me. You brought me here to mock me? I have a bad temper, compared to some. It gets out of hand sometimes. They say Vashanka is the berserker god, so beware."

Now there's blood in that face, hot flush in the cheeks, nostrils flaring white. Knuckles pale, grasping helmet with one hand, belt with the other. *Good. There's life in you. Maybe a god in you. Some real god, with real power to replace the absent Stormbringer and a dozen lesser deities who never heed the sacrifices left for them on the Street of Temples. A god to help us. Take our part. Take mine. The wizard blood within me says it's so. Just give me a sign.*

"So *beware?* If you're truly the storm god's son, I am your humble servant. Vashanka was our state-cult here once, revered above all other gods. His name was on the palace dome once. And could be again. Come with me, Gyskouras. We need to prove just who and what you are."

"You doubt me? My word? My heritage? Question me and my father, the god? Test me? Ask for proof at your peril, priest." The boy is livid, holding on to his temper with every skill he has. Outside, distantly, lightning flickers and thunder rumbles.

Molin turns his back on the young fighter (now with blood lust and surging anger in his eyes) and walks to a wall of shelves, where he pushes a shelf and a passageway opens. *Will you come, Gyskouras? Come test your fate? Meet it? And if you're worthy, will you be all we need?*

He hears the Stepson, behind him in the passageway that's nearly dark but for a square of light down at its end. "Tell me, Gyskouras," Molin asks, taking a chance, hearing the footfalls of the angry young man, closing up the distance between them, "can you stop the rain? Start it? Bring the storm?" *Can you?* "That's the only test you face, the only proof I need." *And if you can, can I get you away from that accursed Tempus and his Sacred Band?*

"Can I? I can start the rain. Bring thunder. Bring lightning," came a growl from nearly in his left ear. "Want to see?"

*Oh, yes I do.*

Then the young Stepson glimpses the statue of his father, the storm god, four cubits high. The statue of Vashanka crawls with sparks as, outside the little palace chapel and all over Sanctuary, a fierce storm breaks, driving rain before it. Storm winds howl their fury and lightning snarls from the east of heaven to the west and thunder shakes the ground. Rain pelts down from heaven. And in the storm god's chapel, Gyskouras crosses his arms and stares defiantly at the priest while lightning flares and thunder cracks and peals like chariot horses under the god's own whip, running down the sky.

*

"What say we let that fat horse-trader run away home?" Straton proposed, trying to get Crit's attention in their Shambles Cross hidey-hole. "My shoulder hurts from pushing all that blubber up the stairs. And it's not easy, hitting hard enough to make an impression through so much fat. Your hand just sinks in.... If we kill him, we've got to dispose of the body, which means getting all that dead weight back *down* the stairs. Because he's not going to fit through the window, so we can't just drop the corpse onto the street."

Critias, sitting under iron shutters tightly closed, just grunted. The table before him was overflowing with paperwork, confiscated drugs, truncheons, slingshots, and dirks. Behind Strat, in the other room, the horse-trader moaned theatrically. Crit rolls a smoke, broadleaf laced with pulcis and krrf they'd taken from some locals: the privilege of command.

"The fat man thinks it was a tall, pretty youth masquerading as a girl, who sold him our horses. Sounds like Sham to me." Strat waits for Crit to respond.

Nothing.

The sword-slice on Strat's thigh, a souvenir from Chaeronea, still itched. Strat scratched at it. "*He's* certain he doesn't know any more, I know that for a fact. Fatty will do us more good than a recruiting poster, sporting all those miles of fresh bruises. Get us a little respect from those citizens who don't remember us from last time."

Around them, like familiar old clothes, was the Shambles Cross safe house – where Crit once kept an office and now did, again. The iron shutters, like the rest of the place, were the worse for wear but still good enough. They took field reports here, ran covert agents when they had them, and sometimes slept in shifts on a narrow bench that doubled as a couch.

Strat poured cheap wine from a pitcher into chipped cups for both of them: water here spilled your guts. "Say something, before my prisoner dies of heart failure or old age, or both."

"What? Maybe it was Shamshi, who sold those horses to the trader. Maybe not," Critias said absently. "What's the difference, unless the trader knows where the seller's gone – or where he lives? Go ahead, if you're satisfied – let him run back home."

*Preoccupied.*

Braving the reek of so much terrified flesh and loosened bowels, Strat went into the other room and freed the prisoner. Released, the ponderous trader pounded through both doorways and down the stairs. "Hope those stairs hold under all that weight," Strat said, gazing after his subject before closing the door.

"Now, left-side leader, what's the problem?" Strat picked up his cup from the table, watching Crit over it. "You're a hundred miles away."

Crit doesn't say a word. He gets out his pouch, where his flints are, and his luck charms. He strikes a spark on a bit of parchment, lights two smokes, extinguishes the burning parchment with a loud slap from his palm, and gives one smoke to Strat. Then Crit says, "Ace, maybe we have a problem."

"Only one?" Strat says, nodding sagely. "That's a good day in Sanctuary." But it isn't going to be just one problem. Strat knows that tone.

Crit scoops up his luck charms and throws them, a personal divination rite he tries only when consternation overwhelms him. His single die lands with one dot up, half atop an old field star on a rotted ribbon; a little silver cavalryman falls atop that; his gold amulet of the Storm God leans against the lead fighter; Crit's shell-and-claw fishhook has its claw over the amulet. Crit shakes his head, staring at his personal omina, pulling at the dirty bandage on his right arm. "Tell me *how* this could be worse. The last time I saw one dot up, Ace, your damned ghost horse and I had to rescue you from that loft at Peres House, just before it burned."

"Fancy that. Those trinkets may tell you something; they don't tell me a thing. I'll ask you a second time: what's wrong?"

Crit scoops up his charms, pockets them, and gets to his feet. He goes to the window and opens the iron shutters to the muggy night. They squeal, in need of oil. "Rain's stopped. Good thing. Every piece of gear I've got is moldy; you can imagine what the local crops are like." Then he faces Strat. "Ace, I have half a dozen reports of rapes and murders, the usual mischief, nothing special. Any of that could be Shamshi – or none of it. Nothing definite. The Riddler wants results."

"We trained Sham. He knows every tactic, technique, and procedure we use. We'll get him, Fox. That's not the whole of it. What's bothering you?"

"Ace…." Crit turned to Strat and said, hands out, palms up, as if forfending something: "I know you'll not like this, but it's beyond my control." He dropped his hands to his sides; they slapped against his thighs. Crit hated anything beyond his control.

Strat crossed his arms and waited for whatever would come next, knowing now he *really* wouldn't like it.

"We're having a party," Crit said, his fine Syrese face screwed up, raking a hand through his dark hair in frustration.

"A *what?"*

"A party. A fête. A celebration. Call it what you will. They call it 'Evening Parade.'"

"I call it stupid."

"There's that. The Thebans want to throw a party to thank us for the rescue. Charon spoke to the Riddler and Stealth and they've agreed. Team building. Molin Torchholder's heard about it somehow and he's supplying women, musicians, and shellfish…from the palace."

"You jest."

"Deadly serious." Crit sighed and puffed on his broadleaf until it underlit his face, making his mouth seem too cruel and his eyes too puffy. "And everyone who's anyone in this scabrous town is invited. Torchholder wants to introduce the Thebans – and *re*introduce us, so I'm told – to polite society."

"I think we're doing a pretty good job of introducing ourselves." Strat hugged himself. "He's bringing *women* and he wants to introduce us to *polite society?* At the same time? Can I assume that you mean these aren't brothel women?"

"This is a Theban event. We're doing it the Theban way."

"What's the Theban way?"

"We're finding that out as we go. So far, it's this way: You play games, you eat, you drink, there's music, and *then* they bring on the women. Not whores – or at least not all whores; some temple virgins looking for a good start in life; and… willing women, maybe fancy, maybe some dancers. That's all I know."

"This is going to get very prickly, very fast. What are we supposed to tell our Sacred Banders about dealing with these women? Or not dealing with them?"

One mistake could be as bad as the other. "I don't know yet. That's what I'm saying. I do know we've got to deal with…" Crit starts ticking off items on his fingers, "…invitations from our side – people who'll be offended if left out; food; drink; horses, prizes and weapons for their games; logistics; security – liaison with the city guard." Then adds: "Oh, I forgot: firewood. Lots and lots of firewood." He taps ashes from his broadleaf into his hand, crumbles them to make sure they aren't still burning, and scatters them on the floor.

Strat repeats, "Firewood. Why firewood?"

"Because we're doing it at the lighthouse spit, where the jetty is, where their goddess appeared. We're going to make some big bonfires and cook all the food on the beach. Do everything there. They want to dance and sing and pretend they're back in Thebes."

"They're *not.* That's an indefensible position. Molin's in this. Let's do it at the nice, safe, walled palace." Strat's mouth goes dry.

"Defending ourselves doesn't worry me as much as spending an evening outside on the lighthouse spit near Vashanka's Rip with a bunch of drunken townies and Thebans. Sure as the gods make kings of fools, some drunk will fall off that jetty and get swept out to sea by the riptide there. And it'll be our fault," Crit says glumly. "If nothing worse happens."

Strat blows smoke out of his nostrils and says, "That 'worse' is Shamshi, for one thing. And me and Ischade, for the other, in your estimation. I can understand that you're worried about Shamshi showing up – a public event will draw him out. So let's use it. Lay our own trap for him."

"That's my thought, too. I could use a little help with planning. As for you and the witch…. I didn't say anything. You did."

Strat mutters, "Going to be too damned busy for women or witches or anything else." He drops his smoke and grinds it underfoot.

## *Chapter 19: Test of Fates*

Sham was shadowing two Thebans in the Maze when a fetching harlot strolled off to work, blond hair shining in the late-day sun. *Be calm. Don't chase her where everyone can see.* His hair had been that blond, before he'd dyed it black. She passed the Vulgar Unicorn, heading for Triumph Gate. *She'll keep till later.*

He was learning about whores, these cheap treats from the streets, and about the well of dark retribution in his soul: how far to push, when to wait, when to loose his passion. He was learning where to take his girls, what to do afterward, if power slipped its bridle and things went too far. Whores were legion in Sanctuary, an endless parade of flesh that no one valued highly.

The Sacred Band was his obsession now: Thebans and Stepsons. He would grind their leadership to dust under his heel for what they'd done to him. But not yet. *Not yet.*

Today, he hunted Thebans most of all: softer targets, still reeling from relocation. If not for the Sacred Band of Thebes – cowards who'd fled their fate in Chaeronea – no evil would have befallen Sham: he'd still be a Stepson in good standing, never shamed before the greater Sacred Band. Those doomed Thebans ruined everything, fleeing into the Riddler's arms instead of staying on the battleplain and dying as was their destiny.

Sham had failed only one study on Bandara, and that was *maat*: once personified as a goddess, *maat* in secular Bandaran lore was the principle of balance and justice, righteousness, truth, and law…and some accursed feather which must be weighed against all a man has done. *Maat* made no sense to him: why seek equilibrium, when change was the engine that drove all things? But Sham now has an inkling of an imbalance to be put right: this Sacred Band of Thebes must surely die, here if nowhere else. *They're overdue in hell,* soft voices in his mind whisper like a chorus.

Nikodemos was Shamshi's ultimate target, his preordained enemy. Stealth was an adept of *maat*, this one skill Sham couldn't master – the one degree of training he'd failed to attain in all those years on the misty isles: this elusive, cosmic justice. He would show Niko, and his beloved Tempus, justice in the world of men. Since none could kill the Riddler, destroying Tempus's favorite would be Sham's greatest triumph. But Stealth was strong, in the world and in his mind, too strong to try…yet. Too formidable to assault…yet.

First, to soften up his quarry, he must destroy everything prized by the Riddler and his right-side partner.

Sham had just begun his reprisals. So far, he'd killed only two little-known Theban fighters (along with Ari), and wounded Lysis. He'd destroyed no heroes, no great warriors, none among the Stepson leadership. Still, it had felt like fire in his blood to see his victims scramble and fall.

These two Thebans he was following today, nondescript cavalrymen without a Stepson escort, now turned right, toward Processional Way, bantering intimately. One of their horses was the blue roan Sham used to ride. He wished he had it back. But he couldn't keep it, even if he killed both Thebans to get the horse. He'd had to trade his stolen Sacred Band horses for a less identifiable mount and money.

Two Thebans on patrol, no Stepson nanny with them, meant that Tempus was letting down his guard. *Time to strike. Past time.* Since he'd waylaid Lysis, Sync, Gayle, and Kouras in the dark, he'd withdrawn, awaiting his moment. He'd stirred them up too much. Sham knew about getting stirred up, about losing control, about letting go all thought of the future – about letting his present and his passion overwhelm him.

He'd been trying his skills on the Sanctuary locals. It was like shooting carp with crossbow bolts in a shallow pond. He'd been studious, practicing (in the Maze, in Shambles Cross, and in Downwind) what the Stepsons had taught him. How to plan a mission. How to kill a target from hiding. Sync told his trainees: *Distance is your friend. If it's worth killing, it's worth stalking.*

Stealth once cautioned, while schooling him alongside Arton and Kouras: *You don't want or need a reputation; reputations are deadly. Be good at your job, but don't sign your work.* This advice was much harder to follow than Sync's.

Sham wanted the Riddler to know that his precious Band was being stalked by one of their own, whom they'd trained and then expelled. He wanted the Band to know that all his training hadn't gone to waste.

He dreamed of retaliation. He craved the most succulent vengeance that hell could serve up. And he was working on it, bit by careful bit. He'd dyed his skin as well as his hair. He'd sold every piece of recognizable gear. He'd found lodging and taken a job guarding produce carts offloaded from the docks. He'd grown a respectable short beard. The job wasn't much, but he already had money: he just needed an excuse to have that money and to move around the city unremarked, with weapons.

Lessons from his naïve days with the Band still served him here in Sanctuary, where rivers swallowed practice kills and swept identity away. Sham understood discipline and self-discipline: he'd been drilled his whole life long, first by the monks of the misty isles and then by the best of the Stepsons – before the Sacred Band had taught him the greatest lesson of all, sewn him in a hideous shroud of meaty hide and left him for the Fates or gods to find and save, or cast away on fortune's shore.

*Trust no one. Take revenge; take it slowly, slowly. Again and again.* Whispers cautioned him, like female voices dimly heard or a sighing wind from deep within his soul. Sham savors his growing power, tending the place in his mind whence inspiration comes: Chaeronea. Sham is learning, in this school the Riddler has made for his Theban band of lovers, how to kill the unwary, the overweening and the undeserving.

Do the Riddler and Stealth think he died, or fled? He hoped not: of all the precepts learned from Critias, their intelligence chief, lying low was the hardest. But he must lull them until he couldn't bear it any longer.

It is so tempting to make sure the much-vaunted Sacred Band of Stepsons knows he can slip up on them anytime, have his way with them, take away what they love the most: each other. They were vulnerable because they were many. He was only one but that one was schooled by his old mentors and new enemies, the Sacred Band.

He'd built a mental rest-place that was a replica of Chaeronea, and more: *Long spears, thunking into flesh; men staggering back, impaled, howling.* Darkness here was overcoming everything, eating up the light on that battleplain, in this place where he could look through each dying eye as if the battle were today.

What would the Bandaran monks think of that? Of him? He sent those images of Chaeronea to far Bandara – his calling card, notes from his field trip. And he sent these same images to all his intended victims, hoping to dishearten them – not knowing if he did; if they saw what he projected, or not.

Let the Riddler and his precious Stepsons think he'd gone away. Let them think Kouras's bolts skewered him: one almost did. It had whickered past so close it holed his cloak and nearly his neck. That quarrel almost made an end to him in the dark of night. Kouras was too lucky by half. He'd hit Lysis, he knew he had. But he'd badly wanted to kill them all: Kouras and Lysis, and Sync and Gayle, who had shot at him as well. *Nearly time to try again.*

Now, he must decide on this night's entertainment. Thebans, or the blond whore, or both? He'd waited long enough. He ached to make his passion felt.

He struck out for the Vulgar Unicorn to get a drink and then decide. If he was going to take down Thebans, he'd need his horse from the livery stable. Above it, Critias had a hideyhole, a station, where the Sacred Band came and went, swapping information and getting orders.

So he must be careful. Notwithstanding, it titillated him to be so close to the Stepsons, right under their noses. He was Bandaran: he could change the way he carried himself: the way he walked, the way he stood, the set of his shoulders, a raft of small details that make one man recognize another.

He'd been busy in his bay's stall, saddling up two nights ago, when Critias and Straton walked right by him, talking about wood and provisions. He could hardly breathe. Critias looked right at him but there was no recognition on that face, in the gloomy stable where he and his partner went about their business. So near, he could have killed the two of them right there and then, surprised them where they stood. *Walk out of the stall, pretend to trip, stab a finger into one chest, an elbow into a sternum, and it's done: death touch – corpses walking for a few hours, just long enough to walk away.*

But he hadn't tried it. He wasn't ready…yet.

*Wait, wait,* voices in his mind whispered, a chorus of women's voices, far away.

In his inner sight, he could still see Crit's face, and his partner's, that night they overpowered him, weapons on the ground behind them. Straton had kneed him in the groin and he couldn't think, couldn't recover fast enough from the pain. He'd learned all a man needed to know that night about not fighting fair, about honor held in abeyance and calculated cruelty, from those men he'd once respected above all others. Someday soon they'd know how well he'd learned his lessons.

Now he needed a place to wait for the moon to rise. Inside the Unicorn, with its sawdust and its board floors and its promise of anonymity that had kept it in business all these years, he bought a beer and leaned there, where he could watch the door and listen to the chatter of a dozen customers. He was a regular, but here no one asked your name.

The day barman, raw-boned and swarthy, hardly looked up from his stock and his bar-rags. Sham wasn't paying attention to the patrons on either side of him. He was daydreaming about going after those Thebans tonight (or another pair of fighters, or a threesome) when they reached the Hill with its clean and landscaped streets, its hedges and wrought iron gates.

Someone said, "Two-Thumbs, did you hear about the party next full moon? Are you invited? Everybody who's anybody is."

The barkeep raised his head, "I'm not anybody, Enas. You mean the Theban beach party? That's the palace crowd, Hill folk, Sacred Band, and that sort. Not for such as me."

Very slowly, without betraying any surprise or more than casual interest, Shamshi turns his head to face the patron, a man with a tattoo on his forehead, who seems of indeterminate age.

"Well, too bad," says the man with the tattoo. "Walegrin's going. The whoremistress at Phoebe's is going, and so's Myrtis from the Aphrodisia House. You'd think the Unicorn's owner would be invited."

"Why? Because the city-guard captain and two madams are on the guest list?" asks the barkeep sourly.

Sham isn't listening any longer. *This changes everything.* He has preparations to make. But first, he needs to get his horse and his weapons and see if he can reduce the guest-list by a Theban or by a Stepson – or two, or more. The die is cast, in this wager with providence. The stakes are on the table.

Time to up the ante.

*

A seer and a son of the storm god ride through Sanctuary in twilight: young heroes-to-be, alone on patrol, looking to make their reputations, policing vicious streets.

These two have new orders, new urgency, in light of all the preparations for the fête: find Sham, the renegade, their former friend, before he kills again. Something else is new, changed: Arton's foresight catches clearer glimpses of the future. In every vision is Kouras with his green eyes and red hair: the god Vashanka's image on the earth.

Tonight the air licks your skin like a dog. Light from adjacent buildings spills out here and there, making city streets into a game board: bright squares and dark under the scrutiny of wagering gods.

Hours ago at the barracks stable, Kouras had said: "Arton, I can get us a night patrol. Just us. No Stepson chaperone, no minder. You can see your mother, if you want. I can see Shawme. Nobody needs to know. *Deal?*" Thunder had murmured, far away.

"I haven't finished cleaning these saddles…." Arton looked Kouras in the eye.

"Let them clean their own tack for a change." More thunder, closer at hand.

"I'll go. I'll go. Just don't make it rain, please?" Arton teased. "All this mildew is so hard to get off…."

So out went Kouras, swaggering in long strides, right up to the Riddler's door. Kouras had knocked. Arton had wanted to hide.

But the door had opened. Nikodemos slipped outside, said something, and inclined his head in that way of his that made you think your soul was on display. A moment later, Stealth was gone, and Kouras was jogging back across the courtyard to Arton.

Now here they were on two experienced warhorses, crossbows hanging from their saddles, prowling city streets. They hadn't completely mastered the skill of firing crossbows from horseback but they'd had some practice. Or Kouras had. Arton hoped he didn't have to shoot his. Crossbows in the night were tricky.

Arton's foresight was restless. He kept imagining what it would be like to have your crossbow trained on these shadows, like Kouras and Lysis had done when they'd been ambushed with Sync and Gayle. Their close call was still the talk of the barracks. He was jittery; probably not seeing the future, just his own worries. Their mounts walked side by side up

Processional Way, widest street in Sanctuary, leading to the palace.

"I was there," Kouras told him, pointing up the street. *"In* the palace. Don't say I told you."

"Has it got anything to do with how we got this duty?"

"Maybe," Kouras dropped his reins and crossed his arms, showing off his horsemanship.

"Fine. *Don't* tell me. This patrol better not be trouble. My foresight doesn't like it out here tonight." Best remind Kouras that Arton is now recognized for his own special skill. The long twilight paints the city walls with blue and crimson; deep purple shadows spill off the palace dome. For a moment the skyline of Sanctuary is almost beautiful.

At the north end of Processional, where they should turn left on Governor's Walk (to go to the Bazaar, where Arton's mother was; or to the Red Lanterns district, where Shawme, the prostitute, could be found), Kouras turned his horse to the right instead. Blocked, Arton's mount turned too.

"I thought we were going to Illyra's...?"

"Let's just patrol first. We have to do our jobs. Who knows what we'll find up on the Hill?" The voice of the storm god's son was purposely portentous. "Honor. Glory. Women."

Not far up the road, where you bear left at Promise of Heaven Park, they heard shouting. Their helmets were hooked on their saddles' off sides; crossbows on the near sides. Kouras grinned at him and clucked to his mount. "See? I can see the future, too."

Arton's horse leaps forward. Then they're running down the middle of the street toward the commotion. Pedestrians scatter. Men shake fists. Women squeal and hike up their skirts, scrambling off the street to safety.

Arton couldn't get his helmet on and his crossbow in position while his horse was galloping under him. Kouras had his shortsword in hand; it caught the light, gleaming. "Get your throwing stars," yelled the son of the storm god. They still couldn't see the fight, if fight it was, around the blind corner ahead.

Then two horses came thundering round that corner, straight at them, riderless and wild-eyed. When horses have that look, they don't stop. The runaways parted Arton and Kouras's horses and kept running, thundering by.

They both saw the Sacred Band gear on the runaways.

Kouras raised his hand and they reined down to a walk. All around, shadows were deepening. The shouting had stopped. Their horses blew and jigged.

Arton's blood pounded in his ears. He hissed, "I *told* you so." His horse didn't want to walk; it spun around and around: it wanted to chase the other two, running pell-mell home to their barracks stalls. Maybe his mount was right and they should recover the bolting horses, but somewhere up ahead were the Stepsons to whom those horses belonged. He struggled with his mount; it danced and fussed; he slapped it on the neck, hard. "I *said* something wasn't right." He pulled on his reins, slapping the bay again, but it wouldn't quiet down.

"No, you *didn't.* Tell me what your foresight says – *right now*." Kouras's voice was brusque. One hand upraised in the Stepsons' caution sign, Kouras peered all around: left, right, up, into the tricky light and down the manicured street.

"It says 'Watch your back, and mine,'" Arton retorted, finally getting horse calm and crossbow ready.

"Careful," Kouras warns. Then he whispers, "Whatever was happening, maybe it's not over."

Arton peers into the light and shadow, looking where Kouras is looking. His horse goes where Kouras's goes. It's a relief to point his horse's face into Kouras's mount's tail, so the beast will settle down. But it's a warhorse and it doesn't stay settled long. He needs both hands on his reins: it's heard action, and it wants to join the fray.

In a dozen strides, Arton sees a crowd forming around two men with Theban panoplies lying in the street. Those Theban breastplates are unmistakable. Arton's horse had heard the fight, smelled the blood, known better than he and Kouras what was happening. Arton's fingers are clumsy, holding too much: reins, throwing stars, crossbow.

They slide off their mounts and drop their reins. Arton shoulders his bow. He and Kouras draw their swords, brandishing them at the twilight. Striding over to the knot of well-dressed folk, Kouras orders, "Make way. Make way. Sacred Band business." Kouras barges through the gathering crowd, disappearing as it closes in his wake.

"Business that would have been better served if you'd been here earlier," grouses some anonymous critic from the middle of the throng.

Clatter echoes down the street: hooves pounding; closer, closer; then shouts, maneuver codes, all the sounds of cavalry approaching fast.

"Let's go, people. There's nothing to see here," comes a sharp, commanding voice from an armored man in a helmet, riding up and sliding to a stop, with the sounds of more horses close behind him. "Clear out, you. We don't need more targets where danger might still be. Get out of range before you're next." In a flurry of chlamys, the lanky Stepson dismounts, shoving his way through the gathered folk, cursing fluently at every soul in his path.

Arton is nearly dizzy with relief. "Sync."

Two mounted Thebans push back the retreating crowd, weapons in hand, threatening the onlookers – urgent and adamant with downed comrades bleeding on the street. A second pair bangs on adjacent doors, threatening to break them down, searching for the sniper; obdurate, they'll ride their horses right inside if people don't cooperate.

Now Arton can see Kouras and Sync, bent over two fallen Thebans in the beautiful dusk. Kouras looks at Sync and shakes his head.

Another Theban, herding civilians, calls out: "Agis and Archias – are they dead?" More Banders are arriving, horses slip-sliding to a stop on cobblestones.

Sync has his head close to a fallen man's chest and doesn't answer. One wounded man moans.

"Not dead," Kouras calls back. "We got here in time." Proudly. "But bad. Throwing stars – poisoned, probably: that kind we have. And crossbow-shot for good measure."

"That's more porking detail than anybody needs right now, porker," critiques Gayle, as the veteran Stepson struggles to hold two skittish horses, nervous from the smell of blood.

"It's great you happened along, Sync," Arton says into the awkward silence, trying to sound brave in the face of yet more unreasoning violence come from nowhere. His eyes search every shadow, every doorway, every hedge and iron fence. There are so many Sacred Band fighters here now: the citizens are pressed back against the buildings by a wall of men and horseflesh but still want to gawk.

"Great," Sync repeats dryly, hands pressing around a crossbow bolt in one man's chest. "Damned hellhole; damned kids; damned mess," Sync curses, gentle and regretful, a softer tone than he'd used to curse the crowd. He cranes his neck, judging the men standing by, awaiting orders. "You two pairs, bring me water, blankets if you can; keep searching house to house, roofs and cellars. Go, go, *go.*" He points. Two teams move off fast, blustering to console themselves, toward the hedges and well-kept homes. "Gorgias, Sciron, get a cart.

These men aren't riding out of here. Strat, is that you there? Help me. We need to stop some bleeding here. Bring any packing you've got." One pair rides off to get a cart. Other pairs are stalking, creating a perimeter with their horses, looking everywhere, shields up, swords out, snarling at passersby and onlookers still lingering.

Now Straton shoves through: "Bleeding's good if there's poison, Sync. Arton, don't just stand there staring. Track the shooter. Kouras, you too. And get these civilians *out* of here, unless they're volunteering to be victims. *Now.*" That battlefield voice clears the street of the last curious like a wind blowing leaves.

Strat joins Sync, kneeling over the wounded, a saddlebag in his hand. Flint strikes; flare and flame; knife glittering, heating. Then a soft sizzling sound. Someone moans and someone coughs too wetly. Arton, sword sheathed, crossbow up to his face, is searching every shadow with narrowed eyes. Wood cracks and snaps, as if a shaft has broken. A shout of agony rings out – just one. Then silence.

Strat is leaning low over one wounded man, listening to his breathing. Sync stands up and wipes his hands on his hips, saying under his breath, "Our shooter is trying to make a statement. Nice of your necromant to warn us, Strat. Maybe a little sooner, next time?"

Strat says, "I'll be sure to tell her you said so."

Gayle calls out, "Where's that porking cart? These boys can still bleed to death out here."

Kouras, hands and knees bloody, eyes wide in the fading dusk, is craning his neck, turning in place, staring all around, looking for the enemy in every deepening shadow. Arton could nearly hear him worrying: *Sham's still out here.*

So Arton says, "*We're* targets, out here. Just like they were. The shooter's still here, somewhere – watching us."

Sync shrugs, sucking blood from his thumb. “Right you are. Put on your damn helmet. Want to get shot in the head? This pud’s out to scare us, and the locals. If he were looking for more kills tonight, he’d have struck again by now. Plenty of easy targets.” His grin flashes in his helmet’s narrow slit.

Strat spits over one shoulder. “He’s not going to risk getting caught outnumbered by an adversary on the alert. He’s having too much fun.”

Sync says: “Anybody want to guess who our shooter might be? In case the necromant’s warning’s not proof enough?”

No one does. Everybody knows.

## *Chapter 20: Divine Lovers and Beloveds*

At the barracks amphitheater, sunlight was breaking through the clouds. Charon saw it as a good omen. All night thunderheads had threatened, their lightning pulsing somewhere far away, with only a few stars shining like beacons on a wine-dark sea. He'd had his wounded brought in secretly, under cover of darkness. Few of his knew yet (a trusted few who'd brought them home) about the injured Theban fighters in the barracks. Soon they would hear. He had to tell them carefully.

In this country where weather told the temper of the gods and prophesied men's futures, Charon was grateful that the sun was shining bright this morning: weather and events on earth and in heaven echoed and reechoed here with preternatural results. A storm on the night his wounded were brought back bleeding and bandaged to their barracks, even a Theban knew by now, would have predicted hell to pay. But no storm broke last night or this morning. Therefore the storm god, Enlil, was not affronted, or wroth, or worse. Impossibly, unappeasably, he wanted to go home to Thebes, to the world that spawned him. Stand on the cliffs, walk the hills, work his sheepdogs, eat grapes from his own arbor. Loss overcame him with a wrenching homesickness so deep he couldn't see anything but the green hills of his farm. Then it was gone, leaving sudden weakness in its wake. So how must they feel, all of his, trusting his word to lead them on?

Before anyone was allowed near the wounded, Charon called his Band together in the arena: his twenty-one pairs healthy enough to sit in the amphitheater and his injured son, Lysis.

"Brothers," he said to them, "once again, beloved friends among us have been saved from perishing: Agis and Archias were brought home last night by Stepsons after being attacked in the city. Give thanks that they live."

He paused to let angry mutters crest and break like swells on a beach. He'd known they would take it ill, this violence come from nowhere. Again.

"There is too much disrespect brewing here, too little gratitude, when Harmony and the Stepsons who saved us once from death keep saving us…again…and again," he said into the morning light, where his pairs sat shocked, some with arms around each other, on the primeval stone slabs encircling the ruined arena. "We are who and what we are, because Harmony has given us consonance and order, mollified our strong and impetuous natures, brought our warriors' force and courage into train with the divine love we share with one another. Let us recall how fleeting life is. Here we are one step farther away from our fallen brothers and one step closer to Elysion. With no Thebes to serve here, our service is due to our goddess and one another – and the memory of our lost land and companions. Cleave closer to your friends and that friendship inspired by our goddess. Pay respect to her, and to your comrades, the Stepsons."

He waited a moment. No one said a word. The Theban Band now sat closer together, by twos and fours – not huddled, but not at ease.

"Today we give thanks – without breastplates, without swords girded on, without anger at our lot. Give thanks today, I say, instead of curses, that Lysis, Agis and Archias will live to fight on other days." He crossed his arms. He wore a kirtle, sandals, and a cord knotted at his waist. His head was bare and the wind blew through his hair, so short yet from when he'd shorn it to honor his brothers fallen at Chaeronea.

Gorgias, one of his best warriors, said in a low growl, "But we're dying here." Gorgias and his partner had helped bring home the wounded pair.

Charon replied, "Gorgias, men die everywhere. It is man's nature to gain life and to lose it, as it is to give life and to take it."

As he'd asked, everyone had come unarmed. There was a hidden danger here – among these strange warfighters in this unforgiving land, with their uncompromising honor and their harsher definition of heroism – that the unique nature of the Sacred Band of Thebes could be lost.

Sciron, Gorgias's fiery partner, said, "Why is it *we* are always the targets of the angry Fates? Twice as many men of ours met harm as did theirs, since we've come here."

There it was, said aloud. Charon looked at Lysis, his young hero in the first row with his maple crutch, and beamed. His son stared back at him, sober and proud. Inspired by Lysis's brave young face, he said, "Sciron, there are more than twice as many Thebans here as Stepsons. Can you count? Or ask my son, who remembers all we've done, if we Thebans fall easily." *Long spears, thunking into flesh. Men staggering back, impaled, moaning.* "Ask yourselves if the gods are angry, you who have seen Harmony come among us, walk among us, touch us, look kindly upon us. We are the Sacred Band of Thebes. We fight in the forefront, therefore we bleed first. We live, therefore we die."

He bowed his head and knew the others would. "Our goddess, Harmony, has appeared to us here. She blesses us and our sojourn – and forgives us for leaving our brothers on the battleplain. *Forgive yourselves* – although so many of us are dead – that you still live. We bring suffering upon our own heads when we are ungrateful to the gods that we yet live to fight on other days." It couldn't have been said a moment sooner; hearts were still too sore, grief too fresh. *But now, we end the grieving. We have a new enemy, Chaos, here, and we will fight this foe with our new brothers and all our might, put to work once more in a worthy cause.*

And then began the questions and answers, the flood of hidden tears he'd known must someday come.

He stood silently while men and boys spoke freely of all they'd lost, and comrades slain, and let their tide of sorrow flow until it ebbed.

When they were quiet and looked with red and swollen eyes to him once more, he said, *"Now* you are fit to welcome our new heroes, Agis and Archias, and to thank our Stepson brothers for a rescue once again. We plan a formal Theban feast, some already know, at full moon to show our gratitude and celebrate life with the greater Sacred Band – with whom we share our passion and our allegiance."

Lysis was looking at him proudly, with shining eyes. Charon didn't need a better omen of how this effort was received. "Cherish one another. And if some die, or some are wounded, or all die between now and the fête or thereafter – are we not still the Sacred Band of Thebes? And are we not now all Stepsons? Our adopted brothers fight by our sides and together we will continue to meet our enemies with sharp eyes and firm resolve. Between now and our feast day, all of you think how you will show your thanks and share your joy that life yet resides within you: show it to Harmony; and to the storm god Enlil, whose place this is; and to the Riddler and the greater Sacred Band of which we are now a part."

Men whooped and clapped their partners on the back, and chatter broke out. Some embraced as if they would hold on forever.

Charon left the center of the amphitheater and joined his son, helping Lysis cope with his crutch. The boy put his left arm around Charon's shoulders. Charon slid his right arm around Lysis's waist and said, "Now, Lysis, you're fit to see Agis and Archias and praise the goddess for their survival, and them for their bravery."

With Lysis hobbling along, the others surged ahead. He'd lost one pair of his; the Stepsons had lost a pair, and he had three wounded since coming to Sanctuary. Graver wounds still showed this day on bodies and in hearts, but the men were right to be concerned: it seemed as if they'd come here accursed.

When he and Lysis climbed out of the amphitheater at last, fighters were queued up to visit the wounded in their sickbeds. He wanted them focused on tomorrow, not on yesterday. He wanted the feast to heal and unify them. If fighting for Thebes was denied them, then fighting for each other, for memory and for their goddess must be enough.

He wanted another sign from Harmony, if the goddess would allow.

Gorgias, brown of hair and eye and skin, who'd been on the scene when the badly wounded Thebans were found, came up to him and said, "Charon, can I speak to you alone?"

"Lysis, hold a place in line for me."

They watched the youth hobble off to join the queue. Soon he wouldn't need the crutch.

"So? How are you, Gorgias? It's time to play our pipes and flutes and tend our wounded heroes. And to thank you for all you did, getting them back here alive, to heal."

Gorgias said, "Let's walk."

They did, up toward the altar of Enlil.

"Do you think we could have an altar to Harmony here?" Gorgias asked.

"I think they would allow it. I'll ask, at the feast." Gorgias was not a forthcoming man, but a worthy warrior, so Charon prompted: "Have you a problem? A question?"

"I have information and questions."

"So, say."

"We have twenty-two pairs left, one of which is wounded; and Lysis, nearly healed: forty-four fighters, you included. Why do they tell us what to do?" Gorgias had a face of broken bones knit roughly, a scar from his right eye to his mouth.

"Because we agreed it so. Theagenes did, for all of us, the night before the battle." *Because we are here, in their country, and so we abide by their rules, their gods.*

"But we never all agreed, man by man, pair by pair."

"We are the Sacred Band of Thebes, and now the greater Sacred Band. I have said to their leader that we are all Stepsons. We will keep our word, as honor demands."

Climbing this gentle hill was difficult today. Charon's lungs labored. But sometimes breath can bate from words, not deeds. Above was only Enlil's modest altar, a pile of stones hardly dressed, and the deep blue sky wearing fluffy clouds of white.

"Equality must be maintained, if it is promised."

"Within order, and rank, and clear chain of command. Don't do this, Gorgias. We have too much to learn from them yet."

The smashed profile of Gorgias, beside him, moved inexorably up the hill. Gorgias sighed deeply. "As you wish, then. For now. Do you know that their commander, their Riddler, is cursed, some say: those who love him die of it, and those he loves are bound to spurn him? Where does that put us?"

"Don't get too friendly with him, I'd advise. If you believe in curses. I've heard the tale. I, myself, don't think any curse can withstand a god." *Tempus nearly is one – would be, in Thebes.* "Anyway, I've heard the curse is lifted, if there ever was one. They say he's eternal. And I know some of these men – Niko, Straton, Critias, Sync – have been with him sixteen years or more. If his men die of loving him, it takes a while."

"So, you don't think we should worry? You don't think it's true?"

"If you don't love him, what difference does it make?"

On the hilltop, they turned around and looked down the blue-green slope at the estate and the training field, where white walls and fences and buildings sparkled.

"If I don't love him – none. And I don't. But if it's true…. what if he loves us?"

## *Chapter 21: Evening Parade*

*Tat, rata tat. Tat rat tat tata tata tat. Tat, rata tat. Tat rat tat tata tata tat.* Hidden behind the lighthouse on the sandy spit, marching drums ring out. *Tat, rata tat.* Louder than the surf and as compelling. In the full-moon night, drums beat and bang; wooden sticks clack. *Tat rat tat tata tata tat.* Stepson horses, rattled by the persistent drumbeats, neigh and neigh across the sand-spit, calling to each other from black shadows, bright moonlight.

Tempus calms his mount, making the Trôs halt in place, out near the jetty: parade rest. *Tat, rata tat. Tat rat tat tata tata tat.* Ten bonfires, crackling, blaze on the beach; logs stand on end, head-high, painstakingly propped together at the center; conical fires, carefully constructed and controlled: flames reaching heavenward.

*Tat, rata tat. Tat rat tat tata tata tat.* The rhythm beats louder now: drums approaching. One hundred and sixty male guests crane their necks, peering toward the drum-rolls in the moon's uncanny light. *Tat, rata tat. Tat rat tat tata tata tat.* This cadence (sharp as swords clashing), so mournful, so angry, so brave, so proud, can force a rank to war or a bridegroom down the aisle or bring a body to a funerary pyre. Or ten. Or a hundred. Or more.

Tempus has heard it often: it's in his pulse, it's in his soul. *Tat, rata tat. Tat rat tat tata tata tat.* Although he'd helped make this plan, knows what's coming, the rhythm raises every hair and makes his heart beat fast. He touches his chest, a customary gesture, one he's made so many times before – before the wound was there, scar pulsing under his hand. Before Chaeronea. *Long spear, thunking into flesh.* Before this Theban ceremony on a Sanctuary shore. *Tat rat tat tata tata tat.*

A melody rises above the drumbeat, bright and fierce and lonely on the beach as flutes and pipes take up this ancient song: *Brum rumpa pum pum. Brum rumpa pum pum.* Tempus looks for Niko but can't find him among the shadows and so many guests.

He can see the Thebans now, marching toward the bonfires, four by four with empty litters on their shoulders. To the death with honor, these men are saying: they won't need litters to bring their wounded home – there will be none, just their dead. *Brum rumpa pum pum. Brum rumpa pum pum.*

Flames dance over the armored fighters, reflecting from shields and greaves and arm-guards; helmets glisten; horsehair crests wave and pennants snap in a wind blowing off the sea. Tonight this Sacred Band of Thebes wears its best armor, polished and oiled. *Tat, rata tat.* Cuirasses gleam. *Tat rat tat tata tata tat.* Toward roaring bonfires, at regimented pace, come the men, by fours. *Tat rat tat tata tata tat.*

Now the rhythm is hypnotic; hearts beat fast and heads are high: *Brum rumpa pum pum. Brum rumpa pum pum.*

All the guests are mesmerized, transfixed, until the Thebans reach their designated bonfires. *Tat, rata tat. Brum rumpa pum pum.* The warfighters halt before the flames. So does the rhythm.

Silence rules, unexpectedly. So abruptly does this march end, which has been with men in battle for eons, the quiet seems too loud. From behind the lighthouse, naphtha fireballs arc high, out over the sea, and fall, green tails streaming out behind like arrows from the gods. Assaulted, the sea seems to stop pounding the beach. At the fireball signal, in perfect synchrony, one man before each chosen balefire adds a wicker litter to the flames.

Hungry fires roar and spit, sending sparks aloft. Drums roll again; flutes and pipes call anew: *Tat, rata tat. Brum, brum rumpa pum pum. Tat rat tat tata tata tat.* The Sacred Band of Thebes, stepping crisply back, turns in unison at a shout from its leader, and marches toward the lighthouse and the shadows. *Tat, rata tat. Tat rat tat tata tata tat.* Now the rhythm fades – flutes, pipes and drums receding, ever softer in the night while the men march away as they had come: proud and perfect, this band of brothers, drilled and ready, marching off to heaven or the lighthouse on the spit (whatever the gods decide) in strict formation.

Then all that can be heard are one flute and one drum; then that single, lonely drum, until the last Theban warrior is swallowed by the dark. *Tat, rata tat. Tat rat tat tata tata tat.* Then silence. No sound at all. Nothing.

The surf decides to swell and pound once more. It crashes on the jetty, rustles up the shore. As guests begin uncertainly to talk and wander toward food or drink, Niko finds Tempus.

Niko's mare and Tempus's stallion nicker greetings as Niko brings her alongside. "Riddler, where were you? What will we do when the dignitaries appear, without you close at hand?"

"I've been right here, the whole time. Watching for uninvited guests from the sea." Although he hadn't been, really. "Don't fret, Niko. If you must, you can handle this without me." There is something in the water tonight, coming in from the sea. He feels it but doesn't tell Niko. Whatever it is, they'll face it, by and by.

"No, I can't. It's you our guests have come to see. Not Thebans, not me."

A wind gusted, fanning the flames of ten bonfires. Touched by fire and moonlight, Niko's face is somber, jaw set and eyes piercing: feelings stirred by the Theban play. "Stealth, everything flows," Tempus reminds him gently. "Our Thebans like a bit of drama with their justice."

"Those Sanctuarites just got more than a taste of Theban justice – more truth, less party, than expected."

"It's not our feast, not our agenda. Let the Thebans have this moment. They paid blood for it. We need only keep a balance. You know how to do that, more than any other." This one, of all he had – of all he'd ever had – was the best, but the most complicated.

"We're on it," Niko says impatiently, raking back hair from his face as the ocean wind tousles it. "But please come. If you snub them, if you don't grace this ceremony with your presence, then what?" Niko gestured toward the celebrants starting to feast from laden festival boards here and there among the dunes. "Even Enlil is giving us a bright full moon." He glances at the heavens suspiciously.

"I'll come," Tempus says with a sigh, regretful at leaving the seashore. His best fighters are mixed with the city guard here, doing double duty: pretending to be celebrating while patrolling, protecting, and hoping to draw out Shamshi, the renegade preying on them like a panther from the dark. "And *you* will have some fun tonight – and yours."

*"Fun?"* Niko repeats doubtfully, as if he's never heard the word.

"Fun. That's an order. You are bows strung too tight, all you Stepsons. We have the city guard to watch our backs.

Keep your weapons handy, but join in. As I must. Now that the Evening Parade is over, circulate. Get yours fed, but not drunk, before the women arrive from the city."

"Oh, I see. I promise," Niko said, "it's taken care of." That quick canny grin comes and goes. "Fun. They'll like that. Crit, Strat, Sync, and Walegrin's best, Torchholder's palace guards: everyone has orders. They didn't think it fair, but they're doing what we asked them."

"The fairest universe is but a heap of rubbish, Niko, piled at random. It's all right to eat a little, drink a little. To ride – and walk – among them. The palace is sending dancers, priestesses, high-born girls, to accommodate the men after the feast is done: Molin's pick of those in Sanctuary."

"But the perimeter –"

"Unbreached, so far." He knees his Trôs sideways, ending the discussion: "Whatever waits, we'll meet it head on. Together."

Stealth doesn't answer, just looks at him askance as their horses amble side by side toward the brighter light of ten bonfires and the celebration, getting raucous now as men drink wine and beer and ale.

In that relative quiet, broken only by hoofbeats and the sea, Tempus still hears the rhythm and the tune, though no marching band is playing now: *Brum rumpa pum pum. Tat, rata tat. Tat rat tat tata tata tat.* Dirge or stirring march to call warfighters to their destiny, it rings in Tempus's head, matching cadence with his horse's hooves as they ride down among far too many soft and powerful men from the city, now meeting pairs of armored Thebans (helmets in hand, shields still upon their arms, mantles stirring in the sea breeze) as equals for the very first time.

And the sea laps the shore, whispering behind his back of things to come.

*

*"Fun,* by the Riddler's order," Stealth told Crit. Three goblets of wine are all Critias can dare, on duty. Ivory-screened wagonloads of women and more musicians arrive, and Crit thinks three goblets may have been too much. Fun, for Crit, can be defined as an evening where nothing goes wrong and nothing's out of order. There are too many people, too many vulnerabilities on this indefensible sand spit for Crit even to hope for that.

Keeping mayhem at bay here will be impossible, if mayhem wants to come out to play. And come she does, soon enough: Mayhem incarnate blows in on wind and wave – a bronzed apparition arising from the sea, coalescing out of riptides and whitecaps, wearing fish-scale armor. Tall and as muscled as any man, she has a tiny waist and upturned breasts.

Then she's striding toward them, up the beach. "Strat, look to the shore," he said in Nisi, elbowing his partner (who is busy trying to explain to a palace oligarch why the Thebans threw their litters on the flames if no one died today). "Do you see what I see?"

Strat looks square at Crit over the oligarch's balding head. "Where? What? Oh. Damn this fun to hell," Strat curses in the mercenary argot, hand on his shortsword's pommel.

Nothing should be able to swim inland from that direction, through Vashanka's Rip, a tide so fierce it scours the bottom, making an aqua stripe in the sea. "Don't let on anything's amiss…." Crit advised. His stomach knots.

"By Enlil's third and fuzziest ball, it's Jihan," Strat swears. "Unless there's another one…."

The little oligarch looked between the two Stepsons speaking an amalgam of foreign tongues, and then said, "You're Critias, I presume. We haven't been introduced, but

I've long wanted to meet all you senior timocrats, you who rule and are ruled by honor, and understand this ethos of the Riddler's Sacred Band…."

"Gods forfend," Crit said in court Rankene.

"Pardon me?" the oligarch responded, drawing himself up to his full height.

"Please don't take offense. I didn't mean you, Oligarch."

"Timo*what*?" Strat spits, already stalking away toward the shore.

"Oligarch, I must go. See to my partner. You know how these things are…. Be right back."

But he wasn't going to be back anytime soon. Crit had to hustle to catch up with Strat. "So, what do you suggest we do about her, Strat?"

Jihan – Froth Daughter, child of Stormbringer the Unbegotten, father of all weather gods – was a sprite of Tempus's long acquaintance and the last thing anyone needed at a seaside gala in Sanctuary.

"Whatever she says," said Strat sensibly. "We're supposed to keep order here tonight. *You* are…."

Then she was upon them: a copper-skinned, inhuman beauty – her long hair blowing around her, not even wet; her eyes filled with glowing red flecks – wearing brown/green/bronze scale armor down to her muscular thighs and nothing else.

"Straton. Critias." She grabbed them both and pressed them together and against her so that for a moment Crit couldn't breathe and his skull knocked against Strat's. "Where's the Riddler? Niko walked into my father's sea and said he needed help. Am I too late? Time is so…fluid…where I live."

*"Seh,"* swore Strat. "Everybody's fine here. No need to trouble yourself. You know how Niko gets.... We've got everything under control."

"Jihan," said Crit, casting a look over his shoulder to see if anyone was watching, "we're having a little fête...."

"An open house, or 'open spit,' so I heard. Well, lead on, Critias. Take me to the Riddler."

Now they were in for it. Crit would be lucky if they got through the evening without Jihan freezing somebody solid or stripping the Riddler and having him in the sand in front of their guests.

But you couldn't control Jihan. He and Strat had trouble pacing her in the shifting sand and firelight. So it took Crit a moment to realize what she'd said.

"What do you mean, you 'heard?'" Crit asked. "Heard from whom?" Strat asked simultaneously.

"From Aškelon, of course," came Jihan's voice, floating back to them as if on her copper mane. "The dream lord. Isn't he here yet?"

"He's coming?" Strat asked dolefully.

"Aškelon? From Meridian?" Crit asked, but didn't need to hear her answer.

If there was one power, one personage, who could upset all applecarts and skew all plans for an uneventful fête here tonight, it was the dream lord. Aškelon, entelechy of dream and shadow, was once nearly killed by Cime, their commander's mistress, a sorcerer-slayer of renown. Stepson legend said that Aškelon's heart was not in his breast, but around his wrist in an obsidian bracelet called the Heart of Aškelon: that he could only die if the bracelet was destroyed.

After Cime had tried to kill him and failed, she spent a year as his wife in punishment. Tempus had been enraged, but was powerless to stop it. Aškelon had intruded into the

Band's affairs for years: courting Niko like a lover; once even spiriting Jihan herself away to Meridian, his nightmare realm.

But powers such as Jihan, Aškelon, and Tempus tolerated one another (if uneasily), since they couldn't overcome or obliterate each other. The entelechy of dream had even made the Riddler's hell-wheeled chariot and given it to Tempus (along with a pair of priceless Aškelonian horses) when he took Cime to wife on Wizardwall. Critias had been there. And Crit knew what he saw on his commander's face that day.

If Tempus profoundly hated anyone, it was the dream lord, regent of the seventh sphere.

The last time Crit had seen Aškelon walk the earth, Ranke's emperor had been assassinated and the wizard wars ended by that act. Whenever the dream lord appeared, push came to shove, the mighty fell, empires crumbled, and blood was shed among puny humans like the Stepsons.

*Oh, crap.*

## *Chapter 22: Playing With Powers*

The women arrived in a throng, gilded and perfumed with gleaming skin and shining eyes and Kouras was captivated as soon as the first ankle, with bells on, poked out of the first ivory-screened wagon.

Musicians followed with their lyres and lutes and harps and bell trees, with their horns and pipes and flutes and tambourines. Kouras and Arton were told by Stealth to stay near the leadership. "Arton, you're to find me and tell me immediately if you have any premonitions," Stealth had said. "Kouras, you'll make sure it doesn't rain, and stay away from Torchholder unless the Riddler's with you, or I am." Stealth's quietude took the sting from it, and Niko was gone, chlamys swaying, weaving through the crowd in his custom- made enameled armor and his sword and sheath with the elder gods and the bulls of the storm god that seemed to writhe like living things in the light of the bonfires. *How does a man get such a panoply? Or warrant it?* Kouras was wondering when a tug came upon his arm.

He turned and there was Shawme, her eyes ringed with kohl and laughing. He thrilled, standing by Arton behind the Riddler's receiving line, where food and drink were laid out for the senior staff. "Kouras," she said demurely, "will you dance with me first?"

A sly challenge came and went on her beautiful lips in the moonlight. He looked at Arton, who was facing the other way, where musicians were getting ready to play.

"I would be honored, Shawme. But drink with me… we have the best food and drink right here." And it was so: clams and scallops and crabs and lobsters, corn and yams – all cooked in the sand – were piled upon that table, and wines from places with names Kouras couldn't pronounce.

No one had said the women couldn't eat or drink, although they weren't invited to the feast but were, themselves, the dessert.… He'd already heaped Shawme's plate and gotten her a goblet when he saw Arton watching, chewing his lip and staring disapprovingly at them.

Kouras ignored Arton. Here was the most beautiful girl in Sanctuary, and here was he. With so many swords to hand here, and sellswords from the palace besides, he could slip off with his Shawme, into those soft dunes with their grassy crests, and no one would be the wiser….

Turbulence began in the throng, and then it was in the receiving line: something scaled and armored launched itself at the Riddler before shortswords could clear scabbards or spears be aimed or crossbows nocked.

Its copper-colored legs clamped around his hips, its arms around his neck. Only the Riddler wouldn't have staggered back when this thing accosted him….

Kouras was launching himself toward the fray when Niko's hand caught his shoulder and jerked him back. "Easy, warfighter. You don't want a piece of that," he heard Niko say. Then the hand was gone, and Stealth with it.

Next he realized that Tempus's arms were about the impossibly small waist of the attacker (a molten-looking female of more-than-mortal proportions), cradling her to him. And the Riddler was laughing, turning in place, holding her while she was holding him and folk gave back. Had he ever heard the Riddler laugh before? Had he ever seen a woman wrap her legs and arms around a man with such abandon? In front of everyone?

He found his cup and drained it. All around the Riddler, his cadre was closing in. The receiving line was reforming, but still Tempus didn't let the woman go – or she didn't let him go. Practiced Stepsons realigned the throng, Nikodemos taking Tempus's place, greeting those who waited in line as if this happened every day.

"Who *is* she?" Shawme asked.

Kouras couldn't admit he didn't know.

The Riddler lets the copper beauty slide down to the ground, turns her halfway round, one arm across her chest, and holds her there, her hips to his groin, his left hand around her right wrist and nearly on her breast.

Someone behind him spoke up. "That's Jihan, Froth Daughter, Stormbringer's child – call her a sprite, a sea goddess, or demigoddess, as you will," said Molin Torchholder, nearly in Kouras's ear.

Torchholder was the one person whom Kouras had been warned by Stealth to avoid tonight. He hadn't seen the priest since that strange interview in the palace, when the god had come up in him so high that for the first time he didn't doubt that Vashanka was really there inside him. Someone refilled his drink. Kouras took his cup, Shawme on his arm. "Shawme, this is His Eminence, Priest of Vashanka, Molin Torchholder. Eminence, this is my…beloved friend, Shawme."

In the firelight, Molin's face seemed to fall as, behind, musicians started tuning up. He looked Shawme over in a way Kouras found offensive, and then said, "Dear, join the other dancers. You've work to do tonight."

Before Kouras could object, Shawme flushed, dropped her head and scurried away.

"We can do better for you than that, Gyskouras."

"Better? What if I don't want to do better? What if I want her and no other?" He shouldn't have drunk so much. He took a step toward Torchholder, the Froth Daughter and the Riddler forgotten.

Out to sea, the sky lit fitfully.

Torchholder gives back, one step. Kouras takes another step, and the priest takes two more, backward.

Now the music starts and it's heady, as fast as a racing pulse. Women run into the open, bells on, little cymbals on their fingers tinkling. Stripping off veils and cloaks as they go, they form two lines and begin a dance of leaping and bending, of racing by pairs down between two lines of other girls, hand in hand. Twirling, whirling, some girls are raising arms to heaven, leaping so high they seem to hover in the sky before landing on their toes or on their knees. One girl lifts another, and then all go through the line, arms high, two by two, skipping through the sand.

Someone pushes him once, and then again. It's Shawme. How has he gotten into the dancers' midst? Kouras doesn't know these Theban dances. But other young fighters are joining in, clapping hands, grabbing girls by the waist and lifting them high, turning with them, rolling them over their backs, back to back, letting girls leap over them. In the line of dancers, skipping down between the rows of men and girls, he grabs Shawme by the hand and twirls her, then lets her go. She spins and spins around. Then another girl leaps toward her and both of them skip with him between the line of men and girls.

Everyone starts swirling through the gauntlet: take a girl by the waist, spin her once, let go. Take the next, hand on her waist. Her right hand to your right hand, just a touch and you go on. And now some couples are pivoting one another, their feet nearly touch each other, fingers entwined, leaning back and out: round and round. He and Shawme are spinning, feet moving so fast they're blurry to his eyes, so fast he's nearly mesmerized.

As they whirl, he sees Tempus, with the copper-colored sprite beside him. From his cavalry training, Kouras can spin and watch what's around him and not get dizzy, see what happens in a spot each time he goes around. Another man comes up to Tempus, pale and darkly mantled. Kouras and Shawme spin and spin some more. When Kouras comes round again, all three of those – the Riddler; the copper-colored sprite, Jihan; and the pale man, who seems to pull shadow around him like a cloak – are gone as if they'd never been there.

Now Stealth, called Nikodemos, appears, over where the bonfire light is chancy. Kouras stops twirling Shawme, stands still, and stares. The music is going faster than his pulse has ever raced. It's inside his head and all around. Girls spin like tops, whirl and swirl; men join now from everywhere: fighters, nobles, palace folk, taking girls in their arms and skipping down the line with them while others clap a rhythm so fast that Kouras's breathing can't keep up.

First he thinks Stealth is dancing by himself, one arm held high, spinning in place. Then Kouras notices a woman there, under Stealth's hand: long, long hair, fanning out behind her; long legs flashing in the firelight. Niko puts both hands on her waist and lifts her and turns with her. She wraps her legs around him and still he turns. And turns. Stealth puts her down and twirls her.

It's unaccountable, that this fierce fighter would dance there like a boy, with this girl who seems nearly weightless. Kouras has never seen anything so beautiful but disturbing. Then they're skipping, coming through the line, as anyone else might do, hands clasped. And out they come, dashing toward the edge of the firelight, like deer or wild things, paying no heed to anything but each other.

Nikodemos spins her, lifts her, holds her high, and lets her down so slowly that every inch of her slides down every inch of him. Now he sets her gently on her feet and she springs away from him, then back, leaps again into the air and flutters down like a leaf or a bird. The two join hands once more and spin around and away, feet nearly touching together, bodies arched back, hands joined, whirling into darkness, as if the gods spin them upon invisible strings.

Shawme says, "Kouras, do you want to dance anymore? Or not? Or do something else?"

Kouras has been dumbstruck, stock still, all this time. He asks the storm god to give him such grace as Stealth has. And the god growls, inside his head: *We will do better.* Before he can respond to this inner voice, Critias comes up, saying, "Kouras, say good evening to your dance partner. We have someone for you to meet."

Shawme left behind, he goes with Crit, back to the post that Kouras had deserted. Crit whispers, "Don't do that again. I want you where I put you," and cuts the line of folk waiting to meet the commander.

He and Critias come up behind Tempus, where Straton stands guard, alert. The Riddler and another big man are talking, very low, their bodies stiff with opposition, a respectful distance apart. But Kouras hears them, as if the god's ears are his:

"…Ash, I can't help you with Niko. I won't. He doesn't want help, least of all from you." "Let me see him." "I can try to stop you." "Someone needs to step in." "He's not a boy anymore. You've had your chance. Find another acolyte. He chose Enlil." "The gods are worried, overworked. The Fates obey no rules of gods or men." "Neither do you. So what?" "All things are connected, Tempus – you know that. You and I have too much at risk to make a wrong decision with Nikodemos." "It's his decision, Ash, not yours or mine – what he wants from life." "Let me see Nikodemos, Tempus. Whatever you think, he needs my help." "No, he doesn't." "Heaven thinks you too arrogant. Want proof? You're not healing like you used to do. I could help you too, old warhorse." "You're too expensive for my taste. Help me by staying in the seventh sphere, on Meridian, and leaving us on this mortal plane alone." "I'll stay here until I've talked to Nikodemos." "So? Then go ahead. See him if you must. And then leave. He'll tell you what he wants. But you respect it, Ash, or you and I will come to blows. And you don't want that, angry Fates or not." "You're right, I don't. Your honor blinds you, Tempus, to what's right and wrong these days." "Good and evil? Come now, Ash. From you? I'll manage as I am, without your moral compass as my guide. Now go on: if he'll meet with you, that's between you two. I'm not his keeper. But you're an uninvited guest here. Be polite."

In a voice much louder, the Riddler says, "Critias, take Aškelon and Kouras with you and go find Niko. Let them talk. But stay with them. Unless you need me to step in."

Crit jogs Kouras's elbow roughly, saying under his breath, "Be very, very cautious, Kouras, if you want to own your soul by morning." And pushes Kouras forward.

The man called Aškelon looks his way. He looms large, with silver-shot hair and deep gray eyes like javelins in a pallid face with an inner light. This shadow-wrapped man looks Kouras up and down and twitches lips slightly cruel, cynical. Everyone else has moved away. Kouras catches a glimpse of Torchholder in the crowd, arms crossed, shaking his head from side to side.

"So," says the pale man, "Critias, introduce me to your young friend," as if Aškelon, not Tempus, rules the Band.

Crit is already moving them along with gentle pressure, away from Tempus and the guests standing around, curious. "Gyskouras, son of Vashanka, meet the entelechy of dream and shadow, regent of the seventh sphere, Aškelon of Meridian. *Not* a friend of the Band. But if you're nice to him, the dream lord might make you a panoply like Niko's, which kills and saves when mortal arms and armor can't. You can chat with Kouras while I find Niko for you, Lord Aškelon." Crit's voice is wry, careful. "Come right this way, now."

The dream lord says through those haughty lips, "And what do you think to be, Kouras, when you grow up? For whom do you labor? And in what cause?"

Over his shoulder, Kouras can see Torchholder shake Tempus by the arm.

*

Flash of thigh, body heat, silken hair along his diaphragm; smooth, smooth skin; the softest sigh. His breath comes fast. Grass kisses them. They kiss each other. There's nothing to say; there's everything to say. She reminds him of someone. But he can't think with her skin along the length of him, her blazing heat firing up his blood. He's as gentle as he's ever been; so careful, until he can't be. His head spins like they'd spun together to the music. Music as fast as his heart was beating while they joined hands, weights counter- balanced, and whirled to the rhythm in the sand.

She won't let him speak. Her finger shuts his lips whenever he tries. She can't be real, so perfect is she: every line and curve of her fits him like a glove. And yet she's the most real thing that's ever happened to him, out where the sea grass makes them a bed and the sand is soft and the moon shines down and the sea surges like his passion.

He hears a man's voice, then another. She's gone like a witch, right out of his arms, leaving him half-naked in the sand, alone and reeling. Not one word exchanged. Not a name, not a token. He scrambles into his clothes and gear: sand, so soft before, now abrades him; it's in his linen loin-guard, in his tunic, in his armor. When he's dressed, he just sits there (where they'd lain together) breathing, elbows on his knees, sword out.

If it's Shamshi, he has no doubt he can kill him now. A fight to the death with honor would be just the thing to quench his heat, and fair payment for this unwarranted interruption.

Stormbringer's ocean is very near. They'd ended up out behind the lighthouse. Offshore, two boats lurk: the Riddler has hired two tenders, to watch for incursions from the harbor.

Those voices – that had chased the girl away and left him empty-armed and angry – keep on coming.

Three men top the rise. In the full moon or under no moon, or in heaven or in hell he'd recognize the one man. He considers using the poisoned blossoms, most lethal of the throwing stars in his belt, but it would do no good. He doesn't rise as they come over the dune: two men and a boy, he amends.

Deep shadows swathe the dream lord: they always do, would in brightest day.

The three come up to him. Crit says, "So sorry, Niko. Riddler's orders."

"And the boy? Kouras? Why is he here?" Niko says. "Get him out of here." *Too harsh a tone. Balance. Equilibrium. Take deep breaths.*

Kouras hangs his head.

"Riddler's orders," says Crit, merciless.

"Fine, but back off, Stepsons." Nikodemos won't get up. But he has to look up to meet the eyes of the entelechy of dream. It's as if Aškelon wears the moon atop his head. Niko waits until Crit and the boy go back down the dune.

"One more time, Ash: *go away*. And *stay* away from me. You had me once, for a while, when I was weak. I'm not that weak now."

The dream lord sits cross-legged in the sand, facing him.

"You underestimate your peril, Niko."

"Are you sure? Or do you mean, from you?"

"You and Tempus brought these Thebans here. Do you think the gods are pleased?"

"Never mind what I think. And how would you know what the gods want, dream lord? Go away. Leave me be." Like Tempus seeking Vashanka to offset a wizard's curse, Niko had come to Enlil to counteract the dream lord's unsolicited favor. But Niko had only his *maat*, while Tempus had immortality to tip the scales his way.

"I've helped you before. That panoply you wear has saved you – how many times?"

"And got me in deeper, every time, where I don't want to be. You want it back? Take it." He starts to gather the dream-forged weaponry – and hesitates: for fighting Shamshi, it might make all the difference….

"Don't be a fool. You're too bold and too angry. You'll need that panoply, for combating greater fools and Fates. Those are fated men, you saved. You know it. Your *maat* knows it. Don't contest with higher forces – not on your own. And not poorly armed. You're not that strong. No one is."

"I'm as strong as I need to be." *Soft skin, sliding against him on the sea grass. Long spear, thunking into flesh. Man staggering back, impaled. The Riddler, fallen between his legs in the car of that hell-wheeled chariot in Chaeronea, long shaft sticking out of him.* He shivers. Tempus and he had chosen that chariot without enough thought to its maker, the lord of dream and shadow. So Aškelon could know all about the battleplain, might have had a hand in the way things went there. "Ash, get out of my head and out of my sight. We did what we did." He shrugged. "For honor. For righteousness. To restore a balance. You wouldn't understand."

"You and the Riddler cheated the Fates. Flouted the heavens. I understand that. And you think to walk away, free and clear, no repercussions?"

"You've done it, time and time again." There was no use in telling Aškelon that the storm god Enlil had been with Tempus at Chaeronea, and therefore with the entire Sacred Band. He probably knew, just didn't care, since any truth for him must be convenient. "Begone. I never should have let you teach me what I did. My rest-place has been a battleground ever since, worse than Chaeronea."

"I can help you fix it. Look what you and Tempus wrought, with your ancient remedy: one more problem under heaven."

So Ash did know all about Sham. And about Niko's hesitancy to confront the youth in metaphysical realms. "Please, no more help. No more anything."

"You're halfway to where you need to go. It's the most dangerous time. And all the gods and forces have a stake in you, Hero. Or do you want to be just a memory, a cult somewhere, with people sacrificing horses to your name?"

That got him on his feet. "Ash, I don't want to go anywhere, become anything. I don't want any higher forces taking an interest in what I do. I'm just a weapon of the god. That's all I signed up for. I'm telling you: no more. I'm not the Riddler's sister, to make a deal with you for earthly gain. I just don't care enough which way it goes: death follows life; it's all the same, if it's honorable. And honorable, you will never be."

He'd never been so bold, but he was too angry these days. Aškelon was correct in that assessment. Niko had Sham to deal with, a wizard's son. He knew Aškelon could help him with the travesty that was Shamshi – perhaps even destroy Sham with a wave of his hand. He just couldn't pay the price. And Ash had come here and chased the dancing girl from his arms….

And when he thought that thought, the dream lord rose up, and seemed to shimmer, and began to fade away. "If you change your mind, my door is always open to you. What difference, if I help you, or all the jealous gods contend to do the same? You know how to find me." And the entelechy of dream was gone with a little puff of wind and a soft *pop.*

Niko got up and went to where he thought the dream lord had stood. He knelt there, to see if there were any real footprints left behind, or depressions in the sand.

He was still kneeling there when Crit and Kouras peeked over the top of the dune.

"Well, brave heroes, how much of that did you hear?"

"Nothing at all," said Crit, clapping his hand over Kouras's mouth.

"I lost something out here. I'm going to try to find it." Niko turned away. *Where could she be?*

"No, you're not," said Crit. "The Riddler's expecting us to bring you back."

Niko collected his remaining sandy gear while they waited and, as they trudged back, he lagged behind Crit to walk with Kouras. "So…Kouras?"

"Why didn't you let this Aškelon help you?" Kouras whispered. "Sham's so dangerous. So many more might die…."

"I've been down that road. I don't like where it leads. And neither will you, storm god's boy, unless you want to be like Sham. You can feel him, can't you, Bandaran: eager to share some pain, pass some fear around? Don't be afraid, and don't be impatient to be a hero. There's no *maat* – no righteousness, no balance – in unbridled power, or in perverting the natural order to serve selfish ends. I don't want to live forever or die a hero enough to trade my soul."

What could Niko say to a boy who's seen the entelechy of dream solicit a mortal's patronage?

Kouras was quiet for a time, then said, "Yes, sir. I see, or I think I do. But that kind of help seems so tempting…."

Catching up to Critias, they walked on in silence, until they began to hear the music of the feast over the crashing of the waves.

"Who was the girl you were dancing with, Stealth?" Crit asked after a long and uncomfortable silence.

"I don't know," he admitted. "I wish I did."

*

Straton was failing in his duty to have 'fun' tonight. Music swirled around; dancers whirled around; power players slithered hither and thither through the crowd of Sanctuary's finest: civilians who wore no armor, no unit designators, nothing to let you know who was who. Niko had told Strat that they were required to have fun, by the Riddler's decree. Tempus was having 'fun' somewhere in the shadows with Jihan. Crit was off with Aškelon and Kouras, having 'fun' seeking Niko.

That left Straton in command, with responsibility for everything that happened here: Thebans, groping Ilsigi priestesses; priests meddling where priests never should; oligarchs and whoremistresses and people who seemed vaguely familiar, regarding him sidelong.

He rode around the perimeter on his ghost horse, which had a spot on its withers where you could see into hell (or somewhere else full of fire and shadow) and another spot on its hip where you looked into nothing at all. The ghost horse wasn't afraid of anything, couldn't be hurt by anything. The bay horse had loved him enough to come back to life for him. It loved him still. And he returned that love with all his fervor: it was the only creature on this earth that had never disappointed him.

He kept one eye on the shoreline. He was on the lookout for the Riddler. Jihan was loving Tempus, somewhere in the dunes. Torchholder was venting to Charon, apparently over his dual furies that Kouras loved a whore, and that Tempus would send the storm god's boy off with the dream lord – and Crit. Charon's son, Lysis, was discovering women with Arton: those two might make a pair someday, if Lysis could outgrow his father.

The music was so loud here you couldn't hear the sea. The smells of roasting food had drawn feral dogs, skulking near the tables, occasionally bold enough to jump up, grab a bone or chunk, and dart away.

He turned the ghost horse toward the lighthouse and heard wings above his head, felt the air flapping. Maybe it's an owl, he told himself, looking for scraps, like the dogs.

But then he knew it wasn't an owl.

Ischade coalesced before him in a flutter, a swirl of sand, and a popping of Strat's ears.

"Straton, good to see that you and the bay are getting on so well," she said; first eye to eye with him in the moonlight; then floating down, settling on the sand so that her face was level with his hip. "I've been wanting to see you alone."

"Ischade." He got off the horse. Nothing less would do. He stood in the sand before her, remembering everything – those mad days of love and death and aching hearts.

The compulsion she exerts on him remains, unabated after all these years.

She says, "Good. I owe you this," and raises her hand to his left shoulder. She touches him there. Her eyes are all black, as big as apples – then all white, and floating off her face. His shoulder pings and blazes. His badly mended bones and aching joint snap with pain so that a moan escapes him and he's dizzy.

The next thing he knew, he was on his knees in the sand and she was holding him, her arms around him. He'd never smelled anything as heady as the musk of her neck.

"No, Straton, no. No, no, no," she crooned.

"Ischade," he managed, strands of her hair on his lips.

"It's all right. It's all right. Things as they once were will never be again, but it's all right." When she took her arms away, he was weak as a kitten, shaking, sitting on his haunches in the sand. "Your shoulder will not pain you. Now, get up. We need to find the Riddler, alert him. The youth you seek comes near."

He didn't want to find the Riddler. He wanted her to put her arms back around him. He wanted to put his arms around her – but she wasn't letting him. He knew what she was doing; he just couldn't stop her.

She arose, more floating to her feet than using human legs, all black cowl and white face and red, red mouth tonight. She didn't say another word aloud.

In his head, he heard her voice, repeating what she'd just said: *We need to find the Riddler, alert him. The youth you seek comes near.*

Then his strength returned, and his reason with it: "Alert him? The Riddler? The wizard boy is coming? Sham?"

So he put her up behind him on the ghost horse. And they rode together, one more time, her arms around him. He could feel her breasts burning into him, her chest rising and falling. She breathed, just as he did. She lived, her own kind of life. A life he once had shared and now could not, because of too many broken dreams and promises.

Searching for Tempus, they jogged past celebrants coupling enthusiastically on the sand. Straton took his time, with her up behind, because now he wondered if this was the last time, as it always was and might be with Ischade – the last time he'd ever feel her heart beat next to his.

Before they found the Riddler, a big dog began to pace them, black and wolfish, tongue lolling out, bolder than a dog should be.

He had a suspicion, then, of just what kind of dog this was.

And Strat was afraid for a moment that this dog was going to jump at the ghost horse's throat. As had happened once, so long ago – and after which, for so very long, he'd had nothing left: no ghost horse; no Ischade; nothing but his own guilt and estrangement from the Band and Critias and the pain of a pairbond stretched nearly to breaking….

He and Ischade and the ghost horse were over near Vashanka's Rip, on the opposite side of the spit from the lighthouse, where the remains of the old summer palace lay tumbled down. He stopped the horse. He felt her stiffen, behind him.

"Be you cautious, Straton," warned the witch.

He said, for both their sakes, lest she misconstrue, "Dog, if you're Randal, stop playing games. And no biting, this time."

The dog sneezed and wiped its nose with its right front paw.

Ischade slipped down from the ghost horse about the same time the dog became a man, to shrug off her cloak and throw it over the naked, white-skinned mage (so bony and frail), who should have stayed back home in Lemuria tonight. Beneath Ischade's cloak was only more dark, more shadow: her own sort of armor – no jewel-toned gown or beloved swell of hip…not for him to see; not this night.

"Randal," Strat growled. "Not a good time. We're off to warn the Riddler – there's a wizard boy, stalking, hereabouts."

Randal straightened up, clutching Ischade's cloak around his slender form, and tugged on one ear: "I might be able to help you with that. Just wait till I manifest something else to wear. Not that I don't appreciate the cloak, dear lady…."

"Is every creature from every plane and hell coming in here tonight?" Strat demanded impatiently, as Randal started making passes with his hands over sand that eddied, and changed, and became a pile of clothes in the blink of an eye.

"It's an open house." Randal shrugged bony shoulders. "Be more careful what you call things, if you don't like the results. Please turn around, you two. Modesty forbids me to dress before a lady."

"She's not a lady, she's a necromant, Witchy-ears," Strat said, and then felt loutish. The Stepsons' warrior-mage knew exactly who and what Ischade was. "And hurry up. The Riddler's been praying for a chance like this, to catch this plaguing Shamshi."

"Your own plague, isn't it?" Ischade says softly, hands out to him to lift her up behind him.

Now Randal has his clothes all made, and something vaguely horse-like is trotting from the shadows, with a sandy coat and sandy tack, but good enough.

"Now, hurry. *Run.* Let's hope we haven't delayed too long," Ischade whispers in his ear. And run they do, across the whole broad spit, sand and civilians scattering in their wake.

*

All of them – so many hunting him. Sham walks among them, proud that he can slip by, unnoticed; sipping their wine and touching their women while he's picking out a target. Then he sees too much and, seeing, drinks too much. Jihan, the copper sprite from eternal seas, is here to help the Riddler make an end to him. And a more daunting power, Aškelon, walks the sand with Kouras, seeking Stealth: this entelechy is very dangerous, once a sorcerer, but now more than most gods can claim to be. Sham recalls Jihan and Aškelon from a sojourn on Meridian, when Sham was just a child. And the dream lord feels Sham's presence: in his mind, Shamshi sees a face smirk, an eyebrow lift, and a hand raise – in greeting, in warning, or to mark him prey or strike him down…. Which, he doesn't know.

These powers gather here to chase him, so many ranged against him: the fearsome necromant and a shape-shifter (sometimes dog, sometimes mage, never only man). He drinks another wine, and then another. Around him, paired Stepsons and Thebans celebrate each other – their unit pride, their warrior bond, their camaraderie stronger than death itself. From which he is forever banished. He is nothing, anathema, shunned and under a sentence of death.

They are united in their hunt for him: far too many seek him for one young fighter to withstand. The music swirls around his ears, teasing him. What had he thought to do here? Pick them off, before their very eyes? Have their women, send their souls to hell? Foolish, to risk so much to make a point.

He's marked for death by every one of them. The enormity of it overwhelms him. It's all he can do to walk, not run, out of the balefires' light, out into the dunes and the cloaking night, before his fear betrays him and he curls up in the sand: alone, helpless before his sudden panic, trying to find his rest-place and his courage.

*Hide. Hide until you're strong enough. This fight is no part of fair, nor will it ever be. Long spears, thunking into flesh. Men staggering back, impaled, mewling.*

No fight is fair. The Sacred Band of Stepsons had snatched forty-six souls from the jaws of hell and got away with it. Shamshi would send those same souls back to hell and have his sweet revenge upon upstart Stepsons who presume to dice with destiny. But not until his terror ebbs and his limbs stop shaking and loneliness takes its constricting fingers from his throat.

## *Chapter 23: Gods and Fates*

If cities have souls, Sanctuary's was troubled long before Tempus got here, and will be troubled long after he and his are gone. Now the Fates are here on the beach, three shadows blacker than black, walking through the dunes and looking for their own. Just shadows, lamb-white hands beneath black robes spun of tears, glide among the celebrants on this night wherein the spirits of Thebes have found a home, if serendipitously.

What do they hear and see, these travelers from another realm, so silent, moving in a half-light (or a half-life) where only they can be?

First they find Stepsons from the Riddler's Sacred Band: "We'll let Torchholder and Aškelon dice for Kouras, but the winner has to kill Shamshi to own the storm god's son," Critias, hard-bitten soldier, proposes to Sync, horse-tamer, only half joking where he stabs a bonfire with his spear to stoke the flames.

The horse-tamer replies, "May it please the gods," and that entreaty spins up to heaven, to be proposed and considered. "I found a woman, Crit. She's not a girl – more my age, or yours…Dianna. She's just what I've been looking for. She rides like a goddess." He throws a piece of bread soaked in wine, with a little oil on one corner, into the bonfire's flames.

Critias asks, "But how is she on a horse?"

The Fates move on, considering the horse-tamer's wish for something other than war, from a taciturn man who's led a most warlike life in a unit called 3rd Commando, without conscience or pity, famed for its brutality throughout this land.

Not far away, before a food-laden board, the Fates find a priest named Torch, not praying: "…dream lord be damned, and the Riddler with him. The storm god's son and a *whore*? 'It's *customary'* the Riddler says. 'Gyskouras is the *son* of the Pillager,' the Riddler says. 'What do we *expect?'* the Riddler says. So I ask him, 'And if Gyskouras rapes her and kills her because Vashanka wishes, will you then sew Gyskouras up in a hide and let the Fates cast him adrift?'"

Hearing their names spoken in a foreign tongue, the *Moerae* peer closer at this priest with wizard's blood, and then exchange knowing looks with one another. This one is already a tool of heaven. And useful to Fates. This man with a foot in two realms (natural and supernatural) takes forward little dooms and untangles strands of destiny dependably, if unwittingly.

Beside this priest called Torch, an oligarch gazes at the bonfires, still burning high, and so many men and girls yet fondling one another in the sand. "None of us realized what the Thebans do with their women," protests the oligarch mildly. "Let alone the Stepsons. These Sacred Bands…or this unified one…may be worse than the chaos we hope to regulate. My wife will not be pleased about this debauch. We can't have these customs here, in Sanctuary. We're civilized."

The Fates cock their ears.

The priest continues, ignoring the oligarch's digression, "So then I say to the accursed Riddler, 'Why did you humiliate that youth, Shamshi? You'll not do anything like that to Gyskouras, no matter what the god disposes him to do, or you'll face my wrath. We put up with *you*, when the god took you up and lay about with your sword arm, beyond restraint or reason. You've sacked and pillaged your way across a dozen empires, you and your so-called Sacred Band. I don't see the difference.' And that Niko's standing by him with those guard-dog eyes. And do you know what *he* says to me? That….second-in-command to the lord of bloodbath? That *familiar* of the Riddler's…?"

The oligarch doesn't. Neither do the Fates, who lean in close: "…that Nikodemos pipes up (without a hint of regret): 'We've all been rough on occasion. Everything in war is rough. For his crimes, we disciplined Shamshi as the gods prescribe. Not for rape, though we might have. For running away – for desertion, for dereliction of duty – when he was told to wait his night out, to face his punishment. Withstand it, prove himself worthy of redemption. Now, we need to find him before he kills again.' And off he goes, sword in hand. No 'excuse me.' No 'by your leave.' At least they're not pretending any longer that the necromant is responsible for all Shamshi's crimes."

When the necromant is mentioned, the Fates look away and go away – away from any chance encounter with such a one, whom neither gods nor Fates or Nature can sway. They have a mission here, and a necromant is no part of the threads they've spun.

Events occurring on this sand-spit are an affront to the intelligible light, which steers all things. The laws of gods hold no power over Fates. The fated dead of Thebes have drawn them here for this night, only. The Fates are here to see that universal order rules unswayed.

Now they spy a man the gods immortalized, and a creature of froth and wave. These two look straight at them. And see them. One Fate snarls. Another shrinks back. The third counsels a decorous withdrawal. And withdraw they do, before the red-flecked eyes of the Froth Daughter grow too bright and the power she can wield traps them in eternal ice, between realities.

At last, the Fates find a Theban youth, brave and true, hobbling on a crutch, with everything worth saving in his eyes and in his soul. He and his companion, a budding seer, are sneaking through sand dunes on foot, intent on finding and killing an evil that all the Sacred Band hunt here tonight in the full moon's light. This pair nearly softens the hearts of the heartless, so pleasing are they in the sight of Fates and gods. But these boys must not be allowed to interfere – and are close, so close, to doing so. In the bright moonlight, the Fates pause. They have been seen once, tonight, by creatures more than human. In this benighted Sanctuary, inhuman and human mix too easily together. In Thebes, it has never been this way.

"We're near," the youth named Arton whispers. "I can almost see him. I can almost smell him." And he's right. The Fates can see what mortal boys cannot: their quarry huddles one sand dune away, weeping softly, his great sobs muffled by his hands over his face.

"I've got the dart tube," says the Theban, Lysis. "We're ready. I just need to get closer." Now the Fates are taken aback. A Theban should not carry such a weapon, which could down a god, or a power even greater; which came out of the sea and should go back there, soonest. It has driven gods from temples, demons from hoary caves, and even struck down such as Fates in its time.

The Fates give back and glide away, over one more dune, where a youth named Shamshi huddles, paralyzed with loneliness and regret. Stalked by more than sixty men (and arcane powers too), this youth is shivering, cold, terrified and repentant. And repentance is a sacrifice that all forces, gods and Fates, revere. But the Fates' wrath at human hubris must not be denied.

Interference is forbidden, too directly. Perhaps a touch of wind, a bit of sand blown in a stalker's eye, could be overlooked. Or a stumble, on uncertain ground. This weeping, disconsolate wizard boy is an unknowing ally; an instrument of theirs; a child of destiny meant to bring the haughty low and make the fights fairer when gods too boldly intervene.

The Fates are here because of supernal anger, celestial imbalance, and arrogance of men and gods that must be curbed. They can touch this Shamshi once, and once again, and a third time: coil him round with the wool of their devising, make him stronger, and let him grasp the threads they weave.

Up they sweep, in a storm of sand. Into the eyes of their own Theban, who holds the weapon that could undo all plans, they blow their sand. In its swirl, in the moonlight, the young Theban nearly sees them – three dark shadows, robed and hooded, sliding together: no faces to see; no feet to walk; no hands, now, to grab. The seer sees the future, not the present. Hence his sight is easier to confuse.

Boys crest the dune, coughing and stumbling. Their quarry, Shamshi, still sobbing, breaks away, scrambling through the sand down to the shore.

Only so much can be done to make things as they should be. The running youth heads for the surf, where the sand is packed and wet, and sprints for his very life. The lame Theban youth gives chase, aiming his little tube with its ancient poison darts. The Theban runs hobbling, as fast as he can.

Faster, faster, catching up in long hitching strides, heels pushing into the hard-packed sand. And closer still.

Lysis puts the tube to his lips, and blows.

The Fates themselves all blow another way. And that gust of wind blows the dart off target – down, down, away from the neck and back of the running Shamshi. The dart grazes his calf but doesn't hit its mark or stick, or puncture, or wound to kill.

Into the water, the fated Shamshi blunders and then, deeper, dives. And the Theban, wiping sand from his eyes, doesn't follow. He's not sure why: he's a good swimmer. Except that the other boy, the seer, is telling him he can't. The riptide is too strong. It will carry him away, with his thigh still wounded.

They watch the swimmer in the moonlight – the Bandaran seer cursing that he doesn't have his crossbow or his horse; the young Theban feeling a touch like gossamer threads on the back of his neck. The Fates can't resist; they must bless their own.

The Theban shudders. Then the two boys head back across the sand, up into the dunes, to report.

And the Fates go another way, now that the moon is tiring of its journey through the sky: their time is up, tonight. But their work is never done. This Sanctuary is not a place for such as they, except on very special evenings, when stars pause in their orbits and worlds can whirl away; when time can stand still, for just a few moments, and Fates can work their will, more directly.

## *Chapter 24: Wake of the Dream Lord*

The dream lord's visit had thrown Niko off balance. In its wake, wherever he turned, all things on the beach felt wrong. Arton and Lysis had come running up from the water's edge, claiming they had found, chased and wounded Shamshi with a poison dart – where so many more experienced scouts and snipers had failed. His trainees were sure it was Sham, despite their quarry's black hair, dark skin and beard.

Niko believed them. Ignoring the revelers and the fête winding down, he swung up on his Aškelonian mare and patrolled the shoreline all night long. His sword and crossbow ready, he went seeking Shamshi, alive and well; or a corpse washed up on the wet, packed sand, in the phosphorescent shoal or the waves. But he found neither.

Eventually, the sun rose in a cloudy sky. This new day unfolded without a single casualty, except from drunkenness and debauch – and some wounded pride, since so many had bet so much that this celebration would flush Sham from hiding. Without proof, the Stepson leadership was unwilling to believe the trainees, who claimed they'd found Shamshi and given chase.

Surely his *maat* and the boys weren't wrong: Shamshi had been at the fête. Surely Ischade, the necromant, wasn't wrong: Shamshi partook of the feast. Surely Randal, fresh from Lemuria, wasn't wrong: he could smell the wizard boy on every dune. Surely Jihan wasn't wrong: the combined strength of the Sacred Band and its allies had this determined youth on the run.

Yet wherever he looked, Niko could find no track or solid trail. He got glimpses. He could feel a chill and shadowy presence in his mind; but Niko always felt an abysmal cold, whenever he had a brush with the dream lord.

Now that Niko was ready to kill Shamshi, he couldn't find him.

"Let's declare victory, since there were no mishaps at the fête," Tempus said, over breakfast in the ruddy morning light, and ordered the Band home to its barracks.

But now Jihan and Randal were among them. The witch hovered nearby, incensed that her warning had yielded no wizard boy's corpse on a litter. Aškelon had annoyed Torchholder and Tempus, chasing after Niko where priest and Band could see. And Niko couldn't find the girl he'd danced with on the beach.

How and why he'd danced with anyone that night was disturbing: he couldn't remember ever having done such a thing before.

Yet duties press. Niko has too much to do. Charon had come to him during the feast and asked to build an altar at the barracks to their Theban goddess. Niko has persuaded Tempus to agree. The Thebans now want their altar on the hill next to Enlil's and must be satisfied. Lysis and Arton must be congratulated for flushing Shamshi, whether or not they really did.

Both things bother Niko. Enlil is a jealous god, and vengeful; crowding a foreign altar onto his hilltop may not be wise. Shamshi is twice as canny as Arton and Lysis; if those two found the wizard boy and chased him, then Sham allowed it, or some other power took a hand.

Something rings wrong about the trainees' encounter with Shamshi and Niko feels it: if Arton and Lysis had been mounted, surely they could have run down Shamshi on the hard-packed sand. Neither boy could explain why they'd hunted on foot, when Lysis was lame: "It seemed the right thing to do," Lysis had said, "with my leg wound and all. But we *hit* him. I know we hit him with the poison dart – exactly the way you showed us, Stealth."

Young Arton had said nothing, just looked at Niko like a rabbit surprised on a country road.

"Then we ought to find a body, unless the riptide took it out to sea," Niko mused. But there was no body; not even a finger or a piece of cloth. "Lysis, tell your father he can build an altar to Harmony, next to Enlil's on the hill, just where he wants it – only not so large that the war-god will be jealous." He'd meant it humorously. Neither boy chuckled, just looked at him with big, round eyes.

Jihan caught Niko at the barracks in the open before the noon meal. "Stealth." She crushed him close and then pushed him back, hands gripping his shoulders. "The Riddler says he needs no help…that you didn't call for me. Why is that?"

He rubbed the back of his neck and tried to remember, watching the play of light in the eyes and upon the skin of the Froth Daughter, and on her scale armor, finer than mortal hands could fashion. "Jihan, I was at wit's end. Tempus was blind, his chest wound wasn't healing: I walked into the water off Lemuria and asked for help helping him, that's all."

"Harrumph. And what did you think would happen next? I've seen that wound. It's closed." She was exquisite, more than human and twice as fierce as any man.

"I assumed you had, by now." The Riddler and Jihan's exploits in love and war were legend among the Stepsons – and now throughout the greater Sacred Band. "Jihan…" He must be careful: the Riddler was the proudest man Niko had ever met. "Is he… failing? Fading? Or is he truly well again?"

Jihan cocked that head and her pinwheel eyes spun, sparking fire. She said, "I'd forgotten how you love him. He's well enough, better than any mortal could think to be. And always will be." She folded shapely arms, so muscled she could lift him off the ground. "You pretend to balance, but you love him too much for that. Look to yourself, young fighter." She tapped her booted foot.

"It's been a long time since anyone has called me that." He smiled a slow smile at her which always got him far with women. "There was a girl, out at the feast…I lost track of her…."

"Better than losing track of yourself," Jihan said and flounced away, scale armor shining on that high rump in the sun. "And stay away from Aškelon," she called back over her shoulder. "The Riddler is not pleased with you for bringing the dream lord down upon us."

He knew that. He got his dream-forged panoply and their second-best Trôs horse and a long-handled rake. He was going back out to the seashore.

But Tempus caught him before he was out the gate. There was hell in his commander's eyes. "Off the horse."

He slid off, butt to horse, and stood. In front of everyone, would the commander chastise him?

The Riddler looked him up and down, and up again and said in a voice like whispering gravel: "Where are you going, without telling me? I have Randal and Ischade still hunting Shamshi – not good here, where sorcery's outlawed and necromants don't exist – and Critias trying to keep track of them while keeping track of everything else."

Niko stood very still, just waiting, meeting the Riddler's savage glare, holding the rake in one hand and the Trôs's reins in the other. "I haven't seen Randal yet. He'll find me, when he needs to."

"And will the rest of us? Torch is furious about exposing Kouras to Aškelon."

"Is Kouras a slave to this priest? Have we sold him to the palace? Last time I looked, he was a Stepson…ours to deploy."

That tight-lipped mouth told him the trap was sprung: "Then take Kouras with you, until all his questions are answered and he remembers he's a trainee. Make him hold your rake."

"I'm going down to –"

"I know where you're going, and what you're trying to do. A witness would be helpful, if you get yourself killed or mortally wounded out on the sand spit, to come back and tell me where to look for a body. If we can't find Sham's, we can at least find yours. And call in no more reinforcements of the nonhuman sort. I've enough to do, without more 'help.'"

The Riddler dismissed him with a wave of hand. Niko mounted up, the back of his neck hot. At least it had been quiet. But then it wasn't: "Kouras. *Here,*" bellowed the Riddler.

Kouras must have been waiting on the big blue roan, for the youth trotted right up, pale and bleary-eyed.

Niko reined the Trôs around and didn't look back to see if Kouras followed until the gates had closed behind them.

Not till they were out at the spit again, deep in the dunes, did Niko say a word to Kouras. He was too busy preparing himself as best he could. "You'll keep watch, Kouras," Niko told the storm god's son.

The Riddler had been right, of course, as he always was. If Niko must attempt this thing, someone should be with him; be his sentry, his guardian at the gate.

He stopped his horse where the sand was flat, between two dunes. Was this where he'd come with the dancing girl? Perhaps, but the wind had scoured the sand clear of tracks and marks of human passage, overnight. The cleanup crew was far off, on the other side of the lighthouse. The sea smoothed the shore, slathering bubbly foam inland and leaving shining wet sand behind.

Kouras knew enough to be quiet and simply hold the horses while Niko chose his spot and began raking a pattern in the sand. The sun was high before he finished. He'd made a perfect circle, mimicked by gulls overhead and one lone osprey gliding, curious, above his design.

Still Niko was not calm, although he knew what to do and how to do it. "Kouras, take those horses over the next dune and wait there." The trainee was too full of '*when*' and '*if*' and '*might have been*' and '*might be,*' looking for Shamshi, fanning his own young senses out wide. Trying to help.

But that wasn't the kind of help Niko needed. Niko kept silent, so Kouras did too: Kouras, bursting with questions, voiced none, and did as he was told.

Then Niko was free to step into the middle of his circle, with its spiral to the center, and sit down there. He wore his dream-forged armor. He had his swordbelt girded on. If Aškelon was right and this fight could be won by force of arms, he was ready.

He breathed deeply, until his breathing changed and welled up from his diaphragm, a different rhythm. He composed his mind and let his body's tension drift away. Overhead, seagulls cried like babies. The osprey's shadow circled, round and round, across the spot he was watching where tiny, pale sand crabs burrowed industriously among the grains of sand. Some errant breeze stroked his cheek. The rustle of the waves grew louder, roaring; then crashed against the beach.

That primal cadence caught his soul, finally, and he was floating, and then riding on those waves, and propelled toward shore: Almost there.

Almost there.... Niko is almost home, where his soul can be refreshed; where his meadow, star-shaped and ever green, meets the sea with its stream and its blue sky like eternity.

This is where he wants to be, where he wants to meet Sham, if there must be a fight. Let this battle take place here, in his rest-place, where time doesn't matter and age is not an issue: where any fight is fair but no fight is fairest. Where his heart always longs to be, in the ankle-deep grass; where wildflowers grow and a fragrant breeze touches his skin....

Without warning he is snatched away, flung into another place. In this other place, nothing exists but shrieking and bleeding and dark death hurtling through the skies. *Arrows arcing. Long spears, thunking into flesh. Men staggering backward, impaled, screaming.* Arrows whiz by his head. Long spears piercing, glittering in the sunlight. Men and horses bellow. Maneuvers, carefully drilled, impossible to complete. Waves of death breaking on the Chaeronean plain. So many falling, piled one upon the other....

Now Shamshi comes striding – not a youth, but a force as old as death, familiar with wearing boy's faces and men's faces and the faces of all the gods.

Armed and armored, crest on a blood-red helmet bobbling, this thing wants battle: long spears thunk by him, just softening him up. Now it has a sword, and has minions behind it: first a unit, then a cohort, then a phalanx. Niko can die, can be spitted here, can bleed out his life here as easily as he could in his own rest-place, or on Sanctuary's dunes.

This young adept has pulled him from one reality to another, into Shamshi's chosen battlespace where severed heads roll, bloated tongues sticking out through purple lips. Sightless eyes stare him down, their eyes-whites greenish, their skin mottled blue with death.

Shamshi and Niko will both have to step over bodies, for this contest to be joined.

Niko uses his shield to call the battle to order, pounding twice on it with the flat of his blade: it's the shield that Aškelon made him. "Ready, Sham? New drill, today." This Shamshi wants to fight hand to hand.

But the boy, or the image of the boy, doesn't answer. *That's fine.* Niko has taught Sham to stay focused, keep quiet, never to betray your intention with your eyes, your body, or your mouth. And it's difficult to keep your mind and your body focused in two places at once: a man can lose it all here, trying to attempt too much before mastering the lessons that can keep you alive.

But there are other lessons, more advanced: "Come on then, boy. Bring me what you've got," he calls, not knowing if he's saying it here, or there, or in both places simultaneously.

"Gladly, for what you did to me," spits a voice from inside that bronze helmet. "Traitor." So Sham *can* speak, here. Impressive. Not encouraging. Revenge is never the best driver for a battle, but a common one. Niko knows that Sham may have made an error, choosing this kind of combat. For a moment, Niko wishes with all his heart that Sham had come to him on Sanctuary's sandy spit, in the clean sunlight. There was nothing more he'd like to do today than hack some problem limb from limb, disembowel something unequivocally. But for real. In practice, not *for* practice.

*Careful, you could die here.*

He had nearly died once before, fighting in a place like this, and that place had been nowhere near as awful as this one.

Had Shamshi been coming here, time and time again? Eviscerating corpses, practice foes, again and again? Not good.

Bowstrings hum. Arrows whisper through the bleak light in this dreadful place where the stench of death is all around – though nothing truly lives here, or ever has lived here.

The thing that is Sham leaps over two corpses to get to him and comes down fighting: no quarter asked, or given. Grunts and thumps and parries and the screech of iron on bronze: swords and shields are all that matter now. Archers, if ever they were there, have fled or disappeared. Hoplites too… javelins are no part of this fight. This youth wants to feel muscle against muscle, pulse against pulse.

But battle here is as real as battle can be, and Sham's foot slips on gore. Lunge. Slash. Lunge. Parry. Riposte. Parry; slash. Thrust. Parry, riposte, and parry again. Disengage and try to dislodge the other man's grip on his weapon. Smash him in the helmet with your shield. Parry and thrust. Now push: knee against overbalanced weight, a screech of short-sword's edge on cuirass, and Niko has – for one second – a clear strike at an exposed, pale throat.

And doesn't take it. Instead, he kicks a greaved leg out from under his adversary as Sham grabs for purchase and catches his shield arm. They both go down together in the gory mud. His sword hand is caught under Sham's shoulder momentarily. Then he grabs the youth like a lover and rolls them both over. His shield and sword, behind Sham's back, are nearly useless for an instant as he does.

Between them are just wordless grunts as two men roll in the mud and blood. Niko lands on his back. Sham's legs are trying to get around him, scissor him, roll him once more. Niko gets a knee between Sham's and jams it upward, using his shield under Shamshi's chin to force the other's head back, and back: a second chance. There's no reasoning with this *boy*, his trainee that he has, perhaps, trained too well – and those before him on Bandara may have trained too well.

They slip and slide and roll amid the gore, coming to rest with Niko on top of Shamshi. This time, Niko takes his opportunity, slamming with the point of his shortsword deep into Sham's neck in a stroke that could be mortal – would be, should be, if what happens here today is reflected on the earthly plane.

And getting stabbed himself, in return, up under his cuirass: a deadly strike, if executed flawlessly, into vital organs. But today, not perfect enough: his cuirass catches the guard on Sham's sword, stopping the thrust short.

As Shamshi's corpse-to-be begins shuddering and coughing under him, Niko says, "This is taking far too long. I don't suppose you'd like to talk about it? The dream lord thinks we should." If this battle is one of wills, not flesh, and the combat here symbolic, there is still time to compromise. It's what they should do; what Bandaran practice requires – what Niko feels he must offer to a fellow initiate, no matter how lethal a turn their combat takes.

Then Sham's shield smashes into Niko's helmet and consciousness explodes into colors.

Along with everything Niko can remember, that battle-plain dissolves.

Now Niko sees sand, tastes it in his mouth; has a face full of it, and a headache that makes his eyes tear.

He half expects to be bleeding from his kidneys, from his bladder or his right buttocks or his hip, but he isn't. Yet. Pain rushes over him in waves. Sweat covers his face – running in rivulets into his eyes, down his cheeks, to his chin, and dripping from his jaw. Pain pounds harder at him, crashing in on his consciousness like surf swamps a jetty. Perspiration breaks out all over him from the pain in his back, down his hip and his flank: he's sweating behind his knees, in the creases of his elbows. The cold sweat is running down his breastbone. So much pain is never good. He starts to shiver. The edges of his vision go black.

Sham was vicious, but inexperienced. Niko should have ended it at the first opportunity – could have: would have, if the youth had been a man, or the battle joined on Sanctuary's sand.

But he's in too much pain to think clearly. He can feel the damage now, far too real for the wages of symbolic combat. Every chunk of ripped flesh, every bit of skin that's split asunder, flares agonizingly. He's wounded worse than he'd first thought. Or expected. His injuries shouldn't be this bad. Shamshi shouldn't be this strong. He doesn't understand it.

Now Niko bleeds. He's bleeding down the leg from some thrust that struck home and sliced him, all the way from there to here. He doesn't see the blood until he staggers to his feet: it's dark blood, venal; not bright red. It's dripping, not spurting out of him. That's good. However much these wounds hurt, they're survivable if he doesn't lose too much blood. He stands with legs widespread, weaving just a little on his feet.

He'd underestimated Shamshi. Underestimating an enemy is an error most fighters don't have a chance to make twice.

He'd meant to kill the representation of Sham quickly on that simulacrum of a battleplain, as an example of what could happen in Sanctuary if Shamshi didn't quit and run. Or kill him altogether, unequivocally, as a final result, if the young fighter was talented enough to make what happened there

– and here – one and the same. He had *not* meant to give an exhibition of how not to kill someone you're trying to reason with. He was ashamed of his indecision: if it happened again, it could kill him, even there. If it happened here, he'd deserve to die.

"Kouras, you can bring the horses now."

Kouras saw the blood and his eyes widened. "Sir? I mean…?"

"Bandage. I must have rolled on my sword when I dozed in the sand just then. It's been a long night."

The boy brought the wadding and they got the sand out of the wounds, stanched the blood enough for him to ride. It's not going to be easy, getting on that horse. He doesn't want Kouras to see how hard it is, to stand on his right leg and then swing it over that horse's back in order to mount. He needed to stop getting damaged where a man sat a horse.

When they both were mounted, Kouras said, "Did you kill…?"

The sand is bright around him but his vision is full of clouds.

"Maybe. Probably not. But if not, I bet Sham's thinking hard about what's worth what."

So is he.

## *Chapter 25: Weapon of the God*

First comes the wolf's call: one of the Wizardwall veterans, giving the old Nisi signal for incoming wounded from atop the barracks wall. To fix disorder in his house, Enlil always reaches for Tempus. He's out of the barracks like the wrath of gods – which he sometimes is, and is today. Bareback on the Trôs, barreling at a dead run toward the two approaching horsemen, he's through the opening gates before the others even gather in the courtyard.

Now the ululation is picked up by the Stepsons inside the compound. Jihan comes racing on foot, frowning. Straton and Crit, bawling orders, are marshaling the Sacred Band: *someone's coming in, badly hurt.*

The gates draw back. Some bring litters on the run to others scrambling for horses, medicine and bandage. Randal stumbles down the stairs.

But there's plenty of time. With the gates open wide, everybody waits there. There's *too* much time. The horsemen are coming very slowly. The commander's mount, reaching the incoming horses, wheels and comes alongside. Three abreast across the dirt track, they ride on, just single-footing: two gray Trôs horses and a blue roan, ambling down the road.

Jihan looks at Randal and Straton, at Critias, and heads shake. There's more than time enough to get prepared. Crit and Strat ready their mounts and weapons, but not hurriedly. The Riddler is out there, and signals them to stay where they are: a young wolf's yip. Once, twice; it echoes, forlorn. So it's not that kind of fight, today.

No one doubts what it means, three horses coming so painstakingly, so slowly toward the barracks.

Tempus should have known: whenever Aškelon appears, the wager is always more than you can afford to lose.

He paces the two incoming riders. He knows what he sees: Niko, with Kouras close beside him and blood dripping down his side, his leg, off his foot; a blood-trail of dashes and dots, stretching out far behind them on the ground. Niko is swaying in his saddle, shocky, helmet by his knee, shield dented. His skin is pallid and translucent: veins stand out sharp and clear. Niko has the grab-strap on his saddle in his right hand, reins wrapped around his left. His head is down, his lips pale.

Tempus's Trôs strikes out with a forefoot at the smell of blood and screams a belly-shaking protest. Niko's gray answers, side-stepping, nearly unseating his rider.

"What happened, Niko?" Tempus says above the hoofbeats and the squeak of leather, snort and blow of horses. *"Niko?"*

Stealth doesn't respond, then knits his brow and turns his head, so slowly. "Nothing much. Inconclusive." He rocks too much in that saddle, trying to keep the weight off his bloody right side. Tempus can't see where the blood is coming from. There's too much of it, soaking the blanket, meandering in rivulets. He reaches down and snatches Niko's right rein.

And gets no argument.

"Kouras, *where* were you?"

Vashanka's son is on Niko's left side, face dirty, eyes wide. "Where *he* told me to be. Holding the horses, over the dune." Nearly in tears, the young fighter looks helplessly from one man to the other. He scrubs his face with a grimy hand. "It's a long ride home…. It didn't seem so bad when we started."

Tempus sidles his horse close enough to grab the bleeding Stepson if Stealth starts to slide off his horse. Blood drips down Niko's leg, so slowly; and dribbles down, more slowly yet, onto the sand. Careful strides take forever to cover any ground. His Stepson sways too much one way, too much the other; right arm braced: side to side, forward and back. Head nodding down, snapping upright.

They've been through this too many times before. The worst is going so slowly, carefully, with so much at stake.

But Tempus knows his partner: if Niko is able, he'll ride into those barracks under his own power. *We could have done without the armor, this whole long ride back from the lighthouse spit. We could have done without this wizard-spawn, Shamshi, in the first place.*

When they've nearly reached the gate, the Sacred Band starts calling out. Tempus lifts one hand and drops it: *stay back.*

Niko raises his head and stares; then catches Tempus, eye to eye. Niko has a feral look, desperate and demanding, like a panther in a trap: "I got on this horse by myself. I'll get off it by myself." That voice is barely audible, but Tempus knows what Niko is going to say, knows what's going to pass those lips: "Don't you let Jihan help get me down, or put her hands on me where the men can see…or try to heal me. Or let *any* of them."

*Damn, not again.* He can see the Froth Daughter, pacing at the gates, hands on her hips.

"I'll do it," Tempus says. No argument possible on either side. "You dismount, and I'll help you the rest of the way." He never should have let Niko go out there with only a trainee, Bandaran or not. *Never should have let Niko take Shamshi to Bandara to begin with.* "My quarters. Just me, you, Strat, and Crit."

Niko nods his head, just slightly; furrows deep on his forehead, as if he's struggling to remember something.

Kouras is looking back and forth between them.

"Kouras, ride ahead, tell Crit we don't need a litter. Just him and Strat. Clear everyone else out of the yard."

Kouras rides off, first slowly, cautiously; trotting until he's far enough away and then galloping.

"Niko…"

"We won this round, if it matters. Couldn't bring myself to kill him there," the fighter mumbles. "Took a while. Wound's not really that bad," and almost falls off the horse's near side before Tempus grabs his arm.

*Now, God, what have You to say? One more sword, Enlil; one more body spilling blood – does it matter in Thy awful sight? This time, and from now on, no mercy for these enemies.*

And Enlil swears: *On this and every day hereafter,* loud as thunder in his head so that his ears pound with it. The sky above takes up that thunder and shakes the ground.

Tempus agrees with the god's anger, expressed by the tremor and distant lightning, coming close. Today he wants thunder, lightning, blinding rain, to wash everything and everybody clean. Not even in Chaeronea did the god have anything to say. This one fighter, this weapon of the god, has shaken Enlil awake, got the storm god's holy attention. But is it worth the cost? Ever?

The day has no shadows left by the time Tempus gets Niko inside the barracks gates.

Everyone stands well back. Men will watch whatever they're told not to. Tempus slides off his Trôs and comes around to help. Straton takes Tempus's horse. Crit takes Niko's by the bit. Randal peeks out from behind a half-closed stall door, his eyes glittering with tears; Jihan is beside him, glaring. No one says a word as Tempus waits by the gray's left side.

"Niko, drop your shield."

Niko squints down as if at a hundred-mile drop over the gray horse's left shoulder. Shaking the shield from his arm, he lets it fall. Tempus catches it and hands it to Strat.

Niko sighs and nods his head just once. Then he swings his right leg over. Gasps for breath. Tempus already knows what's coming. Niko lets himself down too fast, too hard – or loses his grip. One grunt and his right leg hits the ground. It doesn't hold him.

Tempus hadn't thought it would. He's ready: for once the god's speed means something. He gets his shoulder under Niko's right arm and hoists him. They walk that way together into Tempus's quarters, Niko's feet barely dragging the ground.

Tempus has seen the wound. He knows what to do now.

So does Critias. So does Straton. They've been here before.

With Enlil's help, they'll be here again.

And the god is being kind today: as soon as they get Niko on that bed, he passes out.

*

The sky is pregnant with rain, promising a torrent – nothing new for storm-wracked Sanctuary, just a portent of Enlil's divine attention. Tempus wants the rain today; usually wants it, except when it's flooding a battleplain, when mud is all around, chariots sinking in, and horses slipping.... *Long spears, thunking into flesh....*

Tempus is known by many epithets, collected over countless wars: the Riddler, the Obscure, the Sleepless One, Favorite of the Storm God, the Black, and more. Today, he is Tempus the Black. He is furious and focused. He needs to get Niko some more help; he just doesn't know what kind yet: the wounds to Stealth's body should heal – can heal. As to Niko's deeper wounds, who can say? And Niko asks only for some girl he met on the lighthouse spit. Maybe it's just delirium. Men, wounded as grievously as Niko, often do and say strange things when dream and waking mix with pain.

Those wounds shouldn't have been there. Shamshi shouldn't be this strong. Something happened on the battleplain in Chaeronea that no one understands. And Niko is paying the price. Again.

Gods colliding, ethos and mythos trying to combine. The Sacred Band caught up in a whirlwind not of any god's devising: he and Niko had wanted to save twenty-three pairs of fated Theban fighters. Now everything feels fated and fighting overruns its boundaries of time and place and plane.

Niko lies bloody and wounded from a struggle in a battlespace that exists only in the minds of those who fight there. Aškelon, from a plane away, a place that exists only sometimes, shows up unbidden: his manifestations always cost more than anyone can afford.

And Enlil, close and hot-blooded now, roused by so much ravaging of body and soul, is impatient, growling wordlessly in his ears, ready for revenge, looking for culprits to slay. Enlil is proprietary these days, with foreign gods running loose, and wants it made precisely clear who belongs to whom and whose loyalty lies where: battle lines, being drawn. Theomachy: battle among gods or against gods. Tempus has seen it, time after time; been on both sides of it, time after time.

He heads toward Processional Way and the palace – and the meddlesome priest, who has summoned him to talk about Kouras.

"Priest, we got your message. You want to talk about Kouras?" Tempus tries not to snarl. And partially succeeds.

"Yes, Tempus, I want to talk about Gyskouras," says Torchholder, smooth as silk.

"Let's talk. What *about* Kouras?" There's a stone bench in the courtyard. They stand there, in the murky half-light of a sullen afternoon, the bench between them. Over-watered fruit trees rot in pots lined up like sentries along the walls. Tempus finds that fitting.

The priest is dressed in brown, looking monkish and credible for a man on the wrong side of everything Tempus believes in.

"Commander, we can't have you putting Gyskouras in danger."

"You can't? He's a Stepson. What do you think Stepsons do? Sing hymns?" Tempus puts one foot on the stone bench and one elbow on his knee.

"Let me clarify. We don't want Gyskouras exposed to pernicious influences like Aškelon of Meridian," says Torchholder.

"Kouras belongs to the Sacred Band, not to you," Tempus replies. Kouras was the answer to the priest's prayers but

Tempus meant to use the boy for his own purposes, not let Torchholder abuse him. "Kouras is a Stepson, not a pawn in the games of the gods – or their stewards." Kouras was born to a berserker's life of sack and pillage in Vashanka's name; only his training in Bandara and the Stepsons offered some faint hope that he'd outwit his destiny.

"Tempus, Gyskouras belongs to Vashanka, not to you, or your precious Band, or your god Enlil. And especially *not* to the dream lord." The priest's doughy face screwed up, then smoothed. "What were you thinking, exposing that boy to the regent of the seventh sphere? You were Vashanka's instrument during Gyskouras's begetting. You ought to know better than to tempt the dream lord with a god's son like Gyskouras. Don't we have enough problems without the lord of dream and shadow confusing your fighters and my congregation?"

"Whenever you think you can order Aškelon around, I'll hold your mantle and cheer you while you try it." *Whenever Aškelon appears, bad things happen. But the dream lord can't be controlled. You should know that by now, fool.* "And you didn't have a congregation, or much of one, until Kouras came along. Perhaps you still don't. You've had a drought in your believers' hearts, and in your treasury, and in your fields. Now you've had some small relief. But it'll take more than a little thunder and lightning to keep your coffers full. And what happens when the rain won't stop, and flood and famine come?"

"Gyskouras will be Vashanka's avatar and the resurrection of all our hopes. You know that boy won't be able to resist it," Torchholder insists, approaching the bench.

Tempus warns him one more time to tread carefully: "You think Kouras can't resist? Care to bet your palace on it?"

But Torch doesn't want to bet. Tempus wishes Torchholder were the right enemy at this most wrong of times. Torch doesn't really want to fight: he simply wants access to Gyskouras; he won't try to take him by scheme or force. This arrangement between the palace and the Sacred Band is too useful to them both.

This audience is over. The priest has had his say. So Tempus asks casually, "Speaking of the fête, you chose all the dancers. We want to find one of your dancing girls again. Do you have a list?"

"We must, somewhere. And I think your cadre has one as well.... I'll try to turn up a guest list. It will take some time. I'll walk you out...."

Thus, having given all the warning he must for one day and gotten no information he can use, Tempus the Black goes on his way with thunder, lightning and the promise of rain at his back, whipping like a cloak.

He rides south on Processional, looking further for a worthy foe, hoping he'll find Shamshi or Shamshi will find him down on Wideway, past the docks. Here a warehouse that made naphtha incendiaries once stood and now does not (where Stealth's first partner was killed in an explosion, long ago, when Aškelon's wizard weather roamed the streets).

*No sorcery hereabouts. Nothing to worry about.* Just a few hundred ghosts in various degrees of uneasy rest, in a thieves' warren struggling to become a reputable city-state. He checked in at his guard stations, at Critias's hidey-hole in the Maze. The god was restless, up in his eyes, looking everywhere with unmitigated suspicion. He trotted the Trôs through more memories than he'd thought he had here, grateful to be alone and riding, waiting for thunder to clap and lightning to split the belly of the rain clouds overhead.

Waiting for Shamshi, if he was abroad, to make a try at him.

*Please. Oh, please.*

He rode the day into night, he and his good Trôs horse that Abarsis had brought to him here, when the ghost was still a man. Nothing jumped out to challenge them: no obliging street fighter or silent stalker emerged from cover.

So he doubled back, as torches were being lit on narrow streets, thinking to go over to the whorehold and ask in the Red Lanterns district about Niko's dancing girl from the fête. Every time Niko is coherent in his sickbed, he asks for her. It seems a modest comfort, one that Tempus should provide.

Quiet streets in Sanctuary are like two-headed calves or harlots turned to goddesses: unnatural, out of balance, traps for men and gods alike. Wherever he went, he could find no sign of something wrong enough to put to rights: except in his heart, wounded once by spear and now again when his right-side partner went out, without him, and got hurt. *His* miscalculation, in these dank and ominous days filled with Thebans and skies that wouldn't rain but wouldn't clear.

He was nearing Triumph Gate when he saw two men on a corner talking to a mounted Sacred Band pair. He stopped his horse, observing till his Stepsons trotted off. Then he kneed his Trôs: a horse walking forward, nothing intimidating; a fighter with both hands in sight.

"Hakiem," he said, "is that you?" The elder of the two men there was as old as the hills of Azehur and as scraggly – a storyteller and once a confidant of the palace; an information monger.

"Tempus?" said the rheumy-eyed man through a mouth with a half-dozen teeth. "You're really here?"

"No, old one, it's your imagination. Anything I should know tonight?"

Next to the storyteller, a man a fraction of his age was trying to melt back into shadow: an Ilsig with a flat, dark face, one he might have recognized if the torches hadn't been so sparse hereabouts.

"There's a change in the weather," the storyteller said. "But you know that. The Stepsons and their friends have brought more trouble to town that anyone bargained for. Gods and Fates and wild boys run amok in the streets." Hakiem raised his face and it was a thousand years old. "But you know that too, don't you?"

"Tell me something I *don't* know. Something worth a coin or two, old friend, so you'll have a better bed tonight."

"There's a goddess moving in, hereabouts – a real one. And she's making converts, here and there. And some of those are in your boys' beds, so beware."

"Is that all?" The Trôs stamped, blowing restlessly through its nostrils. Tempus was trying to place the younger man, half in shadows, who didn't quite dare to run.

"Not all. But sometimes a fellow doesn't want to tell the Riddler what the Riddler doesn't want to hear."

"Try me, uncle."

Hakiem sighed, a phlegmy sound. "I just told your men, so this tale's free: There's a youth living low in Downwind with too much money and too little to do, who's always where the action is: there were a few arrows loosed in Shambles around sunset, aimed at your Stepsons, which hit nothing. But your Stepsons don't know where to look." The old man grimaced at Tempus appraisingly.

He tossed Hakiem a copper coin. Now he thought he knew who the younger Ilsig was. "But you told them? Where to look?"

"Of course. We always aim to be of service to the palace."

"Who's your Wriggly friend?"

"You know Zip, or your men do…used to be the revolution – when we had one. He made the naphtha fireballs for your party on the spit."

As in former times, there was nothing worth knowing here that Hakiem didn't know.

The man in the shadows, taut and spare, raised a hand but came no closer. A voice he recalled vaguely said, "I'm respectable now. A businessman. Doing nothing to interest you or yours besides selling the occasional legal fireworks…."

Tempus urged his horse up on the shoulder of the street, off the cobbles: "You know Downwind, Zip. Let's go hunting."

So he spent the night hunting shooters with Zip, turned up nothing, and didn't get back to the Street of Red Lanterns until the lightning finally ripped the clouds apart just before dawn, and the rain came pouring down.

*

Sham's fever was spiking again. He'd gone out to shoot Stepsons with his crossbow but he was too sick to hit anyone. Too dangerous out there for someone unfit to fight, with the Riddler's whole Band swarming, chasing him.

He'd already died once, or nearly so, fighting Niko in his rest-place, and been resurrected by some pale and awful hand. His throat was pierced, his larynx stabbed; he'd been choking in his own blood. Gasping. Dying. Wrestling with Stealth, called Nikodemos, a better fighter than he'd ever met before. His lungs had emptied, sucking shut. His heart had stopped. Then something colder than cold touched him, started up his heart, cauterized his wounds and blew breath into his empty lungs. Then he could fight again. Then he was saved, somehow. He could still feel the slices from Stealth's sword, the ridges on his neck; cuts that reminded him that the battle in his Chaeronean rest-place had results quite real in the here and now. He wouldn't waste this new life, this second chance. Wherever it had come from. Only a fool questions his own revivification.

Now that he had a new life, he needed a new plan. He'd been saved, but he was wasting away, wracked with fever and with pain. Saved by some coldly purposeful hand, only to suffer on alone. He wished he knew what providence desired of him, but he was too sick to understand.

Shaking and nauseated, Shamshi snuck back to his third-floor garret. He heated his knife over a candle in his wretched Downwind room and lanced the infected gash on his calf one more time, then squeezed pus out of the long, angry red cut. Once merely a scratch, this wound was getting worse day by day. He was covered with sweat. He'd made a deep hole out of this scratch he'd gotten somewhere – perhaps before the fight to the death with Niko on the battleplain of his rest-place; perhaps before that, on the beach that night he'd drunk too much and cried himself hoarse in the dunes.

This 'scratch' just wouldn't heal. So he dug deeper with his knife: even though it hurt to excise this flesh that smelled and was too whitish, it was worse to let it suppurate. His gut spasmed; he couldn't keep food down. This scratch may have been the problem, the reason he'd been slow to parry Stealth's attack: he'd been sick even then.

At the fête, at the edges of his sight, shadows had hovered: figures like hags under blacker than black veils; alchemical forces, who found him once on the beach and might again. He knew they'd come and gone and could come again: they had their own agenda. His father's blood stirred in him, showing him more than mortals saw. Despite his sickness, his wizard blood nearly triumphed over the Riddler's partner. Oh, how sweet it could have been. He'd been winning over the

Stepsons and all the divine friends of Thebes. Then the fever came.

He would win again. His Nisibisi heritage would see him through. It always did; it always had. When he was just a child, he'd outmaneuvered Tempus's Stepsons, during the fight for Wizardwall: he'd killed his white pony, but gained entry to the misty isles. He'd gotten away with murder then and never been discovered or suffered retribution for anything he'd done – until the whore. Until the Stepsons sewed him in that hide. From a moment's fun with that worthless slut at Aphrodisia House, unremitting evil had entangled him and the Sacred Band of Stepsons in a web of unknown forces and bound them all together, exacting some price that everyone must pay….

How dare Arton and Kouras chase after him, with their puny weapons, their boyish skills? He would make them regret it, soon enough.

But for now he would stay inside, be safe, and let the fever burn through him. Be safe, while something inimical prowled the streets outside, whispering vengeance sharper, bloodier than his own; while some intimidating force tried his most secret mental doors, rattling his defenses like shutters closed against a gathering storm. He wasn't ready. Losing a battle in his rest-place had proven that. If he had been prepared, Nikodemos would be nothing but a memory.

He took a sip of soup, using all his skills (enough to whirl between the worlds) to keep it down. On the beach that night, shocked by so many ranged against him, he'd been frightened, sad and lonely. They'd marched to their chilling music, through the night upon the sand, that fated Sacred Band of Thebes: unflinching determination; unwavering devotion – to one another, to their honor, to their creed…. *Wanting neither too much to live nor too much to die: bravery beyond comprehension.* He wasn't like that, could never be. His allegiance was to himself alone. But he could be bold. He'd be bold again, when he was well.

The soup sours in his stomach. It sloshes. His stomach rolls and cramps and expands until he cannot breathe. His head spins. He closes his mouth tight, squeezes shut his eyes, but that just makes him dizzier. Hot water, then acid water, jets up from his innards, into his mouth. Swallow. *Swallow.* Take deep breaths. *Don't* lose the nourishment. But his head spins, and something hits the back of his throat. He falls on his knees, retching miserably, stomach heaving all its contents, and (empty now) still heaving more, and more. Hideous sounds come from his gut; he can't stop the sounds, or the nausea, or the convulsions of his innards. He retches until he can retch no more.

So Sham has a different fight to fight today; against some enemy he doesn't understand, already inside his body. In his head, something otherly whispers how sweet death can be – away from pain, away from battle, away from this body, when it lies bereft of life. This fire in his veins despises him. It wants to burn through him and burn him out, leaving a cleaner universe behind.

So he fights a grisly battle here, upon his knees, where none can see, against a primeval poison he does not, will not, and cannot hope to understand – a force that judges him and finds him displeasing, and will eradicate him if and when it can, and cleanse his stain from off the land.

## *Chapter 26: No Mercy*

No mercy goes unpunished by the angry gods. Niko lives yet, but with injuries far worse than simple flesh wounds. Crit knows too well how it feels; knows too much about fresh wounds over old scars: proud flesh, hardest to heal; deep sword thrusts – ragged meat where a blade has sliced back and forth inside.

The commander promised Niko that no incantation from Ischade, no potion from Randal or poultice from Jihan will touch him. With so much otherworldly help at hand, Niko refuses mystic aid: he'll heal on his own – or not, if *maat* so decrees. Since Tempus has promised to abide by his right-side partner's wishes, that promise binds the Band like iron.

If it were Crit in that bed, with those wounds, he'd take all the help he could get – from heaven or from hell. And if Crit were demented from his injuries, he'd expect his friends to tie him down and force a cure on him. But Tempus would never do that to Niko, not again.... They'd done it once, long ago. And those old wounds had never scarred right, never healed right.

Jihan and Randal stand guard outside Niko's door with accusatory looks. Meanwhile Tempus himself hunts Shamshi, scouring Sanctuary in his moth-eaten leopard-skin mantle,

Stepson and Theban squadrons thundering in his wake night and day, getting lessons in expedited urban warfare from the master.

This leaves Crit to oversee the building of Harmony's altar, out next to Enlil's, and explain to Thebans why the Riddler does what the Riddler does – an impossible task for a god, let alone for Critias, a simple soldier.

So he doesn't try. And everyone is tired and testy, save Straton. Ischade has healed his shoulder, Strat says. Crit should to be thankful to Ischade and let her come and go into the barracks and into their confidence as she pleases, Strat says. Jihan throws tantrums, calling down ice-storms on the barracks in this fey summer, until Tempus takes her with him on his forays in the town.

The search for Shamshi has become a full-fledged obsession for the Sacred Band, Thebans as well as Stepsons. But whenever Crit encounters Charon, Charon's face is drawn and distant: in Thebes, they don't hunt all day and all night, and they don't kill what they find with impunity.

Up goes the body-count in Sanctuary, with Tempus and his Stepsons out policing, seeking anything to fight, anything to smite, any poor fool making mayhem who's too stupid to know he ought to bide his time. Doors are barred, tents rolled up or tent-flaps tied. Anyone with something to hide (and in Sanctuary, that's nearly everyone) skulks guiltily through overflowing gutters and flooded byways, cursing Stepsons, their god and his rain. Crops are irretrievable: famine looms this winter, but there is no mercy to be had from the weather. Not these days, while Niko lies abed; not today, while Shamshi still eludes them and the commander is so angry.

Now Tempus stomps into Crit's lair in Shambles Cross, rain pouring off his leopard-skin, which stinks when it gets wet, and says: "Find that girl for Niko. The one he danced with at the Theban fête. Get her out there if you have to buy her or tie her. He's still asking about her and he's asked for nothing else."

And stalks back out into the driving rain, slamming the door behind him so hard it hits the jam, flies back against the farther wall, and swings back again....

So – along with building the altar and dispatching his teams in the city and running his few pitiful covert agents; along with Thebans snatched from doom; along with jealous gods and capricious fate; and along with theomachy under heaven that has everyone watching how they go and how they swear – Crit has to fix the damned door and find some nameless woman.

Niko and his women will be the death of all the Stepsons yet. A man that badly wounded ought not to be thinking about using the parts of him too near the parts of him that hurt. "How are we going to do this, Strat? Find her? When we don't know who she is or where she came from?"

"Ischade," Strat suggests, with a wink and a sly grin that says Strat knows Crit will have to do it Strat's way eventually. *Predictable.*

"Better, let's ask Jihan." But Jihan has the Trôs mare and she's on the hunt with Tempus tonight. The Riddler is keeping her away from Niko the only way he can, by keeping her with him. "Better, let's get Randal."

"Fox, you know Randal won't leave the barracks while Niko's hurt unless the Riddler gives him direct orders," Straton reminds him.

Randal is sure that somehow, one of these days, Niko will relent and accept his aid. They'd been paired once. Randal had even skulked into the sickroom in his dog's shape and licked Niko's hand and arm until Stealth realized just what kind of dog it was and called one of the Thebans to chase Randal away.

"Crap," Crit says.

Strat says, "How about sending Kouras to the palace to ask Torchholder nicely for help? You can bet that sly old priest vetted every woman and girl at the party. The Torch likes Kouras. He'll want to show off his power."

So they sent someone for Kouras, and they sent Kouras to the palace in the pounding rain, and they sat in the Shambles station and waited for the rain to stop and the other shoe to drop.

At third watch, the soaked trainee returned, Arton trailing in his wake and shivering. "We think we found her, Niko's girl. But you won't like it…sirs," Kouras announced.

Crit offered the boys the cheap watered wine they kept here, where water must be boiled or mixed with alcohol. Both drank and made faces, but some color came back to their cheeks. "What won't we like, Kouras? Go back and get her. Take her to the barracks."

The two trainees stood tall with rain dripping off their mantles; off the helmets under their arms, their cuirasses and their muddy greaves – shuffling their feet, saying nothing, exchanging glances.

Strat unfolded himself from one of the drop's two chairs, saying, "Speak when spoken to, Stepsons. Answer when queried." He towered over them, bigger than both boys put together.

"She's…in the palace. Molin says, come ask him yourselves – Critias, that is. Or Tempus. And he wants something in exchange for her."

Crit didn't remember standing up, or moving around behind the trainees, or even kicking shut the door. Habits, so ingrained; second nature. He looks closer. These two aren't just cold and wet; it's a summer storm tonight: *They're scared.*

"What's got your skirts ruffled, girls?" he says from behind them.

Arton spins to face him. "Critias, sir…we're trying –"

*"Trying?* Arton, Kouras…you're Stepsons, sent on a mission. You don't come back and tell me you can't do your jobs, or that I have to do them for you."

It's just one more thing: one more unfortunate, small annoyance that tonight isn't small. Tonight, forgiving any infraction is out of the question.

Straton says laconically, "Just what, precisely, did Torchholder say?" Crit's interrogator will save these boys a thrashing or buy them one.

Arton looks at Kouras and Kouras gives a nod. The two young fighters position themselves back to back, training taking hold. Arton facing Strat, Kouras facing Crit: the youngsters know they've pushed too far, without meaning to push at all. Crit gets out his belt-knife and starts cleaning his nails, waiting for his pulse to ease, wondering whether these two would die this way, back to back, for something as inconsequential as this.

Kouras says, very carefully and clearly, "The girl's new at the palace, a temple dancer in training. The priest says he'll trade her services for mine for as many days as you need. The palace just bought her from Phoebe's. She came to Phoebe's two days before the feast. Molin saw her there. She's a…."

"We know what she is." *Damn priest. A temple dancer, a slave whore, swapped for Kouras? One who'd been at Phoebe's, Sanctuary's most infamous and specialized brothel, until the feast?* Crit didn't have the authority to agree to that – or any intention of trying to *get* the necessary authority: "Maybe we'll talk to Ischade after all."

But they didn't. They went up to the palace, boys in tow. Kouras swore he'd recognize the girl Niko danced with, if he saw her again.

When they got there, it was fourth watch and the moon was trying to find a dry place to set among the soggy clouds. They had to locate Walegrin to get Torchholder out of bed. Bleary-eyed, the priest came padding barefoot in a silken paisley robe down to the front hall, where they were dripping puddles on his marble floor.

"So let's see her," Crit said. Mad as a wet cat didn't half cover it.

"What *is* this, Critias? Surely the girl can wait…?" Then Torchholder noticed Straton, Arton and Kouras, and something in the bearing of the Stepsons made him pause and hike himself up. "Your commander didn't deign to join us?"

"He's deigning somewhere else," Strat said.

"Where's this girl, the one you say danced with Niko?" Crit said.

"Kouras, what are you doing back here?" Torchholder said, ignoring Crit.

"Eminence, I'm here for the god," said Kouras and everyone stopped posturing to look at him. "Vashanka wants to know if this is *his* girl you're talking about…one destined for his temple." Arton shoved Kouras, but it was too late.

Torchholder's face suffused with rage. As stiffly as a territorial old stoat, the priest stalked over to Kouras and Arton: "*Vashanka* wants to know? Getting a bit presumptuous, are we, Stepson?"

Kouras widened his stance and said, "My cadre wants to see the girl. The god does. You did say you had her, didn't you?" Everything about Kouras dared Torchholder to call him a liar.

Torch didn't. Instead, with a glare and a grumble, the priest waddled off to get the girl and left them waiting. An awkward silence fell in the black and white front hall, during which Kouras looked at his sopping boots until Strat said, "What's this *'Vashanka wants?'*"

Arton rolled his eyes and snorted. Kouras faced Arton and said, "The god *said....*"

Crit moved in between the two young fighters, thinking that maybe things weren't as simple as they seemed.

"The god said *what?*" Strat asked in his practiced way, before Crit could say anything.

"Sirs, please don't make fun of me," Kouras nearly pleaded. "Vashanka *said....*" His tone brought Crit and Strat both to full alert – that and Kouras's young hand on the wet hilt of his shortsword.

"This girl *will* be Vashanka's. Never mind that it sounds daft," Arton prognosticated, protective of his friend now. The seer crossed his arms, glared at his superiors, and then stalked over to examine paintings of long-forgotten potentates on the marble walls.

"Then why the pork are we here in the rain at fourth watch to look her over for Niko?" Strat asked succinctly.

Before either young Stepson could answer, Torchholder brought them the slave-girl: even right out of a sleep, she was beautiful, like a startled deer. She clutched a wrap to her throat. Torchholder said, "Show them, young lady," and she started to drop her wrap.

Crit caught Kouras's eye. Kouras shook his head: *no.* Crit didn't really need confirmation; he remembered Niko's dance partner well enough. "That's not necessary, Eminence," Crit said. "Unless she's cut her hair, dyed it, and shrunk a foot in height, this isn't the one we want. Sorry, Torchholder, for getting you out of bed." But he wasn't: the fact that Torchholder fetched the girl himself probably meant she'd been in the priest's bed, not in the slave quarters.

Thinking he'd adroitly extricated them from this chariot wreck in the making, Crit expelled a long-held breath. Strat looked wistfully after the girl as, dismissed by the priest, she scampered away, up the stairs. Definitely not returning to the slave quarters.

Then Kouras said, in a voice deeper than his years, "But the issue remains, Eminence, that this is Vashanka's girl, one you were willing to take from the god – *are* taking from the god…."

"How can you possibly know that?" Torchholder said, sputtering; vehement, disquieted.

And Kouras said, "The god tells me what I need to know. And he says he's not happy with you, treating his property as your own…."

*'The god tells me what I need to know.' Crap. Not another one.*

"Where have I heard that before?" Strat muttered. For far too long an interval, no one risked saying another word. The priest smoldered with ire, staring at Kouras. The young Stepson stared back. Finally, Strat reminded Crit that they were due at the Maze safe house. It wasn't true, but it got them out of there without more awkwardness.

When they'd been let out the horse gate by the palace guards, Crit slammed Kouras up hard against the wet and slippery wall, his forearm under Kouras's chin, his left hand grasping the youth's shoulder: "Don't you *ever* surprise me like that again. And don't you come to us with information until you get your information straight. You've wasted half my night. Clear?"

Kouras grunted 'yes,' but Crit didn't release him. Kouras's green eyes flashed in the predawn like a cat's. Crit should let the boy go, but he was just too angry.

Rain was falling gently; the moon had set; the night was threatening to turn into another sodden day. Arton, hovering, didn't move a muscle, but then said desperately, "The storm god *is* angry at the priest – or will be. You've all told me to let you know, when my foresight –"

"Changed my mind, Seer. Don't want to know," murmured Strat absently, watching Crit pinning Kouras against the wall. "Critias…" he said placatingly, "*Crit*ias…."

Strat's voice sounded far away. Crit's pulse was pounding in his ears. This one needed to learn some humility. Crit still had Kouras in a hold that could kill him…so easily. The youthful fighter did not struggle, merely waited, breathing raggedly, ready to die if he deserved it. Kouras was brave enough, for a fool. That decided Crit. He let Kouras go. But it wasn't easy. "You two, go back to the barracks. Clean stalls and tack all day tomorrow. Kouras, let this be a lesson to you: don't believe a palace priest – about anything. Ever."

Kouras had one hand to his throat and was trying not to gag or cough. But he said hoarsely, as Strat and Crit got their mounts, "Critias, I couldn't help it. There'll be no mercy for that priest…. The god *is* angry."

"What's wrong with that? Just let the god pick his own fights from now on. And watch out for Torchholder: you can bet he doesn't think you're fetching anymore," Crit said, swinging into his saddle, and kneed his horse out of there, wondering how they were going to deal with a Stepson who thought the god was telling him what to do.

*

As the sun rose and Charon finished with the consecration, the rain stopped. A pair of rainbows arced high over the Stepsons' barracks walls and over Harmony's newly sanctified altar to disappear behind the hill.

Whether it was better that the rain had stopped, or that the rainbows had shimmered into being when the altar was dedicated to the goddess, Charon couldn't have said. He had performed the rite personally, playing his flute. His song was the oblation, as ritual allowed. He wished all his Theban brothers had seen this pair of rainbows for the goddess of consonance in love and war. So many of his paired fighters were still on duty, few were here to witness this most auspicious sign.

He was walking downhill to the offices, taking many backward looks at the red-to-violet rainbows, when a woman's voice said, "A very pretty tune, you played. Help me, please?" and he almost stumbled over her.

The Stepsons' barracks seldom housed women, though some came in for an evening, or a morning…. But none of those were this sort, noble and proud. The gates were closed. Two sentries watched them from the barracks walls. She could only be here because someone had brought her, or invited her.

Hereabouts now were witches and shape-shifters and Froth Daughters, all manner of dabblers in the blacker arts, sucked into Sanctuary along with his Theban Band. This young woman was none of these, but something different. He was mesmerized, looking into eyes that reflected the rainbows like bronze mirrors.

Her mellifluous voice sounded again: "Can you help me, kind sir? I seek Stealth, called Nikodemos. I heard he was seeking me." Nearly as tall as Charon, she had long hair glistening like honey and a basket on her arm. He thought he remembered seeing her at the feast on the lighthouse spit.

"Certainly I can. Come right this way," he said and reached out to take her arm.

She met his eyes.

He pulled back his hand, which had begun to tingle; the tingle ran all the way up his left arm. He rubbed it. Somewhere in the distance, he thought he heard a dog barking furiously – but there weren't any dogs allowed in the barracks, just a man who changed into one from time to time. "Right this way," he repeated. No one crossed their path as they walked through the yard and up onto the covered porch that led into the building where the officers' quarters were.

As they entered, she stopped and said, "You're from Thebes, so I hear. How do you like it here?" Out of the sun, in the hallway, she seemed insubstantial, nearly translucent, until his eyes adjusted to the change in light.

"We're fortunate to be alive. The Stepsons rescued us and protected us. Now we make our home with them, and our way with them. They pled us mercy from the gods, and the gods agreed."

"Fortunate? And these Stepsons…protected you? Fancy that: the gods agreed? You are adherents of Harmony, are you not? Of a goddess? The gods will show no mercy this season, so it's said. The fated, so it's said, get only what's deserved. The wool is already spun on their spindles."

*Strange, so knowledgeable of the Fates and the spinning of mortal destiny, for someone from Sanctuary.* "Yes, we serve the goddess, Harmony. We have an altar now, dedicated to our goddess; right next to theirs, to their war god." Although it was modest by Theban standards, with no pediment or columns, it was the equal of Enlil's altar in every way. Charon was proud of it. He pointed, and when he turned back, she was already disappearing through Nikodemos's door, although he hadn't shown her which door that was.

## *Chapter 27: Bright Sky, Fated Share*

Niko saw the door open: diffuse, bright light, with someone coming through it. He couldn't lie on his back yet. He was lying on his left side. "Nothing," he said. "I don't want anything." It was too early to eat. His head hurt. His backside hurt. And he needed to wash himself. He must get ready for the arduous dressing of wounds, changing of bandage. Without discipline, he'd be lost, he knew. But he was so tired; he just wanted to sleep.

The door closed. He thought he was alone again. Then a woman's voice said, "You asked for me. Here I am. Now don't move. Let's see you. Let's see…."

She was leaning over the bed. Her long hair tumbled across her shoulder, obscuring his sight of her; onto his face, along his neck, his arm. Soft, honey-colored hair, and eyes as wide as the sky peering through it.

He tried to reach out, to say something. He didn't want her to see the mess, so much ravaged flesh back there yet…. She had a bowl, a cloth, some water. Where did all this come from? He couldn't fathom any of it.

"Lie still," she said, and it was like a command from heaven.

"I...wanted to see you so," he managed. "Ever since that night...."

"I know. It's fine. I'll tend you. You'll be well again. I promise."

He didn't have the strength to argue. Her touch was like cool water. Except when he was in his meadow, star-shaped and ever green and not of this earth, he'd never felt so peaceful. Not even on Bandara. When she peeled the bandage off his hip and touched the worst of his wounds, it didn't seem to hurt. Or it hurt, but he didn't care.

Once he thought she whispered, "Go carefully, child of *maat*, where no mercy can be had, and let your faith lead you on."

But he was sure he imagined it. Her hair kept draping over him and everywhere it touched, it soothed him. Her hair was so long it could wrap around the world. It smelled like a sunny meadow. He took just the end of one lock in his hand and wound it around his fingers, as if he could hold her by that means, as if the hair was a piece of his beloved mare's mane.

And he went back to sleep, though he was trying so hard to stay awake (because there was so much to say, and so little time in a man's life to say those things), holding that lock of amber hair between his fingers.

When he woke, she had gone, and two Stepsons were waiting to help him dress his wounds. Between his fingers were a few soft fine hairs, as long as his arm. And the room was filled with the smell of oranges.

*

"Where could these oranges have come from?" wondered Agis to Archias. The two convalescing Thebans were in Stealth's room, paying a call on their fellow casualty.

"They're out of season, back in Thebes." Agis, swarthy and bearded, limped over to the basket of blood oranges and fingered one.

Archias, his blond, square-faced partner, followed, upper arm tight against his bandaged chest. "Or anywhere, by now," Archias added huskily.

The whole room was redolent of blood oranges.

"Generosity is never out of season," said the badly wounded man on the bed in a voice barely more than a whisper. "Take them with you. Share them with your brothers. There are too many, anyway."

Agis knew they were being dismissed by the Stepsons' second-in-command. With a quick glance at his partner, he grabbed up the basket and they left.

Another Stepson, Cassander, lean and lithe with curly brown hair clubbed back, was waiting in the hallway and slipped in after them, closing the door. Outside the officers' quarters, in the bright daylight, they were met by Charon: "How did it go? How is he? Nikodemos?"

Agis, already peeling a firm little blood orange, said, "He didn't want these. Wonder where they get them? In the middle of summer?"

Archias answered Charon's question: "Nikodemos is badly hurt. Their gods will have to decide, with that one, how he is."

"Like they had to decide with you, Archias?" teased Agis. "Makes you wonder if the gods are always right." Agis had taken a throwing star in the thigh and one bolt in the meat of his left breast, lesser wounds than his partner had sustained.

"Give me those." Charon reached out and tugged away the basket of oranges.

"Stealth said we could share them." Archias grabbed one, before it was too late. "Where are you going with those?"

"Out to Harmony's altar. Any who want them, while they last, can come up the hill: give half of this bounty to the goddess. And don't gobble those. You give half of each orange you have to her – small thanks for your lives."

They had duties, but you couldn't argue with Charon when he had that look.

Their leader swept away, off to the new altar. They followed after, the lame man and the halt, not really minding very much, helping one another up the slope to the altar of Harmony. As they climbed, Agis put one hand under Archias's arm to help his friend, who'd gotten one crossbow quarrel between his ribs, a second too close to a lung during a sneak attack in Sanctuary. On this beautiful sunny day, Agis thought, giving thanks to the goddess was a good idea.

*

For three days, it hadn't rained. The sky was bright each and every day, full of puffy clouds, and the sun beamed down as if there was something to celebrate. Randal didn't give a fig about the sky, or the crops, or the water levels, so high that the White Foal River, below him down a steep incline, was brown and half out of its banks, frothing dangerously as it raced to the sea. He was tired and lonely and distressed as he waited for the necromant to meet him. He wanted to go home to Lemuria.

Now the sun was setting, radiating exquisite color everywhere but on the black shadow that detached itself from other shadows under the White Foal Bridge and glided his way. Randal's former partner, Niko, loved the sky; especially sunsets, which he said the gods decreed were never twice the same.

"Ischade," Randal greeted the witch. "I'm so glad you're here. I just came from the barracks. Niko says that the dancing girl from the beach is taking care of him."

"So, is she?" came Ischade's voice from deep within her black cowl. Beyond her blackness, the beautiful sunset reigned.

"I don't know. No one knows. Imagine, a woman supposedly comes and goes among the Sacred Band, in their sanctum, and *no one but Niko knows.* The Riddler is irate, and he's taking it out on whomever. He wants answers. No one has any. No one else has seen her. Who is she? How would she get in there? How would she get out again? Charon met a woman, asking for Niko, three days ago. But he only saw her once. And no one can account for *that*. Critias is frantic at the very *idea* that someone could be breaching barracks security. I think he'd rather that Niko imagines her. Tempus has everyone who isn't looking for Shamshi out looking for this dancing girl from the beach. No one's found her." It all came out of him in a rush. His nose was running: damnable allergies. He wiped it with the back of his hand.

"Maybe Nikodemos *is* imagining her."

"Could you…ah…find out?"

"Not unless I'm asked by the Riddler. Perhaps not then. I don't know how badly Niko's hurt. But they say he's healing." Ischade was matter of fact. "They don't want my services in that regard – yet. I shall not intrude."

"The Riddler would be very grateful…."

"He says not. If Tempus changes his mind, he'll come to us. Or send Straton, or Critias. If Nikodemos starts slipping away, they'll want both you and me. I know the Riddler that well."

"You don't understand. Niko has forbidden it. He won't let me help him. I'm going back to Lemuria." Despite himself,

Randal was sure he was going to weep. Ischade was not any man's comfort, not on a dark night or in brightest day. But Randal was a mage, the Band's only sanctioned link with the arcane; and Ischade was the arcane incarnate. "Something's going on out there, but they won't listen to me. Three days ago, I found myself locked in a tack room, and I wasn't even in the barn before it happened. Just...*whooooosh.* As if something picked me up and threw me, but not through the air. I had to be a dog and bark my head off until someone came to let me out."

"Perhaps you should go to Lemuria. Perhaps the Riddler's sister should hear of this." Ischade floated up closer.

"She won't care. She's no friend of Niko's."

Black necromant and white mage down by the Foalside, watching the flotsam and the occasional rotting corpse float by: by Tempus's order, they were supposed to be hunting for the accused, Shamshi. But Randal needed to talk to someone, and Ischade was his hunting partner.

"If we find the quarry, then everything will change for the better. One more night, Randal. Your ear and my nose. We promised that much to the Riddler. That one, I'd as soon not disappoint."

"Another night, then, as you wish, my lady. But something *is* going on out at that barracks," Randal said glumly. "Something I don't understand."

"Something is going on everywhere, most of which no one understands," Ischade said, cowl so far over her face that only her white chin showed in the gloaming. "Since the Stepsons came back. Since they brought the fated dead, those Thebans and their foreign goddess – and Vashanka. I liked this town the way it was before. With only powerless dabblers in the occult and power-hungry fools, what *I* need was here in plenty. Now we've gods and goddesses vying and jousting with each other…. And other things, roaming the night. Things I'd prefer not to need to take account of."

Ischade's cowl shifted as another corpse floated by, but when it came abreast they both saw it was deer's carcass, not a man's. It had been in the water so long that it was barely identifiable.

"We should talk to the Riddler," Randal sighed.

"Before you go, then? You'll stay long enough for that?" She started up the bank, which was treacherous for Randal but easy enough for her.

Could it be that someone – that *Ischade*, a power in her own right as formidable as any, anywhere – wanted him to stay? "If you think so, my lady," Randal said and looked up the bank, where the cloaked necromant was already a black silhouette against the blazing sunset. "If you think I can be of some use."

"Oh, I do think so, Randal. For what's coming, I do think so."

But she would tell him nothing more, and what she'd said set his teeth on edge, all night long.

*

This time, when she came, Niko wouldn't fall asleep. This time, he would ask her to stay. He was stronger, strong enough to be angry at himself for getting bloodied in a confrontation in a metaphysical realm. In the world, those wounds were making him pay the price for a hubris he'd thought he'd outgrown.

He could sit up without grunting now, though he still couldn't lie on his right side. Something back there was very sore. He wanted to stand up. He wanted to walk across the room. He wanted to dress himself and tend his own wounds.

He wanted to go outside under the sky, hitch up a chariot and go for a drive, since he couldn't ride yet.

But he was still too weak for that. He could sit up, on his bed, and that was the best he could do. Then he had to wait until his vision cleared and the red-gold flecks went away that danced before his eyes when he tried too hard or moved too fast. *Lost too much blood on that long ride home.* He knew all the signs. He saw blood in his urine from bruised kidneys, swirling in his chamber pot; and a bloody mist before him whenever he closed his eyes.

The Sacred Band came to see him as if he were some dead body on a bier, Stepsons filing in and out of here. Strat came. Crit came, with his worried look. And Tempus came, twice a day, every day, hell in those long eyes, to make sure he ate, or that he let Gayle and Cassander change his bandages. He was not a child. But sometimes he didn't want to let them touch him. He just wanted to sleep. And into his sleep snuck the dream lord, edging around his consciousness, peeking here and there with that commiserating look that said, *"I could help you, stubborn fool. You have only to ask."*

Thinking about Ash made him angry; and anger made him impatient, and a little stronger. Abarsis had warned him from the pyre's flames: '*Niko, it is hard to battle anger, for whatever it wants it pays from the soul.*' And the goddess Harmony had warned him, that day on the jetty: '*...take care, or lose all you've won at such great cost.*' But he hadn't listened, or he hadn't known how to listen. He'd gone up against Shamshi too early, for the wrong reasons and had, finally, been bested by himself.

*Stupid.*

He would stand up today, on his own two feet. He was a Bandaran adept, the Riddler's right-side partner, a Stepson. He wasn't an invalid.

So he swung his legs over the bedside in one movement meant to be smooth and fluid, and his right side stabbed him so hard it took his breath away. If there was an abscess building in there, under the closing wound, then he was dead and simply didn't know it yet. *Long spears, thunking into flesh....*

He hoped the pain was merely flesh, sealing, and the wages of lying too long abed. But this pain burned too much, felt too wrong. For one blazing instant, he saw poor dead Ari, bloated body turning beautiful again as Abarsis held the dead Stepson in his arms amid the balefire.

Now he had his feet planted firmly on the floor. *Good.* And if there was cold sweat breaking out all over him, then that too was good: he could sweat out any poison that remained. He was going to get up. Then his body began to shake uncontrollably and he couldn't. His heart skipped and pounded in his ears in staccato rhythms, like the Theban march on the beach. *Tat, rata tat. Tat rat tata tata tat.* He gripped the mattress, head down, trying to breathe through the pain, with his sight going grainy and a tunnel in front of him into which he was going to fall if he wasn't careful. *Brum, rumpa pum pum,* pounded his heart.

He was pushing himself too hard. He needed to lie back down. If he could lie back down, he could reach his blanket. If he had his blanket, he wouldn't be so cold. Shivers wracked him.

He didn't hear anything, or see the door open. No light from the door poured into his room, not this time. But someone was in here with him: far, far away; but here, outside the pain and the cold.

There was a blanket now, over his shoulders; a touch, on his arm, behind his neck. Hands helping him do something: hands under his knees, on his hip...*lie down.* Then he smelled her, meadow and sunshine, and that soft hair brushed his face.

"Bad boy," she said. "Bad boy. So impatient. Why? To go out and get your fated share of war and pain once more? Join the fray? Shed more blood, yours and theirs?"

He heard her words; he just couldn't really process them. He said, because he'd planned it and because he knew he wanted it, and because everything else he wanted was too far out of reach: "Will you stay here with me?" Once he'd said it, he wasn't sure if he'd spoken aloud or not.

Cool hands moved across his back, down his side, where the worst wounds and the burning pain were: "Oh, I see," she said. And: "If I stay, Stealth called Nikodemos, what will your friends say?"

"That I'm lucky," he thought he said. But by then she was doing something behind his back that took his breath away, so he wasn't sure she heard him.

And sleep was dragging at him. He'd promised himself he wouldn't fall asleep. But he did.

Only this time, when he awoke, she was still there, sitting beside him on his bed, a basket of bloody, pussy rags by her feet. She smiled a sunny day at him, and the light came in his window and found her long, long hair, stirring in a breeze from somewhere, so it brushed against his arm. And this time, he caught her hand and held it. So he went back to sleep, because it didn't hurt so much now, and slept a different kind of sleep, holding her by the hand.

*

When Tempus came back from town, he went straight to Jihan's quarters and spent a short but athletic interval with the Froth Daughter (to prove to her that life trumped death, every time). Then he exchanged his arms and armor for hillman's trousers and a loose tunic, and went to see that Niko ate his supper.

A knot of people crowded the hallway. *Oh, no. No, no.* Thebans, mostly: dark Gorgias and the wounded pair, Agis and Archias; Lysis; and Charon. Three Stepsons: young Arton; solid Gayle and lithe Cassander, the veterans charged with Niko's daily care.

"What?" Their stances said he should have brought his sword – not that they were preparing to take a body to a pyre. *"What?"* Louder, perhaps, than absolutely necessary this second time, with everyone staring at him and breathing shallowly.

They all looked at one another. Everyone but Charon put their backs against opposing walls as if he'd called the *'sides'* signal during a house assault. He moved through the gauntlet. There were swords aplenty here, if swords were the answer. The day was falling toward dusk, playing with the light. Outside, a waning moon was rising in a sky yet blue; he could see it through the hallway window.

Only Charon stood between Tempus and Niko's doorway now. "What? I'm not going to ask you again, Charon."

*"She's* in there," Charon whispered. Men were flattened so tight against those walls they might have been expecting a chariot to come barreling down the hallway: hands on swords; chins up; heads pressed back against whitewashed boards.

He considered grabbing a shortsword from the nearest scabbard (which would be Arton's), kicking down the door, and dealing with this incursion in the time-honored way.

*So, someone's gotten past every one of them.* They were embarrassed. That explained some of this. But not all. *"Tell* me. Who is *she?"*

Charon wasn't moving out of his way. Tempus took one step forward: another step and they would be flesh to flesh. Then Charon said, "Niko's girl from the beach, we think."

"You think? How many men, standing around here, and you don't know? *One* girl? Has she got weapons in there, a juggernaut? A demon? A dragon?" All of that, said aloud – but as softly as he could speak and still be heard, because if his voice got out of control here, then everything else was going to follow summarily. "Stand aside. Or I'll move you."

Charon got out of his way.

Tempus walked up and opened Niko's door very slowly, very quietly, just a crack. He'd opened a door like this once and nearly been incinerated by what waited on the other side. This time, no fire came blossoming out, no whirlwind from heaven or hell. He opened the door farther, put his head in. He wore no armor, no helmet; carried no shield with him, no sword. Whatever this was, which had eight Sacred Banders nearly paralyzed with trepidation in a hallway, it couldn't be *that* bad…could it?

Then he saw the woman in there with Niko. And he slipped through the door, closing it quietly behind him and leaning back on it. She watched him from where she sat by Niko on his bed. Tempus stood very still. She inclined her head, putting one finger to her lips. Niko seemed to be sleeping under a blanket. This woman who perched on Niko's bed had honey-brown hair full of light, like a wheat field when the sun hits it. She was holding his hand and her shimmering tresses spilled around her and over him.

"Get away from him," Tempus suggests quite softly. "Now."

"He asked me to come. He asked me to stay." She has a heart-shaped face, wide amber eyes. She wears a simple gray linen dress. Her voice is melodious, as quiet as his. "He needs help. An abscess…I opened it up. It will drain, but I must tend him. Too many different hands."

"He said you've been coming here. How do I know this abscess isn't your doing? Get away from him. Come outside. Come talk to me until I'm satisfied."

Then Niko moves, and raises his head, saying, "Riddler, please…."

And Tempus is undone, at that moment. His vision is swimming. He slides down the door at his back and hunkers there, elbows on his knees.

"You're staying?" she asks.

"As long as you do. Who are you?"

She doesn't answer his question. "We'll have him right in no time, now," she says.

"From your lips to the gods' ears," he growls, so low, still struggling for control.

"That's not very far, today," she says, and smiles like the first light of dawn.

## *Chapter 28: Shock Troops of the Gods*

The war in heaven has reached the streets of Sanctuary: overhead, the sun shines bright; in the distance, clouds form up to attack the daylight. Right here, right now, Crit needs to keep control of the Sacred Band and of Walegrin's city guard, both units frustrated by their elusive quarry and angry at this hellhole town. Maneuvers, carefully planned, painstakingly apportioned among two forces, must be precisely carried out. Or this sortie won't work at all, and their sweep will sweep only discipline away, become a rout. Theory put into practice – not perfect today. Not smooth enough by half: Sanctuary city guard and Sacred Band are out of step, not meshing. At least not so far.

Through the twisty byways of Downwind, both contingents thunder. Walegrin's city guard leads, bent on showing off their local savvy. Crit knows that mere familiarity won't win the day…or would have won it by now, on other days. Behind Walegrin's men come the fierce shock troops of the Sacred Band, ranks formed up for war and spoiling for a battle where only much less will do.

*Ladies first, all you city guard....*

Too many weapons gleam under heaven in the bright sunlight. Too many horses' hooves clatter on cobblestones. Too many jeers and taunts and war cries resound. Too many fighters look to redeem themselves in one another's flinty eyes. Too many.

Strife is justice; justice is strife. Crit can feel the reins of command slipping through his fingers. Squadrons riding too fast; talking too loudly; sneering at each other: rage and rivalry out of hand. Somehow he needs to hold them to the plan, to their orders. But he's one man, in putative charge.

The Riddler isn't here today. Their commander's got too much brewing, with Niko hurt, and Jihan and Randal hunting Shamshi, and some girl or woman (or something *else)* in the barracks who comes and goes as it pleases, unmindful of walls or gates or doors or locks.... *Too much.*

So no ancient intelligence guides this mission, no wiser eye constrains the troops.

With the Riddler absent, Critias is in charge – trying his damnedest, but just a Stepson. Even with Strat steady on his right, they're jostled, bumped and crowded by city guardsmen who think pairbond is a dirty joke.

Straton can't help Crit with Walegrin. He doesn't offer. They have more than enough to do, taking care of their own half-integrated Band, under Crit's leadership for the first time. Factions make friction: different cultures, different customs, and disrespect – a recipe for disaster when cavalry and populace come face to face.

Disputes, unresolved, are breaking loose. Crit and Walegrin have two conflicting visions of how a sweep through here should be planned and executed, and what the definition of this mission really is. Crit wants to find Shamshi; Walegrin wants to clean his stopped-up city drains of all their flotsam and jetsam.

Chaos is one name for what they field today. Crit has been in full-fledged assaults with less screaming and shouting and cursing and rousting than in this sweep of Downwind. All to catch one wizard boy? To grab the reins of discipline in Sanctuary, where things already are spinning out of control?

They cordon off the Downwind, ranging it round, all the Sacred Band and city guardsmen. Two chains of command; two voices guiding them; two sets of loyalties that cannot be combined. House to house, attic to attic: systematically and without quarter they search, leaving wreckage in their wake.

The raid heats up. Things get rough. Things get rougher. Walegrin's teams are far beyond Crit's control. And free to choose their own rules of engagement: this is their turf and they sortie first, with heavy hands where Critias would have come, hands off, weapons sheathed, with a lighter tread.

Hooves pound; doors fall down; windows break and culprits quake behind their secret panels, in their hidey-holes and root cellars. The Sacred Band catches everyone who flees, cleaning up in the city guard's wake: Crit's fighters, too, have their orders: no one escapes; no one slips away unnoticed.

Except, it seems, Shamshi, the wizard boy. Where is he today? Running for his life, trying to find a place to make a stand? Crit recalls that Lysis and Arton thought they saw Sham on the beach. Was it really him, in the dark, in the water off Vashanka's Rip? Lysis had told Strat that the youth on the beach had dark hair…he thought. Same fugitive? None could say. Was Shamshi a wraith, a figment – long gone? And all this an unnecessary show of force?

Jails fill up and holding pens ring with wails and lamentation. Caravan Square and Farmer's Market lie deserted; Shambles Cross takes refugees until it can't hold one more soul. Nowhere is Shamshi to be found.

"Somebody's protecting him," growls a city guardsman, forcing past Crit and Strat on a wall-eyed red horse, its nose in the air and spattering them with froth. Ahead, two more guardsmen drag a weeping woman and three screaming brats out of her hovel's door. "We'd have him by now, otherwise," the guardsman tosses back, cantering away.

"No you wouldn't, porker. Not this way," Strat says in an undertone. And rolls a smoke amid the turmoil. There's nothing to be done about the problem of tactics out of hand: different command chain; different orders.

Crit and Strat ride on, and Strat scoffs dourly as they watch Walegrin's city guard tear another hut apart, shortswords drawn, capturing pigs and dogs and cats and cowards, but no crafty ex-Stepson on the run.

This next group of four from the city guard is better trained: they advance upon each house side by side, shields up and nearly touching, clearly knowing urban combat can be most dangerous. A fence obstructs them; they use their horses to pull it down. Crossbow bolts from somewhere whisper through the air: *one, two, three, four.* Two men fall. *Five, six.* The same two men die: one shot through the eye, and dead in an instant; the other, shot through the throat, has little more time to live.

*"Cover,"* bawls Strat, calling out a Stepson maneuver code to bring the Band. And: *"Crit. Go, go, go: there!"*

Their horses leap forward, toward the buildings where the bolts seemed to come from. But there are too many obstacles of flesh and blood in their way: hysterically screeching children; ponderous women; city guard – finally waking up – milling, taking cover. Two warhorses, riderless, now scream and rear and tear around, biting and kicking at anyone and everyone until two other riders capture them. Crit and Strat roll off their horses, first running for cover and then on into the street, crossbows ready. They shoot where they think the bolts came from, then dash for building walls. A mud-brick corner hides them; flimsy doors push open. They climb flights and flights of stairs, trying to engage an enemy, a target on a rooftop – and find no one.

Crit and Strat scuttle back to the dead men and hunker down beside them, looking around: if a body hasn't staggered too much in any one direction before falling, you can estimate the source of fire, and return it, based on the angle of the arrow in the corpse and where that arrow might have come from if the corpse were standing. Take cover again, return fire if you can; if you can't, give chase; find someone to shoot back at: do something; counterattack in support of your dead comrades. But there's no target, no one who wants to play shoot-me, shoot-you.

Whoever it was, they've gone on their way. Up on a third-floor landing of the fourth house they search, Strat finds a crossbow, discarded. They come back down, their skin crawling: somebody's awake out here, and picking targets with skill and taste.

They reclaim their horses about the time Walegrin canters over on a jumpy mount, five men behind him. The city-guard captain dismounts, takes off his helmet and stands above his two dead fighters – corpses barely bleeding any longer, fallen among fence boards. Walegrin puts his hands on his hips and turns to Critias and Straton: "I'm telling my guard to stop, *now.* This assault is more than we intended. Agreed, Critias?"

*Now, you ask me. Past time, but it's bad form to quit because you've been hit or lost fighters. It makes the enemy bolder, next time. He knows just how to stop you.*

Without a helmet, Walegrin's blond head is a perfect target for someone in these buildings whence the hostile fire might have come. Crit doesn't mention it. He'll be happy to get out of here before more crossbow quarrels *whukka whukka* through the air. Maybe someone will shoot Walegrin and that will wake up the palace. "Agreed. We stop. Got more trouble than we need from this, and less value."

Strat adds sourly, "This little cluster won't win the palace any hearts and minds. Or find us Shamshi."

"Not my problem. Not my mission," Walegrin grunts, swinging up on his horse; and rides away, back into the fray, leaving his men to deal with fallen comrades while he makes sure his new orders are understood and followed.

Crit and Strat form up the Sacred Band, counting heads: everybody's here; nobody's critically wounded. But nothing will excuse this debacle. When a situation degenerates to this point, there's nothing you can say. Not until the Riddler asks them how they let Shamshi get away, if they don't find him today.

By then, they'd better have an answer.

*

Lying flat on his stomach behind the peak of his garret rooftop, Shamshi hears the cavalry officers talking. He watches everything through bleary eyes. With those orders to withdraw, the cordon eases and the frightened youth makes away, scrambling down back stairs in practiced fashion. Down, down, and farther down: taking well-planned escape routes, slipping into flooded tunnels to get away. But so many boys and girls and mendicants and whores are running out of Downwind that even the tunnels, full of sewage, are overcrowded. There is no safe place left in Downwind for Shamshi. The fevered youth huddles in the tunnels long past sundown, shaking, too tired to flee any farther. He is running out of places to hide.

Sitting in the dark, knees pulled up to his chest and burning with fever, crossbow discarded long ago, he's nearly given up. Boots are sloshing nearby. Men wade closer. Torches flicker off rough-hewn walls. He hasn't got the strength to break and run. He sits, pretending to be dead: he will be soon, at this rate. At least he took down two more of his enemies. The city guard brought the fight to him: left on his own, he'd have stayed there in his little room; but the cordon was too tight. They were going to find him. They had run him out of his garret, right into this new and deeper hell.

The torches are closer now, throwing wild shadows, grotesque and misshapen, on the old stone walls. Curt voices echo. Sham can't decipher what they're saying. He's too sick, or they're speaking in a tongue he doesn't know.

Then he's shuddering, caught.

Three tall, heavy men in armor, each with a torch, look down at him. One kicks at his legs, splashing the water. "Get up, boy. Let's have a look at you."

But he can't do that. He's exhausted. Slipping down into the stinking sewage, he doesn't say a word: one death, or another, it's really all the same after the first few seconds. Isn't it?

Hands pull him up. He's already thrown away his weapons, afraid to be identified by them. He can't fight them off. One of them drops a torch and it gutters; the water is so oily that whorls of grease ignite upon its sludgy surface.

As they drag him along, their hard hands under his arms, he eludes all things by going to his rest-place. *Long spears, thunking into flesh. Men stagger back, impaled, moaning.* So far away is he from his captors, he barely knows that they drag him out and up, into sunlight, or that they callously throw him in a wagon on top of a dozen others, or that one man says, "That's enough of them. We'll see what Torch wants to do with these."

Sham knows he's not dead yet. But he's not coming out from hiding: he huddles in his rest-place where, as long as breath can be had, fortune can be turned around and any game is fair, so long as you win it. He remembers Sync, the 3rd Commando horse-tamer, telling him: *Cheat, if it's the only way to win.* If he can cheat death, then victory can still be his.

But the fever is burning high in him, and he has no more thoughts to think. He sinks down among the gore and corpses of his Chaeronean rest-place, and sinks some more, into a deeper, darker rest than even that place can bring.

When he wakes, he's in a crowded cell with a dozen others, where everyone else is clustered back against the bars. A guard comes by and a street tough calls, "Hey. *Hey.* This man's sick. He's burning up with fever. Get him away from us, before every one of us in here – and you – get the plague."

The next thing he knows, the cell door opens. A burly man with a frightened look throws him a cloak and says: "Go on, pud. Get out of here. No, don't thank me. Don't *touch* me. Two right turns, one left turn: *go.* Get out on the street before we decide we'd better burn you and your sickness alive, to cure it."

He can't go very fast, or very far, without stopping to lean against a wall. He vomits twice as he goes. Two guards follow him at a safe distance as he staggers through some dungeon or other, following directions. The men behind him talk in low, worried voices, using words he can't understand.

There's a barred door, and one more guard – one more gate, between him and the night. And freedom.

At last he's standing outside that high iron gate, on a street he doesn't know, somewhere on the Hill, where the city guard keeps a station.

He has no money, no weapons, little in the way of prospects, but he's alive: he'd been dreaming that they'd free him; he'd been looking for a door to open, in his rest-place. It hadn't looked like this, but never mind.

He walked until he couldn't walk another step, and curled up under a well-trimmed hedge. He was a little warmer under the hedge, a little safer. In the morning he'd sneak back to Downwind, try to reclaim his money, his weapons, and his horse.

No city guard is rousting citizens up here. He curls up tighter, making himself as small a target as possible, praying no one will find him. Something is watching over him, some fortune or providence. He has another chance, now, at everything he'd thought was lost. If he can just make it through the night.

*

Straton watches Tempus and Jihan ride up like avenging gods, just before first watch of the night under a young moon seeking cover, their Trôs horses blowing hard. But there isn't any cover to be had, not from the Riddler. Critias is taking this too hard, Strat is sure. Tempus won't blame him. The Riddler will understand…Strat hopes. "No serious Stepson or Theban injuries, no casualties," Crit reports to Tempus crisply. "No sign of Shamshi yet, as far as we can tell, unless you count a couple of crossbow bolts shot into the city guard. Walegrin's forces fared worse, but that's not our problem. And nothing else useful turned up during the whole sweep. There's precious little left of Downwind, Commander, that we haven't searched," Critias sums up for Tempus with a sigh, patting his tired chestnut's neck as their mounts shift from foot to foot at the rendezvous on the corner of Processional and Governor's Walk.

Strat says, trying to protect Crit as best he can: "There's precious little left of Downwind, period. At least, that's habitable. It's Walegrin's city guard who got out of hand – they, not we, are going to pay to clean up this mess."

Strat's ghost horse isn't tired. It paws the cobblestones: it likes this game, even better now that the shadows are getting longer and night is making its customary promises to such a horse, of breakneck chases through ill-lit streets and wild rides aplenty that lesser horses can't survive. Everybody else, including Strat, is spent, stinking of Downwind: garlic, onions, garbage and sewage.

Unless he's among the prisoners left to interrogate, Shamshi's slipped away again. The Riddler won't be pleased if such turns out to be the case. Strat wants to defend his left-side leader and the Sacred Band's performance, but he shouldn't have to: they were flawless. None of theirs had turned their backs to a loaded crossbow; they understood offense and defense where crossbows were in the mix.

Tempus doesn't comment. Jihan merely stares. Crit says nothing more. So Strat adds, "Commander, we need Ischade, and Randal – and Jihan, of course, dear lady – for this. That boy's a Bandaran initiate, Stepson-trained; he's got wizard blood. He's not predictable."

Crit scoffs derisively, hawks over his horse's shoulder, then wipes his thigh, making no excuses, waiting for the Riddler to give him a dose of the retribution in that stare. Tempus still doesn't respond, just regards them pensively: Crit, Strat himself, their horses, as if taking stock of what he has here. It's hard to breathe under that scrutiny.

The commander's eerie companion, Jihan, takes their measure too, unabashedly. You can hear crickets, horses breathing, soft sobbing somewhere nearby; farther off, an owl questions everything. Jihan's Trôs reaches out to take a bite out of Straton's ghost horse, thinks better of the plan, and backs up two steps.

When the silence is unbearable, Jihan finally breaks it: "If you're serious, Riddler, about catching Shamshi, *let me* help you. We won't get him this way," she says, dismissing Crit, Strat, the Stepsons and Thebans – the whole Sacred Band – as if they are nothing. She sniffs, one hand on her scale-armored hip. For a moment, Strat wonders what the Riddler sees in her, then answers his own question: indestructible, with appetites matching his own, this primordial creature was often the only company their commander craved – especially now, with Niko bed-ridden. Every man needs companionship; it is the bedrock of pairbond.

"Critias," the Riddler says, in a measured tone he usually reserves for announcing some remarkable slaughter in the offing, "deliver the prisoners we've taken to the palace – all but those you want to interrogate." Now his voice turns chillingly gentle: "Tell Torch we're not interoperating with his forces again until they learn to take direction: one mission, one leader – under our command. Tell him I said to let Vashanka sort out these detainees. Let him figure out what the god wants to do." Tempus rubs his jaw. "Strat, before you hand over this lot, you and Crit take one more look at those we've caught – just in case Shamshi's among them, or someone who knows him is."

Just that flatly was the Sacred Band's official position articulated. Command had spoken: Strat and Crit weren't going to take the blame for this fiasco. Strat felt foolish. He should have known better than to worry for Crit, or himself: Tempus was always fair.

Strat takes a chance: "Commander, it's about Ischade and Randal…?"

"I'm handling it. Now, I have another meeting."

The Riddler's horse rears as he wheels it. Jihan follows in a clatter.

"Gods, I'm glad they're gone," Crit mutters. "When he's that angry, I begin wondering if any of us are safe. If you want to see Ischade so porking much, when we're done with the prisoners, I'll go with you."

But they never got there, not that night. There were too many fish in their net.

*

Tempus had been to the witch's house before; Jihan never had. Soon she would see what was to be seen there. Jihan recalled an old rhyme about a witch, but not where she'd learned it or when or why: *Trouble, muddle, spoil and rubble, lightnings flash and passions double; balance measures out the thing, and valor fades where death is king.*

A storm had blown up out of nowhere, pushing at their backs as she and Tempus rode across Sanctuary to their meeting with Ischade. A fierce wet wind was skirling; they were both soaked with rain. The little house beyond the White Foal Bridge had a low iron fence around it, where rosebushes sported black blossoms and thorns the size of wolves' teeth.

"Remember, Jihan, we need Ischade's help," Tempus said. They tied their horses to the fence and its gate swung out of their way as if it saw them coming.

"No, we don't," said Jihan. Tempus was too close to this situation. "Let my father help us."

"One more meddling demiurge or force of nature, unbegotten or not, Jihan, and Sanctuary will sink to the bottom of the sea of its own weight."

"In the sea? My father's domain?" The Riddler had his hand in the small of her back and she could feel him through her scale armor as they approached Ischade's door. His touch had lured her back to human form more than once. She'd thought he was wounded. He said not. She was reserving judgment: there are wounds of the flesh, and wounds of the spirit. His body still intrigues her like no other; the puncture wound is all but gone. But his soul is more armored than ever. He cares for all his fighters too much, each one bound to die and leave him grieving. "In the sea we can have a proper sorting out of all these pretenders to power."

He said, "I didn't mean that."

"Then say what you mean, Riddler." Of course, he never does. But now the door was opening before them and, inside, this house was very much larger than it looked, full of color and light and shadow. And Randal was with the witch.

"Let me assure you, Ischade, we only want your opinion," Tempus said, once inside, moving around a silk-covered table to pull out a chair for the necromant. "And Randal's."

Tempus had never pulled out a chair for Jihan. "Randal," Jihan said, "pull out a chair for me. I wish to sit down."

Randal scurried over and obeyed, whispering in her ear as he did so: "Please, Jihan, help us with this." Then he went to his own seat.

Jihan didn't answer Randal. She dragged her chair forward three times to splay her elbows on Ischade's little table. Jihan would make up her own mind as to what needed to be done.

The famous witch stared at Jihan; Jihan stared back. Although Jihan was the most famous Froth Daughter – indeed the only one – ever to have taken human form, this creature Ischade was…finer… more delicate…more feminine…smaller…almost fragile. Until you got to the eyes, which were of no particular size or shape and soulless like a shark's. They'd met before, but never been this close.

"Perhaps a drink?" Ischade suggested, as if this were some mannered affair with all the leisure in the world available and nothing whatsoever at stake. She reached over to the table's center and poured blood-red wine into goblets from a pitcher fit for a queen.

Jihan didn't care about earthly things, though this place was overrun with them: every surface was layered and strewn with velvet, lace and satin, with all colors ever devised, and a few she could not name.

A silence stretched too long once the wine had been passed. Ischade had her goblet to her lips and the way the witch looked at Tempus made Jihan uneasy. There was history here, but what, the Froth Daughter did not know. And Randal, watching Tempus watch Ischade, was twisting a handkerchief in his fingers.

"Since none of you will start, let me," Jihan said. "We need to decide how to find and kill this Shamshi. Agree a plan. And we need to decide whether we should kill that creature that's got into Niko's bed, as well – whether she's helping him or hurting him, and how to make sure he gets well again, with her or without her. And then we must decide what to do to calm the heavens, whether a universe bereft of mercy and waist-high in theomachy has anything to do with the Riddler's Thebans. Just those three things. It should be easy. In my father's domain, we could remedy these few minor, vexing problems between two surges of the tide at new moon."

"Really?" said Ischade with a raised eyebrow. "Just decide remedies for those few minor, vexing problems? Now? Here? Tonight? And if other forces are having similar meetings to decide some different solutions? What then?"

Jihan replied, "Then leave things to me. I can handle this alone, if the Riddler will but let me."

"Thaumaturgy," Randal said decisively, his ear-tips turning red with passion: "Miracles. Wonders. It's that or send those Thebans back where you – where we – got them, Riddler."

"No."

Everyone turned to Tempus, who sat quite still, looking into his wine with shadows playing at the corners of his mouth. And then he said, "Randal, Jihan, Ischade, we will agree on a joint endeavor. Only those here can know this plan, for each of us can keep invaders from our minds. We need to balance our combined and different strengths. There is harmony in the bending back, as in the bow and the lyre – we will harmonize our purpose, restore balance. We will bring justice, if there is any to be found. Niko would want that. But not mercy – we're done with that, for now: it's too expensive this season. Now, start again."

And, as they began anew, Jihan remembered why Tempus was called the Riddler, and loved him all the more.

## *Chapter 29: What You Pay For What You Pray For*

Sometimes when he woke she was here; sometimes not. Niko could stand up today. He knew he could. Perhaps she'd gone away.

He pushed himself up in bed and swung his legs over. Some triumphs are for others. This one was for himself. His feet on the floor, he took a deep breath, raising himself half-way up before his right side betrayed him and he had to sit back down. He wanted to get to his window, to watch the eastern sky get lighter and lighter, watch the stars fade away.

So he tried again and again, and eventually he stood on his own two feet, forehead against the wall by the head of his bed, just breathing, eyes closed because he couldn't see anything but whirling colors, anyway.

Then he heard a sound, felt a touch on his back.

And she said, "Stealth called Nikodemos, not yet. Not yet."

He wanted to see her. He felt her hair brush against him. He knew if he raised his head and his hands from that wall he was going to fall on his face in front of her.

Then she touched his arm, his neck, and ran her hand down from his shoulder to his flank. That thick, straight hair brushed against his naked skin. Her shoulder came up under his arm. "The sunrise, is it?" she said. "Then look."

Now he could raise his head. Somehow they were close enough to the window that he could see outside, see the sky. He didn't want to lean on her, but he could. He did. And he was steadier, with her shoulder under his arm. He could smell her. She was like a sunny meadow, or maybe it was the breeze coming in with the dawn. Her hair tickled his back, silked along his arm, his side.

"Thank you," he said, "for coming. For staying."

"Isn't it beautiful?" she said.

The sun was rising over the altar of Enlil, and next to it was something else. "What's that?"

"That? Harmony's altar: war and love, balance and justice and all things righteous and true. They finished it and consecrated it while you were…resting. Isn't it beautiful?" she said again.

"It's beautiful." He shifted, turning toward her. He was sure he could stand on his own. He had the wall for support. Looking at her took his breath away. He was dizzy. "So are you," he managed, and then she had to help him sit back on his bed.

When she sat beside him, her sweet hair fell over his wounded side. She said, "I must tend you. Soon you can go outside again. See the sky again. You want that."

He had to lie on his side, or on his stomach, for her to do it.

"Can we sit and just talk, where I can see you?"

She tossed her head and her hair brushed him like a butterfly's wings, over his shoulder, along his ribs. She said, "Lie down. I'll help you."

But when he lay down, he couldn't see her anymore.

"Stealth called Nikodemos, your commander worries for you. Your friends worry for you. And they are not wrong to be concerned. You need to let me help you a little more."

He was on his left side, and he knew what she was going to do there would hurt. So he took a deep breath. He wouldn't flinch in front of her. A cool touch came down his ribs, along his side, along his flank. No pain came, even when she touched him where the abscess was, where he'd been hurt before.

She said, "You need to let me help you more. Agreed?"

So he said, "Please. It's fine. Do whatever you want to do."

"What I need to do. For you, child of *maat*, Stealth called Nikodemos."

Now there was pain: a deep, dark river of it. But he was so tired, and her touch was so cool, he didn't mind. He needed to lie down flat. His breath came fast. He thought she was on the bed, on her knees, leaning over him, hair cascading down from above him. That long, long hair spilled over him and everywhere it touched, he tingled.

He took some in his hand and said, "Call me Niko. Just Niko. And this time, I'm not letting go."

But sleep stole her away from him again, and when he woke there was a blanket over him. The Riddler was there and sunlight was spilling in the window.

Sometimes he forgot how big Tempus was; but not today, with his commander towering over him, armed and armored. "How are you?"

"Better, every day," Niko said, and started to push himself up. "How are you?" He tried a grin, but didn't manage to ignite any humor in those eyes.

Tempus's big hand pushed him back and stayed curled around his right shoulder. "Better. But you save your strength." The Riddler hunkered down by the bedside, and looked and looked with those slitted eyes that had seen so much. "Where's your friend, today?"

Again he wanted to sit up, but Tempus wouldn't allow it. "She…comes and goes. In her room?"

"She doesn't have one."

"Oh. How goes the battling? Did you find Sham?"

"Everything is fine, Niko. What's her name?"

"I…keep forgetting to ask."

"But she's the one you danced with, on the beach?"

"I…. Yes, the one."

"You know who it is," said Tempus, a sound like coursing gravel, but not angry: a different octave of concern. "And I can't just let this go on happening."

"Why not?" He struggled to focus on Tempus's face. Now those eyes were looking at him from afar. "Please, Riddler, she's helping me. I prayed for her to come…"

"Ask her at what price. And be careful what you pray for," said the Riddler. That hand was still on his shoulder, gripping hard. "I need you back the way you were, Niko. Not half in one world, half in another. Not dreaming; not unmindful of what you do while you're awake. Whatever she wants with you, she hasn't said. And you, and I, both need to know. You asked me to allow it. I've allowed it. Now she needs to state –"

"– state what, Favorite of the Storm God?" she said, long legs, long hair, sweet meadow, somehow in the room with him and his commander.

Tempus stood up: "What are you doing to him?"

"Bringing him back to you. His balance is upset. He was so far, far away. Farther than Enlil's altar from Harmony's. Surely you want him back, if you think to win the day? Fight on other days? If you wish, I will leave him…."

The two of them seemed to loom over him – so large, so full of vitality, and he was still so weak. Nevertheless, Niko knew he had to do something or she would be gone, lost. He got his legs under him. He grabbed the wall and pushed against it, made it to his feet.

Niko said, with all his strength, "What about what *I* want?"

The two of them looked at him as if he were a child. Tempus's gaze caught his and shocked him. He'd never seen that face before, full of storm and hardship and something much, much older than his commander.

"Do you wish to choose between us?" she said, very gently, not more than a rustle of leaves in the grass.

Tempus didn't say a word, just folded massive arms and kept Niko's eyes locked in his.

"No. No, I just want…" She was only a girl, after all; the most beautiful girl, whose feelings were hurt. He didn't understand what the Riddler was doing.

"I have a bit of a situation," the Riddler told her, never looking away from Niko, "that requires him. If you can heal him, then don't delay on my account. Otherwise, we need to reach an understanding, or bring these escapades to a close."

"You invited me." Her wide eyes sought Niko's. "You asked me to come. I never would have intruded." Then, to Tempus: "Life to you, Riddler, and everlasting glory."

And she was gone, a quick retreat of flowing hair and long legs and eyes like the sky. He could never remember if she went out the door or through it, because his commander was standing in the way.

After a wordless interval, Tempus helped him to his bed and went away, and he fell asleep again.

His sleep was restless. His heart beat fast. *Brum rumpa pum pum.* His side hurt. His flank ached. His buttocks burned.

*Tat rat tata tata tat.* He slept all day and into the evening. He didn't want to think about what had happened. *Long spear, thunking into flesh.* If the Riddler wouldn't let her be here, then what would Niko do? *Man staggers back, impaled, groaning.* What could he do? His heart was aching. *Rat, tata tat.* And then he felt her, in the dark – the softest touch, the sweetest sigh, breath on his cheek, long hair sweeping over him like heaven.

He said, "What? Why?"

She said, "Ssh, Niko. Just take this blessing for us both," and touched him with those hands – this time everywhere, not just where he was torn and healing, and something in him gave up, gave way. The sounds and sights bedeviling him faded away and were gone. For a single instant, in all the universe of right and wrong and up and down and who and why, nothing mattered but the touch of her, and her lips, and her soft, soft skin, and that silky hair all around him. Her breath in his nostrils, sweet meadow in the curve of her neck. It was as if the two of them lay in his rest-place, on the blue-green grass in his star-shaped meadow, where his stream ran clear and his body was everything he needed it to be.

He said, "Please, please."

She said, "Of course, of course. Never fear. Be brave, my love, young hero; steadfast, and everything will work out aright."

And everything, in that one moment, was so perfect that he barely knew he breathed.

He remembered a strange white house, down a little path, as she slipped one long thigh over him where he lay on his side. Where he'd last done something like this. But that was so long ago. He wasn't sure he could remember what he'd done there or who that was he'd done it with. It didn't seem to matter.

*

Randal was fetching his ball when three boys came by his barracks quarters and he had to turn back into a man.

"Master Randal," called Kouras, the storm god's son; "Master Randal," called Arton, the seer; "Master Randal," called Lysis, the Theban, as all three stood outside his quarters in the late afternoon gloom and the rain came sheeting down.

"Yes, yes," he said, opening his door to them as soon as he was dressed in his hillman's green trousers and low boots. He was very pleased at how quickly he'd been able to manifest clothes and don them, this time.

"Sync says we can go to Aphrodisia House if you go with us," said Kouras, trying to hide his excitement.

"And if there's time, perhaps go see my mother, Illyra, at her shop first. I'd like her to meet you. She'd be so impressed," said Arton, bashful but determined.

"First?" said Lysis. "I want to introduce Master Randal to my father.... We'll lose the light soon enough. Master Randal, my father is Charon, the Theban. He's doing the evening oblation at Harmony's altar. If you could just wait until he's done...."

But Randal couldn't wait. "I'll be honored to meet with Charon, but some other time, Lysis." He tossed the ball up and down in his hand. "The Riddler said something about this foray. I recall now. Well," he said, "if we're going to do this, go get some horses, Kouras, while Arton and Lysis tell me about their adventure on the beach. I've been wanting to hear."

And so they began on it, this sensitive endeavor, Randal guiding three unwitting young fighters, guileless and clear-eyed and brave. Randal almost felt sorry for them, but he remembered when he had had stars in his eyes and dreams of glory in his head. He couldn't tell them more than they needed to know. And he must learn all that they knew, even what they didn't know they knew, for things to turn out right.

After Kouras left to get the horses, Randal kept tossing the ball up and down in his hand and asking the two remaining boys questions about their encounter with someone on the beach – someone who might have been Shamshi. The ball was only a little bit special; any ball, really, would have done for Randal's purposes. But he particularly liked the texture of this one, made of sea sponge. It was full of wonderful holes and tunnels where you could send a soul to learn a trick or two, and keep it there awhile.

Arton was a Bandaran and he knew induction when he saw it. He didn't fight it, but he gave Randal a knowing look and said, "In there?"

"Unless you think you can remember everything you saw and all you did, out here. After all, this isn't magic. You learned it on the misty isles. There's nothing to fear, is there?"

In front of Lysis, Arton agreed, "No, nothing to fear. Lead on, Master Randal," while Lysis looked between them, uncomprehending but trusting, and let his mind go where Randal led. Just as the boys' induction was complete, Randal's nose began to itch. Rather than sneeze, he rubbed it with a charmed handkerchief given him by the dream lord.

When Kouras came back with four horses and a disgruntled look, the rain had stopped. By then, Randal had a good idea what the chase after Shamshi in the sand had been like. Only a few details eluded him, but those would have to wait.

This plan was carefully calibrated, cunningly arranged, and he had his part to play. Even if it meant riding an actual horse, he was willing to do whatever he could for his one-time partner, Nikodemos, sequestered in his sickroom and seeing no one but the Riddler – and the dancing girl. Or at least, not seeing Randal.

Kouras and Arton were Niko's trainees. Randal had been honored that the Riddler had chosen him to take charge of them for this evening's foray.

"Now, Stepsons," said Randal, girding on his swordbelt before he swung up on an old, brown gelding, "there's danger about, these days. While we ride, I want everyone to stay together. And if I give an order or a signal, or a maneuver code, you obey me as if I were the Riddler. Is that clear?"

All the boys agreed and looked fierce.

"I am, you should know, the only warrior-mage ever to serve with the Sacred Band of Stepsons. Any difficulties with this? Any hesitations, questions, or problems? If so, say them now, before we leave the gates."

There were none, not from the strapping red-haired Kouras, the blond and handsome Lysis, or the dark, compact Arton, as the four of them splashed out the gates and into the Riddler's plan. The trainees mustn't know, or even suspect, that ahead lay a different kind of adventure than most boys ever have – and perhaps a different kind of peril. And manhood.

"Old enough to kill means old enough to die," the Riddler had reminded him, when using the young Stepsons to lure Shamshi was discussed by the four of them who could shield their planning from the quarry: by Tempus, Jihan, Ischade and by Randal himself. Their adversary was a mind invader, Bandaran trained. And deadly.

Randal had Arton ride beside him, all the way to town, since Arton was the seer, the most interesting. The Riddler wanted the measure of these youths taken by an objective observer. If there was a hint of things to come, a future to be glimpsed tonight, Arton was most likely to see it.

As promised, they stopped by the sad little scrying shop of Arton's mother, Illyra, and Randal was at pains to be polite. The matron was heavy-set, ill-used, and stooped from her burden of regret. Even so, she loved her boy and lit up when she saw him.

Arton said, "Mother, this is Randal, the Stepsons'…"

"Hazard," said Illyra, and curtsied, a rather awkward sight.

"I…you…I didn't think there were any Hazard-class mages practicing here in Sanctuary." She ushered them in, offering tea at her little round table.

"There aren't," Randal said. They sat. Kouras looked at the ceiling. Lysis peered around with huge, excited eyes. "Sorcery is proscribed here, as you well know, Illyra – its mechanisms turned to dust. I'm allergic to dust. I'm visiting with friends. Your son is making quite an impression…."

This woman might be poor, but she was no fool. "One of your students, Merricat, apprenticed here for a time," Illyra told him carefully. Unlike Arton, Illyra could glimpse the present and the future but feared her own talent. "I can't *see* Arton, I've told him that and I'm telling you…."

"Your son just wanted to visit," Randal said kindly. "Sometimes, we do things simply because they are the right things to do – at least we do in the Sacred Band."

Illyra made a warding sign. But she must have known where her son was apprenticed. So it wasn't the mention of the Sacred Band that caused her concern, though it could have been. It was something else: this woman had foreseen something, despite no cards on the table. Perhaps in her tea. Her level of skill required a focal point.

Randal said, "I will buy each boy a quick reading, and then we must go."

So she read cards, the typical this-upside-down and that-crossed-over-the-other, for Kouras, who would have "long life and prosperity," and for Lysis, who would "write history, be a leader," until she got to her son, and then her cards seemed to betray her: "Three of Swords, reversed; Death, reversed; the Citadel…" She stopped.

Randal was glad she did.

Then Arton's mother said, "My son and his two friends have a destiny. These three portents together make a greater reading. But you know that."

Randal did; he'd known it before he came, but he hadn't expected this blowzy, worn-out fortuneteller to see it. He paid her, murmuring polite inanities, and suggesting that since the Thebans were looking for an oracle, Illyra might apply for the job.

"Oracle?" Illyra said.

"Sibyl, Mother," Arton said, proudly. "A seeress. You would make a wonderful one."

Illyra walked them out. At her threshold, she caught Randal's arm and held on. He let the boys go ahead to the horses. "What are you doing to my son, Hazard? What awful danger? What horrid sacrifice? What?"

"What did you see? I though you couldn't *see* Arton?"

"A mouse can see a cat stalking up to its hole," she said scathingly. "If you harm that boy, I'll curse thee. And that, Hazard, I still can do."

He wasn't worried. He didn't say he lived a plane away, or that she didn't have the skill. He said: "Never fear. We are in a bit of a spooky patch, but the entire Sacred Band will protect Arton, if he needs it. And I, myself. You have my word."

"Your word, Hazard? I'll hear it now."

So then he had to vocally, formally, give his word, and promise to protect Arton on his Hazard's oath and his Sacred

Band oath, which he really would have preferred not to do, heading into the maw of destiny with these three unknowing boys tonight.

*

The mild summer evening was fragrant now that the rain had stopped. With friends clustered around him, Simias could nearly imagine he was back in Thebes. Two gods' altars crested the hill. On the flat below, they had built a modest cookfire. Here under the sparkling stars, Simias waited with eight of his brothers for Charon to arrive.

Simias's partner, Perses, was summing up his tale of atrocities in Downwind: "The city guardsmen were like the *keres,* doom-bringers of merciless vengeance." Finished, the curly-haired young poet leaned back against Simias and sucked from his wineskin.

"You just like the simile, Perses," Simias chided his right-man. "Thank the goddess there are no *keres* here. But you're right, that city guard bears watching. As all our new friends bear watching – all the Sanctuarites and the Stepsons." Simias had called this meeting. He was a gray beard, an aristocrat, a seasoned leader. They listened when he spoke. Only Charon had a tighter hold on Theban hearts.

Gorgias spoke up, his shattered face just angles in the firelight: "We suffered no casualties during the sweep, but the city guard lost two, so how fearsome can they be?" Gorgias was even more sour than usual: his partner, Sciron, stayed behind in the barracks tonight. Sciron had fallen from a horse and hurt his hip today, an evil omen, and no one knew how long the hip might take to heal. "And the Stepsons' enemy escaped – again."

Dark Agis and fair Archias sat side by side, both with chests wrapped. Agis said, "The Stepsons have more blood oranges today."

Archias said, "Let's make Charon get us some of those oranges, even if we must give half to the goddess."

Simias said, "There are more mysteries here than oranges. Before we left for the Downwind sweep, I dreamed I died in that sortie, with an arrow through my throat; and that you died beside me, Perses, shot in the eye. It didn't happen, goddess be praised, so now I'll tell you. But those two city guardsmen died that very way, that very day, during the sweep. There are stranger things here than Thebans know about…."

Now Charon, their warrior-priest, arrived and sat, cross-legged, where Perses made room for him. "So?" Charon asked. "This august body all together? Why are we here, Simias?"

"We're here," said Simias with great care, "because we don't understand what we see. Who is that woman, going in and coming out of the sickroom of the Riddler's second-in-command? All the Stepsons claim they don't know her. And why does it rain all the time except when *she* tends to Stealth, called Nikodemos? And where do the blood oranges come from? Not from the kitchens."

Charon raised both eyebrows; in the firelight, the lines on his forehead deepened. "We're not in Thebes anymore. It doesn't rain all the time, but their storm god has his altar here above us: it rains when he wishes. As for the rest – you know," he said. "You all know."

Nine men swore they didn't. Simias, who'd kept company with some exalted minds in his time, said, "She could be Thetis, savior of Zeus, mother of Achilles, whose son was greater than his father. Or perhaps not." He looked about him archly. "If not, then who else could she be?"

"It *could* be Thetis," Perses agreed, who liked this game and played it with glee. "But she could also be Themis, mother of Prometheus, holy prophetess of righteousness and justice."

Others joined in, suggesting goddesses from far and wide and one side of heaven to the other, proposing to name the one who brings the oranges and stops the rain and tends the hero lying in the Riddler's bed.

Eventually Charon tired of the game and said: "We *all* know. If none of you dare say, then I will, lest we anger all the gods and goddesses from here to there."

Everyone looked at Charon, and this time no one was off-handed, or flushed with wine, or pretending to be either: "So *say* then, Charon – if you say you know and say you dare," said Simias.

"The one who appears in a girl's or woman's form here is Blessed Harmony, our tutelary goddess, and I say it so because I know it so. And now, that said, a prayer is in order, to keep mouths and eyes and hearts pure, since a goddess walks this earth with us, watching everything we do and hearing everything we say. Remember, she is Justice. So be just in all you do and all you say. And be circumspect. Pay respect to her, for respect is the coin that deities most crave. And you all know I speak the truth, for each and every brave soul here has been afraid to speak her name in the same breath with that Stepson's name, or any other heathen, lest we offend our generous goddess of balance and righteousness."

With that said, the prayer begins. And Simias wonders silently, as mercy is requested from the goddess and forbearance sought, if any of them have already committed some offense they might soon regret. Their goddess seldom walked among them in their homeland. Until Chaeronea, he'd never seen her in the flesh. Then in Sanctuary, on the lighthouse spit, she had appeared in all her divine glory to Charon, to his son, to the Band's commander and his right-side partner. *Long spears, thunking into flesh. Men staggering back, impaled, moaning.*

The dream of death by crossbow bolt is still clear in Simias's mind. He will make a substantial offering on the altar up the hill tomorrow. He will sacrifice the finest lamb he can find, to pay for any wrong he may have done, to buy his way out of any unknowing or unwitting slight to his tutelary goddess, Harmony.

But slights aplenty will be here, where Stepsons serve a wild god of war; where more than flutes are needed to calm savage hearts. And where many a Theban may take it amiss that their beloved goddess, Harmony, visits Stepsons, and graces their rooms, but not the hearts and company of her very own.

In Thebes, as everywhere else civilized, it is well known that gods and goddesses only walk the earth to test the faithful and to punish the failings of humankind. So Simias wonders aloud as he hugs young Perses close (this poet like a son to him): "Have we already earned our fate? Is our wool carded, the spindles of our days all spun round? When gods and goddesses walk disguised among men, the wise don't celebrate. They cower. They bow their heads. If they can, they run. If they can't, they hide. If they can't hide, they purify themselves for trials to come."

Shrewd Charon looks up from the fire and says, his face underlit and solemn, "And if they are pure of heart, and balanced, they count their blessings, which the goddess has bestowed and will bestow. But thank you, Simias…I was just getting to that part."

*

"Ischade," Straton calls, outside the low gate which once opened for him and now does not. There's no rain. The young moon is bright, casting teasing light upon the odd little house where his love still lives, and where so much had gone so very wrong in former times.

The ghost horse nuzzles delicately at his shoulder: touch of velvet lips, nudge of muzzle. *Jump the fence,* the ghost horse nickers. *She won't mind. She loves us. We love her. She'll have sugar-beet in there, and carrot. Jump the fence. Or I'll do it for you. There's no time to waste.* It stamps one forefoot, stamps the other, swishes its tail, and pushes Straton forward with its nose: once, twice, until Strat's knees touch the gate. Beyond that gate is everything forbidden, everything he longs for: everything that had nearly killed him, and had left him with a crippled shoulder, years ago.

"She healed my shoulder, you know," he tells the ghost horse. "Look." He raises his arm above his head and tugs on the ghost horse's long forelock, which never gets longer, never loses a hair. But the horse already knows. Those wise eyes with their oblong pupils shine a deep, blood red tonight.

*There's no time to waste*. The ghost horse paws with its forefoot. *Let's go get her, go for a ride.*

But Straton can't do that. Crit would be so angry, so disappointed. Straton had promised not to come here alone. But tonight, he has good reason...he has business here....

The ghost horse whickers again. *We love her. She loves us. The night's still young; the rain's stopped. Think how far and fast we could run together, away from everything, away from everyone, just we three.* And whickers low, soft lips picking insistently at his chlamys: *Just we three...*

Then a square of light appears, beyond that little gate, beyond the twisting walk, up those stairs he's trod so many times. Strat thinks, *She must kill to eat, kill to live. She takes life, to have life. So do we all. Everybody kills for food. No apologies necessary. But she kills people (souls old, weak and sick, deserving and foul)... so she's unclean – and here we are....*

She's right in front of him, not bothering to cross the distance in between – but on her side of the gate, not his. "What is it?" she breathes. "Nothing is finished yet. We are just getting under way. Straton, why are you here?" Then her eyes grow huge and she floats so close he can feel her breath and the heat of her against his chest.

The ghost horse snorts and pushes him forward, muzzle at his back. He's dumbstruck. He has no answers, just trumped-up excuses. Then he seizes the one he'd used to brave this path and stand here: "The commander said, 'Randal's started.' You need to know that, the Riddler said. But *what* has Randal started*?"*

*"You* don't need to know *that.* Tempus shouldn't have sent you."

He reaches out a hand to touch her cloak, to feel something, to prove she is really here with him – not just an apparition, a simulacrum she's sent out to meet him in the garden in her stead.

Now he's caught up in her cloak and she's caught up in his passion and there's nothing in the world that matters as much as Ischade, and the ghost horse standing guard at his back.

"Straton," she sighs. "Straton, not now. When I call, I'm not always calling you." She breaks away and backs away, but their lips have touched and his breath comes fast and he knows: the ghost horse is right. He doesn't say a word. He must not grab for her, or in any way compel her.

"Not now, not now," she croons, as much to herself as to him. "I'm occupied. You need to go. Don't ask a single question, not even of yourself. Just go. Forget you came tonight. And come another night. Oh, come another night. I'll have something for you, I promise. And a carrot for your horse." Next, she reaches out and touches him, just a soft tap upon his forehead – from somewhere far inside that house, across all the empty space of her gate and her yard and her steps, and now he doesn't remember why he came here. But he knows he's welcome back here with his ghost horse…here where it all began for him and for the horse who'd died and come back to life for love of him.

Another night.

Although she never once stepped beyond her gate, never let him inside her yard with its black roses and thorny bushes and its nightshade, he's now sure she will.

Another night.

And the ghost horse is rubbing its head against his chest, saying, *Another night. There will be another night. For all of us. Just we three…to ride, forever.*

## *Chapter 30: The Blessed One*

In the cloying embrace of Aphrodisia House, Lysis stared around, alert for danger close at hand. Sanctuary was still reeling from the Downwind sweep. All three trainees were determined that nothing untoward would happen to Master Randal on their watch. Sacred Band protocol prompted Lysis to empty the big salon before letting Master Randal enter, but he couldn't do that tonight: they had orders not to disrupt the brothel's business unnecessarily. He and Kouras made a circuit of the main room, as Critias and Straton had taught them, taking note of everyone and everything. Arton stayed right next to Randal, in case the Stepsons' mage became a target.

Well-dressed men with fancy clothes and fancy hair and fancy beards drank at the bar: caravan masters in silks and brocades; expansive fellows, some in flashy cloaks, some in robes and lace; a few with the sterner garb of men hoping to look pious. Perfume and seduction; diffuse light and suggestive laughter: perhaps thirty people were in the salon, all told. What would his goddess, Harmony, think of this place, where Lysis, her Blessed One, stood now among drunkards and harlots, perverted priests and libertines and thieves? Menace and dissipation were everywhere.

*Be ready to kill any and all,* Sync would have cautioned. Lysis was in a strange city, on an oddly ill-defined mission with no other Thebans here to help him, only Stepsons. At least his bolt-shot thigh no longer hurt; he used no crutch, wore no bandage. He could ride as well as walk. His scars were turning decorative. He will always carry those scars, reminders of how close to death he'd come in this exotic, erotic, and dangerously unpredictable place called Sanctuary.

The bordello assaulted his senses, titillating him. Harlots slid and rubbed and wriggled sinuously among the men, like cats waiting to be fed. Women and girls displayed themselves on burgundy sofas and sat in little groups at tables: so many girls, legs never together. There were very few male prostitutes here, just the occasional kohl-eyed boy approaching puberty.

"Master Randal," Lysis said, "I don't…I've never…. The last time I was here, I was on duty. My father was with me. Stealth was in command...." Master Randal had a sharp face, large ears, and fine bones like a nobleman, with no hint of brawn or swagger about him. Not Lysis's image of a fighter, but this *was* the Stepsons' famed 'Hazard." The mage seemed in no way hazardous to Lysis, who was a head taller and nearly a third heavier. "Just what's expected of us here, tonight? What should I do?"

"What should you do? What's *expected* of you?" the mage echoed. "What do men usually do in houses of prostitution, Lysis? Didn't you…take a woman out on the beach, at the Theban fête? Or someplace…?"

"No," said Lysis flatly. His father would have had his hide for fraternizing with loose women, but he didn't say that. He said, as brusquely as he could, "I was working – tasked, like Arton, to find Sham. I told you in that trance. I answered your every question about chasing Sham on the beach. At our celebration on the spit, we danced a little, that's all – all us young Sacred Banders." It was important to Lysis to make sure Master Randal knew he wasn't holding himself aloof, as some of the older Thebans did. He wanted to be a full-fledged Stepson, accepted and included.

"Let's get you something at the bar. Tonight you can remedy that problem, if you wish," the warrior-mage said gently, his ears flaming red, guiding Lysis toward the men and girls, drinking and smoking. "Or not, your choice. The Stepsons expect to pay for your evening, one way or the other."

"Oh, I see." He did not see. Why would virginity be a problem? Lysis was armed and dangerous, ready to do his job. Nothing taught in Thebes suggested that prowess with harlots was a requisite for a fighter.

"Of course you see. Or you will." Randal guided him over to the bar and ordered for them both, then turned to face the room. Lysis wasn't sure he wanted to let down his guard – or could. He drank the wine that Randal chose while pipes and lyres played sensuous songs. Aromatic smoke curled around his brain as Kouras came up to them where they stood, a black-haired girl in tow.

"Lysis, this is Shawme," Kouras announced proudly, as if he were introducing a queen. But she was a whore. Nothing special. She was a few years older than Lysis, with guarded blue eyes. She held out her hand to him.

Beside him, Randal shifted; if he didn't know better, Lysis would have thought that Randal was checking his weapons.

He took Shawme's hand, let it drop. "I'm Lysis, son of Charon, son of Thebes, of the Sacred Band of Stepsons, Blessed of Harmony," he said, introducing himself to Kouras's girl. And all that was true. The goddess Harmony had said to him on the beach, where the Riddler and Stealth and his father could hear, *"You are truly mine."* Everyone knew.

Thebans called him 'the Blessed One,' some even said it to his face. And he *was* changed, since then. Truly blessed. Guided. Protected by Harmony.

When Shamshi – and he *knew* it was Shamshi – had tried to kill him from ambush that night on the road, a supernatural hand had knocked the crossbow bolt away, so it skewered only his thigh, not his heart. Then Stealth had given him the dart tube. He'd used one of those ancient darts on Sham when he and Arton chased the fugitive through the dunes. He knew it was Sham then, just as he'd known it was Sham who shot at him in the dark. Sometimes, he could sense the Bandaran reaching out to touch his mind. *Long spears, thunking into flesh. Man staggers backward, impaled, sobbing.*

Balance was not just for Bandarans, but also an attribute of Harmony, his goddess. And Harmony herself was here in Sanctuary with her faithful. Perhaps even here with him right now. Her grace had brought the remnants of the Sacred Band of Thebes here, saved them all....

Kouras's harlot finished appraising him with her big, blue eyes: "You have so many titles, so many names. I'm very impressed. No one calls me anything but 'Shawme.'" Her breasts were showing; her eyes were ringed with shimmering blue powder. She was bolder than a Theban wench. She added, "I'm happy to meet any friend of Kouras's, Lysis, son of Charon." Her expression was practiced, welcoming; but not too much so.

Lysis could feel Master Randal stiffen, could see the warrior-mage watching intently.

Kouras said, "Lysis, Shawme has a friend here tonight, Merricat, who wants to meet you." Kouras gave him a conspiratorial look. "Shawme's the one who found the dart tube." Leaning back with his elbows on the bar, as he had seen Stealth do, Lysis ducked his head to meet Shawme's blue eyes. Perhaps he needed to show these Stepsons that Thebans were not all 'divine friends,' and nothing else….

Master Randal jostled his elbow, then shifted close and whispered, "Be still." Then the mage took a step away from the bar, approaching the girl. "Shawme? Shawme who found the…item? Ten, eleven years ago, it must have been."

Shawme said, "That's me," fetchingly. "But let's not talk about how long ago it was."

Master Randal said, "Do you still have it?" and moved in on her.

"No, Hazard." The whore backed up, right into Arton, coming up behind her.

"What's this?" Kouras asked in his 'son of the storm god' voice. Arton touched Kouras on the arm. Thunder rumbled outside.

"Who *does?"* Randal's voice popped like a bullwhip.

Shawme's head was level with Randal's chin, but she looked up at the mage as if he towered over her. "I did what you told me, Hazard. I gave it to the Stepsons when they came back to town. I couldn't…get to the Riddler. I'm just a…."

Kouras said, "Master Randal, Shawme gave it to me. I gave it to Stealth. Stealth gave it back to me, then took it away again when Lysis got shot and gave it to Lysis. So what?"

*"So what?"* The mage whispered in that way the veteran Stepsons had, which screeched in your soul like fingernails on a slate. Now Lysis saw the fighter in this mage. Iron, whetted to kill. Anger, held very tight. And something else: chagrin.

The warrior-mage whirled on Lysis. *"You* have it? Give it to me."

Lysis almost flinched. "No." He took his elbows off the wet bar.

The Stepsons' warrior-mage might as well have caught a dog stealing dinner from a cook pot. In front of Arton. In front of Kouras. In front of the girl. And in front of all these Sanctuarites.

"I said, *give* it to me." Fire seemed about to issue from the mage's thin nostrils; they quivered.

"No. The Riddler's right-side partner gave it to me. After I was wounded in the line of duty. He said it would serve me well if Sham came at me again. I used it on Sham, when we chased him on the beach. I told you."

"No, you didn't tell me *that.* You said you shot him with a dart tube. Not *that* dart tube. Give it to me. *Now.*"

Lysis was embarrassed. He was angry. He didn't know what he'd done wrong. He said, "Stealth gave it to me. If he wants me to give it to you, he'll say so." Too many ears were cocked. He said, "I'm going over there to a table, where it's not so crowded."

He wanted to say, *I'm getting out of here.* He wanted to go back to the barracks. He wanted to talk to his father. He was 'the Blessed One.' This foreign sorcerer shouldn't be scolding him like this, in front of everyone.

Arton, Kouras and Shawme were looking helplessly at one another. The whore seemed about to cry. She tugged on Kouras's arm, whispered in his ear. The warrior-mage stared at Lysis, black murder in those eyes, his face so white that freckles showed on it, a muscle jumping in his jaw.

Lysis headed for a table. It wasn't empty when he reached it but girls scattered, seeing his scowling face and his hand on his shortsword's hilt. Then he was alone there.

And then he wasn't: "Lysis, we're supposed to obey Master Randal's orders as if he were the Riddler, remember?" Arton murmured urgently under his breath.

"Well, he's not, is he?"

Arton pulled out a chair and straddled it, eyes round. "You'd better give that dart tube to him."

"No." Now it was too much of an issue. He couldn't back down. Anyway, he'd left it in his room. Leaving it behind was obviously a bad mistake, but he didn't want to admit it. Not to any of them.

Then Kouras came. Shawme stayed behind, joined by a prettier girl, and they were talking with animated gestures to the warrior-mage.

Kouras said, "You're in trouble. But you know that." He sat, stuttering a chair under him.

"How can he be?" Arton said tremulously, rubbing his arms. "He didn't do anything wrong."

"He's doing it now." Kouras leaned forward, elbows on the table. "You want to be a Stepson? You want to be accepted? You want Stealth and the others to respect you? You're… what…two, three years older than I am, and you don't know when you're porking up this bad? Doesn't say much for your common sense – or mine, for being seen with you. You're messing everything up for everybody here. I want to spend the night with Shawme, not escort you to the barracks under guard." Kouras scraped back his chair and got to his feet in one quick move. Lightning cracked and thunder rolled, closer now.

*"Don't* make it rain," Arton called after Kouras querulously. "Especially if we're leaving." But Kouras stalked away, over to the mage and the girls.

"He can't make it rain," Lysis said. "That's just talk and coincidence."

Arton looked at Lysis pityingly.

Over by the bar, the warrior-mage and both girls spoke with Kouras, who took Shawme under his arm. Then Master Randal left the group and approached the table where Lysis and Arton sat. Somehow, everyone else had moved away:

there was a circle of emptiness around them. Lysis was miserable – trapped, exposed.

The mage had more freckles on that thin face than Lysis could ever remember seeing on a grown man. They looked like mud, or blood, spattered there.

"Lysis…." Randal sat. "You need to give me the tube. You don't know how powerful it is, or what to do with it."

"I did fine with it. I did as Stealth taught me." And now he had to say it, before things got any worse: "I hid it. After I used it on the beach. I don't have it on me." Lysis had been told by his father to give the tube back to Niko when Lysis could ride again; he'd meant to do it, but by then Stealth had been injured, hard to reach, sequestered in the commander's quarters.

"Then let's go get it. Now," the warrior-mage decreed.

"Kouras doesn't want to leave," Lysis said, crossing his arms.

"Kouras doesn't have to leave. He'll have different orders," said the Stepsons' mage, already striding toward Kouras and the door.

## *Chapter 31: Proof of Heaven*

Waiting for trouble to come. Tempus has to solve this, now. Two forces, or more, at odds over this man, Niko (who'll always be a boy to Tempus), who faces every horror and evil that man can do and never flinches. Listening to Niko's breathing as he sleeps. Aškelon is right: these are dangerous days for this hero half-made; for this Nikodemos over whom, above all other men, the worst and best contest.

Tempus never sleeps. He keeps his vigil over Niko, impatient, brooding. With his god-given sword beside him on the floor, propped with his back against the door, Tempus is waiting for the wizard boy or the Theban goddess to come.

Too many forces are stirred up tonight: on purpose; by his design; at his command. Flush the abomination, Shamshi, to kill it or send it straight to hell. Confront that other power; drive her hence. He wants to grapple with enemies this night as he's seldom wanted anything. Wait much longer, and Stealth would be well enough to insist his fate was his own to choose – and perhaps choose wrong. Or die trying. Tempus would not allow that to happen.

He needed no second bed for himself in this little room of his. He needed something stronger than a door to keep out the damned and the celestial. He wasn't sure which was worse.

Niko's breathing grew fast, then steadied. Tempus looked out the window. Almost time. Dawn was reaching up pale fingers to pull down the night.

He forsook the door. He walked over to the bed. He touched the forehead of his injured fighter with the back of his hand. No fever, now. No cold sweat. No clammy skin. Time to take control.

"Stealth," he says to this fighter who might be dying; might be healing; might be healed; might be damned; might be fated – but was, in the end, just a man. "Wake up. Time to go outside."

All night long (on this night he'd chosen to poke sticks into holes too long undisturbed), he'd expected a pounding on the door, a slithering through cracks, a visitor who could not be forfended.

And got none.

Niko's hair is too long. In the gray light of morning's first promise, it falls into his eyes. A week's growth of beard shadows his face. "Riddler?" He struggles to sit up, half on his left side.

Tempus doesn't help him, just stands there, judging his strength. "We need to get you out, moving. Get dressed, Stepson. We're going up the hill today."

It's chiaroscuro in the little room. Niko sighs, and nods, brushes his hair out of his eyes. "You're right. Too long in here." He swings his legs over, chary of his right side but game. And sits, breathing hard, elbows on his knees, back bowed. Tempus throws his clothes, his panoply, on the bed. And waits.

Color steals into the room with the daylight as his partner struggles into his gear. No questions, no protestations, no accusing looks. Loinguard. Chiton. Linen and leather. Swordbelt girt. Soft high boots fastened on. Now, finally, Niko takes his helmet from the bed's foot. "Ready, Commander."

It's costing him, but Tempus needs to see it. It costs them both.

And then, just as Tempus says, "Good. We'll take a chariot…"

...*she* arrives. Not in a flurry; not with clouds conveying her and not with pops of disturbed air to mark her passage.

Just *here.* Unwilling to face Tempus by herself, without Niko looking on?

She stands, tall and lithe, between Tempus and his right-side partner. She's all a man like Niko could ever desire: long limbs, long amber hair, smooth arms and a face to fight a war for; eyes as deep as the sea at the edge of time.

"What's this?" says the goddess, sweeping a gaze across both men that seeks out your soul and weighs it.

"He needs to work. He needs his strength," Tempus says. "Look at him, after all you've done."

She does: a long, long look. Then regards Tempus archly: "Avatar, what is it that you want from him? From me? Has he not given you enough?"

And Niko says, on his feet now, one hand against the wall, "Don't argue, please. Whatever my commander wants, I'll do it. I always have. I always will. Always. I'm fine."

She doesn't move toward Nikodemos, or toward Tempus. There's a leather cord twined at her waist. She fingers it, but no sword or implement of heavenly justice appears. She peers between them. "Is that so?" she says. "And me?"

Niko doesn't answer.

Tempus almost takes a step toward her, toward Niko. His shortsword is on the floor. She has none, so he has none: balance. It's the hardest thing he's ever tried, to stand there, stock-still. Evince no threat.

"Niko?" Tempus says. "You need to tell her."

His rightman lets go of the wall, squinting as if in bright, bright daylight. "Tell her what? Tell you what? I need to go out. I want to see my mare. That's all."

She says, "Your mare is safe in foal." Tempus says, "How can you know that?" She says, "You'll see."

And Niko says, taking a step, then another, fully armed and armored, and coming up on this entelechy of a goddess: "I…love you both. Where's the harm?"

But before another word can be said, she's gone – just an eye-blink of motion, as someone comes pounding on his door: "Riddler, are you in there?"

Niko reacts as if he's been slapped backhanded.

"Randal, come," says Tempus.

And with a flurry and an awkward jangling and bumbling and stumbling, in come Randal and the Theban youth, Lysis, bodies bristling and opposed.

Niko seeks the wall and then sinks down on the bed, elbows on knees, chin in hands, staring at his booted feet.

*The worst conceivable time.* The worst possible imbalance between these two visitors, so wroth with one another you can nearly see sparks flying.

"What is it, Hazard? Quickly. You're supposed to be doing…other things." Why is Randal here with one of the baits, not watching all three at the bordello and at their duty in the town, as he was told to do?

Lysis can't wait until he's asked to speak. He blurts: "Commander…Sir, I'm sorry. This is important." Bold Lysis, golden and Theban as can be, has both fists on his hips, standing tall and unrepentant about something.

Tempus ignores the youth. "What, Randal?" Tempus says.

Niko sits with eyes downcast, waiting for the intruders to leave, body curled up as if all his strength is spent.

"Riddler, Stealth needs to tell Lysis, here, to give me the dart tube that Stealth gave him," Randal says. "And why didn't anybody *tell* me about it? Everything we're doing should be different. Nothing you told me was right…if *that's* the dart that hit Shamshi, then everything about our response needs to change…."

At this moment, Tempus couldn't care less about darts and tubes and Sham.

"Stealth *gave* it to me," says Lysis, eyes blazing.

Barely comprehensible, a chattering nearly inaudible above the cataract of the Riddler's overwhelming anger: Not the time for excuses from the one, a lecture from the other. "What possible difference could it make?"

*"All* the difference, Riddler." The warrior-mage accuses each man in the room with that statement, as if everyone here but Randal is incompetent.

Niko sighs, "It doesn't matter. Let Randal have it, Lysis. And get out of here, both of you," without raising his head, a catch in his throat.

Randal stares at Niko in disbelief. "We're trying to help you, Niko. Look at you…pale and thin and…"

*"Out,"* Tempus says. "Now. If this is so important, go make sure those who need to, know it. And don't come back here till you have. Leave."

Tempus steps quickly between Niko and his erstwhile partner, and chases Randal and Lysis bodily out the door.

Then he goes and sits down beside Nikodemos, who's trembling, bent over. Weeping? Or on the verge of it. Has Tempus seen Niko weep since his first partner died? He doesn't think so. He doesn't want to see it now.

"What? Do the wounds hurt so much?"

"Wounds, no," says the fighter, face averted. "But, Riddler, why are you doing this? Chasing her away? My oath to you is binding…my faith is strong, my loyalty unswerving. Why? I just need a little help right now."

"Come on, Stealth. Let's go outside." *Too fragile, by half.*

Niko was a man who cherished nature, the wind and the rain, the sun and the sky, everything that crawled and swam and flew and slunk and raced across the world. What this one needed, Tempus must find a way to provide.

Outside, one of the Band's training chariots waited. He offered to help Niko into the car. Niko declined, and used its safety rails to pull himself up. The fighter kept looking around, as dawn bloomed rosy and the sun shone golden and white clouds blushed with every color the gods had made.

Tempus realized he'd not seen the state of Niko's wounds this morning, in all the comings and goings of the supernal and the wizardly and the mortal. But then, he could still judge Niko well enough. Wounds are not auguries. The state of flesh is not always a harbinger of favor, or disfavor, from the gods. His own wound from Chaeronea had been recalcitrant and slow to heal in this strangely fated time. Now he was as strong as he needed to be, perhaps as strong as ever. Nikodemos would be, too.

He handed the reins of the black team to his partner, motioned the two Stepsons that held the horses' bits to step away, and said, "You drive. Up to the altar of Enlil."

He would see, today, what Enlil thought of this forward hussy of a goddess, intruding into pairbond and oaths to the storm god taken under heaven.

Right now, he couldn't care less about dart tubes or ancient poisons. If the trust was poisoned between him and his right-side partner, it was a greater loss than any other Tempus could sustain.

*

On the hill, with the team held by men whom his commander had ordered to wait there, Niko walked with Tempus to Enlil's altar. The black char from recent pyres was almost all blown away on the wind. The primeval stones were black and gray and silent. Niko wanted to sit down in the grass but was afraid to try. Wrong thing to do, for body and mind.

They had put the hide-wrapped Shamshi on this altar, and look what had come of it. He didn't want to touch the stones. He knew Tempus needed some sign from him. He couldn't think of one. Something more than words from him. Niko had never gone on his knees to any force, man or god or greater. He couldn't do it now.

Would Enlil give Niko a sign? An intimation? Some touch, some nudge or nod from heaven? Enlil was a stern, fierce, incomprehensibly powerful god: Lord Storm, in every way, on every day. What kind of sign could he expect, the poor avatar that he'd been (in name only, for convenience and to please the Riddler)?

Niko needed some sign from the god, some hint of what he was supposed to do, if Enlil had a plan in which he figured. He and his left-side leader looked at the stones together while the sunrise faded into blue and a soft wind, aromatic with summer, blew his hair into his eyes. Neither touched the stones.

No sign came, not from man to man or man to god or god to man. Nothing happened. No storm cloud gathered. No lightning struck. No bear came barreling out of the woods toward them. No bull charged them from nearby fields. No god rumbled war chants in Niko's ears. No eagle flew over, or hawk, or even heron.

"Commander, what do you require of me?" he finally said.

"No more than I ever have; no less. These moments are precious. Everything flows, Niko. Let your feelings do the same. Remember what Abarsis said, 'It's hard to battle anger, for whatever it wants it pays from the soul.'"

"I'm not angry at you, Riddler. Only at myself. And Sham. I should have told Randal about the dart tube. I was… self-absorbed."

"You were hurt. Don't blame yourself for any of this. There's too much pulling and pushing from the heavens for that."

Niko looked at Tempus sidelong. That profile, on his left, was the most comfort he had ever had in life. All the proof he needed of heaven was in this man the gods immortalized, who had picked him up and made something of a lost boy with no pretensions, trying only to stay alive or die with honor. He needed to keep seeing that presence there, on his left, for as long as he drew breath. "After Chaeronea…I never thought to see you so wounded. I...it frightened me. Then I miscalculated…too much of that, lately, from me. And she's so…sure, so balanced. There's so much *maat* in her. She can't be hostile."

"I know. But you need to keep a clear head. Let your duty guide you."

"She's helped me heal."

"If we thank her for that, pay her respect as due, will you be content?"

"Yes." His heart leaped. It was so difficult, watching the two he loved most, opposed. "Yes, if you will…make a truce between you two…"

"Then we shall do it."

Tempus called the chariot. The Stepsons walked the horses over. They rode the short way to the new altar, Tempus at the reins. "We're here," said his commander.

"Where?" Niko said.

"At Harmony's altar."

"At Harmony's altar? For what?"

"So you can thank her personally."

"Riddler?" At first Niko thought his partner was chiding him, teasing him. But Tempus wouldn't. Niko didn't understand, didn't want to understand, and then he did:

"No. Oh, no…" His heart broke. He could feel it come apart in his chest. He loved that girl. He loved his dancing girl completely and without reservation. *His hands go around her waist, on the beach, lifting her high in the air, to that music faster than his heart, and she's weightless….* "I didn't want it to be that. I don't. I didn't see it," he confessed. "She never said her name."

A goddess. The Theban goddess. A cold came into the places in his heart where it had shattered, and the cold was such that everything bleeding there seared. He'd been the plaything of too many forces greater than himself, too many times. He was still bedeviled by Aškelon. He'd been in thrall to a witch of godlike power once: his son had died because he'd let it go on too long.

Tempus got out of the chariot. "Come on. Get down." His commander's voice was brusque.

He got down from the chariot's car. This was a work chariot, not the Band's dream-forged chariot made by Aškelon, decorated with demons and familiars of the elder gods. Both of them had taken favors from the entelechy of dream and shadow, ruler of the seventh sphere, most treacherous of unearthly powers. The Stepsons had played fast and loose with demiurges, with gods and the children of gods, and worse. Tempus's lover, herself, was far beyond the rules that bound mortals in their orbits.

He looked up at the sky, so beautiful and calm. And down at the altar, modest and clean, with its white stones shining softly, and offerings of flutes and fruits and oil and water. Not an ant dared climb those stones; no spider made a web there.

He said, "Commander…Tempus, we've taken help from gods – you still do. We've asked for, and gotten, aid from heaven so many times… Why is this different?" He sounded too desperate, to his own ears: like a boy who's found a wild horse and wants to keep it, with his father saying it will never become obedient to any man's hand.

"Yours to answer, Niko. Are you healed? Enlil's healed me in a heartbeat, when he's so chosen. And, think: does the storm god come to walk among us, lie in with me, and tend my wounds with his own hands?"

"She's…so balanced. You know I'm not a man for gods; I took up with Enlil to please you, but my heart is with my *maat* – with the god in man."

"I know. Thank her, Niko, as a man ought to thank a goddess. I will not oppose this further. But keep in mind, she's changing you. And I need you, just the way you are."

So he thanks her. And Tempus thanks her too, but in that voice of his that calls the ranks to war. And they drive away, then, down and around the whole barracks, outside the walls, and in again: the venerable circuit, used by warrior-priests from time immemorial, to keep safe those within.

When Tempus left him, the Riddler promised they'd make the same circuit of the barracks tomorrow. And the next day, perhaps they'd ride together on their horses.

He stripped and exercised until he was wet and seeing sparks, trying to sweat out goddesses and infernal interference – pushing himself against the wall and against the floor and against the limits of his strength. It hurt, but pain was what he needed, to wash the cobwebs from his brain and the cold from his heart.

Eventually the Stepsons came to dress his wounds. He'd long ago gotten over the humiliation of lying on his stomach with his vulnerability exposed to others. He usually kept silent. Knowing his wishes, so did they. But this time he said, "Gayle, how is it, back there?" When he had touched the places where he'd been hurt the worst, he couldn't tell, today.

Gayle answered, "I wouldn't have said unless you asked but you should know this: everything is gone – the abscess, the new scars, and the old. I've never seen it, in twenty years, that new wounds, healing, can take old scars away."

"We'll tell the commander you don't need us anymore," added bristly-jawed Cassander, coming around and wiping his hands on a clean white cloth. "Stealth, congratulations. You're fit to fight."

He doesn't answer, just waits for them to leave. A day ago, or five days ago, he'd have been so grateful. Now he is uneasy.

Fit to fight. Just weak. The pain he felt was only unused muscles, complaining when pressed back unexpectedly into service.

He washed himself, dressed again, and walked down to see his sable mare. The sun would chase the paleness from his limbs. It felt good on him. He's breathing hard when he gets to the barn, but he gets there. His mare trumpets her welcome; her ears track him, pointing to him. He's missed her; she's missed him. Her head butts him in the chest: *don't stay away so long.* He won't, again.

Dressed for duty, he eats with his fighters, letting the men come up to him as they wish. This is a time for building confidence, for gaining strength.

Later, Tempus comes to see him. He's heard about the wounds and how they took old scars away with them when they healed.

"So, is this our sign?" Niko asks. "And if it is, from which one?"

"It's what you wished for," says his commander, clapping him on the shoulder. "I've got to ride into town. You'll be safe enough, with Harmony watching over you."

The Riddler's rebuke – subtle, teasing – still galls him. And he isn't safe: not from his fears, or his doubts, or from his guilt.

Not from the goddess, when she comes without warning, simply there in the room with him. He wants to say to her that she could have told him, should have told him.

But she is still his dancing girl from the beach. Her long hair enthralls him. Her long limbs slide over him.

"Thank you," he tells her. "Thank you. I feel so much better now. You've done so much –"

"So you do. So you will. Now hush."

And those cool hands move over him. Her soft sweet breath is in his nostrils. The meadow is in her eyes. She kisses him. And he can't imagine why he'd been afraid.

## *Chapter 32: Ancient Weapon*

Young Stepsons, in Crit's Shambles office. Big eyes. Chests out. Fondling weapons like women. Scent of danger. Critias gives them orders: strike from hiding; roust anyone who looks wrong. Kill anything that threatens. Find their old friend and bring him down.

No argument from the thin-lipped boys, each trying to outdo the other's bravado.

"Life to you, Stepsons," Crit called after them, "and everlasting glory." *Live till evening, if you can.* Out went Arton and Kouras into the morning, under Strat's command – with Straton trying to hide his amusement, not even complaining that he should be sleeping now, with the sun coming up.

Covert is different. Twice as hard, ten times deadlier. Lots duller, until you're fighting for your life. No swagger. No advantage except surprise. It takes a special kind of operator: command of detail, street control, self-control, the sharpest eye. Boys don't have self-control, or eyes for anything but glory. At least they'd keep Straton away from the necromant. Or so Crit hoped. He didn't want to fish their corpses out of the White Foal.

He got some sleep, to ease his running deficit in that regard. Randal and Ischade and Jihan and Tempus were up to something, but Crit wasn't privy. Yet. When Tempus wanted him to know, he'd tell him. Crit hated the numinous: it made him itch all over, as if ants were crawling on his skin. Hard enough to deal with mortal fools. At least he was free of the fated dead for a while: he had no Thebans under his wing right now, not like during the Downwind sweep.

He dreams of Chaeronea: *Men stagger backward, impaled, screaming.* He has this dream too much. It isn't like him. If he believed in sorcery, he'd ask Randal to take the dreams away.

He goes back to sleep, determined to get some rest. A pounding like a runaway chariot team, coming up the little Shambles stairwell, wakes him when the sun is high.

"Now what?" It's the two boys, alone, white-faced, crossbows armed; waving their weapons, huffing and puffing as if they'd run all the way here on foot. "Where's Strat?"

"Critias," gasped Arton. "It was awful."

"It was foolish," Kouras growled, his hands no steadier, looking every whichway.

"Point those weapons at the floor, not me. Where's Strat?"

"We lost track of him," hawkish Arton admits, shuffling his feet.

"You lost *track* of him. I can believe that. I'm not sure I believe he lost track of you." Hair is standing up on the back of Crit's neck. He starts gathering his own weapons. "What happened?"

"We were in Ratfall with Strat. We ground-tied our horses outside a bar Straton thought we should investigate. And…" Arton spread his hands. He was shocky. Crit noticed some superficial wounds: scratches, blossoming bruises.

"We went into the bar with Straton. Somebody tried to steal Straton's bay horse, I guess," Kouras picked up. "We were inside. A man started yelling outside. The horse started screaming. We looked outside. Strat's horse had pinned a man face down on the ground, its forelegs on the man's shoulders, and it was biting the man's neck, his back…. The horse was killing him."

"That's what Stepson horses are trained to do. So then what happened?"

"A bunch of men ran out with knives and whatever they could throw at the horse. We ran outside. So did Strat. They were trying to get the horse off the man. Straton told us to protect the other horses. There was a scuffle…. The man wasn't screaming any longer. Strat's horse got up. There was more fighting…. Strat said get the other horses out of there…. We came back here."

"And *left* him? Strat?"

"We did what Straton ordered us to do." Kouras's breathing was still ragged. His fingers on his sword's hilt were white. Both boys were spread-legged in the open doorway. "You two, ride those horses of yours out to the barracks. Have Sync look them over. And *stay* there." Crit split the pair on his way out the door.

*

Sham walked unsteadily up Runeway, then up the Street of Arcana, until he came to a place that was overgrown and dark, with a high gate hanging by one iron hinge. Beyond the gate, everything was wild, choked with vines and moss-hung swamp giants. The place was full of shadows, even in daylight. It looked as if no one lived here anymore.

He'd gone back to Downwind. His horse was gone. Just as well. He'd managed to retrieve his money, change his clothes. He'd redone the dye that kept him disguised. But he couldn't stay there. He could feel the wrongness: it was too dangerous; he was too exposed there.

So he'd walked and walked; he'd slept, when his fever got too bad. He'd bought a meal here, a drink there. He was looking for some safe place. No place had seemed safe, until now. This Street of Arcana had very few buildings on it; and this one, before him, was large enough that if anyone else was squatting in there, they probably wouldn't mind if he moved in.

He needed to go in there; he was sure he'd be safe there.

He stumbled through the gate, askew and old. It squeaked. He dragged himself up the uneven walk, where grass was cracking stones and weeds were trying to take back the pavings, turn them into pebbles. This place had been elegant once, impressive; perhaps a fortress.

Like Sham, it was now a little run-down, in need of care. And like Sham, it wasn't getting any help from Sanctuary.

He felt an increasing kinship with this building, the closer he got. All around was a swampy smell; the trees had cottony creepers hanging from their branches; everything was moldy and dank, like his rest-place, like his soul.

He was too tired to look much further, anyway. The steps were wide; yellowed old marble, cracked and crazed. Atop them, a pair of huge doors latched at their center.

For a moment, Sham was afraid he couldn't open them, couldn't get inside. If not, he'd have to walk all that way back to the gate. And it seemed so far. He turned and looked. It seemed even farther away than when he'd started down here, toward the big stone house. Like a mansion. Like a palace, even.

The doors had lions on their front panels, corroded and green, with rings in their mouths. And other symbols, covered with too much verdigris for him to tell what kind of creatures they once had been. He pushed one metal-bound door: it complained, but budged; he pushed again and forced it open wider.

In he went, squeezing through, stepping onto huge stone tiles, tan and black, each as long as his forearm, in a diamond pattern that seemed to go on forever. Twigs and branches and garbage littered the foyer. He felt sorry for the big house, which once must have been so grand. A chandelier over his head had more candles than he could count. Who could reach so high up, to light them?

He walked and walked across those tiles. He wanted to lie down. But a curvy staircase drew him. Upstairs, there might be beds. He put one foot upon the first stair, and somehow he felt stronger.

*This is right. This is where I'm supposed to be.* Sometimes the whispers in his head made no sense. But this makes all the sense in the world. He climbs and climbs, and climbs some more, up winding stairs so wide you could sleep stretched out on any one. On the landing, he sees old pictures in frames, rotted and torn, hanging down. He doesn't stop for those. There's a door half open. He steps through.

In here, everything is dim and once was rich. Deep colors, soft furnishings, ripped and tattered, still gleaming with gilt here and there. And he finds a bed here, as if he's been guided to it. He shakes a coverlet, and moths and crawling things scatter, jump and fly and scurry off.

He's too tired to worry about it. He pulls the coverlet off the bed and sees a bloodstain there. It's old and brown. He doesn't care. He wraps the coverlet around him and climbs onto that big bed.

And sleeps. And sleeps. And dreams of Chaeronea, and long white fingers. And a wrist on which an obsidian talisman, white and black, gleams softly among the corpses of his rest-place.

He wakes, shivering, clutching his coverlet to his throat.

He blinks sleep away. There's something in here. Here's a white hand with long fingers. Here's a black robe, enveloping something that's looking out at him. It's sitting on the bed, next to him.

He's sure he's dreaming, delirious.

As his vision clears in a brighter light, he sees a pale face with silver-starred hair and eyes as gray as a winter storm. He scrambles away, until his back hits the headboard of the bed.

It was risky, coming here: he was in someone else's bed. He should have realized he couldn't be so lucky.

"I'm sorry," he says to the man who stares at him with eyes grayer than his own, their irises ringed with black. A pale hand stretches out to him, with an obsidian bracelet on its wrist. "I'm sorry," Sham says again.

"You won't be," says the man sitting on the bed. "Perhaps you do not remember me, since we were never introduced on Meridian, in the archipelago of dreams, my domain. I am Aškelon. Some call me lord of dream and shadow, regent of the seventh sphere. And you call yourself…?"

"Sham," he says. And he does remember, hazily.

"Sham. Once, when you were a little boy, you spent some time as a guest in my realm with a sprite named Jihan. Since then I've been watching over you in your dreams. I may have saved you once or twice, from this death or that. From a nightmare here or there. From a meaty shroud on an altar and humiliation that no youth should suffer. Are you here to thank me? Or is it something else? Just what are you doing in my house, Sham?"

"I needed a place to sleep."

"I think you've found one," says this pale-skinned man, so elegant and haughty, as his penetrating stare goes deep into Shamshi's soul. His finger reaches out to touch Sham between the eyes and everything fades away.

*

"Ischade, you *cannot* call Sham, if that poison's in him," Randal huffed, biting at a fingernail. They were in Ischade's little house, cool and gloomy in brightest day – the only place left in Sanctuary safe enough from infernal intervention to have such a meeting. Sitting once again at her round table. Waiting for Jihan to arrive.

"*I* can call him," says the witch.

"*Ischade,* he won't hear you the way a normal boy would. Oh, he'll react, all right, but he won't react normally. I'm right, aren't I? He hasn't been responding." Randal needs to be careful, tread softly here, with this necromant of ageless power. "This poison's meant for taking gods and demons to their final rest. It's far too much for a pesky youth, a half-ling: unless he *is not* just that, and we've been underestimating him."

Ischade says, "Randal, you've been away a long time. Things are different here now, attenuated. I hunt. I get along. But all your high-flown sorceries may not avail you here."

"This isn't sorcery." *Please, listen to me. This isn't about your power, or mine, or who's stronger, or who's right and who's wrong.* "It's not magic. It's not heavenly, or even hell-ish. It's…from a different rulebook. From the time when the world was young and only Unbegottens roamed, part of an arsenal that was buried at the bottom of the sea at the edge of time before men wore clothes." *It's not supposed to be here.*

"We have more darts of that poison." The little tube, silvery and unprepossessing, lies between them on Ischade's tablecloth, atop the paisley silk. "Perhaps a second dose for this Shamshi…"

*Don't use it again. Don't anyone use it again.* "Before we use a second dart, we need to make sure we know what we're doing. This isn't just a boy, anymore – if he ever was one. Not if he has got that poison in his system and hasn't died. Something wants him dead, or *alive,* more than we do."

"I never thought I would see a Hazard cower like a child," Ischade says wonderingly, staring past Randal, farther away than eternity.

"Please *don't* call him, Ischade, until we know just how to deal with him and what we want to do with him, if we do catch him. Niko's involved, and Tempus, and all the Stepsons, and you and I."

"The Stepsons sentenced him to death. I gave my word to the Riddler to call this wizard boy, to help catch him. But should we wait, he may die on his own – assuming you are correct. *If* the young Theban is right, and his dart hit Shamshi, and the poison's really in him," Ischade hisses.

"Even a scratch should kill him. It…should have done it, by now. Or he's already dead, or dying a different death: what he *once was* might be dead, or dying, and something else is taking its place. Or has done. Something mere mages ought not to fight. No wonder the Stepsons couldn't find him."

Ischade says sensibly, "I can feel him. Therefore he's still alive. He knows who he is, or was, or will be. Or so I think. I am not so afraid of this…" She reaches out and pokes the tube. It rolls a little, and then comes to rest on its flat side, where the darts are stored.

Then she looks up, past him, over his shoulder at the door. "Jihan comes."

The door opens without a touch. The gate, beyond, does the same. And down the walk comes the Froth Daughter, alone, her scale armor shining in the sun. And the gate and the door close after Jihan, just the same way, with no human touch. Inside the little house, even Jihan's glowing person seems to darken, her glimmer to fade away.

Ischade is not a power to call up lightly or something easy to call back once it has been unleashed. The hunting fever is in those black eyes. Quarry does not elude Ischade.

It cannot happen. It never has. It never does. It must not.

Randal's skills are not akin to the necromant's. He's refused every chance to make his power great like hers: he protects his soul; hers is long gone where she can barely glimpse it, like a kite on a long string, and she has no more control. She kills to eat; she kills to live; she is far too potent for a measly thaumaturge such as Randal to challenge. Nevertheless, here he is, embroiled with this power once again.

Ironically, they never should have involved the witch at all. The weapon on her table can destroy even an ancient force such as Ischade with a touch or a scratch. This dart tube is stronger than the will of heaven or hell. It needs to go away, where no man or mage or god can find it.

So he says, "Jihan, we are so glad you're here. We need your help. No one else can do what's needed."

Jihan straddles a chair like a soldier, muscular arms gleaming, elbows wide upon the table. Her change-color eyes spear him: "Finally, someone realizes. So, Hazard, what may I do for you today?" Her oval face is full of childlike hubris. Nevertheless, she is a power who is up to this test, and neither he nor Ischade can say the same.

"Look at this," Randal says, and taps the little tube.

Jihan's copper brows knit. She says, "How did *this* get here? Does the Riddler know?"

Ischade says, "Apparently, it's been here a decade. Randal left it in the safekeeping of a whore, in case the Stepsons returned. And why was that, Randal?"

"At the time," he said, feeling a flush crawl up his neck, "there was a wizard war, if you remember. It came to light as the last Stepsons were pulling out. I left it in the hands of the girl who was chosen to find it."

"Can we risk giving it back to the whore? It chose her, after all," Jihan asked.

Randal realized that Jihan needed no tutorial. "I don't think so."

She knew just what she was looking at, this weapon to bring down gods and powers ungodly. "It's a tool of greater dooms, a plaything of the Fates," Jihan said to Randal. "And some, if not all, of this mischief, from Fates is surely sprung. I saw three of them at the Theban ceremony on the beach…the sort that don't belong here…the sort that interfere."

"Nevertheless," said Ischade with a sigh, "we have this current problem…"

"I will take it to my father's ocean and bury it so deeply no harm can ever come from it again, in the volcanoes on the very bottom of the deepest trench in the sea at the edge of time."

"Good plan," Randal said. "Excellent idea," Ischade agreed.

"But not yet," said Jihan. "At our peril, we must act. Slowly. Carefully. We have so much at stake. No one can risk angering the Fates."

"Some can. Some do," Ischade said under her breath, but no one answered.

And they sat that way in silence a long time, until Ischade continued, "But, Jihan, can we give it into your care, now? Will you take it?"

Randal could have kissed the necromant – for a moment. He wanted this thing as far away from him as it could get. He wished fervently he'd never left it with the whore. But she was the one to whom it came, and it had been the right decision at the time.

*This is a different time.*

The Froth Daughter sighed, "I will take it. The Riddler will not be pleased, however. You know he hates arcane interference in the lives of men. You two must say to him what you have said to me."

"For fury's sake," Ischade muttered and got up, and went out through a door that banged open, and a gate that did the same, in a rush of pique that Randal could feel, as if a lyre were popping strings. Since the door stayed open, they could see outside. Up rode Straton at a gallop, leaning low over his bay horse's neck. And half falling, half sliding off.

Randal saw the necromant step back, then forward, and take the Stepson in her arms. He couldn't see the damage from here, but Randal could tell Strat was in trouble from the way Ischade folded around him like black salvation.

Jihan was staring. Randal said, "This is not for us to see, Jihan. We have bigger problems."

"But Straton is not supposed to be here…."

"Neither is this," Randal reminded her, nudging the tube with his fingernail, redirecting her attention to the business at hand.

And with Ischade outside, out of earshot, Jihan said very softly, "Randal. I'm not as sure as I pretended, what to do. You will help me?"

*With what? Interfering with Fates? No.* "With protecting the Sacred Band? As best I can."

What Randal could do, and Ischade could do, and Jihan could do, might not be good enough to forestall the kind of havoc those darts wrought – always wreak – when in the hands of men or gods. But Randal had taken the Sacred Band oath.

He looked out the door again, at Ischade with Straton in her arms, holding the fighter, doing what she could to help him with no thought to who should be where, or what this one or that one would say or think. That's what love is. And always will be. As it was with Ischade and Straton, so it would be with Randal, who loved the Stepsons, and one particular Stepson, so much.

Love would help him find a way through this, for all of them.

*Must. Or the Fates will have their day. And might have it, anyway.*

*

Critias rides as fast as a man can go through Ratfall, asking here and there and everywhere for Straton. He alerts every man he's got on the streets. He even sends a runner to Walegrin to ask about unidentified bodies turning up. The sun sets and he's got one place left to look. He must find his partner: his pairbond is on the line.

Crit has the big dun horse tonight: seasoned, powerful – the right tool for this job. A light wind blows; no rain; a trail of stars is bright above. They make good time, searching. Dun horse blowing; sides heaving; hooves loud on cobbles, soft on dirt. Sanctuary is all turns and twists, like his life. At high moon, he heads the dun toward the bridge. He needs to know. *If Strat is there with the witch, what will I do?* This one thing, above all, Crit fears.

Iron-shod hooves ring on boards. Across the White Foal Bridge and down the little cart-track he trots the dun. The horse is breathing hard; he's worked it to a lather. If he were less worried, he'd be ashamed of sweating up his mount.

And now he sees it – just what he doesn't want to see: Strat's ghost horse, tied to her little iron fence, beside the gate. He almost turns and rides away. But the dun needs a rest, needs to catch its wind. Crit might as well be back in Chaeronea: his heart beats fast, his tongue feels frozen.

Ischade and Straton, alone together: recipe for disaster. Last time. This time. Every time.

Crit needs to make an end to this witchery somehow. Here. Tonight.

So he halts the dun at the witch's gate, dismounts; loosens its cinch and feels its sweaty belly, its heaving sides. He thinks to walk the horse in circles, cool it out. But that would be just putting off the inevitable.

Her gate won't open for him. *That's fine.* He vaults the gate, one-handed: it's only as high as his hip.

Gripping his shortsword's pommel, he walks up to her door, incensed, embarrassed. Strat is not his son, his brother. Straton is a grown man, Crit's age. But pairbond requires loyalty with no exceptions: you do your best for your partner. Sometimes, you do better than your best. Letting Straton slide into Ischade's corrosive embrace doesn't fit.

He takes out his belt-knife and pounds with its butt on the door. Once. Twice. Three times. Will she let him in?

He finds he's holding his breath. When the door opens, the necromant is standing there, not even cowled. He can't see beyond her, into the little house.

*What a pretty face.* He's never seen it out of shadow.

"Yes, Critias?"

"Straton. Is he here? There was a problem in town."

"Yes, he's here. Come inside. All your friends are here. Perhaps we'll invite a few more Stepsons, have a little party..."

She sweeps around, floats back inside, leaving him to follow. Within, this house is much bigger than he'd thought. He's never gotten this far into her sanctum before. It's a riot of color, fabric and bauble. He follows her, and now here's Strat, but not alone: Randal, the mage, is here; and Jihan, the Riddler's talisman, sitting at the witch's table with Strat. Straton has bloodstains on his mantle near a tear at the left collarbone, but no visible wound (not even a scratch) after a confrontation in the street that sent Lysis and Arton running for their mothers.

Crit is so relieved he almost staggers; then he's livid. He needs to grab Straton's reins. But this is not the time.

Strat gets up, a wry look on his face, and comes to meet him. Straton and Ischade pass in the narrow doorway between rooms. Strat leans on the doorframe between her front room and the next: "Did the boys get back to you all right, Fox?" His face says, *Don't make a fuss.*

What can Crit say? Strat's not streaming blood from that street fight over the ghost horse's manners. All his limbs are intact. Except for the ripped wool of his chlamys and the bloodstains, there's not a mark on him: not with *her* here to spellbind everything to her taste and everybody to her will... "Those young fighters were pretty spooked. Are you hurt?"

"I'm fine, Crit. I skinned my knuckles." A dry smirk flashes. Strat shows Crit his fist. "We were just talking, here." Straton motions vaguely toward the others. Jihan and Randal stare their way.

"Arton and Kouras said you ran into trouble. I was worried."

"Just a little show-and-tell in Ratfall. More than boys could handle. My horse and I did fine. Nothing serious."

*Nothing serious? The ghost horse killed a man, or close to it.*

"What's going on? What's the meeting?" *Why wasn't I invited?*

"Come sit down and you'll find out. But you won't like it."

He should count his blessings: his partner is in one piece, not wounded, not being sucked dry of heart and soul and sense by the necromant. Whatever's going on here, Crit presumes to think, it's better than what he expected to find: partner and witch in some unholy sex-fest. But that doesn't turn out to be the case.

"So these Fates are in the mix. So what? Why does that mean we can't do anything?" Critias asks incredulously, when they've explained. "Can't kill Sham? Not because he won't die, but because some superstition says we'd better not interfere? *I'm* not trying to explain *that* to the commander by myself."

"We can still kill him," Straton assures him, canting his chair up on its back legs as if he lives here.

"With different tactics, a new approach. It'll be harder than wc thought, that's all," Randal adds.

"How does knowing about this tube make anything harder than it was before?" Crit says, exasperated.

"It may already have done everything it's going to do," says Jihan, eyes pinwheeling. "It won't do anything on its own. It's *who* does what *with* it, not what *it* does."

That starts a free for all, about how and when and who, and should and can and can't, which makes Crit's head spin.

Finally he says, "I've got to take this to the Riddler. It's above my rank to decide."

Silence drops over them like a hawk plummeting from the clouds to strike a rabbit: immediate and terminal.

They take stock of one another, these more-than-mortal helpers of the Sacred Band, and then of him and Strat.

"You don't understand," says Ischade, damning Crit succinctly.

"I think I do, Witch. However you plan to help us, all you wiser beings, it is and will be the Sacred Band's mission. We do the fighting and we do the bleeding. If you're wrong, we'll do the dying." Tone too cynical, retort too sharp, but Crit can't help himself. "And it's the Riddler's to say, whether any of our tactics or procedures change because of some old dart tube that washed up on the Downwind beach a decade ago. If it's so damned special, with all these attributes, why hasn't it done anything until now?"

He reaches out and takes the weapon in his hand. It's cool to the touch, as metal will be; well made; nothing extraordinary: a tube with a slide compartment.

The unearthly powers assembled here draw back like parents watching a toddler grab a loaded crossbow. He lets it drop onto the tabletop. It thumps like metal does. They relax.

Randal said, "Jihan's holding onto it, for now. She'll take it to the Riddler."

"Fine," Crit agreed. "*We'll* take it. Let's go. Strat, Jihan – now."

There was a pause as everyone considered.

"It's the middle of the night," Ischade observed.

*"He* doesn't sleep. And I think he's going to *love* this one, when he hears it," said Crit.

They hesitated.

Crit's pulse pounded. He was the Riddler's executive officer, the senior Stepson present. He'd given an order, one that Straton, if not Jihan, should obey, in front of the witch.

Strat shrugged. His chair's legs hit the floor. He rose and came over to Crit. "Shall we?"

That was good enough, all Crit had really wanted: to get his partner out of here. He expelled a breath he must have been holding for ages.

Jihan accompanied them to the threshold and said, "I'll meet you at Tempus's quarters. Go straight there." In her hand, she held the metal tube, which couldn't possibly be the force multiplier of doom that everyone thought.

Could it?

Then Strat and Crit walked out the door, which opened and closed without a touch or a sound, into the moonlit night. When they reached their horses, Ischade was somehow there first: black eyes and black cowl in the moonlight; faint keening of wind at her back.

"Straton," Ischade asked conspiratorially, "who is in the Mageguild now?"

"The old Mageguild? On the Street of Arcana? Now? I don't know. Crit? It's abandoned, isn't it?"

Crit said, "Ah…I can't say. As far as I know, it's derelict."

The cowl seemed to flicker: no face beneath the hood, just a slash of mouth and those infernal eyes like an owl's eyes in the dark. "Not tonight, it isn't."

Before Crit could ask the infuriating witch if that was a hint, or what she meant, she was gone in a flutter of wings and a *pop* that made your ears ring. Behind, the house was dark, empty, as if no one had been there in years. The little gate swung askew on its hinges, back and forth, creaking every time it moved.

So, just to be thorough, they went by the old Mageguild on their way back to the barracks. It was deserted, locked up tight.

*

"Life is short. Death is simple. Dreams are complex," says Aškelon, stepping over bodies in Shamshi's rest-place, corpses of men slain at Chaeronea.

And the wizard boy beside him says, "Show me."

"Nightmares are the stuff of legend," says the lord of dream and shadow.

And the Bandaran youth says, "Teach me."

"Meridian is my realm," says the regent of the seventh sphere, as the archipelago's main island coalesces out of a pastel sea, its crystal quays manifesting beneath their feet.

And the former Stepson says, "Do you need a son, an heir?"

"Could be," says the entelechy of dream.

## *Chapter 33: Dreams of Immortality*

She hadn't come to him since the night he and Tempus had made their first circuit of the barracks together. Niko and his commander made that same circuit the next day, in the golden air of summer; Tempus let him drive the chariot. He'd worked his body all that day, getting ready for this morning, when the Riddler had promised him he could ride. His thighs ached from the back of his knees up, blending their complaints with the soreness of his flanks and of his back.

*What if she never comes to me again?*

He had practiced swordplay with Sync yesterday, and wrestled with Straton hand to hand when Strat came out from town, unhappy about something and unbeatable because of it. He'd run three laps around the barracks, making his lungs recall their job.

His commander watched him too much. Stayed at the training field too much. Those hooded eyes took his measure and slid away, or caught his and shocked him, probing deep, when he missed a parry or went to his knees in the dirt or was knocked off his feet by Strat.

*What if the Riddler has driven her away somehow?*

All last night, Tempus worked at his table in the little room they shared, lit by a single candle. Now the dawn was breaking through the clouds. Somewhere, thunder rumbled: for the first time in many days, it was going to rain. And the Riddler still sat there, working, when Niko said, "I'll get the horses ready. My mare and your big Trôs stud." The horse Abarsis had given Tempus was his favorite.

"Do that," his commander said. "We'll get it done before the rain." Thunder grumbled. Outside, the sunrise had a lurid cast: towering cloudbanks, nearly purple; crimson rays and golden spears slicing through. Rain from those clouds would pour when it came. Before nightfall, the thunder promised.

They hadn't talked about the goddess since the day on the hill. He didn't want to talk about it. She'd come to him after Tempus left for town and when she'd gone he felt like a boy who'd skulked off into the woods with his first love and later fears to be discovered.

He took rain gear down with him to the stables, a waxed mantle and his most duty-worn leathers, oldest swordbelt; with all of Tempus's gear, just in case the heavens opened up while they were riding.

Doing simple things, too long denied, would help him regain his equilibrium. He couldn't wait to feel his mare between his legs. He took extra care with the horses: grooming, bitting, picking pebbles from hooves and combing burrs from manes. Stableboys came and he chased them away. This was his to do: the pleasures of life shouldn't be handed off to others.

But Tempus hadn't arrived by the time both mounts were gleaming, saddled and bridled and stomping in their stalls. Something had happened to delay him. He unbridled both, unsaddled them and went up to the loft to get the horses some hay to munch while they waited.

She finds him there, amid the sweet hay and the straw.

He feels her before he sees her. Though he's fully dressed, it's as if her hair slides along his back. He's on his knees in the hay. He looks behind him. She's standing over him, so tall, so perfect in every curve and line.

"Niko," she says, and the hayloft smells like meadow, sweeter than it's ever been.

He doesn't know what to say to her. What does he call her? He says, "You could have told me." Does she shimmer in this light? He sits back on his haunches.

She kneels down too, tossing her head. "It makes no difference. Why should it?" She reaches out to him, just a light touch of her finger on his cheek, on his mouth. He kisses her fingertips. Her hand runs down his neck, to his chest, to his hips, and up again. She pushes him backward with one finger on his chest. And he's helpless, weak as a newborn foal, vanquished and surmounted in the hay.

Too much panoply; too much gear. "Let me see you," she says. "My work; your body." She won't touch his armor or his loinguard. He doesn't know how he knows, but he knows she won't. He does it while her eyes hold his, the whole time: he strips naked in the straw before her, his body out of hand, making suggestions inappropriate to a goddess. "Turn over, on your stomach."

Her honey-colored hair sweeps across his back, his flanks, and those cool hands soothe every aching muscle.

He says, "I want to look at you."

She says, "Is that all you want?" He rolls onto his back and those eyes take his breath away – again. Her green dress is soft, caught with two pins at her shoulders; linen draping, then not: there's nothing between them. He can't hold back.

On his knees, then on his feet. He puts his hands around that waist and lifts, as if he were lifting his dancing girl on the beach. He hasn't been strong enough to be so bold since then.

She wraps limber legs around his waist and he lowers her, so slowly. And catches her. She's enflaming every inch of him, wherever their skin meets. Long thighs, slipping over him; long legs, locked around his hips. He looks up. Their lips are searching. He's lost again and again, whenever their mouths meet, lost in amber eyes and hair like summer.

Her arms are around his neck. She catches his lower lip in white teeth when he tries to speak. She's light as a feather. Limbs entwining. She sets him afire wherever their bodies meet. Perfect flesh touches his chest, his waist, his hips.

He tries again: "This can't go… We can't keep… I don't know what…."

"Of course it can. Of course we will. Of course you do. Lie back down."

He barely has enough control to do as he's bid. But he does it: long legs unwinding. He can't help himself – doesn't want to try: he makes an abject and complete surrender. Whatever else this may be, his body knows what love is when it wraps around him.

He must be very still now. He knows the rules. She lies atop him, slips along him.

The heat of her makes him dizzy. He lives forever in those sky-wide eyes; in that smile; in that meadow of silken hair. She's the wind on his face; the softest grass, caressing him, his neck and his chest. Puffs of breath make him shiver – here, there, everywhere. She's so soft, so strong; so gentle, so insistent; so abandoned, so joyous. She enfolds him.

Then it's over. She stops. She sits up.

He reaches out and takes a lock of hair in his fingers, not pulling, just wanting to hold on. He's never feared more in the heat of battle that a wrong move might lose the day. "Don't go. Please, stay," he says: he can't help it.

She looks around at him and says, "You'll be stronger. All you were, and more," and her eyes sparkle as if tears might be there.

"What is it?" he asks, sitting up, desperate for one more embrace. One more moment of forever…one more breath with his face buried in her neck…one more instant with that body, so sinuous and smooth, in his arms: it's all he can think about, all he's ever wanted.

But she's standing over him. That green dress, falling from her shoulders to her ankles, hugs every curve the way he wants to do. Bits of hay are stuck to its linen hem.

She looks down at him. "You may call me by my name," she says, "next time." Then she's gone in a flash, slipping like a deer through the hay and the straw and away.

Now he's naked in a hayloft, and hoping no one chances upon him. Why can't he talk to her? Why can't he make her answer his questions? Why can't he make her stay? *Get dressed; get out of here, before the stableboys come.*

He slides down the ladder using just his hands, boots tied by their laces over his shoulder.

Then he sees Crit's chestnut and Straton's bay ghost horse.

And he knows now why the Riddler didn't come.

It's uphill, just a slight incline, to the Riddler's quarters. He jogs there, testing his wind. *Better.* He's always better, once she's come and gone.

When he reaches the commander's quarters, he hears them talking. He knocks. Tempus, Jihan, Strat and Crit are all inside. One look tells him this isn't a social call.

"Life to you, Stepsons, and everlasting glory," Niko says. He hasn't seen Crit in far too long. Neither Stepson speaks. "And to you, Jihan."

"And to you, Stealth," says Jihan in that husky voice. "Riddler?"

"Let's walk up the hill," Tempus suggests, "while we talk. There's too many in here now." A voice like shale sliding, today.

Crit and Strat are looking at Niko askance. Jihan is not looking at him at all.

They file outside, Niko on his commander's right; Jihan on his left; Strat and Crit behind. "What's happened, Riddler?"

"The tube you gave to Lysis – our mage and Ischade think it's a problem. And Jihan agrees," Tempus says, not looking at him, watching where he walks. The others don't speak.

"What kind of problem?" Niko asks as quietly as he's able, with Stepsons and Thebans all around, eyeing the senior staff out for a walk in the sullen morning light.

"Wait," Tempus says. And he waits, just pacing his commander, glad he's stronger, glad he has his swordbelt. He knows that voice the way he knows his own soul. The Riddler is not happy today.

Tempus leads them to the hilltop, but not to either altar. They hunker down in a circle out near the brake. "Now," the Riddler says. "Again. Jihan first. Then Crit. For Stealth. *All* of it."

Crit looks at the grass centering their little circle. Strat stares at Niko, a distant look as if he's staring at the dead, and then away, past Jihan, toward the horizon and the building storm.

"As you wish, Riddler. Niko," Jihan says, "when the Band sewed Shamshi in that skin, something started that can't be easily undone. Or stopped. That youth has a hand on him, guiding him, a destiny that must play out. You gave an ancient weapon to Lysis, the Theban. That poison is very old, not for men to wield. Nor should a mortal be struck down with it. If Lysis is right, and this Shamshi was wounded by that dart, he will die of it or be changed by it. And if he does not die, he will be a terrible threat – to men, perhaps to gods. The whole Sacred Band has tried to catch and kill him – and failed. If he lives still, he is very angry."

Niko has to say it: "I tried to tell the commander, anyone who would listen, that there was something wrong about that one...." It sounds like an excuse. Niko had taken Sham to Bandara, long ago. "He's my problem. I helped make him. I *will* kill him. I said it before; I say it again: he's mine. I should have killed him, when I had the chance. As you say, he's angry. If he lives long enough, I'll have that chance again."

"It's not so simple," Crit says flatly. "If I understand the threat – what Jihan, Randal and Ischade are saying – it may be *only* you who *can* kill him. But you didn't fare too well against him last time, however and wherever that battle was joined. He hurt you badly. And now, with this ancient weapon, if we haven't killed him, we've made him stronger."

Niko's mouth dries up. *I won that battle, Critias, or close enough, but you can't comprehend it.* Shamshi's rest-place, so like Chaeronea, flashes before his inner sight: *Men stagger backward, impaled, moaning.*

He considers how much discord the Riddler will tolerate here today. If Crit needs to test Niko's fitness, one on one, Niko will be happy to oblige. *Now or any time.* In the face of insult, it's hard to stifle anger, betray nothing with eyes or body. He sits very still and fixes Crit with his emptiest stare.

A silence reigns, too long. The Riddler doesn't intervene, just watches, one hand on Jihan's arm.

*"Crit,"* says Strat curtly, "tell him the rest."

Crit scoffs. "I don't believe in destiny, but I'll tell you: Randal and Jihan think the boy – Shamshi – is protected by some powerful ally. And *you're not,* Stealth."

"Commander, Stepsons, Jihan...Shamshi is a Bandaran who could not master *maat*. He's inexperienced. He has weaknesses. And we have this ancient weapon…." Niko's mouth is still dry; he's cold. *Long spears, thunking into flesh.* "Ever since Chaeronea, I've been seeing that battleplain in my mind."

"So have I," Crit says reluctantly.

"And I," Strat admits, looking over his shoulder and all around at the approaching storm, rubbing his arms.

"Meaningless," Tempus growls like a bear.

"Not so, Riddler, my love," says Jihan. "When you feel that, you feel Shamshi: reaching out. Guard your minds. And I will guard the tube. It must go back to my father's ocean. If it falls into the wrong hands, then woe unto men and gods."

Niko doesn't want to hear this, or believe it. "We'll get him. I will. I'm committed. I have been, for a while. I need to get my strength back, is all. It's mine to do, before the gods."

"Not gods." Jihan slaps the ground with her hand. "Angry Fates. So different, Niko. So different…."

Lightning forks the sky in the distance, as if the gods agree; thunderheads are massing: *Here comes the storm.* The thunderclap comes rolling, finally, on a wind that whips back Jihan's hair.

"Commander…." Niko pleads for understanding, for the Riddler's wisdom. How can the best of the Stepsons be so cowed? And how can Jihan, more powerful than many gods, be so full of dire warnings?

His commander's eyes, blazing, catch his and hold, setting Niko's brain afire: He sees ranks upon ranks in that gaze, war after war, dying and crying and carnage and bloodbath that make Chaeronea seem like a child's playground.

"Commander?" he asks again, when Tempus doesn't answer. And then Niko thinks about the wound that Tempus sustained on that battleplain; and his own, so hard to heal. And he begins to feel a cold leaching into his bones. Probably from sitting too long in the morning grass, he tells himself, after being so long abed, with a storm blowing in.

Tempus looks them over, each in turn, and says at last, "This world, that neither gods nor men have made, is an ever-living fire, with portions kindling, and portions going out. We are either the portions kindling, or the portions going out. Which do you want to be, Stepsons? Jihan? We will not give up the Thebans, if that's what the Fates are angry about, and we will not give up our lives. We will meet this enemy, whether mad youth or maddened tool of destiny, and we will best it in single combat or vanquish it by other means, if the god allows."

Crit starts to speak; Strat elbows him. Neither says a word.

"And if this enemy has *help*, Tempus?" Jihan wants to know. "Help from forces stronger than you've met before? Help from destiny itself? Help who'll bring down gods, if they can…? You are not the only one who teaches lessons, Riddler."

The commander gets to his feet, estimating the inbound storm: "I've fought gods before. I'm still here. We all are. Gather the shards of your courage. Patch together what resolve you can. We'll find this thing – and kill it. Jihan, give me that dart tube."

He holds out his hand.

"Tempus, no," says Jihan. "It needs to go away."

*"I'll* decide that. Perhaps it can go away another day. If it's all you say – if it can bring down gods and destinies and even Fates – it may have a part to play in this yet."

Jihan is on her feet now, so everyone rises up. The uncanny Froth Daughter – child of wind and wave; mother of the Riddler's changeling son – meekly hands to Tempus this little tube about which too much, to Niko's mind, is being made:

*This fight coming is not a battle of weapons, but a battle of wills.*

"Please let me take it to my father's sea," she pleads with Tempus.

And the commander says, "In Enlil's good time. I'll give up no advantage out of hand, not for this battle."

Back down the hill strides the Riddler, Jihan half running after him, grabbing him by the arm. And Crit hurries to catch up. Niko won't (can't, yet) go so fast.

Straton paces him: "So, Niko? How shall we defeat this Shamshi who's too shy to come out to play with all the other boys?"

Once, Straton had been the most talented fighter in Tempus's Sacred Band. He might be, again, with Niko weakened and Strat's shoulder healed. The ethos of the Sacred Band decrees that no man fights alone, but Sham won't risk being outnumbered. Niko says, "I can take him. You or I can – one on one, man to man. If we can just lure him into the open."

"I think so, too," says Straton. And the two fighters walk down the hill together, agreed in principle: "We're not letting the Riddler take on this enemy, if Sham's as dangerous as they think," Straton growls. The two vow to practice with each other, every day from now until the foe is vanquished. "It's you or me, Niko, who'll best him."

"I know," Niko said. "According to Crit, it's mine alone to do. I go first, if the goddess allows."

"The *goddess?*"

"Slip of the tongue. I've been stuck here with Thebans too long," Niko says with his best boyish grin as a wind ruffles his hair and blows it in his eyes.

Strat says, "I need to look more closely at this goddess of yours. I hear you've been seeing her regularly," and both men laugh, relieved to find something to joke about in all of this.

"It's *maat*, for me, that will make the difference, Strat," Niko confides, as they near the Riddler's quarters. "A discipline Shamshi couldn't master."

"It's Ischade, for me, but don't tell Crit," says Straton and winks at Niko in the morning's gathering storm.

But both of them, and Critias too, have admitted they see Chaeronea in their dreams: all but Tempus have confessed to seeing it. And perhaps their commander sees it as well: Tempus is not a man to admit to weakness, even among his closest friends. Chaeronea haunts the others: that revelation chills Niko to the bone.

*

Jihan takes Tempus away to her quarters in the sulky morning light. The Froth Daughter will not be denied. She wrestles with him in words and deeds: sparring with Jihan is always his pleasure. Baiting her has always made him glad. But today, she is petulant. She is nearly as strong as he – or perhaps, after Chaeronea, just as strong.

He finally gets his knees on her shoulders and her scale armor off. "Don't bite," he advises. She bites. She kicks and scratches and throws a tantrum worthy of a hurricane. They almost wreck her quarters before they're done, and he's nearly panting.

She sees it: "See? You are not yourself. This war with destiny has debilitated you."

"You think so? Let's find out."

A long and demanding interval later, when they lay on the floor amid the ruins of her bed, she turned in the crook of his arm and said, "Riddler, I could not bear to lose you."

"If you keep destroying property and throwing tantrums, I'm going to send you back to Stormbringer, finned tail between your legs." But his heart isn't in it. She is right: he should be able to best Jihan in any wrestle, any love play, any fight. And he couldn't, today – not quite.

She slaps his stomach, hard, with her hand. "Stubborn Riddler. That partner of yours, your Niko, is in deep trouble. If not for me, then for him, let me take the tube back to the sea at the edge of time. Before it falls into the wrong hands – again. Or its darts get stuck into the wrong flesh – again. I can drop it into an abyss, down a vent where there is no sunshine, or into a volcano on the ocean floor. No meddling forces will ever bring it up again."

"Let's see, first, if we need it. Or are you so anxious to get away from me? In such a hurry to leave?" Once again he takes hold of her, and it does him good to spar with this creature, more than human, which can't be hurt by whatever strength he might bring to bear in passion or frustration or rage. The storm god likes this game, and adds his lightning and his thunder above their heads – storm horses running free on heaven's endless plain of cloud.

But when they both lie flat, sated and exhausted, she comes round to it again: "What of our son, Cyrus, if the Fates smite you and yours for your impudence? He'll be fatherless. Even now you know he's difficult to control, or you would have brought him with you."

Their son wasn't a conversation for today, or for any day but one on which a man faces his mistakes and tries to fix what's gone wrong. Such talk reminds him of how big the smallest error can become, with repercussions at first undreamed, then long lamented. Here, now, they face Shamshi, another youth gone bad – a threat that lay dormant among them till an ancient remedy went wrong. "Our son stays in Lemuria till he's grown in body and mind. And he has you, if I should shrivel away like some thistle plucked from hell's gate. Are you truly worried?" He came up on one elbow and scowled at her. "I thought you had more courage. Afraid of the Fates? Those geriatric crones? Shamshi the wizard boy? He's barely old enough to shave. What fun would life be, without worthy enemies?"

"If you love life, then having enemies may be worthwhile. But not if all you do is grieve. What about your mortal fighter, Nikodemos, that so many think so much of? Are you willing to risk him? He thinks this Shamshi is *his* foe to face."

Tempus lay back down, watching the darkening sky through her window. "He always does."

"The storm god immortalized you, and *you* are having second thoughts about this battle brewing, looking for any edge you can find. And Niko, not you, must surmount this halfling, this wizard's son, this tool of destiny. Even your Critias agrees."

"We'll see about that."

"Riddler, you can't keep him from it. You and he cheated the Fates. Can your god not help Niko, give him strength?"

Lightning ripped the sky and lit up everything in Jihan's little room. Was Enlil volunteering aid? Or just laughing?

"Niko won't ask, and won't accept. I *asked.* I knew when I needed help." So long ago, to balance off a curse…. He hoped his curse was gone. But he could never be certain. "Remember, Jihan, take care: those who love me die of it…."

*"Ha.* As arrogant as ever, Riddler. Those you love are bound to spurn you: *you* remember *that.* If any of it were true, would I be here now?"

"But I don't love you, just your body," he teased her, and she slapped at him. He grabbed her wrist. "Be careful this time, Jihan. Truth be told, I'd miss you: who else could take care of that ill-tempered Trôs mare of yours and survive?"

And they wrestled with each other once again, this time with embraces longer and more fervent because even they might not have forever.

They clung together until he remembered he had told Nikodemos to get their horses ready, hours before. Then he left her alone there in her fit of pique, that he should think riding with Niko was more important. But that was Jihan: everything her way, or no way at all.

He found Niko and Straton, slicked with sweat and dust and bits of grass, just bringing a training session to its close under a threatening indigo sky. Niko had dirt in his slate-colored hair and Straton's Rankan-blue eyes were sparkling. Niko's quick, long limbs offset Straton's greater strength and mass. If Niko had been on the muscle, the two were well enough matched, rolling around in the grass in just their loinguards: despite Strat's reach, Niko was never quite where Straton thought he was.

A few Stepsons and Thebans stood around, leaning on the fence, yelling time-honored Sacred Band advice and catcalls, and daring Niko to show them where his famous disappearing scars had been.

"Which one did you bet on, Sync?" Tempus asked as he slid in between the horse-tamer and Gorgias, the Theban whose face had been smashed once, long ago.

"Straton," said Sync, cold and analytical. "Niko's still too weak."

And it went that way, in the end, although both fighters declared the match a draw.

Just as they were coming through the gate, arms over one another's shoulders, the sky turned black; lightning smote the earth and thunder chased it. Next came the rain: first a few fat drops, then a spattering, then a torrent.

Niko stood there with Straton, both looking up at the sky and laughing in the pouring rain as it washed the sweat and dirt from them. And Tempus thought then that nothing was more worthwhile than what was growing in this whitewashed barracks, where he has come to build a force such as men or gods have never seen – a force worth reckoning with, if you were of a mind.

And something was of that mind. And something else opposed it. He should have expected that. Battle in the heavens, battle on the earth: Sanctuary.

He got his favorite Trôs, despite the rain, and Niko got his sable mare, and they rode bareback, in just loinguards, outside the barracks walls; and inside them, until the mud was too deep; then brought in the horses, dried off, dressed, and tended to their mounts. Normal men, on a normal day, doing normal things. This was what men fought for, what men died for: a chance at life, and to fight on other days – the battle of your choice, of the body, or the heart, or the soul.

Then Niko said, "Riddler, I need to tell you. She's still coming to see me." He was rubbing down his mare with a finishing cloth.

And the day wasn't normal after that.

*Go carefully with this boy, now a man, who could be so much more. Now, of all times, he must understand what is at stake. I need to help him find his way, even if it is not my way. Everything he is, and can be, hangs in the balance.*

Uneasiness overcame him. He heard a restless rustling from the god within; the fundament shifted under feet greater than his own. The very air he breathed was tainted with a strangeness he couldn't name as somewhere, something very old and very strong assumed a new proportion. All his senses sharpened, as if he were going into combat: every rustle of straw, every gnat, every mote of dust and breath of man and horse came clear. So maybe he was going into battle here, if a different kind.

"Niko," Tempus said, wishing it hadn't come to this, "if she still visits you – if you're still seeing her – ask her for help." Niko's mare was between them; her freshly bedded stall smelled sweet of horse and hay. Tempus leaned back against the stall boards. "This is a troubled time. You're vulnerable."

"And you aren't?" Niko's angular face was impassive; hazel eyes, empty; his arms hung loosely at his sides; his hands flexed, then quieted. The finishing cloth floated to the straw.

"You know I'm not vulnerable in the way that you are." Horses chewed their hay. This rhythm that bound man and horse together through so many centuries always soothed Tempus's heart (so sorely wounded but now, surely, healed). Always. But not today. "After Chaeronea, are you so certain, Riddler? I can*not* ask for any more help – not the kind you mean." Soft voice. Steady gaze. Undaunted. "Even if I were worthy, I don't want it. It's not for such as me." Resolute, with all the strength and beauty of that mystic calm.

"Why not? You want to battle more-than-human foes. How can you tell yourself you're up to it?" Tempus grabbed a brush from a box in the straw and began grooming the mare's near side all over again, watching Niko across her back.

"I have my mind, my body, my soul – my *maat*. I'm not trading any of it away for special favors. You've taught me that nothing can be had without cost. What difference, asking or receiving more than is fitting from a goddess, or from Aškelon, or from the rest?"

"When you die, will you let Abarsis come and take you to your place in heaven? Is that not more-than-mortal help? And what of me, and those who love you, once you've fled to eternal rest and left us all here to struggle on without you?"

Niko's mare gave a warning squeal: Tempus was currying her too hard. He stopped, put his elbows on her back, and caught Niko's distant eyes.

"Riddler…." Niko just shook his head, picked up the cloth, and rubbed his mare. Reserved. Watching his own hands. "I don't know…. Even if I asked, why should the goddess help me…more? She comes and goes, does as she wishes. She's a real goddess. I'm just a man. Who am I to make demands?"

They were skirting the issue, neither willing to say flatly that this struggle might be one no mortal man could win. And if so, Tempus must try his best to shield his right-side partner. But only help from a god such as Enlil – or perhaps this foreign goddess, Harmony – could truly protect Nikodemos now.

"You are a weapon of the god," Tempus said. "A weapon has a right to be properly cared for. I have died…or close to it…how often for the storm god? I don't even remember how many times. I'll fight beside you; protect you if I can and however I can. But we may need more, this time, than I can provide. If you won't ask Harmony, then ask Enlil – you are still his avatar. To fight on other days…it's worth everything."

"Not to me," said Niko, without looking up. His damp, dark hair fell around a face too carefully composed.

"Not yet," said Tempus and left his fighter alone, to think things through.

Either Niko asked, or Tempus would ask on his behalf. And the result of that, not even Tempus could foresee.

*'You, fighter, adept of mind, avatar of Enlil in name but not in soul: take care, or lose all you've won at such great cost,'* the goddess Harmony had said to Niko on the jetty. Her words kept ringing in Tempus's head.

If he asked Enlil, could he *get* help for Nikodemos? And if he could, should he? What would be the result of asking Enlil to save a fighter whose true allegiance was to *maat*, to justice, to balance? *Wanting neither too much to live nor too much to die,* said the code of the Sacred Band of Thebes, whose tutelary deity was Harmony, not Enlil. Niko, a secular adept, a child of *maat*, seemed sometimes more Theban than the Thebans. So perhaps this Harmony might be useful, after all.

He knew Niko wouldn't accept help at any price, as Tempus once did, even to live to fight on other days. And he knew just what kind of help he wanted for Niko, but it was costly, and of a rarefied kind.

## *Chapter 34: Son of the Storm God*

After the storm had passed, when the air smelled fresh and wet streets were bathed in sunlight, everyone in town heaved a sigh of relief. This bright, clear day made Sanctuary preen her feathers. On the Avenue of Temples, the best of the city gleamed. Sunrays spangled all: the finest buildings, gilded and domed; the most piously tended lawns; and the rich facades, where neglected gods held palsied sway.

Kouras was leading a mission here today. He was flushed with pride. He had two Stepsons supporting him: Arton and Lysis. They were armed and armored, full of the importance of it all. "See," Kouras said to Lysis and Arton, riding on his right, "I told you I could make the rain stop."

"Of course you can, Kouras," Lysis called back politely, over their horses' hoofbeats clopping on slippery cobbles. Lysis didn't believe, Kouras knew.

They rode three abreast up the Avenue of Temples, headed to the palace through the Gate of the Gods: Kouras on the blue roan, Lysis on a hair-trigger chestnut from Crit's string, and Arton on an old brown gelding that Sync swore was as good a warhorse as the rest. Kouras wanted to make sure that the Theban, Lysis, saw Vashanka's largest temple in all its majesty and understood the respect due to a son of Sanctuary's one true storm god.

Up to the gates of the palace they jogged. Kouras gave the guard a bi-fold of wood with wax inside that bore Critias's seal: "Three to see the high priest," Kouras said.

And they were "sirred" right through, gates closing behind them with creaks and thuds. The first time he'd come here, he'd been alone and intimidated. The next time… well, everyone knew about the slave girl Molin had tried to pass off as a goddess.

This time, a runner outdid their horses, beating them to the wide palace stairs.

Inside, the black and white marble hall was as splendid as ever. Kouras had heard altogether too much of Thebes: no place could be as grand as Lysis described, no architecture unparalleled in the whole wide world. Surely, Sanctuary's palace, hypostyle halls, and statuary, were as fine as any, anywhere.

Tight-lipped doormen kept them in the foyer, waiting for Molin to arrive. When the priest came down, he was all Kouras could have wished for: imposing brocaded robes flowing out behind him, a careworn doughy face that wrapped sharp eyes accustomed to command. The priest was followed by a small man with a balding head in oligarchs' navy and maroon raiment.

"Gyskouras," said Torchholder expansively, sweeping over to embrace Kouras as if Torch were not a warrior-priest with a war name, but just some cozening palace fop, "so lovely to see you. And…Arton isn't it? And your friend is...?"

"Lysis, the Theban," Kouras said, not waiting for Lysis to give his string of trumped-up titles.

The priest rubbed his bejeweled hands and introduced the oligarch, saying, "I've been telling Oligarch Reton, here, about your heritage, Gyskouras."

The little man darted forward to grasp Kouras's hand in his. "So good to see you, Gyskouras. Son of the storm god, Vashanka.... We're so honored. Could you ask the storm god in heaven to intercede for us in a little matter of rainfall? Not that we don't appreciate an end to the drought – of course we do, we do. It's just that this much rain isn't helpful...."

Torchholder interrupted, "Reton, this is no time for statecraft. The message said your Critias is looking for the keys to the old Mageguild? Well, Oligarch, give them to Gyskouras, if you please. These young men have things to do."

The oligarch rummaged in his robes, saying, "I know I've got them. Ah, here they are," and came up with a key ring big enough to lead an ox by the nose. The oligarch sorted through the keys. Arton stared at portraits on the wall. Lysis craned his neck at frescoes on the ceiling where naked deities cavorted. Torchholder watched Kouras with a commiserating air. The priest was watchful, like a man who has let a lion into his house to win a wager.

"Here you are," said the maroon-sleeved oligarch. "These three keys: outer gate, front doors, back doors. What do I call you, Gyskouras? Godling? Demigod?"

"Kouras," he said, "Just call me Kouras."

"He's a Stepson," Arton said, hands hooked in his belt. "Call him what he is."

"Sacred Bander," Lysis spoke simultaneously. "Just like us." "Well, not really," the priest purred. "Thank you, Oligarch.

Gyskouras wants to take his friends through the chapel. You're welcome to join us."

"Oh, yes," said the little oligarch, rubbing his pate. "I'd love to see: no one gets in there but the priests except on very special occasions. Will you make it rain on demand, Gyskouras? We've heard you do."

"You've *heard?" Priest be damned.* Unexpectedly, this wasn't fun for Kouras anymore. The walls seemed to close in on him. He couldn't wait to get out of there. He remembered Critias telling him to trust no palace priests. "I don't know what His Eminence told you, Oligarch, but Vashanka alone decides when it will rain." Arton hooted; Lysis smirked. Kouras stabbed them with black looks. His face felt hot: "Let's see the chapel then, but quickly. We have orders. Our business here is concluded. We haven't time to take any grand tour."

Not fun at all. But up the stairs and down the hall and in they went, through a different door than the shelf-wall door in Torch's library. Once inside, where the huge statue of Vashanka hulked, gilt and majestic and looking a lot like Kouras, his discomfort eased. Let them see, his unbelieving friends.

This time, as before, the statue called silently to Kouras. He walked up and looked up, straight into its abalone eyes. It seemed to look back at him: *Welcome, my son.* Its arms and legs bulged with muscle. It had an adze upon its shoulder, a jewel-encrusted sword in its right hand, and a scabbard covered with heads of slain demons on its hip.

Kouras didn't hear a word anyone said in that chamber, where sounds echoed and reechoed and the sun spilled in to halo the god's conical crown.

His breathing seemed much louder, because the god was breathing, too, inside his skull. He could almost feel the heft of the adze on his shoulder, the hilt of the shortsword in his hand.

Eventually, although it couldn't have been as long as it seemed, Arton touched him. "Kouras? Kouras? If you're not going to bring thunder and lightning, it's time for us to go."

"Thunder and lightning come at Vashanka's pleasure," he said in a voice deeper than he'd known he had, and backed away from the statue of his father, the god, all the way to the door.

He didn't notice how disappointed the oligarch was, or how irritated Torchholder was, until they were back in the foyer and the priest whispered, "You *could* play along," as he ushered them personally to the front doors, Oligarch Reton hustling behind. The oligarch bid them farewell from the bottom steps with a regal wave, slight and practiced, of the sort seen in parades.

"Let's get out of here," Lysis muttered, when their horses were brought up by men clearly glad to be rid of them, "before it *does* rain."

Muted thunder rolled, far off, as they rode out the gates, headed for the Street of Arcana, though there wasn't a cloud in the sky.

At least they had the keys to the Mageguild. All the way over there, Lysis and Arton teased Kouras unmercifully: "Oh, what do we *call* you, Son of Vashanka?" Arton quipped, mimicking the oligarch's dissipated manner.

"Godling? *Demi*god?" Lysis nearly howled. "You'd be beaten black and blue in Thebes, and staked out overnight for claims like that. In Sparta, the secret police would ambush you, violate you, skin you alive and use your skull for a drinking cup."

That silenced everyone. Being staked out overnight was too close to what had happened to Sham. They rode in silence the rest of the way to the Street of Arcana while the sun went down with a struggle and twilight stretched out her arms in triumph over the day. Old trees made a pergola above this long, straight avenue hung with vines and lined with bushes and shrubs and marsh grass.

By the time they'd reached the high iron gates, a gibbous moon was rising in the dusky vault of heaven. They took off their helmets and hung them on their saddles: the night was too hot for helmets that made it harder to see and hear.

And Lysis said, "It's getting late. We've lost the light. We only have one torch each. How are we going to search this place, the way Critias ordered?"

"We'll unlock the gates," Kouras decreed. This was *his* mission; he was in charge. "Go to the doors, try the keys: that's all we have to do. That's all Critias said. 'Get the keys and see if they work.'"

Arton said, "I don't like this." He stopped his brown gelding in the middle of the deserted, vine-hung way. There wasn't a light anywhere to be seen. If there were other houses near, the creepers and overgrowth blocked them from view.

"What do you mean, Arton… you don't *like* this?" Lysis demanded. "Is it your foresight? Do you have a portent? Guidance? A prophecy?" Lysis halted his horse too.

"I don't like it," came Arton's voice, his hawkish face turned away in the twilight. "I see…. Never mind. I don't like it. That should be enough."

"So, Lysis, you don't believe in the storm god, but you believe in seers and oracles and sibyls and all sorts of prophecy," teases Kouras, but he halts as well.

Lysis says, "I told you once, it's too late – we've lost the light."

Kouras doesn't want to go down there to unlock that gate by himself. Then he wonders why not. "I'll light my torch. You keep yours in reserve, Lysis. And yours, too, Arton…in reserve. It'll be fine."

"With a torch, Kouras, you're half-blind at night, from the light too near your face. Do you really want that torch in your left hand, on your shield arm? That's too clumsy, unless you let go of the antilabe – what Stepsons call the hand-hold – and slide your wrist through it…but you lose shield stability that way. You can't use a crossbow with a torch in your other hand, either. Plus, horses don't like fire, heat and smoke. Not helpful if you run into trouble," Lysis critiques.

Kouras ignores him, but recalls that Lysis is several years older, with more experience in the field. "When we get there, Arton will hold the torch. I'll try the lock. Lysis, you'll keep watch." Command was his only if he exercised it.

So exercise it he does, and the other two do as they are ordered.

All around, mosses and vines hang down, huge trees sway, and the high iron gate seems alive with ivy waving in a light wind. At least it's not raining. Usually, Kouras wanted it to rain. But if they had to run their horses out of here, dry footing would be best.

Arton holds Kouras's flaring torch. It blows right, then wavers, then blows right again. Lysis has his quiver and his crossbow, but slings the crossbow over his shoulder, preferring his shortsword.

Kouras forces the key into the old, verdigris-encrusted lock and turns it. The key works. They push back the gates and lead the horses through, closing both gates behind them. All three mounts are skittish: shying at shadows, ears flattened, eyes rolling.

"Who's staying with the horses?" Arton asks as they reach the front stairs. "We'll lose them if we leave them here on their own."

The horses could run only as far as the gates, Kouras thinks but doesn't say. Arton is superstitious. So is Lysis.

Together, they are twice as difficult. But there is a brooding presence about this monumental old mansion, a gloom deeper than twilight. "You stay with the horses, Arton," says Kouras.

"What do you think has them so nervous?" Lysis mutters, leading his chestnut with some difficulty. All three horses plunge and bellow.

"It's a Mageguild. Maybe they smell black magic, sorcerers, evil spells." Kouras means it as a joke, but no one laughs, here where overhanging swamp-giants creak in a soughing wind and no light shines but the moon and their single lighted torch.

Someone needs to take control of this situation or the deep menace of this mansion will be their undoing. Kouras says, "Come with me, Lysis. Arton's got the horses." He and Lysis start up the stairs.

Kouras looks back once and sees Arton, face wide-eyed, struggling to plant the torch in the dirt while holding all three mounts. Lysis, not Arton, is talented with horses. Kouras knows that, but he forgot to consider it when he issued his orders. He should have left Lysis the Theban with the horses, and brought Arton the seer with him. But Lysis had more combat experience, and those weren't the orders Kouras gave, and it's too late to change his mind.

The double doors are decorated with lions holding rings in their teeth and lumpy, misshapen demons of neglected brass.

Kouras feels around for the keyhole. Finding it, he tries all three keys in the lock. The last one turns. The mechanism clicks.

From somewhere, a gong or a huge bell tolls twice. It's so loud Kouras can't tell where it's coming from. It sounds again. And again. The entire house seems to shiver and settle. Kouras grips the ring in the right-hand lion's mouth. The door opens inward, pulling him off-balance.

He stumbles forward, across the threshold, into the dark. And now he's all alone.

Something inside screeches like an angry owl. He nearly falls to his knees inside the partly open door. Something runs away: he hears footsteps, scrambling. Then a grating sound sets his teeth on edge.

The whole mansion flares alight, as if there's a grand event inside, which would require a thousand candles and accommodate a hundred guests. Music wafts toward the door, and fragrances of food and drink and women and more.

He staggers back a step.

A man is standing there, wearing a scowl. He's large and severe, with salt and pepper hair, a pale complexion. Everything in the mansion except this man is undefined, wavy, insubstantial.

Kouras says, "I'm sorry…to intrude. We were just… checking up. We heard there'd been a disturbance out this way and we were sent to investigate."

"To investigate," repeats the man. "A disturbance? And you'd know one, if you saw one? Or would that disturbance be you? Who are you? Why are you breaking into my house?" asks this man whose eyebrows are fierce and whose profile is haughty. He resembles a temple carving more than a man, but one of inestimable antiquity.

Blink. Look again: this man's no older than the Riddler. "And why," continues the man severely, "do *you* have a key to this door? Surely, there's been some terrible mistake. Go back to your master, familiar, and tell him if he wants to see me, come in person." Gray eyes bore into him. This man has one hand on an ornate sword in a scabbard at his hip.

"We're from the Sacred Band of Stepsons, sir. Dispatched to investigate," Kouras blusters. "We thought this place was empty: that's what the palace said. That's what the oligarch who had the keys said. We always have keys, sir, to empty dwellings of…value." An utter fabrication, a desperate lie.

"Well, this dwelling isn't empty. And no one should have keys but me. So give me the ones you have there."

Kouras couldn't think. Those gray eyes impaled him, then impelled him. He had to give the man his keys. It was clearly his duty to drop the two keys to this house into that outstretched white palm.

For a moment Kouras exists alone in a bubble with just that palm and those keys – no other sounds, no other sights or smells or signs of life can reach him. He drops the two keys into the man's waiting hand.

Some spell is broken. Kouras can move again. He's alone, in total darkness.

He scrambles backward, bumping his way out of the foyer, across the threshold, out of the door, heart pounding. He turns and bolts down the front steps, desperate to get away from the man in the house. Something in his head is growling and hissing. He ignores it.

Now he's face to face with Lysis, spread-legged, staring at him across a sighted crossbow.

"Where were you, Lysis? You were supposed to be with me."

"I *was* with you. But when it looked like something pulled you inside that right-hand door, I came back out here. Somebody has to be left alive to report what happened."

"Very funny. Go back up there and pull that door shut. We've got to check around back before we leave."

"Do it yourself," Lysis said. Beyond him, Arton was still struggling with three jumpy horses, milling and casting reproving, wild-eyed looks at the three young Stepsons. "I'm not going around the back of this place. You stuck your head in. There wasn't anything there."

So Lysis hadn't seen the lights flare in the mansion. Somehow, Kouras wasn't surprised. "Let's get out of here." He chose not to make an issue of Lysis's refusal to follow his orders: it wouldn't do any good. Kouras looked all around.

"When we tell them about this, Critias will send a bigger team back. Probably in the morning," warned the Theban.

Lysis was correct. When Critias investigated this, Kouras daren't be found wanting. Kouras gritted his teeth and, marshalling his courage, ran up the front steps again and pulled shut the door. Something brushed his hand. He yelped. *Long spears, thunking into flesh. Man staggers backward, impaled, screaming.*

They threw themselves on their horses, barged through those gates, and locked them with their remaining key before Kouras relaxed. Then, at his order, they set off at a jog, turning left at the corner onto Runeway, headed toward Governor's Walk and safety.

*Whoosh. Whoosh.*

Throwing stars came out of nowhere. One lodged high in Kouras's right arm. It burned like hellfire. He yelled, "Run," when he should have yelled "Cover," and kicked his horse. Then another star struck his cuirass over his heart, penetrating the laminated linen between bronze bosses with a force he didn't think a star could have. Yet he felt no pain.

Kouras never remembered the rest of the gallop through Sanctuary's moonlit streets to the Shambles station, as he never remembered realizing that his neck had been grazed by a third star. Or that Lysis and Arton had also been hit.

The worst casualties of the evening were Kouras's reputation, and his pride: Lysis and Arton had seen him flee from that Mageguild door and the hidden attacker like a scared little boy.

Critias looked at him skeptically when Kouras explained what had happened to two of the three keys. "Give me the third key, Kouras." When Kouras held it out, Crit took the remaining key to the outer gate: "I'll have to follow up on this, you realize, Stepson. A man, you say? In the Mageguild mansion? And the palace didn't know the house was occupied?"

At least the Bandaran throwing stars that wounded him, and Lysis and Arton, didn't seem to be poisoned. Though these injuries might pulse and burn and need to be cauterized and dressed, none were bad enough to keep them bedridden, Strat decided, once the boys had stripped to the waist and most of the blood was washed away.

Arton had his wounds tended first. Then it was Kouras's turn. "This will sting," Straton warned, slapping him companionably on the back when Kouras sat on the corner of the room's wooden table. "Get ready." Then the big man pulled the throwing star out of Kouras's pulsing right biceps and held a heated blade against his three wounds, one by one: first his neck, then his arm, and then even cauterizing the shallow wound on Kouras's chest where one star had penetrated his cuirass. Pain flared. Kouras nearly cried out, but managed to keep silent in front of the other youths as Straton applied dressing and bandage with surprisingly gentle fingers. Kouras's wounds hurt more after Straton tended them than before. The smell of burning flesh and bacon grease caught in his nose and made his eyes tear.

The throwing stars gave Critias and Straton pause. Crit wordlessly examined the stars Straton took from Kouras and Arton before tossing the weapons onto the table. Kouras thought he knew where throwing stars like these came from – who had them, and who didn't.

"The stars are Bandaran, like the ones we use," Straton confirmed, wiping blood and bits of flesh off the next throwing star he unceremoniously pulled from Lysis's arm with tongs. "You Stepsons are lucky. Maybe too lucky. These stars were thrown with skill, in a situation with a high degree of difficulty: multiple targets, moving in the night. Three of you, each wounded but not seriously, in nearly the same places. Throwing stars, but not poisoned. Your playmate's telling us he could have killed you if he chose."

Lysis, who'd had a throwing star embedded in his cuirass as well as one in his arm, was pressing a cloth to the bloody slice on his neck where a star had kissed him and sped on; blood ran down his right arm where Strat had pulled out another.

"Come on, fighter, let's get this bleeding stopped," Strat said. "Sit." Strat patted the table, where he expected Lysis to sit, and took his blade back to the hearth to heat it more. Handsome, golden Lysis blanched.

"At least he took the bait," Critias said with a contented sigh, brushing his thin nose with his knuckles. "We know he's still out there."

"He wants us to know, Crit," Straton said, poking the blade in the flames. "He's playing with us. Or *they* are. He's got a friend or two, looks like. It makes me irritable when people come around asking for trouble and I don't have any ready for them. Now I'll have to go find them and deliver some." He came toward Lysis. "Better grab something, Stepson," he advised, just before he firmly pressed the blade against the Theban's neck. Lysis, his fingers curled around the table where he sat, grunted angrily as his flesh sizzled.

"Who's 'he?'" aquiline Arton wanted to know, glancing from Critias to Straton. His wounds already tended, Arton was struggling back into his blood-stained gear.

"Who's *'he?'* Shamshi, you dolt," said Kouras.

"Who's 'they?'" Lysis asked. "And what's this about 'bait?'"

Nobody answered.

Critias and Straton just walked out of the room, side by side, heads together, talking very low.

## *Chapter 35: God and Goddess, Oath and Honor*

"If, as you teach, the universe has no beginning and no end, why should we?"

"We shouldn't; we needn't."

"How can I become like you?"

"You can't. You must become like yourself."

"My enemies will hunt me down and kill me."

"Only if you let them."

"I don't have time to become anything."

"Here, time has no meaning."

"I need help now."

"You have my help, I swear it."

"Against all of them? Just us two? I'm still so sick, weak."

"You get what you expect. Expect to heal. Expect victory."

The wizard boy said nothing more, thinking over everything that Aškelon had told him.

*

Randal circled over the Mageguild on the wings of an eagle. Soaring on updrafts, swooping on downdrafts. Sad to see this once mighty citadel brought low. He'd fought here, taught here. Even become First Hazard here, long time gone.

Tonight it is a husk of its former glory. Randal could recall so many days: tented clouds, pink and lit from within, arching over feasts and fêtes held on the lawn with luminaries from plane and time immemorial in attendance; Tempus, riding his Trôs up the stairs when the First Hazard here had been a fool among fools; and those foolish sorcerers playing tug of war here, nearly destroying house and home with their hubris and their paltry skills.

Down he circled, and down, and down. He'd promised Crit he'd do this. He'd gone to Ischade, to make sure someone would know if he were felled here. He could hear her, feel her, this necromant high above him, on her own black wings: watching, waiting. She is adamant that she will not intervene. Unless....

Unless something catastrophic happens. Unless Randal himself is in deathly peril. Then she will. She *will. Ischade will.* She's promised. She's deadly, without remorse or compunction, indefatigable on the hunt. And no lesser can help him, if this Mageguild is the trap it seems. If what the storm god's son saw is what Critias thinks; and what Straton thinks; and what Randal himself thinks: Aškelon.

If Aškelon, lord of dream and shadow, regent of the seventh sphere, has come back to Sanctuary for a stay at the Mageguild...then what? What will avail them, this Sacred Band of mortal fighters? Brave beyond measure, risking everything. What can save them, if the entelechy of dream takes a hand?

No one had asked the Riddler or Niko if Randal should do what he does tonight. He knows Strat and Critias well enough to be sure of that: these two labor to protect their commander and Nikodemos, both wounded by ineluctable forces no simple fighter understands. But Randal has a glimmer. And what he sees, he fears: the dream lord.

The only way to face a problem is straight on, so the Stepsons had taught him. Tempus lived that maxim. Niko followed in his commander's footsteps. And Randal, too, must always find the strength that courage needs. Crit had asked him, never looking Randal in the face, to do this for Nikodemos: get two keys out of the Mageguild that three boys have lost here. Simple. Go in and get the keys. And live to bring them out again.

There are too many heroes in the Sacred Band these days, all trying to save one another…after whatever happened on the Chaeronean battleplain.

Randal didn't argue that keys were meaningless to Aškelon, regent of the seventh sphere, who could twist eternity to his will and make reality itself a different shape. Or to angry Fates, if any such roamed here.

But Critias asked, and Randal must rise to the occasion – to the challenge. He belonged to Tempus's Sacred Band, body and soul. His oath to his former left-side leader, Nikodemos; to Tempus; to the Stepsons, was on the line.

So down he swept, a great black eagle of a man, decided, wings fighting air. Updraft rushing by his keen eagle's ears. Wings slowing his descent. Making order out of chaos as the wind skirled and he dropped like a stone from heaven.

Crit had sent a contingent here and they'd broken out some windows with their crossbows, got in the gate but couldn't breach the mansion's wards.

Randal will – or die trying.

To the death, with honor. For his one-time partner, Nikodemos, who wouldn't even speak with him, or meet with him. Because the Stepsons asked it. Because the Sacred Band was the best that a man could do. Try your damnedest in the face of everything. Never falter in your loyalty or betray your oath. Live and die, shoulder to shoulder, back to back. For the honor of serving by your partner's side. For the glory of dying by your partner's side. Honor and glory meant everything to these men. And whatever else Randal might be, he was a man. And one of them. And bound to them, howsoever long his life should last.

And proud to be so.

Ischade had said to him, standing by her little gate, "You don't owe them this. No mage owes any man this: your life? Face Aškelon? When you're bound to fail? Can't possibly prevail? For what?"

"For Niko," Randal had said. "For my left-side leader. And for myself."

"Ah," had said the necromant, "I see." Just before she and Randal took wing, finally Ischade had understood. Between her and Straton was a bond, perhaps different – witch and man – but still one that neither time nor life nor death (so far), could break. "But how long has it been since Niko's called you partner? How long since you fought on his right? Lives are coming apart now, Randal; empires falling away. Foul days, darker ages, bleaker times approach. Death is in the air. And intolerance, and venality. Good for me. Bad for you. Save yourself. This is no place for a white magician – not in Sanctuary. Go back to your aerie of Lemuria, out of jeopardy, safe from time. The Sacred Band will never accept you. They never have. *He* never has."

"He does. He loves me, in his way. And I am the better for it. My oath is binding. My loyalty, beyond question," he says those ritual words to her, knowing she will never comprehend, with her black wings beating, bird head cocked. Ischade lives to eat. Randal lives for love – not a love of flesh, but a love of spirit, of humanity, of a future never quite here but always on its way. So different. Too different. If not for Straton, no one ever could have reached the witch, let alone claimed her aid, secured her help or depended on it. Straton was the bridge from her lonely world to the world of men who were not cattle, not fodder, who had value enough as they lived and breathed.

The wind roars now, in his head. Down and down he streaks, going where he has promised Critias he can go….

Into the Mageguild, through one broken window he flies. Randal's feathered wingtip skims razor-sharp slivers. Crossbow bolts have shattered these windows to make an entrance, a path for Randal: the handiwork of Crit's archers lies all around. Carefully, so carefully, avoiding so much sharp and deadly glass, Randal soars, and flaps only when he must.

He glides his eagle's body as quietly as he can…. All these crossbow bolts were strewn here because of him and him alone; so he could get in and out: the Sacred Band's bowmen, taking care of one of their own – they had prepared his way, and his escape route. Escape might be his only salvation, in this place that once he loved, now languishing under an inimical hand.

And if he couldn't get out again, on his own, now that he was in? If Shamshi, the fearsome youth with wizard's blood, or even Aškelon himself, reached out to destroy him, took him prisoner, or worse? Then the Sacred Band would come to find him, lend its strength. Critias and he had agreed.

Below him, his eagle eyes glimpse what he's come to find.

He swoops closer. Now here they are: the prizes…two keys, lying on a dusty floor. His eagle form wants to grab them. Two keys, lying forgotten, discarded on wooden boards? Or a lure? Are these keys a trap in plain view for a foolish mage who thinks to flout (if rumor is truth) the very entelechy of dreams? Or worse, angry Fates?

He spreads his wings and guides his descent. Arches his back. Stands up tall upon the air, flapping hard, feet out before him, claws ready. His eyes are so good when he is eagle. He screams in joy. He can't help it. It feels grand to use an eagle's throat.

Then his talons grab up the two keys, lying close together, and curl around them.

Now, *fly*. Beat wings. *Beat.* And *beat!* And beat away, and up, and out. *Up.*

Soaring up. Alive into the dark and the moonlight. Alive. Heart beating. Wings beating. Up, and up. *Still* alive. Pushing on the air for all his eagle's heart is worth.

And high above him glides Ischade, a soaring shadow before the moon, a speck that no human eye can see.

Nothing comes chasing after, but Randal flies as far and fast as an eagle can.

He flies all the way to the Stepsons' barracks, flapping his mighty wings with Ischade high overhead, shadowing his wake.

Triumphant, he flaps down to the barracks walls. He alights on those familiar battlements where he can change, and make some clothes, and become a man.

He conjures garments from dust, simple trousers and a tunic, before he's discovered by the guards. And when discovered, to their shouts and curses, he raises both his hands. When spears and crossbows sight him, he says his name – and men step back, respectful, and make an honor guard to take him to the Riddler. But not to Niko. Well, Niko didn't want to see Randal, anyway. He'd made that clear.

Crit wants Niko, not Tempus, to have those keys. Nevertheless, the sentries cannot be dissuaded: they will take him to the commander. No fault of Randal's: chance, or predestination, holds sway. Soft boots scuff on wooden stairs; leather creaks; men whisper: sentries look sharp about them, taking an intruder to the commander, no matter how famous that intruder might be.

"Life to you, Tempus," says Randal, when the Riddler slips outside his quarters, motioning sentries away. Primal eyes, so long and sharp: look of eagles, some men call it, that intense gaze that marches ranks to hell and back, and worse: until you've seen it, you never know what makes fighters give up their lives at another's command. Having been so recently an eagle, Randal feels some kinship on this fateful night; just a taste of what it must be like, to live on but outside life, to bury so many whom you love so well.

Tempus takes his measure in the moonlight – a momentary focus that strips him to his soul. Overhead a shadow circles before the moon: Ischade won't interfere, only waits and watches, far above. "Hazard, what is it?" says the Riddler, a tender voice that gives Randal chills.

"I need to see Niko. I have something for him."

The Riddler shakes his head: "No."

He knows the Band's commander as he knows his own doom.

"I have to see him."

"Tell me what you want," says Tempus, in a gentle murmur reserved for the dying, or his horses, or the bereaved.

"I have two keys. Crit wants Niko to have them."

"Keys to what?"

"Keys to the old Mageguild." *Critias, Straton, I'm sorry. I tried.* Crit and Strat do *not* want the Riddler to have these keys – not these two, nor the third, which Crit has kept. Randal's heart beats fast. He sneaks a glance above: Ischade still circles.

The commander's gaze follows his. "Moral support? Or immoral?" He knows what he sees, what soars on high. "Get her down here. Or send her away."

Then the outer door to Tempus's quarters opens and Niko is standing there in a chiton, one hand on the lintel. "Randal? Life to you, and everlasting glory," says Nikodemos, very softly. "It's been too long."

"And to you, Stealth," says Randal, feeling as if his heart will burst.

"Good to see you," Niko allows. "Thank you for all you've been doing."

"Inside," says the commander. And there is no other option.

Randal wanted so much to talk to Niko on his own. But Niko is Tempus's partner now: moral strength to immortal strength, they're bonded; and a terrible strength is the result.

Within the little room, there are only two chairs, a narrow bed, and a board table. Niko sits on the table.

At least he's well enough for that. Candlelight flickers over Niko, nestling in the hollows of his cheeks, in his deep-set hazel eyes. "What is it, Randal?"

So he must tell them. Critias and Straton will understand. These two can't be lied to, or temporized with, or denied. "The god's son, the Theban boy, and the seer got three Mageguild keys from the palace, then lost two of the keys in the Mageguild itself. Crit kept the third key and sent me to get the other two keys back and bring both keys to Niko. Something's in the mansion – or someone. Maybe Shamshi. Maybe…."

"Maybe what? Maybe who?" Niko asks, as if he's asking about the weather.

Tempus steps in front of Randal, his hand out. "Give them to me," and Randal must obey the Band's commander. He drops the two keys into the Riddler's hand.

Now Niko's up beside them. He squeezes Randal's shoulder, then pats Randal on the back familiarly. "Thank you, Randal. Commander, let me have those."

"Not yet. When you're ready," says Tempus, enfolding the keys in his fist. The commander brushes past Randal and goes outside in a rush of air and silence.

Niko looks at Randal from a world away. "Better those keys had come to me. But you know that. It's mine to do. Even Crit agrees, or he wouldn't have sent you to me with them."

"Stealth…let us help you."

"Us?"

"Me, Ischade. Everyone."

"No. Go on – go somewhere safer, mage. This is no place for you. Go back to Lemuria with Cime. Unless you know something I should know…?"

One candle isn't nearly enough light for this night, for talking to this man, who's led Randal far beyond the limits that the mage once thought he had.

"Stealth, please. The Mageguild…no one's supposed to be in there, but someone is. Many are, perhaps. And then no one is. It might be…Aškelon."

Niko didn't flinch, or even blink. "Why not? Everyone else is here. Aškelon. All the more reason for you to go someplace safer." Niko's gaze caught him and held him like a hand around his throat. No sign there of all their years together, of all the loss and all the gain.

Randal was going to cry if he didn't speak: "Stealth… Niko… if it's Aškelon, you must let me help you."

"Must? Never again. I don't want or need that kind of help."

Something showed in Randal's face, or Niko saw him bite his tongue. Stealth looked away, out the door where Tempus had gone. Too much pain, too many battles, too many lost souls haunt this man: Niko's son, murdered by a witch, not the least of those; and his body, battered and broken too many times, and patched up by Randal and other well-meaning friends who had a bit of magic, but not well enough.

"Stealth…my heart is with you. Why won't you let me stay, let me help you?"

"I don't want to hurt you, Randal, or see you hurt. It's not anything you did. It's everything that's gone before. Too much that's unnatural. Things need to balance. I have to do this on my own. And I don't want the Riddler hurt again. None of us do. No one understands what Enlil has in his mind."

*Theomachy: the preoccupation of the Sacred Band now, these pawns of gods at war with everything – themselves and men and Fates included.* So Randal wasn't surprised when Niko chased him out of there, with all due Sacred Band respect and Stepson formality, but with those distant eyes that damned him: Randal's offered aid is far too little, far too late.

Above Randal's head, Ischade still circled, awaiting him, a dot before the moon. And he almost left then. He climbed up on the barracks wall, thinking to make away.

Tempus was there, clinking keys in his left hand and looking at the night. The commander didn't turn around. "Well, Randal, what did he say?"

"He doesn't want you to have those keys. Neither do Crit or Strat."

"And what else?" came that hoarse voice, blown back to him on a rising wind as lightning flared so distantly that no thunder followed.

"He wants to do this on his own."

"I know," sighed Tempus, shifting like the settling of the earth. Errant torchlight caught his face and turned it into wrath incarnate.

"He needs *some*one's help," Randal insisted, braving the commander's displeasure. "If not mine, then yours. In the Sacred Band, it's said, no man fights alone…"

"Randal, I want you to seek Cime in Lemuria. Tell her I have something she might like but she'll have to come here to get it. If she won't come, don't tarry. Come back straight away. Clear?"

"Yes, Commander." His heart leapt.

"And tell your winged friend to come down here, out of the sky, if she has a reason to be here. Or leave. Or I'll shoot her down myself," said the Riddler, and left Randal alone, on the barracks wall, in the middle of third watch.

So all the things Randal wanted to say to Stealth, called Nikodemos – about love and honor, about how one man can make another's life so much better, about trust and loyalty, remained unsaid. At least Niko had acknowledged him.

But some nights, one wants to tell beloveds everything that's been waiting to be said. Some nights, a man needs flesh and blood and warm breath and a loving heart. Some nights, valor and cold purpose aren't enough.

So Randal stripped on the wall and took eagle's wing once more. Then he told Ischade what the Riddler said and flew back into Sanctuary.

He landed in his eagle form on the doorstep of Shawme, near the Promise of Heaven park. There he dressed, using shrubs to make some modest clothes, a tunic and pantaloons, and knocked. And when the door opened, Merricat, Shawme's housemate, greeted him.

"Merri," said Randal, and took the girl under his arm. Merricat had been Randal's apprentice long ago in Sanctuary's Mageguild. She was Shawme's closest friend. Randal knew she'd always loved him. But first she'd been his student; he, her teacher.

Then pairbond had intervened. Tonight, Merricat was the perfect comfort for a mage who wanted no carnal pleasure, only honest affection and perhaps a little more....

Merricat looked into Randal's eyes solemnly and her heart reached out to his. She knew just how to soothe him. She returned his hug and brought him inside. There she fixed him a cozy place to sit and something warm to drink, since a storm was brewing, both agreed, such as Sanctuary had never seen. And eventually the love this girl had harbored for her mentor, so long denied, came out in a husky confession. She knew what he was. She knew what he wouldn't do: Randal's was a celibate order.

So later, when they sat on her step together, looking at the stars, they went venturing into fields of mind where few mortals ever go. The two mages, the thaumaturge and his best student, shared themselves there – their hopes, their fears, their burdens – and made their plans there, to help and protect those they loved from whatever was coming in on the rising storm.

Tonight Randal wants to forget, for a while, all about the Riddler, and Stealth, and even about bringing Cime, the Evening Star, from Lemuria. Time enough for all of that, tomorrow, he thinks. The universe forgives those who give until their hearts are aching and their spirits weak, and finds a way to renew all strength and cure all ills, in this world or the next, if a soul can just have faith.

*

Just before sunrise, Tempus rode out on his favorite Trôs, north of the barracks, where he'd made a pyre for Abarsis, so long ago. Storm clouds massed in the distance, threatening rain. He slipped the gray horse's bridle over its ears and let it graze. This one would never desert him. Everything around was wild or ruined. There was no one to hear him and no one to blame. He could say what he pleased to the storm god, or to all the gods of heaven. He could curse or beat his chest or yell his rage at the sky.

He didn't. He stood very still and waited to see if Enlil would come. In the distance, lightning was sheeting: it was a summer for storm and fury. That suited him. He had some of his own to add.

When Tempus had intercepted Critias coming in from Shambles to the barracks, Crit had surrendered the third Mageguild key on demand, explaining defensively, "Sham, or someone of his, attacked Kouras, Arton and Lysis with Stepson throwing stars, coming down Runeway last night. They're not seriously hurt but it's demoralizing, being attacked from shadows by an adversary you never see and can't engage. We think the wizard boy is hiding at, or in, the old Mageguild now. We must hurry, before Sham disappears again. I sent those keys ahead with Randal. We all agreed Shamshi is Niko's to dispatch, so he'll need the keys. It's time, Commander."

"When it's time isn't yours to say. It's mine. We're done here," he'd told Crit summarily, too outraged to say more to this intense fighter whose errors came from loyalty, not deceit. *More* attacks. Not Crit's fault, however infuriating. But Crit, trying to go around him, straight to Niko with the keys; Crit, setting battle tempo – that, he wouldn't tolerate.

*'Niko's to dispatch.' If* Niko can. *When* he can. Certainly not yet. Not until Tempus finds some help for his partner, still intent on facing Shamshi, or vengeful destiny, alone.

Tempus had fought too long and hard not to know the stench of oncoming doom when he smelled it. But this time, he didn't know where to strike, or what to strike, or even how to strike against this insidious enemy who thought to get at him through Niko.

This opponent overestimated Tempus, judged him stronger and more canny than he was. The spear to his heart had taught him he was not invincible, not omnipotent, not almighty.

Here today was just a man the god immortalized, and a horse somewhat more than a horse should be, and a sky full of gods above. All his Stepsons felt the danger. They wanted to protect their commander. But from what? In times gone by, the god had always told him what he needed to know. But not now. Not today.

He sat down where he thought he'd sent Abarsis up to heaven and looked out over the uplands and abandoned farms, just beyond Sanctuary's northern reaches. Farther north than the eye could see were Ranke and Tyse and Wizardwall. To the south was Sanctuary, broken away from a failing empire, trying to be a city-state on its own. He'd fought hard for each and every regime in its turn, before Niko came to the Band, and after.

Niko had been little older than Shamshi was today when Aškelon had appeared in Sanctuary and given Stealth the dream-forged panoply – cuirass, dirk, shortsword and shield – whereon all the elder gods and demons played. Niko wore that panoply and carried those weapons through countless clashes with enemies mortal and immortal. Still carried them to this day.

Sage and heather dot the hillside, spilling down toward the valley. And wild roses, white with yellow centers, climb where bees are busily at work. He doesn't recall any of these being here before. But he hasn't come up here since he'd sent Abarsis's soul to heaven. When Abarsis died, they'd been sacking the slaver's compound that became the barracks. After that, they'd sent their dead to heaven on flames from their own wood, from pyres made on their own ground.

Soon enough, the Band went north for the wizard wars. Niko was still so very young. Stealth carried scars from that conflict, where a man least needs them, until these strange days of Chaeronea and the Theban goddess who took those scars away.

He and Niko had planned the Chaeronean sortie, for its justice: to wheedle a bit of mercy from the gods, to save twenty-three pairs whose bodies would never lie beneath a granite lion for later men to find. Where was the harm? Of those twenty-three pairs, only one pair was lost to them thereafter. A better record than most could claim, trying to save the fated dead. They'd given no thought to cheating the Fates, if cheat them they had.

As for the whispers in all their minds after Chaeronea, Tempus had lived for ages with voices in his head.

Very quietly, though only the Trôs was near, he said aloud, "Enlil, hear me. I've asked for little, done a lot. This fighter of mine, this Nikodemos, is an avatar of yours, but too beset by ungodly forces to triumph on his own. Give him what you've given me: the strength, the fortitude, the flesh to match his will."

He waited for the god to answer. Far off, a fork of lightning ripped the sky. But overhead, no storm clouds gathered. Where he sat, no rain or wind whipped him. It was sunny. It was dry.

From behind him came a voice: "Why do you ask the storm god in that boy's behalf? He's mine, you know."

He knew who spoke, before he could turn to face the sound, so he didn't turn. He'd known, when Harmony started to speak, just what she would say, so he didn't answer. He sat very still, to see what the goddess would do. His weapons were on his horse: they'd done for gods before; but weapons were not the answer, today.

She came closer, barefoot, with lavender linen rustling around her ankles. She sat beside him. "Speak up, Riddler, for him and for yourself."

"I need help for him. I'll give my life, if that's the answer – if I can trade it to keep him safe."

"Safe for how long?"

He could see her out of the corner of his eye: her proud profile, her full lips, her body that his Stepson couldn't resist. "For as long as I would live, otherwise."

"For eternity? You want immortality for your Stealth, called Nikodemos?"

He took a chance, a breath; then said, "Don't you?"

Harmony laughed like a stream over rocks, like a bird in a tree on a fine spring day. "You arrogant creature. Who gives you the right to petition such a thing?"

"Not who. What. What he is, and what I am, and what we've sworn to one another – these give me the right. What would the world be without him, and those like him? I have the right to ask."

"It's not up to you," she said.

"But is it up to you?" he asked.

The goddess stood up. He stood up. On her feet, Harmony was nearly as tall as he. He saw the Trôs horse, uncanny beast, staring with its ears pricked, every muscle bunched: it sensed how dire was this circumstance, this quiet meeting on a hilltop whence the original Stepson had gone to heaven, unmarked and unremarked by any but Tempus.

She stared down at feral fields, abandoned farms, wild horses and deer running free. "He loves the world so much. I agree it would be a shame to take that love away from meadow and tree, stream and sky, and all that lives in nature, and leave them lonely."

"My thought exactly," he said, although it hadn't been, going very carefully: this was not only a goddess of love, but a goddess of war, of order and balance and justice. Make an enemy of her, and what was difficult could become impossible.

"He belongs to you and your storm god, he thinks."

"He, of all men, belongs to himself," Tempus said honestly.

And that honesty turned her face to him. Eyes wider than the heavens weighed him. And blinked: "I cannot give what he will not ask for, or accept. How would it be, then? How was it for you, when you took on curse and god?"

"I got used to it. I lived to fight on other days."

"Wanting neither too much to live nor too much to die.... I have given him all he asked for. I should not – perhaps cannot – do more."

"And if we lose him?"

"He will not be lost to me, whatever happens."

Anger roared up from his bowels and caught in his throat. *Gods and goddesses, all alike.* With every iota of discipline he had, he sought composure. "So, you will leave him to fight alone?"

"He has you."

"By my oath, and ours, and all of mine: he has me; the Sacred Band of Stepsons; and all your Thebans. But you know as well as I, no man will prevail in unfair battle. Fine, then. He and I will face whatever is in store. You don't mind if I tell him what you've said? Perhaps the storm god will do better for him."

But she was gone by then, dissolved into flax on the wind.

In Tempus's belt pouch, when he went to get his horse, the three keys to the Mageguild clinked.

As he swung up onto the Trôs, a voice in his skull said, *"Art thou finished, avatar, pleading with a foreign goddess instead of begging My Majesty to aid one of My own?"* Its reverberations, so loud, made him dizzy astride his horse.

So the storm god of heaven was present and accounted for, after all. And, after the inconclusive way his meeting with Harmony had gone, Tempus was more relieved than he could ever let Enlil suspect: the god was waxing jealous, even proprietary, where Niko was concerned.

Thus began the haggling over Nikodemos, which was difficult, since Tempus was trying to offer Enlil a soul that, by rights and oathbond, the god already had.

But he must do something. Niko is his greatest vulnerability, perhaps his only one.

## *Chapter 36: Grace of the Goddess*

The three keys to the Mageguild were in Niko's pocket, ceded him by his left-side leader. They weighed on him like lead as he and Tempus rode through the city while rain poured down and thunder thrashed the air. They put their two Trôs studs in the stable behind the mercenary's hostel, out of the downpour, and went indoors, to sit drinking possets by the fire in the rufous common room. And they were welcome there.

Men drifted in, by ones and twos and fours, hoping to approach them: eager fighters, who'd heard about the Downwind sweep. Wondering what was in the offing. Looking for glory and tales to tell.

Wolfish mercenaries studied claret walls hung with antique weapons. They'd glance at Tempus and Niko, and then away. Sellswords lounged at a polite distance, talking together before they approached the guild-master to ask about the Stepsons' commander. They'd fill their bowls with watered wine, add wheat and cheese or nuts and honey; and eat, biding their time, calm and predatory: it never pays to be too anxious to sell yourself or your sword.

The quiet in the common room made Niko's ears ache as unknown mercenaries appraised the two of them, at their corner table, again and again. These were calculating men, looking for hire. Some wore their most storied gear, complete with unit devices and decorations won in conflicts known throughout the land.

They'd heard the tales; they wanted to see the specter: Tempus in his leopard-skin and boar's tooth helm, readying a new cohort, preparing a contingent for some unspecified operation – and soon enough, off to war.

Niko had been one of those men once; a rightman whose leader wanted to serve under Tempus, come down from Ranke looking for adventure and spoils – a last campaign together, his partner had said, before the older fighter took a wife, raised a family, put in a crop of wheat. And his left-side leader had died here, in an explosion down by the docks, leaving him devastated and alone.

Up they came, these fit, harsh men, professionally reserved, asking to meet, wanting to sit, hoping for hire. Some of these fighters were younger than Niko was when first he came here; some older than Straton or Charon now; some showed their scars, some didn't. They'd say, "Heard you're hiring for the Stepsons."

Tempus would say, "If you're good enough."

Lips would quirk, legs stretch out, bodies lean back slouched with both hands on the table or in their belts: exposed bellies and hearts and throats saying all that needed to be said about courage and skill. "What's the mission? How long? Where?"

And Tempus would say, "The battle of your dreams."

They hired a dozen on the spot and sent them out to the barracks to see Sync and get fit up. Reinforcements, for whatever Tempus thought was coming.

Then they went to Marc's weapon shop and ordered armaments: iron-tipped short flights and bolts, longer quarrels and barb-pointed arrows; crossbows and cavalry bows of sinew composite; short, medium and long spears (javelins, dories, and sarissas butted with bronze and tipped with iron); daggers and shortswords, curved and straight; Bandaran throwing stars by the case. And armor: cuirasses of bronze and leather and linen; linothoraxes; scale corselets; mail shirts; bronze-faced shields of wood or wicker with leather arm-bands and cord handholds; helmets, some with horsehair crests; arm-guards and bracers; greaves and boots and sandals. Enough to fight a long campaign.

All day, the Riddler had been fey: preoccupied, secretive, as if the god was whispering in his ear, leaving Niko to sort out men and weaponry. Out in back of Marc's, the practice range was still there: straw-stuffed cuirasses, torsos, and ox-hide targets were strategically arranged against a tall wooden wall atop a berm. Niko wanted to try the new high-torque composite crossbow with its rope springs: it shot farther in the rain, nocked more bolts quicker, penetrated deeper, than other crossbows could. When he'd come back in with it, Tempus and Marc were waiting. Tempus leaned back against the shop's wall, weapons hanging all around him. Raindrops still stippled his mantle.

Marc had aged; his pulchritudinous blond wife had died; his rough complexion was rougher; his thick black hair shot with gray, his hairline higher. Marc said, "Your commander says you need a whole new kit, Stealth. I have some special arms and armor…."

Niko's summer duty gear was plain and worn, but he didn't want any changes to his war panoply with battle in the offing. "Commander…?"

He looked at Tempus, who said, "No dream-forged arms or armor. None of it. Nothing given us by Aškelon. Go downstairs with Marc and find what suits you. If it's not here, we'll have it made. When we can drive it down here, Marc will take the chariot in trade as well."

The ground seemed to lurch under Niko's feet. Not until then had he realized how serious Tempus judged Aškelon's involvement to be. Talk is talk, especially encamped, with no warfare looming. Men make much of little. But this....

He'd used that dream-forged panoply for a decade, maybe more. His head spun. Tempus really thought Aškelon was taking sides. And not *their* side.

"I don't have any of it with me...." Stating the obvious.

"The Sacred Band's credit's fine. I know that panoply of yours as well as you do. I can sell it before sundown, sight unseen. Why you don't want it... that's not my business."

"You're right. It's not," Niko said, and went with Marc to try to replace the irreplaceable.

He found pieces and parts. A cuirass of quality must be measured to a body, custom-made to flex and give. A sword such as his dream-forged one was unobtainable at any price. Eventually, among the best gear downstairs he found a western shortsword, forged by a Bandaran hand from the way the exotic metal was folded and the tang was set. It had a leather-wrapped hilt, and its length and balance were nearly perfect.

When he'd finished, Tempus was leaning in the doorway, watching him. "Time to go, Stealth."

Marc's sturdy legs pumped as he accompanied them up the stairs and out to their wet horses, standing in the mud with their tails to the wind. "Ten days. Best I can do, for Stealth's cuirass and the rest."

"That's fine," Tempus told Marc, and they rode out of there without another word to the weaponer. In ten days, what they'd get could never replace what Niko was giving up.

He kneed his Trôs closer to Tempus's as they headed across Downwind. "Why?" he asked Tempus.

"You know why. You can't trust that panoply from now on. You can't trust the hand that made it. I can't. We don't need his chariot and we don't need his weapons."

Tempus had god-given weapons, older than Niko was. But arguing with the commander would be fruitless. Especially since Tempus was right. Niko used that dream-forged panoply sparingly because Aškelon had made it: only for the direst of circumstance, or ceremonially. He'd tried a dozen times to lose it, throw it on a pyre, or bury it. It always ended up back in his hands.

They rode in silence for too long. You couldn't see the angle of the sun; the sky was dark gray and grayer, like wet slates. Just before they turned into the Street of Arcana, the others began arriving at the appointed rendezvous.

First to join them were Crit on his white-faced chestnut and Strat on his ghost horse. Crit fell in on Niko's right, Strat to his right. Jihan took her position on Tempus's left, on her Trôs mare. Behind them came Thebans, right to left: Archias and Agis, both on Stepson bays; Gorgias, on Niko's black colt; Perses and Simias, on a sorrel and the big dun. Each of the second rank had crossbows, lances, shields, and long horsehair ropes coiled on their saddles.

The precision of the ranks made him proud; no horse or rider misbehaved. All knew their places, knew their jobs. Five abreast they trotted up the Street of Arcana as, behind, the third rank closed up: Kouras on the far right; Arton, next; then Lysis in the middle; then Charon, with Cassander on his left.

The Street of Arcana was longer than Niko remembered it: its trees were taller, bending lower over the road, shedding rain that fell on the Band in streams as wind shook the branches. Rainwater puddled across the road so that horses stepped with care.

But no horse jumps a puddle, or bites, or calls; no rider curses or talks. Everyone knows the plan. Or did know it, until the Mageguild came into view, ablaze with lights, far down at Arcana's end. How many were in there, where no one was supposed to be?

Lysis, Arton and Kouras had come here and left unharmed, then were punished for their temerity with a shower of throwing stars – party favors from an enemy they couldn't see. "Commander?" Niko asks.

"Straight in, Niko. All the way to Meridian if we can," says the Riddler, and draws his god-given sword. It's tinged with a ruddy glow – the sword's reaction to unnatural opposition: sorcerers, gods, demons, or worse.

Tempus holds his shortsword high for a moment – a signal for all; a warning to veterans, who know the tinge on that blade means infernal or supernal enemies are near: *Look close about you.*

Then the Riddler brings his sword down sharply. Fifteen horses break into a canter, each keeping distance and spacing on the slippery wet cobbles; each far enough from the other that no man's weapon will pose a threat to the fighter next to him. Mounted, a shield-holding line can still drift right. Drills and skills prevent it: if it happens in these close quarters, where bushes line the street, obscuring iron fences on either side, real problems will arise.

Horses thunder down the Street of Arcana. Weapons clank and crossbows crank. Metal jingles. Swords gleam. Snorts mask cadence. Leather slaps. Hooves splash in puddles. All are perfect, by the book. Even the three young Stepsons in the third rank are where they should be; holding steady, keeping pace.

Niko can hear a flap of wings above, he thinks: Ischade, keeping watch through the trees, among the rain squalls, mist and clouds.

Mist is moving in now, as if it is alive, straight toward them through the rain. Veterans look at it askance. Aškelon had once unleashed a killing mist in Sanctuary: mist like this had crawled these streets once before, shredding limbs and leaving flayed carcasses frozen where they fell.

This uncanny mist and rain unnerves the horses and the fighters. Riding through your fear is part of the mission today. Even without his helmet, Niko's breathing sounds too loud. He slides his oldest shortsword, service-worn and plain, out of his scabbard. Crit, beside him, watches Niko too much.

Anxious for a skirmish, pulling on their bits, warhorses toss froth on everyone and everything. On they canter, but the Mageguild gets no closer. They ride under the trees and out of the rain, deeper into the arcane mist: fetlock high; knee high; foreleg high; barrel high.

Niko feels the cold mist lapping around his feet, his calves, his knees. He is careful where his hands are. This chilling mist in summer is Aškelon's doing, without a doubt.

Wind, whistling, catches up the mist and slaps them with it. When it touches Niko's face, it stings, making his eyes burn and tear. He can no longer see the lights of the Mageguild. There's nothing ahead, nothing behind – just pearly mist, crawling up the bushes, into the trees. He wishes he'd worn his helmet but he wanted to see everything, hear everything. He has a shortsword in one hand, reins in the other. From the feel of his Trôs, if he slacks his reins to put on his helmet, this horse will bolt, trying to find a way through the unnatural mist – and out of it.

Niko knows how bad this kind of sortie can get: a battle without a visible opponent; no clash of skills, no test of valor

– just an opaque mist, impossible to fight, killing all the horses and men, pulling everyone down on the road to die….

He chances a look to his right – at Crit, in the flat, shadowless light; at Straton, beside him: both helmeted, steady in their saddles.

He looks to his left, where the Riddler rides, face unreadable under that boar's tooth helm, dragging his sword-point through the mist as if trolling for fish. Wherever the commander's shortsword drags, the icy mist turns dark and curls away.

Their mounts sound louder than he's ever heard them: laboring but plunging on. He wants to call a halt; or charge; or retreat and regroup. If it were his mission, he would have. *Get the horses and the riders out of the mist.* Or through it, before it drops down on them from above and men lose hearts and souls….

"Commander," he calls softly, leaning left in his saddle, hoping Tempus can hear him above the hoofbeats and the clank of armor, through the boars-tooth helmet, "let's run through it, or back out of it, or…" The Stepsons have no maneuver codes for "maybe" or "what if." Niko can call an order to charge or halt or retreat, but his left-side leader is right here….

Before Tempus can respond, a lone figure appears, riding toward them down the middle of the road from the direction of the Mageguild. And behind that horse and rider there is no mist now, just a clear street and a patch of unaccountable sunshine. Beyond, the Mageguild squats, smug but dark once more in the afternoon light.

The lone horse and rider keep coming, single-footing. No menace, no weapons showing but one long spear with a pennant tied to its butt, snapping in the wind: a makeshift standard for an undeclared war. This horse approaching is as good as any of theirs: black as night, with gold dapples; big-chested, big-crested, big-boned; moving squarely with effortless impulsion, fixing them with proud and fiery eyes.

On come the horse and rider. Back scurries the mist, as if lifting up its skirts. Then the rider pulls up the big black and halts, one hand on thigh. Black armor; black and gold helmet, crested with red horsehair blowing in the wind; almond-eyed; nothing to be seen within: only a flash of pale lips and chin showing through a vertical slit.

The rider waits for them; the horse stands still as a statue. The mist in the bushes and the trees hisses as it shrinks back. The sound is eerie. When they are almost close enough to call to one another, the black-armored rider raises its fist with the standard in it and casts that spear with its pennant: straight at them.

The spear flies through the air in a silence that seems to stop every horse, though each is moving, and every rider's sound.

Breaking formation, Niko reins his horse halfway around, raising it up and pushing it sideways, his legs and hands demanding; forcing it across and in front of Tempus and his mount – covering their bodies with his horse and his body. His shield angles high to protect his partner as the spear arcs up and down: *Not again. Not ever again.*

Both Trôs horses squeal angrily, bumping one another, biting.

The standard strikes a few lengths short of them, its spear-point driving deep between the cobbles. The shaft quivers there as he rolls his horse back into place on the Riddler's right.

Who is this sole rider, challenging them? Shamshi's panoply, when last Niko fought him, was very different from this fighter's gear. Niko has never seen the dream lord ride to battle except by chariot, so it can't be him in that black armor. Can it?

There is stirring in the ranks behind him: he hears Charon whisper something unintelligible to his son.

At that moment, Tempus raises his sword: *halt.*

Everybody stops. Horses bugle and stomp. There's no chilling mist now, not even around their horses' ankles. It's back in the bushes or hiding in the leaves or curled like snakes around the boughs overhead.

The black horse walks forward. Beyond the horse and rider – not near, not far; or both, or neither – the Mageguild wavers: now it is dark, shuttered; now it is lit, every window blazing.

Tempus says, "Niko, now." Tempus and Niko ride forward alone as, behind them, Crit closes up the rank.

They walk their mounts slowly, neither brandishing a sword, toward the spear with its pennant – black and red, gold and white – flapping in the rising wind.

The armored rider on the black horse comes closer now, curved shortsword in hand. Sunlight breaks through the cloud and rays down around horse and rider.

The rain has stopped – or is held in abeyance. A few drops splatter from the pergola overhead. Niko hears too loudly every rustle of leaves, every breath he takes, every clop of his horse's hooves. Between his legs, he can feel his mount's heart pound as it struggles to walk when it wants to run.

They reach the standard – Tempus on the left of it, Niko on the right – before the other rider does. His commander motions with the sword in his right hand and says, "Niko, pull up that standard and cast it down."

Niko tries to do as he's told, reaching with his shield arm, his rein hand. To his rear, he can hear the Stepsons on their horses, thirteen men and mounts: riders shifting in their saddles, taking better hold of their weapons; horses champing at their bits and snorting. But he can't grab the spear on which the pennant whips in the wind – not without moving closer; not without letting go of his reins.

So he says, because it's important, because Tempus needs him to make this symbolic gesture, "I'll get closer," and knees his horse left. He grabs the standard's shaft, that long spear stuck into the street. And tugs. And pulls, while the armored rider on the black horse continues its measured approach.

But the spearpoint won't come out of the road: it's in too deep. He's not wearing his helmet: the pennant snaps in a gust of wind and nearly slaps him in the face. "I'll have to dismount to free it, Commander."

Tempus is watching the black-armored rider narrowly. Eye-whites gleam within that boar's-tooth helm. "Never mind. Leave it."

After one more yank, he lets go of the shaft. He needs both hands for whatever's coming.

The other rider stops before them. The big black horse has a golden muzzle: it stares at them as brazenly as any soldier and chews its bit.

"Why would you pull up my standard?" asks the rider. "Rather, get off your horses and bow your heads. Or kiss my pennant and ride on by to glory, brave fighters." Then the helmeted head turns to Niko: "All but you. *You* stay."

*What's this?* He can't move. He's rooted to the spot. A heartbeat overwhelms him; the next one comes infinitely slowly; then another pounds against his brain.

*Is this Shamshi? The dream lord himself? Or some other enemy? Is this where it will be? How it will go? A final confrontation in the middle of the Mageguild street?*

Beside him, Tempus slowly turns his head and stares at him for what seems like forever. Then the commander raises his sword without a word, pointing it forward, motioning to his left: *Go around: go on by.* Obedient, Crit calls a maneuver code. The Riddler leads the Stepsons on.

The squadron moves along, their horses walking single file to funnel past Niko. Some Thebans reach out to touch the pennant with their fingers or brush their lips against it as they go: Charon, Lysis, Gorgias, Agis, and Perses. *Superstitious. Or hedging their bets.*

No one looks at Niko, not even Critias or Straton, not Jihan. The Riddler has made his decision. Only Niko's horse objects, neighing loudly as it's left behind. His horse wants to go with Tempus's, and cannot. The last Stepsons ride slowly by him, looking neither right nor left. But ride they do.

Past him and on toward the Mageguild they go. Leaving him behind, with this armored apparition confronting him in the street. He watches his Sacred Band ride into the patch of sunlight and onward, horses' rumps swaying, tails swishing.

He shifts his grip on his shortsword and flexes his shield arm, his wrist, shaking slack rein through his fingers. *Ready when you are, Sham. Or whomever.*

The opposing rider sheathes the curved shortsword. He sheathes his straight one.

The rider on the black horse says, "What's fair in love is fair in war. Why so solemn? You'll live to fight another day. That's what your commander wants for you."

"Harmony?" *Goddess of balance in love and war.*

If it is Harmony in that black armor, he's misunderstood this whole encounter.

But she's not like this: she's beautiful and gentle and kind. If this is the goddess, he's probably the only one who has misconstrued. And, misconstruing, let his commander ride on, with the thirteen other Stepsons. He should have gone. He should have ridden on by. But that voice had bid him stay. He hadn't recognized the timbre, yet there was a hold on him he couldn't break.

He wants to say, 'Is that *really* you?' Or is it Sham, skewing his perceptions, making him weak to strike him down? On Mageguild ground, nothing can be trusted. He says, "Harmony…if it's you…I have to go."

"No," says the rider, as if disciplining an unruly horse. "You stay here a little longer. If you go now, you die now. Right here. Right now. Today." The big horse paws the ground. "Your Band was an odd number, imbalanced: fifteen. Now they're fourteen. Much better."

Now he's sure it's Harmony. He nearly claps his mount into a run. But he doesn't dare. "And what about them? The killing mist? The threat *they* face? What have you done?"

"You think their fates are up to *you?* You'll save them all, will you? The mist won't be killing anyone – not you, or yours, or mine – today. They'll be fine, without you there. It's not a trap for them now. It *was* a trap for you."

Now the rider takes off that helmet and long amber hair spills out. Those wide eyes take his measure. Again. "You may go *now,*" says Harmony. And her horse walks forward, until she can put her own gloved hand on the standard stuck in the Mageguild street.

Her fingers curl around it. "Your commander asked me to help you. Did he tell you?"

"No." He's embarrassed. He should go. He should be with his left-side leader. He wipes his sword-hand on his thigh; his palms are sweaty. He's not sure if he believes her. She's a goddess. All deities are tricksters, twisting lives and hopes to their own ends. "I have to go. I have to help him. If you want to help someone, help him."

"He says the same of you," she tells him.

Then the standard goes away, as the magnificent horse goes away, and the goddess with her honey-colored hair goes away. And he kicks his horse and runs it all the way to the Mageguild (farther away than it could possibly be from here to there), frightened of what he'll find.

But when he gets there, the Sacred Band's ropes are on the Mageguild gates and archers with crossbows are shooting out windows – windows they'd already shot out, according to Critias, once before. And no traces of the mist remain.

Tempus, safe and sound astride his Trôs, is hacking away with his shortsword at the lock on the Mageguild gates. The sword is glowing hot but the lock doesn't break. The lock sparks blue, gleaming with wards. Jihan, beside him, touches the gates to freeze the metal, make it brittle. The lock doesn't crumble. They try the sword again. No combined force avails them: the lock still holds.

Niko's horse comes around the corner just as Tempus reins his mount away from the gates, toward Crit. The commander sees Niko and signals him to approach them with a motion of his god-given sword that has won so many days. But not this day. Niko heads that way.

Straton, crossbow ready, and his bay forsake the bushes by the side of the road. "Glad you could join us, Stealth," says Strat, riding up beside him. "I'd tread softly, were I you, right now. We can't get in there. Commander's not thrilled with how this mission's playing out," Strat cautions.

"I still have the keys. I was…detained."

"Tell it to the Riddler." Strat snorts and spits over his shoulder. "That's your little dancing girl, the Theban goddess on her big black horse?"

Niko says, "Strat…." He won't apologize, not for staying behind, not for the pennant, not for Harmony or anything she's done here. But he must say something. "That's her...my dancing girl, on the big horse."

As he and Strat ride up to Tempus and Critias, Crit pulls off his helmet and calls out, "Stealth, before I kiss that goddess's pennant, *you* can hug my crack. And you can tell her I said so." Black look, aimed Niko's way.

"Ready now, Niko? Keys? This isn't over yet," the Riddler says.

"Ready." Ready to go in there. Ready with the keys. Ready for whatever trap awaits – or remains. He remembers what the goddess said, but he can't say such things to Tempus. And yet he must tell Tempus what his commander needs to know.

"Commander. She said the mist won't trouble us again today," Niko reports. He shrugs. If there's still a trap in the Mageguild meant just for him, if the Band is in danger because of him, if the balance is restored if he dies…then maybe that's the best thing. Maybe his *maat* wants an end to all this. "At your pleasure, Commander."

Tempus waves him on. He dismounts and tries the keys in the lock. The Riddler had been hesitant to give him the keys, and now he was late bringing them to bear. Men and horses have tried – still try – to pull down a gate that a key should open easily. But no key is working in that lock today.

They can't get the gates open, no matter what they do. No matter how the horses strain, the gates won't be pulled down, not with five ropes and five rumps and every horseman cursing and pushing, slapping and cajoling.

The Mageguild sits there, squat and blank-eyed, dark once more and seemingly empty – daring him to come alone, come again, come another day.

When they're losing the light, they prepare to ride out. Not a pane of glass remains in any window, yet not a single section of iron fence has been brought down. The Mageguild taunts them, as impregnable as ever.

Bareheaded, helmet bumping by his knee, Charon rides up. He looks appraisingly at Niko, where he sits his mount between Critias and Tempus, then at the commander. And Charon says, "You know who that was, don't you, in the black armor?"

Tempus finally takes off his helmet. "I think we do," comes the gravelly voice.

Charon says, "You have no idea how blessed we all are. We live by the grace of the goddess. We should all go immediately to her altar and give thanks."

Crit says, *"Thanks?* For what? Did we get in there? Did we find and kill the wizard boy? You call this blessed? What happens when you're cursed?"

"Then you die," says Charon, and rides away to help form up the third rank.

Niko offers Tempus the keys to the Mageguild: "I shouldn't have these."

"Keep them. Souvenirs. We're not coming back here."

Jihan rides up, always too bold by half, ungovernable. "Niko, what were you doing back there so long, with the Theban goddess?" She grins lasciviously.

Crit scoffs and looks away, his face full of critique unspoken.

Niko says, "I did what the commander wanted." Not precisely true, but true enough. His face feels hot. The teasing has just begun, and it will be unmerciful. The goddess singled him out during a public encounter and made him stay behind like a child kept after school, and everybody saw.

"Jihan, I'll handle it," says the Riddler, and hooks his helmet on his saddle.

When the ranks are formed up, the commander tells Critias, “Make sure everyone remembers that the most dangerous part of this mission begins now and lasts until we reach the barracks. That’s when Shamshi has struck before.”

And they rode out, five abreast, the way they rode in, all present and accounted for. The back of Niko’s neck prickled, waiting for throwing stars to hit or crossbow bolts to fly or spears to thunk into flesh.

“Niko, what else did Harmony say?” Tempus asked when they turned off the Street of Arcana without further incident.

“She said it was trap for me, not for any of you.”

“Then so it was. We’ll deal with it.”

“She said,” Niko added reluctantly, looking between his horse’s ears at the street ahead, free of mist, “you asked her for help…for me. Is that true?”

“It’s true.”

“You know I don’t want that kind of help. Why would you do that?”

“Because you’re going to need it,” Tempus said.

The Sacred Band rode carefully through Sanctuary in the failing light. Niko had cavalry all around him: his reserved and wary Stepsons; volatile young fighters marveling that they’d seen a goddess in armor on a great black horse; older Thebans, who should have known better than to chatter while in formation, exulting that they’d been in the presence of their tutelary goddess, fitted up for war.

Niko was, thanks to Tempus’s forbearance, still second-in-command here, and it was his duty to keep order in the ranks. That responsibility had never seemed as precious as it did tonight in the gloaming, riding back to the barracks: he’d missed it so, while he’d been healing.

For some reason, or no reason at all, the whole time they’d been at the Mageguild he hadn’t felt Shamshi’s presence or seen the battleplain of Chaeronea or heard the screaming of the dying from that carnage, sounds that scraped his very soul.

And then, as if he'd summoned it, he did feel Sham – a cold, pure touch; a glance from the corner of eternity; a moment of being eye to eye with something he almost recognized but didn't understand; something sitting on a pile of Chaeronean corpses, that looked at him and promised, "Your gods and lovers can't protect you forever. Not from me."

## *Chapter 37: Echoes of Chaeronea*

The third-quarter moon casts teasing light. The cityscape seems dreamlike. Back and forth through Ratfall, Shamshi chases first one girl; then another; then a boy. Catching all with speed and skill. Finding the fear in each mind. Feeding that fear, making it paralyze and choke his victim. Tearing away clothes and courage and hearts and souls, until his ferocity ebbs. Until his hunger is sated; till his wrath is slaked.

Then, one more: he slips up on this target from behind, grabbing it deftly around the neck, catching its chin in the crook of his arm, his other hand over its mouth. Even in Ratfall, too much screaming isn't wise. He drags this writhing victim into an alley, and there he takes his time. He knocks it off balance deftly. When he has it on its knees, he pushes those knees apart.

This one fights hard: it's stronger than the rest, wanting to live, wanting so badly not to take a final breath. He shows its mind how its death will be, in the most flawless unrest he has yet to find. It screeches into his hand, bites his palm. It doesn't matter: it's terrified now, a better way to die than any – at least, for him, as he hugs it from behind.

He has found a formula for those who struggle: still with one hand on its mouth, he drops his own body on top of it in the most perfect intrusion and then slowly strangles it until it dies.

As long as it wriggles, he rides it. When it stops convulsing, he moves out of its mind and body, satisfied with his work.

Cruelty having cooled his ire, his frustration, he kicks this one only once when it rattles out its dying breath. Then he goes on his way, thinking how much stronger, how much better, how much fiercer he is than he had been, last time he was down this way.

Sanctuary denies him nothing. It is a town for late night dying, for alleyway crying, for skulking under bridges and sliding corpses into rivers where a body will float away. Sanctuary is not like Chaeronea, whose echoes haunted him but whose substance, so far, remained elusive and whose nature, unlike Sanctuary's, he couldn't grasp or control. Yet.

He'd learned not to draw too much attention to his playthings, or to his kills. He'd learned that the unremarkable is written off, while the artful brings search parties and the city guard and the accursed Stepsons from their barracks.

He needed to practice. He needed strength, built of exertion. Finally, his compulsion ebbing, he can seek more delicate fare. Uptown, cross-town, to the Street of Red Lanterns; that's where he'll go, as soon as he gets back to Wideway and reclaims his horse.

When he had walked as far as the dockside, along the swampy marsh, he saw a flash of leg, a gleam of skin. It was too tempting. He gave chase. He chased and chased it, into the Maze and through a warren of alleys and hovels. He was about to give up when he caught sight of it again: a flash of skin, low cursing, heavy breathing and a clatter in an alley.

He gave chase once more, heart pounding, and when he saw that the alley was blind and that there was a black shape crouched where the alley ended, he sauntered toward it, fingers on his knife. A little variety might be nice tonight. The day had been so long, so lonely, and the days before so frustrating: he wanted to talk to Aškelon about all that had happened; but the dream lord was elusive, lately.

Down toward the crouching black shape Shamshi went, whistling tunelessly, a military air, and reaching for the mind crouched in that body.

And recoiled.

Something rose up, huge and black, with great white-rimmed eyes that came swooping at him: *'Mine,'* it howled between his ears. *'Mine.'* And it sprang at him, fingers like claws; long nails; and eyes so far out in front of the rest of it, they seemed to have no face in which to dwell. *'Mine.'*

He just had time to see, beyond it, as he turned to run, a body crumpled there: the one he'd chased here. The one he'd wanted.

But from this thing, which needed no feet to run, he fled with all his might. From this creature, beating wings upon the air and keening with a wildness he'd never have and a single-mindedness he'd never known, he sped with all the strength his body had, screaming. Not even knowing that he screamed. For that mind had caught his, when it went questing, and grabbed his sanity round and squeezed it, and showed it horrors of hell such as he had only glimpsed: a gate, rotting flesh on moving bones, fluorescent maggots in eyes that saw, and teeth that cracked skulls like candy.

*'I'm sorry,'* his mind blithered to the thing chasing him. *'I'm sorry; I'm sorry. Please let me go. I didn't know.'*

*'Now you know,'* he heard its voice, clear words ringing in his head. *'If now's not too late. Run fast, baby horror. Run off and practice till the morrow. This is my hunting ground. These are my cattle. Run before I tell the Sacred Band where*

*and how to find you. Curl up in a hole somewhere, because they will – they will. I have your scent now. And you have affronted me. Stealing from me? Stealing from Ischade is something you'll only manage once. Go dream about the deeper hells. I can send you there. I can keep you there. I can call you up, time after time, and send you back again – and again. You'll beg for death, you who fear it so. Now, run. Run back to the dream lord and tell him he can't protect you from me. Not from me, if you come again to my hunting ground, or touch one fool who's mine. And mind you who those may be, foolish boy. Scat. Come back when you're older, and bolder, and we'll have a tussle. Now run – and only to the dream lord. Run and carry my message. Flee. Flee while you still have any legs at all or arms at all or eyes at all with which to flee.'*

Sham tore down that street, running as he'd never run before, not even from the city guard or the Sacred Band. He ran until he passed Runeway, until he reached Wideway, and ran some more.

He ran into the stable, paid the liveryman and flung himself up on his horse, air cutting like knives in his throat and lungs, mouth too dry for speech.

By the time he got to the Mageguild, the Street of Red Lanterns forgotten, he was chilled and shaking and weak all over.

The gates opened before him and Sham threw himself off his horse. Someone always came to take it. And to bring it when he asked. He never saw them otherwise.

Up the steps he charged, and inside. In where the walls were high and thick, and the silence deep, and Aškelon of Meridian ruled over staircases that went into nowhere and galleries overarching nothing, and room after room where he still dared not go.

He ran up the marble staircase he knew led to his room. Its door opened for him. He threw himself on his bed and broke out in sobs he couldn't muffle by burying his head in his pillows.

Eventually, his terror subsided; his panting eased. He was sure now he wouldn't vomit; he was sure now this fit of chills would pass. He was so much stronger. He was so much better. Behind him, in the doorway, a light flickered. Then a candle lit his room.

The dream lord stood there. "Shamshi," said the regent of the seventh sphere. "I have something for you."

"For me?" He could barely find the strength to sit upright, but he must. The gray eyes of the dream lord looked him over; the arrogant lips drew back over teeth that gleamed too white. His savior came to the bed and sat there for a moment, then put a hand on his clammy brow.

"For you. If you're well enough."

He must be. He had to be. Shamshi was learning about Aškelon and he'd learned a very important thing: one didn't disappoint the entelechy of dream. In the single candle's light, the shadow of his benefactor danced upon his bedroom wall.

Then other candles lit, without a touch of flame. Aškelon said, "Look in the trunk at the foot of the bed."

Sham pulled himself to his feet and staggered over there.

Aškelon saw him struggle but didn't move to aid him.

The lid was heavy. The candles flickered and played. He couldn't believe what he saw. He reached in and took the first piece piled there in the trunk and brought it to the bed. "For *me?*"

"For you. I made it long ago. I've made no other like it."

It was a cuirass, with wrought demons of the elder gods, and snakes, and bulls and lions and a god or two, and lightning, all enameled and touched with gold. "It's magnificent."

Would it fit? He was afraid it wouldn't. He'd seen one very like it, but he didn't remember where. He tried it on over his tunic. First it was too big. Then Aškelon said, "Come here, boy."

He went, and the dream lord touched the cuirass and adjusted it somehow. Now it fit him. "Turn around," said Aškelon. "And turn again. You be careful until you learn its power: it has the lightning, and bulls and lions: all sacred to the storm gods."

Then Shamshi remembered where he'd seen a cuirass like this. But one was very careful with this entelechy that had caught him at death's door and poured life back into him. Sham went again to the trunk and pulled out the shortsword and dirk, and then the shield. At last he was certain.

"This was Stealth's. This panoply belonged to Nikodemos. Is he dead? Have you killed him? Have we…? You promised me that *I* could kill him."

"He's not dead. And that's not so: I promised you that you could *try* to kill him. This came to me another way. If you don't want it –"

Sham gathered up the sword and dirk and held them against the cuirass, near his heart. "Oh, I want it. Everyone said it has charms and powers…. Does it?"

"A few. The odd this, and that; and a bit of mischief in its soul."

"Thank you so much," said Sham, now utterly exhausted, a cold sweat once more breaking out on his brow. "You've saved me and saved me…. Oh…. Dream Lord?"

"Yes, Sham?"

Was that a paternal grimace on the regent's arch face? "I…was practicing in the town, as we agreed I could. And I ran into something that told me to tell you we had met: it calls itself Ischade."

The dream lord's friendly face dropped away. The candles in the room winked out, all at once.

A voice said out of blackness, "Tell me all about it."

When he had done that, the bass voice in the dark said, "You need to be more careful. We do."

"I was so…I'm sorry. None will miss the…victims – would have missed them – but her. She wanted one of them for herself, that's all. I was so disappointed. After nearly getting the Stepsons and Thebans caught and killed in the mist, and then losing them. Every one of them is still alive…. I was frustrated. Careless. I wasn't thinking."

"We need you to do more thinking, less slaughtering, Shamshi. These aren't sheep. The souls of these beings are the best part, the most covetable part."

"I'm sorry. I want to learn. I want to be good. But the fever comes over me and I get delirious. Then I'm so hot, and I need to run, to find a destined fool…."

"Immaterial. Now, we will have a lesson about protection from one such as Ischade. And about protection of the mind and soul when dealing with more potent forces. So listen well, and repeat after me, or you won't survive long enough to wreak the havoc that animates that half-dead body of yours."

Now the blackness around him deepens. Sham has come to know this feeling, this place: halfway between his Chaeronean rest-place and eternity, with Meridian on his right, a wish away, and hell upon his left.

But here he is stronger. Here, he is as strong as Aškelon allows. From that blackness (so warm, so welcoming) the lord of dream and shadow speaks, tutoring this weepy, disconsolate wizard-boy who is an unknowing ally of the Fates – a tool of theirs; a child of destiny, meant to bring low the overweening and make the fights fairer when gods and unchecked powers too boldly interfere with best-laid plans.

So Aškelon enfolds this weapon from another realm. And speaks to him. And speaks again. And shows Shamshi what such a youth must see, to serve desired ends: "Now here is Death. Death is your friend. Death is a minion at your gate. Death guards your house and keeps it safe."

"Safe from what?" Death, to Shamshi, was still an ending, a fearful ravener, a king of terrors.

"Safe from the meddling of gods and Fates. Safe from the wants and needs of men. Safe from right and wrong and good and bad. Safe.... Eternal."

Shamshi wants to be right. He wants to punish wrong. He wants to triumph over gods, have doom on his right hand and destiny on his left. He wants to go back to Chaeronea, to his rest-place.

But all around is only dark; this deepest, velvet dark made up of shadows, where the dream lord's fearsome power dwells (long out of all proportion to what a being, once an archmage and now so much more, should wield).

"I want to go back to my rest-place, to the echoes of Chaeronea. Where I can draw the power of the dying and the newly dead. Where I am strongest."

"You will. But you must be strong wherever you may be. You must earn dominion over place. With that skill comes control of plane and time. Without it, fear can still destroy you. If fear paralyzes your mind, you cannot think; if you cannot think, you cannot prevail. Look what happened with the witch: you feared her; she had power over you from the first moment you were afraid. When you are afraid, you are emasculated. Learn to overcome your fear."

"If we do not fear, then why did we not destroy the Sacred Band when it rode into our mist? That mist can kill, you said – has killed here before. Why didn't it kill them?"

"With three gods there? Two storm gods, and the Theban goddess, ranged against us and actively defending them? Don't fight the gods, student, when men will do."

"So we are afraid of something – some gods?"

"The universe craves not justice, nor vengeance, or satisfaction. The universe craves only knowingness. So know yourself and know your adversary. This is the path to power. Know the difference between fear and prudence. Study strategy, and tactics, and knowingness: together, they sum infinite power. Know when you are up against an enemy too terrible to defeat, out-manned if you still are a man. To live on in the seventh sphere is one thing. To live on in the world of men, quite another."

"How will we defeat our enemies if their gods protect them? I want to kill my enemies there, in Sanctuary, and have them know me as they die. And know why they die. I must. *Must.* It is my destiny. I know it is."

"And you may. When the time is propitious. When your fear lets go of your heart. When your thirst for revenge no longer blinds you. If and when the Fates take a stand against the presumptuous gods. Until then, wait. And learn. And grow strong. When the day comes to fight in such a battle, the echoes of Chaeronea will not be all you have to strengthen you. But until then, even you and I are vulnerable."

And the dream lord went away, leaving him floating in the shadows and his wrath and his fear, to find his way to safety on his own. To find his way back to his Chaeronean rest-place and browse among the perpetually dying and the almost dead and the restless dead he kept frozen there, poised between this world and the next, where Shamshi most liked to be. And he gloated there, among those bodies with their memories of honor and glory, in the place he loved the most.

He had made an error, lost his courage and cravenly fled a power he might have bested, were he brave enough to face the witch and try. This, he thought, was what Aškelon was trying to teach him. So Shamshi studied hard all the wisdom of the lord of dream and shadow: wisdom of fear, and courage in the face of fear, in that shadow realm where nothing was, or is, or will be, except mind. And, studying, learns to know when fear creeps in, warping hopes and dreams.

And, learning, grows strong. And stronger. And stronger yet, day by day, as he masters the lessons Aškelon has set for him. And he tries hard to please his mentor, his savior. In the process, he is becoming something more and something else (much greater than a boy, a youth), in this noplace where days and nights are meaningless, and time itself can fade away. Here he grows strong enough to control his fears – strong enough even to challenge a witch, or more. Strong enough to surmount the poison firing up his blood, which turns his mind to its dark purpose and impels him onward, toward fearful doom. Strong enough to free himself from even the threads of destiny that bind him.

Sometimes.

## *Chapter 38: When Gods and Men and Fates Contest*

"I found him," came Ischade's disembodied voice from no particular direction.

Straton was trying to wrap up his duties in town so he could get out to the barracks to practice with Niko. Ischade materializing here in the middle of Sanctuary in sparkling daylight, in front of the two trainees and Lysis, was the last thing he needed. Ever since Niko's Theban goddess had shown up on the Street of Arcana, the youths went around with eyes the size of saucers. And the Theban Sacred Banders weren't much better.

But in the Stepsons, you do what's in front of you. And right now, what was in front of him was about to be Ischade. "Halt," he said laconically to the three boys trailing him. "This is Ischade, ladies."

A smoky whirlwind was forming in front of the ghost horse's nose. From the whirlwind, the witch's voice issued like fire crackling on a blazing hearth: "When Shamshi's here he is in the Mageguild. When he's not, he is in his battlespace of Chaeronea. Try to catch him here, where he is weak. There, he's too powerful. And he has the lord of dream and shadow for an ally, so beware shadows. But now I have his scent. No more will he elude me," the witch advised Straton, materializing on the street before him with a little *pop*.

The best conceivable thing at the worst conceivable time. He couldn't dally with her now – not here, not with the young fighters in tow. And dallying with Ischade was all Straton thought about, in between battles with sorcerous mist, helping Crit interrogate this one and that one, pulling quarrels and throwing stars out of wounded, and getting the ranks ready for something the Riddler wouldn't discuss. Today he must finish escorting Arton, Lysis and Kouras up Processional and into the palace.

The day had been sunny, beautiful and mild. Now it wasn't: a miasma came with Ischade as if she rode it into town, settling over them in the middle of the street like a tent. Too overt: drawing too much attention here in brightest day. But this news was important, so she came to him in daylight in the finest part of Sanctuary.

Black robes swirled about her on a wind all her own, which whirled round her and out from her and pulled the horses' manes. When Ischade was moving, you just gave up and accommodated her. Ischade was the only force in Straton's life that he'd ever given in to, and he did so whenever he could. Straton's bay ghost horse nickered and pricked its ears at the disturbance in the air. The boys' horses spooked and shied.

The witch hovered there, in the black tent of cloud she'd made in the middle of a busy street in broad daylight. Her huge eyes floated level with Strat's, then zoomed up before each boy's face in turn.

"And you three," came her disembodied voice once more, thin and reedy, floating on the air from a mouth that was further from them than her eyes, "remember – there's nothing *you* can do." And she *popped* away again, whirling in upon herself in a sinkhole of black upon the air, leaving nothing in her wake but wings that flapped up and away: no dark tent of cloud, no whirlwind, no sign she'd ever been there.

"Now what?" gritted Kouras, struggling with his rearing roan as, around them on the street, civilians gawked unabashedly.

"Ride onward. To the palace. Smartly," Straton told them, unwavering. "The commander says we aren't going back to the Mageguild to look for Sham. Niko has the keys, in any case. We continue on with our mission. We find out what Molin means about a coming-out party for Kouras at the palace and see if the Riddler will approve it."

"Straton," Arton called, jerking his brown gelding's reins, "something awful's going to happen. And soon. My stomach's sick from it."

"Something awful is always going to happen, Arton. It's Sanctuary. You're a Stepson. Awful is a big part of your job," Straton told his youngest fighter as the foursome formed up (Lysis beside Straton, Kouras and Arton behind), promising himself that tonight he was going to go back to the Street of Red Lanterns with this boy, Arton, and buy him a proper start on his manhood.

While they made their way toward the palace, Kouras asked Arton, beside him, "What is it? What do you see?"

Before Strat could silence him, Arton said, "It's incomplete – my visions always are. But it's just as bad as Chaeronea. Awful."

"No talking," Straton decreed. But by then Arton had already said quite enough.

When he finished with Arton tonight, Strat decided, he would find time to pay a visit down by Shambles Cross, to the necromant. In the line of duty.

Soon enough they were in the palace and Molin was telling Strat all about his cunning new plan: "We're going to publicly welcome our long-missing storm god, Vashanka, back to Sanctuary. We shall celebrate the Pillager in the body of his avatar, Gyskouras. Embrace syncretism. Of course we'll invite the best and brightest. And most powerful. All the oligarchs. And we'll perform the requisite ritual."

"Wait. What's this ritual?" Strat asked: priests will be priests. They were meeting with Torchholder in his most private sanctum, full of parchment scrolls and tablets on shelves and priestly paraphernalia, astrolabes, and frescoes of rutting gods and deities striking down terrified worshippers with lightning bolts.

"Ritual," said the priest innocently. "Tempus has performed the ceremony here many times. And it would be nice to have a thunderstorm, Gyskouras…if you would be so kind. With lots of lightning. A mighty storm, at the very *end* of the evening, of course…not during the feast. We begin with a feast on the lawn and then bring the privileged inside – *that's* when we want thunder and lightning – for Gyskouras's ritual copulation."

"For his *what?*" Straton asked, too loudly, while Lysis burst out laughing and Kouras flushed as red as his hair and Arton stared open-mouthed. Then Strat recovered. It wasn't that bad. Maybe they could just show a bloody sheet. Or maybe it was going to be the whole, protracted deific marriage ritual, with too many people in attendance. "I'll have to ask the commander. That's more than he may want to make out of so junior a Stepson. Who's the lucky girl?"

"Oh, we have several candidates. Don't worry about that. But, Gyskouras, what about the storm? Do you think you can manage one, on Ilsday next?"

Kouras was looking past the priest, to Strat, eyes frosty; not boyish, not embarrassed now. *"Man proposes, the god disposes.* Vashanka will consider your request. About a ritual. About a storm. The will of gods holds sway. There are other gods to be considered, other wills. Or have *you* not considered *that,* Priest, with Enlil here, and the Theban goddess, and the Fates in play?"

Torchholder said smoothly, "I…have considered it, Gyskouras. That's what we mean when we speak of celebrating syncretism: combining different beliefs and practices harmoniously. And I'm sure the gods will welcome you with open arms, as will all of Sanctuary. As do we, here." The priest spoke softly, attempting a conciliatory tone, meeting the young fighter eye to eye.

A long pause stretched to the sky outside and back again. Somewhere far off, thunder grumbled. This red-haired youth with legs spread wide and green eyes flashing was not the Kouras that Strat knew. Even to Straton's ears, Kouras had sounded convincing. Or convinced: his voice came from deeper in his throat; he seemed taller, stronger; more authentically Vashanka's son.

Straton said, seeing his chance: "So you'll be inviting the entire Sacred Band, as the son of the storm god's retinue, and Jihan, of course?"

"Yes, the entire Sacred Band, including your Thebans and any special guests. Ilsday next. At sundown." The interview was clearly over. "And thank you so much, Gyskouras, for your sage counsel on this matter." Sarcasm dripped from the priestly voice so that Kouras turned on his heel and left the room without another word.

Straton got the remaining two boys out of there, down the stairs, and outside. By then, Kouras was already mounted, holding the other horses in the forecourt. They rode in silence out of the palace compound through the Gate of the Gods, and halfway down to the park called Promise of Heaven, before anyone said a word.

And then that word was preceded by a break in formation, as Kouras urged the blue roan up and crowded Lysis, who was trying hard to be the taciturn Stepson, but having trouble keeping a straight face.

"Ride with Arton, Lysis," Straton said, and heard the scoffs, chortles and whispers behind as Lysis's mount fell back and Kouras fell in beside Strat.

"What am I going to *do?*" Kouras demanded in an urgent whisper, sidling the roan as close to Straton as he could. Overhead, clouds rolled and lightning arced across the sky from horizon to horizon, as if the east of heaven were fighting with the west.

"About what?"

"About…ritual copulation in front of *people,*" came Kouras's tortured voice, boyish now. No god talking, this time.

"If the Riddler agrees to it, you'll do fine. It's the god who's going to do the deed, anyway – not you. Just using your body. Right?" Straton said, dead-pan. This arrogant youth needed a lesson and, if the commander agreed, he was going to get one.

But Straton was uneasy. And so was the sky above: overcast blowing in, cloud-cover boiling up, thunderheads racing and scraping the top of the heavens.

Perhaps Kouras *was* the son of the storm god, conceived here long ago with Tempus's body as the god's instrument. Some said Tempus was conceived this very way; was himself a storm god's son. The commander certainly didn't treat this boy as if he were Tempus's own blood. If so, and if all this talk of Vashanka was true, then they might have another god in play. Two storm gods in one city-state was one storm god too many, to Strat's way of thinking.

But in blew the storm and down came the rain, as if the lightning had opened heaven's underbelly. In the cloudburst, hands slipped on reins and a man could barely see the road ahead between his horse's ears. All things seemed full of gods, every tree, every field, every stream they passed.

And all the way out to the barracks in the downpour, Strat kept thinking that if the Pillager was truly back in town, then this thieves' world would finally suffer its due: Vashanka was the berserker god, untrustworthy, vengeful, hungry for blood and careless of his faithful. However, if someone woke him to his former glory, the Sacred Band might benefit.

When Tempus and Vashanka had been one flesh, blood had flowed like a river. In those days, the armies said that any battle in which the Riddler fought was as good as won, every enemy of his defeated; every cause he championed reigned supreme. Strat had fought under Vashanka's blazon then, and the Pillager was hell on wheels in any fight. They could use as much of that unconquerable force as they could get, these days. But now the Band was sworn to Enlil; and this foreign war goddess, Harmony, had shown her standard.

Whenever gods fought among themselves, men suffered. Still, the Sacred Band could use a little bit of Vashanka's kind of luck right now, and his fated glory, if killing mist and the lord of dream and shadow were creeping about Sanctuary's streets again. Strat had been here the last time Aškelon unleashed his lethal mist. The aftermath of that, no man could easily forget.

When Strat got to the barracks, soaked and dripping, he went to the officers' quarters, in search of Nikodemos and the Riddler, to report. But he couldn't find them, either one. They'd left no word with the sentries, or with Sync, where they'd gone. And neither of the Trôs stallions were in their stalls.

Strat was here to practice with Niko. Niko was unlikely to go off without leaving word.

With both of them gone, Strat was the senior officer present. There was plenty for Strat to do at the barracks. Especially with Tempus's twelve newly-hired mercenaries standing around. Each had to be outfitted and evaluated, as did incoming shipments of arms and armor, half a dozen chariots, and incendiaries from Zip, arriving by the wagonload.

Sync said, "What are we going to do with all this naphtha?" Sync hated anything flammable: he was responsible for the horses. The first crate they opened was filled with naphtha amphorae, with blown glass bottles (the right size for throwing), and smaller ampoules for arrow points.

Strat said, "Build a shed for all this, across the compound from the horse barns. Near the cisterns, in case we need more water than the gods are giving." It was still storming. Rain was running down their faces, dripping from their chins.

"Do you know what the commander is planning?" Sync gestured around, at the wagons up to their spokes in mud.

"No," he said. "He'll tell us when he's ready."

Then he happened to look up at the crest of the hill and saw two mounted figures out by the altars, nearly invisible in the torrential rain.

He considered getting his horse and riding up there, but something told him not to do it. He'd been listening to that something (not a voice, but an instinct) for years. It had kept him alive this long.

So he said, "Come on, Sync, I'll help you," and off they went to divvy up the workload among the new fighters and the veterans not otherwise engaged. If he got done soon enough, he could still take Arton to Aphrodisia House and ride out to Shambles Cross this evening.

*

Cloudburst, overhead and all around.

"Niko," said Tempus, "when gods and men and Fates contest, any help is welcome." Trying to be heard through the blinding rain, he shifted on his horse. His mount and Niko's were side by side, one facing east and one facing west, between the altars of Enlil and Harmony.

"It's not that. I'm putting everyone at risk. The goddess said the Mageguild was a trap meant for me. Give me leave to go back down there, call Sham out for battle – one on one." Frustration rode Niko's words. So dangerous, with a fighter like this, when patience slips away. Wet hair hung nearly to his shoulders, not long enough to club back, too long to stay out of his eyes.

Tempus needed to retake control of his partner. Anger, eroding discipline, corroding everything so painstakingly built, was throwing Niko off balance.

"No. I said before, we're not going back there." Earlier, the day had been bright and sunny. They'd ridden out to the spot where Tempus had sent Abarsis up to heaven, so long ago. Niko had never seen it. He'd hoped the ride would help his partner focus, put events at the Mageguild in perspective. It hadn't. The outcropping bore no marker, no sign that Abarsis had been dispatched from there to heaven.

Now that they were back on the hill above the barracks, the storm god's lightning was tearing up the sky. His Trôs stallion pawed the ground, impatient, standing so long in the rain; he stroked its neck.

"Things aren't as simple as you insist, Niko. Killing one wizard boy isn't the answer to all our problems. Gods are moving; forces shifting. You don't understand the threat."

"I do, Commander," said Niko, rain running down his face like tears, dripping from his hair in the torrent. "It's better to face Sham in the Mageguild than in my rest-place, or his. I know what to do. Give me leave to do it. Now." Lightning snapped above.

"Not if you won't make peace with that goddess and take any help she offers you." Combating Sham in some mystical Bandaran battlespace, Niko was nearly lost to them once. How do you tell your best fighter he's not ready, when such a man must believe he can win against all odds on any day? "I can't afford to lose you." Thunder pealed.

"First you tell me to stay away from her." Niko had to raise his voice to be heard over the storm. "Now you want me to give her my soul. I don't believe I need…more help than you and the Sacred Band provide. Or that the Band needs… her. How will Enlil take it, with a goddess vying with him for adherents?"

"You needed her help to heal; when you were hurt, she was *all* you wanted. For the healing, I'm grateful and you should be. As for Enlil, are you asking for your own sake? Or for the Stepsons? Enlil will do as he pleases." Wind caught the rain and whipped them with it, whistling.

"She's upsetting things." Exasperated. Humiliated. "Thebans kissing her pennant, making pennants of their own. Crit's offended. Others are." Thunder rolled again.

"Those Thebans are hers. Her adherents." Strange, to be taking the goddess's part, but truth was truth. "She's here because of them. Not because of you. She has an altar here; she has rights here now. She lost two-hundred fifty-four fighters on the Chaeronean battleplain. Then she lost two more here. How would you feel?"

"I can't answer that. Perhaps you know the minds of gods. I don't. But I know what *we* need. It's me doing what I said I'd do. We need this to stop. I'll stop Shamshi. He's a symbol of all that's wrong. And if Aškelon is really here, in this with his mists and all his tricks, it's not going to stop until I stop it. I can talk to him. He'll meet with me." He raked strands of sopping hair back from his face.

*Not 'we,' but 'I.'*

"It's past time for talk, Niko." His rightman seldom told him to his face that he was wrong. At least Stealth was stronger now. His fighter sat his horse without thought, without favoring his right side, without leaning left, or using his right leg gingerly, or weakly.

"We need to do something. I do."

Lightning flashed again. Tempus said, "I'll make a deal with you. I'll ride down to the barracks. You stay here and talk with the goddess, Niko, if she'll talk with you. Talk with Enlil, if he'll listen. You'll be helping me: I need to keep the gods off all our necks, with Aškelon here." *Go carefully: gods contest here, and Aškelon is beyond the laws that men and gods obey.* "Then I'll ride with you into Sanctuary. And we'll try, one more time, at the Mageguild. Just the two of us. Agreed?"

Niko looked at him through the rain, his eyes flat and empty now, his face composed. Not a good sign, with this one. "I'll try," he said.

So Tempus rode down the hill to wait and watch from a distance. And Straton was waiting for him there, wet and muddy, on foot in the courtyard where men wrestled with crates and carts in the rain.

Strat said, "Commander, Ischade came to me in the city. She said Shamshi's joined up with Aškelon. She says when

Sham's here, he's in the Mageguild and when he's not, he's in some Chaeronean 'battlespace.' She says try to catch him here, where he's weaker. She thinks he's too strong in that other place – wherever it is – even for us." Strat spread his arms and dropped them. "Not my opinion – hers. She says she has his scent."

"I'll deal with it. What else?" Tempus asked, seeing more left unspoken in Straton's eyes. Niko had just said nearly the same thing to him: '*It's better to face Sham in the Mageguild than in my rest-place, or his.*' Treacherous ground, today, and not only because of the mud and the storm.

Rain slicked Straton's face. "Riddler, Torchholder wants to throw a feast for Kouras on Ilsday – full moon. And he wants Kouras to perform one of Vashanka's copulation rituals, with luminaries in attendance. You'd know which rite...."

God of sack and pillage. He knew Vashanka's rituals well. One of them had produced Gyskouras. *He's too young.* If Tempus let the boy perform the rite, the god would be fully in Kouras forever after. And fully in Sanctuary, if the Pillager wasn't already. It had been a long time since Vashanka had spoken to Tempus, who'd cursed Ranke and all its gods, who'd left Vashanka's service and taken up with Enlil. They were estranged, the man and his former god. The rain chilled him.

Vashanka was a jealous god, and the Sacred Band of Stepsons had once been his to command. And was not, now...but for this one youth, Kouras. "Perhaps the mating rite is not so bad a thought," he told Strat. "If Kouras has the god inside him, let's see what happens when we acknowledge the fact formally. At least we'll know. And afterward, if the god is pleased, Vashanka may fight for us once again. We'll do it. Tell Torchholder we'll attend. And tell Kouras he may come to me with questions if he has them."

Strat grinned at him through the buffeting storm, "Can I be there for the tutorial?"

When Tempus looked around, Niko wasn't on the hilltop any longer. Too much anger, and only one place Niko would have gone.... Tempus clapped his legs around his horse and galloped out of there, hoping to intercept his fighter before things went too far. The sentries barely got the gates open in time.

But Niko hadn't disobeyed his orders. On foot, head down, he was walking his mount toward the gates through the rain, which was finally letting up.

"So what happened?" he asked, riding his big Trôs in a circle around his Stepson, and then coming alongside.

"Nothing," Niko said, looking up at him, soaked and dripping. "I stood there in the rain at their altars. Neither Harmony nor Enlil spoke to me. I tried. I'm not like you, not what's needed for talking to gods and goddesses. And I've got to rub down this horse and clean all this tack." Wet hair, down in his eyes; wet beard, close around his face; gaze remote and colder than Tempus liked. He'd let this one have his own way too much, and now they were at odds over gods.

So Tempus got off his horse and walked together with Niko through the gates and back toward the stables as the rain stopped at last. "You need to cut your hair," he said. "We're going to a feast at the palace at full moon." *Change the subject.*

Tempus wasn't going to tell Niko what Ischade said right now, or let Niko go to the Mageguild by himself. He wasn't going to soften. His gut told him that if he did, he could lose his partner.

*

Back in his own quarters, not the Riddler's, Niko cut off all the hair he could reach. It wasn't easy, but his helmet would fit better; his hair wouldn't fall into his eyes. He shaved his beard. He cleaned up after himself. He'd moved back in here two days past. He needed to sleep. The Riddler was up all night, every night. Niko needed to meditate. He needed to spend time in his rest-place.

He needed to decide what to do. His anger, aimed at the gods themselves, was spilling over, even polluting his contact with the Band and the Riddler.

There is always a correct path. There is always the right solution. There is always balance, equilibrium, and calm. If he could just find it. His body was no longer betraying him. He was as good or better than he'd ever been.

When the goddess said the Mageguild trap was just for him, she'd made it clear that all the harm Sham had done was on his account. Riding with the Sacred Band through a mist that chilled, but might have killed, had shown Niko how great a threat the wizard boy could be.

Shamshi had help, that was clear. From Aškelon. No one else could call down wizard weather. Aškelon wasn't being fair. But then, the dream lord never had been.

He sat on his bed. Then, stripped down to his loinguard, he sat on the floor cross-legged, to see if he could. His right flank didn't scream at him; his body was better than it had any right to be. *She* had done that for him. Or to him.

He sat until he couldn't sit any longer. He couldn't stay in his rest-place; he wasn't calm enough. He could reach his blue-green meadow, his clear stream, his blue sky – but two figures moved among the trees at the edge of his copse, intruding there, lurking. And that made him angry. He could see them in the distance. And whenever he tried to chase them away, the specter of Chaeronea intervened, opening up under his feet like a chasm.

He wasn't going to Sham's battleplain. Not again. He couldn't face that battle, that parody of Chaeronea – not unarmed, not from here. Not yet. Not while his *maat* eluded him. Fury was eating at his composure, eroding his hold on his soul. This intrusion into his rest-place was intolerable, a violation of sanctity that kept him from finding equilibrium. Was it the dream lord lurking there, with Sham?

He still had only his shabby duty gear; none of his new equipment had arrived but the crossbow and the shortsword. He strung the sword on his old work belt. Tomorrow he'd practice with it, with Strat.

Then he remembered he'd missed his practice with Strat today.

And that made him even angrier with himself. This had to stop. He got his gear, his work belt, its belt-pouch, girt on the sword, and went outside to the stables. He'd go find Crit and work the town tonight. He needed to attack something; dismantle something; find a target and dismember it, piece by piece; push the rage through him. There is no balance in an angry soul.

He took out the black colt and tacked it up. He wasn't taking his mare, who might be in foal, for this foray, or one of the good Trôs horses. This was his colt. No one could disapprove of him taking it.

He swung up on it while still in the stable and rode it between the doors into the night. A light rain was falling, hardly more than a drizzle, soft and mild. The stable doors could stay open.

Sentries saw him coming and pulled back the gates before him, closed them behind. Then it was done.

All the way down to Sanctuary in the dark, he sought his *maat*, that mystic calm that gave him all the peace he ever knew. He'd hoped the ride would lull him: the cadence of his horse, the patter of the rain, the sounds of night creatures all around. He would make a gravel pond out at the barracks. Tempus wouldn't mind. Arton and Kouras could use it too. He could give them lessons more advanced than they'd yet had.

The black colt was rambunctious, hot-blooded, petitioning heaven for mares. As long as the colt kept his head down, Niko didn't punish him: he was a young horse, after all, looking for love wherever he could find it.

They forded the White Foal just above the fork; it was good for the colt to wade across. So they came into the city through Triumph Gate. It was fourth watch by then; few were stirring. The rain had stopped. He ran his palm over his slick saddle, over the colt's sweaty shoulder; its muscles twitched under his hand. Crickets chirped somewhere close.

He wasn't paying much attention to his route; he didn't realize he was near the Street of Arcana until he got there. He halted the colt at the intersection.

His commander had told him not to do this alone. He knew better than to disobey. But that long, empty street called to him, taunting and sinister. He put his left leg on the colt and it ambled toward the Mageguild. They'd just walk up there to see if any lights were on. Tempus had said he couldn't go in there, not that he couldn't ride by there.

There was no mist, tonight – at least not that kind. The air was wet, heavy; wisps of fog lay about, like steam floating above the ground. He rode to where he thought Harmony had cast her standard, that long spear. He couldn't see the hole that the spear-point had made in the road, but he knew it must be there.

He couldn't let this go on, not this way; not with Sham picking off his cohort, trying to get to him. He wasn't afraid of that wizard boy. One youth, causing so much trouble: he couldn't excuse it. Ari dead, and Deon, and a pair of Thebans. Lysis wounded, twice; and Kouras and Arton, once.

Enough. The youth was big and strong, and lethal. This time, Niko would give no quarter. He was looking for something to hack to pieces tonight and Sham was just the right thing.

He closed his legs on the colt. It snorted but did as he ordered: they jogged straight up to the Mageguild gates. He had the keys. Tempus trusted him. His commander had let him keep those keys: souvenirs.

He would solve this problem of Shamshi and his commander would be pleased. The threat would go away. The youth would go away. No one else needed to be hurt.

He slid off his mount, rump to horse. He drop-tied the colt, telling it, "Stay," then thought better of it and tied its reins to the Mageguild's iron fence. He slipped his shield off its saddle thong and onto his left arm; from the colt's off side, he got his helmet and settled it on his head.

In his belt-pouch, the keys clinked. He got out all three and tried them. Tonight, the second one opened the lock on the gates. He pushed the gates open, then slipped inside, putting the keys back in his belt-pouch.

He drew his new shortsword. It felt unaccustomed in his hand. He tried it against the air, slashing back and forth. It would serve its purpose. The colt called plaintively: it didn't want to be tied there, all alone.

He'd just started up the walk, setting one foot in front of the other, when the Mageguild's double oak doors banged open. Something came flying out, screeching so loudly his ears rang, launching itself through the air at him.

Nothing human could leap so far. He couldn't make sense of the form it had, distorted and misshapen, streaking at him through the dark. But it did have a shape.

He tracked the center of that shape with his sword: whatever it was, if it had bowels, he could disembowel it; if it had a head, he could decapitate it; if it had a heart, he could skewer it. It certainly had a mouth and lungs: it screamed like a banshee, a long burbling scream, coming on.

It hit him faster and harder than he thought it would: it hit him and his shield with the force of a falling rock, knocking the wind out of him. He staggered, almost going down. His sword stabbed into something soft and he pulled his blade up, twisting: he felt a body, some indescribable carcass that might be ribbed, grating on that shortsword; other things that might be arms, around him. But there were too many limbs for them all to be arms.

Too many arms and legs were grappling him. This thing was screaming and sobbing and it definitely had teeth: teeth were sunk in his shield arm. The embrace that held him didn't have bones where bones should be and the thing that hugged him close didn't smell like a man. It smelled like a dead thing. He'd once embraced his undead partner, Janni, and he knew what long-dead things smelled like close at hand.

It was slimy. Its fetid breath was puffing against him; spittle rode each gasp. It caught up his legs with some part of itself and wound around his arms with something else.

He hit the ground.

Then it began tearing at him, biting at his cuirass, wrenching and pulling in a battle he didn't understand.

He was rolling on the ground with it, his shortsword and sword-hand stuck up inside it. He couldn't get his sword free, couldn't use his shield; he couldn't get its teeth out of his shield arm.

And it had another way to cut and rend and tear, although he couldn't see a sword or a knife or even a head or an eye.

He couldn't get to his belt-knife, couldn't get his sword arm free with this adversary clutching him like some hellish lover. The only chance he had was his sword, stuck up there, inside its body, while this thing screeched and howled around a mouthful of his arm. He wrapped his legs around whatever was grabbing at him.

On his back with the wailing thing on top of him, he tried to push forward with his sword, then pull back with his shield-arm, hoping to sever or break something – a spine, a limb – while he dug around with his shortsword inside a body that was slippery and screaming.

His stomach caught on fire. It hurt, a white hot pain, coursing across him from side to side. It was hard to breathe. He couldn't get this amorphous, ravaging thing off him. He couldn't get a grip on its arms (if it had them) or neck (if it had one) or head.

And then it was gone. No more banshee howling, no more keening, no more growling or munching.

Abrupt silence.

Not even a final grunt when it disappeared. It just *wasn't there* – its weight was no longer on top of him.

He was lying there, flat on his back on the Mageguild walk, alone, with a white-hot pain in his stomach and a chewed shoulder. But he still had his sword and something wet was all over it, and all over him. He thought he'd get up, now; take stock. His sword arm was lying across his chest. He could feel his heart beating through his cuirass.

At first he thought he was just too weak with relief that this incomprehensible battle was over. He'd studied battle all his life: every nuance, every form, every nicety. Fighting something that flickered in and out of being with no particular shape was a test of faith, a test of *maat* – a test of every skill he had…and some he didn't have.

It was gone, now. Whatever it was, or had been, its suffocating weight wasn't on top of him anymore. His chest was heaving. He took greedy breaths, happy to have the privilege and lungs that could still breathe air.

But he couldn't get up. He couldn't move. He was lying there in a wet patch, in the dark. And he couldn't move at all.

He took a deeper breath. He could breathe as deeply as he pleased. He was alive. He could feel his heart pounding in his ears.

But he couldn't move his arms or legs. And beyond the white-hot searing pain in his stomach, he couldn't feel anything. He tried to shift his head but he couldn't do that either.

Behind him, the colt gave a plaintive, mournful whinny. And another. And something whinnied back.

*Now I'm in for it. It's sent a friend to finish the job.*

But he still couldn't move, not yet. He was too exhausted. As soon as he could roll over, he'd need to deal with whatever this was, coming in on horseback.

He wished the dawn would break, so he could see better. Helmets were tricky that way: you couldn't hear, or see, the way you'd like.

His breathing was very loud in his ears, so he wasn't sure if he heard footsteps, or if he didn't.

Stones scraped, clacked together; scraped again. And then he was sure: someone was coming. Or something was.

*If I can just move.* But he couldn't. He still couldn't feel his arms or legs.

And yet the pain in his stomach was very clear: the pain was so intense it made him want to retch, but he couldn't do it. He could feel every flap of ripped skin across his stomach, every iota of cut muscle and slashed flesh. That pain washed over him in waves, as if it was his pulse, as if whatever hurt in his stomach was his whole being.

But he still couldn't move an arm, or leg, or turn his head.

*Bad way to die. Helpless, belly up on the ground, like a beetle waiting for someone to come along and crush it underfoot.*

He went seeking his *maat*, his rest-place, and this time it opened to him, welcoming and full of joy: his meadow rolled eternally, star-shaped, ever green. The grass was thick; butterflies and hummingbirds fluttered there; clouds like mares' tails floated across a clear blue sky. Here he could move. He walked over to his stream and saw a current of blood in the middle of clear water, with a blue tinge of sorcery winding it round: his faith and fate; the will of gods. There were pebbles in his stream bed, worn smooth with the passing of time.

If he could just retreat, just hide his soul here, then he was safe. He could sit down here. Gain strength here. Watch the blood and colors in his stream. Abarsis would come and sit with him. And everything would be as it was meant to be.

Then something hit him – hit his body on the Mageguild walk. It pounded on his chest. He could feel it strike him: *once, twice, three times.*

*Again.* And *again.*

So he had to go back there: he had a body to protect. And now it hurt like very hell.

After the sunlight in his rest-place, the dark of night was impenetrable. Through the eyeholes in his helmet, in that dark, he couldn't see who was bending over him; still, he knew someone was there.

He wanted to say something, but he couldn't. If it was Sham, his enemy, he wanted to acknowledge an end to fighting, salute the victor; make a proper finish to what was so poorly begun. If it was the Riddler, he wanted to explain. He wanted to say how much he'd loved their life together, how much he loved the Stepsons, how much Tempus and all he taught had meant to him. He was the richer for it all.

But he couldn't talk. He couldn't move.

He felt his neck snap back when the helmet was pulled off his head. He felt the moist summer air kiss his face. He tried to make out the figure above him but there was too much darkness, tinged with red.

A jolt tore through him; he knew he was being dragged: the pain in his stomach spiked hotter, curling around his spine and ribs, his kidneys and his heart. The pain constricted his gut; muscles cramped; breathing was harder; his stomach was blazing. Anguish pulsed in waves, breaking across him in sparks that caught fire wherever they met his muscles, spasming his flesh. He could barely breathe for the agony of it.

Then his head fell back on something softer than stone. Someone was bending down over him. He could see a vaguely human form, just an outline in the lifting dark.

Hair fell in his eyes, and then away. He heard a voice say, "Niko, let me help you, one more time. Please. Or you'll miss all your beautiful battles yet to come." And lips sought his own, kissing him, caressing him, blowing breath into him. "Please say yes. Say…yes. And then lie still – don't fight, for just another moment. Just lie still, and then you can get up."

He couldn't move. He couldn't fight. He wanted to, so much. He had nothing left to fight with; lying still was all he could do. He could smell her, that summer breeze of her. But he couldn't say anything. He tried. His body wouldn't obey him. He thought, *Oh, please. Please, yes.*

And she kissed him again, with his head in her lap, on her armor. There was a moment where and when he hung suspended. Far below were her thighs, his head resting there, and life. And all around, there was red anguish, and dark numbness, worse than pain – pain held in abeyance, with no body to hurt, or take a breath, or know it hurt, or be in any way alive. Then feeling returned.

And with it came a deeper, more excruciating agony, a more abiding pain, and he groaned despite himself. “Please,” he said out loud, “Please, help me if you can.” *Don't leave me paralyzed here for it to find....*

“Oh, I can,” said Harmony’s soft, sweet voice. And the goddess kissed him once more and blew her breath of life into his mouth and every inch of him caught fire. Her breath burned hotter than the white-hot pain in his stomach. It burned hotter than the sun. It tingled colder than the space between the stars, or the place where his heart should beat like a drum. *Tat rata tat.* He remembered how a heart could beat, what it should feel like. What it should sound like. *Tat rata tat. Tat rata tat.* He remembered lifting his dancing girl on the beach, in the sand, with the music pounding so fast in his head and her silken hair swirling around them.

That fire consumes him and remakes him. *Tat rata tat. Tat rat tata tata tat.* Lightning courses through him, igniting every sinew, every nerve, and searing deep into his flesh. When that fire passes, his stomach doesn’t hurt. His legs and arms obey him.

“Thank you,” he manages, ashamed and relieved and free of pain, but still content to lie there, breathing the meadow of her, trying to find her eyes as dawn begins. Is she real? Or has she come to his rest-place to find him? Abarsis had come there, once, when death was near.

She still cradles his head in her lap. And behind her, dawn’s first colors preen, surrounding her with all the fire of nature. She is the most beautiful sight he has ever seen, wrapped in the dawn, as if the world itself exalts her. She is illumined by heaven’s glory.

And she says, "Beloved, you'll never be hurt that way again. Not now. Come, get up. We need to get you out of here. You can ride. Trust me."

He trusts her. He tries his arms. They move. He tries to sit up. His spine works. He tries to get his legs under him. They hearken and obey. She stands up first and holds out her hand. He takes it, not ashamed now, but glad to have her help. Their dawn is turning gold and blue and peach and fiery, reflecting from her armor.

He looks down once, and back again: where he lay is now an empty pool of blood, too big to be survivable if it came from just one man. His cuirass is chewed on the left side, ripped open across the middle by a claw or blade whose strength he can't fathom or begin to estimate. The two of them leave bloody tracks as they walk slowly together to the open Mageguild gates.

His colt and her big black snort reprovingly at the smell of blood. He is shaky, but strong enough. She paces him. Somehow his arm is over her armored shoulder. He thinks that he shouldn't get blood in that beautiful hair. She walks him to his horse.

First he thought he couldn't swing up there; the saddle seemed so far away.

She said, "You can. You're just shocked. You're fine. Get on your horse."

He did, because she said so. And he could sit the horse just fine. She untied his reins from the gate and gave them to him. "Heinous place, full of heartbreak and hubris," she said, tossing her head. "We'll not come here henceforth. Your commander was correct, not to want to do battle here again. This is no place to meet such foes as these, on their home ground."

"I'm not supposed to be here now…."

"Then you were never here, if you wish it so."

But he couldn't ask her that. Not to lie. Nor would he. He said, "Will you ride with me to the barracks?"

And she rode beside him, all the way home.

*

"It's done," said the Theban goddess to Tempus, at the barracks, outside his office. "What you asked." The goddess wore her black armor; it gleamed in the morning sun. Her helmet was under her arm.

"Done? What's done?" Niko must be with their horses. He could see hers at the stable door.

"He accepted the help you asked for him. I thought that you should know, before your next battle." Her voice was grave. Her amber eyes searched his. "Use him wisely. Few have been given such a weapon by the gods or Fates before."

And she walked away, toward the barracks stable where her horse was tied outside.

When Tempus got there, he found no goddess, no big black horse tied there.

In the cool stable, Niko was rubbing down his black colt, his back to the stall door, wearing just his tunic of mossy green linen, old and threadbare. The tunic was stiff and torn, dark with stains like mottles all down its side and across its back. His cuirass and gear lay on a bale of straw outside the stall.

Tempus fingered the cuirass: the leather and linen of the armor was sundered across the diaphragm, crusted with blood. He could put his fingers through the slash and spread them. The whole left shoulder of the cuirass was badly chewed, sticky with clots. The new shortsword was nicked and its blade blackened.

Niko had cut his hair; it stuck out and up and every whichway, clumped together.

Tempus knew Niko had seen him come in. He waited, leaning on the stall's partly open half-door, but his partner didn't say a word, just brushed and rubbed on the black colt. Niko's tack was slung over the half-door, smeared with mud or blood or both.

"What happened, Stealth?" Tempus asked at last.

Niko untied the colt from the wall and turned to face Tempus. The whole front of his tunic was dark, stiff and torn. "She left," said Niko, coming toward him until only the half-door was between them. "She was coming to see you, she said. Her horse left too."

"Before she left." Tempus licked his fingers and ran them across the saddle, then tasted his fingertips. Blood. He reached out to touch Niko's stiff tunic, where the long slash was. "What happened?"

Niko retreated a step, away from his hand, then slipped out the half-door and closed it behind him. "I…ended up down at the Mageguild. I apologize for disobeying orders. Whatever punishment you decide there is for that, I deserve it." He stood face to face with Tempus, head high, eyes a world away.

There was too much dried blood mottling that tunic, on his arms, on his legs. *I should have told him what Ischade said. When I realized he was gone, I should have gone after him. I knew where he was going.* Far too much dried blood. But his partner wasn't shaking, or pale, or dripping fresh blood, or holding his entrails in place.

"Come to my quarters. Now." This was nothing to discuss in public. Men were coming in, changing horses, choosing tack. Niko gathered up his cuirass, his swordbelt, the rest of his gear, and paced him.

The sun was smiling bright; birds were singing. He watched his Stepson as the two of them walked across the courtyard. Three times men approached them. He waved them off with hand-sign. This fighter of his had been through something that not even a tunic meant to minimize blood-stains could hide. Niko's long limbs moved easily. Tempus scrutinized every detail. His partner showed no sign of pain or weakness.

Niko paused on the threshold to put down his gear.

"Bring it," Tempus said. "Inside – you and all of that."

Here it would be easier, whatever they must say to one another. He took the little chair behind his table. Niko stood with his back against the door he closed.

"Now, tell me."

"I'm sorry. I…I thought she'd tell you."

"She told me you accepted the help I asked for you. Now you tell me. Look at you. You're lucky you aren't dead, from the state of you and your gear. *Again.*"

Niko leaned his head back against the door and stared at him so hard he thought his heart would break: resignation, loss, and sadness so deep a man could drown in it. *"Never* again, she said. Commander, forgive me. I can't face that Sham thing in my rest-place, or his. I need to do it here."

"I know, Niko. Ischade told us. Yesterday. I should have told you. So we will forgive each other, today."

"Thank you," sighed the fighter, leaning against the door, and sagged a bit. "Thank you."

"Now tell me."

"I…ended up at the Mageguild gates. Used the key. Something came flying out of the doors. I grappled with it. It won. I couldn't even move. Lying in my own blood. Paralyzed. She…came along. Told me to ask if I wanted help. I didn't want to live like that or die like that. I should be braver, but I'm not. I asked. She *did* something to me…. I'm not wounded. *In any way.*"

Nikodemos came away from the door and reached him in three strides. He sat back. The Stepson stripped off his tunic with a pull that ripped it from his body. "Look. Just dried blood: mine. Not a scratch." He turned slowly, full around, examining his own body as if it belonged to someone else, his face expressionless. But his voice was trembling. "My whole stomach was on fire – ripped open, I think. Look at the cuirass. I couldn't move – my head, my arms, my legs. Couldn't talk at first. I was lying in enough blood for two men. I…don't understand. She…."

Tempus was up before he thought about it. Came around the table. Took his Stepson in his arms and just held him, feeling Niko shudder and shiver and shake, feeling that spiky hair matted with blood against his shoulder.

They stood there that way until Niko's breathing eased. Then Tempus let him go.

Niko sat on the table and said, "What now?" looking up at him with naked entreaty for an instant. Then the expressionless countenance returned, and armored eyes narrowed. In only the bloody loinguard, his breathing was easy to judge: this one wanted to fight, or flee. "What do you think, Commander?"

"I think you're very lucky. I think the next time you disobey my orders, I'm going to treat you much more harshly. I think you're going to promise not to go off alone – for any reason – until we get this matter sorted out with Shamshi and Aškelon. Agreed?"

"Yes, Commander." Hazel eyes locked on him like salvation. "But now what?"

"Now what? Not much has changed. You're still a Stepson. Still second-in-command of the Sacred Band. You have duties to attend to, that can't be attended to half naked and covered with blood. Clean yourself up and we'll go into the city. And thank that goddess, every day, that you came through this so well."

"Thank you, Riddler." Niko got off the table and headed to the door, fluid and fit and strong. There he paused and looked over his shoulder, and said, "Am I…?" He shook his head and opened the door, shrugging into his ripped tunic and grabbing up his ruined gear. And paused.

"Are you what?" Tempus asked softly. He knew what Niko wanted to know. He simply didn't know how to tell him. When it had happened to him, it had taken him ages to accept it. He'd slit his wrists and watched how long it took for them to seal. He'd done that more than once, over time, testing the gods and himself. With Vashanka. With Enlil. And neither god manifested outside him, but within him. This thing between Harmony and Niko was different.

Niko stared at him wordlessly, waiting for wisdom, absolution or intimations of immortality.

Tempus sighed and said, "My right-side partner needs to be able to withstand more than the average fighter. Now you can. Or so your goddess says." Stealth, called Nikodemos, had suffered enough, repented enough, and now needed something to hold onto, desperately. So Tempus added, as gently as he could, "You're still what you were: a weapon of the god. Perhaps more than you were. Your goddess told me that few have been given such a weapon by the gods or Fates before. And for that, I'm grateful to her. I need all the weapons I can get."

He saw his Stepson nod as the fighter slipped out the door without another word and into a different kind of future than Nikodemos had faced before. Or than he had.

How will it be for him, this Nikodemos, this simple fighter of few pretensions, so young in body and in mind? Fighting with his goddess beside him, not with a god inside him? Will he still be so just in battle, this balanced force, now that grace relieves his soul?

Niko had been Tempus's greatest vulnerability for so long. If things were really as they seemed, if the goddess were truthful, then not only Niko was changed.

Everything was different now: they could bring the fight to their enemies. Fight on other days without number. Forever.

## *Chapter 39: God to God, Man to Man*

"Love sees all; hate is blind," says the goddess Harmony to Enlil and Vashanka, where they walk among purple heather and sage, on feral fields below an outcropping of rock. "We will mend this rift among us through harmonious action in war, if hate cannot blind us. Celestial order must be restored."

"Why bother? Only from chaos does order come. The angry Fates bring death where they will, when war is king," says Enlil, storm god of the armies, and the tip of his crown rends the clouds above their heads. "Wheresoever I rule, death comes shambling after. So it has always been, is, and will be."

"True. Strife brings all things into being on her battlefield. This I know. I have been there many times," says Vashanka, lord of sack and pillage. "I have died before."

"Gods cannot die while love lives. In knowing hearts lies eternity," the goddess of harmony in love and war rejoins.

"Speaking of eternity, Harmony, you saved a lowly avatar of mine twice from death and then resurrected him. Each soul has its appointed doom. How is it you dare to raise a mortal boy so high – high enough to flout the gods? Bring godhead where a man may reach out and take it?" growls Enlil, and lightning splits a clear blue sky.

"Yes, how? Why? I have never done so much for any mortal, lest power tempt lowly humans to vie with gods," Vashanka adds, in his voice of thunder that shakes the ground beneath their feet.

"He asked for help for another – not for himself. We all heard him, when that young fighter walked into the Lemurian sea and prayed for help…to help his partner – to help *your* favorite avatar, Enlil – an act of love in war. Any of us could have answered. But you didn't. So I did. And do. Surely, all agree, from that one selfless act, all this has sprung. To right a balance still upset."

"That mortal fighter begged you for the life of his partner, and then for his own life. And you had mercy. Mercy is not in favor in my heavens today," says Vashanka, unforgiving and combative, folding vast arms and spearing Harmony with lightning that crackles from his gaze.

"Nor in mine," Enlil agrees, adding thunder of his own.

The goddess of love in war entangles their aggression in her hair, as long as infinity; ensnares it, holds it till it fades away. "Balance drives all things through all things," Harmony reminds them. "You upset the balance, Vashanka, and died of it yourself, and lost adherency, and loyalty, and the love of souls. Now, reborn, you start anew. Beware the same cycle overcoming you again: spend souls profligately and they'll not love you. Then what have you? Empty altars, empty temples, empty threats of power you no longer wield."

Vashanka's lightning forks to earth and thunder rolls once more. Harmony waves her hand and thunder ceases; black clouds split, and sunshine bathes the fields across the whole of heaven.

The god Enlil says, "Vashanka, you lost Tempus thus, your greatest earthly avatar, and now he's mine. I have raised him up far beyond what you ever did for any man. The goddess is correct in that."

"And look what comes of all this," Vashanka rumbles, calling back his thunderheads around him like a cloak. "We three are disunited in the face of angry Fates and killing mist, fighting among ourselves over frail mortals when we should be fighting greater dooms and malignant powers not subject to the rules than men or gods obey."

"You have nothing to fight a war and win with, Vashanka," declares Enlil, shaking out his yarrow-honey hair to tangle up with Harmony's and blow across his high brow, free from lines. "You have no true believers among the fated dead, and no souls who love you, no empire raising up your standard when it fights, no armies going down to you on bended knee. You are a puny god, ignoble and cowardly, all but forgotten. The Missing God, they called you once, these mortals. Was that Missing in Action? Or Missing in Heart? Harmony is right: it takes love, to war. It takes passion to fight. And you have no love, no passion besides your own passion for yourself. Come back when you have an avatar and walk with us again," Enlil decrees, and ends the summit unresolved with a flash of lightning that blows all knowingness away, and gods away, and time away, with no pact made by these three against greater enemies of men and gods. So theomachy reigns in heaven, still. Until another day, when a better balance may come into play, and men and gods unite.

*

Lysis couldn't help teasing Kouras. Nobody could.

When Kouras walked by Sync to get his mount, Sync called out, "Look, Kouras, it's easy. Just like riding a horse," rotating his hips, fists out, grasping the air. Stepsons catcalled and Thebans broke out laughing until they cried and staggered, hugging one another.

Charon wanted Lysis to stay away from Kouras, whose black rage was evident and mounting, but that was impossible: they were teamed for duty with Arton.

Then Critias came out to the barracks, his fine Syrese face determinedly impassive, and said, "The Riddler thinks you need to have a lesson, Kouras. This ritual involves a chariot. Sync, get it ready. You're going to teach him."

And nobody could be pried away from the training field for that lesson. By the time Sync and brown-haired, brown-skinned Gorgias brought out a training chariot, rolling it with no horses, lifting it by the centerpole, everyone was gathered there but the new mercenaries, who didn't quite dare walk away from their appointed tasks.

Gorgias, his smashed countenance betraying no amusement, straddled the chariot's centerpole. Sync, beside him, said, "We need a volunteer." This flat statement started everyone up again, elbowing one another and waxing scatological.

"Volunteer for what?" Perses, the young curly-haired poet called out.

"You just did. You're going to be the girl. Get in here," Sync decreed. Nearly twenty men, around the rail, howled gleefully. "You, too, Kouras. The Riddler wants you trained on this. Just think of it as a tutorial on tactics, techniques and procedures."

Suggestions rang out. Simias, Perses' gray-haired partner, sidled up next to Charon, perhaps the only man who wasn't laughing, and said, "What's the drill?" deadpan.

By now Kouras was out there, in the middle of the training field, stiff-legged, red as a beet, and men were clapping and sounding long, plaintive wolf-calls, while Gorgias and Sync strung ropes from the chariot's rails and through the rings on the car's floor and back to the front of its rim, where the centerpole attached.

Then curly-haired Perses bent his dark head to Sync's. Sync whispered in his ear. Kouras glowered. Gorgias put one foot on the centerpole to keep it down. Sync led Perses by the uplifted hand, like a bride, around to the back of the chariot's car and handed him up into it.

Perses grabbed one rope in each hand and hopped up, backwards, onto the chariot's forward rim, saying, "Come on, big guy. Let's see what you've got," wriggling his buttocks suggestively. Perses leaned back against the ropes, dropped his butt further over the car and made a kissing noise. Even Charon was laughing now.

Kouras bolted, running through the gate, toward the stables.

Perses, linen-covered buttocks hanging provocatively over the chariot's rim, looked over his shoulder at Gorgias and asked, "Was it something I said?"

"Go after him, Lysis," Charon decreed. "Stay with him. And don't laugh at him."

Lysis found Kouras saddling up the roan. "You'd better go back out there. They don't mean anything by it. The Riddler wants…"

And then a shadow darkened the stable doorway. Tempus stalked in and said to Lysis, "You. Outside."

Critias was right behind the commander. As Lysis hurried to obey, Critias said, "Everyone's going back to his duties. You, too, Lysis: whatever you were scheduled for, get about it."

Lysis had never heard that tone from Critias, but he was scheduled to ride with Kouras into Sanctuary. Lysis stopped in the stable doorway, uncertain, faced with conflicting orders.

So he heard Tempus's gravelly voice saying to Kouras, "They're trying to help. You wouldn't want to face that chariot for the first time in the palace. You're a warfighter. How did you think the god of sack and pillage would take a maiden? In a bower of flowers, with garlands all around? This is a different kind of battle, but battle it is. Get out there and plan your strategy, your tactics. There's more than one way to accomplish this mission. From inside the car, or outside. Think it through, son of the storm god. Don't leave everything to Vashanka or your life will be hell."

And the Riddler passed by Lysis, long eyes flashing with displeasure. And stopped: "You, Theban," Tempus said to Lysis. "You're Charon's son? The one who got the dart tube from Stealth and wouldn't give it up?"

"I am, Commander."

"And you ride with Kouras?"

"I do, sir."

"Then get your horse ready, and his. And take that other boy, the seer. Once Critias and I give Kouras his lesson, we're going to Phoebe's to get the bloom off you three roses, before you wilt in public." Tempus strode away.

Critias came over to him, glaring, before Lysis could digest the shock of being singled out by the commander: Tempus still remembered Lysis from the fracas over the dart tube. Lysis wished he'd never seen that tube, or blown a dart at Sham, or tried to keep the tube when Randal came for it. Some said the commander had the dart tube now.

Critias growled at him: "Why are you standing around? Get Arton. You heard the commander. Saddle up. And soldier up, for this. If you think Sacred Band honor isn't at stake next Ilsday, you're wrong."

Lysis was struck dumb and numb. But he had his orders. So he got Arton, and they went into the stable to get the three horses ready.

When they came out, it was as quiet in the barracks as any grave, as deserted as a pyre when the flames have burned down.

And when they rode out, the Riddler was in the lead, with Stealth, on their magnificent dapple-gray Trôs horses. Critias, all prickly and stern, was riding beside Lysis, with Kouras and Arton bringing up the rear.

Out at the training field, there was not one Stepson; no one from the Theban Sacred Band was in evidence – except for Lysis's father, who waved at him and signed a blessing as he rode past. But the training chariot still sat there, balanced on its two wheels and the tip of its centerpole in the middle of the bullpen, ropes dangling over its rim.

Lysis had heard about Phoebe's Inn, and what went on there. It was the smallest and most esoteric of the brothels on the Street of Red Lanterns. None of the young Thebans had ever been there. Older Stepsons dropped their voices low when they talked about it, if the boys were near.

Lysis wished he was riding with someone other than Critias, Tempus's executive officer. "You're the Blessed One, the Theban who's supposed to have some goddess-given gift with horses?" Critias asked him. "Show me." From then on, Critias critiqued Lysis's horsemanship, correcting everything Lysis did, the whole long way into the city.

At Phoebe's, Lysis and Arton were left to take the horses to the stable-nook before going inside. Arton said, "I don't want to go into the brothel."

Lysis said, "We'll be fine." Just leading the Trôs horses was enough challenge for one day. The big stallions had sized up Lysis and Arton and decided that horses, not Stepsons, were in charge.

When they finally got all six horses safely inside the stable nook, Arton came up close. “Something awful’s going to happen.”

“Stop *saying* that. Nothing ever does,” said Lysis, but his skin crawled. It was whispered that something terrible had happened, the night Arton had predicted it, but no one knew just what: something about Nikodemos and the goddess and the Mageguild. Nevertheless, Stealth seemed fine, although he’d cut off nearly all his hair. “You know, Arton, Thebans set great store by prophecy. You need to tell me more. What do you see?”

They left the dark stable nook and went around to Phoebe’s front door. At least it wasn’t raining. It hadn’t rained for two days straight. But clouds were massing again.

“First off, there’s going to be an awful storm.” Arton craned his neck at the late afternoon sky, where a wall cloud was coming in off the sea. “Kouras is furious.”

“Something better than that,” said Lysis.

“Just make sure you have your weapons ready,” Arton said.

“Can’t you be more specific?” Lysis always had his weapons ready. He was a Theban Sacred Bander.

“I hate to jinx us….”

“I’ll take that chance.”

“It’ll be like the battleplain at Chaeronea. Just as bad. So many men. So many dying.”

“Today? There’s no room here, no battleplain….”

“Not today. Today, just you watch out. We need to make sure the horses are all secure in the stable. Something’s going to happen here. You’ll need to keep your ears and eyes open.

You're going to distinguish yourself… or die trying. So be very careful."

"In a whorehouse? With the senior staff here? I don't think so." And then they went up the steps and inside, where a fat woman daubed with too much paint and powder leered at them as if she were a man and they were the harlots, and Lysis forgot all about Arton's reluctant prophecy. If Arton had been Theban, maybe he would have been easier to credit.

Arton was clearly frightened of this mannish woman covered with paint. Lysis puffed up tall. The senior staff and Kouras weren't anywhere in sight.

Half a dozen girls lurked there, posturing suggestively. The bordello mistress said, "You're lucky young men, Stepsons. Critias picked out your girls for you personally. Now, just come with me."

Thereupon the two Sacred Banders were led by Madam Phoebe herself, their guide on this descent into whoredom, to two waiting strumpets who were giggling and took them each by the hand. Arton was dragged off, looking backward at him helplessly, by a black-haired beauty in sparkling blue veils. Lysis's companion suited him better: willowy and soft-eyed, all in gray linen as if she were a priestess, with long brown hair falling to her waist.

"I promise, Lysis, this isn't going to hurt a bit," she said, and led him up the stairs. It wasn't even dark outside yet.

Thus it wasn't dark in his tart's room. He was shy, but she was slow and engaging. He noticed the ropes on her bedstead, and other things that gave him pause: a lash whip, some chains, and a strange low amphora upended on its mouth with its point up in the air. But there was a big bed there, with silky covers. She led him to it.

"What's all this?" he asked, motioning around, still in his armor.

"Not for you," said the girl, putting her hands on his cuirass, on the pin of his chlamys. "You're going to be fine. Let's take all this off…."

He didn't want to see her; didn't want her to see him. He wished it was dark. "Close the curtains," he said. Then he was glad she didn't, when his head started to spin as she stripped off his armor and pushed him down on the bed and wrapped herself around him before he had time to pull off his tunic.

Her legs were around his waist when he heard a stallion scream from the stables. He knew that sound. He scrambled off her, grabbing his gear while she fussed at him.

He'd never dressed so fast. He was running down the stairs, buckling his swordbelt as he went careening out the door. Around the back. He got there just in time to see the commander's big Trôs stallion on its hind legs. Someone with a drawn sword was brandishing that blade at the horse's soft underbelly.

Lysis yells, drawing his own shortsword, running as fast as he can. The man with the stallion's reins in one hand and a sword in the other looks around, sees him, and lets go of the horse, retreating.

The stallion, furious, stalks forward on its hind legs. Lysis could see some blood against the gray coat, but the horse wasn't giving any ground. *Easy, big horse. Easy.* The Trôs just keeps on coming, retribution in its fiery eyes.

The man with the shortsword hesitates and then makes a choice. He runs toward Lysis – away from the horse, who's gotten one foreleg tangled in its reins. The stallion is pulling on its own bit and fighting to get its head free, but still coming on, ears flattened.

Lysis holds his ground, calling out, "Come on, coward. Come fight me, not a helpless animal." But the big dappled stud isn't helpless. The horse is down on four legs and preparing to charge, pawing the ground. Beside the stable nook there's a fence, an alley, a jumble of trash. The Trôs horse breaks the bridle: first the browband hangs from one ear; then the leather and the bit fall away and are gone, under the horse's legs. The man, sheathing his sword, takes one more look at Lysis and runs up the trash heap to vault over the fence. The horse leaps forward.

Lysis must make a choice: either chase the would-be horse thief or try to keep the stallion from bolting up the ally, onto the Street of Red Lanterns.

He chooses the horse even though, enraged, it's still coming on; ears flattened, teeth gaping, roaring and squealing.

Lysis sheaths his shortsword. Its rasp is very loud as it settles in its scabbard. Spreading his arms wide, he starts walking toward the horse – knowing it is going to run him down; seeing the glowing, oblong pupils in those hard, wild eyes. These Trôs horses are trained to kill and Lysis is the only obstacle between the stallion and the way home. The stallion wears no bridle to grab, but Lysis knows exactly what he must do.

He must stop the Trôs horse. He can't let Tempus's horse get loose, run off down the street. He is the Blessed One, whom Harmony has given an affinity for horses. He will stop this horse or die trying.

The world slows down. Every stride of the oncoming stallion takes an eternity. Hoofbeats pound. Snorts and neighs sound too loud. Clarion calls blare as the runaway horse bears down on him.

Just before it tramples him, he thinks, '*O Harmony, You blessed me, gave me skill with horses. If I still have it, please let it save me now. Otherwise, O Harmony, beloved goddess, please take my soul, because that horse is going to kill me and run on, and I'm not going to try to stop it with a sword.*'

A blurry shape moves up beside him – and past him, so fast he's not sure if it's a man. Now that shape is in front of him.

The gray stops in its tracks. Raising its frothing muzzle, it screams a challenge to the clouds. Its ears flick: forward, back, forward again.

Lysis's commander stands in front of him, stripped to the waist. The Riddler says, "He won't hurt you, Lysis. Not with me here. Go on by me and get me a rope or a halter or a strap from the stable."

Without thought, Lysis unbuckles his swordbelt and strips the gear from it, sliding everything through his hands, letting his gear drop to the dirt. "Here, take this," he says.

His commander takes Lysis's belt and walks up to the infuriated Trôs, talking to it, very low. The horse takes a step toward the Riddler. The Riddler takes a step toward his horse. The stallion lowers its head and puts its face against the half-naked man's chest. Tempus fastens the strap around the stallion's neck: there isn't much leather to hold onto, but there's enough.

Then Tempus runs his hand down the horse's chest. His fingers come away smeared with blood.

Lysis walks carefully, slowly, up to the commander and his horse. "What else can I do?"

"Just stay behind me. We're going to walk him in there and get him cleaned up. He won't die from that wound, unless it's poisoned."

In they went, Lysis still with his arms spread wide, following the dappled rump of the Trôs, who left little drops of blood behind as he walked calmly beside his master into the stable nook.

Not until they had gotten some hot water and cloths, and dressed the shallow sword-cut on the stallion's lower chest, did Lysis remember that his gear and his weapons were lying in the dirt outside.

By then, Critias was there, holding everything that should have been strung on Lysis's swordbelt.

And Arton was there, staring around. "I told you," Arton said.

Critias squeezed Lysis's shoulder, saying, "Nice, Stepson. Really nice," and actually grinned at him as he handed Lysis his sword and scabbard, his belt-pouch, and his dirk. "Now, describe him – the fellow you chased off."

Then Lysis really understood that he'd saved the horse. And he began to realize how much that act meant to the senior Stepsons. He told Critias everything he remembered, and then he repeated for Straton everything he'd said to Critias.

Critias and Straton wanted to know if it could have been Shamshi, but Lysis wasn't sure. The swordsman was big enough, tall enough, young enough to make that vault over the fence; but it might have been anyone: it all happened so fast. And the thief, or would-be horse-murderer, was dark, as Shamshi had been on the beach – before which time, Shamshi had been fair. So Lysis couldn't say for certain. Still, Critias and Straton were pleased with him. All the tension over the dart tube he'd refused to give to Randal seemed to melt away, as if it had never been there. He wished he could say for certain whether the would-be horse thief had been Sham. They wanted him to say so.

But he was the Blessed One, Harmony's chosen, and he wouldn't lie, or fabricate. Especially now, when finally the awkwardness over the dart tube that Stealth had given him, and Randal had taken back, seemed to be behind him.

Despite the fact that Lysis couldn't say whom he saw at the stable nook, Critias and Straton shimmied over the wall to take a look, coming back empty-handed, with clenched teeth and muttered curses that the stallion's assailant had gotten away.

As they all stood around watching the horse (tending it; hoping it wouldn't die from poison or tie up from stress), Tempus came over to Lysis. By then it was storming outside again, lightning flashing and thunder boxing your ears. Kouras was still enjoying the brothel's amenities. Arton was standing quietly in the doorway of the stable nook, looking up at the sky.

The Riddler said, "That's the best horse I've got. You have done me a great service, Lysis. You deserve a reward. Name it."

Until then, Lysis had been sure that the Riddler still disapproved of him: Lysis was the fool who had made Randal take the dispute over the dart tube all the way up to Stealth, in his sickbed – and, as the goddess had willed, to the commander himself.

*I want a colt by that dappled stud.* But they would never give him one; he was just a Theban. The senior stallion's get were too highly prized. Many Stepsons coveted one, and still had none. Stealth's wonderful black colt was one of the few. *No, they won't give me a colt.*

Then he knew what he wanted…if they'd let him have it: "I'd like to be paired, sir. With Arton, here." He couldn't believe he'd had the courage to say it. If Tempus granted his request, Lysis would be the left-side leader of the first Theban-Stepson pairing ever; his father would be very pleased. He wasn't even sure he liked Arton. But Arton had been right: his foresight, his seer's gift, was real. Lysis was a Theban who respected prophecy above all other gifts. And he needed to have a real partner, a partner who was not his father.

Now the commander appraises him and Lysis understands what the men mean when they talk about the gaze that weighs your soul. Tempus's long, hooded eyes, so ancient and wise, stare at him and into him and all through him. And the commander slowly says, "You have my approval, if Arton will agree. Arton?" Tempus's hoarse voice rang out, sharp and clipped.

Arton comes over to the commander. Behind Tempus, by the big Trôs's stall, Critias is all attention, arms akimbo. Straton, next to him, whispers in Crit's ear. Critias nods at whatever Straton says and smiles.

"Commander?" quavers Arton, craning his neck to look up into those disconcerting eyes.

"Will you pair with Lysis – shoulder to shoulder, to the death, with honor?" asks their commander.

"I…. I…. Oh, yes. Yes, I will. I mean, I can. I mean, of course I will. Be honored to."

"Then here, before my officers, I say it to you: Life to you, Stepsons, and everlasting glory. May you be steadfast and loyal to one another, and to the numinous fraternity of the Sacred Band."

"Life to you, Commander," says Arton.

"And to you, Commander," says Lysis. And it is done. Lysis is a left-side leader among Stepsons. He has achieved this dignity on his own merit and he has chosen a right-side partner that his Theban brothers will esteem – a seer. He is no longer only Charon's son, dragged along by happenstance and fortune into this strange and demanding land.

Lysis knows he is worthy. He is Harmony's Blessed One. And the Riddler's Trôs stallion knows it too, for it whinnies and bugles and charges around its stall, as horses will when they know something important is afoot.

*

"Why can't I kill him?"

"Tempus? He's beyond your scope. What you tried today was foolish. You're lucky you survived. He's protected. You will have your day."

"I couldn't even kill the accursed horse."

"The horse doesn't deserve to die. Learn what can, and cannot, be asked from destiny."

"Why couldn't we kill Nikodemos at the gates?"

"We did."

"I *saw him,* riding through town with the Riddler and their Stepsons."

"Then, if you want him dead *again,* we will have to kill him *again.* It may be that, to kill him, you will need to risk your own death more directly. Do you want to kill him that much? Do you want to kill him as much as you want to live? Sham? Shamshi? *Answer me.*"

"I…want to kill him very much. I want to kill them all, but so far, so few of them have died, no matter what I try…."

"They are fighters. They are the Stepsons. They are the Sacred Band of Thebes. They are skilled. They are many. You are one. If you keep this up, reinforcements may be needed."

"But you said they are among the fated dead."

"They are. That doesn't mean it is *your* fate to kill them – any, or all of them. It means only that they have a destiny, that men are born to die. And die they do. Each man dies at his appointed time."

"*I* didn't. You saved me."

"That is another discussion, in which life and death become relative terms."

"I want to kill them. I must keep trying. It's what I live for. It's what got me through the sickness. After what they did to me, I must. It's what I dream."

"Then you will keep trying. Until you or they are dead. We have been invited to a feast. Perhaps your dream will come true there. Perhaps not. If we choose to act there, we must plan – to act successfully. It will not be easy. And the risk will be great."

"I'm not afraid."

"Then learn to be afraid. Learn when to fear, and how to fear, and how much to fear, before you squander all you have left."

## *Chapter 40: Three God Night*

"Identify yourself," demands the palace sentry sharply, a single pale youth in too much braid and armor, nervous and uneasy. The sentry checks his slate and peers at Crit in the last heat of day, while a full moon shines down from a blue sky turning red over battlements bristling with guards. Thirty of the palace guard stand watch – above, behind, and all around – but this lone sentry can still make a crucial error: let the wrong people in; keep the wrong ones out, on this momentous night when Vashanka and his avatar will be welcomed to Sanctuary officially. "What are your names?"

"Critias, the Riddler's executive officer. We're the Band," Crit replies, looking for a glimmer of recognition or relief on the sentry's worried face now that the Stepsons, armed and ready, are here in force. And doesn't find it. The palace is another world, the sentry's world: his to guard; his to save; his, the blame…if something goes wrong.

Sunset sparkles off the helm and hilt of this anxious sentinel, guardian of the Gate of the Gods. Of the Sacred Band's seventy-four, Crit has brought fifty along with him and Strat – hardened fighters, uniformed in dark green linen and light wool chlamys, bronze and leather and iron girded on, ready for whatever comes their way. This checkpoint is miserably understaffed, and unprepared for so many armed Stepsons in a group.

The sentry looks left, then right, craning his neck at all the formed-up Sacred Band watching patiently; hounds of hell before the hunt, waiting only for Crit's command to spring – and making no secret of their readiness with their promissory stares.

"But *who's here* from the Sacred Band? I have to have the names." The sentry taps his stylus on his slate. "Or you don't get in."

*Better you'd have thought that through before, young soldier.* Because this palace guard will need some help, if every name is not on that list.

"Walegrin should have taken care of this. Listen closely then. One time through." Crit doesn't like this sentry, who's too defensive, too intimidated: flustered men make errors, sometimes deadly ones. And Crit doesn't like delays – not on any day, but especially not today. Behind him, his Stepsons come to ready. Crit hears the smallest signs of patience wearing thin (clinks and rustles; terse whispers; shields shifting).

Straton nudges Crit with his hip: *Let's move.* Twenty-six Sacred Band pairs need to get through this gate and onto the grounds, where their commander expects them to deploy.

Their horses are already in the palace stables; Crit regrets the necessity of leaving mounts behind. Can't be helped. He knocks his own hip against Straton's in return, harder: *Wait.* The Sacred Band pairs are strangers all, to the palace guard. Finesse is vital, here and now.

Crit calls the roll, in formation order: "Critias. Straton. Sync. Gayle. Cassander. Delios. Charon. Lysis. Arton. Perses. Simias. Agis. Archias." Crit stops. He coughs and spits, too near the sentry's feet. Ari should have been here; and his partner, Deon. But they weren't – casualties of this war that wasn't one: absent friends, with Abarsis up in heaven. He spat again, nearer the sentry's sandaled foot, this time; sometimes you had to make a statement. Sometimes, words weren't enough.

To his credit, the sentry didn't jump back, or threaten, or curse. So Crit continued, calling out his men by name: "Dolon. Memor. Menander. Periander. Gorgias. Sciron. Simon of Athens. Simon of Thebes. Epani. Zitos." And on, through all his stalwarts, his Stepsons, his Thebans and the new mercenaries Tempus had so recently hired, until fifty-two names were recited, for the record.

And the sentry checked them off, each and every one. Of the fifty-two of them facing this young sentry, better than half were Thebans, the fated dead whose brothers' bones lay under a granite lion, a world away.

"Sentry, we have senior officers waiting inside. We have orders. If trouble starts, you'll be glad we're here." Crit's patience, never great, was coming quickly to an end. "Now let us pass, before my commander, Tempus, wonders why we're late."

Crit has said the magic word: *Call that name, and every gate opens wide.* The sentry closes his slate, gives way with an exaggerated bow, and the Sacred Band files by – not asked to give up their weapons.

This sentry has been forewarned, then, by Walegrin, by Torchholder or the palace prefect. Because no Stepson was relinquishing weapons tonight. Not with Shamshi on the prowl, picking them off like festival prizes at a charity booth. Not with Aškelon abroad, an otherworldly threat. Onto the grounds the Sacred Band flows, smooth as water, perfectly rehearsed and spreading out among the throng, each to his assigned position, casual as you please.

Even so, obvious doesn't half cover it.

So be it. The Sacred Band has a job to do: maintain order where chaos is intrinsic. Not easy. Two storm gods will be here tonight. Enlil is always with Tempus. Vashanka will claim Kouras this night, inhabit their young Stepson; take back what is his – or some of it.

Critias has been happy enough without Vashanka calling shots or setting battle tempo. Tempus was terrible in his wrath and temper when Vashanka was his patron god. Enlil is harsh, but just. Better. Fairer. More apt for fighters in a Sacred Band. Enlil, storm god of the armies, is a cannier war-god than Vashanka, to Critias's way of thinking; always subtle, never crude.

And Tempus had said darkly, giving Crit his orders, "We'll see the gods tonight, Critias. And a goddess, I'll bet. See how heaven battles for the loyalty of men. And see the lord of dream and shadow. So watch where you step, lest you step into something that sticks to your feet."

So had Enlil told Tempus something? Warned him? Or was it only the black humor of his immortalized commander, twisting Crit's soul up with worries half understood – or plain truth that Critias, just a soldier, couldn't understand?

Whatever Tempus meant, the Band was here with complex orders: whom to watch; whom to guard; how, and when. What to guard against. When to show your blade. Whatever Tempus thought was in store this evening, watching Kouras prove his manhood wasn't the whole of it.

But with Straton on his right and his contingent deployed in perfect order, Crit felt ready for anything. Now, to keep things that way: that's the trick, the test, the task, when gods are invited out to play.

Next, Tempus comes up to them, parting the crowd, with Niko on his right. The commander is wearing Stepson issue, no leopard-skin and boar's-tooth tonight. Stealth too wears summer armor, no dream-forged panoply.

Niko has been strange these last days, reticent; looking out from under hacked-off hair; brooding. Yet Stealth is strong and fit this evening, moving with unconscious grace, effortlessly poised, like some fighting noble who'd never languished at death's door: not so thin, not with burning eyes sunk deep, but with enough muscle gliding over flesh to win a fight.

Here tonight Niko is all business. He squeezes first Strat's shoulder, then Crit's: "Good you're here, Ace. Fox, no trouble at the gates? Or in the stables?"

"None," Crit says. War names, this evening, from Niko: that choice speaks volumes.

Stealth looks past Crit at everyone, everywhere. Looking for something. Looking for someone in the throng.

It's hard to pick out individuals in the courtyard. Too many people crowd the celebration on the lawn. Oligarchs in riotous brocade and priests in claret velvet and lace; women with copper beads weighing down multicolored skirts and veils that veil nothing clutched to up-thrust breasts; diners queued up at festival boards laden with crusty lambs and glossy pigs with open mouths; musicians playing flutes and lyres, drums and bells, horns and harps; powdered whoremistresses and demure noblewomen; tattooed sailors and decorated soldiers: corpulent and sepulchral, ascetic and indulgent, dark and fair, short and tall, all are here tonight.

Niko fixes Crit with a penetrating stare: "Call if you need us."

Unnecessary and bold, for Niko to speak so, with Tempus by his side.

The Riddler doesn't say a word. There's no need. You can feel the god residing in their commander this evening, stronger the closer you get to him. And Tempus, like Niko, looks askance at everyone and everything, Crit included.

Is the god talking to him now? Whispering in his skull? Peering through those ancient eyes? A chill walks over Critias's skin. He rubs his arms.

At last the Riddler inclines his head to Crit and says, "Fox, watch the boy tonight – Kouras – very closely. Ride back to the barracks with him. He doesn't stay here, no matter what. Send Lysis and Arton to us when you don't need them. Clear?"

"Perfectly clear, Commander," though it wasn't. Not why, or how. Above the walls, sunset flares, incendiary. Palace guards light torches, here and there and everywhere.

"If you see Aškelon or Shamshi, bring *us* to them," the Riddler orders, and he and Stealth stride away, larger than life, a pair of heroes stepped off some marble temple wall. Stealth gets more like the Riddler every day. Tempus says over his shoulder, "For the rest, you know what to do."

This time, Crit hopes he does. *What is he expecting?*

And Strat says, "The Riddler still has that dart tube, you know," for no reason Crit can fathom. Except that Ischade is whispering in Strat's ear too much lately. If Strat hadn't been his partner for so long, with the necromant in his blood again (despite all Critias had tried to do to keep them apart), Crit would be wondering if he could trust Strat, should push come to shove here.

And on this night, of all nights, Critias needed to be able to trust his partner implicitly.

Now Jihan comes swaggering up, scattering the crowd effortlessly, wearing a long skirt under her scale armor, hair and eyes and skin gleaming like molten copper. The skirt seems somehow out of place with greaves and armor, but Jihan makes her own rules. Stormbringer, father of all the weather gods, had sent her to Tempus to learn humanity. She cuts a swathe through lesser women and wistful men, destroying beyond redemption any attempt by Critias and Straton at anonymity.

"Crit. Straton," she says, too loudly, in that voice like waves crashing on a beach. "Life to you, and everlasting glory."

So they return the Sacred Band greeting. All around, people gawk at the glimmering woman with the impossibly beautiful body, at her tiny waist, her high rump, her pert breasts and muscular limbs. "Jihan," Crit whispers, "people are staring at you."

"Yes, the skirt. I shouldn't have worn it. It keeps sticking between my legs when I walk." She reached behind her rump and pulled at the fabric. "Isn't it fascinating? About Niko and the goddess? Where are they? Does he look different? Can you tell?"

Crit is dumbstruck. *What?*

Straton says, "Tell what, Jihan? What's fascinating?"

Crit says, "Never mind. Molin's coming. Don't talk about it, whatever it is."

"Randal is back," Jihan murmurs under her breath as she sidesteps Molin's hand, about to slide around her waist from behind.

*

"Look, Charon. Do you see the Riddler's wind-charmer, Jihan, over there, dressed like Athena fitted up for war?" Gorgias muttered. "Why, do you imagine, is such a dangerous creature among us, if this is merely a social gathering?"

Gorgias was followed closely by Agis and Archias, shoulder to shoulder; the Theban fighters gaped, speechless, at the best of Sanctuary, arrayed in the torchlight on the palace courtyard's extensive lawn. A moist breeze blew, promising wild weather to come, fluttering the torchlight and casting it hither and yon.

Since the young Sacred Band pair was near enough to overhear, Charon responded to Gorgias in an undertone: "Because, Gorgias, Jihan is the commander's…" *What? Plaything? Mistress?* "…friend and companion." Gorgias was among Charon's most suspicious fighters, and many other Thebans were leery of Jihan, daughter of an Unbegotten. In Thebes, the powers of wind-charmers had been greatly feared. "This Jihan fights at the commander's side. Therefore, at our side. Rest easy, Gorgias. She's no menace to us and ours, but a potent force against adversaries of the Sacred Band. Can it be, old friend, that you want too much to live, these days?"

"No, but I might want too much to die, in this strange place where nothing is as it seems and an honorable death may be elusive." The night breeze stirred Gorgias's hair. "Tell me, Charon, why do you think this Sacred Band of Stepsons needs so much help, and against what echelon of adversaries?" Musicians played softly somewhere, lilting melodies, chromatic and plaintive with semitones, as if chosen by a knowing ear to ease all hearts. But not Gorgias's: "At the barracks, some Thebans hide when the wind-charmer shows her face or brings her icy storms. And these Stepsons have more unnatural allies than just the Froth Daughter. Witches and worse, changing to dogs and birds. Men who need such friends face daunting enemies. Meanwhile we Thebans have no oracle to guide us. Only this Riddler, decreeing all, unopposed."

Gorgias stomped determinedly through the celebrants with Archias and Agis trailing behind. Charon must keep up or let these accusations go unanswered.

"Gorgias, we owe these Stepsons our lives. They are audacious, but that audacity saved every one of us." Many Thebans were uneasy, living cheek by jowl with the supernatural and the inexplicable. Hard-faced Gorgias is always the naysayer, the voice of dissent in any council. There is no formal Theban council here. Inevitably, the Sacred Band pair tagging along behind Gorgias will repeat this conversation to all the others. Charon must win this point, nip dissonance in the bud to preserve their loyalty, stave off doubt. "Our goddess wouldn't be here with us if what we are doing was displeasing to heaven."

But Gorgias is dogged, plowing on. "These Stepsons tread where mortals don't belong, some of us think. They seek out battle high above their station. Who knows what powers may yet take them and their mystic allies to task, bring them their comeuppance? And we'll bear the brunt of it. Even if their commander is truly what he's rumored to be – a demigod, son of the storm god of the armies – that's no protection. Gods have been cast down for hubris before."

They walk past a festival board loaded with shellfish and savories, toward a firepit where a lamb turns above hungry flames and fat spits and sizzles as it drips into the fire.

"Our patron goddess agreed that we should come here," Charon reminds Gorgias in a voice meant to carry to the two behind them. "Not to safety, but to carry on. Blessed Harmony girt on her sword and donned her armor and came to sanctify our mission at the Mageguild. She saved us all from the chilling mist that Stepsons say can kill. Would you gainsay our own goddess? This matter's closed." Admonishment, oh-so-carefully delivered. "Harmony has shown us the way. We're here, to fight on other days, by her will, more than any other's. So fight we shall, when and how the commander and his Stepsons say. We've settled this. Let it rest." Agis and Archias, too quiet at their backs, are hanging on every word. "Yes, Charon," Gorgias sighs. "We've settled this. We've agreed." And Gorgias does, at last, let the matter drop as he and Charon circulate among the partygoers, Archias and Agis yet following along behind. The four Thebans eat; they drink; they listen to the talk of storm gods and floodplains, of ruined crops and trade missions, of oligarchic decrees and weather to come. And above their heads, the full moon rises among silvered clouds.

The palace priest, Torchholder, seeks him out. Charon knows he should be flattered. He tries to explain to Torchholder that he is not ordained, not a real priest. When the Thebans came here, he was proclaimed leader by vote and priest by default: somebody had to fill the clerical role.

"Let's not be coy, Charon," says Torchholder. "As one warrior-priest to another, let's admit we both know what's happening here tonight." The Sanctuarite priest's mouth twists irreverently.

Charon puts on his wisest face but doesn't understand. He must tread carefully among these heathens.

Up came a slight, balding man, and Torchholder introduced them: "Reton, Second Oligarch of Sanctuary, this is Charon…of the Sacred Band of Thebes…. I'll let Charon further introduce himself and his fellows…."

"Oh, more timocrats. Glorious. I'd love to discuss with all of you what you recommend when honor cannot be the sole criterion for governance and still benefit the populace as well as its rulers and its military…. And who are your colleagues?"

Charon introduced Archias and Agis and brown-skinned Gorgias, thinking that the best pair to match wits with this oligarch would be Simias and Perses, not Archias and Agis – or Gorgias and himself. "Gorgias, let's take Oligarch Reton to meet Simias. He's our intellectual. He's kept company with some of the best minds in Thebes, and even Athens…."

Gorgias knew what Charon wanted: rescue. Obligingly, as if making amends for his earlier antagonism, Gorgias led the little man away, with Archias and Agis in tow. But Torchholder was still standing there.

"Don't you want to meet Simias, Eminence? He's very intelligent…."

"I want to talk to you alone," said Vashanka's priest. "Alone in crowds is always best," and he started to walk, forcing Charon to keep up, headed toward the feast board with the lamb and carrots and rice, where most Thebans were congregating. "I've heard your son has paired with our home-grown seer, Arton. We're very pleased for them both." The music faded.

Charon stopped in his tracks. So much had happened. This priest was treacherous, he knew. And Molin knew too much about Sacred Band business. Charon was still adjusting to the news of his son's pairing. He should have been consulted. But he hadn't been. *Different land, different customs.*

So Charon said, "It was a field promotion. By the commander himself. I didn't know until it was over. And yes, we're pleased. Our goddess is very proud of Lysis. As am I." What does he want, this lizard-eyed man with his darting tongue and his devious heart? He gave Torchholder his most pious smile and waited for the man to speak. Several guests approached, but went away when they weren't acknowledged.

"I'd like your assistance," Torchholder said carefully, "in making sure that the introduction of your worshippers to our culture goes smoothly." The moist wind picked up, tugging on the priest's velvet vestments.

Then Charon thought he understood what Torchholder wanted. "Our goddess makes her own way. We can ask. But we follow. We do as she commands."

"We'd be very grateful if she'd command you and yours to stay within the laws of Sanctuary, not go around attacking private property that's empty, ransacking expensive estates, and generally running amok."

*The Mageguild.* Not until then had Charon realized that Torchholder might not believe in the god he served; or, believing, might think that he alone could interpret the will of the god. In Thebes, this had been a very perilous circumstance, whenever it arose.

"We go where the commander orders us; we fight where we're bid; we attack the targets we're given."

"Yes, but I'm paying your salaries, and I don't like having to apologize to Reton for breaking out every window in a property under his stewardship. Someone has to pay for all that damage, you know. And I want to take you over to Reton once more, and have you tell him that you and yours are sorry, and it won't happen again without prior consent from us."

"'Us?' The Riddler pays us Thebans. We are the Sacred Band, loyal to our brothers and our commander."

"Yes, well, loyalties to your Band are fine, so far as they go. But you need to remember your first loyalty must be to the palace. *Me.* The oligarchic council. Or the council's representative – *me.*"

Charon said, very carefully, "I think we should go find your Oligarch Reton. I'll apologize for shooting out the windows."

"And the rest?"

"The rest you should take up with our commander. How is Kouras doing?" Charon didn't really care how Kouras was doing. This priest was insidious.

As they moved among the celebrants, toward the festival lambs turning slowly on their spits above the firepits, he thanked the goddess, one more time, for bringing him and his to this place where Lysis could live to become a man – not die surrounded by Spartans or Macedonians and doomed, one way or the other, but in a land with neither. Here, where their goddess had come and blessed them all.

The worst thing about this Torchholder was that he had chattered at Charon throughout their whole, glorious twilight stroll. The priest was still nattering when they found Perses regaling the oligarch with poetry while gray-haired Simias looked on fondly and Agis and Archias heaped wooden plates high with lamb, rice and carrots.

Torchholder was immediately drawn by Simias into the crowd gathering around the poet. Gorgias, grinning, slipped away and met Charon over the wine service. Thus, Charon didn't have to apologize to the oligarch about the damage to the Mageguild.

"Just think, Charon, we could be dead, instead of eating all this delicious bounty in the moonlight on such a night as this," said Gorgias, sipping his wine.

"Thank the goddess," Charon advised sternly. And they did, finding the lamb's two eyes, a bit of oil and some fresh bread, and making an offering to Harmony over the firepit before they themselves ate a bite.

Charon looked up at the moon. Some night-bird flew across it. The moon was full and clouds were building.

So he said, "Storm's coming," and Gorgias agreed.

*

Ischade found Randal before Randal found the Riddler or Stealth. The necromant was slipping along the wall, out of the torchlight, wrapped in a velvet cloak of midnight blue. Randal was shocked to see her but, of course, she'd be here: Straton was here, somewhere.

Randal had thought he'd need a horse for this. So he'd conjured a rather nice one (if smelling a bit loamy), from the lawn, and then realized that no one else had a horse inside the palace walls tonight. So he'd had to dispatch it. He'd chosen his customary hillman's trousers and the mottled tunic of Free Nisibis, and ankle-high boots; thus he was decent and, if he wasn't dressed like a Stepson tonight, he was dressed well enough.

"Ischade," he whispered. She shrank back in the bushes and then realized who he was. She was so beautiful. He was sad for her, that she felt the need to hide. Out from shadows she came, nearly creeping, looking around cautiously with her luminescent eyes. Randal offered her his arm. "Shall we? The food will be good, if you're…hungry." Wrong thing to say, but the necromant took his arm and let her hood fall back, a sure sign she wasn't hunting for her dinner.

"I've already eaten," she confirmed. "But we must find the Riddler. Shamshi is here. I can smell him." Those delicate nostrils quivered; that whitest skin, nearly incandescent, seemed to pale even more.

"I'll help you find Tempus." Randal patted her arm. He was grateful for her company. The palace lawn was huge, surrounded by high walls, crowded with celebrants. One hates to walk through a throng of revelers alone, unaccompanied, when everyone else has friends and lovers by their sides. "Now where would the commander be…?"

And then Ischade stopped quite still. So Randal did. The necromant pulled on his arm: *back up; retreat.* Ischade was afraid of nothing in all creation, as far as Randal knew.

So when she asked it, Randal retreated with her. She pulled him by his sleeve over to a feast board with a haunch of bloody meat on it. At Ischade's urging, they each took plates, while Randal stood between Ischade and whatever frightened her.

"You can't be seen through me." Randal stood up tall. He was a warrior-mage. He could protect her, if she needed protection from discovery – but beyond that, only up to a point. "What *was* it? What *is* it?" he whispered, leaning so close to her he could see the blood throb in a vein at her right temple.

*"Them,"* she hissed.

*"Them?* Which *'them'* do you mean?" he whispered back. "Shamshi. And Aškelon. And if I'm not mistaken, Shamshi wears Niko's panoply."

"Oh, Furies. Oh, by the Writ and my soul's worth – oh, no," Randal groaned. The Riddler, not anywhere in evidence; Niko, nowhere to be seen. And here on the lawn come the regent of the seventh sphere (the nearly omnipotent dream lord) *and* Shamshi, manifesting in Ischade's path.

He sneaks a look, dares a glimpse. A tall graying man and an indolently beautiful blond youth are standing in full view, looking away, into the crowd. The man had the height, the dignity, the regal bearing appropriate to the regent of the seventh sphere. The youth was…not completely present, not wholly what a youth should be… more, and less, and not at all what Randal expected of a Bandaran initiate who'd trained as a Stepson. The bone and muscle were wrong, somehow: preternatural, ethereal. But the youth wore a panoply the like of which only Nikodemos – and Randal, due to Niko's generosity – had ever worn.

Was this the same panoply, made by more-than-mortal hands? Moonlight was cuddling up to it, caressing it; demons and gods at play were chasing across it, cavorting on it as if alive. Lightning bolts and the bulls and lions of the storm gods were emblazoned there. That panoply had saved Randal's life when he'd worn it. How could there be another like it?

Was it the same Aškelon, standing before him, shoulders broad enough to heft a world; strength of deepest dream, darkest nightmare, animating flesh once belonging to an archmage, now demiurgic? And that flesh with its own unearthly glow, its strength beyond transience – how could it belong to anyone else?

Firelight haloed the two of them, as if flame were tame, as if they were not mere flesh and blood, but reflections of some higher octave of being, some resonance of desire animated and strife harnessed – as if their forms were crafted, like Niko's panoply, from bloodshed and inferno not entirely of this place or plane.

Randal fought panic so deep it froze him mindless. Then he gathered his courage, lying all about in pieces. He stared over his shoulder, trying to get his bearings. He breathed deeply, as Niko had taught him, seeking composure. He yelled with his inner voice to his twelfth-plane guide for help. Then, despite his pounding heart, he said, "Ischade…. Perhaps it's not really them. Perhaps that's not Niko's panoply. Aškelon made Niko's. Perhaps he has made another. And are you sure that's Shamshi? It didn't look like him."

"I'm sure. I said, I can *smell* him. I need to find Straton." Over her shoulder, as if a world away, men in robes and armor were drinking and laughing; women were parading in their finery, eating and teasing men to come and dance with them.

"Come with me, first," Randal asked, trying not to plead. Her sorcery was stronger than his; he was a mere thaumaturge. "Come on, Ischade," but she wouldn't. She stepped back and *popped* away in a rustle of wings.

Then he was utterly alone.

Alone among a host of celebrants, witnesses by the score if any mischief was afoot. Alone in the crowd, so close to the dream lord and the fearsome wizard boy, on the palace lawn. He wanted to flee, the way Ischade had fled. But Randal was a Stepson. He was the Riddler's warrior-mage. He mustn't be afraid. If Shamshi had Niko's panoply, what could it mean? And why would Aškelon attack Randal in front of all of these?

Randal had flown into the Mageguild and out again with the keys. If Aškelon were after Randal, he could have struck him down there and then. No place or plane was safe enough to hide Randal from the dream lord: Randal was a mage, vulnerable to all the sortilege that had raised Aškelon up so high. Aškelon could have him any time. So what was he afraid of, here and now? Stepsons face their fears, and their destinies, straight on.

So up he went to confront the dream lord (oh, so politely), to see if Ischade was correct, to see if it really was Shamshi, wearing Niko's panoply. As Niko would have done. He would stand eye to eye with Aškelon of Meridian, and face up to this power that had chased Ischade away. And if Shamshi was beside the dream lord, then Randal would brave even that danger. By himself, since Ischade had deserted him. Without running for help. Without quailing. As a Stepson must do. And if evil came of it, then his commander and his partner and his brothers would have fair warning.

Randal knew it was the right thing to do.

The man upon whose shoulder he tapped was tall, and gray-haired, and wore a luxurious mantle. But when he turned around, the man didn't look like Aškelon and the youth with him looked not at all like Shamshi, and wore no panoply whatsoever, just velvet and silk.

Randal apologized and stumbled away through dancing, happy people on the palace lawn until he found one Stepson, who sent him to another. Who sent him to another. And another. And another.

When he was almost losing heart, he saw Straton, with Ischade, in a shadowed corner near the palace cisterns.

He strode right up to them. Ischade stepped back. Straton looked around and said, "Randal, your timing is getting worse every day. What is it?"

"It's what it wasn't. It wasn't Aškelon. It wasn't Shamshi. The younger man wore no panoply. It wasn't them."

"Fine, Randal," said Straton. "Go away. Go find Crit. I want a moment with Ischade, alone." Muted pipes played, soft and low. Lutes joined in, strings plucked and strummed.

Ischade murmured to Straton, touching his brow. Straton blinked, shook his head, and took a step toward Randal. Just then Ischade spun away in a flap of wings. Straton growled, "Now look what you did, Witchy-ears. She's gone."

"I'm sorry," Randal replied, and he was. These two were as doomed as lovers can be.

"If you're sorry, go tell Crit what Ischade told you. And that you think she's wrong, if you must." But Straton wasn't angry. He was…bemused.

Straton was always bemused after Ischade had had her hands on him. Randal hoped, tonight, that Ischade's effect on Straton wouldn't be a problem. He told himself that Ischade wouldn't let her personal feelings, or Strat's, interfere with the hunt. By the time he found Jihan and Critias, such worries no longer seemed to matter.

Randal hadn't remembered how forceful Jihan could be. She had Critias by the arm and was pulling on him. Her fingers were digging deep into his biceps.

"Critias, please, come with me," Jihan said. "Let's go get something to eat…. Oh, Randal. Critias, tell Randal what you told me."

"If you let go of my arm, Jihan." She did. Crit rubbed the finger-marks there. "Randal, we're on alert. Watching out for the dream lord and Shamshi."

"Ischade was here, Critias. She smelled Shamshi here. Now she's left."

"Ischade was here and left? *Why?*" Crit ran a spread hand through his short, feathery hair, a habitual gesture of frustration.

"I'm not sure. She thought she found Shamshi and Aškelon. First I thought she did. Then I thought she didn't… at least, the two I saw didn't look like them –"

*"I'm* sure," said a voice from behind him, as Straton came up and towered over him. "She said Sham's here. She said they're both here. And I believe her."

"They *are* here," Randal nearly shouted, realizing finally that Aškelon had tricked him.

*

Kouras is still chary of the rite to come, so the Sacred Band must see to one of its own. Tempus waits for Kouras, Niko, Arton and Lysis to arrive, thinking that the god should prepare his own avatar. But the god won't, so Tempus must: sometimes a man does what he'd most like to avoid.

Vashanka's private chapel enfolds him. The chapel is dim, full of the god. So many of Tempus's own ghosts are here. He bows his head and greets them one by one. Shades and revenants from years gone by crowd in, murmuring like the dead he carries in his heart. The gilded chariot gleams in the chapel's soft light: a prop for a show he disdains, in these days when it is so hard for him to keep man and god separate, distinct from one another; when so many, many wraiths come with him, walk with him, ride with him from battlefield to battlefield, war to war.

He hates waiting. But the Stepsons are late. And he must tarry. As he waits, memories engulf him, collected over centuries, tokens from fated souls who died for reasons long forgot. Reasons never matter, once Death comes cold and bold and takes the living by the hand. You count up your dead, every one. Always. He recalls them, each and all – every face, every heart. Ritual rapes and slaughters and sacrifices: so many rites performed in this chapel to sate the hungry god, from former times till now – most, far crueler than what the Sanctuary audience will see tonight.

In the glory days of Vashanka's armies, a girl was raped in a chariot on the run, buttocks up, bent over the front of the car on her stomach by two men and thrown out the back or off the side when the deed was done. As a marriage bed, the stationary chariot with no horses came much later (along with a girl's backside dangling above the centerpole, her knees hooked over the car's rim), in these gentler times on this climb up from slime.

Now even that is too real for these genteel folk, voyeurs of celestial passion hoping for a brush with godhead. Tonight there will be golden chains, velvet ropes, a willing wench privileged to be ceremonially ravished by a youth who may, or may not, truly hold the god. They'll crown an avatar this evening, warp a boy's future and think they've brought a god to life. Those who are praised to the heavens live a life of fantasy.

Yet here was Tempus once again, laboring in Vashanka's chapel for this god whom he'd deserted for another. Or who had deserted him. He hoped that Kouras would have better luck than he'd had with Vashanka, lord of sack and pillage. When Kouras had been a babe, Vashanka had disdained him.

Fled. Went missing. Was cast down. Or died, only to be reborn. To gods, all things are good and just. There is never only one truth – if there is ever any truth in terms mortal men can grasp.

Kouras came in alone, still in duty gear, shoulders hunched, head down, shuffling his feet. "Commander. Thank you for being here…."

"Kouras," said the Riddler, "you'll be fine." Kouras was here to chase his jitters and inspect the preparations for the ritual. Tempus was here to inspect Kouras.

As promised, the gilded chariot awaited this son of the storm god, its centerpole fastened to the stone floor by an iron ring. Tempus said, "Accompany me, Kouras," and they made their circuit: examining the chariot with its golden chains strung through rings in the car's floor; chairs arranged in a circle around the chariot; the great statue of Vashanka, frowning down.

Niko comes in and goes straight to the chariot without a word, kicking at the wheel chocks, straddling the centerpole, leaning first against the rise of the chariot's rim and then pulling back: testing the chains, the steadiness of the wheels, the car. Finished, he turns and looks at Tempus, arms crossed.

Lysis and Arton hurry in and flock to Niko, struggling to keep their composure as Stealth says, "The chains are strong. The brake is set. The centerpole won't budge. The chocks on the wheels will hold the chariot still. It won't roll left or right. Unless you want to shim the undercarriage, it's done. Safe as it can be."

Although Niko stated his verdict emotionlessly, it's clear to Tempus that his rightman disapproves: it's in his every move and in his eyes.

"Kouras, you heard Niko. If you want to straddle the centerpole, it won't roll away from you. If I were doing this, I'd step into the car. Not enact the rite from outside. But it's your choice," Tempus said.

"If you say so, Commander," said Kouras doubtfully.

Lysis put his fist to his lips, but snorted a gust of laughter.

Arton punched him, and Lysis hit him back.

Niko silenced them with a sharp hand-sign. Both boys sobered.

Tempus said, "Arton and Lysis, you Stepsons stay with Kouras until Torchholder comes to get him. Arton, we hear your gift of prophecy is real. Is there anything you see that Niko and I should know tonight? Or that Kouras needs to know?"

"No, Commander." Arton had been staring first up at the statue of Vashanka, and then at Tempus. Some resemblance remained between the man and the statue of his former god. Arton gulped, and reddened. "I mean…I keep seeing Chaeronea. But everybody does, who fought there." Standing tall, Arton shifted his weight from foot to foot. No levity now, no giggles, no dancing eyes. "I can't foretell on command. It comes, or it doesn't." Arton spread his hands, palms up. "I hope you're not disappointed."

Niko stepped over the centerpole. He came to Tempus's side, shaking his head almost imperceptibly: *let it be.*

"Thank you, Arton. Come to me any time." And they left the boys there, exiting through the shelf-wall passage. Tempus and Niko both knew this palace too well. Tempus had climbed up and down these marble stairs many times when Niko was sequestered here during the fight for Janni's soul. And after.

"We all see Chaeronea," Niko remarked when they'd descended to the foyer with its floor of black and white marble squares. And those words called it to Tempus's mind: *Long spears thunking into flesh. Man staggering backward, impaled.* Sometimes, his heart still hurt, a beat would skip, a muscle would cramp somewhere. At Enlil's pleasure.

"What do you think of Arton, Riddler?" Niko asked when Tempus didn't speak, as they headed for the double doors leading out to the festivities on the lawn.

"It's understandable that Arton sees Chaeronea," Tempus said. "It was his first battle. That so many see it? Perhaps it's Shamshi, reaching out to touch their minds, as Jihan and Randal and Ischade think. This seer is young and untested. We'll learn what he is, in time."

There were no sentries waiting. Tempus thought it strange, with so many guests outside. But when they pushed open the double doors, he saw the sentries on the outer stair, talking with each other, eating from wooden plates.

Beyond was merriment in the night. He counted his Stepsons, moving through the crowd, professional and polite. Torches flared. Music wafted. He saw Jihan and Critias, with Straton, at a feast table, talking to some Theban Stepsons. Niko was walking toward them when the music stopped.

Everyone on the vast lawn was stock-still. Frozen in word or deed. Asleep between blinks.

Tempus had seen this happen once before. So when Aškelon came wending his way through a crowd of stationary, unknowing revelers, he wasn't surprised. The last time this had occurred, Niko had been new to Tempus's service, and was saved from the dream lord's temporal suspension because the young Stepson had been meditating.

Jihan was frozen in place, unmoving, with a bite of food on her dagger, halfway to her lips. Randal, beside her, had his mouth open, and the rest of the Sacred Band – Critias, Straton, and the other Stepsons – were ensnared by Aškelon's spell as if time itself had stopped.

The dream lord could twist time, hold it in abeyance selectively; and at night, the lord of dream and shadow was strongest. But Jihan was Stormbringer's daughter, a power in her own right. Despite himself, Tempus was impressed that Aškelon could reach Jihan and stop her in her tracks. The first time he'd ever seen Jihan, she had been on Aškelon's arm, swaggering across the training field at the barracks, past all his unknowing Stepsons, halted between breaths, not realizing that they couldn't move, or see, or feel.

Yet Niko was wide awake, beside him. Not frozen, like the rest. Not unknowing, not caught in stasis between heartbeats. Stealth said, "Commander, what do you want me to do?" under his breath.

Tempus touched the dart tube in his belt-pouch. Niko's fingers tightened and relaxed on his new shortsword, lifting it slightly and sliding it back into its scabbard.

*"Don't* draw that sword. No fighting, unless they start it." *They:* Aškelon had someone with him tonight, as he had had that day, long ago. Only this time, it wasn't Jihan: it was a young man – or something young and like a man.

Up came the dream lord, with his friend matching him stride for stride. This younger man was gray of eye and dark of mien. Tempus wasn't sure it was Shamshi, or even human, from the way its substance flickered, until the two were right in front of them and he saw Niko's panoply on the younger man.

Niko took a sideward step toward Tempus. Both of them had left their shields inside the chapel, but this was not a battle that their Stepson arms or armor would win.

"Aškelon," Tempus said. "I trust you're well. Introduce your friend."

Both wore dark raiment; both were tall. A breeze blew softly in the dream lord's gray-starred hair: he was really here, not an illusion.

"Shamshi, this is Tempus and his rightman, Nikodemos. I think you've met before." Ash's haughty sneer was under wraps. He too spoke carefully. He had a hand on Shamshi's arm. The youth glared at Tempus with pure hatred in his eyes, ignoring Niko as if he couldn't see him.

Now Tempus couldn't quite take Shamshi's measure. The youth and the dream-forged panoply he wore seemed only partly visible, as if Shamshi were behind a waterfall or in a heavy rain. Or only partially present.

Then Shamshi took on more substance: "Riddler. I will destroy you yet. You and your favorite. For what you did to me. I *will....*"

Aškelon raised his hand from Shamshi's arm and the young man was gone. Not frozen, not held in abeyance, not invisible: expelled. Tempus could feel the absence of the youth's hatred, as if a wolf had slunk away into a pitch dark night when lightning struck.

*Pop. Whoosh.* Air clapped transiently where nothing now was but something man-sized just had been. Tempus's ears felt as if they had been boxed.

"You must excuse Shamshi," Aškelon began, "he's young and full of vengeance…."

While Aškelon spoke, Niko drew his sword reflexively, a reaction to the youth's disappearance and the booming, disturbed air rushing in to fill the void.

"No," Tempus warned, but Aškelon was quicker: Niko's shortsword clattered to the ground, obedient to a wave of the dream lord's hand. Aškelon raised an eyebrow: "Nikodemos, after all I've done for you, you lift a blade to me…?"

"Ash, don't do this," Tempus says, as close to pleading with an adversary as he can remember. "Don't start this, between you and me." With the fingers of his right hand, he delves into his belt-pouch, where a weapon lies that might skew all plans, or might win the day. He doesn't know for certain. He doesn't really care. He has a courtyard full of unseeing Stepsons, an entire Sacred Band of reasons not to let this malicious demiurge do more harm.

But Aškelon ignores Tempus. "Nikodemos, do you really think to threaten *me?*" asks the dream lord sardonically. "I make you a panoply worthy of a god, and you sell it? I offer you the secrets of the universe –" Ash is pointing his finger at Niko, and Niko is stock-still, shortsword at his feet. "– and you reject me, time after time?"

Niko's eyes are moving now, and his left hand is inching toward his belt, where his throwing stars nestle.

Then Aškelon brings his finger slowly down – and Niko down, onto bended knee. The entelechy of dream takes another step toward Nikodemos. And Ash says: "I promised Sham I wouldn't kill you – again. He wants that pleasure for himself. And I had thought that your mentor, here, cared more about you than to let you suffer the way you will from now on."

At that, Tempus pulls out the loaded dart tube. He puts it to his lips. He blows. The dart flies straight and true, into the dream lord's neck, above the dark cloak, where the pale skin is thin. Aškelon slaps at his neck but does not stagger. Doesn't fall down dead.

Instead, the dream lord howls, a sound that pounds eardrums across the lawn: "Tempus, it is between us now. Eternally," Aškelon snarls as he melts away, as fast as he had banished Shamshi to some other place.

In the dream lord's wake, people stir. Clap their hands to their ears and, with shocked expressions, wipe their bleeding noses and one another's. And stagger once or twice.

Niko, still on one knee, picked up his sword. Tempus put out a hand to help him but was rebuffed by an open palm. "I can do it. I'm fine." Stealth scrambled to his feet, shaking his head to clear it as Molin came running up to them.

"What was *that?* Such a thunderclap. Everyone has nosebleeds. We wanted the storm god, but perhaps not quite so *much* of him." The priest rubbed his nose and smeared dripping blood around his upper lip.

Nikodemos swiped the back of his hand under his own nose and inspected the hand that came away unbloodied. He sheathed his sword, his eyes downcast.

Tempus had to answer the priest: "You asked for thunder. We'll see if Kouras can moderate himself. He's only a boy, after all. Go hand out cloths and water to your guests, and tell them how fortunate they are: that blood, shed from the nose, on the occasion of this ritual, ensures good fortune for the enterprise – and those who give this blood-sacrifice to the god Vashanka are doubly blessed."

"Of course, of course. I knew that," huffed the priest, wheeling on his heel in a flurry of claret velvet, and hurried off to instruct his staff.

Leaving Tempus and Niko, eye to eye. "So?" he asked his partner.

"I'm…so sorry," Niko said, "I should have waited. But all I could think was that Sham was attacking, when he disappeared like that; that he'd reappear, right in front of me or behind me, and I needed to be ready to engage him…."

"Think nothing of it. They came here to make us angry, goad us. We must pick our battles as we always have. With care, whenever possible. Not fight on someone else's terms; not haphazardly. Are you hurt?"

Niko flexed his sword hand. "No. I'm fine. The dream lord just…pushed me down. With his little finger. I didn't think…he would." Then he turned to Tempus. "And Shamshi…wearing my old panoply, coming and going and glaring and flickering. Was he here, or not? Would it have mattered if I put my sword into him?"

*Good, Niko. You're learning.* "What was here was something under wraps, held very tight, much different from the Sham we knew. Ash didn't dare let Shamshi manifest completely: that boy is out of control. Good for us; bad for them. Control may make all the difference, on the day. But make no mistake: the battle is joined – with the dream lord, not just the wizard boy – till the end…of them, or us. I've avoided this conflict for more years than you've been alive. And now it's here."

"I brought this on us." Niko ducked his head. "But the poison dart will kill him, won't it?" he asked hopefully.

"It didn't drop him on the spot. Remember, time is *his* ally, not ours. Poison works in time. It will have an effect. Make him angrier, for certain." Shamshi and Ash weren't his most pressing concerns right now. "We need to see if all of ours are well," Tempus said. But it was Niko he needed to judge. Too much was happening, too fast, to Nikodemos. Stealth wasn't sure what to expect – of himself, or anybody else.

They went among the revelers, all talking about the mighty thunderclap that made so many noses bleed and so many ears ring. Niko was steady on his right, ready to strike at anything that moved, hand always on his sword hilt, as if he could still seek out and destroy this foe who'd come, threatened him, dropped him to bended knee in front of Tempus, and then gone.

Instead of an enemy, they found Jihan, the only one who had an inkling of what had really happened. She soothed, "Stealth, don't take it badly – or not worse than I. I am a Froth Daughter, strong as the tides. And he froze *me.* Ash does not fight fairly. He dared to lift a hand in anger against Stormbringer's own begotten daughter, when I almost wed him once? We will have our revenge, Niko, I promise."

"We may already have had it," Niko said in a low voice as Randal came toward them across the lawn, with Critias and Straton not far behind, walking backward, scanning the crowd.

"What do you mean?" Jihan whispered.

"The poison dart," Niko said quietly. "The tube."

"Riddler? You didn't…. *Did* you…?" Jihan murmured, aghast.

Tempus shook his head: *not now.* Not with Critias approaching, and Straton, and Randal close by. "Jihan, Niko means that with you so affronted, the problem's surely solved. Ash has offended a Froth Daughter. Certainly his days are numbered."

The Froth Daughter huffed a bit, but when Randal arrived, greeting her with a hug, Jihan beamed like sunrise and began tending to the mage, whose nose was still bleeding.

Randal said, sniffling, with his face toward heaven and Jihan peering up his nose, "Riddler, I saw Aškelon and Shamshi. Ischade did. I warned Straton and Critias, but when we looked again, we couldn't find them. We all tried and tried…. Shamshi had Niko's panoply."

"It's not the weapon or the armor that makes the man, Randal," Tempus told him.

Then Niko shifted on his right, reaching around Jihan to touch Randal's arm in greeting: encouragement given by the tall fighter and received by the slight, big-eared mage without a word.

Crit and Strat bore down on them, a phalanx of two; bodies angled left and right, peering at every shadow, every stranger. "Life to you, Riddler," Crit said wryly, "and everlasting glory." Strat's sour face said he doubted much glory could be found here tonight, among the throng of fat men and powdered ladies on the palace grass.

"And to you both. And to you all." Tempus said, "Critias, Straton: the dream lord and the wizard boy have come and gone, with no one the wiser. The battle is joined. Redouble your precautions." And Tempus thought, in that moment, that these five were the best he'd ever had. Only the gods knew how many more nights like this they'd have – how many more times they'd stand together like this and talk together like this.

Crit said, very quietly, looking all around this public place for prying eyes or pricked ears, "I'll be damned and roasted. Our fault, Commander, but all mine are trying their best…. How are we going to stop Aškelon and Shamshi – united?"

Strat grimaced. "We're not. This fight will be on their terms, not ours," he said fatalistically.

Crit couldn't let it go at that. He whistled a maneuver code. From all directions, Stepsons gathered, crowding around Critias for new orders in the wake of the thunderclap that was all anyone remembered. None of them had seen the dream lord or Shamshi. But they knew Crit, curt and cold; knew his face like they knew their own nightmares. Knew his urgency for what it was.

Crit ordered, "Bring me a dream lord. Bring me a wizard boy. *Now.*" Men moved off, hunting for shadows they wouldn't, couldn't find. Trying the impossible, with all their might.

From the corner of his eye, Tempus kept watch on Stealth. His partner was obedient beside him; first suspicious, then wary, then vigilant as his senses quested through the crowd. Was Niko seeking Aškelon, Shamshi, or his goddess?

Above their heads, real thunder rumbled as the lightning promised by boy and god began to flash. Guests headed for the shelter of the chapel or their homes.

Tempus stayed by Niko, alert as his Sacred Band sorted out the crowd: some to leave, some to stay and file indoors. If Aškelon or Shamshi, or both, were yet among the throng, this was when the danger for his Stepsons would be the greatest.

Scrutinizing everything, waiting for Critias and Straton to signal them, Niko said to him, "Commander, I…let Aškelon take hold of me. Let him put me on my knees. You told me not to start anything." He shrugged.

"You didn't. They did. You did what I ordered you to do. There'll be chances enough to be a hero in the days to come. You're not a berserker. Unthinking rage is not a strength; it's a disability. You'll have your opportunity to face Shamshi, when his protector turns him loose – or when Ash is dead. Ash held onto Sham. I held onto you. There's a balance in that, some degree of *maat*."

Niko's quick canny grin came and went. Seeing it made Tempus think that perhaps he, himself, had not overstepped tonight.

He had never meant to challenge Ash directly. He'd avoided it so carefully all these many years. The lord of dream and shadow was not an opponent whom any man, immortalized or not, would choose. But it was time to make a stand, for the sake of Niko's soul, and his own, and everybody else's.

He hoped Jihan was right about the ancient weapon having deadly results, even on gods and those who were beyond the laws that gods and men obey. Because Aškelon was one of those. As long as Ash had coveted Niko, there had been rancor between Tempus and the dream lord. But now, enmity had changed into something far worse.

If Aškelon had angered destiny, and Shamshi was just an instrument, then the Fates might yet have their day. Greater dooms bring greater destinies.

He couldn't have been more grateful to Niko's goddess. At this moment, when the risk surpassed any he'd known before, his right-side partner could hold his own. Tempus was now certain of it.

Niko was just learning who and what he was, but Tempus had seen the future, tonight, clearer than Arton ever could. Did Niko realize what it meant that he wasn't frozen between blinks, helpless before the dream lord? That he *could* draw his sword? Even Jihan had been entrapped by Ash, this time.

Lord of dream and shadow, entelechy of the seventh sphere: how much more havoc had Aškelon hoped to wreak? More. Getting up off your knees, to fight another day, so far as Tempus was concerned, was still winning. In any battle.

In Tempus's head, something rustled and growled and shifted: Enlil had come to the party.

*So, Enlil, what do You think of my partner now? Perhaps You should have kept him closer, done more for him when You had him to Yourself. Fighting the lord of dreams, I'll need him – and all the help I can get.*

And the god Enlil, so silent for so long, rattled in his skull and came up in his eyes and looked all around, and said, *What was Mine is still Mine. Vashanka is a child. Harmony is a female. Whatsoever is thine, is Mine. And you, arrogant servant, best not forget it. For I am always with thee, wheresoever thou art. Have faith in Me, rely on Me, and only Me, in the battles yet to come. Forever and ever.*

*

Poor Kouras. For once, Lysis felt superior to this Bandaran-trained Stepson, god's son or not: no Theban deity would ever require such an act from a believer. There were so many people in the little chapel – too many. Oligarchs and priests and noblewomen and priestesses sat and stood against the walls.

In the front row, on chairs carefully chosen, Arton sat next to Lysis as a drum began to beat and Kouras entered in slow and measured strides, wearing golden armor and the conical hat of Vashanka's kingship in heaven.

Lysis stuffed his hand into his mouth far enough to bite his knuckles. Critias had warned him what disciplinary action awaited him if he laughed aloud. Arton kicked him in the shins and it hurt right through his greaves.

Pipes played. Lutes strummed. The rhythm picked up, pulsing, as Torchholder strode in, pigeon-breasted, chest stuck out, a golden mace in his hand. The priest pumped the mace up and down, conducting the music and the procession behind Kouras. Then the priest stopped the music with a loud rap upon the marble floor.

*Silence.*

"Gyskouras, son of Vashanka, Favorite of the Storm God, Lord of Sack and Pillage," intoned Torchholder, while behind him red smoke belched from censors.

Lysis hugged himself. His stomach hurt from trying so hard not to laugh. Kouras looked as if he'd been caught trying on his father's best panoply. Then in came the priestesses, beautiful young girls spiraling like tops in only veils and chains, and Arton elbowed him. "Look at *them.*"

But Lysis could hardly see through his tears. He wanted to tell Arton to look at fat old Torchholder, strutting like a peacock, but he couldn't get out the words. Then he chanced another glance at Kouras, who was doing some sort of two-step with the foremost priestess. Kouras was now half naked, his golden armor discarded, wearing only a shiny loinguard and ceremonial sword.

It was too much for Lysis. He bit his hand to keep from laughing. Priestesses came swirling around Kouras, touching him all over. Arton said, "Look. Look, oh *look*. Look at *that.*"

And Lysis saw what Arton meant when he said *'that.'* "It'll never work. Never fit. I mean.... Oh. O goddess, he's *not* going to get up *in* there...."

From directly behind them, Straton growled, "He'd better get up and get in there, or we're all in a lot of trouble," and hit Lysis's tailbone with his knee.

"That's just exactly what he's going to do," Lysis whispered to Arton, taking a chance. "Get *up in* there."

Music played, louder this time. The chosen nubile priestess had gold paint on her breasts that made her nipples look like eyes and she was up in the chariot, clinking her little chain bracelets. Her delicate veils did nothing to hide any part of her; her rump was against the highest point of the car's bumper. And it was a very shapely rump, Lysis had to admit.

Kouras was handed up into the car by Torchholder and some old oligarch and an aged priestess, and that beautiful girl draped herself over the chariot, bent nearly double, stomach on the bumper's rim, arms reaching for the centerpole.

"Look, look, look," Arton whispered wonderingly. "He's not. Oh, he is..."

With a great rumbling flash, a thunderhead appeared inside the chapel, as if it had issued from the head of the storm god's statue. Lightning crackled and crawled along the chapel walls. Women yelped. Priestesses scattered.

Lysis rubbed his eyes. And looked again: the thunderhead had descended over Kouras and the girl.

Inside the cloud, lightning flashed. Lysis could see two shapes, then one shape in the cloud. From the cloud came girlish wails, and sobbing and begging and moaning and groaning. Now a man growled in a voice too deep and fierce to be Kouras's, saying things that Lysis wasn't allowed to say, and reciting some hymn which included the phrase, "lettuce is your hair."

And that did it. Lysis doubled over in a fit, laughing silently until his eyes ran with tears and his stomach convulsed and Straton, from behind, cuffed him soundly on the back of his head.

But he couldn't help it. The creature in the cloud-cover was eight-limbed and thumping. The chariot rocked as if it would break loose from its anchors.

Then it was still.

As the cloud dissipated, people began, first politely, and then enthusiastically, to cheer. And when Lysis looked at what they were cheering for, he started laughing all over again.

"Someone ought to bring him a rag," Straton groused to Crit, "or a robe."

Now priestesses were taking around a piece of red-stained cloth, showing the result of the ceremony, pride in their painted eyes, their breasts heaving.

Arton had fallen silent. Lysis looked over at his new right-man. The seer wasn't laughing anymore. Arton said, "Lysis, what am I going to do?"

"You? Nothing." Lysis didn't understand, and then he did. "Don't worry, Arton. I promise, when it's your turn, no one will be watching you."

The blood on the ceremonial cloth clearly attested to success. After the cloth was retrieved, the priest spoke loudly of how important this ritual was for Sanctuary and its Vashankan congregation. Gyskouras was marched away, surrounded by dancing virgins. The guests got up, congratulating one other. And Lysis was free at last to laugh.

But by then Critias and Straton were wondering how that thunderhead had massed inside a building; and how it had been cajoled to descend and cover the ceremonial mating, or to illuminate the copulating couple.

And no one had an answer for that question, or so many others. Was the storm god Vashanka really here, in this chapel? Was the god inside Kouras now? And if so, was this god really the berserker god, lord of sack and pillage? Whatever that might mean for Sanctuary, it might not be good for Lysis's friend, Kouras, who had seemed so depleted and dazed when the priest pulled a robe around him and led him away, amid whirling priestesses and rejoicing spectators.

*

Niko was dead. Now he's not. He's nearly certain of both. He's nearly sure that he's alive, not in some unending dream of immortality. The night air is so soft, now that the rain has stopped. The breeze seems so sweet to him, as they get their horses from the palace stable: all the smells of horse and straw and hay and life – treasure beyond measure, gifts beyond price. He'd almost died before. Almost. Abarsis, the Slaughter Priest, had come to sit with him, tousled his hair, and Death had gone hungry that day.

But he'd never taken a last breath before. Never hung between heaven and hell before. Until she came into his life and changed it. Came all the way from Chaeronea. *Men staggering back, impaled, moaning.* Came with the Thebans. She was on the Chaeronean battleplain, the Thebans said. Came from heaven. Now everything was different. He was. And she didn't come tonight.

Sync, the horse-tamer, had a woman with him at the palace stables as the celebration was winding down: thick hair, blond and gray; a weathered face once beautiful, now regal; a vital body, muscled and strong. She was helping Sync get the Band's horses, this tiny woman before whom kill-trained stallions dropped their muzzles and came along, meek and mild, at her command. A deadly wench she must have been – but better now, with so much wisdom; so deep a soul, as his *maat* sees her…golden, shining like the sun. He is happy for Sync – the loner, the 3rd Commando colonel who had no friends outside the cohort, has found someone at last.

Life comes, and then departs. He'd always known it, expected no reprieve from death. A secular adept of *maat* looks for god in man, seeks only balance within and balance without. Live every day, accountable for what you do and what you say. Show heaven your respect for the intelligible light, for supernal order. Try to make things better if you can.

The Sacred Banders had wagered their hard-earned money on who would be the target of malice and opportunity tonight: the majority chose Kouras. The majority was wrong. Crit profited. So did Strat.

The gift of life is given once, no more. The Riddler didn't die; he healed.

Aškelon had looked into Niko's eyes tonight with a disdain and rage that froze his soul and made his flesh uncertain. Even when Ash had followed Niko to Bandara, the dream lord had never threatened him. Or shown him what there was to fear in shadows.

Now he knew. Now he had Aškelon on his track, not just Shamshi. But he had his *maat*, and the Riddler on his left. And he was different somehow, in his body, if not his soul.

Sync's woman brought Niko the second-best Trôs stud, her eyes blue as the sky when the moon rises early. Behind her, horses milled as fifty-four Sacred Banders in the palace stable-yard got ready to depart. She said, "I'm Dianna. I like your horse."

He thanked her earnestly; he had to stoop to meet her gaze. He took his reins and watched her stride away to get the next mount; she rode like a goddess, Sync had said.

Niko knew about goddesses now. The Theban goddess had told him, '*...you'll never be hurt that way again.*' What did she mean? What could she mean? Tempus knew. Niko didn't want to ask.

'*My right-side partner needs to be able to withstand more than the average fighter. Now you can,*' his commander had said. *'Few have been given such a weapon by the gods or Fates before,*' the goddess had told Tempus.

So he is still what he had been, a weapon of the god. Perhaps he is more, but not enough more to keep the dream lord and Shamshi at bay.

Strat swung up on his ghost horse. Strat had seen Ischade this evening. Critias knew and let it pass: Ischade was useful to them now. Crit's wild-eyed chestnut fussed and whinnied as he and Strat started sorting the Band for the ride to the barracks. Highest alert, now: forming ranks as if for battle, Crit is laconic, demanding, abrupt. But they know him, they trust him, and everyone obeys.

Aškelon had dropped Niko to his knees without a hint of effort. The goddess had brought him back to life, not made him impervious to harm. He was in too deep with powers far beyond his ken, his commander not the least of them. He chides himself.

But Niko's *maat* knows its instrument: knows he is stronger, changed in ways he cannot yet comprehend. His *maat* must recalibrate the weapon that once was Stealth, called Nikodemos – and is again. He'd hoped that Harmony would come tonight. He looked and looked, but didn't see her. She came and went as she pleased.

Dianna sashayed back with the big Trôs horse and handed the Riddler its reins. Her head reached no higher than his heart. *Long spear, thunking into flesh*: into the Riddler's breast; one barbed spear pierced the heart of the whole Sacred Band that day. If Niko could have stopped that spear with his shield on the Chaeronean battleplain, everything might have gone another way.

But what happened, happened. So Tempus is changed, since then; even bolder, closer to his Band.

And Niko is changed now, too. Niko's skill has always been in his body and his soul, in his discipline, his mystery: he's struggled to restore balance, bring justice, find refuge in mystic calm – time after time. Nature bred man to die. No one knew it better. He'd never asked for more than life and death with honor. He was not like Tempus, more than a man, living on, seeing more than men could bear. One life, one chance, one test of faith: he'd always known his limits. Now he doesn't. Now he is so different, a stranger to himself. He feels the strangeness in every sinew, every muscle, in the way he draws each breath. His commander knows it, too. Sly looks and sidelong glances from the Riddler: *welcome to the club.*

Thunder pealed, from nearby and far away; the skies opened up; rain came falling down. Kouras had let the storm god into him tonight. Everything was changing.

Tempus kneed his horse and off they went, by fours, out through the Gate of the Gods, the way they'd come: Kouras behind Crit on the big blue roan; Jihan and Randal riding to Tempus's left. With Tempus and Niko, that made fifty-six mounted fighters, headed to the barracks in the pouring rain.

Niko kept waiting for Harmony to show herself, for her black horse with its golden muzzle to join them on the road. But she didn't come. Perhaps she'd only been in his life to save it.

What can he do, now? Go to her altar every day? He's not a man for gods. But he's a man for that goddess.

They took the General's Road, up where he'd found his sable mare when she'd been lost. He'd tried to find that house again, with its white columns. And he couldn't. He'd ridden this road with Kouras, after the fight in Sham's battlespace. Kouras had thought it was the shortest way back to the barracks. Niko hadn't cared, by then, with so much blood running out of him, down his leg, leaving a red trail behind.

Tonight, he wanted to ask the Riddler to help him, tell him what it meant to be saved by this foreign goddess…again. Lying on the Mageguild pavings – without a hope, paralyzed – he'd wanted so badly not to die that way or live on that way. And she had come. Resurrected him.

He wished Harmony would appear and explain herself; explain what she did to him. His heart beat strong; his right flank didn't twinge. Old aches he'd lived with so long, from this injury or that, no longer pained him. But Aškelon had dropped him with a pointing finger, put him on his knees in front of his commander. Best not to expect too much from this resurrected body of his, or risk it profligately, until he and it had come to terms.

When they turned off the General's Road, there was a glow on the horizon, low in the sky, like the torches of an army encamped on a battleplain. They were nearly to the barracks and deep into third watch when a horse and rider came running the other way, flat out through the rain: one horse; one rider, headed their way as if Death himself were chasing after.

Tempus launched his horse into a gallop. Niko rode apace, calling to the others to keep formation. They'd closed half the distance when the rider called out, "Commander? Riddler? Fire at the barracks!"

And Niko didn't need to signal the men behind: everyone raced homeward, as fast as their mounts could go.

They were nearly there when a horse leaped out of the underbrush and dashed across the road, coming up on Niko's right.

He recognized the big black with its armored rider instantly: Harmony.

But there was no time for talk. There was only time to run their mounts as fast as horses would carry them, toward the barracks, toward home.

*Fire!*

## *Chapter 41: Death Comes Shambling After*

"Gods damn you, Kouras, bring more rain. *Now!* All you can," Crit shouts.

*Please, please, let my mare be safe.* Niko can't find her. Stables afire, and Niko's sable mare is in the flames, somewhere, with so many other Stepson horses. The heart and soul of the Sacred Band, burning together, screaming together. Each of them has horses – and partners trying to save horses – in the stables: if everybody charges in, willy-nilly, to save only their beloveds, all will be lost.

Critias organizes a bucket brigade. Men tear linen masks from chitons, blindfolds for their mounts.

Niko does his best, heeding Crit's hoarse orders, but this fire rages beyond mortal control. Stepsons tie wet linen around their noses and their mouths. Everyone risks death under falling rafters, collapsing lofts, crumbling and lethal as they tumble. Flames breed more flames wherever they land on horse or man or straw-bedded stall.

Fire just kept on falling from the haylofts, from the rafters, from the roofs, and nothing they could do would stop it.

Tempus, like a god himself, raced into flames and out again with this blind-folded horse or that, with one staggering man and then another, again and again.

Jihan, right beside him, tried her gift of cold and sleet on screaming horseflesh and blazing timbers, even holding a burning rafter high while Stepsons scuttled under and got safely by with terrified mounts. But sleet won't quench this Greek fire; naphtha sticking to whatever it touches, setting flesh and wood and hay ablaze.

She and Straton, mighty strengths, wrestled tirelessly with rearing horses and stricken men, clearing pathways from the burning stables.

Randal ran alongside them, his magic parting fire where it could to make path after path out of the inferno.

But it wasn't enough. Not the rain, pouring down in torrents. Not the Riddler, braving fire that would char a man. Not Jihan's gift of ice and cold or Straton's strength or Randal's magic or the storm god's rain cleared the way to safety. There was some strangeness in the proportion here, some balance out of whack.

*Where is she? Velvet muzzle, tipped-in ears, liquid eyes that see his soul and soothe it. Please, don't be dead; don't be hurt.*

Niko's *maat* looked at this world of pain and flame, and looked away again: unnatural pain, unnatural flame. His mare was in there, somewhere, in the inferno. But so were so many other horses – and so many men, Stepsons, Sacred Banders. Over and over, Niko told himself that his job wasn't just to save his own, but to save them all, as many as he could.

And his mare was deep inside the west stable, hardest to reach. Or perhaps not: maybe she was already safe, outside. He couldn't get to her stall from where he was: there were too many other stalls, other horses, in the way. He had no time to mull it.

Horses screaming. Men running. Water in buckets; never enough. Black smoke billowing up from the barracks, making men and horses cough and wheeze. Lurid flames; evil, awful light from hell as hungry fire eats up men and horses, hopes and dreams.

And Tempus, striding through the chaos with piles of sopping bed sheets, ripping them as he went, to rescue terrified horses from the fiery stables. Eighty stalls: four barns, twenty horses each; two barns ablaze.

*My mare is in there, somewhere.* He has other horses, rides other mounts. He should love them all the same, but he doesn't. No one does. Your horse saves you; you save it; and that love is a partnership like no other. Your horse lends its strength; you lend your purpose; and together you are so much more. With the right horse. With that love unlike any other.

Black clouds like charred flesh. Choking smoke searing eyes and noses, closing throats, dropping men to their knees who breathed that smoke too long. Lightning flashing in sheets of rage. More icy rain, whirling, skirling, gusting through doors and windows and cindered roofs and rafters. The storm gods pitch in, bringing torrents; rain storms in a deluge. Thunder masks the screams of horses still in their stalls.

Niko couldn't count how many times he went into those barns, or how many burns he had. No matter where he went, he never saw his mare. So many rafters fell, and shingles fluttered down, aflame like the stalls and the hay. Men ran in with sheets, swathed horses eyes and heads; dragged them out, kicking and screaming, to lead them outside the barracks walls.

*Mare, where are you?*

He'd grab a horse. Fight it. Push it by the rump. Beat it, if he had to, to get it to move forward. Blindfold it. Halter it. Drag it from its stall. When he doesn't have enough rags, he uses his chlamys, his chiton. He's stripped to the waist, soaking himself each time before he runs back into the conflagration. Even wet linen and wool can catch fire in this heat.

Stepsons are everywhere in the pall of noxious smoke, stamping out flaming chunks of wood and hay, soaking embers when they fall, beating out sparks and flakes of burning straw on horse and man and wood.

Finally, there was no man or horse left alive in the westmost barn. The in-line barn next to it still smoked. But the worst of the fire there was out, thanks to Kouras and Jihan and the gods for the rain in gusts, on a wind that drives that rain everywhere, soaking everything, man and horse alike. Now there was nothing left to save except the offices and the living quarters: everyone pitched in, trying to stomp out each spark and ember on the west side of the compound.

*Where's my mare?*

Niko couldn't unravel what had happened until Sync told him: the shed they'd built for the naphtha had exploded (no one knew how or why) and blazing naphtha fireballs, arcing high, had landed on the roofs of the stables, of the living quarters, everywhere. Or so the Stepsons said, who'd been here. And the new mercenaries and Thebans all agreed.

Unlikely story, Niko thought: they'd purposely built the shed of earth at the farthest east end of the barracks compound, so this couldn't happen.

But happen it did. And the rain still pelted down as if the gods themselves were trying to help drown the fire. Jihan took that rain and chilled it, adding sleet of her own in gust after gust; calling on her father, Stormbringer, for aid. Soon enough the inner courtyard was treacherous to man and beast, but the roofs were soaked, and the last blaze in the stables finally went out.

Tempus was counting the horses – and the men – they'd saved, by then. Jihan was right beside him, with her unguents and her Froth Daughter's touch to help man and horse, freezing naphtha cold where it stuck to flesh. And with her was Randal, fielding those healing powers a mage could bring to bear.

Niko didn't know how many bellowing horses he'd dragged outside to safety. Sacred Banders staggered and stumbled, wet down, stripped down, covered with soot and ashes and burns bad enough to gleam liquid red, white and angry in the last of the flames or in the torchlight where they treated the wounded.

When Niko closed his eyes all he could see were burned manes, flaring tails, sparks and showers of flaming hay landing everywhere. Red, raw flesh; white melted skin and serum seeping, with blackened hide all around. Men and horses, dying together. Because of a spontaneous explosion of naphtha, carefully stored away by men conscious of the risk and trying to preclude it? He couldn't credit it. Perhaps lightning had hit the shed. How many dead men? How many dead horses? How many badly injured? No one knew, yet.

*Please, not my mare.*

The only thing worse than the sound of terrified horses and men trapped in flames was the smell of the dead ones, roasted alive in there. One of the side barns had been completely engulfed; the west barn parallel to the gates smoldered. Some of the best of the Stepson horses were in the west stables: it was lucky that fifty-four mounts had been at the palace. Lucky for all but the horses left behind.

*Please, please let her be safe.*

When he could, he needed to go through the stable and identify the dead horses and any bodies of men they'd missed. Nothing left in there now could be alive. But even with the torrential rain, it was too soon for that. He walked across the compound, where muddy ground mixed with char, and over to the main gates. The Band had improvised some horse lines. Tempus and Sync and Critias were taking stock of what remained.

Some new mercenaries and younger Thebans were holding on to mounts that had come back from the palace. Niko can't assess this loss. It's too horrendous. But he has his job to do: he's grateful not to think too much. He starts with the first horse line, where men are picking ashes out of open burns, applying bacon grease and salve where they can. Kouras and Lysis and Arton are sitting on the ground, tearing sheets into bandage. There are tears streaming down Arton's face unheeded, mixing with the rain.

*Where is she?*

Thunder peals and peals and peals again, as if heaven stamps it foot, enraged.

Niko can't bring himself to ask if anyone has seen his mare. He'll find out soon enough. The Band has torches stuck in the ground all around; it's hard to keep them lit in the rain. His burned hands, his arms and shoulders and torso sting when raindrops hit melted skin, liquefied flesh and blistered wounds. He walks the first line and sees his black colt. It calls out, a frightened whinny. He goes over to it where it pulls upon the rope line. They haven't gotten around to treating this horse yet. He's got open wounds on his croup; his tail is singed half off, but his eyes are clear and there's nothing here that can't heal, in time, with luck.

Niko starts to move on by and steps backward, bumping into Lysis. "What is it, Lysis?" he asks absently, still evaluating the damage to his colt.

"Oh, Stealth, he's such a wonderful colt." The young Theban's voice trembles; the boy is shivering in the downpour.

"Can I take care of him? I'm sure I can get him well. He's not that badly burned. And he's so talented."

*Mare, don't be dead, please.*

"Tend him as if he's your own. He may well be, someday," Niko managed, not really thinking about what he said. Lysis was the one who'd been given a special gift with horses by the Theban goddess. And that reminded him: the goddess had come to ride with them, just before the messenger reached them and told them of the fire.

Now he wanted to find Harmony. But first he needed to go through the horse lines. First he needed to find his mare. And then it hit him – what life would be like if she'd burned to death in that barn, with her unborn foal inside her, while he attended a meaningless celebration on the palace lawn and riled the dream lord.

And the rain keeps pounding down.

*My mare is here. She's alive,* he promised himself. *She's somewhere on the horse lines. I'd know if she were dead.*

But she wasn't there. His sable mare was not among any of the horses rescued from the stables.

He found Tempus, eventually, working by torchlight on a horse with a badly burned eye. "What do you think, Commander?" Niko called out, over a rain so fierce it came down hard and loud and sluiced everything clean, bouncing off the ground when it hit.

"About what? This horse's eye? Maybe we can save it. Or about what happened here?" his commander growled. Any man of sense would back away from this voice. This was not the Riddler who was reasonable. This was the Riddler of old. That voice was shale sliding into hell and Niko, despite himself, retreated.

"About what happened here," he had to say. He suspected, now, what Tempus meant: and he took one long, backward step, right into wrath unending and revenge reserved normally for gods: "You mean you think someone *set* this fire?" He could barely get the words out. His fists balled until his nails bit his palms.

Tempus looked away from that horse to Niko with eyes that blazed like the fire in the stables. And said, "Your *maat* doesn't know? Enlil knows. I know. Let's get these burned horses treated, and see if there are any that can't be saved. Then we'll see about taking this war back to the dream lord."

*Some strangeness in the proportion. Please, please, mare, don't be dead.*

The smell of roast flesh, burnt timber and hay was fading, washed from the air by the rain. He stood silently too long, watching the Riddler.

"So, Niko? What is it? There's plenty for you to do on this horse line."

"I…was looking for my mare." There, he'd said it. The rain stopped. Above their heads, clouds scudded away.

Tempus put down a jar of unguent and wiped his hands on his naked sides. He ducked under the rope and came to Niko. "I haven't seen her. Not out here – *or* in there." His chin jutted to the stables.

Niko didn't have the stomach to look among the dead horses quite yet. There was still a chance she'd escaped somehow. He said, "I'm going to finish up here and then go look inside," very softly.

Then he heard hoofbeats behind him, and faced the sound.

Lit by torch and moonlight, the goddess seemed huge on her big black horse.

She said, loudly enough for Tempus and Niko to hear her quite clearly, "Stealth called Nikodemos, you want your Aškelonian sable mare?"

"I do," he said. "You know I do."

"So does your adversary, the dream lord," the goddess said, and began to ride away.

"She's not dead?" His heart leapt. "Did you see her?"

The goddess's big black horse stopped. She turned in her saddle. "If she's yours, she's dead. The dream lord will kill her if he can't get her back, rather than let her succor you. If she's mine, she may yet live. Your choice, Niko."

And Harmony rode on down the horse line, leaving Tempus and Niko staring at each other.

He asked Tempus, "What does she mean?"

"She means your mare is alive. Perhaps she means that Ash set this fire merely to take your mare away, to punish you. If I were you, I'd give her the mare – no matter what shape the horse is in."

The Riddler had told Niko to keep nothing Aškelonian – no sword, no cuirass, nothing made by the dream lord. He'd never thought that included his sable mare, bred by Aškelon. She'd been his for so long. "Your sister brought that mare to me," he reminded

Tempus. He didn't say, *'as a gift from the dream lord,'* when Aškelon still courted him, long ago.

Niko remembered Straton's ghost horse. He didn't want a dead horse brought back to life. And he knew that Tempus might be thinking the same, as his commander, hands on hips, watched the goddess disappear into the moonlit darkness.

No rain now. The moon shone down, clear and bright, running along the goddess's armor as she rode into the night.

Niko hadn't even asked Tempus if anyone knew, yet, how many men had been hurt or killed in the fire.

When they found out, he was ashamed that he'd been thinking only of himself, his loss: six of the new mercenaries had died in the flames; three Thebans; and one veteran Stepson, overcome by smoke. A dozen more had significant burns.

They would make pyres tomorrow, or the next day, when the wood and ground dried out.

They pulled the remaining bodies out of the rubble as soon as they could touch them. Nothing is more frightening than a corpse burned beyond recognition but still intact: just teeth in wizened skulls, blackened flesh stuck to bone and holes where eyes had popped. At least they could take all of these to the pyres and burn them again, to pure ash. And Abarsis would come and take their souls away. But it will be much harder to drag out the horses…those sorry, sad carcasses….

Men have choices; horses go where men demand; trusting, always, in the hands that guide them.

He went looking for the goddess then, beyond the final horse line. From what Harmony had told him, there was no use in looking for his mare. All was quiet but for soft groans and mutters of men and horses, stomping feet, swishing tails and the occasional crack and thud from the ruined stables as weakened timbers tumbled down. She'd come and ridden with them, and then she was gone. And come back again….

At last he found Harmony, astride her black stallion, outside the gates, looking at the burned stables from beyond the horse lines.

He said, "So much destruction. Surely not only because my mare was here. If you can save her, she's yours." He wanted to ask, '*How will you do that? Is she dead? Will you bring her back from beyond death's gate? Don't let her suffer. Don't make her suffer.*'

He said, instead, "Is she here? With you?"

The goddess wore no helmet. Her wet hair was heavy from the rain, dark and slapping in strings against her as she moved. She slid down from the big black and came toward him, holding out the reins. "Here. Take him in trade. I'll ride her. And don't worry for her."

He took the reins of her black stallion. First he was so relieved he couldn't speak. Then he wanted to ask her what she had done to him, whether he was still the man he'd been before. He didn't. He just looked into those eyes of hers, reflecting torchlight or moonlight. He asked, "Can I see her again? And you, again?"

Harmony said, "We will be where you came to find your mare when she was last lost to you. In the house off the General's Road." Until then, he'd never really connected the woman who'd found his mare and his dancing girl. He remembered now. "Look," she said, and held out her hand.

Out of the darkness into the moonlight ambled his sable mare – or her sable mare. Or the ghost of his mare. Or his immortalized mare. If his life hung in the balance, he couldn't have said which one this mare was. The mare stopped between them; saddled, bridled, no sign of burns or harm, and snuffled. Took one step toward him. He held out a hand to stop her: she wasn't his mare anymore. If this mare came up to him, put her head against his chest, shoved him softly with her nose, then he might be unable to give her up. And then his mare would be truly lost – lost to the lord of dream and shadow.

Harmony said, "Go to her, Niko. Say what you wish to her.

She's a warhorse. You'll see her again in the days to come."

He didn't. He couldn't. "No, you take her. She's yours now." He had the black stud's reins in his hands.

She swung up on his mare. "So are you," he thought she said. Then, loud enough that he was sure she spoke: "No one can harm her. She's with me now."

And he wondered if it would be the same for him, as she rode away, the sable mare's long tail swishing from side to side in the light of the moon.

*

Now it is bright. Now it is dry. Now there is not a cloud in the sky. Now the sun shines down at midday. Tempus thinks it unseemly that the heavens should make such a display of themselves today.

"She gave you *what? Him?* In trade for that old pregnant mare? Would she like one of mine? Has she got another one of *those?"* Strat asks Niko. Everyone is half naked, hauling charred chunks of horse out of the ruined stables.

Tempus has to stop himself from trying to protect Niko. But Straton means well. Bravado is all there is to hold onto, in the face of so many men and horses dead for no reason, or for reasons no one wants to face: the dream lord, and Shamshi, striking out with cowardly battle, hurting innocent animals to hurt the Sacred Band.

And Niko says, "Breed to him, Ace. You, Crit, the Band – you can bring mares to him as you please, at no cost. It's still early in the season. If he's really a horse, not a figment, maybe he'll breed true. He's got everything a horse should have: thin mane, thick tail, and back broad enough for any one of you." Walking away from the little group clustered admiringly around the black stallion, Niko calls back over his shoulder, "Try him out."

Tempus half expects to look around and find the black horse gone. With the goddess astride him, that stud had often vanished in the blink of an eye.

Beyond the goddess-given stallion, outside the charred stables, Randal has been working with four Sacred Banders, levitating horse forequarters and horse haunches and floating them toward the gate and through it, to a mass gravesite prepared for fourteen horses: too many carcasses; too much flesh for the funerary pyres. So the Band will bury their mounts, all together, in the earth: a herd of ghost horses for the afterlife.

Niko has almost nothing of his own now, Tempus is keenly aware. His right-side partner had few enough possessions, before. With his sable mare and his panoply from Aškelon gone, Niko has very little to anchor him: a few young horses, not ready for war; bits of arms and armor, trusty but old and worn. Niko has never collected trophies; he uses mostly service panoplies, Stepson issue. Tempus knows his second-in-command needs a tether, while his soul spins in the winds of change. And Tempus must provide it, somehow. But what will stabilize Nikodemos won't be in the realm of the body; it must be in the realm of the soul.

Niko came over to him, where he watched the cleanup, arduous and just beginning. His rightman fixed him with an unblinking stare: "Why don't you take that black stallion, Commander? I've been riding yours so long. I don't need a horse like that."

"Don't give away a gift from your goddess, Niko. For your sake, and ours, don't insult her." *Not now, with theomachy raging.*

"I…didn't think of it that way," Niko whispered, chary and withdrawn, wearing a tunic despite the heat. The burns on his hands, his legs, and his arms were healing fast – too fast, scabbing up at an unnatural rate. Hence, the tunic, to hide the flesh already healed on his torso. Niko scratched at his left forearm absently. Flakes fell away from new pink skin bright against his deep tan.

"How did you sleep, Stealth?" Tempus recognized the signs. He understood healing – a real gift from Niko's goddess, one that a man couldn't give away…or even wish away. So Niko had the gift of healing now. Good. And this Stepson of his, who for so long had had nothing, wanted nothing, asked for nothing, now had this great horse, fit for a general or a conqueror or a deity – and a goddess who favored him. But could Niko sleep, in his rest-place, or in his bed?

"Sleep? I didn't. I couldn't," Stealth replied. "Too much to do, too much going on."

Tempus wondered if that was the only reason Niko hadn't slept, but let it go.

A third of the Sacred Band prepared the training field to hold the horse lines until new stalls could be built; another third worked clearing the ruins; the rest readied the pyres for ten dead men, lost to fire and smoke and fury. A sad day, this, for one and all. But reconstruction already was beginning.

Tempus's three Aškelonian horses, and eleven others, had burned to death in the flames. Too many warhorses and warriors lost, when real war loomed. It takes so long to train and season cavalry: each horse and man is impossible to replace. Everything in life is borrowed, but Tempus grieved for lost warhorses in a way he never did for men.

The only good thing that had happened was the addition of the black stallion to the Band's string. When Sacred Banders came in from burying grisly quarters of horseflesh or dragging branches or building stalls and paddocks, they joined the crowd around the big stallion tied in front of Niko's quarters.

Sync came up to Tempus and said, "Is that a real horse, do you think? Can a horse *be* that good? And will it breed true?"

And the Thebans came by, admiring. Charon said, "My son is in love with that gold-muzzled stallion, and Niko's colt as well. And, by the way, Torchholder says let him know if we're going to wreak any more havoc in his town – or his Mageguild. He was complaining."

"Molin always does. Lysis is doing a good job tending convalescing horses. Let's hope we do as well healing our

Sacred Band's wounded and putting our dead to rest," Tempus told the Theban.

They had scheduled the rites for tomorrow night at sundown. Charon wanted to add games, with prizes dedicated to the newly dead. "You can have your games, Charon. Two or three events. Crit will help you. Tonight, you can do as you wish after sundown, in honor of your dead." Three dead Thebans; six dead mercenaries, just hired; one Stepson of long standing. It wasn't going to be easy for anyone to say goodbye. "Niko and I won't be here."

Brown-skinned Gorgias, face like a battlefield, came up behind Charon and said, "Won't be here? The goddess will miss her favorite when the songs are sung."

For a moment Tempus didn't know what Gorgias meant, but then realized: Niko had that stallion, a gift from their goddess; she'd healed him in the barracks where all the Thebans could see. Thebans were starting to think of Niko as an avatar of their goddess.

"Charon, Gorgias – don't let your Thebans start worshipping that horse, no matter whose horse it is now or whose it was before." *Or its new owner: hero-cults complicate everything in a Sacred Band.* Tempus knew from experience. "We're going to the city. We'll be back before the night is done."

The Thebans went their way, rejoining the crowd around the big black horse with the golden dapples.

Tempus called his best together: "Straton, get Ischade and bring her here; while you're in the city, order what replacements – tack and carts, materials and supplies – you may. And hire some laborers: we need stables in working order. Critias, you're in command here. Kouras goes with us today; get him now. Jihan, go up to Wizardwall and borrow a dozen horses from Bashir's Successors. Get them here as fast as you can

– use cloud conveyance if you must. Randal, try once more with Cime, to make her come. And bring Sync's Third Commando back here, and their mounts, all but ten."

With the storm god's favor, he and Niko will be back in time to smell the smoke and burning flesh of his ten newly-dead fighters on their pyres. Enlil is hot within him now; fuming; swelling up inside his skin, against his flesh; pushing him back inside his own skull so that his head throbs. When Lord Storm is angry, swirling in him, he must go very carefully until a battle worthy of the storm god is joined. Enlil is an impatient god, pushing Tempus to go faster, shoving his humanity aside and hungry for the fight.

But this is a cannier enemy than they have faced before, who must be drawn in, lured, made to come to them. Or else, he must find a way to Meridian, straight on, past the ground and sky.

From Sanctuary, it just might be possible to reach Meridian. Sanctuary has always been a border town between mortality and immortality, its feet in hell and its fingers stretched up to heaven – a place where anything may happen, and sometimes does, when wills are strong and mysteries invoked.

All of his go running to their tasks, hearing the god in his voice, taking furtive backward looks. Thebans have only seen Enlil come to ground one time before – out on the jetty, when the god took their pretty little goddess in the sand. They may see the storm god of the armies in all his glory yet, before this fight is done, if Enlil's wordless fury is any harbinger of war to come.

*

"Now they feel the pain," said the wizard boy to the dream lord.

"Now you be careful," said the dream lord to Shamshi, in a dark place in Sanctuary, in the Mageguild, where borders between realities are thinnest, and shadows play.

There is ancient poison in the dream lord's veins, blazing. If he were flesh and blood like Shamshi, he'd be dead of it by now. But he's been alive so long, and traded off so much, that his flesh and blood lie thinly over his entelechy.

This boy, Shamshi, has brought such ruination and damnation upon everything and everyone he's touched that even Aškelon is appalled. But this youth, this wizard boy or what is left of him, is Aškelon's creature now. So much substance of the mortal boy has been replaced with the stuff of dream and nightmare, even the regent of the seventh sphere is unsure of what he's got. "Be *very* careful, Shamshi, whom you see and what you do and what you say when you're abroad tonight. We've hurt them badly. They're hot for war."

"We can destroy them. If..." A flicker shivers over remade flesh that once was Shamshi and now is something else, something darker, not quite comfortable among the likes of men. "...if you still wish it so." The youth didn't see Aškelon struck by the poison dart. But he knows something is amiss.

Aškelon doesn't trust this wizard boy; he knows Sham now, too well. "We'll destroy them, if destiny allows. Meanwhile, we go to Meridian, to prepare."

Aškelon waves his hand in the warmth and dark, his fingers spread. Shadows between those fingers thicken and trails begin to form. Those trails make light, and heat, and stream out behind his hand, forming into azure sea and softest sky above Meridian, whose crystal quays, golden streets and shining spires are more beautiful than man can make.

And they are there, in a heartbeat. The regent of the seventh sphere has been lord of Meridian for thousands of years. It is inconceivable to him that he will not be here for thousands more. At his arrival, lutes are strummed and pipers pipe and horns begin to play. His lion-rammed barge is floating at its dock, ready. Down the wide and perfect streets, his welcoming throng approaches.

Things are mostly as they should be: sea lions bask and seals cavort and dolphins ply his waters. Yet there is a rustiness to his skyline, a smudge around the edges of his island chain, a decay in streets beneath his feet that should be smooth and straight along his route.

Clouds above are tinged with gray, where he wants sunlight. Lutes are slightly out of tune. Pipes sound spitty, tentative. Denizens seem more dazed than even their dream-life warrants. And Meridian has never tarnished before. The archipelago of dreams only touches reality once every thousand years, unless he so commands it.

Is the poison in his blood leaching into Meridian itself? Can it be so? After so long a reign, can rot set in? Can dreams rust? Can acid eat at the foundations of the land of dream?

He mustn't let Shamshi know he is weakened. But he is. And, weakened, he is worried. For the first time in millennia, he feels a remote, corrupting pain that will not leave him. It's in his substance, eroding the glue that holds his person fast. It's in the world around him. How sad it would be if Meridian and the seventh sphere dissolved, leaving dreams unmanaged, nightmares out of hand. As a palanquin arrives to take them to his palace, he pensively regards the youth beside him: blond and gray-eyed and fair today, as handsome still as ever he was – when he's here. When he's elsewhere, he's a specter, disconcerting: sometimes manlike, sometimes not.

Dissolution is in the air. Aškelon can smell it in his nostrils. For the first time in eons, he must prepare for war. It is inconceivable that with all his skills, a physical encounter could – might – be needed. But Tempus is a fool, and rooted to the earth and all its violence. And every edge of every building on Meridian is wavering; every comfort being eaten away by dark where light should be, and light where dark should be: dissonance is here. Some strangeness in the proportion afflicts his inner ear, throwing him off balance.

And lest dissonance be here to stay, Aškelon must hasten to protect Meridian, this timeless, perfect place of dream and shadow.

So he raises up his hand and calls his multitude to war: so many who have been here forever; so many who have died in sleep or dream; so many whose dreams are violent, retaliatory, or worse.

Here they are, coming up the causeways and out of the buildings, even tramping up from the quays with measured tread.

Ready for combat, for hostilities, for conflict or confrontation, for warfare of any sort he might decree.

If an army is required, he can field one. If the rules are changing, then no rules apply. So it may not matter that so many who serve him are already dead.

Dying in dreams is still dying. And dreaming on, they dream what dreams Aškelon commands.

*

"You'll pay *how much?* To raze one empty building? You're on," said Zip to Tempus, outside Zip's warehouse down on Wideway. "You'll clear this with the palace? I'm not looking for any trouble with Walegrin or that lot." Zip is dark, hawk-faced, thin. This Ratfall boy has grown up in the margins of Sanctuary, and midnight dealing is his stock in trade. "I suppose there's no use in me telling you I don't do this kind of job anymore – that I don't have the men, or the muscle, or the heart for this?" Zip scoffed in a meager pool of light beneath a single torch and leaned back against the warehouse brick.

"No, there's not."

"I'm just a businessman, Sanctuary style."

"Come see me when it's done. And remember, none of yours needs to go inside. Just burn it down and collect your pay."

Zip still wore a sling-shot at his hip. Old habits die hard, when they die at all. This warehouse is purposely ill-lit and well positioned for a man needing to watch his back and the street in both directions.

Zip looked away from Tempus, at Nikodemos, on the black horse at Tempus's right, and said, "I see you're still here, pretty boy. Still coat-tailing your way to glory. I liked the Riddler's daughter better. Do you do for Tempus what she used to do for me?" Zip grinned, teeth flashing in the torchlight.

Niko's new horse took a step forward and snorted: undue pressure from his rider's calves. Niko said, "If I were you, wanting to keep those white teeth in that cut-throat's head, I'd be about my business. Now." Niko's black took another step forward. Two more, and Zip must dodge to one side or the other or be pushed against the wall.

Tempus said, "Niko, give him the keys."

From astride his big black horse, Niko tossed the keys: one, two, three. Zip caught them all, but had to lunge clumsily to do it.

"You're both better than this," rebuked the commander, and wheeled his Trôs. Niko followed on the black, who might as easily have pushed Zip into those bricks or chased him down the wall.

"He may be, but I'm not," Zip called after them. "But thanks for the compliment. I'll remember that you're sweet on me, yourself, big fellow. But it won't reduce the cost of this little gambit one bit. Not one bit."

The cost of this was liable to be lives, not coins, but Tempus didn't answer.

Offer made and accepted. Bargain duly constituted. In Sanctuary, lives were cheap and fools died often. This Zip was smart. He'd lived a decade longer than he should have. If Zip was as smart as Tempus thought, he'd live through this. If not, then that was part of the cost of this customary thieves' world contract, arranged in the traditional way: in the dark of night, on a nondescript street where a midnight mover ruled over a crew of hand-picked unfortunates who'd dare whatever they must, to keep their bellies fed.

Tempus had warned Zip not to go inside the Mageguild, or let any of his street fighters and brigands go in there. More, he couldn't do. He felt a little twinge of pity for Zip, who'd lived long enough to become cocky about what he could survive. But prudence was in short supply this season.

In his head, Enlil growled and ramped, impatient for blood to spill and battle to be joined. Gods live forever; men die in multitudes. So despite all this encouragement from on high, Tempus was proceeding with caution. For the first time in a long time, the god rode through Sanctuary with him, peering out of his eyes, his hand on Tempus's reins, wanting to rend and tear and devour and flatten all he saw.

But this was no longer Enlil's territory. This beleaguered city belonged to Vashanka, rival storm god.

*Burn the whole town down, cowardly servant. Lazy avatar, they don't deserve you, or Me, or life itself. Make an end to this place, with your fighters. And I will meet Vashanka on the battlements of His temple, a blasphemy in My sight. You do not need that girl goddess – or Her unfaithful avatar, once My own. You need only Me.*

*Enlil, You let the dream lord set fire to my barracks, kill my men and my horses,* he retorted as silently as the god had spoken to him. *Where were You then, Lord Storm? Where was Your might against that blaze from hell? If You think to push me into battle prematurely, You think wrong. You are not the only lord of war, these days. There is the Theban goddess hereabouts. And Vashanka rises. Look to Your adherents, and treat them better – me and mine. And bide Your time, Ravener. This battle will be one to sate even Your hunger. Now get out of my head, so I can think. Be Thee quiet. Be Thee patient. And all that Thou wills shall come to Thee.*

His breath was bated; his pulse beat fast. He wanted to ask the god to heal his heart, make it beat as once it had, but he didn't: when you asked something from Enlil, you needed to know what you would trade.

*

Down past Shambles Cross, where the little house nestled by the riverside, Straton tied the ghost horse to Ischade's low iron fence. And waited, respectfully, to see if the witch would come.

When she didn't, he tried her gate. It wouldn't budge. But it wasn't hanging askew on its hinges, either. "Ischade," he said under his breath, "let me in or come out here to me. It's the Riddler's business."

The ghost horse whickered behind his back. He wheeled around: this place was full of undeads, tortured souls. No one knew that better than he.

He remembered watching Niko embrace Janni here. Of all he'd seen and all he'd done in life, that image of two Stepsons, the living and the dead, embracing by the White Foal, still haunted him the most.

Straton wasn't like Niko, afraid of nothing in this world or the next. The ghost horse raised its head, calling out again. What was coming? You could meet your doom here in a heartbeat; end up in the White Foal River where corpses floated till they waked.

Cloying darkness surrounded him, as on so many other nights when he'd come to her like this, waited for her like this, ached for her like this.

Then she was there: no wings, no flutter this time, walking out of the bushes as if she'd been for a stroll by the river. But the ground was treacherous there, where the swollen White Foal lapped stones from neglected graves and altars and worse…stones you didn't want to disturb on a summer evening when the moon was just waning.

"Straton," she breathed, and he thrilled to her voice. Her eyes didn't float off her face. She was his beauteous Ischade tonight, smelling of nightshade and jasmine. Her dark cloak enfolded him as she put her hands around his neck and drew his head down. He hoped she'd eaten already. Then he didn't care, so sweet was the kiss she gave him, soft as a spider's web.

"Ischade," he said when her lips left his, before he couldn't remember why he'd come here or what he wanted, or anything but the touch of her and the love for her which was the greatest love he'd ever known – but for the ghost horse. That horse stomped a foot and made those soft, short noises that horses make when greeting their loved ones: not whinnies, not even whickers or nickers, but softer sounds, right up from their souls.

"Ischade, I…." He couldn't recall what he wanted, except her touch. He couldn't remember why he was here, except to drown in her eyes, content. "Ischade…."

'*Get her. Convince her. Here I am. This is our night. It can be,* 'the ghost horse told him, pawing the ground with one forefoot.

"Yes, Straton? Yes, what is it? We'll go inside...."

'*Boost her up on my broad back and we'll have our ride. Across the fields; through the streets; and on we'll go, just we three. Ride away, we can. Far as the eye can see. Away from all of this, just you, and her, and me...forever. Just we three,* ' urged the ghost horse, shifting from hoof to hoof.

And he couldn't remember what he had to say, with his arms around her and her hair tickling his nose. Then he did: "The Riddler said to get you. Right away. There was a fire at the barracks last night. Ten men dead, twelve badly burned. Fourteen horses killed. He's planning something. We're moving. The commander wants you with us."

"Ah, I see. That explains all the disturbances. All the unrest. So many spirits discommoded." She took a step back, no longer pressed against him.

Now he can think. "Please, Ischade. I'm here for you..."

The ghost horse whinnies, *'Right now. Come for a ride. Out of here and away...forever. My strong hooves can carry us wherever love wishes. We can go another way, just we three...before it's too late.'* And the horse paws the ground again and snorts impatiently, craning its neck at them, imploring with its eyes.

Ischade moves quickly now, decided: "Get up on him then, and give me a hand. We'll ride out there. Just we three."

Ischade glides over to the ghost horse and pats its neck and croons to it as Straton has never seen her to do to anyone or anything, man or beast.

He'd never known whether the ghost horse talked to her, or was really talking at all, or whether that horse's voice was only a whisper in his head.

But he swung up and reached a hand down. She grasped it: her hand was cool and dry and strong. When he swung her up behind him she was lighter than air, hardly there at all.

And the ghost horse let out a loud whinny of joy as it trotted, then cantered (oh, so carefully with Ischade up behind him), toward the barracks and whatever Tempus had in mind.

*

Kouras was on his own, on the big blue roan, waiting for Torchholder in the forecourt of the palace, watching clouds scud across the moon.

When the priest arrived, Molin was frowning. "It's the middle of the night, Gyskouras. What do you want? What do you need?"

"My father, Vashanka, needs you to do as we instruct," said Kouras, and it was true: the god was moving in him, sharing his sight, sharing his body, whispering around in some part of him he'd only suspected was there – until last night. He had been scourged, enflamed, encompassed and reborn as if he'd walked into the stable fire and out again. Which he had. Unharmed, for the most part.

"Listen, Gyskouras, this is not a ceremony. You're carrying things a bit too far. There's no one here to be impressed…." Then the priest glanced up at Kouras's face, and amended: "I'm sure we can help you – and Vashanka. Just what is it?" The priest's eyes darted around the courtyard where guards stood, leaning forward, trying to hear. Molin took another step toward the big blue roan. "What *is* it?" he whispered.

Kouras would have gotten off his horse, if it were yesterday, or the day before, or any other day. Now, he stared down at the priest and said, "Fire at the barracks. Horses and men killed. We need resupply, and labor. The Riddler's sent me with a list of what you must provide us. Now."

*"Must? Now?* You and Tempus are entirely out of control," blustered Torchholder, and then thought better of it, seeing Kouras glare and realizing how many eyes and ears were on them.

"Give me your list," Torchholder sighed. "We'll see what we can do."

"Good," said the Stepson, and the god in him agreed. "One more thing," he added as he handed Torchholder the parchment the Riddler had given him. "Two, actually: First, there's going to be a problem at the Mageguild and you're not to interfere – tell Walegrin …stay out of there. Second, the girl, from the ceremony: I want to see her. I want to know her name. I don't want her dying like my mother. Is that clear? You're responsible to keep her happy, and to have her here for me anytime. Any mishap that befalls her, that same mishap befalls you. We decree it."

"Gyskouras…? I can't be responsible for every temple dancer and slave and concubine…"

"Of course you can. It's part of your job: you're Vashanka's priest. You do as the god decrees. Mark us: if she dies, you die. When and how, the same."

And he reined his roan around, the way Sync had taught him, a full ninety-degree turn, and kicked it into a lope. And rode out of there without a word. When the guards had hustled out of his path and he and his horse were through the Gate of the Gods and headed for the Hill, he slapped his thigh as hard as he could: *"Yes,"* he told the horse and the night and the god chortling within him. "Vashanka, being your avatar is everything I could have dreamed, and more. Now, Storm God, let's get that Shamshi, just you and me."

*Come on Sham, come out and fight. Come meet me. Or run from me and my god, if you're too afraid. Are you scared? You should be. Run then, Sham. Run and hide. We'll find you.* Kouras was exultant, full of a strength he'd never known before.

So he didn't see the fluttering shadow that darted across the street in his path, or hear the crossbow letting arrows fly, over the blue roan's snorting, until it was too late.

A quarrel hits him in the right side of his chest, rocking him back, puncturing his armor. A quarrel pierces his gut, just above his thigh, stopped by his hipbone. A quarrel penetrates his back, between his shoulder-blades. He screams in outrage and pain. The blue roan leaps forward.

Frenzy overwhelms the pain engulfing him. With a strength he has never known and a speed he's never had, he spins his horse in its tracks and drops the reins. "Seek," he tells it. With his left hand he works one crossbow bolt out of his armored chest, and the second from his gut, unworried that he'll break off the iron points inside him. The quarrels come away whole. He's so angry, and so fast, that he can think and move between the waves of far-off pain.

He can't reach the third crossbow bolt, in his back, but he can reach his shortsword and his throwing stars. And Vashanka is one with him, pouring strength into him, filling him with wrath and lust for reprisal.

He has his sword in one hand and his throwing stars in the other. Shooting a crossbow from a saddle is always difficult. It's hard to aim at a moving target when the weapon being aimed is moving as well. So he leaves the crossbow on his saddle.

He doesn't know that he's crouched down along his horse's neck. He doesn't know that he's bleeding. He can see the enemy flickering; a shadow, moving. It's too fast to catch, although he tries to speed up his horse. This horse has never gone this fast.

The shadow is faster. Too fast.

They chase it through alleys, better streets. This is the Hill, and soon he knows he's lost this antagonist: the streets are too well lit for anyone to hide from him. He has god-sharpened sight in his mortal eyes.

He has the hearing of the god, keener than his mortal ears. He holds his breath, thinking he hears the enemy – breathing hard, panting. But his horse is blowing; hooves are pounding, louder than his quarry's sounds. Now he hears his adversary; now he doesn't.

Then it's gone, too far away.

Kouras can't track it farther. His head is spinning. He needs to stop.

He halts the horse. There's wetness everywhere: his blood.

The quarrel in his back is bobbing there: the weight of the quivering shaft hurts worst of all, a bruising throb whenever he moves.

He wants to go back to Crit's hidey-hole, but no one is there tonight. He sits on the blowing roan in the middle of the street. It's too late in the evening for many to have seen him. The horse is heaving; they've run a long way. Chasing something so elusive… even Vashanka isn't sure how to find it.

He tests the god, to see if Vashanka will speak. Silence. He's getting dizzy, lightheaded. The dizziness and the pain seem to belong to someone else: there, but far away. The god is still in him, propping him up, guiding him.

He knows he has to get that arrow out of his back. If he can get the arrow out, he'll heal. He knees the roan. It goes walking through the streets. He's not directing it.

But something is. They find themselves at the Promise of Heaven. There's a house nearby. The horse stops there. Kouras knows he can't ride much farther. He needs to get the arrow out. He slides off the horse and drops its reins. He winces when his feet hit the ground and the shaft in his back bobbles. There's a door in front of him. He knocks on it. It doesn't open. He pounds on it with the pommel of his sword.

Now someone comes. And blinks, and puts hand to mouth. "Oh, gods. Kouras. What's happened?" asks Shawme, her robe hanging open, forgotten, as he staggers a step, covered with blood, and sinks forward. Sinks toward her. Sinks toward the robe. Sinks toward the floor. Sinks into a place where there's only the god, and his wounds, and Shawme's hands and voice.

"Oh, gods, Kouras. What happened to you? Merri, get me some hot water and some clean cloths."

He wants to tell Shawme not to worry: he knows he'll heal. The storm god is taking care of him. Didn't Vashanka lead him straight to her door? But he can't find his voice; not right now – or even his tongue. It's so good to lie still and rest. He feels women's hands on him. He feels the crossbow bolt as it is yanked out: a grunt escapes him, nothing more.

Vashanka is inside him. He tells them so, these women tending him: "The storm god loves you," he grits out. But it's not really true. Kouras loves Shawme; always has. Even Vashanka knows it's true and lays his avatar down in the arms of his beloved as the world reels away and consciousness leaches away with his blood and the pain goes with it.

Kouras thinks the god is standing over him while he sleeps. He can see the storm god, Vashanka, yarrow-honey hair clubbed back, high brow free from lines, one foot on each side of him, brandishing his glowing shortsword. The god won't let him sleep: nightmares have a special sting this night, like vipers from the deepest pit of hell. He mustn't dream, the storm god tells him. And keeps watch over Kouras, his new avatar, until the dawn.

*

It's not yet sundown when they begin the ceremonies. This time, at the pyres on the hilltop, it is *so* different. Niko expects an exalted calm, an intimate remembrance, subdued, formal. Instead, the bereaved call their gods to earth, believers trying to rebalance, desperate to reestablish equilibrium in tragedy's wake. The way up and the way down are one and the same, Tempus often says. Here, on this late summer afternoon, it's true. The road between heaven and earth is open wide: what goes up, comes down, and goes up again.

Niko thinks he's imagining it, at first, but as dusk approaches there's a feeling none have felt before: a presence of more-than-mortal nature.

Grief-stricken fighters contest in funerary games, on horseback and on foot. Cavalrymen catch rope rings on their swords. Hoplites cast javelins at oxhide targets. Charon and other Thebans play their flutes and pipes and sing songs to Harmony. And the sky is clear, full of early moon and stars. A milky road to heaven seems to beckon, yet the sky stays blue. Daylight won't lose its battle against this night without a fight.

Smoke curls around the mourners and wafts upward. So many have come to honor the Sacred Band's dead: priests from the town, laborers, carpenters, armorers, horse-traders, and more. Sync's woman is among them, blond and small and quick: pitching in, helping where she can.

Niko and Tempus see to the burial of the fourteen dead horses. At Tempus's order, Niko begins the ritual but can't finish, so Tempus says the rest. Niko's throat closes up: fourteen horses died for their masters, not knowing or caring why, but that men asked them.

And now all of these are in one hole in the earth, together. Some few Stepsons attend this graveside funeral, among the grasses and the weeds: Niko watches his commander, unflagging, willful lips drawn tight, enduring every trial with that expression all Stepsons know so well. This massive strength, shoulders pushing forward into a future no man can see, tireless, relentless, and inexorable as the dawn: if he could become half of what the Riddler is today, he'd be content.

Tempus claps him on the back when the rite is done and says, "Next time, Stealth, you'll do it all." Next time. He hopes there won't be one. His burns are healing, scabs itching, nearly gone – so fast, too fast. What is he, now? Not a horse in a grave or a man on a pyre, but something else – something that heals like his commander does…. He doesn't want to think about it, not today.

As they prepare to head back toward those grieving for dead fighters, Niko notices that Arton – thin, intense and hunched with sorrow – has come to the horse grave with Lysis, his Theban partner, to honor their equine dead. And Sync is there with his woman by his side.

Niko and Tempus lead their horses from the gravesite, side by side: they won't ride them here today. Behind, in solemn processional, the other Stepsons follow. The two stallions, the silver and the black, represent the equine god (whomsoever horses pray to) in this ritual so ancient that no one knows what god to thank. Thank Poseidon, say the Thebans; and Epona, the Greek goddess. Thank Stormbringer, Jihan says. So many gods claim the horse, perhaps the finest creation under heaven. Man and horse have worked together longer than either can remember. But these two stallions know their brothers, and paw the ground and trumpet their grief and thanks to heaven. It must be enough. It always has been: horses know what to say for horses; men know what to say for men, when life has fled and spirits soar and the bereft are left behind, tethered to the earth.

So all of them walk together in a somber group, back through the copse and up the rise, where the games have ended. The rites for the Sacred Band are getting under way. Stealth watches the young pair – the seer and the Theban who has the blessing of Harmony and the love of horses in his soul: new Stepsons, new blood for a new Sacred Band.

Atop the rise, they can see the altars of Harmony and Enlil and hear the rituals proceeding. The pipes play sad songs, then sweet songs, and the flames roar high. Three Thebans; six mercenaries from Syr and Machad and Tyse; one Stepson who'd been with the Band for years: all these dead are ready for their sortie into heaven on plumes of smoke.

But Abarsis doesn't come to take the souls of the Sacred Band as he's always done before, materializing in the balefire. Abarsis thunders down from the sky in a chariot with blood-red harness and two white horses. This is Enlil's chariot, come down from heaven on a road of cloud: Everyone is choosing sides, in this world and beyond.

By then the goddess Harmony is there in her black armor. Into the flames the goddess walks, and lifts up her first faithful man of Thebes tenderly. Arms around her neck, the soul is smiling as he goes his way. Then she returns to get another.

Niko's own soul aches to see her walk into that inferno, and out again. This goddess is his dancing girl from the beach? She's so much more than Niko should aspire to. His body wants to stop her, keep her from the conflagration, from all harm, but it's she who's kept him from harm, time after time. No part of frail flesh and blood is she. Each time she braves the flames he holds his breath, but she's not mortal. And because of her, he no longer knows if he is.

He can't reconcile love and trepidation. Doubt wracks him. What has he been doing, dallying with her, a being of such power? What has he been thinking? His heart thuds in his chest as he watches her take the souls of the Theban Sacred Band to their rest.

There is no music now. No pipes play, no flutes.

And Tempus is watching him closely, gauging his reaction to the goddess standing in the flames.

When the Theban souls have all gone, Harmony steps back and to one side and stands with head bowed, Niko's sable mare attentive beside her.

Now comes Abarsis to Enlil's altar: the original Stepson, the Slaughter Priest, patron shade of the Sacred Band. Fiery-eyed white horses of the gods stand stock-still as Abarsis walks into flames. He takes Stepsons, old and new, lifting up each soul in turn, and then comes out again.

The Thebans may not know what they see, but they sense godhead in Abarsis, heaven's emissary come on a mission. Every Stepson there recognizes the gravity of this honor, that Abarsis would appear in flesh to take their dead. People drop to their knees, heads pressed to the ground, in fear and awe. Even outsiders bow down, all these folk from Sanctuary who have never seen a funeral for fighters of the Sacred Band.

Abarsis walks among them and no one looks or raises up a face. The goddess walks beside Abarsis, and people close their eyes and cover them.

Tempus looks at Niko and Niko spreads his hands. "I didn't call him. I didn't pray to him for help," he tells the Riddler. "Or to her."

Howsoever, the Slaughter Priest, full blown, envoy of the gods, treads their barracks ground while chariot horses with coats white as snow wait, motionless, for their driver.

At her own altar Harmony lingers, spread-legged, her armor gleaming as if she hadn't walked through flames for three Theban faithful. She stays awhile among the throng, touching a Theban here and there, lifting them up and talking to them softly: She is their tutelary and their faces shine with joy and thanks, to see Harmony there and touch her and speak with her.

Niko's black stallion sees its mistress and wants to go to her. He swings up on it, and Tempus mounts the Trôs, and they wait. This ceremony is in hands more exalted than theirs, in this dusk fading into night.

Niko is more and more uneasy, and sees the same in Tempus. He feels as if something is ending, something else beginning. Change of this magnitude is never easy. Tempus wears a wary face. Niko sits this strange horse as calmly as he can. This black horse is better than any he's ever had, but this is no time to exult in the treasures of the living, when so many of theirs are newly dead. And he doesn't like this ceremony. His *maat* is restless. Too many powers are here. Abarsis has only come to them this way before in the direst of times.

Abarsis mounts Enlil's chariot and drives it over to Tempus and Niko.

"Tempus, Niko, life to you, and everlasting glory," Abarsis says in a voice like clear water running over pebbles.

"And honor to you, and glory, Stepson," says Tempus, and Niko says the same.

Abarsis is fully here, real as blood, not a ghost or shade this night: upswept eyes so wise, black hair glossy on a young bull's neck, flaring cheeks and tawny skin as beautiful as ever. "You two, take care in this battle coming," says Abarsis. "Too many forces are aroused. I will be with you. Enlil will. The gods want to bring a better day, and you are their messengers. Trust not in all you see. Trust only in your hearts. And in us, who love you both," says Abarsis, and shakes his reins, and drives between their mounts and away, as those white horses climb a ramp of cloud up to the sky. The chariot rattles like thunder from the heavens but the night is clear: no mist obscures the moon.

And as Abarsis disappears, there are more stars above than Niko has ever seen.

Even the Trôs horse is skittish now, watching Abarsis and that chariot of white stallions swallowed by the sky. It dances and prances. Niko's goddess-given black tosses his head and challenges heaven as Niko sidles it over to the Riddler.

Then Harmony comes riding, on the sable mare, her helmet by her thigh. "So, Stepsons. Are your reinforcements all like him?" She gestures with her hand to where Abarsis's chariot had left the earth, where no wheel ruts remain, no hoofprints mark the ground.

Her question hangs in the air. Niko doesn't know what to say to her. He's looking at his mare. So are many of their fighters. All around the grounds, wounded men wear dressings; horses too: open burns are slick with unguents and grease. But this sable mare is free of burn or scratch or blister. Touching each other on the arm, Thebans whisper, clustered together. Even Critias and Sync stare at the mare askance.

And Harmony is so different today: all war goddess, armored and brave, embracing the fallen, encouraging the wounded. *Reinforcements*, the goddess says lightly, for a battle that Abarsis warns is coming. Niko knows all too well that it is never good when Abarsis comes to earth outside a pyre of flame.

Tempus finally answers the goddess, "There is no other like Abarsis in all of earth and heaven. Do we need reinforcements? And if we do, will you provide them?"

Harmony looks from Tempus to Niko with those sky-wide eyes and says, "You have enough, with those committed to fight by your side. If you and yours are steadfast, this battle coming will go your way."

*...this battle coming...* Abarsis and the Theban goddess have both said it, now.

Niko slides off his horse, thinking to give the goddess a hand down from the mare, take Harmony away and talk to her by himself. He has so many questions to ask. But the goddess is gone when he looks again, with nothing to show she's ever been there, not even a gust or a breeze left behind. And Niko's sable mare is gone with her.

## *Chapter 42: Echo of War*

Fated fire rages: Aškelon has called down such a firestorm upon the Stepsons' barracks that it blows back upon him and his Mageguild. An infernal imbalance puts itself right: action and reaction, law of nature. A risk he took. Circumventing caution and the gods to inflict witch-fire revenge has left him helpless to extinguish the blaze. A loss he'll take. He's too late to block the path of fire leading to his earthly door.

"Now," says the wizard boy, sobbing in the burning manse. *"Now* we will kill them *all. Promise."* He coughs. He stares around with tearing eyes among the cinders, smoke and blaze. He darts from one window to the next, smudgy with soot, looking more like a youth and less like a wraith, covered with ashes, dodging the flames.

"Now," agrees the dream lord, waxing wroth as his Mageguild flares around his ears. *"Now."* All about them, naphtha fireballs are exploding, flaming arrows whizzing by, draperies catching fire, galleries collapsing.

He takes the wizard boy by the hand, and bids farewell to this place that has served him so long. And with that promise, made in a single word, Aškelon bids farewell to reason – farewell to hopes of lesser conflicts brewing or to lesser retribution ahead.

With strength eroding, with ancient poison in his blood, with Shamshi's hand in his, he waves the Mageguild away. Not another word to say. Not another thought to think. After all is said and done, it comes to this. Brute force. Brutal last resorts. Brutality in all its guises at last will have its say.

All because of Tempus and his clan of Stepsons, his Sacred Band? Not so. In truth, because of Nikodemos. For a score of years, men and gods and mages and demons have struggled over this one pure soul. This one hero in the making, Nikodemos, has caught up so many powers and undone them all with his balance and his steady gaze.

Perhaps not even Niko can be blamed, Aškelon ponders with his last shred of humanity as he whisks Shamshi away to Meridian, his stronghold, his sphere. Perhaps the fault is with Aškelon himself, and not with enemies he's made or souls he's coveted to take and train and mold.

He's been a force unsurpassed for untold centuries. Once a mage, he'd risen to rival gods themselves: Demiurge, and arrogant; not the originator of evil, but close enough in some philosophies. Regent of the seventh sphere; entelechy of dream and shadow; ruler of Meridian, the antithesis of Bandara, the dark that balances Bandara's light – if he had been content with what he had, then all he'd had would still be his. But greed and hubris crept into him, and pride that was unbending.

What doesn't bend must break, when dooms are apportioned and destiny takes the lead.

As it will now, and as it must, until this struggle ends.

*

A great funnel arched over the sunny eastern sky, pink and gold and crawling with lightning. The Thebans went running, covering their heads with their arms, but Tempus explained to Charon: "It's only Jihan, coming with the horses from Free Nisibis."

And so it was. The cloud conveyance, borrowed from Stormbringer, father of all weather gods, rose and stretched and sank to ground north of the barracks. All around the funnel cloud, wind whipped. On the barracks battlements, men crowded to see, despite the gale.

Tempus rode out with Niko and five others to take the horses' shanks from the Nisibisi fighters who brought them and hug their brothers, allies from the wizard wars they'd fought together. And to say farewell again.

"You're sure you don't need us? We'll stay and fight with you against any threat, until the end. Can we help?" Bashir asked Tempus, his flat dark face and gray eyes worried. "Jihan said your barracks were set afire."

"Just leave the horses, my brother. You've been as good a friend as a man could ask. This is not your fight. Life to you, and yours, and everlasting glory to all your Successors and Free Nisibis. May it remain forever free."

"Riddler…. Be you careful," Bashir warned low, seeing something in his face or his demeanor. "And remember, you always have a home with us, you and all of yours." The two embraced and clapped one another on the back, one more time.

As dearly as Tempus needed reinforcements, he couldn't ask Bashir's Successors. Not this time. They were too few as it was, guarding their mountain passes against all intruders.

Jihan held open the cloud conveyance, one hand outstretched, copper hair blowing in the maelstrom. Without another backward look, Bashir led his Successors into the funnel. Jihan stepped in beside them, to see them back whence they came. The conveyance swallowed them whole, closing its mouth of pink-tinged clouds, and whirled away.

So now they had spare horses. Niko looked over at Tempus with sparkling eyes: "I missed that man – he'd have stayed.... Free Nisibis was good to the Band."

"No need to involve him and his. Not in this. This is our fight." If things went badly, having Bashir's fighters along would mean spreading the war to Wizardwall. "What starts here, ends here, Niko." He could see Stealth's wistfulness; outside the Band, Bashir was Niko's closest friend. "Let's get these horses fitted up."

But Crit and Sync were already seeing to the horses. This staff he had now was the best he'd ever assembled. They knew his heart, knew his mind, and anticipated his every need. Overhead the cloud conveyance arched back the way it had come, and then disappeared.

When they'd apportioned the new stock amid the commotion of reconstruction, stalls being built and roofs being raised, the day was nearly done.

"There's still some daylight, commander. You should try the new black stud," Niko said to him.

"Later," Tempus told him, as they threaded their way through the courtyard full of wagons (carting debris out and lumber in) and chariots and supplies to replace all they had lost.

A wolf-call from the battlements sounded: someone was coming, fast.

It was too soon for Randal to be back. They stopped where they were. The gates opened. Kouras and his roan galloped through and straight up to them.

"You're a day late," Stealth called out. "You'd better have a good explanation."

The Stepson nearly tumbled off his horse. "Commander, Stealth," he said breathlessly, staggering once. "I'm sorry. I was… detained."

By then the blood on Kouras's cuirass and his chiton and the puncture wound over his breastbone were easy to see. Niko moved to support him, but the young fighter stepped back.

Kouras raised both hands: "I'm well enough. Vashanka is healing me. Look." Kouras pushed and pulled at his cuirass, wriggling, showing them the puncture near his groin. He postured brazenly. "The storm god loves me."

"Out of the courtyard, Kouras," Tempus said. "Not here, with so many watching. If the god is looking after you, how will the others feel? Come to my quarters. What happened?"

With Niko on one side of him and Tempus on the other, Kouras said brashly, "I was coming back from the palace, the long way – hoping to find Sham – and took three crossbow bolts." He indicated the other puncture, behind his shoulder. "I lost some blood. Shawme tended me. It was wonderful."

Niko eyed Tempus over Kouras's head. *Wonderful.*

"Don't depend on the god to do your fighting for you. Stick to your orders. Don't improvise. Be more careful. You should have sent word to Crit," Niko said harshly. "We were concerned."

"It won't happen again." Kouras looked away, to Tempus. "But, Commander, was it like this for you?"

*Like this, when the curse fell on me and I bargained with the storm god for my life? Like this, century after century, debacle after debacle, up to my hips in blood and carnage, unable to give love or receive it or even stop men intent on dying from throwing their lives away?* "Life is different for each of us," Tempus said. "Niko is right. Gods are not dependable. Things that you can see, and touch, and feel – these do I prefer." *Gods are fickle, vengeful and mean, using us to their own ends. Beware, young fighter, the euphoria of a man who thinks he's immortal – a fool is always first to die.*

And Niko said, "I want a look at those wounds. Before we decide Vashanka is omnipotent. In my experience, no god is. Anything else to tell us?"

They were near the door to Tempus's office. Tempus held up a hand to silence both until they got inside. Then, "Strip," Niko said, adamant. Kouras looked at Tempus: "Must I?"

"You must. As you must always do what Stealth orders. Now, what else?"

"Well, I went to Torchholder, told him what you said. And then early this morning the Mageguild was destroyed by fire: burned to the ground, I heard. But I didn't go there: you told me not to go. I came back as soon as I could ride. *Ow.*"

Niko probed in the wound on Kouras's shoulder, and then spun the boy around. "Let's see the rest." Assiduously, Niko prodded at Kouras. Stealth would save every one of his fighters, if he could, from everything. "We'll dress all these wounds again. Reopen the one in your gut. You'd better hope the god truly loves you. It's going to hurt."

Niko rummaged in his trunk, still in Tempus's room, and came up with a clean loin guard and chiton. "I'll get Crit to send Gayle and Cassander to cut you. Stay here with the Riddler until then."

Niko said, "Commander, a moment please? Outside."

Out in the wind, leaning on the closed door, Niko said, "Not good. Too much heat in those wounds. Too much blood lost." As he spoke, he stared around the courtyard. A muscle jumped in his jaw. "This one's the palace favorite. Maybe we should send him there. I don't think he's fit to fight – or will be, any time soon."

"Niko, what is it?" It wasn't Kouras's wounds, bothering Niko: Kouras would mend soon enough. Something else was wrong, something deeper.

"Can't you feel it, Commander? I felt it before he told me. The Mageguild's destroyed. And something's coming. Fast. My *maat*…. Never mind. I want to send out scouts, half a dozen, rotate them through the four evening watches. I'll take the first watch myself."

"Niko, have you been sleeping?'

"I wish I hadn't. When I sleep, I'm back in Chaeronea. Or there's fire everywhere. I wish I was like you, Riddler."

"No, you don't. You're like yourself. Just be patient."

"What about the scouts? Outside the walls?"

"Have Crit detail them. But *you're* not going. You and I have too much planning to do."

So it was that they didn't ride outside the walls during the first watch, or the second. But by third watch, Niko couldn't be put off.

They were saddling their horses to go scouting beyond the walls when the call came.

Crit ran up, breathing fast: "I've got a scout who just came in saying there's something out there we should see." Crit seldom ran anywhere.

"Where, out there?" Tempus said. "Below the overlook, out where the…."

"Where Abarsis went to heaven," Niko said knowingly, checking the big black's cinch. "It was in my dream last night."

*

Torches flared in the camps beneath the overlook, tents stretching out on the feral fields of the valley below. In the waning moonlight, you couldn't judge their number. But Critias knows there are too many. Many, many. Camps like this don't just appear in a valley, with more men encamped a hill away. It doesn't happen. Men moving, horses and chariots and infantry: it takes preparation, logistics; men in a multitude create noise and disturbance. It can't be done in just one day.

But this army hadn't been out here yesterday, or the day before.

Deep blue night all around. Tempus and Niko on Crit's left.

Eye-whites and teeth flashing, horses and men close together, back just far enough from the edge not to be silhouetted against the vault of heaven. His commander's helmet catches a spill of moonlight and a superstitious chill runs over Crit from head to toe. *Been here before. Done this before.* But he hadn't. Not quite. Nothing stirs but the three of them and their horses on the overlook, and too many torches wavering in the camps below.

"Commander, what do you think?" Crit asks, after they've been here too long, stared for too long into the eye-teasing dark, in a silence broken only by their horses whuffling and stamping in the summer night.

"I think we all know what we see," Tempus says softly, voice cutting through the dark like a snake hissing, poised to strike.

Niko says nothing. Stealth is watching the farther hilltop for a glint of movement or a darker shadow of men or horses obscuring firelight in the valley below. Tempus, astride his Trôs horse (too luminous tonight), is still as a statue, one hand on his hip, his reins dangling. Looking for something to show him the identity of this army down in the valley. But only sunrise can confirm what everyone here tonight knows.

Never mind it: this is their adversary, bringing the war to them. Did Tempus know it? Expect it? Entice it? Lust for it?

Niko's black horse shies at something, skittish and surprised, sidling rightward, crowding Crit's big chestnut. Crit feels vulnerable, with so many enemies stretched out before him in this valley and the next.

"I know what *I* think," Niko mutters. "But how can it be?" Eye-whites again: Niko is searching for something in his partner's face, out here in the dark. "Chaeronea."

"Chaeronea," Crit repeats. *But it can't be.* But this *is* what it looked like, what it felt like on the night before that battle. Crit doesn't have enough fighters, not with all his people, to meet this enemy. Not with all his own Sacred Band and ten other bands besides, if he could find them.

Crit's mouth dries up. Of the seventy fighters left to him, twelve were burned badly. He'd come to Sanctuary with sixty-five; lost a Theban pair and a pair of Stepsons, hired twelve, and lost four more. So the Sacred Band totaled (including himself, Stealth and the Riddler) seventy men. Fifty-eight fit fighters to face hundreds, thousands, maybe more? Plus Jihan. Plus Randal, who was off in Lemuria seeking reinforcements.

"Reinforcements for what? And how many?" Crit had asked when the Riddler ordered Randal to go. Tempus had told Crit, "Randal will bring back two hundred and ninety on temporary duty, under Sync." So Crit had learned then that Tempus was bringing in nearly the entire 3rd Commando to support them. Far more manpower than the Riddler had ever brought to Sanctuary. The commander had known what was brewing here. Maybe the god had told him.

How long had Tempus known? And the gods? Enlil? Vashanka? The Thebans' Harmony? What difference, what the gods knew, or when? Better if Crit had known sooner.

*Will heaven even up the odds?* Because the storm god of the armies is surely wherever Tempus is. And perhaps Vashanka is where Kouras is. As for the Theban goddess, none knew what she had in her mind. Some god, or goddess, or power, had let the barn fire happen, perhaps made it happen. Never mind that other powers from on high may have helped to quench it. When the gods are at odds, men die.

*Or are we on our own, this time?* Is this incursion simply the result of snatching the fated dead from Chaeronea? Or of adventures begun by his commander and Stealth, so strange these days and fey, locked in some battle with an adversary you couldn't see to fight?

And the sky above is too full of stars.

*Let's get off these horses. Crawl over to the edge. Present a less tempting target.* Crit is not immortalized, not favored by any god, or any other power – or the mortal enemy of any, he hopes, beyond what honest war demands. *Get a closer look.* He wants to say it, but he can't.

Now the Riddler has caught up all their souls again and put them down in hell again. This time, to face a battle that might be one they can't win. Crit hadn't realized that hell could be so big. No matter how good you are, this many fighters will wear you down, tire you out, overrun you. How many? Too many. Twenty to one, for certain. Maybe more.

"Chaeronea," he sighs, shaking his head as if he could shake away the sight, too evocative, twisting his gut with memory. "Just like before."

"Chaeronea, Crit," agrees the Riddler, gravel in his softest voice, reserved for horses and the dying. "But not like before."

*Clop. Clop. Clip-clop.* Then Niko unwinds from his horse and crouches down at the overlook's edge, reins in his hand,

and speaks so low Crit can't catch the words with the wind picking up and their horses chewing on their bits.

Crit needs to shake the feeling that he's been here before, lived this before, and is fated to live it all again. His hair is standing up all over his body. His mouth is so dry it stings as if he's been eating thistles. Neither the commander nor Stealth says another word for what seems like forever. The silence is eerie, broken only by insects chirping, leather squeaking, tails lashing. Above, the sky starts to lose its gauzy road of twinkling stars: clouds boil up, from a storm building somewhere.

How are we going to fight through this? Are *we* now the fated dead?

On the battleplain at Chaeronea had been three hundred of the Sacred Band of Thebes, and better than thirty thousand others, some said, on either side: Thebans and Macedonians. How many were out there tonight? And *was* this their enemy, or was Crit jumping to conclusions? Could this be some other army, happening by, bivouacked for a night, on their way somewhere?

But he would have known about it. Tempus would. They'd asked for this, snatching those Thebans from that foretold battleplain. So here it comes, some echo of war unfinished, perhaps to take those Thebans back again….

"How can this be?" Crit asks the Riddler.

"It's not what it seems," Tempus says, sighing. "Not the same Chaeronea. Not the same enemy. More like the visions we've all had. You can't fight the same battle twice. Eternity won't allow it. It's Ash's doing, he and Shamshi. They want us to think we're doomed. This is what we'll fight, and where we'll fight, for certain. We wanted this; we courted it. Now it's here. Whatever else it is, it's something far out of balance."

Niko stretches out flat on the overlook and says, "It's surely something. And a lot of it. I've been dreaming this for so long."

"Did you dream how we fight it?" Crit asked Stealth.

"Straight on," replies Tempus's second-in-command, a murmur in the night.

And the Riddler says, "It will look different in the morning. We'll break their pattern. Set the battle tempo. Make them bring their war to us."

Niko gets to his feet and swings up on his horse. "It's winnable. We can do this. We just need to make a plan – decide what's critical and what's not."

"How do you mean?" Crit asks. No one is better at detail than Crit, but he is more tactical than strategic. And this may be an enemy beyond his ken, and beyond the skill of any fighter of unmagical means and mind.

"We know what happened at Chaeronea the first time," Niko says. "This is different. This is the dream lord's army," Niko adds in that off-handed voice with which he always announces the deepest peril. "Isn't it, Commander?"

"These are all Ash's dreamers and his dreaming dead," Tempus agrees. "Souls not saved by any god. Those who live in their sleep and those who died in their sleep; restless ghosts and men collected for ages, from everywhere. Meridian's dreaming dead or living dreamers, it makes no difference. All of them can die, or die again, and if they die at our hands, they'll find a better rest. Aškelon and Shamshi think to overwhelm us with sheer numbers," the Riddler adds. "That's not going to happen. We need to find the dream lord and Shamshi. Kill those two, and this battle's won. All these troops are meant to frighten and demoralize us."

"They're succeeding in scaring me," Crit muttered.

"No, they're not," Niko said wearily. "The Riddler's right. This will look different in the morning. We'll go back, send out scouts to watch here and tell us if these start to move – if you agree, Commander."

Turning his back on enemies in such numbers – so many, many – was something that went against Crit's grain. He prized intelligence most of all. "You two go back. I'll stay awhile. Until the scouts come. I'll want to give precise instructions. Then I'll find you, if you agree, and hear what you want to do."

So they left him there, to lie on his belly and brood, and wonder how he was going to get his Band through this, and safely home to Lemuria. He wished Strat was here. At a time like this, a man wants his partner close at hand.

All he could think was that they'd gotten through it the last time, on the Chaeronean battleplain, with just as many enemies there, or more. He'd brought all of his home, alive if not unscathed, and saved twenty-three pairs of Thebans besides. So it was possible to survive, maybe even to win. The commander and Niko were right.

Possible, but not likely.

And they'd nearly lost Tempus, the last time.

*Long spears, thunking into flesh. Man staggering backward, impaled, groaning.*

*

Straton brought Ischade to the barracks straightaway, though the hour was getting late. The moon was setting; everything should have been sleepy at the barracks. But it wasn't. Torches were blazing everywhere; men were running to and fro, hitching wagons, moving equipment.

The ghost horse – carrying Strat, Ischade up behind – smelled the smoke. It whinnied and grunted and wouldn't behave. Sync came to take the ghost horse to its new stall, saying under his breath, "Still looking for glory in a witch's eyes, Strat?"

Strat gave Sync a promissory look and said only, "We're here at the commander's order." Crit would have been proud of him for holding his tongue. He helped Ischade down and then dismounted.

They found the commander in his quarters. Niko was by his side when Tempus opened up the door. When these two met late, something was always afoot. And Kouras was here, pale and wan but bright-eyed, wearing a tunic that was too big, with lumpy bandages underneath it. Niko whispered to Kouras, but the boy didn't leave.

"Ischade," Tempus said, "please join us."

There isn't enough seating. Kouras is still sitting on the bed; Niko whispers in his ear again and Kouras gets up and leaves at last, eyes averted from Ischade as he goes, closing the door behind him. Niko gets the room's two chairs for Ischade and Straton and sits on the bed. Stealth seems almost serene tonight as he lays his new sword across his lap and begins roughening the leather of its hilt with a rasp.

Ischade sits in the rickety chair as if it were a throne, her cloak pulled around her, her cowl down about her tiny shoulders and her white face delicate. "So, Riddler, you sent for me?"

"We have a number of questions, and an offer you may find irresistible. If you can help us, we're sure we can make it worth your while."

Straton wished he could have advised the commander not to bargain with her: Ischade would act, or not, based on other criteria than what the Sacred Band could offer her. Riding together, so far, so fast, had made him certain of it. What they felt for one another could be invaluable on this night.

But Tempus wasn't asking Strat and his slitted eyes held damnation. The commander said, "What would it require to foray into Meridian? With, say, three hundred and fifty fighters and their horses? And if it can be done, what price would you ask for helping us do it?"

*"Ha.* Now I know you're mad," said Ischade. "In the city, they say you're all possessed. By some foreign goddess. Meridian? *Please.* Be reasonable."

But Tempus never is, not when he stalks around like this, looks at you like this, as if you're already dead. Strat doesn't say a word but words don't matter now. The commander is going through the motions, weighing options. If you know him, you know he doesn't care whether Ischade says yes or no, helps them or not. He's going to tear some enemy limb from limb, and soon, with all the Sacred Band behind him. Battle is in his eyes and in his heart and all of them are in his hands. Last call. Last throw of the dice. Strat shivers, though the room is warm with all of them packed in close.

"*'Please,'* is it?" the Riddler asks Ischade. "If saying 'please' will do it, I'd be willing." The commander paced off the room, fixing the necromant with his most baleful stare. "If you're not strong enough, or skilled enough, just tell me. We'll look elsewhere for aid. But there will be many casualties, one way or the other. Many nearly dead and dying who can't be saved. If you're not around to help save the living, then you won't be with us to help dispatch the soon-to-be dead. A feast will be laid on, for someone of your…tastes."

*Offer on the table. Bargain of the most hideous kind. Or, perhaps not so hideous. Dying men suffer. So do the men who have to kill them out of mercy when lives can't be saved on the battlefield.* Sometimes the commander sent chills up Straton's spine, fielding tactics and strategies that no lesser man would ever dare. Tempus had commanded how many armies? Was hardened in battle over how many centuries?

Ischade replied in her silkiest voice, "Riddler, I didn't know you cared so much for my well-being. I'm flattered. And intrigued. Many dying and soon to be dead? For *me?* As a part of your expeditionary force? Do tell me more."

Maybe there *was* something worth having for Ischade in this oncoming battle, after all. Something she would prize. Where is the honor, the glory, in what Tempus is proposing? What the Riddler was offering the witch still seemed too horrible. But the commander was right: Ischade could save many dying men untold agony in pitched battle, if pitched battle there was to be.

Straton was just a soldier. He did what he was ordered. Crit would understand what was right, what was fitting, how to do what they were asked. Meridian? Where was that, exactly? How would they fight Aškelon and the wizard boy on such uncertain ground? But some battle was in the offing. The commander was readying a strike in the wake of the barracks fire and the burning of the Mageguild. But there was something else here, urgency such as he'd seldom seen in Tempus. Could Ischade help them locate the dream lord and the wizard boy? She hadn't succeeded yet.

Then the Riddler said, with a cold and appraising look, "I need to show you something, Ischade. Straton, get her a horse. We're going to take a little ride."

*

Niko's primary mission is to protect Tempus, his commander. Chaeronea, happening again? A second Chaeronean campaign, with the Sacred Band of Thebes and his commander's Stepsons against tens of thousands of enemies on that gods-forsaken battleplain ...*again?* The Riddler, speared in the heart...*again?*

Could the same mistakes happen twice? Could the same awful destiny repeat itself here and now? A world away? A plane away? Divorced in place and time from the battleplain that dogged Niko in his rest-place and deviled him in his sleep? This was the doom that had been haunting his dreams.

It took everything he had, every skill of *maat*, all his transcendent perception and what was left of his equilibrium, to appear calm and reasoned. He wanted to be alone on that overlook, send his senses out to assess this enemy, soul by soul. But he couldn't. Not now. Too much was in motion. And the commander was too busy for Niko to get him alone.

Niko rode out with Tempus, Ischade and Straton to where they'd left Critias. During the whole ride out there, Niko's stomach had been rolling as if he were on a boat at sea. Chaeronea kept dancing before his inner sight, Sham's battlespace bringing up the rear. He'd not taken those visions seriously enough. Not by half.

He wanted to pull the night around him, go off by himself and think things through. But there was no time. Not with a battle looming and an enemy encamped so close.

When they got back out to the overlook, he didn't see Critias. But he saw the troops camped in the valley below, taunting them to come out and fight.

Battle was what the Band wanted, what they needed – what they all did, what they all knew. Sham would be there somewhere, waiting for Niko, finally ready for death or victory. All the powers agreed that only Niko could kill Sham. Fine. Tomorrow was as good as any other day. Better. And Aškelon would be there: time to make an end to this lord of dream and shadow. Past time.

Here or Chaeronea or Meridian, or all three merged together: battle was battle, men were men. No commander fields a force like the one in that valley and hides himself away. Shamshi and Aškelon would come out and fight.

The big black horse was more talented than any horse he'd ever had. It would be a shame to die before he got to know this stallion. But death would take him here, there, now or on some other day. *Maat* made you ready to live or ready to die. He healed, now, faster than before: a gift from Harmony.

The Theban goddess had brought him back from the dead once and back from deadly wounds once. Was it for this she'd saved him? Was she looking for vengeance for her Thebans, all two hundred and fifty-four massacred on the Chaeronean battleplain? She'd have it, with Chaeronea stretching out before them where it shouldn't be.

Why things were as they were couldn't matter to Niko now. Here he was, and here he'd fight – for his commander, for himself and his *maat*. To make an end to the strangeness in the proportion encamped in the next valley and a hill away, with torches aflicker, taunting them to come out to play.

There was still enough night to cover their party. They rode their horses up to the overlook where Abarsis had gone to heaven, and it was peaceful there. Straton was getting off the bay to help Ischade down from the big dun, but Tempus was quicker.

They stood there in silence until Ischade said, "I see you didn't overstate the situation. And I think I can help you with some…though not all.… You want to take your force to Meridian, you say? Don't bother. For all intents and purposes, Meridian is here."

She gestured to the valley below. "Didn't anyone ever tell you, Riddler, to be careful what you wish for?"

Then the necromant put her arm through the commander's and the two walked away, along the edge of the outcropping, talking very low.

Strat came up to Niko: "You heard about the Mageguild being burned? Do you think that's what set this off?" Ace waved his hand toward the valley below. "How could they get here this fast? What's the plan?"

"Meet the enemy and defeat the enemy. The plan is always simple. Always the same. He'll tell us how he wants it. By might. By guile. By force of will. By force of arms. Or by dint of all, in proportion to the force arrayed against us. What's the difference? They've come to us for battle. We'll bring it to them."

"What if they're already dead?"

Straton didn't know that Niko had died and been resurrected at the Mageguild. No one knew but Tempus and the goddess. "So what if they are, or some are? This is Sanctuary. Death here is a relative term. Your time with Ischade has surely taught you that."

"If I hit it or spear it, or stab it or strangle it, or decapitate it or put an arrow in it, and it goes down and stays down, that's good enough for me," said Straton gruffly.

"And me," said Niko. But it wasn't.

## *Chapter 43: Battle of Your Dreams*

*So, Enlil, lord of war and bloodbath, do you like fighting this fight a second time?* Tempus asked the god in his head and got no more reply than he had the last time he fought on the Chaeronean battleplain.

The god breathes with deep and greedy breath in him, so much a part of him, reaching into every sinew, every muscle. Enlil is in his heart, in his mind, and in his body, remaking him one more time and reaching through him, to his horse. His horse is stronger, faster now than a horse can be. But this horse has fought before when the god rides, and understands its mission.

Purple haze lies all around Tempus and his Sacred Band. With their reinforcements (two hundred and ninety 3rd Commando fighters now under Sync's control), they're fighting for their lives among the dream lord's forces, who attack even one another: Thebans and Macedonians, ghosts and men, are on this battleplain today. *Again.*

And there are no gods or goddesses on the overlook, no lightning bolts or shower of arrows from on high. Just Enlil in his head and so many fighters, shoulder to shoulder, eye to eye....

Reality and illusion, mixing together, lethal together. Abarsis had warned Tempus, *'Trust not in what you see.'*

Iron grating, swords clanging. The wounded yell and curse; the dying sob and cry. Horses whinny, hooves drumming. Orders bellowed from too many throats: too much noise; too much passion. Confusion swallows order on this battleplain today. The purple haze scuds in billows across the valley floor, obscuring fighters' sight, making it hard to tell friend from foe in this ferocity everywhere.

Niko says this battleplain looks like Shamshi's rest-place, when he fought there. Just before they'd brought the ranks onto the valley floor and into this demented war, he'd let Niko address his forces: Stepsons and Thebans and Sync's 3rd Commando, fresh from Lemuria. In case Tempus was felled and Niko survived, command must transfer smoothly. There must be no doubt of his successor.

And Niko had told their fighters, gathered on the overlook, "Restore balance. Deliver justice. That's the mission. Show me you understand." Niko thrust his sword sky-high and howled their wolf-call. And three hundred fifty-eight warriors did the same. "Look around you. It's an honor to fight beside you. Today we choose to fight. For the freedom to fight on other days. So we remember what's worth fighting for." They'd howled again. Stealth had waited, then called out, "Life to you. And everlasting glory." And the Sacred Band all shouted back the same.

Then Niko had stepped back and muttered, "You should be doing this, not me."

"Not today," Tempus had told Niko, and clapped him on the arm, proud of this boy he'd grown into a man whom all of his would follow to their deaths, if need be, understanding why they did. Then they'd ridden away from Abarsis's overlook in tight formation, and down into this valley with its purple haze and combat all around.

Piercing enemy lines, Tempus in the lead. Always keeping tight together, until the enemy's sheer numbers slow their penetration. Tactics and execution, by the Riddler's book: sharp wedge of cavalry; take the high ground; find the dream lord; find the wizard boy. Sweat on the training field saves Band lives on the battlefield. Training makes all the difference on the day. Now it's hack and cut and push and shove and trample. Fight on through, teams tight together, pairbond making two men into so much more. The Band fights well today, outnumbered against this disarrayed enemy busy fighting one another. Amid so much confusion, their practiced battle takes a grievous toll.

And it feels so good, to bring this battle, so long coming. To split line after line arrayed against them, knifing their way through this dreaming host with his rightman by his side and all his beloved fighters charging in their wake.

Tempus gallops his speeding Trôs through the fray, Niko on his right. His mount calls a challenge to every other horse it sees. And Niko, on his goddess-given black, keeps pace.

The battle swirls all around, again – same battle, different day – and the god likes this battle just as well as he did the last time. Tempus can barely keep his right-side partner on the big black horse in mind while Enlil glares down from his heaven and out of Tempus's eyes and everywhere is shrieking and bleeding and dark death hurtling through the skies as the dream lord tries unearthly battle, new and deadly, against the mortal fighters of the god of war.

Enlil is outraged by this sorcery: by unnatural lusts defiling honest battle; by dead and dreaming heroes denied their hard-won rest and glory. The god is snarling so that Tempus can hardly hear the wails and howls of men and ghosts and dreamers dying once again as crossbows change the tempo of this battle and Stepsons try to break the pattern of Chaeronea, a war that was never theirs to win.

*Arrows arcing. Long spears, thunking into flesh. Men staggering backward, impaled, groaning.* War, then and now, so similar but so different: here, today, the name and the work of the crossbow is Death; none can stand before it.

Arrows whiz by his head. Niko's horse jostles his, the Stepson using his mount and shield to protect his commander. *No need, Stealth.* The god of the armies will surely see to his servant. Long, long spears, glittering in sudden sunlight, some with iron points, some with bronze. On this battleplain clash professionals and raw recruits and civilians, every Theban and Macedonian soul caught dead or dreaming by Shamshi or Aškelon.

And Tempus's greater Sacred Band.

Niko crowds Tempus and his Trôs at every turn. Both horses' lower legs are hide-wrapped to protect from swords and arrows. Stealth has his new composite crossbow, loaded and ready, and bolts to spare. His black stud kicks out at the enemy troops with both hind feet and bares its teeth, dealing death wherever it can strike.

Men and horses screaming: the living and the injured, the dreamers and the dreaming dead; men and ghosts, indistinguishable; stricken, about to die – or about to die again. Some fall down cursing, struggling, bleeding – fighting back until the end, more dangerous when wounded than before. Some crumple silently when speared or skewered or sliced; fragile, hardly struggling, quickly bleeding out – easy to hack apart, but adding to the fog of war.

Heads fall like apples in autumn on this battleplain, severed from their bodies; bouncing as they're kicked by horses' hooves; wide-eyed and staring at the sky as they roll in mud and blood.

Now enemies surround Stealth, cutting him off from Tempus. Niko's new horse plants its left hind foot and pivots left, head down; Stealth has his sword out straight. Tempus sees the shock run up Niko's arm each time that blade connects with hostile flesh and bodies topple, jerking; then lie still.

The black horse jumps three corpses freshly made and Niko is with Tempus once again, in time to raise his shield to meet his partner's as arrows fly their way. And the black pushes and bites the Trôs, but Niko's shield is where it needs to be, when it needs to be there: a brace of arrows hit with a thudding trill. Some pierce and stick, some fall away. Niko slams that shield with its bristling arrows into an enemy running at them with a spear, knocking the spear away, and the head away. Arrows splinter in the adversary's face and neck and on his armor.

The black horse bumps his again, knocking the wind from both, pinning Niko's left leg and Tempus's right together. Tempus clears his own shield, scraping down it with his blade. Pushes his own mount left to get some room to use his sword against new assailants charging Niko from the ground. Calls a maneuver code. And Stealth turns in time: his sword arm arcs down and the black horse kicks out sideways at hoplites who get too close.

Above their heads, the sky rolls and snaps. Purple haze hugs the ground, shrinking back. The sun breaks through the clouds, making every detail of the battleplain bright and clear.

Alone, the pair fights its way on horseback through endless foot, broken ranks in stark confusion. They thrust through routed soldiers, cleaving helmets in the press of far too many. Horses kicking, biting. Blades swinging. Blood spurting in close quarters. And he and Niko are still separated from their cadre by these opponents stumbling backward over their own dead and wounded, shoving one another, running from war-horses killing men upon their own. Their horses spin and kick and race through panicked ranks, leaving crushed and mangled bodies in their wake.

Tempus sees no Stepson now except his partner, up too close to him, eyes always scanning for spears come out of nowhere. Hears nothing but men yelling and horses squealing. He and Niko strike at enemies retreating and others coming on, keeping their horses' hooves off dropped swords and arrow points and bodies on the ground as they try to find their cohort in the armored press.

But you can't see far through the low-lying haze.

Finally they break free, on a hillock where no foes are charging, and look around. Chaos rules this battlefield, where every kind of tactic meets terror run amok, where professionals fight amateurs and carnage results.

Maneuvers carefully drilled, impossible to complete. Waves of death breaking on this simulacrum of the Chaeronean plain. So many falling, piled one upon the other. Bloody mud so slick that horses skid and stumble.

And his Stepsons, bright Stepsons in the thick of it: cavalry routing foot, stomping enemies into gory mud, again and again. Such cavalry as this has never been before. Sync's 3rd Commando, two hundred and ninety mounted fighters, add their strength to the greater Sacred Band, trying their skill on Aškelon's living dreamers and his dreaming dead. From somewhere, Macedonian horsemen reinforce Aškelon's contingent: those who struggle here again for another breath, another kill, another victory soon to be forgot.

*Is this what You, Storm God, really want, yet again? Is this what You, Enlil, Lord Storm of the Armies, so long to see and see? Yet again? And want? Again and again? Enough to let unholy battle rage against mere mortal fighters? And want enough that You will let effrontery win the day? Will You let Your brave fighters die before an onslaught of the dreamers and the restless dead?*

No answer from Enlil, god of the battlefield, as spears rip and quarrels thunk and Stepson cavalrymen lay about them with their swords against too many with so much less to lose.

The god won't speak to him today, is too close today, perhaps too angry today, his celestial mind bloody and full of dark purpose. But the god's speed is in him, and he is Enlil's instrument. The god is so high in him: Enlil's mind in his mind; strength beyond mortal comprehension.

Now celestial rage is loosed, as Tempus looks up from the helmets and spears and swords flashing around him and sees so many more ranks coming, hoplites and peltasts, angry ghosts and dreamers never-ending.

Beside him, Niko seems tireless, grimly slashing, striking out at every armed and armored soul who might threaten his commander. Too many, enough to make the strongest tire. Yet Niko circles him, protects him and guards him, front and back, putting himself and his horse between Tempus and all harm with more strength than Tempus thought a man could muster.

He sees the sweat running off Niko and his mount, sees the heavy breathing, the unflagging determination of his rightman. With javelin and shield and throwing star – then with sword and bow and arrow, as light cavalry rushes down upon them – Stealth defends him. Nikodemos meets every assault, parrying every thrust, big black horse roaring between his legs and frothing.

*So, Enlil, what do you think of my partner now?* The storm god says nothing, is just deep growling in his ears. *We could use a little help this day.* Against endless troops and maddened fools. Those with nothing left to lose come on like doom, uncaring, shields close together, long spears flashing in phalanxes and formations from a dozen wars.

As on that other day he fought on this Chaeronean battle-plain, Tempus can't say now where Tempus ends and Enlil begins. This time he must enlist the god. The lord of dream and shadow has gone too far – profaning souls who'd earned their rest, desecrating righteous battle.

Tempus has a rage in him that threatens to tear heart from body, sinew from bone. Enlil crowds inside him now, as he slashes about him once more with his god-given sword. Always watching for Niko, who keeps putting that black horse in his path, trying to save him from everything and anything.

Enlil now takes him over, this primordial force that sees so little difference between good and evil, right and wrong, but loves conflict and change and the steering of all things through all things by strife.

And that force seeks the dream lord, who's reached too high and now must come out and face a god in man. Today, Tempus is surely more god than man, as Enlil takes his flesh and empowers it. It can't be helped. Or maybe it will *be* the help.

But the pattern of this battle is hard to break. Niko is consumed with keeping Tempus safe; his sword is like a scythe; his eyes stay steady, burning in the shadows of his helmet. Like all his Stepsons, Niko knows more about how to use a horse in battle than those they face today. A throng of dreamers, eyes and mouths wide, comes at them like a wave and Niko sinks his mount's pivot foot and spins the horse again, shortsword out, lopping heads from necks and slicing armored chests and limbs as the big black whirls in place.

Beyond them, Sync's 3rd Commando cavalry fight a war whose rules they wrote. Deadly strategies and tactics, fielded against heavy Macedonian horse, just learning what the 3rd Commando knows full well. It takes more than felted armor on the horses of this enemy to protect them from the 3rd's ruthless onslaught. Legs ruined, wounded horses drop on top of riders, neighing. Even Tempus turns his face away.

Critias and Straton have the wings of the Sacred Band contingent (closing ranks upon a conscripted infantry with little stomach for this fight), slaughtering all those in between. Led by Stepsons, the greater Band steps up to this terrifying battle, where the dishonored are dying in a multitude.

Here on this transplanted Chaeronean battlefield, the spirit of Tempus's fighters is invoked and their precision finely tuned. The dream lord's minions cannot be allowed to rout brains and heart and honor.

Still the adversary marches in, where glory takes a shameful face, and war an ugly turn, counting on sheer numbers to win the day. *Long spears, thunking into flesh: men stagger backward, falling, fleeing.*

Mortal strikes from dreamers' hands kill just as dead as dead can be. Swords slash necks and arms.

Randal gallops up, thin face pale and big ears flaming red, on a conjured horse that is not quite a horse, but rears like a horse when the mage jerks its reins. "Riddler," Randal shouts, "I begged Cime. I pleaded. Notwithstanding, she says you must bring her the Heart of Aškelon before she'll forgive you." With battle all around, Randal looks as if he'll weep.

"Not your fault, Randal," Tempus calls from his cantering Trôs, circling Randal's conjured horse, striking at the dreaming dead getting between them. *Slash.* "She sent the Third Commando." *Thrust.* "That's good enough." *Parry. Slash.*

Too many enemies are surging toward them, trying to surround them where Randal has paused to speak. "I tried, Commander…" yells Randal as his mount, squealing like a real horse, leaps into the air and comes down kicking; crushing adversaries – then runs the other way while Randal, holding on for dear life, saws on his reins and fighters scatter.

A unit of Macedonian cavalry, eight abreast, thunders over the hill, and redeploys into a flying wedge galloping through ranks of foot, unmindful that it tramples its own infantry. And is trapped there, when its leaders fall, and mills helplessly until men are pulled from horses and disappear into the fray.

Niko squints at Randal, then at Tempus, shaking his head in disgust. His black mount strikes at enemies, its head snaking out to bite at nearby foes, as Niko closes up the distance between him and the Riddler, thrusting with his shortsword at whatever fool comes near.

No matter how Tempus and Niko try, they can't break this stubborn pattern. Shield-holding lines drift right, each man protecting his open side. Tempus calls Niko close: too much interference from Stealth is not helping as his rightman tries to shield him from all jeopardy with his own body and his horse.

Too many open sides; too much rightward drift among the Sacred Band. Too many hoplites and peltasts ranged against them: a wall of shields and long spears is an unholy menace to men on horses. Spearpoints and edges sharp as blades can cut and maim and kill; bronze butt-caps hold long spears steady, braced in the ground when cavalry charges. Horses bleed and men bleed more as a phalanx of Aškelon's foot bears down on them.

Tempus and Niko race their mounts toward the enemy formation. These fighters won't run; this line won't break. Hoplites crouch, shields touching, long spears overlapping, spearpoints bristling.

*Faster, then.* Tempus signals to his rightman. They must count each stride, judge the distance perfectly before they ask their horses to make this leap. They jump their mounts over the dream lord's array, hoping to come to earth beyond the phalanx, not on top of spearpoints and shields. For a moment, they are floating. He hears shouts and clatter below, grunts and swearing beneath him as men attempt to turn in quarters far too tight, to reorient their line to face an enemy coming from behind. Too late.

Clearing the hindmost rank, the Trôs and the black land on open ground; neither horse stumbling into bodies; neither speared. Wheeling their mounts about, Tempus and Niko attack the exposed rear of the enemy. Soldiers die. Soldiers scatter. Soldiers flee. Straight into the waiting arms of the greater Sacred Band.

Time to regroup.

But Tempus can't see more than Niko and the black horse. Niko has his shortsword in his hand: there are too many hostiles surging around them for his crossbow, when long spears imperil mounts and riders. Niko slashes faces, necks, and groins, when he can.

Breaking free, they race their mounts through ragged lines to smash them, stabbing as they go. Living dreamers feel different than the dreaming dead when swords cut into them: the living shock and stop the blades, flesh and bone holding fast before giving way, fighting back as best they can; the dreaming dead slice like butter, drop like stones. It's unnerving. It's meant to be. It's nerve that wins, today.

More of the dream lord's army crests the hill: new fighters field no strategy but overwhelming numbers. *So, Enlil, will You take a hand or let the ungodly win this day?* Ancient weapons, adze and blade; ancient helmets, more like the gods themselves had worn: these men deserved clean death, long since. Tempus aches to give it to them, each and every one.

And the god in his head doesn't answer. But the god is within him, a greater heart than his own, pounding in his breast.

A crossbow bolt speeds toward him; his god-sharpened ears hear it moving through the air: *whukka whukka whukka.* He knows just where this quarrel is; he can feel it coming at him…see it with Enlil's sight. He reaches out his shield arm with god-given speed and plucks the quarrel from midair, snaps it in two with his fingers, and lets it fall.

Enlil is bright within him on this battlefield today. The god-given sword in his right hand is glowing. Strength pours into Tempus: his battle is yet strong. But even with his god-given sight, so keen, he cannot see the dream lord or Shamshi, the wizard boy, anywhere among this countless enemy.

*Bring them to me, Enlil. Or me and mine to them.*

He must kill those two, to end this conflict. No matter how he tries, he can't find them in the waves of conscripts from the archipelago of dream. But he sees his Stepsons, beleaguered, and his 3rd Commando, and his Theban Sacred Banders, and even Theban revenants, battling every comer – ghost or man, Macedonian, ancient soldier, dreamer, or dreaming dead.

Meanwhile, Niko stays close beside him. His partner's right side is smeared with blood; it's trickling from a dozen superficial wounds, clotting fast. Niko doesn't seem to notice, caring only to protect him, to keep the spears at bay so the pattern can't complete. He finally yells to Stealth above the din, "Niko, you can't step twice onto the same battleplain. Don't defend. Attack."

Black horse rearing up, his rightman salutes him with an empty stare, then brings the horse down, but doesn't try to speak over the cacophony. Just then, Niko takes a quarrel in his right arm. He's reaching over with his shield hand to pull out the bolt when hoplites surge between him and Tempus.

At that instant, from among the press, an infantryman with a war axe, whirling, charges Niko – a mad attacker spinning between horses, spears and arrows. The war axe connects hard, its edge throwing sparks as it skids down the bronze plates on Stealth's armor, slicing across his right hip and thigh, into his horse's shoulder and its chest.

The black horse screams. Niko winces and shudders at the concussion, knifing forward reflexively, grabbing his horse's neck for support. Blood spurts everywhere. His horse blares loudly, rearing, wheeling away from the axe swinging through the air a second time. For too long, Stepson and mount are silhouetted against the sky, Niko's shield arm and sword arm clasped around his horse's neck to keep his seat. Then he recovers his balance. Man and horse come down fighting. Enemy foot scatter from the onslaught of hooves and teeth and blade.

*Not part of the pattern.*

God-given sword glowing in his hand, Tempus claps his legs against the Trôs and his gray leaps on the axe-wielder from behind. He cleaves the assailant's collarbone, then wrenches out his sword. The man stumbles and the Trôs is on him, pummeling him, crushing helmet and skull beneath its hooves. Tempus shakes out rein and lets the horse finish the sorely wounded man: the only mercy today is clean kill. The wounded on the ground cry out for death. Foot soldiers break and bleed and try to crawl away, but can't.

Tempus hardly cares, once the immediate danger to Niko is past. In time so distended that breaths come too far apart, he watches the blood well on Niko's hip and his horse's chest, and slow…then stay its flow completely, and start to clot.

At least Harmony is giving Niko and his horse that much grace.

Or Enlil is. The storm god of the armies succors all his own, today. Until they find the dream lord, Enlil's field blessing must be enough. Until this conflict ends. Until they can break the pattern.

Until they can call the dream lord and the wizard boy out to battle. *If* they can.

*Look to the souls of Your own soldiers, God, who labor in Thine awful cause.* He hasn't come here to lose lives. He's come to save them: all of his, against all the angry dreamers and the dreaming dead.

*Look to the souls of Your own, Enlil.* He's said it before. He says it again, in this battle that will not take a different turn. But must.

*Must.*

*

The Sacred Band of Thebes, valiant fighters all, are holding firm, each pair tight together while the enemy – so many, many, with gross force of numbers – seeks to overwhelm them. Charon had tried his best to inspire them, coming onto the field of battle.

"I have faced worse at the hands of men," he'd told his faithful Thebans, not yet fully comprehending what was to come. Said it with his son among them and Lysis's young partner, Arton, at his side.

Charon spies what he'd hoped not to see – and hoped to see most of all: ghosts of his Theban brothers who'd died here when this fight was fought before.

They'd lost this battle, then; so many of his brothers, massacred. All but his precious few, rescued by the Riddler to fight on other days. So maybe they *can* win today. Against history, against the Fates intention. Foolish hope won't be banished. Snatch all these brother souls away and take them home.

How must he look to them, to his two and hundred fifty-four foredoomed brothers, these fated dead? How must his men – his son, saved from death – look to these souls recalled from Elysion, or from Hades?

He doesn't understand how this could happen, how their goddess could allow heroic souls to be profaned. But Tempus had said to him not to trust what he saw here. Their goddess Harmony had said they had all they needed to prevail here, and everybody knew it. So prevail they would. Or some would.

And some evil older than the gods themselves and darker than the deepest hell would be put to rout.

Or not. If faith had been misplaced, then they would die here, as they had nearly died the last time Theban faced Macedonian at Chaeronea. Meet their fate here, a fate that Tempus and their goddess had conspired to forfend. But this was not the Chaeronea of Charon's memories: this was some other place, some nightmare.

Charon sees a chariot, the first on the field today: Theagenes, their captain, is driving toward Charon and his fighters. He wants to get to Theagenes, say something to this ghost, this revenant. As man or ghost, alive or dead, Theagenes has led them well for so very long. What can Charon say to them (to these shades of the Sacred Band of Thebes), he who has escaped death by Harmony's grace, without ever once needing to beg for mercy or besmirch his honor?

He can say his brothers are remembered. He can say the soul of the Sacred Band of Thebes is alive and well among the Stepsons. He can say dead Thebans are revered by the living and their goddess.

But is that really Theagenes, broad and strong? Is that Charon's own Sacred Band of Thebes, around Theagenes, all two hundred and fifty-four? All his dead friends and comrades, the heroes of Chaeronea? What had they done to be snatched from Elysion and set down here? Whom do they fight for? The Riddler? What do they fight against? The dream lord?

Sick at heart, demoralized, Charon looks back to his own fighters and beyond, where a wave of antagonists is coming on, loosing arrows and waving dories and sarissas, yowling like banshees. Then Theagenes gives a hand-sign and the Theban revenants form up between Charon's little force and the assault of Macedonians, dreamers, and the dreaming dead – braving a rain of arrows, ducking under shields, putting themselves in the way of ungodly harm.

Charon's skin prickles. His breath comes fast as he calls his fighters to the ready. Now the dead heroes of Thebes are clearly defending their living brothers. Shoulder to shoulder, the revenants of Theagenes's fighters join forces with Charon's unit.

The caterwauling is awful. The enemy closes: wild eyes and gaping mouths and long spears attack in a bulging phalanx, then a wedge.

But Charon has been through this before. He knows what to do, how to fight this enemy. This time. And he's on a horse, so much faster, so much more deadly, with weapons and tactics he hadn't had before. He even has a crossbow in his hands. As there are crossbows in the hands of all his living Sacred Band.

Crossbow bolts fly, speeding through the bloody press, short sharp missiles of death, iron points piercing armor, skin and bone. It feels good to fight back, to take the initiative, to break the pattern that had killed so many here before, when this battle last was joined.

And they are holding their own, holding firm; advancing tight together on foot and horse, with their long-lamented brethren going on before, up into the faces of the enemy. Marching forward till the walls made by their shields are all that separate one contingent from the other, each stabbing and pushing and slashing where they can. His cavalry, at the rear, is shooting arrows over precious heads that couldn't be saved before. Might they be saved, this time, these ghosts, these truly fated dead?

Charon flexes his fingers on his sword hilt, knocks away arrows with his shield without a thought. When Thebans fall who'd died before, he watches, awed, but they don't get up again. Don't fight again. They're not immortal. They only die once more, one atop the other, so many bleeding on one another…. Then disappear, as if they'd never been here, bled here, died here…a second time.

The 'fated dead,' the Stepsons call Charon's remnant of the Sacred Band of Thebes. What would the Stepsons call these vengeful ghosts, once left for dead on the Chaeronean battleplain, who now fight again and die again and then vanish, bones and all, back to their shared grave under a stone lion for later men to find? So much more fated, for certain.

Charon knees his horse and kicks it, heading for a knot of enemies, needing to fight back, and rend, and take some just revenge. He's nearly snarling, as he lays about him with his sword, striking at Macedonian heads and necks and arms raised against him with sharp weapons glittering in every hand.

No man should have to fight the same battle twice…so he won't. Tempus had told the senior staff, warned them all: fight a different way today.

Now Charon sees another chariot coming, only the second one he's seen on this battlefield. This chariot has wheels with sharp axle blades that mow down allies and enemies alike, uncaring who is who. The edges on those wheels cut deep like scythes. He first saw this chariot the night before the Chaeronean battle when the Riddler drove it. Its image is etched deep into his soul.

Up beside Charon comes Lysis, on a big blue roan with Arton on his right. Ducking arrows and knocking spears away from his father with ready shield, Lysis is intent on protecting both his father and his partner. He has time to wonder at his son – no boy now, but a man this day, and worthy – guiding horse and partner through the skirmish to his father's side.

Time is so slow today, waiting for Death to pick and choose His way across this foretold battlefield. *Whooshing, clashing, ring, and bellow.* Death is all around.

Charon has felt it before. He's been here before. Horses or no, crossbows or no, dead comrades or no, this pattern reasserts itself, resisting all attempts to change it, as if it were a living, knowing thing.

Theagenes falls, struck down by a long spear…thrown, not thrust. And lies still, as he had lain before, jointed shaft aquiver in his diaphragm. His partner stands spread-legged over him, unwilling to move another step till Death notices, and takes him too with a flight of arrows. *Some strangeness in the proportion.* The pattern from Chaeronea, repeating despite all they can do.

Charon wants to cry. He's seen these two die before, divine friends until the end. He knows they might be hallucinations, not really here; or revenants, not really men – but it rends his heart to see their pain and blood and valor once again. No man should die in battle twice, trying to protect his partner and failing twice. For an instant, he can't see anything.

His strength erodes. His fortitude leaves him. But then he notices his son once more; feels Lysis's knee hit his own; hears greaves clink and horses snorting.

He has something to protect here, after all. His son and heir. A boy at risk, whose future is in hot dispute. And that realization shakes him from despair. For a heartbeat. In battle, a heartbeat can be as long as time itself.

*Break the pattern. Change the rules to change the game,* the Riddler had counseled all his senior staff. So had the storm god Enlil devised this strategy?

Change this pattern, break these rules of history, or fate snaps back like a slingshot. If the pattern holds, then predestination reigns, Tempus has warned him. And then all of his will die as they'd have died if Tempus and his Stepsons had never intervened, never plucked them from harm's way. He knows it for a fact. The Riddler had told him so, in his gentlest voice.

But this was not exactly the Chaeronea of the Theban battle, he told himself. This was some darker, danker place, more like the Chaeronea of Charon's visions – and, from what he'd heard, of everyone else's. Many others had spoken of these flashes of the battleplain, purple and full of shadows, like this battleplain today.

Now Charon sees Tempus, on his great gray horse that moves so fast they're both a blur, across this killing field of mud and blood and fighters locked in mortal combat. And sees Stealth, the commander's rightman, an unearthly look on his face, helmet off and dangling by his knee, hair plastered to his head with sweat.

As Charon watches, transfixed, Kouras gallops up to him, enemies in hot pursuit strung out behind, drawing fire from the gauntlet of the fated dead of Thebes.

"The commander says I'm to fight beside you, till the end," yells the son of the storm god with a death's-head grin, his face pale, his hip already bandaged. And Kouras slides his horse in line on Charon's right, between father and son, because their commander ordered it. Because Charon has no partner. His son Lysis is paired with Arton – and should be protecting his own rightman, not his father.

Relief floods over Charon and strength returns. Trust in his cohort, trust his commander to see them through this battle. His fighters need every advantage Tempus's Stepsons can provide, and more. So Tempus has sent the son of the local storm god to fight by Charon's side, a benediction of the martial kind.

*Long spears, ripping into flesh. Men shoving forward, enraged, bawling*. Charon is sure now: this is not like the last time when long spears slew. Not the same pattern. Not at all.

Kouras catches his eye, reins his horse up even closer to Charon, and screams hoarsely, "My father Vashanka defends us. Hold firm and live to fight another day." So speaks the child to the man, when Death is near. But boys can't comprehend Death, a taste acquired through familiarity, a yoke to which every head someday bows.

It won't be long now until the eerie quiet falls that signals victory for one, annihilation for the other. But it's not over – not yet. The Sacred Band has other plans today.

*

Paired with Randal for this battle, Jihan is engaging the enemy from her Trôs's back, dismayed at all she sees. She calls upon her father, Stormbringer, to strike the travesties dead from heaven this day. Randal chants his strongest incantations, does whatever he can do. But in heaven and on earth and even in Jihan's oceanic realm, order is disturbed, unheeding. Something is wrong with the correspondences of earth and heaven today.

On the unnatural battleplain, Strife is here, bearing down with her awful mouth open wide, keening. Fear follows, stinking, her bowels loose and horrid. And Death rides his own chariot, while Disorder and Chaos flank him, shambling beside. Here Panic reigns. Speech is impossible over the uproar.

Jihan sees it all – what mortal men can see and what they can't – with her Froth Daughter's eye.

She sees Randal, who rides a horse that really isn't one. He's trying desperately to control it as it's overwhelmed by Aškelon's dreaming infantry. Jihan can't get to him fast enough.

The conjured horse dissolves and, with it, Randal is lost to view, swallowed in the press of combat. Jihan fights off pikemen with her big Trôs horse and its flailing hooves. On its hind legs, Jihan's mount stalks among the enemy, while she and it cleave helmets, crush skulls and strike down foes where they may.

Never before has Jihan seen such a test of heaven's mandate. She searches for Tempus. The Riddler is too far off to reach, or even call, above the noise of the dying and the arrows flying and the javelins whispering toward their targets.

She sees Tempus reach out to Stealth, touch Niko's shoulder, both reins in his left hand. Niko's shield comes up and Niko pulls his horse in front of his commander's, his black half-falling against the Trôs, trying to block a long, long spear from Tempus's gut. And succeeding.

What they all feared was a repeat of this deadly pattern. Niko had been adamant. He will stay with Tempus. All will try to change doom to triumph. And Stealth, on that great black horse, has sworn upon his life he will not fail.

Now comes the Theban goddess, riding across the battlefield on a sable mare, seeing to her own. She seeks out the remnant of the Sacred Band of Thebes – these Theban fated dead and truly dead, encircled by Tempus's own Stepsons.

Nearby, a whirlwind is forming.

Jihan cries to out to Tempus with her tidal voice (louder than any mortal could), trying to alert him. But his partner Niko sees it now, and Tempus heads his horse that way – toward the whirlwind.

In that moment, a chariot emerges from the throng of dreamers, Macedonians, Thebans, and other ghosts from battles past. Stepson maneuver codes ring out, called by Critias, by Straton, and by Niko when he can: as soon as anyone sees that chariot, they're sworn to alert all the others.

Jihan calls out again with all the voice she has. In response, the dream lord's minions focus on her, marching toward her, casting javelins before them, waving short spears as they come.

But now the whirlwind is manifesting here. Two forces new to the battleplain are coalescing at the same time: Aškelon in his chariot; and this whirlwind, this shimmer and shiver in the fabric of creation that is a portal to Lemuria.

*Now*…the pattern breaks. At last, the foretold pattern crumbles, shreds its ethereal bonds. The pattern is blowing on the winds of change, picking up in mighty gusts. And remakes itself, begins anew – offering up a strained and strange proportion, a different fate not chosen by the lord of dream and shadow.

Jihan can hear the difference in this war before she sees it. All sounds are louder. Men and horses move at their normal rates. She can smell blood and decomposing flesh and rot. And she smells fear, stinking across the battleplain, wafting over everyone, into every nose. She evades a spear, dodges arrows. She lifts her horse into a lope and away from the tight press of javelins and swords and conscripted dreamers.

Aškelon's chariot makes a wide sweep, turning. Jihan knows the dream lord when she sees him. The regent of the seventh sphere is really here. The horses of his chariot trample restless dead and living indiscriminately. Mortals run from the dream-spawned chariot, yelling. Arrows rain upon it. But Aškelon waves aside shaft after shaft, driving his chariot one-handed.

This is the hell-wheeled chariot Tempus once drove. Sharp blades stick out from each hub and demons and the elder gods shine from its car. The chariot is pulled by two sable horses. Beside Aškelon, in the car, stands a tow-headed youth, handsome and tall, wearing a panoply that matches the chariot, with enameled serpents and gods and bulls and lightning decorating it.

Jihan knows this panoply, once Niko's, as she knows the chariot, which once belonged to her beloved Riddler. Fear oversweeps her, an unaccustomed emotion for a Froth Daughter, child of wind and wave. Are Stealth and the Riddler dead, then – defeated?

She tastes panic for the first time ever. It clouds her mind; she struggles to think.

Where is Randal? When confused or disheartened, Jihan always seeks the little flop-eared mage. Jihan looks for Randal and finds him, not far away, on foot, among the skirmishers in the purple haze.

Before Aškelon and his travesty, this wizard boy with such a taste for war, she and Randal are vulnerable themselves, alluring targets. Yet few of the dreaming dead accost her as she slips among them. She is female: no threat, they think, to such as they.

Spears thunking. Arrows whizzing. Swords clanging. Jihan sees the shimmer and the shiver of the whirlwind at the edge of her vision.

*"Randal,"* she calls out for the mage in a voice as loud as a cyclone.

*"Jihan."* Randal stumbles toward Jihan, arms outstretched, as if seeking salvation.

Aškelon sees Jihan, sees the mage, and points them out to the youth beside him in the car, who has a crossbow in his hands.

Jihan needs to get over there, between Randal and the dream lord's chariot. She asks her mount, and it thunders across the battleplain.

Time tries to reform itself, go back to the beginning of this battle once again. Jihan won't let it: she fights to keep time moving forward. Her horse's hooves mark a cadence that goes onward, from past to future, and from one side of the battleplain to another. She won't be frozen in time by the lord of dream and shadow ever again. Nor will anybody else here, if she has her way.

Jihan raises her hand and sends withering cold to the dream lord. Across the battleplain it speeds as if it were a flight of arrows made of ice and sleet and rain. And catches him and his bowman and winds them round with the cold between the stars.

The dream lord shivers; his partner, beside him in the chariot, freezes. Their horses halt in mid-stride. For an instant.

Reprieve, for a moment. A reprieve long enough to protect Randal from Aškelon as the mage runs toward Jihan through the churning battle: horses stomping, hooves flailing, swords swinging, quarrels flying – while the Sacred Band (Stepsons, Theban remnants, 3rd Commando fighters) and fated dead and dreamers are locked in deadly combat.

Closer Randal runs. Closer.

Then Aškelon revives and touches the tow-headed youth. His team's hooves pound the ground.

And a quarrel glowing blue speeds toward Randal, shot from the crossbow of the youth who is riding with the dream lord. The blue-tinged bolt hits the little mage in the back. Randal's arms outstretch, trying to reach for Jihan. His white face has a quizzical look upon it as he falls flat. Then battle rushes over him and Jihan can't see Randal anymore.

*Randal. Dear, sweet, brave Randal. Randal full of gentleness, with iron beneath it.* Jihan wants to lament. But there is no time for mourning. Not now.

Aškelon has his arms upstretched, asking something of the universe that Jihan knows must be wrong. The purple haze drapes about him like a cloak.

For a moment, Jihan stares around her at the tableau on the battleplain, shocked and sorrowful, unsure of her next move.

Off to her right, with Charon leading them, the Theban Sacred Banders fight beside the pile of their dead brothers, lying just as they had lain before on this benighted battleplain. The Riddler's Thebans surround their slain companions, trying to protect the living and the dying.

Far to her left, Stepsons see Tempus and Niko coming and form up, trying to get to them. Critias signs a maneuver code to Straton. Straton has the ghost horse, and Ischade is riding up behind him, holding onto Straton's waist. Straton heads his horse Crit's way.

*Arrows whizzing by, dropping from the sky like a black and awful sleet.*

Now Jihan notices that the Theban goddess is with her faithful, protecting them as best she can. Harmony touches her wounded with her soft hand – and the remaining Thebans come together over their dead.

The Froth Daughter knows that look on Harmony's face. That expression has been on her own face enough times. The goddess wants to take her Thebans to safety. But this time, like last time, despite all, so few want to leave….

Jihan sees a crossbow being aimed at her – a gray eye sighting in on her from the dream-forged chariot. She knows this enemy is Shamshi, the wizard boy, hoping to shoot her with an ensorcelled bolt as he had skewered poor Randal. She tries to rein her horse away.

But not even her Trôs mare is fast enough to avoid that dream-sped arrow.

She is struck between her breasts. The quarrel that hits her is tinged with blue: sorcerous, sent by the wizard boy. Her scale armor can't withstand this bolt, so sharp, loosed with such inhuman force. The arrow point touches flesh – and changes flesh to froth, to foam, to mist.

From froth came Jihan, daughter of wind and wave. Water is her element. To water she returns. Her scale armor and all her weapons dissolve and splash to the ground, making a puddle there. Her moisture soaks into the bloody, muddy earth.

Her Trôs mare, affrighted, riderless, screams and runs amok until it finds its stablemates among the Stepson horses. A 3rd Commando horseman catches the mare in the melee. There is no blood on horse or saddle, just a bit of foam here and there.

*

Ischade, up behind Straton on the ghost horse, says, *"Now,* Straton. Have your commander strike *now.* Aškelon and Shamshi are as present as they're going to be." He and

Ischade are here together for this very purpose, to tell the Riddler when he can engage Aškelon and Shamshi directly.

Straton, calling the maneuver code, twists in his saddle.

Ischade pushes away from him.

And then she is gone. A swish of cloak. A flap of dark wing. Now he's alone in the middle of battle, with nothing of Ischade left behind – not even a stray breeze against his cheek. He can't see her at all, not a trace of her, not even a bird wheeling high, not a sign in the late day sky.

In the midst of all this chaos, he hadn't had a thought until now for his safety. Or hers. He looks up into the sky, where the sun is sinking toward the west through crimson clouds, trying to see her. At last he thinks he sees a dot. He blinks and peers into the clouds again, trying to be certain she's there – certain she is safe.

An arrow hits him in the chest like a fist, boring in between his ribs. Slapping the wind from him. Slamming him backward. Knocking him from his horse. Searing pain fills his lungs as if all his air is sucked away. He thinks, as he tumbles, how fortunate he is that there are several corpses where he's sure to land, soft enough to break his fall.

*

Lysis saw his father with Kouras, and then he didn't. He tried to signal Arton, but the confusion was too great. He headed the dun toward the Thebans: the living, the revenants, and the newly dead.

Their goddess was here. She was touching fighters, talking to them where they stood over the bodies of their companions, one atop the other. Lysis remembered this sad sight, those bodies, from the battleplain of Chaeronea…the first time. He remembered all of this cavernous moment from the first battle.

This battle was easily as bad as the first, as real as the blood running down his right arm from a jab with a spear; as real as the sweat soaking his horse. But it is *not* the same. Kouras wasn't with the Thebans then. It was brighter then. Now there is haze, lying close to the ground with a strange purple pall, although the sun shines bright above.

It's different now. It's like the visions of Chaeronea that haunt his dreams, but different from the reality. He's sure it is different today, this horrendous war that is as terrifying as it was when he last fought at Chaeronea. And as deadly.

Sadness overcomes Lysis, that those Theban bodies are still here – or are here once again. He must kill as many as he can of these enemies coming from nowhere, or from Macedonia, marching down the farther hill.

He swings with his shortsword at any ghost fighter who comes close enough. Stab them, and they stagger backward, crumpling. Slash them, and they mewl and fall. Hack at their limbs, and they go to pieces, yowling. The Macedonians on the first Chaeronean battleplain had been tougher: they'd fought on their knees, staggered to their feet, laid about with their swords until their eyes went empty, until their every drop of blood was shed. This adversary has everything but heart. And heart is something Lysis has in abundance. He'd used up all his quarrels. He has a throwing star or two, and his sword and dagger – and this horse. He needs to find his father, but there are too many fighters in the way.

He is about to spur his horse through the enemy at a gallop, to clear his way despite their long spears, when something comes up fast and hard on his right side. He nearly decapitates the rider, until he hears a shout and looks into the other's helmet…just before he swings his sword.

Pacing him is Arton, struggling with his brown gelding who is wild-eyed, nose in the air. "Don't kill me, Lysis. I'm on your side. And don't go over there with the fated Thebans. You can't."

"Why?" It is difficult to be heard over the tumult and the snorting horses. "No one said I couldn't. I have no orders to stay –"

*"I* say. *Please,* Lysis. Go over there and you'll die. Right now."

Lysis jerks his horse to a stop. "Right now?" Arton had found those missing Stepson horses, and warned Lysis of real danger enough times that Lysis took Arton's presentiments seriously. Arton's eyes are very wide, peering out of the shadows of his helmet as if looking at something Lysis cannot see.

And at that moment a sword catches Arton from behind, slashing deep into his armor. He screeches in pain. His assailant pulls hard, jerking to get his weapon free.

Arton topples off his horse and into dirt quickly turning red with his blood.

*

Tempus saw their youngest Stepsons distract each other in the midst of peril: his youngest pair, callow youths with tempers flaring, the fire of battle-lust in their eyes. These two were first blooded at Chaeronea, the last time.

He sees Arton fall, slashed right through his leather armor by a Macedonian galloping past, then speared by a hoplite as he tumbles. Lysis jumps off his mount to protect his unhorsed partner. He watches Lysis, standing over Arton with his sword drawn, keeping Aškelon's minions at bay. Lysis helps Arton try to stand. He sees Arton staggering to his feet, sword in hand.

Cut and speared, youth always gets up to throw itself again and again into the fray. Until flesh won't respond. Until swords can't be held and bows can't be shot. Until consciousness ebbs. Why? Always pushing their limits. Testing their courage. Judging their mettle. For the look in the eyes of their comrades. For the black stare in the eyes of their enemies once life has fled. *Don't stare too long in the eyes of the newly dead, young fighters, Thebans and my own*, Tempus thinks again as he'd thought before, the last time he stood here like this.

The pattern keeps reforming – old pattern into new, and back again. *Aškelon knows it. I know it. I can feel it, steering all things through all things. Enlil knows it, too.* Was this the right choice, or only one more horrific moment in the annals of wrong?

Tempus has his sword, god-given, and it glows with sanctification of his battle. He strikes whenever he can, leaning over his horse's withers, long and low, ravaging these enemies who deserve no quarter, who have died once or will die soon, with belly slashed and entrails spilled.

Laying waste where he can, devastating all he may, he seeks the dream lord among the carnage, his rightman at his side.

If anything can break this cycle, he and Stealth can. Aškelon is here now. Ischade has said so. Straton has confirmed it, called out the maneuver code. Niko has seen Ash come, motioned with three sharp jerks of his sword. Niko is determined not to let Tempus take another spear here, not this time. But Tempus needs to get near Ash's chariot, despite the arm-long blades on its axle, twisting and cutting everything as those wheels spin.

The dreamers and the dreaming dead with their dazed grins have heard his shortsword *sussurrusing,* have seen his god-given speed, and decided he and Niko are too costly a target, here and now. But every other man of his is still at risk. *Long spear, thunking into flesh. Another man staggers backward, impaled, crying.*

One of Sync's, this time, takes a spear. All the way across this foretold battleplain, Tempus can feel the shock of it, the rip into flesh, and the cold where point touches heart. And he shivers, on his Trôs horse, with his god-given sword glowing in his right hand.

He must get to the dream lord. He must let Niko have his chance at Shamshi. Otherwise, this war will go on forever. Literally. There seems to be no end of revenants and dreaming dead and dreamers, drafted from Meridian and perhaps deeper hells. But there is an end to the strength of the Sacred Band, of his Stepsons and 3rd Commando.

What then? What if they fall here? Die here? Will they be sent back onto this killing field, eternally? Drafted to refight this war of Sham's preoccupation, forever? It is too cruel a fate, even for the regent of the seventh sphere to decree.

Niko says this battleplain looks like Shamshi's rest-place; to Tempus, it looks like the specter of Chaeronea that has haunted him since the long spear pierced his breast: whichever, it promises devastation beyond anything they have faced before.

With hand-sign, he indicates to Niko where they need to go. First Stealth scowls and shakes his head: *no.* Niko disdains his helmet now, and Tempus can't convince him otherwise: Stealth needs to see everything, hear everything, around him. Must, Niko thinks, to keep Tempus safe from harm.

*No need, Niko.* But there's no convincing Stealth of that. His rightman won't obey his order. Niko's black horse circles in front of Tempus and the Trôs, dodging spear points and broken arrows and a few mangled limbs in its path, trying to keep Tempus from heading toward the whirlwind.

*No. Wait. Stay here,* Niko signals back.

The whirlwind, a portal into Lemuria, beckons. It can take the Band to safety through a shimmer and shiver and a rip in place and time. It offers salvation for the Sacred Band once again – as it did before. His Stepsons are closing ranks, looking first at the portal, then at the adversary coming, and coming, and coming over the hill. They'd drilled this twenty, fifty times. Whenever the whirlwind appears, Straton and the ghost horse, impervious to all, hold the portal open.

But Straton isn't there today. Isn't holding the portal today.

And going from here to Lemuria is part of the pattern. Tempus can't allow it. They'd spent too much and tried too hard to flush this enemy. It is time to engage Aškelon and Shamshi.

Getting their horses over there, where the dream lord's chariot clears a swathe, won't be easy. The chariot is too close to the portal and the Sacred Band. Niko isn't wrong in trying to keep Tempus away from there. Stealth doesn't want to risk recreating the conditions that led to the spearpoint piercing his commander's breast.

*Fear gets us nowhere but stuck in Meridian, eternally. Fear is what Aškelon is selling. Quail, and he wins.* Tempus's ire is too high to brook insubordination. Again, he gives Niko the signal. His grip is too tight on his sharkskin-hilted sword. It might be easier to rid the field of enemies than to get Nikodemos to settle that black horse on Tempus's right and ride across this battlefield.

This time Stealth obeys him. They ride together, strides synchronized, precise: left-side leader and rightman, knees almost touching, both of them looking at the ground and all around. For an instant of sublime relief, this could be any day, any drill, or any battle. But it's not. Enemies and ghosts of enemies still pour over the hilltop, down the slope: ranks in perfect formation, Macedonian style; light cavalry on the right, eight across; infantry in the middle; heavy cavalry by ranks of eight on the left. Soon they will be surrounded. And soon enough, the sun will set. Then Aškelon's power may be too great to counter.

The ground beneath their horses' feet is littered with flesh and blood and bone, arms and torsos and heads – body parts lopped off and skewered and chopped and severed, limb from limb, lying in the purple mud. And casualties sob, groaning, moaning in the midst of it, desperate to move, trying to crawl away.

Tempus sees Critias, brave beyond what any could ask, sliding off his horse, trying to scoop up a wounded fighter in his arms. Behind him struggles a remnant of the Sacred Band of Thebes, covering Crit's back, holding his horse. These few fated Thebans left alive (paired brothers and lovers and friends) all stay together, guarding the corpses of their comrades, slain again today. They are as good as their oaths: battling together, shoulder to shoulder; to the death, with honor unbounded – stronger than death itself.

He has a moment to recognize the pile of dead that was once the greater Theban Sacred Band: a muddle of still flesh and blood, with that forgotten look that bodies have when life has fled.

The day is waning. Time grows short. And behind them the portal to Lemuria shimmers, open again today as his sister had opened it for them when first the Band fought in Chaeronea. Crit has orders to take the Sacred Band of Stepsons through and away to safety, if he and Niko fall today. If they fail today, something will be saved.

If that happens, at least Tempus will not have to listen to Cime tell him how wrong he was.

Some fighter shouts. Then someone else does.

Then there is no sound but from his partner and their two horses. Silence reigns across the valley and beyond.

A way is clear before them.

They have a path straight through to Ash's chariot.

Tempus still thinks his battle plan is correct, even when he looks down that empty way before him – a long corridor where silent combatants, struck motionless, line an expanse of grass and blood and mud – at the other end of which is Aškelon, with Shamshi beside him in their dream-forged chariot.

Are these two paired, in some parody of Sacred Band devotion? The sight makes him angry, despite himself. Only a fool belittles what he wants most of all. The prizes here, over which all contest, are Tempus's Sacred Banders, valiant fighters; honest men, principled and brave; and Nikodemos, the best of the Stepsons.

The dream lord knows it. Even at this considerable distance, Aškelon's arch and haughty face is paler than Tempus remembers it. With his long right hand, Ash motions Tempus to come forward – to ride with Niko down this corridor lined on either side with men and ghosts and dreamers locked in a grisly, mindless truce: each fighter here is frozen; immobile.

*Come on,* gestures that white hand, its fingers curling toward the dream lord's palm. On Aškelon's left wrist is the bracelet called the Heart of Aškelon, where some say his power lies. This bracelet is Cime's obsession, her price for peace between them, if Randal can be believed.

It is too quiet. Utterly still. No swords grate. No arrows carom off armor. No shields thump spears away. No attacker howls a war cry. No wounded scream. No dying weep. No wild beasts or birds or insects dare to make a sound. No god rustles in his skull. Silence pounds his ears, complete but for his breathing, and Stealth's, and the noises made by their horses and the dream lord's.

Tempus keeps waiting for the spell to break, for someone to move or sneeze or rub his nose. He is hesitant to ride down between those ensorcelled ranks. Every fighter lining that empty way is imprisoned in time, frozen between heartbeats. Will he and Stealth fall asleep forever, too, if they brave that soundless gauntlet?

*'Come and meet me, Tempus, you fool. Come and lose what little life you have. As you promised, you and I will come to blows,'* Ash intrudes, taunting him with a voice inside his head.

He recalls when he'd threatened Ash, at the fête on the beach.

So he'd set all this in motion then. He'd known, but just forgot.

He caught sight of Crit, off to one side, asleep on his feet with eyes open wide. Tempus stretched out his arm and pointed: "Ash, turn these loose," he called aloud. "All of mine." The whole hazy battlefield was frozen yet – everyone but Niko and Tempus, Ash and his wizard boy, and their horses. Shamshi was grinning like a gargoyle but kept quiet, satisfaction aglow on his face.

"Turn them loose? All of yours? Why, Riddler? So all your men can see what men should not?" retorted the dream lord. No wounded fighter groaned or cried or whimpered or cursed, no dreamer shifted weight from foot to foot; no revenant moaned.

The hush was so deep that every noise from his horse and Niko's reechoed. Aškelon was flouting nature, flaunting his power: challenging Tempus and his partner to come and fight.

Niko's horse neighed a challenge. One of Ash's chariot horses took it up, screaming, and pawed the ground. Tempus twisted in his saddle to look behind him. On the hill, Aškelon's ranks, descending, were as motionless as statues. Would they blow away in a breeze, when this was done? Or would they return to some deeper hell?

Ischade said this was not hell, not Chaeronea: this was Meridian. The witch was sure this twisted Chaeronean battleplain manifested where Aškelon chose and as he chose, to amuse the wizard boy.

Tempus had asked for this: straight on to Meridian, he'd insisted. He'd had no inkling then that the lord of dream and shadow would – could – bring Meridian to him. But this must be Meridian: it was not any place he'd ever been, not Chaeronea as he'd known it, nor the valley below the outcrop from which Abarsis had gone to heaven. The sky was all wrong; striated; folded.

"Commander. Can we…?" Niko asked under his breath. He had his hand on his sword. It was clear he wanted permission to engage this enemy.

"Not yet, Niko," Tempus muttered back, spreading the fingers of his right hand to make sure his meaning was understood.

And at that moment Tempus sights a spear arcing toward him that he hadn't seen thrown, which Shamshi must have secreted in the bottom of the chariot's car.

Niko's shield smashed into him. Niko's horse nearly climbed the Trôs, pushing it backward. The spear grazed Tempus's thigh and fell to the ground. This time, Niko had saved him from a long spear aimed at his chest.

*"Now?"* Niko pleads, wanting so much to attack he is nearly crouched upon his horse.

"Now." Tempus draws his shortsword and closes his legs around his mount. His horse leaps forward at a gallop.

Niko's follows. Reins flapping loose, guiding his horse with his knees, Stealth sights his new crossbow. He lets three bolts fly in quick succession from that moving horse. Chancy shots, at best. Impossible ones, for most. But the three quarrels fly true, toward Shamshi, where they can do the most harm, aimed by a hand and an eye that knows just where to strike and how to strike.

And Niko, looking first at Sham, then up into the heavens, looses one more bolt, aiming nearly straight up into the air. Nocks another. Cranks and levers that bolt to ready, fits five more in place, then picks up his reins and steadies his horse. And waits to see his bolts hit home.

'*Use him wisely,*' the Theban goddess had told Tempus. '*Few have been given such a weapon by the gods or Fates before.*' Niko is the weapon that Harmony meant, not his bow or sword.

One of Niko's bolts flies straight toward Shamshi's heart. Sham's shield deflects it. Niko's next two bolts sink deep into that dream-forged shield that Stealth knows so well, lodging between two iron bosses.

Sham screams a wordless war cry, exulting.

Unheeded, Niko's fourth bolt speeds straight down from the sky like divine retribution, to drive deep into Shamshi's chest behind his collarbone.

Tempus can almost feel the cold when iron meets heart, feel strength fleeing out of Sham as once it fled from him. When Stealth's bolt strikes Shamshi, when that iron pierces a beating heart, a pattern deforms. A strangeness in the proportion goes another way. A different heart is pierced; a different fate, foreshortened: Sham's heart, Sham's fate; not Tempus's own.

But Tempus has his own target: Aškelon. He asks his horse for speed and tells it, "Seek." His Trôs knows just what target he means, as they head for Ash's chariot.

Then that horse, his Trôs of god-given strength and skill, is frozen between strides, all four feet off the ground. A dead weight, his horse starts falling forward, to the left.

He needs to get his left leg away from the Trôs's left side before they hit the ground together. Perhaps he can, perhaps he has a chance, because time is so slow for him, the god so deep and alert in him.

Tempus is half astride, pulling his left leg aside, trying to avoid being crushed. This is no time to be crippled, no matter how temporarily.

Horse and man hit the ground together, hard. His left knee takes the force of impact. And then he's crouched, pinned down, half astride the frozen Trôs, the lower part of his left leg caught under the horse's barrel as it rolls and then rolls back. His horse lies there, its eyes wide, lips curled back, mouth agape: not breathing.

This horse has been with him for so long; he loves it like a brother. But there is no time for counting up losses, or the lost. Not yet.

Enlil thunders in his head, *No mercy, avatar, on this battleplain. Get up now. Strike. Strike hard.*

And Tempus replies, *So, god of war and blood and death, have you joined the fray?*

And the god, rustling inside him, doesn't say another word, but looks, and looks, and allows him to get his leg out from under the horse so he can finish what he's started.

*

Niko halts his mount when his commander's horse goes down in the purple haze. He sees Tempus and the Trôs hit the ground. Maybe wounded; maybe killed; but taking an unnatural fall: Aškelon's handiwork, Niko is certain.

He'd gotten separated from the Riddler. Niko had been too focused on Sham, his target. Not paying close enough attention to where Tempus was.

Then he sees his partner move, dragging his left leg out from under the motionless Trôs. Next, Niko hears the chariot reins snap as Ash exhorts his team forward.

The chariot horses begin running down the long, long corridor of frozen fighters toward the Riddler. Aškelon is intent on cutting down the commander. Niko heads his horse that way: to intercept, to pull Tempus up on the big black horse with him, to kill Aškelon's wheel horse or grab its reins – to draw attention to himself and away from his partner.

Sham is holding his bolt-shot neck with one bloody hand, the side of the chariot's car with the other.

The Riddler staggers to his feet and runs with long, limping strides, away from the prostrate Trôs, away from Niko – and toward the moving chariot.

*Toward* the chariot? Three strides, four. Four more. Gaining speed with every step, Tempus closes on that chariot, sword in hand.

Niko halts his horse, mystified. He knows Tempus sees him. The Riddler flashes him a hand-sign. The message is unmistakable: *stay back; stay out of this.*

The hell-wheeled chariot picks up speed, rushing toward the Riddler.

Niko knees his horse that way. Tempus may not want his help yet, but Niko needs to stay close.

Tempus dodges the team, jumping the spinning axle-blades as the chariot nearly runs him down. His commander reaches out, quicker than Niko had thought any man could move, grabbing the car's rim and swinging up, into the chariot as it clatters by.

Niko's horse is running as fast as he can urge it. Even so, he barely has time to get out of the chariot's path.

The chariot is speeding, out of control. With three men aboard, it seems that no one is driving. The car teeters onto one wheel. Then it rights itself while Tempus, Aškelon and Shamshi are all pushing, shoving and struggling for control.

At least Niko is staying out of this, as he's been ordered. So far. He has no choice: if Niko fires his crossbow into the moving chariot with three men so close together, he risks hitting his commander; if he shoots the wheel-horse, the chariot will wreck. He can't ride up close beside the car, or the black's legs will be cut to ribbons. He can't pluck Tempus out of that car unless he can get behind it.

But if he can ride up beside the team and cut them off, turn them inward in a spiral, or grab a bridle, he might be able to stop them. The team is running wild. He tries to position his horse to catch them but they're difficult to predict. He sends his mount one way in the chariot's wake, then the other.

Tempus still struggles with Aškelon in the car. The reins are lost as these two powers wrestle, eye to eye, hand to hand, force to force.

Shamshi, with Niko's quarrel buried in him, is bent over the chariot's rim, trying to grab the reins that dangle too low between team and car. The wizard boy's blood is everywhere but he doesn't seem to notice. Sham leans too far over the chariot's rim – toward the straining haunches of runaway horses, trying to recapture the trailing reins – but doesn't fall.

Niko's mount paces the chariot. Now the team of horses veers in the direction of the Trôs, still lying senseless where the dream lord struck it down. If Niko can get close enough, he can jump from his horse onto the wheel horse. But if he can't stop them, he'll have given up every advantage, horse and shield and weapons. And his commander ordered him to stay out of this. He doesn't try it.

He calls a maneuver code to Tempus: *get out of there; regroup*. His commander doesn't seem to hear, or hears and doesn't heed him.

The wizard boy is nowhere to be seen, hiding low in the car, cannily presenting no target – or already dead.

Niko halts his mount and waits, watchful, flexing his sword hand: that chariot will surely overturn when it hits the prostrate Trôs horse.

Tempus and Aškelon clutch like lovers. They turn together, holding one another close. For an instant, Aškelon's robes obscure Niko's view of the fighting. Then the Riddler's sword arm swings up. And down. Aškelon staggers.

A scream rings out across the battleplain, louder than a man or horse can scream: *Aškelon.*

Holding something in his left hand, Tempus jumps down from the chariot and rolls away just before the team shies to the right: the chariot team swerves sharply, refusing to trample the Trôs horse lying in its path.

The chariot hits a bump and overturns. Screaming, the team breaks free from its traces as Aškelon and Shamshi are thrown high and wide.

Lining that broad, long corridor, every fighter is still frozen in the purple haze: uncomprehending, unseeing; asleep between blinks.

Niko urges his horse forward, toward his commander.

Tempus takes a staggering step, looking back at the overturned car. The dream lord and Shamshi are lying on the ground like rag dolls. Released by whatever force had held it still, the Trôs horse shudders, kicks its legs, rolls onto its belly, and gets to its feet.

So does Aškelon. The dream lord heaves himself upright and staggers in circles on the bloody ground. His robe is dusty, dark with gore. He holds the stump of his left arm where a wrist and hand should be, glaring at Tempus from a face as white as ice.

Niko's partner pays no mind. He's staring at something on the ground, hacking at the dirt with his shortsword.

In another stride, Niko can see what Tempus strikes at, again and again with his sword, as a man might strike a snake: the wrist and left hand of Aškelon of Meridian.

*"You,"* Aškelon howls. "Riddler. You *fool.* You murdering beast. You slave of war," screeches Aškelon to Tempus, who never even looks around. "You have lived too long." Ash's chest is heaving. His face pales and pales. Blood is gushing from his stump as he staggers toward Niko's partner.

Tempus ignores it all: Niko; the team of horses careening into unknowing belligerents and away; the overturned chariot; the dream lord, coming up on him from behind, now howling inarticulately with a rage that makes Niko's soul sore; Shamshi, who should be mortally wounded but is crawling toward the chariot.

The Riddler hacks at the severed wrist and hand of the dream lord with single-minded purpose, as if hacking it to pieces will solve every problem for every man alive.

"Commander?" Niko tries to get his partner's attention, but cannot. He heads his horse toward Sham, to finish him, since his quarrel hadn't. The wizard boy is dragging himself up, trying to get into the chariot, its axle broken and its wheels gone, lying on its side. Sham gets a hand on the car's rim and crawls inside.

The Riddler finally turns to face Aškelon. Ash's left arm flops.

Niko slows his horse to a walk, shortsword in hand; then halts, careful not to distract his commander. Sham can wait.

Tempus says to Ash, "For the fitness of the thing, let's end it with our swords."

"Never," replies the dream lord, and raises his remaining hand, pointing at Tempus.

"As you wish," the Riddler says. From his belt-pouch, he takes the little silver tube and puts it to his mouth. And blows.

Turning to run, Aškelon shrieks as the dart hits home – this second dart, for the second time, in the same spot. He grabs his neck. He drops to his knees. He crumples over in a heap. Blood leaks from his stump, onto the ground and all around. He is moaning, but the moaning has a tune to it – an incantation, a spell, damnation from the lips of the nearly dead.

Then the dream lord drops onto his face like a stone. Shivers. Quivers, with the blood leaking out of him, and seems to shrink the way some corpses do. Aškelon's body deflates, bowels loosening, gas escaping as death sings its humiliating song and the dream lord's flesh is humbled to insensate meat.

Niko catches his commander's eye. Tempus nods once, his kill-smile shadowing the corners of his mouth, the smallest sign of satisfaction. The body of the dream lord doesn't move. Tempus walks over to Aškelon and toes the corpse: once, twice. Then the Riddler strikes it with his sword: he cleaves Aškelon's head from his neck and splits the skull apart. To be certain. The remains of the dream lord don't twitch or shiver.

Relief floods over Niko like ecstasy: the demiurge is but another corpse, bleeding in the grass and dirt; vanquished. Lifeless. Dead.

Tempus goes back to hacking at the amputated wrist and hand in the dirt.

And finally everything else starts moving at life's own pace: horses snorting; dreamers lurching; fighters flailing with their blades, resuming battles interrupted. The space between Niko and Tempus starts to fill with combatants. The purple haze thins, dissipating.

Aškelon's warriors are staggering, dazed, confused. Some are still fighting whomever is closest, friend or foe. Some are fleeing, some disappearing over the hill. Some fade away like ghosts; some, wounded, stagger and fall. Most are wandering, dragging their weapons aimlessly in the grass and dirt.

The Riddler is crouched down over the wrist that wears the bracelet, intent on its destruction, concerned with nothing else.

Then Niko remembers Sham. Sham can't be allowed to get away, crawl away, fade away, drift away.

Niko sheathes his sword and unhooks his crossbow from his saddle, nocking a bolt. The wrecked chariot blocks his way. He reins his horse around it, looking for Sham.

And sees the wizard boy. Shamshi is sitting by the chariot's overturned car, on its far side, in a pool of blood, with a crossbow trained on the Riddler.

If he's noticed at all, Tempus doesn't care: he continues sawing at the Heart of Aškelon on the dream lord's lopped-off wrist.

The bolt behind Sham's collarbone was driven deep; only fletching still protruded. That bolt surely skewered Sham's lung, his heart: that wound should be fatal, should have been by now. Aškelon's smithery might have protected Sham from the quarrel – but didn't. Some strangeness in the proportion, skewing all, had spared the wizard boy so far.

"Sham," Niko says, "it's over."

"Is it? Maybe it will never be over. Look at him." Sham motions with his chin to Tempus, crouched and very still.

Now Tempus stares at Sham and Niko through those hooded eyes. Niko sees the dart tube in his commander's hand and wonders if Sham does. Niko judges the distance from Tempus to Shamshi. It's too far to make that shot with the dart tube, unless you have the wind of the god in your lungs. Not even Tempus will try it.

Sham's helmet was gone, lost or discarded somewhere long ago. A lesser foe would be senseless by now. Not Shamshi. He's bleeding, pale; yet he lives, not even gurgling or gasping for breath.

The wizard boy's gray eyes are fixed on Tempus. His skin seems to pulse. Light crawls over it. His face is distorted, and then it's not. "Just because you killed Aškelon, doesn't mean you can kill me. He was sick, sicker than me. What great glory is there in killing an aged, sick man, noble fighters?" Before Niko can respond, without looking away from the commander, Shamshi adds: "Nikodemos, if you and that horse take one more step toward me, your beloved Riddler dies. I can hear you thinking. Don't think anything I don't like."

"Are you done, Sham?" Niko urges his black horse toward Shamshi, stride by measured stride: one; two; three. He needed to divert the wizard boy's attention from the Riddler. He couldn't let Tempus get hurt again; couldn't let Sham shoot an arrow into the Riddler's heart. Not when that arrow might be deadly, ensorcelled, dangerous beyond even Tempus's power or a god's skill to deflect or heal.

*"Stop right there*, Stealth, or the Riddler dies," grits the wizard boy.

"What do you want, Sham? Honorable battle?" Niko asks, halting his horse and holding it steady, making sure it doesn't walk another step toward Shamshi. "One on one? Man to man? Then get up and face me." Niko's black snorts in agreement. Niko drops his reins. Slipping the shield off his arm, he lets it clatter to the ground, as if he were disarming. "I'll make it easy. I'll get off this horse, and we'll settle this." He takes a chance, sliding off the horse, only his crossbow in his hand. *Look at me, Sham. Look away from him. Look away.* "Didn't they teach you anything on Bandara?" *Please, Sham, try to shoot me. Look away from him. Look away for just one instant. Please....*

"Oh, they taught me." Shamshi never flinches. His crossbow never wavers, aimed at the commander's heart. "And I'm going to teach you what it is to be less than you need to be. It's sad, you know. To try and try and never quite succeed. To find there's always someone smarter, quicker. I can't think of anything better than to kill your beloved commander before your eyes."

Niko had his crossbow's butt balanced against his hip. He needs a clearer shot at Sham than the one he has, but this might be the only shot he can get. He must be precise, because that crossbow in Shamshi's hands needs very little pressure to loose a bolt. Sham's crossbow could trigger at any time: out of anger, instinct, reflex, or a spasm preceding death.

Niko's gaze is fixed on his target. He could see Tempus at the edge of his vision, holding a hand out toward his Trôs horse, coming up whuffling where its master was hunkered down as if nothing in the world were wrong.

The Riddler says, "Stealth, just kill him. You heard him; he wants to be put out of his misery. Now."

*Now.*

Squeezing his trigger, Niko takes the shot, into the spot below Shamshi's ear, where the blood would flow free. And nocks another bolt while Sham's crossbow fires.

Sham's quarrel flies toward Tempus as the Riddler throws himself left with all his god-given speed, and then launches toward Shamshi. The quarrel misses, whizzing by, to strike among a few bewildered fighters still contesting.

Niko dives for Shamshi at the same time his commander does. Because he knew Tempus was going to try to finish Sham and somehow he couldn't let that happen.

Sham was still sitting there, his legs curled under him, holding the fresh wound below his ear and the bolt in it. That shot should have been lethal, should be. The wizard boy, or whatever Shamshi had become, looks dazed. Bright red blood is leaking through his fingers, under his hand. Then Niko's body hits Sham's and everything changes.

As Niko grabs for Sham, Sham grabs back, wrapping around him. The grievously-wounded wizard boy has too many arms and too many legs. His bones are not in the right places. Sham grapples him and tears at him. Or something does. It enfolds him, and everything around goes dark. This something rips at him, at his gut, at his chest, as if he wears no armor.

This is the same thing that he'd battled in front of the Mageguild. If this is Shamshi, or something else, it doesn't matter now: it's here and it isn't as strong as it had been the last time. He'd launched himself at Sham with just his crossbow in his hands. He shoots the ready bolt into the part of the thing pushing against it, then slams up hard with his bow. His assailant shudders. Niko's hands are covered with slimy fluids. The crossbow slips out of his grasp. He can't reach a blade to stab this thing. He keeps trying to get one hand free to draw his shortsword or grab his dagger, but it's impossible.

All he can do is wrestle with something wrapped about him, this thing that has no head to lock his arms around, no arms to wrench from sockets, no pelvis to crack.

It gets hold of him behind his hips and around his neck and it bends him backward. Much more of this, and his own spine is going to snap. He still can't reach his weapons. It's pulling him apart, ripping at his gut.

He remembers where its bones had been the last time. He grabs for what might be a neck, grabs what might be ribs, and pries them apart as hard as he can, with his legs wrapped around something and something wrapped around him.

Then something gives. And something gives up. And gives out.

The thing that once was Sham stops moving. Completely stops. It lies on top of him, motionless.

He needed to move. He wants to move. He wanted to get his arms free. He wants to get to his sword. He wanted to hack this thing to pieces. He wants to shove a blade up in between those ribs and cut out its heart, wherever that might be. He didn't think he was as badly wounded as he'd been last time. Nothing hurt him very much.

But the thing just lay on top of him, heavier than rock. He couldn't see around it. The two of them were alone in some tent of night where it was hard to breathe, impossible to move.

Eventually he hears voices and sees daylight. Tempus and someone else are talking. *Oh, no, not again. Please, not again. Not this again.* He couldn't move, couldn't turn his head. Couldn't feel his fingers, his legs, his feet.

Then hands were on him, and on the thing that had been, or was, Shamshi. Hands lifted the dead weight off him.

Then he could see. Then he could move his head, his arms. He balled his fists, to see if he could. His fingers obeyed him. The Riddler was there. And the Theban goddess was there.

Harmony bent down over him, eyes wide as forever, her hair spilling over her shoulder. "Stealth called Nikodemos, you're fine," she said. "I promised you, you wouldn't be hurt that way again. And you're not hurt. There's a bit of poison in your system. It will pass. You can take my hand. You can get up."

He trusted her. He took her hand, so cool and dry against his slimy one. He sat up. His spine worked. His guts didn't fall into his lap. He stood up. He hurt, but not badly. His back was wrenched. He'd pulled a muscle in his groin. His diaphragm was on fire. His head ached. But he could move every limb. The cuts and bruises and strains he felt were simple battle damage, nothing more, he told himself. Nothing hurt worse now than the axe had hurt when it cut into him, and all that pain had faded as the wound closed, somehow, while he was busy with the battle.

"Thank you," he said to the goddess. On the ground beside her, something flickered in a pool of blood. It seemed to him like a meaty oxhide with something wrapped inside. Then it began to change. First, it was the wizard boy; and then it was a quivering mass of flesh, amorphous, with many arms, red and white like meat and cartilage. Next, it changed its shape to Sham's again and collapsed into dust in the pool of blood. And then the dust absorbed the blood and the bloody dust blew away.

Behind Harmony, the black stallion stood. Niko's shield was on his saddle; someone must have picked it up and hung it there. Around, Stepsons were beginning to gather. He saw Sync, holding the goddess's pregnant sable mare: seeing her made his heart glad. She nickered and peered his way.

He looked from the goddess to his commander and back again to her. "Sham's dead, then?" he asked her. "Turned to dust?"

"Dead, yes. You killed Shamshi, brought him his death. He'll never trouble you again," said the goddess: a promise, a pledge. And he believed her with all his heart when she smiled at him like sunrise.

He turned his head to Tempus once more and his neck hurt so much he caught his breath. When he could, he said, "And Aškelon, Commander?"

"We're free of him. You saw his corpse. I have the Heart of Aškelon," Tempus said. He showed Niko the obsidian bracelet on Ash's amputated wrist. The hand below the wrist and the entire forearm above the bracelet were hacked away. When Niko looked up again, the goddess and the sable mare were gone, but the black horse and his commander still waited.

Without another word, watching him narrowly, Tempus brought him his horse. Niko took the reins and leaned against the black stallion while tremors wracked him, and passed: the horse's warmth chased the cold from his limbs, and he was stronger then. He looked behind him and all around. No vast ranks of fighters still clashed upon the battleplain; no dreaming Macedonians refought Thebans for supremacy in a conflict decided long ago and far away.

But there were corpses everywhere, so many piles of bodies, and the smell of fresh blood upon the breeze. The corpses seem uncountable, men lying as men will when killed in battle, in mid-step or mid-cry, limbs askew or detached. The valley was dotted with fighters lying in clusters or sitting still, while others bent over them with spear or sword to make an end to suffering wherever they could.

From the look of the battlefield, many hours of danger and dying remained: hours of searching for the wounded and dispatching the nearly-dead and trying not to get killed while dispensing mercy. How many dead here? Hundreds.

A reasonable number, considering the odds, the forces arrayed on this battleplain. He felt as if he'd killed that many personally….

But there is no good number, no number low enough when counting up the dead. And when the dead are your dead, no casualty is reasonable.

"How many of ours, dead or wounded?" he called softly to Tempus, who was over by the Trôs, hunkered down beside his horse, feeling its legs for damage from its fall. Niko joined his commander there, his goddess-given black horse following close behind him.

"Casualties? Unclear. Ischade's out there. Crit and Straton haven't come in yet. We'll know when they get back. Lots of Aškelon's forces piled up out there…released to whatever hell or heaven whence the dream lord conscripted them," Tempus said, not looking away from the Trôs's legs.

Niko crouched beside his commander. "Riddler? Is there something more I can do?" He was restless, full of questions: who was hurt; who was dead? On the far side of battle, he was always filled with nervous energy: there is always so much left unsaid and so many lessons to be learned.

"Crit knows what to do. Rest a moment, Niko. Stay here with me." And without looking at him, Tempus reached out and squeezed his arm. "This was as hard a battle as any man has fought. Ever." His voice rattled. "A battle that men who don't go to war will sing about for generations. It's good to have it behind us. It's good your goddess came along," added Tempus, very low. "Now we pull all of ours together and see what's left to us. The sun is new each day. On the other side of Meridian and the dream lord and Shamshi, everything begins again. Look around: this is our valley, not theirs. We'll claim it and use it. For Abarsis. For our dead, when we can name them. For ourselves. And for the Band, for many years to come."

*

And so they began anew, in the valley below the overlook where Abarsis had gone to heaven on smoke and flame. In the late afternoon light, the valley looked nothing like Chaeronea. No campfires gleamed from the heather-covered slopes or from the valley floor or from a hill away, or the valleys behind that. Sage and white roses with golden eyes glowed softly on the hillsides. The purple haze was gone.

Niko asked Tempus, "The war we won, the battle we fought…did we fight it in Meridian?" He stood up. The Riddler stood up too. Both of them had taken wounds. Both were healed. Injuries gone as if they'd never been. From this last clash with the wizard boy, Niko had no rips or tears, no ruined flesh. His body now fares better than his armor. Probing in the dusk, he rubbed his right hip and found only a scabby scratch. No cut remained where he'd sustained a bloody slice down hip and thigh from a berserker with an axe. He rubbed his right arm where an arrow had lodged. He found no puncture. Tempus looked at him and shook his head, just long eyes and a flash of teeth in the deepening dark: *Trust in heaven. We heal. Don't question it.* So he doesn't: "How could Meridian be here, Riddler?"

"Ischade says," Tempus answered him, "that this time, the Chaeronean battleplain was in Meridian, but that Meridian was manifesting here, today." Tempus shrugged massive shoulders. "We fought a glorious battle in a real place and time: in this valley on this day. Call it Chaeronea or Meridian or Sanctuary, it makes no difference. Men really died. Fates were really decided. We really triumphed over the dream lord and the wizard boy. I think I've told you before: things I can feel and touch and see, these do I prefer."

Tempus swung up on the big Trôs, and Niko on his new black horse.

Niko could feel the sweet wind in his hair; stroke his horse's muscled neck; see the day give way to spangled splendor above their heads. His commander was right: nothing could compare to riding together through the last of the daylight on their horses as wolves called prayers to the moon and owls began their hunt and peepers and crickets praised this world the gods had made.

Men are fools who forget what really matters while time goes by.

They rode over to watch the Sacred Band of Stepsons and the 3rd Commando putting their casualties and walking wounded in wagons. The sunset was raying out like Enlil's crown and the clouds blazed pink and blue and gold. They stayed there together, unspeaking, until dusk covered the heather and the men and the horses. Then Niko asked, "Are you content, Commander?"

Tempus looked at him sidelong and said, "Niko, this was a test we all had to pass, not just you. Character is destiny. The gods fought at our sides and something very evil, of very long standing, has been vanquished. Perhaps the Fates are no longer angry. Perhaps even Sanctuary can come aright, now that this is done."

"That hellhole?" Niko grinned at the thought. "If it came aright, it wouldn't be Sanctuary."

"Did you see Randal?" Tempus asked. "He brought us the Third, without whom we might not have fared so well. That little mage may have saved the day. He deserves your thanks. So does Jihan. And so does Ischade."

That brought them back to casualties. They wouldn't know, for sure, until they got everybody home. Not until they'd called the roll, praised the valiant, tended the injured, mourned the dead. Niko knew the drill. Fog of war, hard to dispel. Shock and numbness, wearing away, leaving dead and wounded, maimed and ruined, and all the enduring questions. How well did we fight? What did we do right? What did we do wrong? How do we do better next time? And dealing with those for whom there would be no next time; and with their loved ones, every stricken soul. The hardest part in the days, weeks, and months to come was always reckoning the loss.

Everyone must come to terms with sorrow, while fighters recalled what love is worth and what price there is for freedom. Until the next battle raged, and men used the lessons they'd learned here to fight on other days.

Too soon, Crit came riding up, voice sharp and anxious, on his wall-eyed chestnut. "Commander? Straton's pretty badly hurt. We can't find Randal or Jihan."

"Get Ischade," Tempus ordered. "And *don't* argue with me."

*Strat.* Niko felt the news like a slap across the face.

Ischade was already there when he and Tempus found the wagon in which Straton lay. Dusk was fading into deep blue night, torches flaring all across the valley.

Straton didn't move or speak, lying with his eyes closed among the other badly wounded, some moaning and groaning in the crowded wagon.

"Get back," Ischade hissed, eyes afloat and furious, bent over her mortal lover. "I will see to him. Just go away. He'll be well in time for your next bloodbath. I don't need any help from you."

Niko couldn't see what wound she was treating, but her tone was preemptive.

Tempus took Niko by the arm and led him away from the witch and Critias, whose face was so tired and concerned in the torchlight. “If Ischade can’t see him right,” Tempus said, “then he’s deader than the dream lord and the wizard boy. There’ll be more to tend. This wasn’t easy for anyone.”

“What do you mean, ‘deader’?” He needed to know. He didn’t want to worry about Aškelon rearing up in his dreams or Shamshi sneaking into his rest-place.

“Relax, Niko. You killed Shamshi. Believe your body’s knowledge. The wizard boy won’t trouble us again. Trust me. Trust your goddess. I’ve done this all before, too often. As for Aškelon …without the bracelet called the Heart of Aškelon, the dream lord can’t survive death, or be revived. The dart’s poison alone would have killed both of them eventually, if we could have waited.”

*But Aškelon and Shamshi wouldn’t wait. And how many more would have died, if we had waited?*

“Wait? I couldn’t wait any longer,” Niko said. “And let them keep picking us off and roast our horses and make everyone’s life an endless nightmare? I believe you. I believe Harmony. I believe that Shamshi’s dead and gone. But I remember what Abarsis said, that we shouldn’t trust in what we saw. I need you to tell me that the dream lord’s really dead. As dead as dead can be.”

“He is. I promise, Niko, when I get back from Lemuria, it will be as you want it. Both our enemies, destroyed for all time.”

Something in him took a breath, let down a notch. The dream lord and the wizard boy were truly vanquished. His commander had looked him in the eye and told him so.

They walked their horses back up the slope. Somewhere to the west, lightning hopped from cloud to cloud. Thunder chased it inland.

"Storm coming," Niko said, eyeing the sky.

"There always is," the Riddler answered.

When they reached the top of the overlook, Tempus mounted his Trôs and said, "Your goddess will want to see you, when you have the time."

The Theban goddess was gone again. "Commander, did her Thebans fare well…?"

*"Our* Thebans," Tempus corrected. "We need to count heads and wounds and see what our damage is. Your goddess stayed there on the field with her fighters – with our fighters. She was there for them. She was there for you."

Niko got on the big black horse. "Yes, she was there for me." And there for this horse, as well, unscathed now despite so much skirmishing in close quarters. Niko knew Tempus had seen the axe slice the black horse in the chest.

The black stud jigged along, settling in on the Trôs's right side as if he'd always been there. They had many wounded to tend, but they would manage.

"Life to you, Tempus, and everlasting glory," Niko said under his breath, thankful for all he'd learned and all he'd become on this warm summer night, with the deadliest battle of his life behind him.

"What?" Tempus asked, shifting in his saddle.

"I said, we have a lot to do before morning," Niko answered.

And the Riddler agreed.

## *Chapter 44: All Fall Down*

Stormbringer, the Unbegotten, god of wind and wave, searches Sanctuary with a hurricane eye for his Froth Daughter. North and east he blows inland, whirling and swirling his arms to rile the sea and scrape the land. In a pinwheel of storm he rolls past the jetty and swamps the lighthouse spit where a goddess once stood and grappled with a god in the sight of man.

He is the father of all weather gods; no force on earth can withstand his might. His maelstrom arms spread out over Sanctuary, chasing lesser gods and their thunder and lightning before him. He wails around the palace, affrighting priests and oligarchs, absorbing the wrath of storm gods into his more perfect storm. But his daughter isn't there. He rattles windows and batters doors across the city, where two young girls (one whore and one sorcerer's apprentice) hug each other and beg destiny to spare them and their beloved fighters of the Sacred Band.

He spirals outward, lifting roofs in the Maze and tents in the market, looking for his daughter in vain. He finds only an aging seeress, crying for her son (who is fighting for his life in an arcane war she cannot understand) while her brother holds her hand.

His hurricane floods a dockside warehouse full of incendiaries, setting naphtha fire-bottles afloat and sucking them out to sea. The hurricane flattens the gutted Mageguild, stone from off of stone, and tarries there, looking all around Sanctuary through one baleful eye, washing any taint of sorcery away.

Up the White Foal River the tempest howls and whistles, smashing trees and throwing boulders in its indignation, looking for Jihan, leaving devastation in its wake.

Inland roars the hurricane, until it reaches the barracks of the Sacred Band, where it settles with its one great eye.

Here Stormbringer spies the Stepsons, the Theban fighters, and the 3rd Commando, attending to their own. In the face of such unflinching determination and unswerving devotion, the hurricane pauses and calms. Its ravings turn to mutters.

Stormbringer looks, and looks, and looks there for Jihan, keening a sad song. His long arms wash every bit of blood and gore from an infernal battleplain as he goes, leaving only heather and sage and roses climbing its grassy slopes.

At last he finds her, froth and water sunk into the valley ground. Stormbringer rains down harder, to wash his daughter to the river and out to sea where he can retrieve her on another day, another way. For something else is coming, with powers that not even an Unbegotten can sway.

Critias watches the storm's eye from the doorway of the barracks mess hall where their wounded lie. Above his head is blue sky, clouds tinged with pink and cream, like a hole right through to heaven in the heart of this dispersing gale. Around the barracks yard are downed tree limbs and branches and a spattering of puddles.

Time for Crit to report to the Riddler. He hardly has the heart for it. Straton lingers close to death from a barbed arrow that hooked between his lowest ribs. His partner hasn't rallied, despite all Crit would allow Ischade to do since last night at dusk. Now dusk is nearly here once more and Strat still worsens. Wherever he looks, Critias sees Strat's big, broad face crinkled in a smile.

The hurricane continues to abate in heaven, but not in Critias's heart, still spinning with anger and grief. They had fought as good a fight as men can, against killing odds.

The Riddler comes to visit the wounded, Stealth at his side, when day is nearly done. Niko has a scabby scratch on his left thigh, a few bruises yellowing too soon on his arms – and that's all. Lucky, with all the fighting he'd done. Stepsons were whispering about a strange confrontation between Stealth and Shamshi...and maybe with something else. No one quite saw the fight between Niko and Sham, or between the Riddler and Aškelon, but many remember snippets, as if from a dream. The Riddler shows neither wound nor bruise, after battling Aškelon to the death. He has healed from whatever wounds he took.

If only there hadn't been so many enemies, if only the Band could have held formation, there'd be a different tale to tell today about dead and wounded. Even with the 3rd Commando reinforcing them, this fight took a horrendous toll. But things are as they are.

"Crit," says Tempus, here to hear who's dead and who's dying, "how are they?"

Behind Crit in the mess hall, the wounded and the dead lie with just enough room to step in between and tend the one or say farewell to the other. This mess hall, the largest single room in the barracks, is now a hospital and morgue. They had nowhere else big enough for everyone. The weather was too bad to leave bodies outside and no one wanted to put bleeding men in the half-reconstructed stables. They didn't have enough beds and stalls for men and horses as it was.

*Just say it, straight out.* The Riddler wouldn't want it any other way.

"How are they? Or how's Strat? Strat may not make it. Ischade says she's done her best." The words came out of Crit's mouth as if someone else were speaking. Crit wants a way out of this nightmare, into a world where Ischade is not a fact of life among the Stepsons, where Straton is happily cursing by Vashanka's third and hairiest ball or Enlil's prong. But he doesn't know how to make that happen. "Our Stepson Epani is critical: his intestines are dirty and torn and he doesn't have enough uncorrupted flesh for us to sew him up. The Theban Sciron, Gorgias's rightman, has fluid in his lungs from internal injuries: he was run over by those two chariot horses. He may not make it through the night. Arton has a spear wound in his right side and a slash wound across his kidney," Crit says flatly.

"What else?" asks the Riddler as Crit makes room for the commander and Stealth to come inside. Niko puts one hand on the lintel and doesn't say a word, surveying the nineteen badly wounded and twelve dead covered with linen in ranks on the floor. Damned hurricane, keeping the dead indoors. Crit needed the room those bodies were taking up.

Before Crit can answer the commander, Niko asks, so low Crit leans forward to hear, "Casualties? How many missing? Dead? Unfit for duty?"

Crit sighs and replies, "Casualties – Stepson, Theban and 3rd Commando: sixty-one wounded, missing and dead. Jihan and Randal and six others are still missing. As for the known dead, we lost seven Third Commando fighters; three of our new hires; one veteran Stepson – Epani's partner, Zitos; one Theban, Simon of Athens. Simias has the list of the known dead; I'll add to it in the morning. We expect fourteen to seventeen dead, all told. We have twenty-two walking wounded and nineteen seriously injured. With those and the twelve burn cases we're still treating from the barracks fire, we're fairly busy. Simias and Perses, Gayle and Cassander are helping me here."

Niko raises his head at that, watching gray-haired Simias and Perses, the young poet, working on someone at the other end of the long room.

Then he shifts and whispers in the Riddler's ear. Tempus listens, takes one step toward Crit and says, "Niko thinks you should ask the goddess for help with Strat."

"I'm not Theban," Crit rejoins, his skin crawling. "Stealth, don't you to talk to me anymore?"

Nikodemos is silhouetted in the doorway, before a striated twilight of gilded mares' tails falling into a deep blue night. He takes his hand from the lintel. "Fox, it's not up to me to tell a Stepson sworn to Enlil that he should ask help from any but our tutelary god. But...losing Strat...." Niko spreads his arms and drops his hands to his sides. "I shouldn't have suggested it. *You'd* have to ask her. Pay her respect. I can't do it for you."

"And you agree with him, Commander? Just stroll up to this Harmony's altar and ask the Theban goddess to save *our* nearly dead?" Crit had almost said 'to the altar of Niko's goddess.' But he'd stopped himself in time.

Tempus doesn't answer.

Stealth rummages through Crit's soul with those disturbing eyes. "Fox, we're *one* Sacred Band. *I'd* try it, if I were Strat's partner. If it were the commander, lying there. I'd try whatever might save him, no matter how small the chance." Niko shrugged. "I need to see Arton." And Stealth slid by him, weaving among the bodies on the floor until he found the young seer. He crouched down there, elbows on his knees. Arton raised his head.

Tempus, unspeaking, mouth drawn tight, was watching Crit closely.

"You think this will work, Commander? You think I should? Are *you* suggesting that I ask a foreign goddess, rather than Enlil, for help?" Tempus hadn't said that – only said that Niko thought Critias should petition Harmony for aid.

"I have no objection, Crit. We would ask her for you, if we could. Niko thinks it's you who must ask for Strat's life. If you do ask the goddess, nothing about your status here will change. You'll still be ranked the same, respected the same. No one will think less of you. Enlil grants few wishes but for war."

The Riddler left him and went among the wounded, stopping to speak to each injured man in turn, bending down, touching this one's shoulder, that one's arm, until he got to Strat. And there he stayed, till Critias had to join him or look a fool.

"Whatever you need to do or need to say," said Tempus when Crit hunkered down beside him, "you'd best do it now. There's not much time."

Straton's face was pale, his forehead shining with sweat. His eyelids looked bruised, eyes roaming under them. His breath was bubbly, too ragged. "I knew he shouldn't come back here," Crit whispered. He leaned down over his partner and murmured in Straton's ear, "Strat, just hold on. Please hold on." Then, to Tempus: "Will you…can you stay with him till I return?"

Tempus nodded, putting the back of his hand against Straton's brow.

So now Crit has a last resort, one final chance to save the best man he's ever known. Out into the strange yellow light that the hurricane has left behind and up the soggy hill Crit goes, jogging, to the altar of the foreign goddess. When he gets there, he's breathing hard. It's his heart breaking that is making his lungs ache. He knows what grief can do. You can't blame the necromant. She tried. Too much blood was lost inside Straton and too much lost on the ground.

No time now for wondering how things might have been or wondering why he had let Strat come here when he'd known better. He feels as if his body is another's as he kneels down before the white altar stones of this goddess from afar.

He says quietly through clumsy lips, "I am Critias. I pay you respect and honor, Goddess. Please save my Sacred Band partner, Straton, the Stepson. We fought for you and yours, twice. He'll have laid down his life for you and yours, if you can't help him." And then he couldn't talk. His eyes were blurry. He balled his fists and stayed there, on his knees, wondering if anything was going to happen. How long he should wait here while his partner is dying?

After a dozen breaths, no goddess appears. Nothing happens.

Crit's never been one for prayer, or celestial last resorts. He gets up and trudges down the hill. He tries to think what he'll do without Straton, how his days will go. What is it like, without the person who is always beside you? Why do you strive on, all alone? He tries to think of the words he must say, when Strat is on the pyre. How do you praise a life of so much valor, so much sacrifice, so much service? How many lives had Straton saved in his career? How many fates had he changed for the better?

When Crit reached the barracks mess hall, he couldn't go inside. There was no rain around him, to hide the tracks of tears on his face. He stood beside the door, trying to compose himself, unball his fists, calm his racing heart.

When he could, he pushed open the door.

Tempus was still with Straton. Niko was nowhere to be seen. And then he did see Niko, his back to Crit, over in the corner, talking to someone. It was all Critias could do to walk calmly to the commander's side. He knelt down beside his partner.

"How is he?" Crit asked hopelessly. Miracles weren't for men like him and Strat.

The Riddler said, "Look for yourself," and rocked back on his haunches.

Straton's eyes were open. *He's dead,* Crit thought. *Died while I wasn't here. Died while I was wasting time up at that Theban altar. Fool, Critias.*

But then Strat's eyes focused, moved and caught his own. There were footsteps behind him. Crit didn't look around. He didn't look at the Riddler. He couldn't. Strat shifted and his hand came out from under the blanket. Crit wished he hadn't put Strat on this hard floor, but couldn't do differently for Straton than for any other Stepson, though he'd wanted to put Strat in his own bed, so badly.

Crit took Strat's hand and whispered, "Life to you, Straton, and everlasting glory." He was sure he'd never be able to say that again – that Strat would never be able to hear him say it again. He almost couldn't speak the words. Strat's hand was cold and dry. After Strat died, Crit promised himself, he would never pair again. Ever.

Strat sucked a rattling breath and said, "Critias? Riddler? What in…" Strat looked over Crit's shoulder and said, "Stealth?" Strat struggled to sit up. Crit tried to push him back, but Tempus was quicker.

"Stay down, Ace, for a bit," the commander said, and got up. "You need to rest. You lost a lot of blood." Then he added, craning his neck, "Thank you, Harmony."

And a woman's voice behind Crit said, "Critias asked me for help to save his partner. It was fitting to help a worthy soul who labored in our cause."

Strat said, *"What?"* Straton's color was better. His eyes fixed on Crit, and held. "You did *what?* Where's Ischade?"

"Ischade couldn't do this, not without letting you die first and then bringing you back to life." Crit's voice was too sharp. Heads turned in the makeshift infirmary. Nevertheless, this had to be said. Now he whispered: "We all remember Janni. I knew you wouldn't want that, so I forbade it." There, now they all knew. Crit let go of Strat's hand and turned, still on his knees, to face Harmony. The Theban goddess, armored in black, was standing beside Niko. "I thank you, Goddess, for Strat's sake and my own." His voice came out too thick, too choked. He hated deific intervention. Very unprofessional, begging help from heaven, for a man in his position. But then, his position at this moment was one of being immensely relieved, on his knees before a foreign goddess. He started to rise.

"Stay with your partner. Your thanks are clearly in your heart and in your soul," said the goddess in a voice like a breeze through the trees in summer. "And thank Stealth called Nikodemos, and your commander, for making such blessings possible." Crit smelled a meadow. He looked back at Strat, and then to the goddess once again, but she was gone.

Tempus said, "I need to go hunting for Jihan and Randal and the rest of the missing. Straton, you stay there until Crit gives you leave to move."

Niko said, "I'll go with you."

Straton said, "By Enlil's third and mightiest ball, what was all that about?" and tried to sit up.

So Critias now must tell Straton about things Crit himself doesn't understand. About Ischade. About Niko's goddess.

But before he began, he said crisply, “You know, Strat, you never told me who gets the ghost horse if you die before me. Or anything else of yours, for that matter.” He couldn’t let Strat see how shaken he had been, how terrified for his partner’s life…and for his own life, if Straton were no longer in it.

And Straton, his sworn partner whom he loved above all other men, said, “The ghost horse? All that bay horse wants is to ride forever. Ride him as long as you’re able, if you like, and then give him to the Riddler. He’s a great horse for a fighter who’s always in the thick of battle. Of all around you, man or horse, you can on count on him never to let you down.” Straton’s voice dwindles to a whisper, exhausted, shaky. “All I own is yours...like my life.” Then Strat’s expression holds him tight, desperately, as the looks of men retreating from death’s door sometimes can. Insisting on strength. Hungry for days. Grabbing a future he can’t let slip away. There in that mess hall, among the hurt and dying, Straton’s face says so much more: about loyalty and respect and honor; about life and love of partner and commitment greater than death can break; things that can’t be said aloud between these two – so senior, so cold, so bold – but that both men understand.

*

The Stepson Epani joined his dead partner at moonrise. That made thirteen dead, eighteen seriously wounded, eight missing. Such adding and subtracting made Charon’s heart sore. Epani’s wounds, sustained in the campaign against Aškelon, brought such agony to the hardened Stepson that he moaned and cried fearfully before he died. To Charon, his death seemed a blessing. Blessings come in all colors, all sizes, and all shapes.

Sciron, a Theban hero who had fought beside Gorgias for nine years, died soon after: Run over by a pair of chariot horses he swore he never saw coming. No other Theban remembers the chariot wreck, either. Sciron didn't even remember being trampled. It's the sort of thing a man remembers, whether he is watching runaways come on or running from pounding hooves. Fourteen dead, seventeen badly wounded now.

Charon must convince his son, Lysis, Blessed of Harmony, to leave Arton's side for a while. Thanks must be given to the goddess. Prayers must be said. So Charon walks through the softly moaning wounded and the silent dead, to where his son sits beside his injured partner.

It would have been better if Lysis had a Theban partner, but the Riddler has done this. This Sacred Band fights differently, in arcane combat against enemies who are beyond the ken of Thebans. Or were, until Harmony had appeared to them on the first Chaeronean battleplain, and then salvation had come with a flight into a shimmer and a glimmer and a maelstrom and a citadel...and out again, to this unnatural Sanctuary.

Careful not to kick or bump the wounded on either side, Charon knelt down beside his son. Lysis said, "Father, Arton saved me, you know. Came riding up, telling me if I rode another step I'd die, right then. And took a sword-cut meant for me."

"You can't know that," Charon objected, and then regretted it. Lysis was the Blessed One and his partner – so severely wounded, so pale, so wan – was a seer, men said. "But perhaps you're right. Arton, thank you for saving my son," he said gravely, while his heart said that only the goddess deserved his thanks.

Arton peered up at him as if from another world and said, "Fighters find their way to heaven. Sanctuary lies on the border between mortality and immortality. I see it. You must see it now, Thebans." His voice was scratchy, thin. If Arton had been a woman, Charon would be sure he was hearing an oracle pronounce a prophecy.

"You're *not* going to die of this," Lysis said determinedly to Arton. "You're not. Stealth said."

"Come, Lysis," said Charon. "Let your partner rest. You have horses to treat in the stables. Sync was asking for you."

"Arton, I will pray for you," Lysis promised as he arose and followed his father to the door. "We all will."

Critias, leaning in the doorway, made way, acknowledging them with a wave of his hand and a haunted look as they went by.

When they were alone, Charon said, "Our goddess is here with us. Don't burden her with the lives of these unbelievers. We need all the help *we* can get. We have our own wounded and dead for the pyres. Sciron died tonight. Gorgias will be bereft. You pray for them. And thank her that you have only these few cuts and bruises."

Lysis wouldn't meet Charon's eyes as they headed to the stables to see Sync.

*Our goddess is with us.* Men whispered that she saved the Stepson, Straton. Some wondered how this could be if she hadn't saved her own Simon of Athens, who'd died next to the ghost of Theagenes, after they found their brothers from the Sacred Band of Thebes on the second Chaeronean battleplain. And now Sciron, too, was dead.

Charon was neither a vengeful man nor a stingy one, but blessings from a goddess are precious. He needs all her help to shepherd his own through this impious land. He had been afraid, when he first saw Theagenes, that the Theban dead would avenge themselves upon the forty-six of his who'd been led away by the Riddler. But Theagenes himself had arranged for their salvation. And the goddess had agreed.

And now here they are, the remaining forty-two of the Theban Sacred Band, at Harmony's bidding, led by a warrior-philosopher of obscure nature, whose partner is a warrior-monk and favored of Harmony. Blessed be Harmony, for the Thebans had lost as few as any squadron in the battle.

Charon watches his son out of the corner of his eye in the moonlight. None of this numinosity bothers Lysis, whom the goddess loves. Charon is proud of his son, but he is homesick tonight for the seven gates of Thebes and a world he'll never see again. Anyone would be, after fighting twice on the Chaeronean plain. Or was it only that Charon was not young, not adaptable, not like his son, who took everything in stride?

When they found Sync in the east in-line barn, Kouras was there with him.

"Life to you, Kouras, and everlasting glory," Lysis called out before they reached the other two, who were leaning together over a half-door. "And to you, Sync."

*Yes, my son is fitting in among these fighters.*

Stepson greetings rang out to both of them in the quiet stable, where horses munched their evening meals contentedly, proving all was well on earth and in heaven for one more night.

"Come here and look at these two mares, Lysis," called Sync, who had cheesecloth swathing his right arm above the elbow and a long gash on his right cheek.

When they got there, Kouras said, "Lysis, Sync says if we break them to saddle, we can ride them." He pointed toward one stall, and then the next. "I want this one. You take the other."

"They belong to the Band, not to you," Sync warned, and looked slyly at Charon. "You two need to remember that. We lost our other sables. These are the Aškelonians that pulled the dream lord's chariot in battle."

"So won't the Riddler kill them?" asked Lysis. "Since they were bred by Aškelon?"

"We don't kill horses," said Sync sternly. "We breed them. Aškelon is dead. It's not these horses' fault, whose barn they were born into. Kouras, you'll be responsible for the mare you like. Lysis, you'll care for the other."

Lysis ran to Kouras and the two young fighters put their heads together. Sync came over to Charon. "Your son has a talent for horse-breaking. When you see what he does with this filly, you'll be proud."

"I'm already proud." Charon and Sync watched the youths. Kouras showed not a single scratch from battle. Charon's son had war wounds sewn and dressed on his left leg and along his right side.

"Is there something else you want to say, Charon?" Sync asked. Sync's 3rd Commando had been called by the Riddler to join the fight, and nearly three hundred of them had come from far Lemuria. They'd lost the most fighters of any unit in the battle. Yet Sync seemed unfazed.

"Lysis and I are going up to the altars, to pray for the wounded and the dead. You have many of both. Can we say prayers for yours?"

The dark horse-tamer, rangy and angular, leaned back against a stall wall and said, "If you wish. But listen, first. You're new to this cohort. Let me tell you what it means to me. It's an honor to fight where the Riddler fights. I always know I'm on the right side. Doing more than other men can do. Sometimes you think it's more than you can do. Sometimes it is. He knows us, what we all are and what we all do.

He puts us where we matter. We say, 'It's better to die for something than for nothing at all.' If you don't believe in the commander yet, believe in that. You'll fight battles others only dream of, find honor and glory most profound – not for some ruler, or town, or city, but for all men. The Riddler says you make the world better one battle at a time. There is no harder life. There is no better one, for men with a certain bent of mind and body, heart and soul."

"I understand," said Charon.

The horse-tamer, seeing that Charon had some dressed gashes on his right side, clapped him on his left arm, smiling crookedly around the slice on his face. "You've brought new blood we're all going to be proud to call Stepsons in this greater Sacred Band. Give thanks for that, when you're at your altar."

And Sync floated away, another hero among the many collected here, to help the youths and teach them what he could.

When Charon and Lysis finally got to the altar of Harmony, the best of his Thebans were all there, clustered on their goddess's consecrated ground: Gorgias, newly bereft, dark of skin and hair with his craggy face remade by war; Agis, swarthy and bearded and Archias, his blond, square-faced partner; Simias, their gray-bearded intellectual and Perses, the lithe young poet with his dark curls. In the moonlight, bandages on each man seemed to glow. Gorgias was sitting cross-legged, playing a song to the goddess on his flute.

All of these would live to fight on other days. Charon, with his son by his side, felt truly grateful. In the miasmic battle, when he had found Theagenes and the fated Sacred Band of Thebes, two hundred and fifty-four doomed fighters, all he could think was how terrible it was, that these would fight again, and meet their fate again, without hope of reprieve.

But now he saw all of his, alive and well, with offerings of oil and bread and wine to give their goddess, while the flute played softly and insects kept the time, and he knew better. He knew that a great blessing, at a great cost, had been given to them by their goddess Harmony and by the Riddler, and Nikodemos, and the Sacred Band of Stepsons: to have a chance at life; to fight on other days; to carry on; to have some left who remember.

And he remembered Tempus saying this to Theagenes, so long ago on that first battleplain of Chaeronea, the night before the massacre. And his beloved Theagenes had agreed. Theagenes and Tempus had come to terms, while the Riddler and Stealth had stood in that dream-forged chariot and Critias and Straton held the chariot horses by their bits. He hadn't understood it then. Now, finally, he thought he did. Wanting neither too much to live nor too much to die, he sat with his son and the best of his Thebans, and they recalled their dead, every one, and their living, wounded or hale, and prayed to the goddess to grant them grace in the days and battles to come.

And if Lysis, the Blessed One, had the audacity to ask Harmony to heal and preserve his Stepson partner, Arton, then all the older men forgave the youth. For the young believe that anything is possible, if only a mortal soul will be just and true and have faith.

*

In the wake of the hurricane, Tempus and Niko hunted up and down the valley, everywhere they could, in search of the missing and any dead they'd overlooked. They didn't find Randal. They didn't find Jihan. They found no other bodies or wounded, no matter how hard they searched. There had to be some. They had other fighters missing in action. Sometimes men wander off, get lost, forget themselves for a time if they are hurt badly enough or stressed highly enough. The fog of war still hung over the Sacred Band, and would until their dead were put to rest. Finally, for one night, even Tempus had searched enough.

They came back to the barracks before daybreak. But the commander was restless, cleaning his weapons. The sound of his whetstone came too fast, too angrily. Niko knew the Riddler well enough to know that Tempus had something weighing on his mind.

"What is it, Commander? Can I help?"

Tempus's face was turned away. "You've been wanting to see your goddess, Niko. She invited you. Go now, before the rites. I'm going to Lemuria to visit with Cime. I need to give her the Heart of Aškelon. Then this is done. Until I do, it's not. I'll be back before the ceremonies."

Tempus showed him the bracelet with its obsidian center. Not anything the Riddler could do would pulverize that volcanic glass, or crack it. He let Niko try his hand at demolishing it. The obsidian stayed as it was, even when they put it in a vise and hacked at it with Tempus's god-given sword.

He wanted to go with thc Riddler, but Niko would not be welcomed by Cime and he didn't want to force Tempus to say so. The commander rode out on his Trôs stallion soon after. When the gates closed behind Tempus in the dawn, the barracks seemed too empty, despite all the heroes crowded in there – the wounded, the dead, and the unscathed.

So it happened that Niko had this time alone, a few hours uncommitted. Critias must have had orders from the commander, because Crit chased him away, saying all preparations for the rites were ongoing, and Stealth would only be underfoot.

When he started toward Sanctuary at midmorning, he thought he'd hunt further for Jihan and Randal. Perhaps they'd found one another and were struggling to get home. He tried this valley and that hill and the other field, but no Stepsons or Sacred Banders or Froth Daughter or Hazard-class mage could he find. His search took him to the General's Road, where he'd found his mare.

The air was full of birdsong, bright and clear. The skies above were washed clean, sparkling. When he finally admitted to himself that he was seeking out the goddess, he was afraid he'd never again find that white house, down some elusive, winding path off the General's Road.

The goddess must live somewhere near here. Mustn't she? The house with its fluted columns must be here somewhere. Mustn't it?

Niko and the black made good time, headed south. This horse healed like no other, worked like no other, had stamina like no horse he'd ever had between his legs. Its mouth was soft, its eyes were fiery, and it had gaits to please a god.

So when he reined it to the right along the General's Road and it refused, he was surprised. He tried again. It wouldn't follow the road. It wanted to take a fork he didn't recall. Finally, when he was about to get off to see if it had picked up a stone or hurt itself some other way, it turned its head toward him with an arch and reproachful look and bit his left boot.

He thumped its muzzle. It let go. But then he thought that the black horse might know the way to its mistress's house. Perhaps the horse was correct and he was wrong: the stallion clearly wanted to go to the left.

He loosed the reins and gave the horse its head. And the black trotted happily down the road's left fork, past abandoned farms and fields that looked increasingly familiar, until it came to a sheltered lane where bushes with white blooms grew high on either side.

When the horse turned in and started down the lane, Niko looked up. Above his head, leafy trees made a pergola against a sky of cornflower blue. A twist, a turn, and they came upon a big white house.

It seemed to be the same house as before, or one just like it, set back from a circular drive strewn with pebbles. He slid off the horse. He didn't remember the pebbles from the last time he was here, but that day he'd cared only about reclaiming his mare from the woman astride her, who'd led him here.

He hesitated. As he looked around, a grizzled man came from behind the house and walked toward him, whistling under his breath, dark hand held out to take his horse's reins.

He shouldn't give up his horse until he knew if he had the right house. He couldn't knock on the door from where he stood with his mount. The windows, so tall, so wide, were curtained. He couldn't see in; no one could see out.

The dark man had long curly hair. Yellow teeth peeked through his lips as he waited to take the horse.

"I've come to see your mistress," Niko said. It sounded foolish. Of course that was why he'd come. The grizzled man made no reply.

Just then the tall front doors opened and out she came, onto her porch. Had there been only one door, the last time he was here? Now there were two doors, open wide between soaring columns supporting a pediment.

Harmony stood there under the pediment in a lavender linen dress, pinned at the shoulders, draping softly around her. A breeze stirred long honey-colored hair. She said, "I was hoping you would come today, Stealth called Nikodemos," and held out her hand.

He must have given up his reins. He must have climbed the stairs. He took the hand she offered him. Then he was inside the house and cool shadows played a game with sunlight on its white, bright walls. Rooms opened off a hallway flagged with limestone. He couldn't recall if he'd been in here before. It didn't matter. He had her hand in his. Her hair swayed back and forth across her hips as she led him through halls and up stairs, to a room he remembered.

She said, "I hope you didn't come just to see your mare," as the door closed behind them and he leaned back upon it. Everywhere was the sweet smell of meadow. A summer breeze caressed the curtains.

He was dirty and sweaty and he wore his work panoply. He said, "I came because you said I could...."

"Oh, you can, Niko. You can," she said.

He was hesitant. He didn't want to do the wrong thing. He didn't want to assume anything. But there was a bed in this room. She'd brought him up here, in here.

He started to take off his cuirass. She watched him and he watched her and eternity stretched before him in those amber eyes.

He asked, taking off his work belt (with its sword that surely shouldn't be here), "Am I...always going to heal? As I did in this battle?" His shortsword and belt hit the floor. His cuirass followed.

She asked, "How long is always?" Now the goddess was close to him, so close he could reach out and touch her white skin, her silken hair, her linen dress. Her long arms were so beautiful, skin so smooth, breath so sweet.

"I.... Am I...?" *Eternal? Immortal?*

"Ssh." She put a finger to his lips. "You are what you need to be. Be quiet and you can feel it. See? Now, that's better."

They were standing in the middle of his gear. He looked at the goddess. She looked at him.

She ran her fingers down him, from the hollow of his throat, across his breast, down his diaphragm, along the line of hair there and farther down, past his navel, to his groin.

She'd told him to be quiet, so he didn't say a word. Wherever those fingers touched him, heat flared, muscles jumped and tingled.

"Turn around, Niko. I want to see the rest of you."

He obeyed. She ran her cool hands over him. She touched him everywhere he'd been hurt, stroked every place that he'd been wounded: down his right arm where he'd taken a bolt; over his right hip and thigh where the axe had cut him; along his right hip, his right flank, his buttocks, his thigh, where the abscess that nearly killed him had been. Her nails traced across his skin, where new flesh was, over all his old scars, which once were there and now were not.

"Perfect," Harmony murmured, from behind him. "Now turn back to me."

"Thank you, Goddess," he said then. "For healing me. For saving me when I would have died. For all of it. For all you've done." Those hands had brought his body to life when he was wounded, when he was nearly dead, and truly dead. Now this touch makes life burn brighter in him, and his body feels as it has never felt before.

Harmony put one arm around his neck, then the other. He wanted to lift her up, put his hands around her waist. There was linen between them. Then there was not.

Her lips touched his and he did lift up this most beautiful girl. She's his dancing girl from the beach again, light as a feather, cool as a breeze. He didn't know how long they'd been here. He didn't know how long he could stay. He wanted to be with her forever, just this way, with the smell of her in his nostrils and the feel of her in his hands.

He carried her to the bed and she unwound from him, all sunlight and glossy hair shifting in the breeze.

"Nikodemos," she said softly, "come, lie down. We have all the time in the world. The balance is restored. The heavens rejoice with us."

He wanted to ask so many things. Would she stay with him?

How long?

Did he dare to ask? Every time he tried, the goddess put a finger to his lips and he couldn't speak. Her bed was as soft as the clouds in this room painted like the skies above, where they had lain together once before, and now again.

He wants to show her his rest-place: it is what he is and what he has fought so hard to preserve.

Then he's swept away with her. His rest-place is full of sunlight and she is with him there. The grass of his star-shaped meadow is so green it's nearly blue. His stream runs through it bright and clear and clean: no blood or sorcery mars the ebb and flow that is his life. Gravel and pebbles gleam from the bottom of his stream, shapes and colors blending like days without end. Around, his trees are ever green and proud and tall.

He says, "This is my place. How is it you are here with me?"

She replies, "You have brought us here, to this eternal place of yours. Do you want me with you here?"

He says, "Yes. Please. Always." They lie there on his grass together for a time beyond counting, until a cool breeze sweeps them back to her bed again. Everything is melding together as he lies in her arms and she lies in his: past and future, swirling together, exaltation beyond what just one soul can hold. But they are two, now, here and there and everywhere.

"Is this real? This place, this time? Are you really here with me?" He had to know the answers. The bed is just as soft as it had been before, the room still painted like the heavens.

"Yes," says Harmony.

Then he didn't need to know anything more.

But when she rolled on top of him, he said, "I don't know what you want from me...what to do, what to say."

"Just breathe deep, beloved. So many days to come are ours. Love your life. You will be everything you wish, in time. Be patient. All is in proportion, for you and me." And she kissed him so very softly that all his questions flowed away, and his anger at the gods with them.

Then her body wound round him and the day spun round him and nothing mattered more than the glory of those eyes.

And when he rode out to the barracks in the gloaming, Harmony rode with him, on the sable mare, to be there for the funerary pyres of his Sacred Band.

*

On the overlook above the valley where an infernal battleplain had been, two gods and a goddess must meet again. Harmony calls the meeting on this sweet-smelling ground. Theomachy has brought a strange and strained proportion: although the earthly balance is restored, too much anger remains among these three. Too much meddling unbalances even divine souls.

She wears her human aspect, and green linen, in consonance with the sage and heather spilling down the hillside. Enlil wears his cloak of storm cloud. His crown scrapes the sky above. And Vashanka stalks in, down a ramp of lowering cumulus, heavy with rain, ominous with lightning. He is angry. He is young. He is proud. "So," speaks Vashanka, "now we storm gods are summoned by a goddess? What is the purpose of this meeting?"

"After this battle, you have to ask?" Harmony disbelieves. "The Fates were aroused. Stormbringer the Unbegotten vented his wrath. And who was hurt? Not we, but our faithful. And we will bring down worse if we do not cease hostilities among ourselves and tend our flocks. Gods can be struck from heaven for abandoning true believers. Destiny can be changed forever. We need to come to terms, as to which of us will champion what mortals; and how; and how much – not fight among ourselves, now that this battle is won, now that the dream lord is no more."

Enlil growls deep in his massive throat and thunderheads obscure the heavens. He makes himself so big he stabs the sky's belly with his crown and rain begins to fall. "You did well for your believers in that battle, Harmony. Why are you so concerned?"

"The balance, restored at so great a cost, must be maintained," says the goddess, shaking her head until her long, long hair brushes the heather and the roses and the sage on the slope, so that bees take wing and hummingbirds dart skyward and dragonflies flit away. The rain stops. "Enlil, you did little for your own, yet I cannot do what I'd like for them because they are yours, not mine. Vashanka, you did nearly nothing for any fighter in this battle, but you did do *some*thing for your avatar. And now once again you have adherents in Sanctuary, temple-goers and priests. You are therefore implicated in any wrath we may face from eternity. What say you?"

Vashanka takes a breath so deep that clouds rush across the sky. He slaps his chest and tosses his mighty head with its yarrow-honey hair. "Yes, I have adherents. Many, now. You'll no longer treat me like a child here. I have an avatar upon the earth, and he is young and strong."

"As are you," Harmony says gently, to make an ally if she can.

But Enlil is older than the hills, and canny. "Young storm god, you had so few in the battle, your talk is empty, yet. Vashanka, you have a temple, a chapel, some worshippers. But you are nothing compared to me." Now Enlil puffs himself up, until he is all storm clouds with raging, swirling eyes, and glares balefully at the two of them.

Harmony holds her blowing hair at the base of her neck, but it lashes down the slope in Enlil's wind, knocking petals from the roses. "We must cease this prideful fighting across the heavens. If we don't, worse will be forced upon us."

Vashanka says, "Let the Fates come and give me battle." He pounds his fists together and thunder claps and echoes.

"Fool," says Enlil, and shrinks to appropriate size.

"Fool," says Harmony, and pulls her hair back from the valley, winding it around white shoulders like a stole.

So they regard each other, two storm gods and the goddess of celestial order and love in war. The sun surmounts the clouds, breaking through and shining while a persistent wind drives off the thunderheads and rainbows arch from where they stand to the far side of the valley. "Conflict must end, like this rain, in a *good* result," Harmony decrees.

"And how will you enforce this mandate? Who appointed you queen of heaven?" Enlil wants to know, for his own wife bears that title.

"I need not be any greater than I am," says Harmony. "I speak for mortals, exhausted from war and storm; facing famine, next; calling out for help while you two fight between yourselves, ignoring them except as fodder for your battles."

Vashanka laughs and deer break cover in the valley, running for their lives. "Surely you don't seek peace on earth? Are you not a goddess of war? Has your dalliance with a mortal made you weak?"

"Nikodemos should be *my* avatar," she says clearly. "You each have yours. Enlil has two. Cede me Nikodemos, O Storm God of the Armies – completely, not with vengeance in your heart. Then you and I, Enlil, can and shall be allies."

"So it's not peace you want, but merely one fighter sworn to my cause? He has free will. Take him if he wills it. If you and I can come to terms so easily, then so be it." Enlil waves a hand and a storm front pushes against the bright sky all around them. "I have done little for that one, your mortal toy."

"Or any other," Vashanka huffs. "I did more for my faithful in the battle and in the hurricane than did you, Enlil."

"Let's not start this up again," suggests the goddess. "I acknowledge you, Vashanka – your battle and your believers. My faithful choose. I will not pit mine against yours, or my bright heaven against your soggy one. All will have a turn, in appropriate proportion."

"I have so many faithful, Vashanka, on so many lands and planes and worlds. Not like you, with just a few. And you, Harmony: after what you did for your Thebans, you, of all of us," Enlil warns, "are at the greatest risk from angry Fates. Is protection what you want from me, goddess? If so, I grant it…with a few concessions, of course, from your lovely side."

Harmony says nothing. She needs no protection, only cooperation, but this answer will suffice from a potent old god who must be better than all the others in his own eyes.

Vashanka looks, and looks, between the two elder gods, and says, "If you two acknowledge that Sanctuary is mine, and ask before you intervene for the Sacred Band or other favorites, I will bring my lightning, put my sword at your disposal when you come to me. I'll fight beside you against any predation. You will need only to ask."

Enlil and Harmony look keenly at one another. This accord will never last, both know. But nothing remains the same under heaven. This young god wants to be consulted, respected, elevated above his station. Lightning climbs among the clouds but doesn't strike to earth or flare across the sky.

Nature holds her breath in an eternal silence.

"I accept your proposition, Vashanka. I will not rise against you without due notice. I will call upon you, indulge your passion for concurrence. For now," Enlil agrees.

"And I," Harmony breathes and sunlight spreads above while heaven and nature softly sing.

From their mouths comes the power of their oaths. Then it is done: she has her avatar. And a truce reigns, as fragile as rainbows and as robust as storm clouds. For now.

Enlil rumbles away. Vashanka clanks back to his heaven along his ramp of sky. Harmony stands alone in her pool of sunlight for a time. She looks upon the valley, washed clean of sorcery and bloodshed.

Then she too goes her way.

*

On his own threshold at Pinnacle House, Tempus waits while gargantuan dogs stare at him appraisingly from between huge oaken doors and a pock-faced servant informs Cime, Evening Star of Lemuria, of his arrival.

He considers committing various pleasant mayhems. But this is Cime's game, after all. Behind and around him, everything in the citadel of Lemuria is as it should be:

cyclopean walls, forbidding and tall; gate guards and sentries well positioned.

When he hears someone coming, he is counting the red and black stone tiles on the foyer floor. “The Evening Star will see you, Sire,” says the servant, now bowing low. The two dogs growl, and then there are six, swirling around his legs. Even for Cime, this is an ominous show.

He curls his fingers around the sharkskin hilt of his sword and goes meekly behind the servant, although this is his place, more than hers. He fought for it, claimed it, and brought her here to rule as she deserves.

Inside, glass walls still tower. Balconies stretch; angles tease the eye. Indoor trees reach toward the roof above, so high. Multi-colored streamers hang from rafters, battle standards from forgotten wars.

Cime comes to meet him there in silk and leather jerkin, doeskin leggings. Her hair is bound up. Her gray eyes are cold. She stands by the hearth and waits. Her hands are on her hips. She’s armed.

He closes the distance. When he’s close enough to her that he can see the moisture on her lips, he says, “I brought you this. If you had destroyed it when you could, a decade ago, think of the lives we could have saved.”

He digs out his grisly gift from his belt’s pouch: the bracelet called the Heart of Aškelon, encircling a chunk of wrist. The two will not be separated: wrist and bracelet are connected by artery and sinew. The Heart of Aškelon has an obsidian jewel at its center.

She doesn’t say a word, just stares at him, then at the bracelet in his hand.

“You need to destroy it now,” he continues, wishing he didn’t need to say what next he must: “I can’t. I tried. Niko tried. It may be that only you can.” He holds it out to her.

For many years, Cime was a Free Agent, a slayer of sorcerers by profession; now she may be the last of those left alive. If anyone can do this, from knowledge all but lost, it is she.

For a moment he's not sure she'll take it. All their striving, these many years since she's come back to him, has been warped by Aškelon, this bracelet, and this stone.

The look on her face is one he's never seen before. She is the most beautiful woman in the world to him. Down the centuries since they first met, no other touch has excited him as hers does. No other eyes are as wide. No other mouth is as fetching, despite all their years and all their hardship. He always wants to kiss the disappointment from that mouth, erase the shadows from her eyes. He gave her everything he had when they were young. He took on a curse for her, fought a sorcerer for her, and went to his knees before a god for her. He's given her everything again, in Lemuria.

For too long Cime only looks at him, and at the grisly trophy he offers her, and finally sighs. "Hold it out then – but by the flesh, not by the bracelet."

He does.

She reaches into her hair with its streaks and stars of gray, and takes down the diamond rods with which she's done so much good and evil over time. In two steps, she's beside him. She taps her wands together at their tips, three times. They spark and sparkle. "Now, don't touch any of the metal. I know this ritual, but it's been a very long time."

And Cime begins to sing.

The song is older than both of them, so sad and soft and low. She sings as she brings the tips of the wands into contact with the obsidian jewel. The wands seem to tremble. The obsidian begins to bleed. The wands sparkle brighter. The volcanic glass bleeds and bleeds. She sings and sings, this primal song of a world's early dawn, when sorcerers and gods vied for everything and everyone.

He nearly drops the bracelet. It's heating before his eyes, threatening to scald him. The tips of the wands seem to sink into the obsidian, so black. The black glass has veins now, white and red and pulsing. And the quantity of blood coming from that chunk of gemstone clasped around a dead wizard's wrist is far too much for a jewel, or even a man, to hold.

Blood drips and streams, then gushes onto the red and black tiles at their feet.

She stops singing. The obsidian heart cracks and crumbles and drops in shards from its bezel. The silver of the bracelet is too hot to hold. He can feel the heat although he's not touching the metal. The flesh and bone he's grasping grow gooey, grow dry, and at last drop away to powder.

So hot that it's glowing, the silver bracelet clatters to the floor. He kicks it out of the blood and powder. It skitters across the tiles. She still says nothing. She stares at the blood and the powder on the stone. The floor is slippery with so much blood.

Then she looks at him, tears in her eyes, shaking her beautiful head with her hair falling around her face. "So much death. So much pain. So much grief. I'm sorry."

And she comes into his arms, stepping through the remnants of the Heart of Aškelon on her palace floor.

He's astounded. Is this really Cime? No scathing remarks? No cutting tongue, barbed with hurt? No aspersions? No slurs on his character?

He puts his arms around her as gently as he can. And she weeps there, while he holds her. Long, wrenching sobs shake her whole body.

A dog howls in the bowels of the palace. Others take up the cry. The dogs sing a long and complex dog song. Sometimes they're men and women; sometimes servants; but from the number of throats singing, most must be dogs today.

Tempus and Cime stand that way until she slumps against him. He catches her before she falls and helps her to their chamber, with its white bed and white floor. He's left a trail of bloody footprints behind.

She buries her head against his chest. She won't look at him.

She won't speak.

She took Aškelon as her husband once, to save them all from his depredations for a time. She'd given even that, but never was able to destroy him. They didn't talk about the time she'd spent with Ash.

They didn't talk about his lovers. This room had once belonged to a woman named Chiara, the former Evening Star, and it still had the same bed with a white coverlet and a hundred pillows.

Cime lies down on that bed and looks at him at last. "I was so angry when you left with those boys of yours – with your heart still not healed. To Sanctuary, where only a fool would go, I thought. Looking for trouble, I thought."

"I know," he said. If he sat on her bed, he was going to get it covered with the blood that had run down his arms and his hips and his legs as he held the wrist of Aškelon.

Now she has, finally, finished what she started and destroyed the talisman that gave the dream lord his infernal power. She bit her lower lip. He remembered Cime anew: this girl for whom he'd fought a wizard…and lost that fight, so long ago. And from that – when she'd come to him to save her and he'd tried – their shared curses had come. And all the lessons of their lives followed, as the thunderbolt steered all things through all things and everything came into being out of strife for them.

"You're still cursed with me," she said, sniffling, running an unladylike hand under her nose. "You're not getting out of this so easily."

"This?"

"Me. Us." She put her fist to her mouth and bit her knuckles. From behind the fist, she said, "I was so frightened for you this time. That god of yours is senile, careless of you, a wastrel."

"I know," he said. Her grief was nearly overwhelming, so long pent up inside. It washed over him in waves. If he wept before her, shed one tear, his life would not be worth living. He thought of how many times she'd taunted him, taken other men to hurt him, played the harlot to provoke him, even whoring among his Stepsons: it was her curse then, to take any man for pay, to turn away from love on pain of showing all her awful years. Together, they had managed to free her from that curse, and him from his, but it had taken three centuries and more to do it.

"Sit *down,*" she commanded, and slapped the bedside near her thigh. She was shivering. He unfastened his chlamys and tried to put it over her. She struck away his hand. "Now what? Are you finished with your Sacred Band of killers in Sanctuary? Done with warring? Done with slaughter there?"

"No. You know that. We have Lemuria for a purpose, to keep all things in proportion. We will do as we have always done here. Pick our battles. War as is fitting. Restore balance. Deliver justice. Dispense mercy when we can." He chuckled a little, hoping to make her stop shaking. But that made things worse; she knew his kill-smile when she saw it.

"You took so many of your fighters. I thought you'd done with this place, and me. And left me nearly defenseless…"

"That's not true. You never are, or will be."

She sat up. She wound her hair up with her rods. She sniffed. "I want my Third Commando fighters back. You took too many of them, and too many Stepsons. The Evening Star should not be without a force."

"Come down to Sanctuary and get them."

"No," she said. "Not there. Not ever again. What of your pretty Stealth, called Nikodemos? Where is he?"

"Niko? He's where I left him. Doing what he's supposed to do."

"And what might that be?"

"Becoming the hero he's destined to be. He may outstrip us both, in time. Goddesses have been known to make gods of their earthly lovers. The goddess Harmony told me, 'Use him wisely. Few have been given such a weapon by the gods or Fates before.' He saved me several times in the battle with Aškelon, keeping Ash's wizard boy from mixing in – keeping spears from my heart and my head on my shoulders."

"You jest. That delinquent? That street fighter with delusions of spirituality?"

"Speaking of delinquents, how are my son and daughter?"

"Kama and Cyrus? On another mission. For me. You're not the only one with sorties under way."

Then he tired of the game. She was what she was, what she'd always been. He needed to stop thinking about Aškelon, the lord of dream and shadow, and what had been between Ash and Cime. And so did she.

"You're not upset about the Third, or Niko. It's the dream lord that's bothering you. Aškelon is truly and completely and forever gone, with the destruction of the Heart of Aškelon. Correct?" He never should have allowed Aškelon to claim her, even for a year. He had no inkling of what she'd been through at Ash's hands.

Now again she shivers. "Gone. Well and truly gone. Dead beyond resurrection. I was so sure I'd never see you again…."

She flew across the bed into his arms in a flurry. She kissed him with those lips he loved better than any others. She curled into his lap. And she said, "Promise me you'll never leave again unless you're well. Unless I agree. Unless we both concur."

"You know I can't do that," he said.

"I'm going to kill that god of yours, next. Then we'll see what you can do, and what you can't."

"Don't bait the god, Cime. Not now. Not ever. Please."

Then he stripped her and let his body make promises he could keep. She was all he'd ever loved, all he'd ever wanted. They came together and blew apart, over and over. Her passion was a match for his own. It always had been. But sometimes, great passion creates great trials. She climbed him and wrestled him and surmounted him while, outside her window, the sun beamed down and the seabirds wheeled above Pinnacle House.

Not until much later did he try to explain to her why he couldn't stay. And she was at first wroth, then disconsolate, but she wouldn't come back with him to Sanctuary.

"I could refuse to grant you passage," she threatened him as he girded on his sword.

"You would never do that. You are Evening Star of Lemuria, by my good offices. You will do, as you always have, what is right."

"Don't you bring that Nikodemos back here."

"I will. When it pleases me. And you will welcome him. Perhaps you'll meet his goddess. It's about time you met a female you can't disrespect. Or do you not still love all of this?" He waved a hand, purposely dismissive, at the strength and grandeur of Lemuria, out their bedroom window. "Perhaps you'd like a simpler life. You could knit. Raise sheep. Become mortal. Live a short and foolish life with no care for anything but yourself."

"You wouldn't dare."

And that was true enough. "You're correct," he said. "I wouldn't want to have to rescue you from sorcerers again, should you find any that you or I haven't killed."

And she came in under his arm then. She fit him perfectly. They walked together through the halls of Pinnacle House, past the servants and the dogs. Outside, through the tall walls of glass, he could see the stables, the citadel battlements. He could hear the sea beyond.

When they were ready to part, she said to him, "You know it's not the killing, or the warring, that bothers me. It's how high you're reaching now. Please come back to me in one piece, this time. No more cheating the Fates. As you say, greater dooms make greater destinies. We will pick our targets more carefully from now on. I promise." She looked into him, past his eyes, into his soul. "Now *you* promise."

But he couldn't do that. So he said, "I'll send our Third Commando home to you, all but Sync. Be good to my fighters. They were valiant. They fought well, but we lost too many, this time."

She rubbed her arms. "Life to you, Tempus," Cime whispered, "and everlasting glory."

He'd never expected to hear those words pass her lips. So he stopped them with his own, before she could say anything that would make him love her less, since at that moment there was nothing, not even his own life, he loved more.

## *Chapter 45: The Way Up and the Way Down*

When the pyres burned high against the evening sky and the words were all said for the Thebans, and the gifts were all thrown on the flames for her two souls destined for glory, then the goddess Harmony took her honored faithful away to heaven and stood by, head bowed.

Then down came Abarsis from the skies for the Stepsons and the 3rd Commando, all twelve souls. Tempus called the roll of the dead from the greater Sacred Band while Niko stood beside him, with gifts of arrows and locks of manes and tails. One by one, Niko threw the arrows, then the forelocks, then the tail hair on the flames for each of their beloved friends and comrades. And there were tears on the beautiful face of Abarsis, patron shade of the Sacred Band, and on the faces of seasoned fighters, this night, as the original Stepson stood in the blaze with so many of the slain, one after the other.

Seeing tears on the beautiful face of Abarsis made Niko brush his own eyes with his hand.

*Too many deaths, too close together, against an inhuman enemy. Too high a price, even in so just a cause as an end to Aškelon, the lord of dream and shadow,* Tempus thought. No wonder Abarsis shed a tear.

When the shade held the last soul in his arms, Abarsis looked out from the fire at Tempus and Niko, and at Sync, openly weeping for his dead warriors, and smiled through his tears. And the soul smiled too, on his way to eternity, safe now from all harm, caught up in the arms of the Slaughter Priest. From the middle of the flames, Abarsis arose without a word, leaving the Stepsons alone in the night with their grief and their joy that the gods still loved the Sacred Band and sanctified their battle and the spirits of their fighters.

*Godspeed, Abarsis.* It was difficult tonight, Tempus thought, as Niko watched his armored goddess with her faithful crowding around her. Next time, he might let Charon's Thebans have mourners' processions for their dead, as Thebans were wont to do.

For there would be more dead – in the Sacred Band, there always were. *Other dead, on other nights, stretching out eternally.*

Today they had buried the enemy corpses strewn across the valley in limed trenches; mass graves for Aškelon's warriors, and for the dream lord himself: Ash would rest with his fighters, every dreamer, every soul.

This night was not for celebrating or playing pipes and flutes. But Theban pipes and flutes wafted through this gentle dark, where the goddess stood and then did not.

Once Harmony had disappeared, Niko walked among the Stepsons, touching this one and that one, somber and sober or smiling his slow smile, depending on whom he met.

They still had so many missing, presumed dead. So many Stepsons were too weak to walk to the pyres, too badly wounded to participate. Tempus had decreed that Stepsons be brought out on litters in order to attend, if they were conscious and could be moved.

Critias was sitting on the ground beside Straton. Strat was still healing, not yet as strong as once he was; but better, so much better. *Niko's goddess is just and full of mercy for the deserving.*

Next to Strat lay Arton, with Lysis tending him: Arton, the seer, and his Theban partner, the Sacred Band's youngest pair, were wounded but steadfast, with sparkling eyes. And eleven others were there on litters…so many.

Despite the flutes, this was a true Stepson funeral, restrained and solemn because some were still unaccounted for: there were no benches, no feast boards at the pyres. Food and drink and games would be delayed for a week, until the missing could be declared dead or alive. Then they would perform a rite on the sand spit where the lighthouse stood. And his Sacred Banders could make what sacrifices they chose, there and then, say what they felt to men and gods.

Honor and glory wear a righteous face when men go knowingly into battle against overwhelming odds. Even the gods frown down where disorder and imbalance tip the scales, and winning at any price is what the Fates demand.

Tempus still hopes the lost will be found. He must set a good example for his men: no one rests when loved ones still are missing; no comrade is forgotten; no stone left unturned. But his visit with Cime had made his heart ache, as she always could do, for the price that fighters pay, time and again, in lives and souls.

He went to Straton's side and knelt there. "Life to you, Straton, and everlasting glory. I see the good don't die young in the Sacred Band."

And Straton replied, coming up on his elbows, "And to you, Riddler. I could have walked here, if Fox wasn't such a mother hen."

"Not a chance, Ace." Critias made a face and shook his head at Straton.

Crit had organized this night as he saw fit. The wounded were being carried back indoors. "Rest, Strat. I need you back on duty," Tempus ordered, while Critias looked thankful.

"Arton," Tempus said. "So, you're called Hawk. What do you see with your hawk's eye?"

Lysis gave back, making room beside his partner for Tempus. Arton raised his head, buoyed that his commander knew his war name. "I see the Slaughter Priest," said the badly injured youth, whom everyone said was healing better now that the Theban goddess, Harmony, had been invoked. Overhead, lightning flickered and thunder grumbled, far to the west, blowing inland off the restless sea. "I see ranks ready for battle, stretching out. Five, six horses across, ranks in formation. Endlessly." The youth coughed and wiped his mouth. His eyes were black and huge.

"That's the best thing a Sacred Bander could see," said Tempus gravely. "Thank you for this good omen, Arton. Tell your partner. Tell your friends." Beside Arton, Lysis beamed proudly.

Tempus stood up again and Niko was there beside him, with a question in his eyes. "What, Niko?"

"Commander, is it done? The Heart of Aškelon, I mean. Is it destroyed, and him with it? Permanently?"

"It's done. Your rest-place is safe. *Maat*'s justice is served, with the proportion no longer strange or strained, and all things in balance once again. Now everyone's dreams will take a different turn. No more nightmares of Chaeronea, I'll wager."

"How was Cime?" Barely a whisper, guarded.

"The same. Angry and frightened and brave and controlling. She'll be better once the Third gets back there. I'll send them in a fortnight, all but Sync. How is your goddess?"

Niko looked away. "She can help Arton more, if you permit it."

"Choose life over death, Niko, when a choice can be made that puts no soul in jeopardy."

"I needed to know you wouldn't disapprove, that Enlil wouldn't take it ill." Niko's angular face caught a flicker of firelight and Tempus saw his future there: sharp purpose, discipline, and power in perfect balance; love of man and gods, and mercy transcending all. If war ever wore a more humane face, this one would make it so. "I'll tell her, Commander. She'll help us, as you and the storm god will allow." Niko caught his eye and stared hard at him. "But…."

"But?"

Niko's mask fell away for an instant and frank eyes searched his, entreating guidance, beseeching patience, demanding understanding: "Riddler, the Sacred Band, and you and I, are sworn to the storm god. And I'm…just a son of the armies, still content to be where and what I am…learning what I can from you. I'm unworthy, not all the goddess thinks I am – or can be. I'm not ready for more than what *maat* teaches: restoring balance, order, the fitness of things, seeking god in man…."

"You're my partner, more fit to be so than ever." *Thank the gods.* "When you teach *maat* to my fighters, I don't disapprove. You, of all of mine, belong only to yourself. Keep it that way, and serve the balance as you see fit. Be an avatar of Harmony if it pleases you, for as long as it pleases you. It will please the Thebans among us. But don't do it for them. And don't worry about Enlil. Serve the Band as you always have. Remember, nothing endures but change."

*Few have been given such a weapon by the gods or Fates before.* Tempus understands now that Niko knows what's happening to him; he just can't come to terms with so much change, so fast. *Neither could I, when the world wrenched me out of it and back again, different for eternity.*

"Thank you, Commander. I thought as much, but I... needed to hear you say it. And.... Commander?"

"Niko?"

"Did Abarsis speak to you?"

"Not this time."

"Nor me," said his partner, and melted away into the night.

When the pyres burned down and men slipped away to dice or duty, drink or dream, Kouras found Tempus where he watched the embers burning low.

"Commander?" Red hair and green eyes caught the embers' glow as the Pillager's son looked him over.

"Kouras. What is it?"

"Critias says we're going to have a celebration for the dead, with games, on the lighthouse spit. Can I help?"

"I'm sure you can. Ask Crit or Niko how."

"About Nikodemos...is it true?" Behind Kouras's head, lightning forked from cloud to cloud.

Tempus said carefully, "Is what true?"

"That the goddess of the Thebans made Stealth like you – like us?"

*Us? What does this son of Vashanka think the god has made of him?*

"Kouras, no man is like any other. We each take a different path through life. So what do you mean? Niko is Bandaran trained. In that way, he's like you." Niko would want to decide who knew what – in his own time, in his own way. But Kouras was perceptive. "In other ways, you two are nothing alike. You've already given the storm god more than Niko has, or would: you let the god use your body for begetting."

Kouras rejoined, "I can bring the thunder and the lightning. You can heal. I can heal. Nikodemos…has this goddess, and now he heals. What else can he do? What else can I do? Will we be like you?"

"No." This newly-made avatar of the Rankan storm god was too young and impressionable for what awaited him. "Kouras, I was the instrument of your conception, nothing more – as another man, in another time, was the instrument of mine. So what? Ritual matings, on their own, don't make demigods, or sons, or brothers. But since that act did make you an avatar, be warned: exalted expectations make for deep disappointments. Vashanka is a cruel, cowardly, and vengeful god, arrogant and careless of his adherents."

"I meant, how do I control what's expected of me, what I can do, what the god wants?"

"If you're very lucky, you'll live long enough to find out. Gods speak only for gods; men speak only for men. Control is the prize – whether you are in control, or the god is. Make no mistake: your life will be harder now, not easier."

Flustered, Kouras said, "Thank you, Commander. I see…." Too far into uncharted territory, Kouras finally stepped back out of it and away from the fire.

Tempus sat cross-legged there, watching the embers cool and the storm blow in; feeling the moist air lick his skin and the breeze picking up, driven before the oncoming squall.

This was where he needed to be right now, with his Stepsons and the greater Sacred Band. Here the horses stamped in their makeshift stalls and on the horse lines in the training field below, and the men went to their duties with more care tonight. Life is most precious when you nearly lose it. Death is cruelest when it takes your friends and comrades without warning. All about him were his own, the best he could find – the most worthy, the most determined, the most devoted – about their appointed tasks.

In a week they would celebrate life. Now they faced death without the roar of battle: the awful consequences of bloodshed, all the endings and beginnings when friends and lovers are ripped away and silence reigns.

When the rain began to fall, Critias wandered over.

"Commander, have you some time for me?"

"Always, Crit," Tempus said to his executive officer. This one had more on his shoulders than most men ever lift. Crit's fine-featured Syrese face was intense, his eyes circled with dark smudges, his flesh wounds absently tended under damp bandages. *He'll get to it when he's ready.*

Critias sat with him awhile, securing his approval on plans for the celebration and efforts to find their missing and presumed dead, those who had no bodies yet to place upon a pyre. "We'll find them, every one. None of ours would have cut and run."

"I know, Crit."

Critias, coldest and boldest of the Stepsons where everything but his partner was concerned, looked at Tempus almost shyly, and asked, "Were we right, to try to save the fated dead? Was it worth it…in your sight?"

"Yes, we were right. It was worth it. We did more than I thought could ever be done – perhaps more than we set out to do."

"Rile the Fates? Provoke the lord of dream and shadow? Fight phalanxes from a man's worst nightmares?" Crit's voice was sharp, clipped. "All to save twenty-three pairs, this Sacred Band of Thebes, fighters from another place and time? And end up with twenty-one Theban pairs left alive and a foreign goddess looking for converts among our Stepsons here in Sanctuary, where so many of ours were loath to come?"

"We could have done it no other way, from no other place. We made an end to the lord of dream, who had become too powerful and tortured so many for so long. We'll want to mark this battle, give out service medals, pennants, and carry new Stepson standards at the commendation ceremony. Make enough to honor each deserving fighter. We'll use a new device: black feather crossed over gold sword, on a field of green. This was a conflict whose like will never come again. Those few who fought with us have won a great victory, and those lives lost in this struggle were not lost in vain. We must make this clear to all." If Abarsis had not spoken to Tempus and Niko when he came this time to take their dead, the look on the Slaughter Priest's face had said enough: only infrequently is battle truly righteous, but this was such a fight in the sight of heaven.

"Battle standards. Pennants. Service medals. As you say, Commander," Crit said crisply, blinking fast.

"You don't have to stay here, Critias. It's Sanctuary, the witch, and the goddess that bother you. I understand. But you need to decide. If you want to leave, and take Straton, you can go back with the Third to Lemuria and no one will think ill of you. We will reassign you. We have other missions, other squadrons. But this Sacred Band will stay here awhile, and I think it is your Sacred Band as much as mine."

"I'll stay as long as you need me here. I'll always go where you need me, fight where you put me. So will Straton. As you say, Riddler, to die for something is far better than to die for nothing at all," Critias murmured as he got up to leave, brushing wet grass from his bandaged thigh. They were learning, growing, this Band of his. And the young ones would follow what they learned from those whose wisdom had come at so great a cost.

He was just thinking he would go to see Cime again soon, since she was calmer, knowing he was not hurt, when Niko came back to sit on his right.

“Commander,” Niko said, “I need to look again for Jihan. And Randal. They are too important to us both to be left unfound. Living or dead.”

“Now?” said Tempus, getting up.

“Now,” said Niko. “I don’t need as much sleep as I once did.” Tempus understood exactly what Niko meant. And they walked together, with the storm coming on and the embers going out, into the night to get their horses and seek their absent friends.

## *Chapter 46: Life and Everlasting Glory*

Sanctuary's best were invited to the ceremony on the lighthouse spit to honor the Sacred Band – the living, the missing, and the dead. Nobles and traders from town, sages and seers, city guardsmen and seamen, oligarchs and priests: all came out in their formal finery to the beach on this late summer day.

So bright and clear and beautiful a day didn't belong in Sanctuary. But since it was a day for honors and remembrance, it seemed to Crit that the gods must be doing their part: the sun was shining; seagulls and terns swooped; ospreys dove into turquoise waves sighing their way ashore. The breeze was warm and tangy with salt, as if the sea itself approved the occasion.

Everyone on the guest list had to pass Crit's checkpoint. So far, no one had refused to give up horses or weapons. So far, no one had gotten too drunk, too early. All was as he'd planned it. He had Straton by his side – a bit thinner, but walking under his own power. Critias didn't know whether to thank the necromant or the goddess, so he thanked neither. He'd thrown his personal prognosticators for this event, and the fishhook had surrounded the silver figure of a fighter: that little metal fighter had always represented Straton to Crit, lo these many years. So Crit thanked Enlil, who had gotten them safe and relatively sound through so many wars, and left it at that.

They had started celebrating at midday with games that went on all afternoon. Critias had arranged for the same musicians that the palace had sent when last they'd fêted here. Once again they'd erected conical bonfires. They raced horses on the hard-packed sand along the tidehead, and Tempus's Trôs beat Niko's black by a nose. They caught rope rings with their swords. They threw javelins and shot crossbows at oxhides stuffed with straw. Many prizes were given to the winners, and dignities accrued. Celebrants laughed and shouted; horses neighed and thundered down the beach, splashing in the surf; guests sang and poets recited tales of derring-do.

When the women arrived, with the sunset, this celebration would bear more watching. Then the madams and harlots and priestesses and noblewomen and dancing girls would be here, to frolic on the sand and raise everyone's mettle. His Stepsons and city guard knew what to do when someone got out of hand. They didn't want an incident, not here, with Torchholder and all his lackeys in attendance.

Now Crit had a moment, as he seldom did, to take stock. If the Band had been truly blessed, the missing would have been found by now. But they hadn't been. *Seventeen seriously wounded, fourteen dead, eight missing.* The search went on. There was nothing Crit could do that wasn't being done. But this was a celebration, not a time to mourn. So he went to the tall, sandy-haired blessing standing nearby and clapped his partner on the shoulder. "We're winning our share," he said to Strat. "Not bad, so far. Better if you'd been in the wrestling, but good enough." The veteran Stepsons had beaten the Thebans in three events out of five. With Straton fighting for them, they'd have swept the competition.

Strat said, "I know you didn't want to come here," looking away, out to sea, his blue eyes narrowing. "Didn't want me to come. I'm glad we did. The Riddler needs us."

"We're here. We'll make the best of it. We always do." Was Strat looking for the witch? Ischade had said she'd saved him, but she couldn't heal him. It had taken the Theban goddess to do that. So many fighters had died on the battleplain, some men thought the necromant herself had lost control, and supped on souls she might have saved. He hoped Strat hadn't heard the mutters, but someday he would. Someday he should. When he did, Critias would be there to help him.

"Let's walk down to the water," Straton said, in that distracted way he had when he wasn't distracted at all, but tightly focused.

Crit made a sign to Sync to take over for him. Sync was there with his little woman, she of the glorious thighs and thick flaxen hair. All the Stepsons were wearing the gray, green, and brown of the unified Sacred Band. Sync put down his food and assumed Crit's duties at the checkpoint.

The dunes dropped your heels into them and tried to get inside your boots. They'd nearly reached the hard-packed sand, where the tide rolled in and wiped away footprints of man and horse with every surge, when he saw why Straton had wanted to come down here.

Niko and Tempus were standing at the water's edge, looking out to sea, beyond Vashanka's Rip.

Crit came up on Niko's right side, Straton on Tempus's left. "What do you see, Stealth?" Crit asked, peering west, where the sun was arcing toward the horizon and the sea gleamed like molten glass.

"Something, Fox," Niko said, too calm, too composed, every bit the mystic warrior today.

"What *kind* of something?" Crit asked, his gut tightening, his scrotum drawing up. *Niko, what sort of answer is that? What does your precious maat see that I can't?*

"Watch the wave tops there," Tempus advised, clarifying."Something's coming in."

"A boat?" Straton said, straining to see.

Crit looked harder, shaded his eyes, and looked again. He saw no sail, no froth or wake of the sort made by a trireme tacking inward or an oared vessel hugging the shore.

"Not a boat, Ace," Tempus answered Straton, voice shifting like the sand. "Something else."

"Whatever it is, it's still a long way off," Straton said.

"Not so very far," said Niko, head high, hands on his hips.

They stayed there, watching something no one could quite identify. Niko lifted his shortsword slightly in its scabbard and dropped it back down.

"I'll go back, alert the city guard. Come on, Strat," Crit said. He couldn't just stand there, mesmerized, waiting for something so far away to get close enough to be a problem.

"Send me six Stepsons with more weapons," Tempus said as if he were asking for a plate of lamb and rice. "Have them bring our horses down here." The Riddler's horse and Niko's, having raced earlier, were on the horse lines, resting. And none of them here carried more than a sword, throwing stars, and dagger.

As he and Straton went sprinting up the beach, Crit was thinking about where to find the commander's kit, his panoply, and whom he'd dispatch here with mounts and gear before whatever that was, out there, came ashore.

And Straton, pacing him, was breathing easily, running through the sand. Niko's goddess was as good as her word: Straton was fit enough to fight, if he had to fight today.

Strat looked over his shoulder, then stopped running and faced the shore, shading his eyes with one hand. "Hurry, Crit." Even from here, they could see the froth now striping across the waves, through the sparkle of sun on the surf.

*

Jihan came out of the breakers on a horse of spume and tide. Tempus had seen these froth horses before. By the time the horse's withers poked out of the surf, it was a real horse: solid, no longer blue, but frothy gray. When only its hooves were still in the water, it had black stockings. And the Froth Daughter on its back was coming into being, creature of wind and wave, copper as a settling sun, her long hair wet and flying.

Dropping his mantle to the sand, Tempus waded into the surf and held out his arms to her. She dove off the horse into them. He staggered back. "Jihan. Where have you been?" he got out, before her questing lips found his and her arms locked around his neck and they toppled over backward into the brine.

On all fours, Jihan straddled him and then began to laugh. "You should see your face, Riddler."

Niko caught the dappled froth horse and held it while Tempus disengaged from Jihan and got to his feet, soaked and immensely relieved. But Jihan wouldn't be put off. She grabbed him again and nearly took the breath from his lungs, kissing and hugging.

Niko stroked the froth horse's nose as it danced and pranced, trying to get accustomed to being a land horse.

By then Critias and Straton and six Stepsons were approaching, as Tempus had ordered, with weapons and their horses. Tempus said to Niko. "Keep them here." And to Jihan, "Walk with me, Froth Daughter."

Up along the shoreline they went, she in her scale armor and boots that never seemed to get wet, he with his arm around her powerful shoulders. "Jihan, what happened to you? We searched everywhere."

"Riddler, you shouldn't have bothered." Sunlight ran down the curve of her cheek, caressed her ample lips. "I became froth and rain. I soaked into the ground and was trapped there until my father's hurricane freed me to seek the sea. I went back to him, and he gave me leave to come again to you. Stormbringer approves of your Sacred Band. And you know he approves of very little in the world of men." Her fingers sought his.

"We were worried. Next time, send word."

"With what mouth? With what hand? Next time, don't worry. I am always yours to call, wherever the sea can reach. You know that."

"I do know that. I should have remembered. But you were among the missing, and we lost so many.... Aškelon was more powerful than mortal enemies are. He held you in thrall once before; he might have overwhelmed you again."

Her eyes sought his, glowing. "Never fear for me, Riddler. As for Aškelon, that sorcerer with pretensions of godhead, he is gone from you. He never will harm you or yours again. Stormbringer came and cleansed the land. Certainly you understood his hurricane eye, watching over you and yours in your barracks."

He should have. He hadn't thought along those lines. *Much learning does not teach understanding. Nature is wont to hide herself, and Stormbringer and Jihan are among Nature's most elemental expressions.* So much had happened.

"Jihan, this was an ancient enemy, a battle more terrible than I'd thought to fight. I have so many still missing."

"Tempus, you did not waver, surely. Or is it not that? Are you telling me, O Sleepless One, that you really care? Beyond the way you care for your men? My father will not believe it. But I do." She jumped him again, all primal power and passion. He staggered, nearly ending up on his back in the sand.

"Jihan, I have a task, an important one, which only you can accomplish."

"And that is?" Now she lets him go. She knows his voice. She knows his heart. He thinks she may even know what he's going to ask. She nibbles her lower lip and stares at him.

He hesitates. He's not sure, at this late moment, whether he wants to let go of this weapon. Or let go of this creature, so much more than mortal, that the oceans have lent him once again. Jihan can fight any fight, dare any danger, and emerge unscathed, if Aškelon himself could not destroy her. Knowing it, he values her even more. Although he should have known, should not have worried that the dream lord had destroyed her. Too much guilt, obscuring everything, at the end of this conflict whose extent was ages, not hours or days. Too many still missing, even with this one returned to him. Too many dead to tolerate even one more.

*"Riddler? What?* I hate it when you drift away and don't tell me what you say you'll tell me. And no riddles. Straight out, please, or I'll take you down in the sand before all your men. You surely deserve it by now. *What?"*

He sighed, and the rattle of it made her retreat a step. He put his hand in his soaked belt pouch. Had the salt water damaged the tube? Destroyed the darts? Washed away the poison? He got out the dart tube and held it between his fingers. He slid the slide. The darts were dry. He took one and put it in his belt pouch. *For luck.* In case he ever faced such an enemy again. Now there were twelve left, nestling there. Then he held out the tube to her.

"Take this into the sea, Jihan. Right now, if you can. Drop it into the deepest crevice in the ocean floor, as you promised you could do. Where no man will ever find it, or god, or sorcerer put his hands on it again."

"Ah," she said. She took the tube in her hand and reached up under her scale armor with it. She shimmied. Her hand came back, empty. "Now *I* had forgotten. Of course I will. But not this instant. I want to be with you tonight, at your celebration. Taste the wind. Taste the wine. No one can get this tube from me. And you must do one thing for me, to pay me for this service, for I must journey so far again when I have just come all this way."

"And what is this I must do?" he asked cautiously. Jihan was capricious, an innocent, eternally naïve in the ways of men. Sometimes she understood him, sometimes not. Her record of comportment among mortals was spotty at best. She didn't always recognize when enough was quite enough. Which was, of course, what he cherished most about her. "What is this one thing you ask?"

"You must teach me to dance, tonight, in front of everyone – and dance with me among your Sacred Band as Niko danced with his goddess the last time we were here, when musicians played."

"Jihan, commanders don't dance." He took a step back and looked into her change-color eyes. Red flecks sparked in her pupils.

"You will," she said, crossing her muscular arms, so beautiful, so powerful yet feminine. "Or I won't take your trinket anywhere. I'll keep it. Then you'll respect me."

"I respect you now."

"Then *pay* me respect as Niko pays it to his lover, the goddess. Never forget, my sire is Stormbringer the Unbegotten. I am just as much a goddess as she. Dance with me before everyone. Hold me high in the air and twirl me."

"I have not forgotten who or what you are, Jihan. We will do it. But I haven't done such a thing in a very long time. We must go about this cautiously, so as not to embarrass either one of us."

"In front of *everyone,*" said the Froth Daughter, implacable.

Her foot tapped upon the sand. "Promise, Riddler."

So he promised. Then he put his hand around her impossibly small waist and escorted her up the beach, among his Stepsons, where Niko waited with her horse and Critias and Straton and the rest.

Jihan said, "Niko, Critias, Straton. So lovely to see you," and the formality of it made a gust of laughter sputter from between Crit's lips. Ignoring Crit, she inclined her head demurely and added, "Riddler, I didn't tell you. I am meeting someone here. A surprise for all of you. So please don't use those weapons on my guest too hastily…."

She walked backward, away from them, into the sea whence she'd come. She'd left him this way once before; turned back into froth and wave before his eyes. But she'd said she wanted to stay and celebrate; she'd said she'd invited a guest….

When the whitecaps reached her waist, she slapped the waves with her palm. And the waves cuddled up to her, white lacy tops curling over her. The froth makes a gown for her and reaches for her breasts, her hair, her face.

By now she's swimming (a copper face amid the waves; a flash of one arm, then the other) out to sea against the current.

"The Rip," Crit warns.

"It's *Ji*han," Niko says, as if no tide could daunt her and Critias should know that.

Out fifty yards, she turns and heads back inland. Now there's something swimming next to her: perhaps a shark or a dolphin; surely something large and dark.

The sea reflects the sinking sun like a net of diamonds cast upon the water, undulating, sparkling, surging inward as she swims alongside this dark shape, toward shore.

When she can, she stands, and beside her is a burst of wave, a disturbance of froth, an upwelling of whitecaps.

"Commander?" Niko asks. "Shall I go get her?"

Tempus has both hands in the wet leather of his swordbelt. "No, she's in no trouble. Just wait with me."

Now they're no deeper than her hips, and Tempus thinks he knows what comes with her out of the sea.

Jihan's hand trails down. There's a dog beside her, big and black and soaked, with lolling tongue and floppy ears. It cavorts and jumps for her hand, barking. Behind him, Tempus hears the rasp of a sword unsheathed. "No. It's fine. This is our uninvited guest."

He chances a look at Niko, who grins his quick grin. Niko crouches down in the sand beside him, holding out both hands.

The dog, jumping and barking, bursts out of the surf with Jihan and runs up to Niko, licking his face. Niko is laughing. He has the dog by both its ears. It shakes itself from head to tail, showering Niko with salt water. Stealth says, "Crit, get me the commander's mantle."

For this event of commendation and remembrance, Tempus has chosen a full dress mantle, not an abbreviated chlamys. Now he's glad.

Jihan, arms akimbo, is beaming like the sun at her back. Crit tosses Niko the mantle. He drapes it around the dog, but not to dry it.

Niko stands up and steps back. The new Stepsons holding the horses are looking dubious, but Critias, Straton and Niko all know what kind of dog this is.

Jihan laughs delightedly as the mantle fills up and stands up, and Randal greets them as a man: "Riddler, Stealth, Ace, Fox. Life to you, and everlasting glory. And to you all. Sorry it took me so long to get back. Jihan had to find me, in all this water." Clutching the mantle to his chest, Randal gestures at the ocean waves. "Becoming water wasn't something I'd done before. It was Jihan's idea, if something went wrong. And it saved me…."

Niko says, "Get him gear, clothes. Full Stepson panoply," and reaches Randal in two strides, enfolding the little mage in his arms. And Niko holds Randal tight, while Straton says, "Witchy-ears, I never thought I'd miss a skinny runt like you. But I did," joining their embrace.

Jihan looks at Tempus with her change-color eyes and says, "So, Riddler. All is accomplished that needs to be. Except for the promises between us, you and me."

Crit looks between them quizzically.

Tempus says, "Don't ask."

Jihan swings onto her dappled froth horse, bareback. Tempus mounts his Trôs. And they walk their horses inland while men ride off to find Randal attire fit for the fête. Although the mage could have conjured his own, Niko was right: Randal should be in Stepson garb for the honors ceremony this evening.

While Tempus rides with Jihan toward the throng, he looks back and sees Niko and Randal, with Straton and Critias, silhouetted together against the dazzling sea as the sun prepares to set and a bright quarter moon comes early to the sky.

Although he still has fighters missing, unaccounted for, presumed dead, Tempus reads the return of Jihan and Randal as an omen that all who are lost can be found, if he will just be patient and heed his own heart. So he thanks the god, for returning Jihan and Randal unharmed.

But Enlil doesn't answer. The storm god speaks to him less and less on these grueling, fated days, yet seems more a part of him than ever. God and man are merging as they never have before. His heart is finally healed and strong, beating as it always has, in a rhythm that propels him across the centuries. And he thinks, with Jihan beside him and so many of his remaining Stepsons safe and well, that he can truly celebrate tonight as he has not done in a very long time. Then, somewhere overhead, far away and out to sea, thunder rolls, as if the storm god of the armies agrees.

*

In the twilight, the women all arrive, perfumed and glistening, along with dancers and musicians, so gaiety can thrive among the gathered company.

Now the Fates, here on the beach (three shadows, blackest black), travel through the dunes, looking for their own. Come across a bridge of sighs, opened wide once darts began to fly. Counting darts released in battle. They've felt a loosening of the bonds of dream, a wrongness being righted, an affront to nature just undone.

They came before, to find an unknowing ally, untwist some destinies, and guide the hand of men against a travesty among them. Now the deed is done; the snarled thread, snapped. The lord of dream and shadow has been vanquished by this tool they made and game they played, when they chose a wizard boy to lure a haughty demiurge to his deserved end.

Their mandate thus was put in force, their tempers soothed, their righteousness endorsed. All is balanced now but feuding gods and men still guilty for their lives so deftly spared – too few wrongs to right for Fates to shame the valiant, or make more culprits die. For there is only will to live in these, not a sin the mortal sees. Threads are spun; spindles wound; Fates allowed upon the ground to see what glory can be found among those living, once called fated dead.

Only shadows of the dusk, they manifest among the revelers. Lamb-white hands beneath black robes spun of tears are they, not much more. To be twice upon the same ground, so close in time, requires special favors from beyond the stars and planets, from amid the planes where they abide.

Among the celebrants they glide, counting souls of Thebes who've found new homes, if providentially.

Tonight Fates hear and see so much, these travelers from another realm, who may never pass this way again. So silently, moving in a half-light where only they can be, they slip and slide between men and women (among the good, the better, and the best) and look out from their half-life, wondering at what they see.

First they find the Stepsons from the Riddler's Sacred Band.

The Fates have met these fighters once before. Now they are weary. Now they are wounded. Now they are grieving. Now they are heroes, one and all, who helped the Fates themselves bring an enemy of ancient standing to his just reward.

The Fates swoop in, looking Tempus in the eye. And he can see them, this man of so many years, who has beside him a creature of wind and wave. These two are nearly supernal, so the Fates give back, lingering, while the Riddler whispers to Jihan and neither points a finger.

For one instant, when eyes touch eyes and minds touch minds, there is an understanding between the Fates and these two: all is forgiven, destinies and dooms rescinded, among those who labor to help mankind on its way. The Stepsons and their commander have lent a helping hand, and that hand will not be struck away.

The Fates move on, finding a boy with a god inside him and a boy who is a seer, and one more Theban boy, all young fighters: one torn between mortality and immortality; one with an eye that sees as Fates can see; one blessed by the Theban goddess of love in war, and pleasing in the sight of Fates.

So they go another way, sliding through the sand, and find there other Thebans, so many wounded, so many sad who miss their home and the customs of their land. These cannot see them, so the Fates touch a heart here and there, uplift a soul and make it glad. These are their fated dead; the remedy for all disruption began with ripping twenty-three Theban pairs from the cloth of history. One Theban, Charon, led the rest to glory, gave his Sacred Band another chance to fight, shoulder to shoulder beside their doomed brothers on a second Chaeronean battleplain, and win the day when destiny reprised. Thus guilt can be replaced by triumph in the hearts of these, and sadness washed away. And Fates can seal it so, and so they do.

Listen close and you can hear, "Please, bless us and forgive us, and make us good here and strong here. Let us get along here. Let those we love and left behind be blessed. Let us find the proper path and keep to it. Help us act harmoniously, and find work pleasing in the sight of god and man."

All this praying from devout Thebans makes the Fates turn away and go away, gratified. They are not gods, but they understand reverence.

Now torches and bonfires are brought alight, and there are deeper shadows for Fates to slide among, and play. They find a necromant, long cursed and long regretting evil done and doom long spun. They can do but little for this one. Her spindle was wound, her wool carded and spun so long ago that no Fates remember the whys and hows of her damnation. Her curse acts upon her, every day. Her time of reckoning will come, but she has found real love, and love can heal and save. So one Fate brushes this tortured soul with just a finger, to bring a touch of grace where it has been well earned – a few better days, a little respite.

The witch's eyes flash. Eyes blacker than night fly off a bone-white face and zoom up close to hover there before them: she sees them. Her hands before her face are claws, but her eyes before their eyes are wide: "See *me,* do you?" hisses the necromant, nearly as old as they. "Help *me,* will you? I need no meddling from geriatric powers such as you. What you had in store for me, I have endured with no entreaty. And *now* you have pity? Please understand if I'm not impressed. Why now? Save it for yourselves. Throw a dog a bone, a necromant a bit of grace? And how? Please, no more help from you. You've already done your worst to me. Better, have mercy – but Fates don't, do they? You're here with too little, too late," spits the witch, elbows up, forearms crossed before an eyeless face, while those untethered orbs of hers, black and huge, dart from Fate to Fate to Fate, then swoop away at last to return to her countenance and rest within her shadowed cowl. "Get away. Go away. Leave me *be.*"

The Fates get back, and back: startled; insulted. Few see them. Fewer still upbraid them. But this old soul is nearly fearless. And the Fates recall, then, what it means to have nothing left to lose.

Then it's time to spin away, and go away, among the men and women, some with short lives, some with long. So many hearts here, for creatures locked away from tears and laughter to see; so many souls here, not crying, content to wait to be released.

On this beach in firelight there is soft wind and warm night. Fates have no world of weather; they are far beyond the gods and day and night; but only spin, and spindle, and know, and say who will die and who will live to fight on other days.

They see a man who can be a dog or a horse, a mage who is white of heart and slight of stature. He stands beside a goddess in black armor, and she beside a true and balanced soul. This fighter makes them swoop and peer and look into hazel eyes to see how Nature has concocted such a one.

He feels something: a breath, a touch of veil upon his cheek, and brushes at his eyes. Almost, he sees them. Almost, the mage beside him does.

Now the goddess looks, and looks, and looks the other way, taking her beloved by the arm, saying, "Niko, come this way. Let's watch the waves. And Randal, come with us. This way."

Almost, one irked Fate reaches out to remind this goddess – so bold, so brave – of humility and who holds sway among the powers of creation.

But the other Fates have their say, and reason its day: the Aškelonian abomination is gone, because this fighter risked his life; this mage has helped make the seventh sphere clean and new and safe for all spirits. Dreams are freed.

There is nothing to affront the heavens now in this place except the ancient weapon in the Froth Daughter's care; and it will go another way, and be lost to men as it always should be. And can be. And will be soon enough to please even these three Fates, who used it to bring down an enemy of mortal and immortal, a scourge of all the worlds of man.

The Froth Daughter has looked into the eyes of all three Fates and her soul has told them so: this weapon beneath the sea will go, never to be seen by men again. She has promised. They believe her, and spin their wool to make it so. Thus all will be as it should be, once more, above and below.

So their dispensation has come to its close. Twice they have sojourned, where Fates usually cannot come to dwell or visit, among the mortal and the damned and the divine.

And now they are content. The haughty have been brought low. So they slip away, and swirl away, and whirl away into their own timeless realm, content to go where Fates are meant to go: A realm they only could have left to come here once and once again, to be here on this special night when worlds align and destiny takes it time, because mortal souls have called them, called out to heaven and beyond, once and once again.

So they leave here (leave the life and death here) and go their special way, content with what Fates have done and what life will come to these, whom they had caught up in their hands on days gone by, and tested.

Those who are here, left behind where sun and moon still shine, are full of grace. The survivors of this awful purge, when the mighty were brought low and the grasping lost their grip, are pleasing in the sight of Fates. And so, with their leave-taking, they give a gift to those alive who labored, unknowing, in their cause: joy and honor and glory, for all who endure to fight on other days.

Now place and plane shift in their courses, and day and night align, and all things that are in heaven are on earth, in just and right proportion.

*

"What are we doing, Niko?" Randal wants to know.

"Ssh," says Niko. "You'll see." He has the ghost horse, its reins in his hands, and he and Randal are sneaking through the shadows at the edge of the celebration, beyond which Crit and Straton wait, obedient to the Riddler's orders. "She's here. I just need to.... There," Niko says.

Randal nearly bolts.

Niko grabs his arm. "She won't hurt you. You know that."

"But why is she here in the darkness, and not with everyone?"

"Where would you be, if you were she? Hold this horse."

He walks up to Ischade, where she hovers in the shadows. "Ischade, come join us. You're welcome here. I brought Straton's bay horse for you to ride. The commander wants to thank you publicly for your service to the Band."

*"Publicly?"* comes a scathing voice from within that cowl. "Critias suspects me of all manner of crimes to which I would never sink, and says so – *publicly.* And after all I've done for you."

"All Stepsons know how much you've done for us, how many lives you saved. Tempus knows. You're to be a guest of honor. Please come," he said and tried his slowest smile, which had melted women's hearts from here to there and back again. "Please?" He held out his hand. "Strat's waiting. I'll help you mount. I'll lead you both to him. He'll lead you through the commendation. Then this horse wants a ride – just you and Strat and him...so much. All powers rejoice when a noble animal is happy. Give the horse his ride, just you and Strat. Tonight's a night for counting up the living. For rejoicing. Who knows how many more nights like this we'll have, with all of us together?"

Randal murmured, "Stealth, I've never heard you talk so sweetly. Why don't you treat me like that?"

His eyes still on the necromant who could drain his life in a second, Niko muttered in return, "Because, Randal, you don't need so much help." And then, louder: "See, Randal's here, and welcome here, and he's a mage. The Riddler wants you to ride up so he can commend you personally, in front of everyone. With Straton. On the horse. Please, don't make me fail because you won't come with me."

Then out she came, floating. This necromant needed no horse and no help. But Tempus was right to send Niko on this ticklish mission: Strat couldn't have convinced her; her hold on Straton was too great. Ischade took the hand Niko offered, put her slim fingers in his own as if she were a queen, and let him help her onto the big bay ghost horse. He arranged her inky cloak over the ghost horse's croup, over the spot on its hip where nothingness could be seen if the light was just right.

Then he said to Randal, "I'll lead the horse. You get Strat."

Niko blew out a deep breath. Tempus never asked the easy things. Ischade could jump on him right now, from behind, and he wouldn't be able to fight her off. It might take her just a little longer to finish him than it would the average soul. He didn't think his blessings from the goddess could protect him from a soul-sucking necromant, the feared vampire woman from Shambles Cross who didn't bother sipping blood, but drained the very life force from her prey.

Then Straton came up, Critias fuming alongside. "I'll take them, Niko," Straton said. Niko relinquished the bay's reins.

Crit put his hands on his hips and damned them all to hell and back as Straton led Ischade, her black cowl still pulled down over her eyes, to the line of honorees filing up to the Riddler, where he was awarding commendations before the gathered crowd. Straton had freshly-dressed wounds and scabby burns, as did nearly all the fighters in the commendation line. Critias stared after his partner, leading the witch on the ghost horse. The sea wind gusted in Crit's fine-featured face, blowing dark hair around an angry look.

Beyond and out to sea, thunder grumbles, lightning flickers, but Harmony and Kouras both have promised that there'll be no storm tonight, and Niko believes them.

"You think this is smart, Stealth?" Critias asked him scathingly. Crit had asked Niko that same question back in Lemuria in front of the bull pen, before this Sanctuary expedition began. It seemed so long ago, when the Riddler lay abed, sorely wounded: before the Theban goddess appeared on the jetty; before the ancient remedy gone awry; before the fighting with Sham in his rest-place and at the Mageguild; before the goddess healed him; before the fire at the barracks; before the confrontation with Aškelon on the second Chaeronean battleplain. Before they'd lost Deon and Ari and Epani and Zitos and too many others. So much had happened. To all of them.

"I think it is fitting, Fox," Niko replied, very softly. "I think it's what our commander ordered. I think you're lucky to still have a partner and you should kiss the hem of her cowl if she helped to make it so."

"Stealth," Critias said, "you can kiss my pommel."

Niko sighed, "Critias, you and I need to make peace. I'm just doing what the Riddler tells me. All the time. You're better than I am at so many things. Please just let me do my job, and help me do it. And I'll help you do yours."

"That necromant…"

"…loves your partner, as do you. If she wanted to kill him or eat him or whatever she does, she's had chance after chance. Let them have their time. He'll come back to you. He always does."

Crit grunted, but he seemed somehow less angry. Niko stopped trying to fix what might not need to be fixed, or might not be fixable.

He stepped into the dusk to watch Straton lead the ghost horse and the necromant up to be commended. Torches flickered, being lit.

The Riddler was all anyone could ask tonight, massive strength, magnanimity and command, sure in everything he did and said.

"Now," Tempus told the assembly, "I want you all to meet two home-grown heroes: Sanctuary's own, the youngest of our Band, and as magnificent in battle as any of us. First, there's Hawk, called Arton, right-side partner of Lysis and son of Illyra. Illyra has graced us with her presence tonight." Everyone craned their necks to see the teary-eyed Illyra at the front of the crowd. "Hawk and Lysis, come join us."

They had built a low podium, and on it Tempus stood in uniform. Lysis and Sync helped Arton (hobbling, pale but healing) up to meet the Riddler, one on either side to steady the wounded youth. Niko saw Harmony, in her black armor, beside the reviewing stand on Tempus's far side, watching. The commander told Illyra in his battlefield voice: "Illyra, your son Arton saved the life of his Theban partner, here – took arrows meant for Lysis. And this Sacred Band pair fought a valiant fight against more than ten times their number and emerged victorious. We're lucky to have them – and you, Illyra – on our side." Tempus handed boxed commendations and service medals to Arton and Lysis as the audience clapped and cheered and Sync led the two away.

"Next we have a Stepson many of you have heard about: Gyskouras, Sanctuary's own son of Vashanka." Sacred Banders thumped their shields as Kouras let Sync escort him before Tempus. "Kouras distinguished himself in battle, fought off a dozen enemies with all the ferocity of the god in him, shoulder to shoulder with our Theban brother, Charon, and was magnificent in victory. Charon, if you would, come up here and give Kouras his service medal, and receive your own."

Kouras accepted his commendation with an aplomb that suggested to one and all that he was merely receiving his due. Then Sync escorted those two away to thunderous cheers, begun by Molin Torchholder and his palace oligarchs, who swarmed around Kouras as soon as his feet were on the sand.

"And now," Tempus said, alone again on the stand, "we are especially honored to present one of Sanctuary's most esteemed powers and a special guest of the Band who has saved countless lives over battles too numerous to recount here, accompanied by one of our finest officers. Please welcome Ischade of Shambles Cross; Ace, called Straton; and his most valorous warhorse of the Sacred Band."

Straton lifted Ischade off the ghost horse and down, and her cowl fell back as the big Stepson helped the tiny necromant up onto the stage. The crowd gasped. Niko saw Harmony's head tilt, and the goddess drew back – one step, two – then held her ground.

"Ischade, this commendation is long overdue. For a decade or more, you have helped the Stepson leadership unselfishly, whenever you were asked," Tempus said. "When we have faced infernal battle, where sorcery was arrayed against us, you never once hesitated or faltered. Among the heroes here today, you are the largest in stature. In this battle, not only did you help plan and execute a winning strategy, but you went among our wounded and dead upon that most daunting of battleplains and helped rescue all you could. For service such as yours, there is no adequate reward. But please accept our tokens of esteem, our honors, and our everlasting gratitude."

The Riddler handed Straton a service medal hanging from a loop of ribbon. Straton put the ribbon over Ischade's head. The tiny necromant blinked through owlish eyes at the crowd. People clapped cautiously. Straton resumed his position beside Ischade.

Tempus continued: "Many of you know Straton, my valued tactical officer, who commanded the Stepson contingent here in days gone by. Straton was grievously wounded in this fighting, and Ischade's skills were critical to his recovery. Among the heroes of the Sacred Band, none has served more bravely, or performed more superbly, or led more critical missions. If you wonder what a Stepson is, or why we esteem them so highly, look at Straton and see the answer. Here, Strat, is our highest honor, won not once but a hundred times in service to our forces." Tempus went to stand in front of Straton and pinned a gold feather to the shoulder of his mantle, then stepped back. Niko saw Critias, near the dais, blinking fast.

"And now, for our most singular award of the evening, presented to our most unique combatant." Tempus reached down and got the special commendation that Niko, Sync and Lysis had prepared: a garland of sugar beets and carrots. Then Tempus stepped off the podium and draped the garland over the ghost horse's withers.

"No one has saved more lives than this horse, fought more battles, faced more foes. We thank Ischade, and Straton, and the horse himself for his valorous service. And each of you, for joining us here to celebrate these heroes, one and all. Life to you, every one, and everlasting glory."

The ghost horse reached around and pulled off a carrot, and everyone cheered and clapped and fighters thumped their sword hilts on their shields. At that signal, the musicians struck up the martial air Niko had heard the last time they'd feasted here.

*Rat, rata tat. Tat rat tata tata tat. Brum rumpa pum pum.*

*Brum rumpa pum pum. Tat, rata tat. Brum rumpa pum pum.*

All the guests line up to watch as the marching song begins with flutes and drums.

Now, at measured pace, fighters from Tempus's unified command – those who fought the dream lord's hordes on the second Chaeronean battleplain – troop slowly out from behind the lighthouse on foot. Across the sand in double files they come, carrying empty litters from the far side of the lighthouse, each toward his designated bonfire.

This time, following the foot soldiers with their litters representing the missing and the slain, cavalry marches toward the firelight from the shadows.

The hair stands up on Niko's arms, to see these men and horses come across the sand by sixes. As the Riddler has ordered him, he falls in on foot when they come abreast, walking beside the leftmost horse and rider. He's so close he can touch the nearest, hear their timeless sounds above the music: squeak of armor, creak of leather; metal jingling, horses snorting; hoof beats, so many, pounding the ground like Niko's heart against his ribs. He paces the leading rank as they pass before the crowd. Row after row of mounted Stepsons, Thebans, and 3rd Commando, come together to parade past their commander in review.

The Band's fighters know this ceremony for what it is: the aftermath of victory, bittersweet and full of honor for the living, glory for the dead; a harbinger of struggles yet to come, new beginnings. Greater destinies await, born of these greater dooms they'd just surmounted, with the Riddler guiding them, driving them through their fears to feats yet unimagined. The honor guard rides with somber eyes, faces set, taciturn; fit to fight wherever their commander bids. Tonight, once and forever, their differences are subsumed into the greater Sacred Band, cadre honor superseding all.

It's as if Niko is walking into his own future alongside this cavalry as dusk fades to dark and the flames burn high: endless ranks, grim men on tall horses, bound by love and honor to duty and to one another; no illusions, no dreams of sack or pillage, wealth or conquest. Not now, not ever. Stepsons and Thebans, 3rd Commando, thrown together, melded by strife in the crucible of war into something stronger: fighters clear-eyed in the face of danger, seeking a better future for them all.

His commander tells him these men will be his someday, all these fighters of renown, wolfish and keen.

And he will be ready, someday. His *maat* knows it. The goddess Harmony believes it. Tempus has told him so in no uncertain terms. Even now his partner honors him beyond his expectations: the black feather of justice crosses over the sword on the Band's new standard: the Riddler's gift to him. The feather stands for *maat*, for Harmony, for Niko's need to find a better way to fight on other days.

One hundred and twenty horses and riders are filing by the commander in perfect rhythm, perfect time. Soon there will be two hundred and fifty more, Tempus says. *Tat, rata tat. Tat rat tata tata tat. Brum rumpa pum pum.* All wear uniforms of gray, green, and brown linen, leather and wool. The fighters farthest left and right have mail shirts, sparkling in the torchlight. These riders hold aloft the new standards, pennants of the greater Sacred Band of Stepsons, snapping in the breeze. Shields of wicker or wood faced with leather and bronze carry the same unit device. Mantles billow in the sea breeze and horses' manes and tails are flowing.

Out of respect for the fighters being honored tonight, every bit of metal and leather gleams on each man and horse. The commander too has dressed for the occasion, but in the new uniform, not in leopard skin – the Band is praising, not warring, today. When Niko reaches Tempus's position, his commander salutes him. He stops there, as arranged, while the cavalry rides on.

Niko's throat closes up. He wants to go to his partner, but Tempus is with Jihan and the cavalry horses are in between. The Theban goddess is nowhere to be seen. *Tat, rata tat. Tat rat tata tata tat. Brum rumpa pum pum. Brum rumpa pum pum.*

Alone, on this sweet summer evening, with the moon bright in a sky aglitter with stars, he gives thanks for all he's done and all he's become. Inside him, his *maat* is no longer restless: justice has been served and will be served. He has his equilibrium. And if he finds his path solitary sometimes, then so be it. He has his rest-place back again, with its star-shaped meadow; no threat or shadow lurks there, anywhere.

Then she's there beside him on the beach, his luminous goddess wrapped in night, wearing her black armor, her soft hair afloat in the breeze, bringing the smell of his meadow with her to mingle with the wind coming in off the wine-dark sea. They watch the rest of the march together, silent while the music plays as the horses and men pass by and on into the dark.

And then it is done. The last rank passes by them. The music crescendoes and stops. In the sudden silence, the surf crashes upon the shore.

He's so conscious of her standing beside him that his skin tingles all the way down his right side. He leans in toward her. She leans toward him. His hand goes around her, and putting his hand on her armored hip is the most natural thing in the world. The breeze blows her soft hair over the back of his hand, against his naked arm. Will he ever know what to say to her?

"Thank you," he says, watching her as she watches the horses disappearing behind the lighthouse, "for everything. I wouldn't be here to see this, if not for you."

"Your mare misses you. She's here. You should make time for her." The goddess shifts and her left hip brushes his right. "Come this way," she says.

And they walk that way, with his arm still around her, through the celebrants, past Charon and Gorgias and Agis and Archias, past the young Theban poet Perses and his grizzled partner, Simias; and all the Thebans bow their heads before her. They pass by Molin Torchholder, talking earnestly to Kouras.

Kouras looks to Niko for rescue from the clutches of the priest and his oligarchs, all clustered in a festooned heap like presents waiting to be unwrapped. But Niko won't help Kouras tonight. Shawme and Merricat prowl nearby, giggling with girlish glee behind their hands and switching their hips at the boy who is the storm god's son. Niko knows young girls; they'll extricate Kouras from his plight presently.

He's never been with Harmony in so public a situation. So many stares make his skin flush hot. Or being so close to her does it. Sanctuarites and soldiers gawk, unabashed, as they go by, until Niko stares them down and makes them drop their eyes.

A goddess setting foot on earth is too remarkable, by half. She shifts her shoulder into him as they walk. "Don't mind them. They want to see you as much as they want to see me. Smile. Wave if you know them. Just keep moving."

They're heading toward the lighthouse, behind which the mounts are kept, until she leads him astray, into the dunes.

"Here," she says, between two sand dunes crested with grass, and sits in a hollow there.

He sits in the sand beside her and she comes against him. She fits effortlessly under his arm. Even through armor, she sets him ablaze. The wind teases him with her hair. He's sure nothing can happen here and now, between them, on a night like this in a place like this, dressed like this. But she is a goddess and his doubts melt away with the touch of her hand. Their gear is strewn on the sand but it doesn't matter.

All is consonance around her, and grace; nothing untoward can happen when he's in her arms. Even here, she brings the meadow; he smells it, he feels it, he sees his rest-place in her eyes. The sand is softer, cooler than he expects. And she yields to him, this time, as she has not done before, and speaks his name in a voice so melodious that his heart trips and skips a beat. Her lips on his are as soft as the sea breeze and there is only this moment, in all of creation, with her silken hair and her long limbs entwining him.

Somehow he's not afraid they'll be discovered here. She has a way of bringing everything into balance. Her touch is so cool on his heat, and her body so perfect for his, that Nature herself will surely protect their privacy.

When he can see the moon over the grass of the dunes, she lies with her head on his arm, her hair across his chest and trailing down his ribs, and says, "None could ask for more, beloved, than we have here tonight. Don't you agree?"

"When I'm with you, I want it never to end," he says, his voice too husky, his words too brash, he fears. He kisses her forehead; her skin is fine, soft.

"Then it will not end," she says, shifting onto one elbow in the sand, while the stars send light to gild her limbs, "since that is your wish. We will have many nights like this."

And the nearby sea breathes for him, because looking at her lying in the sand makes him hold his breath. "I don't want to lose you," he dares. "I need you to know that. If I die in battle…."

"Ssh." Her finger touches his lips. "You died. Now you live again. You will never be lost to me."

"I'm…trying to understand. I'm not sure what all this means. You give so much to me…. How do I thank you? How can I?"

"It means we go this way together," she says and kisses him once again. "As you have chosen. It is what we both want. No thanks are needed."

Tempus has taught him that all things are reflected in all things. Tonight his rest-place and his destiny are reflected in her eyes. He must stop asking questions with no answers – stop wondering at his good fortune and follow his heart; believe, as he always has, in himself, in his bright purpose, in his *maat*.

He can't bring himself to ask what she has done to him. He keeps trying, and he can't say the words. It is too forward. She might misunderstand. But in his heart, he knows. He'd sliced his arm, cleaning his shortsword: the cut healed as he watched. So in some way is he like Tempus, now, never to age, but still vulnerable? For how long?

What was the difference? Risk is risk; life is life. Meet it quailing, meet it bravely, but meet it you will. Pain still hurts. Dogs still bite. He isn't dependent on her, doesn't want to be. She's not like Enlil, inside Tempus. She comes and goes as she pleases. He needs to stop holding back with her. What she sees in him is what he is, not what he wishes he might be. His body knows just what do with her.

Whether Harmony can do all she says – or will; whether he lives forever or just this one more night; right now he is immortal in her arms and more balanced than he's ever been, except when he looks down from the heights to which her caresses lift him.

So he touches her once more. Music starts to play, its strains wafting round them. And everything is new again, as it always is with this goddess who has him by the heart.

Eventually, they dress and find the horses, and his mare is there. Her sable head turns to him. She sights in on him with her ears and presses her head against his chest. She nickers and he scratches her neck.

And Harmony says, "She will have a great foal for us."

*For us.* He doesn't doubt her word. When man and mare have had their reunion, he walks with the goddess back toward the music and the dancing, where bonfires burn high and flames lick the sky. And he says once more, "Please, accept my thanks for all the blessings you've given me." And he wants to say more this time, so he does: "Stay with me tonight. All night long."

And she says, "Of course," as if that was all he'd ever had to do, just ask. So he walks her toward the feast boards, keeping himself between her and any who might wish to intercept her. It was easy. It was what he did. It was what he knew. He could protect her person from intrusion, now and forever. It's nothing, compared to what she's done for him, but it is his pleasure. He wants to give her something. The commendations included small golden feathers on pins, field decorations from the battle. He gives her his. He says, "It's nothing much, but I want you to have it. It's my medal from the fighting."

She takes it gravely. "It is wonderful," she says. "I am honored."

He brings her food. *Does she eat?* Tonight she will, and he's fascinated by every move she makes when she does the simple things that mortals do: she takes a bit of bread, a drop of oil, a little wine, and throws them on the flames. There is no richer man on earth tonight than he, with Harmony by his side.

Jihan and Tempus find them, soon after, and Tempus makes the introductions. The two most beautiful women here weigh one another with calculating eyes, then bare their teeth and touch hands. And there is no thunderclap, no lightning bolt from heaven, when they touch. The two laugh softly, each more beautiful than a mortal woman can be, each with triumph and exhilaration in proud wide eyes. *Tat, rata tat. Tat rat tata tata tat.*

Jihan says, "Tempus is going to teach me how to dance tonight."

Niko sees that kill-smile tugging at the corners of his commander's mouth on this soft, warm night in which everything is finally right. The Riddler's eyes implore him to do something, but Niko doesn't know, in this odd moment, with dancing and music all around, what Tempus requires of him.

He wishes he could stop time, make the world stay here forever, where he has all his loved ones around him and his wounded on the mend and there is no dying or crying or bleeding, but only music and dancing and beauty and joy.

"Dancing with the Riddler, Jihan? What could be more sublime?" asks Harmony. Then the goddess beams at Niko. The meadow of his rest-place is still in her eyes. "We could help Jihan, Niko. Show her how we dance."

Then Niko realizes what the Riddler wants, his commander whom he'd followed into so many battles and who now needs him on his right for a sortie into a different kind of combat.

"Of course. Jihan, just watch us. Harmony?" He took his goddess in his arms, his hand on her waist, and they spun together across the sand.

And when Niko looked up, he saw Tempus and Jihan doing the same, dancing in the moonlight with the sea at their backs and the stars twinkling down on the waves.

*

Tempus, with Jihan clasped close to him, watches his partner in the moonlight with the Theban goddess; and all his Stepsons, laughing and eating and drinking and dancing. And he sees how life might be with Harmony among them, with all the simple good that this goddess of the balance brings to Niko, to the Band, to everything she touches; this goddess of love in war, helping to steer all things through all things.

At first he feared this change she brought, despite all he was, all he knew, all he'd taught. For he too is different now, with Harmony among them; it is not just Niko who is changed, but all of them. How Tempus feels, where he goes, what he wants now: so much more seems possible tonight than ever before. Change, like war, is constant. He'd always known it, but disappointment and loneliness had long fought on his right hand, and the habit of suspicion had grown deep into his bones after so many years, so many wars, serving the storm gods of the armies, facing the worst that gods and men can do and never blinking.

This warrior goddess has brought a softer hand, sounded a more compassionate note, and her Thebans are with his Sacred Band to stay, bringing all their love and happiness among his fighters. First he'd thought it might make them weak; now he saw it made them stronger. And loneliness (among men and gods, the greatest curse of all), which makes so many climb too high and fall, was kept in balance now. All things were in proportion.

Wanting neither too much to live nor too much to die, he and his had accomplished more than he'd thought men could do. To gods all things are good and just, but the dream lord had been neither, his reign so far beyond the rules that men or gods obey. And Tempus's greatest vulnerability, this soul called Nikodemos, who made him feel too much and want too much and want to protect too much, was at last strong enough for all the trials ahead, with time enough to learn all that Tempus had to teach him.

So if he could not step twice into the same river, he could at least try to keep Niko from making so many mistakes that he had made. Eternity would be the better, for having Nikodemos in it. And the entire world remade, in a better order, once the power that was Niko came of age. Thanks to the Theban goddess, Tempus finally had the weapon he needed in Nikodemos, over whom so many powers contended for so long. *Use him wisely. Few have been given such a weapon by the gods or Fates before.*

And so he would.

The Fates had come here tonight. He had seen them. Jihan had. And Ischade had seen something. And the goddess, he suspected, had seen them too.

The Fates had come, and looked, and looked again, and gone another way. They had struck down none of his. They hadn't cut a thread or ended a life. He'd had a moment when his own life had passed before his eyes as he realized what he faced there, in those black robes.

So much striving, so many days and nights, so much love and death.

Since he was still alive, and all of his were alive, he had to assume that opposition had brought concord, once again. They had done a favor for eternity, at great cost. He had only seen the Fates once before, even in so long a life as his.

But he saw destiny when he looked over Jihan's coppery head at his Stepsons, at Niko, who might be more than ever Tempus had hoped; at Straton and Critias; and at his new blood, Lysis and Arton and Kouras, with so much striving stretched out before them.

The sun is new every day.

He wanted to get his horse, and have Niko get his, and ride through the surf in the moonlight.

So when he could, he got Niko, and they did that, just the two of them, while the celebration wound on and the dancers danced and the musicians played.

With Niko on his right, they rode through the splash of the surf, he upon his Trôs horse who had served him so well these many years, and Niko on the black stallion who had come from the goddess; not talking, just riding together, their horses cantering slowly, synchronized, as if they rode in formation into battle.

And then Jihan came up on Tempus's left side, riding her gray froth horse farther and farther out into the surf. She waved at him and he knew she was going, back to the sea with the weapon she'd promised to take there for him. He waved in return and a breaker covered sprite and horse. Then the Froth Daughter and her froth horse were gone. In a blink. In two blinks. He knew she'd come to him again, if he stepped into the ocean and called, but someday he needed to teach her how to say farewell. The world was always a little smaller after Jihan had left it.

Above his head he heard wings beat, and looked up. He called softly, "Niko, above you," and Niko looked up too. Two winged shadows wheeled on high, masters of the air, dark against the luminous vault of heaven, lazing on the currents aloft, pacing them.

Niko caught his eye: "Ischade and Randal, up there. Look how beautiful they are." And they were, safe and free, the necromant and the warrior-mage, wheeling high above them in the night, watching everything ahead of them from far-seeing eyes.

Next the goddess Harmony joined them on Niko's right, astride her sable mare. And up beside her, to her right, came Critias on his chestnut with Straton mounted on the ghost horse to his right. Now they were five across, Tempus with his Trôs in the surf and the best of his Sacred Band of Stepsons beside him. This first rank of his could lead a charge into heaven itself, or into hell, and never falter, never fail. He felt grace and gratitude at that moment as he had never felt them before.

Now more Stepsons come riding, his Sacred Band, forming a second rank behind, left to right: Kouras on the blue roan; then Sync on his bay; Charon on the big dun; Lysis on Niko's black colt; and Arton, weak but riding proudly, head high, astride his brown gelding. And behind them, from right to left, came Gayle and Cassander, then Gorgias next to him, and then Perses and Simias fell in alongside.

When they had almost passed the lighthouse, Niko craned his neck and called out softly, "Commander? Tempus, they're still with us."

In his ear, so softly, above the sounds of the horses and the surf, he thought he heard the velvet voice of Abarsis say, *Perhaps they always will be, Riddler. If you wish it. Blessings from all of heaven go with you tonight, Sleepless One. Life to you, Tempus, and to all your Sacred Band, and everlasting glory, from all of us who love you.* But perhaps it was just the crash and spill of the whitecaps against the sand.

Above Niko's head, against a deep blue sky adorned with stars and moonlight, Tempus could see the darker shapes of

Ischade and Randal soaring, on the wing, an honor guard such as he had never imagined.

And so he rode on, with Niko and his goddess and the Sacred Band all about him in perfect formation, past the lighthouse, following the tide with its phosphorescent foam, as moonbeams paved a silver road across the waves, stretching all the way from heaven to the shore.

## *Authors' Notes and Acknowledgements*

It is true that three hundred of the Sacred Band of Thebes fought at Chaeronea at the end of August in 338 BCE and two-hundred fifty-four skeletons lie buried today under a granite statue of a lion there. Some still argue about the fate of the forty-six whose skeletons were not recovered. Plutarch says that all died together, and Philip of Macedon wept to see it. Another, later view is that the remainder were taken prisoner or fled.

We tell a different story.

In our text, we have taken Plutarch as our primary source on the Sacred Band of Thebes. We have quoted or paraphrased from Plutarch's *Lives* on Pelopidas, as well as his writings on Epaminondas, Gorgidas, and on the Battle of Chaeronea. We have also briefly paraphrased Plato's Symposia on governments and suggestions as to the formation of Sacred Bands, but followed Plutarch's "Life of Pelopidas" on the creation of the Band and the choice of Harmony as their tutelary. We acknowledge but did not quote Pausanias and Diodorus, as well as Demosthenes, who fought at Chaeronea as a hoplite and fled.

Throughout our Tempus story we have used the pre-Socratics extensively, quoting or paraphrasing Thales and

Herakleitos. We have also drawn upon Hesiod and Homer and all earlier mythology liberally. Our mythical Trôs horses are descendants of those bred by the founder of Troy, given to him by Poseidon. Some references far predate Homer: the ancient storm god Enlil reaches as far back as the epic of Gilgamesh. We have used carefully-researched ancient technology, techniques and procedures, but liberally intermixed them with the fantastic and the mythical. For example, the crank-and-lever crossbow may never have existed, but since the discovery of the Antikythera mechanism, it might have; smaller crossbows and other more advanced military and technological capabilities are continually being unearthed and documented. In the Homeric tradition, our heroes have mythic weaponry and powers. They must contend with gods and Fates taking sides, while curses and the supernatural are arrayed against them.

In this work, ethos and mythos combine; history remakes itself and dimensions are crossed: realities diverge purposely, as the gods and Fates demand. The ancients understood this: Pausanias says that ghosts were seen fighting on the battlefield at Marathon; Homer used painstakingly correct detail in his battles, yet gods were enemies or allies and occasionally walked the black earth, and his heroes fought monsters and shape-shifters and all manner of more-than-mortal females. Historians will find many details of person and place different in the mythical world of The Sacred Band. It has been our pleasure to make it so.

Most of all, we have used the life, temperament and writings of Herakleitos, not only in this Tempus story, but in all others set in the Riddler's world, as the touchstone for Tempus's nature, quoting and paraphrasing Herakleitos extensively, often but not always using Kirk's translations as our starting point.

Tempus himself says that the god long ago thrust him through a dimensional gate, and this is so: the world of the Stepsons exists in an alternate dimension, where Tempus's history and Herakleitos's at times may seem to be one and the same. At times they are. Tempus himself is not only the embodiment of Herakleitan philosophy, but believes himself to be the author of many Herakleitan fragments. He uses them liberally. Tempus is not limited to the pre-Socratics, however; his ontological base extends from the Gilgamesh epic, through Thales, to modern times. Like the goddess Harmony, he comes and goes as he pleases.

Tempus says that someday he may find that dimensional gate through which the god long ago thrust him, back to the time and place where he was born, a world away. Perhaps he will.

Like all mythologies, Sanctuary was created by many minds over a long period of time, at the instigation and invitation of Robert Asprin and Lynn Abbey. Asprin's Hakiem and several of Abbey's characters, as well as Andrew Offutt's god, Vashanka, and C. J. Cherryh's necromant, Ischade, appear in this novel. We thank them, and acknowledge all the other writers who contributed texture to Bob and Lynn's *Thieves' World*™ series.

This book is the culmination of our long-held desire to save what could be saved of the Sacred Band of Thebes, and what came of it. When in 1978 we finished *I, the Sun,* (Janet Morris, Dell, 1983) a novel based on the Annals of Suppiluliumas I, Great King of Hatti, we looked long and hard at writing a second deeply-researched and correct saga on the Sacred Band. Given the inevitable ending of that historical story, even starting with Epaminondas and Pelopidas, we chose not to pursue the project to the Band's inevitable doom.

When we were asked to contribute a story to the shared universe of Sanctuary, *Thieves' World*™, we began the Tempus stories, intending through the mechanism of the series to get as many as possible of Herakleitos's "Cosmic Fragments" into modern print. But the Sacred Band still whispered to us, and in our second Sanctuary story, "A Man and His God," (copyright 1981, Janet Morris, in *Shadows of Sanctuary*, Ace, Robert L. Asprin, ed.) Abarsis brought his Sacred Band to Sanctuary, died there in Tempus's arms, and Tempus inherited the mythical Band, then ten pairs and thirty unpaired fighters. There, for the first time, a Sacred Band appeared in modern fiction, with all the complex social issues of their ancient morality and sexuality intact. The kiss between Tempus and Abarsis was a signal event in fiction of this type, in those days.

The Band wanted to call themselves Stepsons, after Abarsis, their slain leader, and we were off to many adventures with what eventually became the Sacred Band of Stepsons. But even the creation of our own Band did not quell our desire to save what could be saved of the historical Sacred Band of Thebes.

In 2009 we finally gave in, and undertook the rescue of the twenty-three pairs of Theban Sacred Banders not buried at Chaeronea. We knew it would be difficult, but there were additional joys in store if we could persevere: the future of our own mythical Band needed to be ensured, old enemies vanquished, old ghosts laid to rest, our battered heroes reunited and rewarded and set on their new path together. We think we have done that here, and enjoyed every moment of it.

Horsemanship in this book has been informed not only by Xenophon, but by a myriad of horsemen, dead and living, beginning with Kikkuli's Hittite text on horse-breaking and continuing through to the present day – and by many horses, who teach us every day in every way.

Life to you all, and everlasting glory….

www.ingramcontent.com/pod-product-compliance
Lightning Source LLC
Chambersburg PA
CBHW030543310726
48979CB00010B/2013/J

* 9 7 8 1 9 4 8 6 0 2 5 0 1 *